A MATTER OF HONOUR

&

FALSE IMPRESSION

Jeffrey Archer, whose novels and short stories include *Not a Penny More, Not a Penny Less*, *Kane and Abel* and *A Twist in the Tale*, has topped the bestseller lists around the world, with sales of over 250 million copies.

He is the only author ever to have been a number-one bestseller in fiction (fourteen times), short stories (four times) and non-fiction (*The Prison Diaries*).

The author is married with two sons, and lives in London and Cambridge.

www.jeffreyarcher.com

ALSO BY JEFFREY ARCHER

JEFFREY ARCHER

A MATTER OF HONOUR
&
FALSE IMPRESSION

PAN BOOKS

A Matter of Honour first published 1986 by Hodder and Stoughton
First published by Pan Books 2003
False Impression first published 2005 by Macmillan
First published by Pan Books 2006

This omnibus first published 2011 by Pan Books
an imprint of Pan Macmillan, a division of Macmillan Publishers Limited
Pan Macmillan, 20 New Wharf Road, London N1 9RR
Basingstoke and Oxford
Associated companies throughout the world
www.panmacmillan.com

ISBN 978-0-330-54537-2

3 5 7 9 8 6 4 2

A CIP catalogue record for this book is available from
the British Library.

Printed and bound by CPI Group (UK) Ltd, Croydon, CR0 4YY

A MATTER OF HONOUR

To Will

PART ONE

THE KREMLIN
MOSCOW

May 19, 1966

CHAPTER ONE

THE KREMLIN, MOSCOW
May 19, 1966

"It's a fake," said the Russian leader, staring down at the small exquisite painting he held in his hands.

"That isn't possible," replied his Politburo colleague. "The Tsar's icon of St George and the Dragon has been in the Winter Palace at Leningrad under heavy guard for over fifty years."

"True, Comrade Zaborski," said the old man, "but for fifty years we've been guarding a fake. The Tsar must have removed the original some time before the Red Army entered St Petersburg and overran the Winter Palace."

The head of State Security moved restlessly in his chair as the cat and mouse game continued. Zaborski knew, after years of running the KGB, who had been cast as the mouse the moment his phone had rung at four that morning to say that the General Secretary required him to report to the Kremlin – immediately.

"How can you be so sure it's a fake, Leonid Ilyich?" the diminutive figure enquired.

"Because, my dear Zaborski, during the past eighteen months, the age of all the treasures in the Winter

3

Palace has been tested by carbon-dating, the modern scientific process that does not call for a second opinion," said Brezhnev, displaying his new-found knowledge. "And what we have always thought to be one of the nation's masterpieces," he continued, "turns out to have been painted five hundred years after Rublev's original."

"But by whom and for what purpose?" asked the Chairman of State Security, incredulous.

"The experts tell me it was probably a court painter," replied the Russian leader, "who must have been commissioned to execute the copy only months before the Revolution took place. It has always worried the curator at the Winter Palace that the Tsar's traditional silver crown was not attached to the back of the frame, as it was to all his other masterpieces," added Brezhnev.

"But I always thought that the silver crown had been removed by a souvenir hunter even before we had entered St Petersburg."

"No," said the General Secretary drily, his bushy eyebrows rising every time he had completed a statement. "It wasn't the Tsar's silver crown that had been removed, but the painting itself."

"Then what can the Tsar have done with the original?" the Chairman said, almost as if he were asking himself the question.

"That is exactly what I want to know, Comrade," said Brezhnev, resting his hands each side of the little painting that remained in front of him. "And you are the one who has been chosen to come up with the answer," he added.

For the first time the Chairman of the KGB looked unsure of himself.

"But do you have anything for me to go on?"

"Very little," admitted the General Secretary, flicking open a file that he removed from the top drawer of his desk. He stared down at the closely typed notes headed 'The Significance of the Icon in Russian History'. Someone had been up all through the night preparing a ten-page report that the leader had only found time to scan. Brezhnev's real interest began on page four. He quickly turned over the first three pages before reading aloud: "'At the time of the Revolution, Tsar Nicholas II obviously saw Rublev's masterpiece as his passport to freedom in the West. He must have had a copy made which he then left on his study wall where the original had previously hung.'" The Russian leader looked up. "Beyond that we have little to go on."

The head of the KGB looked perplexed. He remained puzzled as to why Brezhnev should want State Security involved in the theft of a minor masterpiece. "And how important is it that we find the original?" he asked, trying to pick up a further clue.

Leonid Brezhnev stared down at his Kremlin colleague.

"Nothing could be more important, Comrade," came back the unexpected reply. "And I shall grant you any resources you may consider necessary in terms of people and finance to discover the whereabouts of the Tsar's icon."

"But if I were to take you at your word, Comrade General Secretary," said the head of the KGB, trying to disguise his disbelief, "I could so easily end up spending far more than the painting is worth."

"That would not be possible," said Brezhnev, pausing for effect, "because it's not the icon itself that I'm after." He turned his back on the Chairman of State Security and stared out of the window. He had always disliked not being able to see over the Kremlin wall and into Red Square. He waited for some moments before he proclaimed, "The money the Tsar might have raised from selling such a masterpiece would only have kept Nicholas in his accustomed lifestyle for a matter of months, perhaps a year at the most. No, it's what we believe the Tsar had secreted *inside* the icon that would have guaranteed security for himself and his family for the rest of their days."

A little circle of condensation formed on the window pane in front of the General Secretary.

"What could possibly be that valuable?" asked the Chairman.

"Do you remember, Comrade, what the Tsar promised Lenin in exchange for his life?"

"Yes, but it turned out to be a bluff because no such document was hidden . . ." He stopped himself just before saying "in the icon".

Zaborski stood silently, unable to witness Brezhnev's triumphant smile.

"You have caught up with me at last, Comrade. You see, the document was hidden in the icon all the time. We just had the wrong icon."

The Russian leader waited for some time before he turned back and passed over to his colleague a single sheet of paper. "This is the Tsar's testimony indicating what we would find hidden in the icon of St George and the Dragon. At the time, nothing was discovered in the icon, which only convinced Lenin that it had been a pathetic bluff by the Tsar to save his family from execution."

Zaborski slowly read the hand-written testimony that had been signed by the Tsar hours before his execution. Zaborski's hands began to tremble and a bead of sweat appeared on his forehead long before he had reached the last paragraph. He looked across at the tiny painting, no larger than a book, that remained in the centre of the Chairman's desk.

"Not since the death of Lenin," continued Brezhnev, "has anyone believed the Tsar's claim. But now, there can be little doubt that if we are able to locate the genuine masterpiece, we will undoubtedly also be in possession of the promised document."

"And with the authority of those who signed that document, no one could question our legal claim," said Zaborski.

"That would undoubtedly prove to be the case, Comrade Chairman," replied the Russian leader. "And I also feel confident that we would receive the backing of the United Nations and the World Court if the Americans tried to deny us our right. But I fear time is now against us."

"Why?" asked the Chairman of State Security.

"Look at the completion date in the Tsar's testimony and you will see how much time we have left to honour our part of the agreement," said Brezhnev.

Zaborski stared down at the date scrawled in the hand of the Tsar – June 20, 1966. He handed back the testimony as he considered the enormity of the task with which his leader had entrusted him. Leonid Ilyich Brezhnev continued his monologue.

"So, as you can see, Comrade Zaborski, we have only one month left before the deadline, but if you can discover the whereabouts of the original icon, President Johnson's defence strategy would be rendered virtually useless, and the United States would then become a pawn on the Russian chessboard."

CHAPTER TWO

APPLESHAW, ENGLAND
June 1966

"And to my dearly beloved and only son, Captain Adam Scott, MC, I bequeath the sum of five hundred pounds."

Although Adam had anticipated the amount would be pitiful, he nevertheless remained bolt upright in his chair as the solicitor glanced over his half-moon spectacles.

The old lawyer who was seated behind the large partners' desk raised his head and blinked at the handsome young man before him. Adam put a hand nervously through his thick black hair, suddenly conscious of the lawyer's stare. Then Mr Holbrooke's eyes returned to the papers in front of him.

"And to my dearly beloved daughter, Margaret Scott, I bequeath the sum of four hundred pounds." Adam was unable to prevent a small grin spreading across his face. Even in the minutiae of his final act, father had remained a chauvinist.

"To the Hampshire County Cricket Club," droned on Mr Holbrooke, unperturbed by Miss Scott's relative misfortunes, "twenty-five pounds, life membership."

Finally paid up, thought Adam. "To the Old Contemptibles, fifteen pounds. And to the Appleshaw Parish Church, ten pounds." Death membership, Adam mused. "To Wilf Proudfoot, our loyal gardener part time, ten pounds, and to Mrs Mavis Cox, our daily help, five pounds."

"And finally, to my dearly beloved wife Susan, our marital home, and the remainder of my estate."

This pronouncement made Adam want to laugh out loud because he doubted if the remainder of Pa's estate, even if they sold his premium bonds and the pre-war golf clubs, amounted to more than another thousand pounds.

But mother was a daughter of the Regiment and wouldn't complain, she never did. If God ever announced the saints, as opposed to some Pope in Rome, Saint Susan of Appleshaw would be up there with Mary and Elizabeth. All through his life 'Pa', as Adam always thought of him, had set such high standards for the family to live up to. Perhaps that was why Adam continued to admire him above all men. Sometimes the very thought made him feel strangely out of place in the swinging sixties.

Adam began to move restlessly in his chair, assuming that the proceedings were now drawing to a close. The sooner they were all out of this cold, drab little office the better, he felt.

Mr Holbrooke looked up once more and cleared his throat, as if he were about to announce who was to be left the Goya or the Hapsburg diamonds. He pushed his half-moon spectacles further up the bridge of his nose and stared back down at the last paragraphs of his late client's testament. The three surviving members of the Scott family sat in silence. What could he have to add? thought Adam.

Whatever it was, the solicitor had obviously pondered the final bequest several times, because he delivered the words like a well-versed actor, his eyes returning to the script only once.

"And I also leave to my son," Mr Holbrooke paused, "the enclosed envelope," he said, holding it up, "which I can only hope will bring him greater happiness than it did me. Should he decide to open the envelope it must be on the condition that he will never divulge its contents to any other living person." Adam caught his sister's eye but she only shook her head slightly, obviously as puzzled as he was. He glanced towards his mother who looked shocked. Was it fear or was it distress? Adam couldn't decide. Without another word, Mr Holbrooke passed the yellowed envelope over to the Colonel's only son.

Everyone in the room remained seated, not quite sure what to do next. Mr Holbrooke finally closed the thin file marked Colonel Gerald Scott, DSO, OBE, MC, pushed back his chair and walked slowly over to the widow. They shook hands and she said, "Thank you," a faintly ridiculous courtesy, Adam felt, as the only person in the room who had made any sort of profit on this particular transaction had been Mr Holbrooke, and that on behalf of Holbrooke, Holbrooke and Gascoigne.

He rose and went quickly to his mother's side.

"You'll join us for tea, Mr Holbrooke?" she was asking.

"I fear not, dear lady," the lawyer began, but Adam didn't bother to listen further. Obviously the fee hadn't been large enough to cover Holbrooke taking time off for tea.

Once they had left the office and Adam had ensured his mother and sister were seated comfortably in the back of the family Morris Minor, he took his place behind the steering wheel. He had parked outside Mr Holbrooke's office in the middle of the High Street. No yellow lines in the streets of Appleshaw – yet, he thought. Even before he had switched on the ignition his mother had offered matter-of-factly, "We'll have to get rid of this, you know. I can't afford to run it now, not with petrol at six shillings a gallon."

"Don't let's worry about that today," said Margaret consolingly, but in a voice that accepted that her mother was right. "I wonder what can be in that envelope, Adam," she added, wanting to change the subject.

"Detailed instructions on how to invest my five hundred pounds, no doubt," said her brother, attempting to lighten their mood.

"Don't be disrespectful of the dead," said his mother, the same look of fear returning to her face. "I begged your father to destroy that envelope," she added, in a voice that was barely a whisper.

Adam's lips pursed when he realised this must be *the* envelope his father had referred to all those years ago when he had witnessed the one row between his parents that he had ever experienced. Adam still remembered his father's raised voice and angry words just a few days after he had returned from Germany.

"I have to open it, don't you understand?" Pa had insisted.

"Never," his mother had replied. "After all the sacrifices I have made, you at least owe me that."

Over twenty years had passed since that confrontation and he had never heard the subject referred to again. The only time Adam ever mentioned it to his sister she could throw no light on what the dispute might have been over.

Adam put his foot on the brake as they reached a T-junction at the end of the High Street.

He turned right and continued to drive out of the village for a mile or so down a winding country lane before bringing the old Morris Minor to a halt. Adam leapt out and opened the trellised gate whose path led through a neat lawn to a little thatched cottage.

"I'm sure you ought to be getting back to London," were his mother's first words as she entered the drawing room.

"I'm in no hurry, mother. There's nothing that can't wait until tomorrow."

"Just as you wish, my dear, but you don't have to worry yourself over me," his mother continued. She stared up at the tall young man who reminded her so much of Gerald. He would have been as good-looking as her husband if it wasn't for the slight break in his nose. The same dark hair and deep brown eyes, the same open, honest face, even the same gentle approach to everyone he came across. But most of all the same high standards of morality that had brought them to their present sad state. "And in any case I've always got Margaret to take care of me," she added. Adam looked across at his sister and wondered how she would now cope with Saint Susan of Appleshaw.

Margaret had recently become engaged to a City stockbroker, and although the marriage had been postponed, she would soon be wanting to start a life of her own. Thank God her fiancé had already put a down-payment on a little house only fourteen miles away.

After tea and a sad uninterrupted monologue from his mother on the virtues and misfortunes of their father, Margaret cleared away and left the two of them alone. They had both loved him in such different ways although Adam felt that he had never let Pa really know how much he respected him.

"Now that you're no longer in the army, my dear, I do hope you'll be able to find a worthwhile job," his mother said uneasily, as she recalled how difficult that had proved to be for his father.

"I'm sure everything will be just fine, mother," he replied. "The Foreign Office have asked to see me again," he added, hoping to reassure her.

"Still, now that you've got five hundred pounds of your own," she said, "that should make things a little easier for you." Adam smiled fondly at his mother, wondering when she had last spent a day in London. His share of the Chelsea flat alone was four pounds a week and he still had to eat occasionally. She raised her eyes and, looking up at the clock on the mantelpiece, said, "You'd better be getting along, my dear, I don't like the thought of you on that motorbike after dark."

Adam bent down to kiss her on the cheek. "I'll give you a call tomorrow," he said. On his way out he stuck his head around the kitchen door and shouted to his sister, "I'm off and I'll be sending you a cheque for fifty pounds."

"Why?" asked Margaret, looking up from the sink.

"Just let's say it's my blow for women's rights." He shut the kitchen door smartly to avoid the dishcloth that was hurled in his direction. Adam revved up his BSA and drove down the A303 through Andover and on towards London. As most of the traffic was coming west out of the city, he was able to make good time on his way back to the flat in Ifield Road.

Adam had decided to wait until he had reached the privacy of his own room before he opened the envelope. Lately the excitement in his life had not been such that he felt he could be blasé about the little ceremony. After all, in a way, he had waited most of his life to discover what could possibly be in the envelope he had now inherited.

Adam had been told the story of the family tragedy by his father a thousand times – "It's all a matter of honour, old chap," his father would repeat, lifting his chin and squaring his shoulders. Adam's father had not realised that he had spent a lifetime overhearing the snide comments of lesser men and suffering the side-long glances from those officers who had made sure they were not seen too regularly in his company. Petty men with petty minds. Adam knew his father far too well to believe, even for a moment, that he could have been involved in such treachery as was whispered. Adam took one hand off the handlebars and fingered the envelope in his inside pocket like a schoolboy the day before his birthday feeling the shape of a present in the hope of discovering some clue as to its contents. He felt certain that whatever it contained would not be to anyone's advantage now his father was dead, but it did not lessen his curiosity.

He tried to piece together the few facts he had been told over the years. In 1946, within a year of his fiftieth birthday, his father had resigned his commission from the army. *The Times* had described Pa as a brilliant tactical officer with a courageous war record. His resignation had been a decision that had surprised *The Times* correspondent, astonished his immediate family and shocked his regiment, as it had been assumed by all who knew him that it was only a matter of months before crossed swords and a baton would have been sewn on to his epaulette.

Because of the colonel's sudden and unexplained departure from the regiment, fact was augmented by

15

fiction. When asked, all the colonel would offer was that he had had enough of war, and felt the time had come to make a little money on which Susan and he could retire before it was too late. Even at the time, few people found his story credible, and that credibility was not helped when the only job the colonel managed to secure for himself was as secretary of the local golf club.

It was only through the generosity of Adam's late grandfather, General Sir Pelham Westlake, that he had been able to remain at Wellington College, and thereby be given the opportunity to continue the family tradition and pursue a military career.

After leaving school, Adam was offered a place at the Royal Military Academy, Sandhurst. During his days at the RMA, Adam was to be found diligently studying military history, tactics, and battle procedure while at weekends he concentrated on rugby and squash, although his greatest success came whenever he completed the different cross-country courses he encountered. For two years, panting cadets from Cranwell and Dartmouth only saw his mud-spattered back as Adam went on to become the Inter-Services champion. He also became the middleweight boxing champion despite a Nigerian cadet breaking his nose in the first round of the final. The Nigerian made the mistake of assuming the fight was already over.

When Adam passed out of Sandhurst in August 1956, he managed ninth place in the academic order of merit, but his leadership and example outside the classroom was such that no one was surprised when he was awarded the Sword of Honour. Adam never doubted from that moment he would now follow his father and command the regiment.

The Royal Wessex Regiment accepted the colonel's

son soon after he had been awarded his regular commission. Adam quickly gained the respect of the soldiers and popularity with those officers whose currency was not to deal in rumour. As a tactical officer in the field he had no equal, and when it came to combat duty it was clear he had inherited his father's courage. Yet, when six years later the War Office published in the *London Gazette* the names of those subalterns who had been made up to Captain, Lieutenant Adam Scott was not to be found on the list. His contemporaries were genuinely surprised, while senior officers of the regiment remained tight-lipped. To Adam it was becoming abundantly clear that he was not to be allowed to atone for whatever it was his father was thought to have done.

Eventually Adam was made up to captain, but not before he had distinguished himself in the Malayan jungle in hand-to-hand fighting against the never-ending waves of Chinese soldiers. Having been captured and held prisoner by the Communists, he endured solitude and torture of the kind that no amount of training could have prepared him for. He escaped eight months after his incarceration only to discover on returning to the front line that he had been awarded a posthumous Military Cross. When, at the age of twenty-nine, Captain Scott passed his staff exam but still failed to be offered a regimental place at the staff college, he finally accepted he could never hope to command the regiment. He resigned his commission a few weeks later; there was no need to suggest that the reason he had done so was because he needed to earn more money.

While he was serving out his last few months with the regiment, Adam learned from his mother that Pa only had weeks to live. Adam made the decision not to inform his father of his resignation. He knew Pa would only blame himself and he was at least thankful that he had died without being aware of the stigma that had become part of his son's daily life.

When Adam reached the outskirts of London his mind returned, as it had so often lately, to the pressing problem of finding himself gainful employment. In the seven weeks he had been out of work Adam had already had more interviews with his bank manager than with prospective employers. It was true that he had another meeting lined up with the Foreign Office, but he had been impressed by the standard of the other candidates he had encountered on the way, and was only too aware of his lack of a university qualification. However, he felt the first interview had gone well and he had been quickly made aware of how many ex-officers had joined the service. When he discovered that the chairman of the selection board had a Military Cross, Adam assumed he wasn't being considered for desk work.

As he swung the motorbike into the King's Road Adam once again fingered the envelope in his inside jacket pocket hoping, uncharitably, that Lawrence would not yet have returned from the bank. Not that he could complain: his old school friend had been extremely generous in offering him such a pleasant room in his spacious flat for only four pounds a week.

"You can start paying more when they make you an ambassador," Lawrence had told him.

"You're beginning to sound like Rachmann," Adam had retorted, grinning at the man he had so admired during their days at Wellington. For Lawrence – in direct contrast to Adam – everything seemed to come so easily – exams, jobs, sport and women, especially women. When he had won his place at Balliol and gone on to take a first in PPE, no one was surprised. But when Lawrence chose banking as a profession, his contemporaries were unable to hide their disbelief. It seemed to be the first time he had embarked on anything that might be described as mundane.

Adam parked his motorbike just off Ifield Road, aware that, like his mother's old Morris Minor, it would have to be sold if the Foreign Office job didn't materialise. As he strolled towards the flat a girl who passed gave him a second look: he didn't notice. He took the stairs in threes and had reached the fifth floor, and was pushing his Yale key into the lock when a voice from inside shouted, "It's on the latch."

"Damn," said Adam under his breath.

"How did it go?" were Lawrence's first words as he entered the drawing room.

"Very well, considering," Adam replied, not quite sure what else he could say as he smiled at his flatmate. Lawrence had already changed from his City clothes into a blazer and grey flannels. He was slightly shorter and stockier than Adam with a head of wiry fair hair, a massive forehead and grey thoughtful eyes that always seemed to be enquiring.

"I admired your father so much," he added. "He always assumed one had the same standards as he did." Adam could still remember nervously introducing Lawrence to his father one Speech Day. They had become friends immediately. But then Lawrence was not a man who dealt in rumours.

"Able to retire on the family fortune, are we?" asked Lawrence in a lighter vein.

"Only if that dubious bank you work for has found a way of converting five hundred pounds into five thousand in a matter of days."

"Can't manage it at the present time, old chum –

not now Harold Wilson has announced a standstill in wages and prices."

Adam smiled as he looked across at his friend. Although taller than him now, he could still recall those days when Lawrence seemed to him like a giant.

"Late again, Scott," he would say as Adam scampered past him in the corridor. Adam had looked forward to the day when he could do everything in the same relaxed, superior style. Or was it just that Lawrence was superior? His suits always seemed to be well-pressed, his shoes always shone and he never had a hair out of place. Adam still hadn't fathomed out how he did it all so effortlessly.

Adam heard the bathroom door open. He glanced interrogatively towards Lawrence.

"It's Carolyn," whispered Lawrence. "She'll be staying the night . . . I think."

When Carolyn entered the room Adam smiled shyly at the tall, beautiful woman. Her long, blonde hair bounced on her shoulders as she walked towards them, but it was the faultless figure that most men couldn't take their eyes off. How did Lawrence manage it?

"Care to join us for a meal?" asked Lawrence, putting his arm round Carolyn's shoulder, his voice suddenly sounding a little *too* enthusiastic. "I've discovered this Italian restaurant that's just opened in the Fulham Road."

"I might join you later," said Adam, "but I still have one or two papers left over from this afternoon that I ought to check through."

"Forget the finer details of your inheritance, my boy. Why not join us and spend the entire windfall in one wild spaghetti fling?"

"Oh, have you been left lots of lovely lolly?" asked Carolyn, in a voice so shrill and high-pitched nobody would have been surprised to learn that she had recently been Deb of the Year.

"Not," said Adam, "when considered against my present overdraft."

Lawrence laughed. "Well, come along later if you discover there's enough over for a plate of pasta." He winked at Adam – his customary sign for "Be sure you're out of the flat by the time we get back. Or at least stay in your own room and pretend to be asleep."

"Yes, do come," cooed Carolyn, sounding as if she meant it – her hazel eyes remained fixed on Adam as Lawrence guided her firmly towards the door.

Adam didn't move until he was sure he could no longer hear her penetrating voice echoing on the staircase. Satisfied, he retreated to his bedroom and locked himself in. Adam sat down on the one comfortable chair he possessed and pulled his father's envelope out of his inside pocket. It was the heavy, expensive type of stationery Pa had always used, purchasing it at Smythson of Bond Street at almost twice the price he could have obtained it at the local W. H. Smith's. 'Captain Adam Scott, MC' was written in his father's neat copperplate hand.

Adam opened the envelope carefully, his hand shaking slightly, and extracted the contents: a letter in his father's unmistakable hand and a smaller envelope which was clearly old as it was faded with time. Written on the old envelope in an unfamiliar hand were the words 'Colonel Gerald Scott' in faded ink of indeterminate colour. Adam placed the old envelope on the little table by his side and, unfolding his father's letter, began to read. It was undated.

My dear Adam,

Over the years, you will have heard many explanations for my sudden departure from the regiment. Most of them will have been farcical, and a few of them slanderous, but I always considered it better for all concerned to keep my own counsel. I feel, however, that I owe you a fuller explanation, and that is what this letter will set out to do.

As you know, my last posting before I resigned my commission was at Nuremberg from November 1945 to October 1946. After four years of almost continuous action in the field, I was given the task of commanding the British section which had responsibility for those senior ranking Nazis who were awaiting trial for war crimes. Although the Americans had overall responsibility, I came to know the imprisoned officers quite well and after a year or so I had even grown to tolerate some of them – Hess, Doenitz and Speer in particular – and I often wondered how the Germans would have treated us had the situation been reversed. Such views were considered unacceptable at the time. 'Fraternisation' was often on the lips of those men who are never given to second thoughts.

Among the senior Nazis with whom I came into daily contact was Reichsmarshal Hermann Goering, but unlike the three other officers I have previously mentioned, here was a man I detested from the first moment I came across him. I found him arrogant, overbearing and totally without shame about the barbaric acts he had carried out in the name of war. And I never once found any reason to change my opinion of him. In fact, I sometimes wondered how I controlled my temper when I was in his presence.

The night before Goering was due to be executed, he requested a private meeting with me. It was a Monday, and I can still recall every detail of that encounter as if it were only yesterday. I received the request when I took over the Russian watch from Major Vladimir Kosky. In fact Kosky personally handed me the written request. As soon as I had inspected the guard and dealt with the usual paperwork, I went along with the duty corporal to see the Reichsmarshal in his cell. Goering stood to attention by his small low bed and saluted as I entered the room. The sparse, grey-painted, brick cell always made me shudder.

"You asked to see me?" I said. I never could get myself to address him by his name or rank.

"Yes," he replied. "It was kind of you to come in person, Colonel. I simply wish to make the last request of a man condemned to death. Would it be possible for the corporal to leave us?"

Imagining it was something highly personal I asked the corporal to wait outside. I confess I had no idea what could be so private when the man only had hours to live but as the door closed he saluted again and then passed over the envelope you now have in your possession. As I took it, all he said was, "Would you be good enough not to open this until after my execution tomorrow." He then added, "I can only hope it will compensate for any blame that might later be placed on your shoulders." I had no idea what he could be alluding to at the time and presumed some form of mental instability had overtaken him. Many of the prisoners confided in me during their last few days, and towards the end, some of them were undoubtedly on the verge of madness.

Adam stopped to consider what he would have done in the same circumstances, and decided to read on to discover if father and son would have taken the same course.

However, Goering's final words to me as I left his cell seemed hardly those of a madman. He said quite simply: "Be assured. It is a masterpiece; do not underestimate its value." Then he lit up a cigar as if he was relaxing at his club after a rather good dinner. We all had different theories as to who smuggled the cigars in for him, and equally wondered what might also have been smuggled out from time to time.

I placed the envelope in my jacket pocket and left him to join the corporal in the corridor. We then checked the other cells to see that all the prisoners were locked up for the night. The inspection completed, I returned to my office. As I was satisfied that there were no more immediate duties I settled down to make out my report. I left the envelope in the jacket pocket of my uniform with every intention of opening it immediately after Goering's execution had been carried out the following morning. I was checking over the orders of the day when the corporal rushed into my office without knocking. "It's Goering, sir, it's Goering," he said, frantically. From the panic on the man's face, I didn't need to ask for any details. We both ran all the way back to the Reichsmarshal's cell.

I found Goering lying face downwards on his bunk. I turned him over to find he was already dead. In the commotion that immediately followed I quite forgot Goering's letter. An autopsy a few days later showed that he had died from poisoning; the court came to the conclusion that the cyanide capsule that had been found in his body must have been implanted in one of his cigars.

As I had been the last to see him alone and privately, it took only a few whispers before my name was linked with his death. There was, of course, no truth in the accusation. Indeed I never doubted for one moment that the court had delivered the correct verdict in his case and that he justly deserved to be hanged for the part he had played in the war.

So stung was I by the continual behind-the-back accusations that I might have helped Goering to an easy death by smuggling in the cigars that I felt the only honourable thing to do in the circumstances was to resign my commission immediately for fear of bringing further dishonour to the regiment. When I returned to England later that year, and finally decided to throw out my old uniform, I came across the envelope again. When I explained to your mother the details of the incident she begged me to destroy the envelope as she considered it had brought enough dishonour to our family already, and even if it did point to whoever had been responsible for helping Goering to his suicide, in her opinion such knowledge could no longer do anyone any good. I agreed to comply with her wishes and although I never opened the envelope I could never get myself to destroy it, remembering the last sentence Goering had uttered about it being a masterpiece. And so finally I hid it among my personal papers.

However, since the imagined sins of the father are inevitably visited upon the next generation, I feel no such qualms should influence you. If there is therefore anything to be gained from the contents of this envelope I make only one request, namely that your mother should be the first to benefit from it without ever being allowed to know how such good fortune came about.

Over the years, I have watched your progress with considerable pride and feel confident that I can leave you to make the correct decision.

If you are left in any doubt about opening the envelope yourself, destroy it without further consideration. But if you open it only to discover its purpose is to involve you in some dishonourable enterprise, be rid of it without a second thought.

May God be with you.
Your loving father,

Gerald Scott

Adam read the letter over once again, realising how much trust his father had placed in him. His heart thumped in his chest as he considered how Pa's life had been wasted by the murmurings and innuendoes of lesser men – the same men who had also succeeded in bringing his own career to a premature halt. When he had finished reading the missive for a third time he folded it up neatly and slipped it back into its envelope.

He then picked up the second envelope from the side table. The words 'Colonel Gerald Scott' were written in a faded bold script across it.

Adam removed a comb from his inside pocket and wedged it into the corner of the envelope. Slowly he began to slit it open. He hesitated for a moment before extracting two pieces of paper, both yellowed with age. One appeared to be a letter while the other seemed to be a document of some sort. The crest of the Third Reich was embossed at the head of the letterpaper above the printed name of Reichsmarshal Hermann Goering. Adam's hands began to tremble as he read the first line.

It began, *Sehr geehrter Herr Oberst Scott:*

CHAPTER THREE

As the black Chaika limousine drove out under the Spasskaya Bashnya and on to Red Square, two Kremlin guards in khaki uniforms sprang to attention and presented arms. A shrill whistle sounded which ensured that Yuri Efimovich Zaborski would experience no delays on his route back to Dzerzhinsky Square.

Zaborski touched the corner of his black felt hat in automatic acknowledgment of the salute although his thoughts were elsewhere. As the car rumbled over the cobbled stones, he didn't even glance at the long snake-like queue that stretched from Lenin's Tomb to the edge of Red Square. The first decision he had to make would undoubtedly be the most important: which of his senior operatives should be charged with the task of heading the team to find the Tsar's icon? He continued to ponder the problem as his driver took him across Red Square, passing the grey façade of the GUM department store away to his left before driving along Neitsa Kuibysheva.

Within moments of leaving his leader, the Chairman of State Security had formed in his own mind a shortlist of two. Which of those two, Valchek or Romanov, should be given the nod still taxed him. In normal circumstances he would have spent at least a week making such a decision but the General Secretary's deadline of June 20 left him with no such freedom. He knew he would have to make the choice even before he reached his office. The driver cruised through another green light past the Ministry of Culture and into Cherkasskiy Bolshoy Pereulok lined with its imposing block-like, grey buildings. The car remained in the special inside lane that could be used only by senior Party officials. In England, he was amused to learn that they had plans for such a traffic lane – but it would only be for the use of buses.

The car came to an abrupt halt outside KGB headquarters. It hadn't helped that they had been able to cover the three kilometre journey in less than four minutes. The driver ran round and opened the back door to allow his master to step out but Zaborski didn't move. The man who rarely changed his mind had already done so twice on the route back to Dzerzhinsky Square. He knew he could call on any number of bureaucrats and academics to do the spade work but someone with flair was going to have to lead them and be responsible for reporting back to him.

His professional intuition told him to select Yuri Valchek, who had proved over the years to be a trusty and reliable servant of the State. He was also one of the Chairman's longest serving heads of department. Slow methodical and reliable, he had completed a full ten years as an agent in the field before confining himself to a desk job.

In contrast, Alex Romanov, who had only recently become head of his own section, had shown flashes of brilliance in the field but they had been so often outweighed by a lack of personal judgment. At twenty-nine, he was the youngest and, without question, the most ambitious of the Chairman's select team.

Zaborski stepped out on to the pavement and walked towards another door held open for him. He strode across the marble floor and stopped only when he reached the lift gates. Several silent men and women had also been waiting for the lift but when it returned to the ground floor and the Chairman stepped into the little cage, none of them made any attempt to join him. Zaborski travelled slowly up towards his office, never failing to compare it unfavourably with the speed of the one American elevator he had experienced. They could launch their rockets before you could get to your office, his predecessor had warned him. By the time Zaborski had reached the top floor and the gates had been pulled back for him, he had made up his mind. It would be Valchek.

A secretary helped him off with his long black coat and took his hat. Zaborski walked quickly to his desk. The two files he had asked for were awaiting him. He sat down and began to pore over Valchek's file. When he had completed it, he barked out an order to his hovering secretary: "Find Romanov."

Comrade Romanov lay flat on his back, his left arm behind his head and his opponent's right over his throat preparing for a double knee-thrust. The coach executed it perfectly and Romanov groaned as he hit the floor with a thud.

An attendant came rushing over to them and bent down to whisper in the coach's ear. The coach reluctantly released his pupil who rose slowly as if in a daze, bowed to the coach and then in one movement of right arm and left leg took the legs from under him and left him flat on the gymnasium floor before making his way quickly to the off-the-hook phone in the office.

Romanov didn't notice the girl who handed him the

phone. "I'll be with him as soon as I have had a shower," was all she heard him say. The girl who had taken the call had often wondered what Romanov looked like in the shower. She, like all the other girls in the office, had seen him in the gymnasium a hundred times. Six foot tall with that long, flowing blond hair – he resembled a Western film star. And those eyes, 'piercing blue' the friend who shared her desk described them.

"He's got a scar on his . . ." the friend confided.

"How do you know that?" she had asked, but her friend had only giggled in reply.

The Chairman meanwhile had opened Romanov's personal file for a second time, and was still perusing the details. He began to read the different entries that made up a candid character assessment which Romanov would never see unless he became Chairman:

Alexander Petrovich Romanov. Born Leningrad, March 12, 1937. Elected full Party member 1958.
Father: Peter Nicholevich Romanov, served on the Eastern Front in 1942. On returning to Russia in 1945 refused to join Communist Party. After several reports of anti-State activities supplied by his son he was sentenced to ten years in prison. Died in jail October 20, 1948.

Zaborski looked up and smiled – a child of the State.

Grandfather: Nicholai Alexandrovich Romanov, merchant, and one of the wealthiest landowners in Petrograd. Shot and killed on May 11, 1918, while attempting to escape from the forces of the Red Army.

The Revolution had taken place between the princely grandfather and the reluctant comrade father.

Alex, as he preferred to be known, had nevertheless inherited the Romanov ambition so he enrolled for the Party's Pioneer organisation at the age of nine. By the age of eleven, he had been offered a place at a special school at Smolensk – to the disgust of some of the lesser Party workers who considered such privileges should be reserved for the sons of loyal Party officials, not the sons of those in jail. Romanov immediately excelled in the classroom, much to the dismay of the Director who had been hoping to disprove any Darwinian theories. And at fourteen he was selected as one of the Party's élite and made a member of the Komsomol.

By the age of sixteen, Romanov had won the Lenin language medal and the junior gymnastics prize and despite the Director's attempts to undermine young Alex's achievements, most members of the school board recognised Romanov's potential and ensured that he was still allowed to take up a place at university. As an undergraduate he continued to excel in languages, specialising in English, French and German. Natural flair and hard work kept him near the top of every subject he specialised in.

Zaborski picked up the phone by his side. "I asked to see Romanov," he said curtly.

"He was completing his morning work-out at the gymnasium, Chairman," replied the secretary. "But he left to change the moment he heard you wanted to see him."

The Chairman replaced the phone and his eyes returned to the file in front of him. That Romanov could be found in the gymnasium at all hours came as no surprise: the man's athletic prowess had been acknowledged far beyond the service.

During his first year as a student, Romanov had continued diligently with his gymnastics and even gone on to represent the State side until the university coach had written in bold letters across one of his reports, "This student is too tall to be considered for serious Olympic competition." Romanov heeded the coach's advice and took up judo. Within two years, he had been selected for the 1958 Eastern Bloc games in Budapest and within a further two years found other competitors preferred not to be drawn against him on his inevitable route to the final. After his victory at the Soviet games in Moscow the Western press crudely described him as 'The Axe'. Those who were already planning his long-term future felt it prudent not to enter him for the Olympics.

Once Romanov had completed his fifth year at the university and obtained his diploma (with distinction), he remained in Moscow and joined the diplomatic service.

Zaborski had now reached the point in the file at which he had first come across the self-confident young man. Each year the KGB were able to second from the diplomatic service any person they considered to be of exceptional talent. Romanov was an obvious candidate. Zaborski's rule, however, was not to enlist anyone who didn't consider the KGB to be the élite. Unwilling candidates never made good operatives and sometimes even ended up working for the other side. Romanov showed no such doubt. He had always wanted to be an officer of the KGB. During the next six years he carried out tours at their embassies in Paris, London, Prague and Lagos. By the time he had returned to

Moscow to join the headquarters staff he was a sophisticated operative who was as relaxed at an ambassadorial cocktail party as he was in the gymnasium.

Zaborski began to read some of the comments he himself had added to the report during the last four years – in particular how much Romanov had changed during his time on the Chairman's personal staff. As an operative, he had reached the rank of major, having served successfully in the field before being appointed head of a department. Two red dots were placed by his name indicating successful missions. A defecting violinist attempting to leave Prague and a general who had thought he was going to be the next head of a small African state. What impressed Zaborski most about his protégé's efforts was that the Western press thought the Czechs were responsible for the first and the Americans for the second. Romanov's most significant achievement, however, had been the recruitment of an agent from the British Foreign Office whose parallel rise had only assisted Romanov's career. Romanov's appointment as head of a department had surprised no one, himself included, although it soon became clear to Zaborski that he missed the raw excitement of field work.

The Chairman turned to the last page, a character assessment, in which the majority of contributors were in accord: ambitious, sophisticated, ruthless, arrogant but not always reliable were the words that appeared with regularity in almost every summation.

There was an assertive rap on the door. Zaborski closed the file and pressed a button under his desk. The doors clicked open to allow Alexander Petrovich Romanov to enter the room.

"Good morning, Comrade Chairman," said the elegant young man who now stood to attention in front of him. Zaborski looked up at the man he had selected and felt a little envy that the gods had bestowed so much on one so young. Still, it was he who understood how to use such a man to the State's best advantage.

He continued to stare into those clear blue eyes and considered that if Romanov had been born in Hollywood he would not have found it hard to make a living. His suit looked as if it had been tailored in Savile Row – and probably had been. Zaborski chose to ignore such irregularities although he was tempted to ask the young man where he had his shirts made.

"You called for me," said Romanov.

The Chairman nodded. "I have just returned from the Kremlin," he said. "The General Secretary has entrusted us with a particularly sensitive project of great importance to the State." Zaborski paused. "So sensitive in fact that you will report only to me. You can hand-select your own team and no resources will be denied you."

"I am honoured," said Romanov, sounding unusually sincere.

"You will be," replied the Chairman, "if you succeed in discovering the whereabouts of the Tsar's icon."

"But I thought . . ." began Romanov.

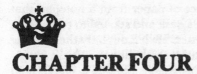

CHAPTER FOUR

Adam walked over to the side of his bed and removed from the bookshelf the Bible his mother had given him as a Confirmation present. As he opened it a layer of dust rose from the top of the gold-leaf-edged pages. He placed the envelope in Revelation and returned the Bible to the shelf.

Adam strolled through to the kitchen, fried himself an egg and warmed up the other half of the previous day's tinned beans. He placed the unwholesome meal on the kitchen table, unable to put out of his mind the slap-up meal Lawrence and Carolyn must now be enjoying at the new Italian restaurant. After Adam had finished and cleared his plate away, he returned to his room and lay on the bed thinking. Would the contents of the faded envelope finally prove his father's innocence? A plan began to form in his mind.

When the grandfather clock in the hall chimed ten times, Adam lifted his long legs over the end of the bed and pulled the Bible back out of the bookshelf. With some apprehension Adam removed the envelope. Next, he switched on the reading light by the side of the small writing desk, unfolded the two pieces of paper and placed them in front of him.

One appeared to be a personal letter from Goering

to Adam's father, while the other had the look of an older, more official document. Adam placed this second document to one side and began to go over the letter line by line. It didn't help.

He tore a blank piece of paper from a notepad that he found on Lawrence's desk and started to copy down the text of Goering's letter. He left out only the greeting and what he assumed to be a valediction – '*hochachtungs-voll*' – followed by the Reichsmarshal's large, bold signature. He checked over the copy carefully before replacing the original in its faded envelope. He had just begun the same process with the official document, using a separate sheet of paper, when he heard a key turning, followed by voices at the front door. Both Lawrence and Carolyn sounded as if they had drunk more than the promised bottle of wine, and Carolyn's voice in particular had ascended into little more than a series of high-pitched giggles.

Adam sighed and switched off the light by the side of the desk so they wouldn't know he was still awake. In the darkness he became more sensitive to their every sound. One of them headed towards the kitchen, because he heard the fridge door squelch closed and, a few seconds later, the sound of a cork being extracted – he presumed from his last bottle of white wine, as they were unlikely to be so drunk that they had started on the vinegar.

Reluctantly he rose from his chair, and circling his arms in front of him, he made his way back to the bed. He touched the corner of the bedstead and quietly lowered himself on to the mattress, then waited impatiently for Lawrence's bedroom door to close.

He must have fallen asleep because the next thing he remembered was the tick of the hall clock. Adam licked his fingers and rubbed them over his eyes as he tried to get accustomed to the dark. He checked the little luminous dial on his alarm clock: ten past three. He eased himself off the bed gingerly, feeling more than a little crumpled and weary. Slowly he groped his way back towards the desk, banging his knee on the corner of a chest of drawers during his travels. He couldn't stop himself cursing. He fumbled for the light switch, and when the bulb first glowed it made him blink several times. The faded envelope looked so insignificant – and perhaps it was. The official document was still laid out on the centre of the table alongside the first few lines of his handwritten duplicate.

Adam yawned as he began to study the words once more. The document was not as simple to copy out as the letter had been, because this time the hand was spidery and cramped, as if the writer had considered paper an expensive commodity. Adam left out the address on the top right hand corner and reversed the eight digit number underlined at the head of the text, otherwise what he ended up with was a faithful transcript of the original.

The work was painstaking, and took a surprisingly long time. He wrote out each word in block capitals, and when he wasn't certain of the spelling he put down the possible alternative letters below; he wanted to be sure of any translation the first time.

"My, you do work late," whispered a voice from behind him.

Adam spun round, feeling like a burglar who had been caught with his hands on the family silver.

"You needn't look so nervous. It's only me," said Carolyn, standing by the bedroom door.

Adam stared up at the tall blonde who was even more attractive clad only in Lawrence's large unbuttoned pyjamas and floppy slippers than she had been when he had seen her fully dressed. Her long, fair hair now dropped untidily over her shoulders and he began to understand what Lawrence had meant when he had once described her as someone who could turn a matchstick into a Cuban cigar.

"The bathroom is at the end of the corridor," said Adam, a little feebly.

"It wasn't the bathroom I was looking for, silly," she giggled. "I don't seem able to wake Lawrence. After all that wine he's passed out like a defeated heavyweight boxer." She sighed. "And long before round fifteen. I don't think anything will rouse him again until morning." She took a step towards him.

Adam stammered something about feeling rather whacked himself. He made sure his back shielded her from any sight of the papers on the desk.

"Oh, God," said Carolyn, "you're not queer, are you?"

"Certainly not," said Adam, a little pompously.

"Just don't fancy me?" she asked.

"Not that exactly," said Adam.

"But Lawrence is your chum," she said. Adam didn't reply.

"My God this is the sixties, Adam. Share and share alike."

"It's just that . . ." began Adam.

"What a waste," said Carolyn, "perhaps another time." She tiptoed to the door, and slipped back out into the corridor, unaware of her German rival.

The first action Romanov took on leaving the Chairman's office that morning was to return to his *alma mater* and hand-pick a team of twelve researchers. From the moment they had been briefed they proceeded to study in pairs on four-hour shifts, so that the work could continue night and day.

The early information had come in almost by the hour and the researchers had quickly been able to establish that the Tsar's icon had remained in his private quarters at the Winter Palace at Petrograd until as late as December 1914. Romanov studied religiously a photo of the small delicate painting of St George and the Dragon. St George in tiny mosaic patterns of blue and gold while the dragon was in fiery red and yellow. Although he had never shown any interest in art, Romanov could well understand why people could be moved by the little masterpiece. He continued to read details of the icon's history, but still couldn't work out why it was so important to the State. He wondered if even Zaborski knew the reason.

A royal servant who had testified before the People's Court a year after the Revolution claimed that the Tsar's icon had disappeared for a few days in 1915 after the visit of Ernst Ludwig, Grand Duke of Hesse. At the time, the inquisitors had taken scant interest in the misplaced icon because it was still on the wall of the Tsar's study when they had stormed the Winter Palace. What concerned the court more was why, in the middle of a fierce war with the Kaiser's Germany, the Grand Duke of Hesse should want to visit the Tsar at all.

The Professor of History at the university had immediately been asked for his opinion. The great academic was puzzled by the request, as the KGB had never shown any interest in the nation's past history before. Nevertheless, he briefed Romanov on everything that was known of the incident. Romanov pored over his report once again. The Grand Duke, it was thought, had been on a secret visit to his sister Alexan-

41

dra, the Tsarina. Historians now believed that it had been his intention to secure a cease-fire between Germany and Russia, in the hope that Germany could then concentrate her war efforts on the British and the French.

There was no proof that the Tsar made any promises on behalf of his people but the Grand Duke, it seemed, did not return to Germany empty-handed. As the reports of the proceedings of the People's Court showed, another palace servant had been instructed to wrap up the Tsar's icon and pack it with the Grand Duke's belongings. However, no one on the palace staff could properly explain to the court how a few days later the icon reappeared in its rightful place on the wall of the Tsar's private study.

Romanov's chief researcher, Professor Oleg Konstantinov, having studied the professor's notes and the other researchers' contributions, had underlined his own conclusion in red ink.

"The Tsar must have replaced the original painting with a brilliant copy, having handed over the real icon for safe-keeping to his brother-in-law, the Grand Duke."

"But why," asked Romanov, "when the Tsar had a palace full of Goyas, El Grecos, Titians and Rubens did he bother to smuggle out one icon and why does Brezhnev want it back so badly?"

Romanov instructed the professor and his twenty-four researchers to turn their talents to the Royal House of Hesse in the hope of tracing what had then happened to the Tsar's icon. Within ten days, they possessed between them more information about the Grand Duke and his family than any professor at any university had managed to gather in a lifetime. As each file appeared on his desk Romanov laboured through the night, checking every scrap of information that might give him a lead to the whereabouts of the original painting. He came to a dead end when, after the Grand Duke's death, the painting had been left to his son who was tragically killed in a plane crash. Nothing had been seen or heard of the icon after that day.

By the beginning of the third week, Romanov had reached the reluctant conclusion that there was nothing new on the whereabouts of the icon to be discovered. He was preparing his final report for the Chairman of the KGB when one researcher, Comrade Petrova, whose mind did not work in parallel lines, stumbled across an article in the London *Times* of Wednesday, November 17, 1937. Petrova bypassed the research leader and handed the relevant photocopy to Romanov personally, who, over the next few hours, read the news item so often that he came to know it off by heart.

In keeping with the Thunderer's tradition, the foreign correspondent remained anonymous. The article carried the dateline 'Ostend, November 16, 1937'.

It read:

Grand Duke George of Hesse and four members of his family were tragically killed this morning when a Sabena aircraft carrying them from Frankfurt to London crashed in thick fog over the Belgian countryside.

The Grand Duke had been on his way to England to attend the wedding of his younger brother, Prince Louis, to the Hon. Joanna Geddes. The young prince had been waiting at Croydon Airport to greet his family when the news was broken to him. He immediately cancelled his original wedding plans and announced they would be rescheduled with a small private service in the Chapel at Windsor.

The Times went on:

> Prince Louis, who succeeds his brother as the Grand Duke of Hesse, will leave for Ostend with his bride later today in order that they can accompany the five coffins on their journey back to Germany. The funerals will all take place in Darmstadt on November 23.

It was the next paragraph that the researcher had circled boldly.

> Some of the late Grand Duke's personal belongings, including several wedding presents for Prince Louis and his bride, were scattered for miles in the vicinity of the crashed aircraft. The German Government announced this morning that a senior German general has been appointed to lead a team of salvage experts to ensure the recovery of any family possessions that still belong to the Grand Duke's successor.

Romanov immediately called for the young researcher. When Anna Petrova arrived a few minutes later she gave no impression of being overawed by her head of department. She accepted that it would be hard to make any impression on him with the clothes she could afford. However, she had put on the prettiest outfit she possessed and cut her hair in the style of an American actress called Mia Farrow whom she had seen in one of the few films not banned by the authorities. She hoped Romanov would notice.

"I want you to scour *The Times* every day from November 17, 1937 for six months, and also check the German and Belgian press during the same period in case you come across anything that would show what the salvage experts had discovered." He dismissed her with a smile.

Within twenty-four hours Comrade Petrova barged back into Romanov's office without even bothering to knock. Romanov merely raised his eyebrows at the discourtesy before devouring an article she had discovered in the Berlin *die Zeit* of Saturday, January 19, 1938.

"The investigation into the crash last November of the Sabena aircraft that was carrying the Hesse royal family to London has now been concluded. All personal possessions belonging to the family that were discovered in the vicinity of the wreckage have been returned to the Grand Duke, Prince Louis, who, it is understood, was particularly saddened by the loss of a family heirloom that was to have been a wedding gift from his brother, the late Grand Duke. The gift, a painting known as the 'Tsar's Icon', had once belonged to his uncle, Tsar Nicholas II. The icon of St George and the Dragon, although only a copy of Rublev's masterpiece, was considered to be one of the finest examples of early twentieth-century craftsmanship to come out of Russia since the Revolution."

Romanov looked up at the researcher. "Twentieth-century copy be damned," he said. "It was the fifteenth-century original and none of them realised it at the time – perhaps not even the old Grand Duke himself. No doubt the Tsar had other plans for the icon had he managed to escape."

Romanov dreaded having to tell Zaborski that he could now prove conclusively that the original Tsar's icon had been destroyed in a plane crash some thirty years before. Such news would not ensure promotion for its messenger, as he remained convinced that there was something far more important than the icon at stake for Zaborski to be so involved.

He stared down at the photograph above the *Zeitung* report. The young Grand Duke was shaking hands with the general in charge of the salvage team which had been successful in returning so many of the Prince's family possessions. "But did he return them all?" Romanov said out loud.

"What do you mean?" asked the young researcher. Romanov waved his hand as he continued to stare at the pre-war, faded photograph of the two men. Although the general was unnamed, every schoolboy in Germany would have recognised the large, impassive, heavy-jowled face with the chilling eyes which had become infamous to the Allied powers.

Romanov looked up at the researcher. "You can forget the Grand Duke from now on, Comrade Petrova. Concentrate your efforts on Reichsmarshal Hermann Goering."

When Adam woke his first thoughts were of Carolyn. His yawn turned into a grin as he considered her invitation of the night before. Then he remembered. He jumped out of bed and walked over to his desk: everything was in place exactly as he had left it. He yawned for a second time.

It was ten to seven. Although he felt as fit as he had been the day he left the army some seven weeks before, he still completed a punishing routine of exercise every morning. He intended to be at his peak when the Foreign Office put him through a physical. In moments he was kitted out in a singlet and a pair of running shorts. He pulled on an old army tracksuit and finally tied up his gym shoes.

Adam tiptoed out of the flat, not wanting to wake Lawrence or Carolyn – although he suspected she was wide awake, waiting impatiently. For the next thirty-four minutes he pounded the pavement down to the Embankment, across Albert Bridge, through Battersea Park to return by way of Chelsea Bridge. Only one thought was going through his mind. After twenty years of gossip and innuendo was this going to be the one chance to clear his father's name? The moment he arrived back at the flat, Adam checked his pulse: 150 beats a minute. Sixty seconds later it was down to 100, another minute 70, and before the fourth minute was up it was back to a steady 58. It's the recovery that proves fitness, not your speed, his old Physical Training Instructor at Aldershot had drummed into him.

As Adam walked back through to his room there was still no sign of Carolyn. Lawrence, smart in a grey pinstripe suit, was preparing breakfast in the kitchen while glancing at the sports pages of the *Daily Telegraph*.

"The West Indies made 526," he informed Adam forlornly.

"Have we begun our innings?" shouted Adam from the bathroom.

"No, bad light stopped play."

Adam groaned as he stripped for the shower. He was ready for his morning game of finding out how long he could last under the freezing jets. The forty-eight needles of ice cold water beat down on his back and chest, which made him take several deep intakes of breath. Once you survive the first thirty seconds you could stay under for ever, the instructor had assured them. Adam emerged three minutes later, satisfied but still damning the PTI from whose influence he felt he would never escape.

Once he had towelled himself down Adam walked back to his bedroom. A moment later he had thrown on his dressing-gown and joined his friend in the kitchen for breakfast. Lawrence was now seated at the kitchen table concentrating hard on a bowl of cornflakes, while running a finger down the Foreign Exchange rates in the *Financial Times*.

Adam checked his watch: already ten past eight. "Won't you be late for the office?" he asked.

"Dear boy," said Lawrence, "I am not a lackey who works at the kind of bank where the customers keep shop hours."

Adam laughed. "But I will, however, have to be shackled to my desk in the City by nine thirty," Lawrence admitted. "They don't send a driver for me nowadays," he explained. "In this traffic, I told them, it's so much quicker by tube."

Adam started to make himself breakfast.

"I could give you a lift on my motorbike."

"Can you imagine a man in my position arriving at the headquarters of Barclays Bank on a motorbike? The Chairman would have a fit," he added, as he folded the *Financial Times*.

Adam cracked a second egg into the frying pan.

"See you tonight then, glorious, unwashed and unemployed," jeered Lawrence as he collected his rolled umbrella from the hat stand.

Adam cleared away and washed up, happy to act as housewife while he was still unemployed. Despite years of being taken care of by a batman he knew exactly what was expected of him. All he had planned before his interview with the Foreign Office that afternoon was a long bath and a slow shave. Then he remembered that Reichsmarshal Goering was still resting on the table in the bedroom.

"Have you come up with anything that would indicate Goering might have kept the icon for himself?" asked Romanov, turning hopefully to the researcher.

"Only the obvious," Anna Petrova replied in an offhand manner.

Romanov considered reprimanding the young girl for such insolence, but said nothing on this occasion. After all, Comrade Petrova had proved to be far the most innovative of his team of researchers.

"And what was so obvious?" enquired Romanov.

"It's common knowledge that Hitler put Goering in charge of all the art treasures captured on behalf of the Third Reich. But as the Führer had such fixed personal opinions as to what constituted quality, many of the world's masterpieces were judged as 'depraved' and therefore unworthy to be put on public view for the delectation of the master race."

"So what happened to them?"

"Hitler ordered them to be destroyed. Among those works condemned to death by burning were such masters as Van Gogh, Manet, Monet – and especially the young Picasso who was considered unworthy of the blue-blooded Aryan race Hitler was grooming to rule the world."

"You are not suggesting Goering could have stolen the Tsar's icon," asked Romanov, staring up at the ceiling, "only then to burn it?"

"No, no. Goering was not that stupid. As we now know, he didn't always obey the Führer's every word."

"Goering failed to carry out Hitler's orders?" said Romanov in disbelief.

"Depends from which standpoint you view it,"

Petrova replied. "Was he to behave as his lunatic master demanded or turn a blind eye and use his common sense?"

"Stick to the facts," said Romanov, his voice suddenly sharp.

"Yes, Comrade Major," said the young researcher in a tone that suggested she believed herself to be indispensable, at least for the time being.

"When it came to it," Petrova continued, "Goering did not destroy any of the denounced masterpieces. He held some public burnings in Berlin and Düsseldorf of lesser known German artists, who would never have fetched more than a few hundred marks on the open market in the first place. But the masterpieces, the real works of genius, were moved discreetly over the border and deposited in the vaults of Swiss banks."

"So there's still an outside chance that having found the icon . . ."

"He then had it placed in a Swiss bank," added Petrova. "I wish it were that simple, Comrade Major," said the researcher, "but unfortunately Goering wasn't quite as naïve as the newspaper cartoonists of the time made him out to be. I think he deposited the paintings and antiques in several Swiss banks and to date no one has ever been able to discover which banks or the aliases he used."

"Then *we* shall have to do so," said Romanov. "Where do you suggest we start?"

"Well, since the end of the war many of the paintings have been found and restored to their rightful owners, including the galleries of the German Democratic Republic. Others, however, have appeared on walls as far-flung as the Getty Museum in California and the Gotoh in Tokyo, sometimes without a fully satisfactory explanation. In fact, one of Renoir's major works can currently be seen hanging on the walls of the Metropolitan Museum in New York. It undoubtedly passed through Goering's hands although the curator of the museum has never been willing to explain how the gallery came into possession of it."

"Have all the missing pictures now been found?" asked Romanov anxiously.

"Over seventy per cent, but there are still many more to be accounted for. Some may even have been lost or destroyed, but my guess is that there are still a large number that remain lodged in Swiss banks."

"How can you be so certain?" demanded Romanov, fearful that his last avenue might be closing.

"Because the Swiss banks always return valuables when they can be certain of a nation's or individual's right of possession. In the case of the Grand Duke of Hesse and the Tsar's icon there was no proof of ownership, as the last official owner was Tsar Nicholas II and he, as every good Russian knows, Comrade, had no successors."

"Then I must do exactly what Goering did and retrace his steps by going direct to the banks. What has been their policy to date?" asked Romanov.

"That differs from establishment to establishment," said Petrova. "Some banks wait for twenty years or more and then try either by extensive research or advertising to contact the owner or their next of kin. In the case of the Jews who lost their lives under the Nazi regime, it has often proved impossible to trace a legitimate owner. Although I have been unable to prove it, I suspect they kept the rewards and split the proceeds among themselves," said Petrova. "Typical capitalists."

"That is neither fair nor accurate, Comrade," said Romanov, glad to show that he had also been doing some research. "Because that is another of the great myths perpetrated by the poor. In fact, when the banks have been unable to discover the rightful owner of any treasure left with them they have handed it over to the Swiss Red Cross to auction."

"But if the Tsar's icon had ever been auctioned we would have heard about it by now through one of our agents?"

"Precisely," said Romanov. "And I've already checked through the inventory of the Red Cross: four icons have been disposed of during the last twenty years and none of them was St George and the Dragon."

"Then that can only mean some unscrupulous bankers have disposed of the icon privately once they felt sure no one was going to make a claim."

"Another false premise, I suspect, Comrade Petrova."

"How can you be so certain?" the young researcher asked.

"For one simple reason, Comrade. The Swiss banking families all know each other intimately and have never in the past shown any propensity for breaking the law. Swiss justice, in our experience, is as tough on corrupt bankers as it is on murderers, which is precisely why the Mafia was never happy about laundering its money through the established banks. The truth is that Swiss bankers make so much money dealing with honest people that it has never been in their best interests to become involved with crooks. There are remarkably few exceptions to this rule, which is the reason so many people are willing to do business with the Swiss."

"So, if Goering stole the Tsar's icon and deposited it in a Swiss bank vault, it could be anywhere in the world by now?" said Petrova.

"I doubt it."

"Why?" sighed Petrova, a little peeved that her deductions were now proving wide of the mark.

"Because for the past three weeks I have had heaven knows how many operatives combing Europe for the Tsar's icon. They have spoken to nearly every major curator, keeper, dealer and crook in the art world and yet they still haven't come up with a single lead. And why not? Because the only people who have seen the icon since 1917 were the Hesses and Goering, which leaves me with only one hope if it was not destroyed when the Grand Duke's plane crashed," said Romanov.

"Namely?" asked Petrova.

"That while the rest of the world is under the illusion that the original still hangs in the Winter Palace, it has, for the past twenty years, been lodged in a Swiss bank waiting for someone to claim it."

"A long shot," said the researcher.

"I am quite aware of that," said Romanov sharply, "but don't forget that many Swiss banks have a twenty-five-year rule before disclosure, some even thirty. One or two even have no deadline at all as long as enough money has been deposited to cover the housing of the treasure."

"Heaven knows how many banks there might be who fall into that category," sighed Petrova.

"Heaven knows," agreed Romanov, "and so might you by nine o'clock tomorrow morning. And then it will be necessary for me to pay a visit to the one man in this country who knows everything about banking."

"Am I expected to start straight away, Comrade Major?" the researcher asked coyly.

Romanov smiled and looked down into the girl's green eyes. Dressed in the dull grey uniform of her trade, no one would have given her a second look. But in the nude she was quite magnificent. He leaned over until their lips nearly met.

"You'll have to rise very early, Anna, but for now just turn out the light."

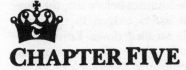

CHAPTER FIVE

It took Adam only a few more minutes before he had checked over both documents again. He put the original back in the faded envelope and replaced it in the Bible on his bookshelf. Finally he folded his duplicated copy of Goering's letter into three horizontal pieces and cut it carefully along the folds into strips which he placed in a clean envelope and left on his bedside table. Adam's next problem was how to obtain a translation of the document and Goering's letter without arousing unnecessary curiosity. Years of army training had taught him to be cautious when faced with an unknown situation. He quickly dismissed the German Embassy, the German Tourist Board and the German Press Agency as all three were too official, and therefore likely to ask unwanted questions. Once he was dressed he went to the hall and began to flick through the pages in the London E–K Directory until his finger reached the column he had been searching for.

German Broadcasting
German Cultural Institute
German Federal Railway
German Hospital
German Old People's Home

His eye passed over 'German Technical Translations' and stopped at a more promising entry. The address was given as Bayswater House, 35 Craven Terrace, W2. He checked his watch.

Adam left the flat a few minutes before ten, the three pieces of the letter now safely lodged in the inside pocket of his blazer. He strolled down Edith Grove and into the King's Road, enjoying the morning sun. The street had been transformed from the one he had known as a young subaltern. Boutiques had taken the place of antiquarian bookshops. Record shops had replaced the local cobbler, and Dolcis had given way to Mary Quant. Take a fortnight's holiday, and you couldn't be sure anything would still be there when you returned, he reflected ruefully.

Crowds of people spilled out from the pavement on to the road, staring or hoping to be stared at, according to their age. As Adam passed the first of the record shops he had no choice but to listen to 'I Want to Hold Your Hand' as it blared into the ears of everyone within shouting distance.

By the time Adam reached Sloane Square the world had almost returned to normal – Peter Jones, W. H. Smith's and the London Underground. The words his mother sang so often over the kitchen sink came back to him every time he walked into the square.

> And you're giving a treat (penny ice and cold meat)
> To a party of friends and relations,
> They're a ravenous horde, and they all came aboard
> At Sloane Square and South Kensington stations.

He paid a shilling for a ticket to Paddington and, installed in a half-empty carriage, once again went over his plan. When he emerged into the open air at

Paddington he checked the street name and, once he was sure of his bearings, walked out on to Craven Road until he came to the first available newsagent and then asked the directions for Craven Terrace.

"Fourth road on the left, mate," said the shopkeeper, not bothering to look up from a pile of *Radio Times* on which he was pencilling names. Adam thanked him and a few minutes later found himself standing at the end of a short drive, looking up at the bold green and yellow sign: The German Young Men's Christian Association.

He opened the gate, walked up the drive and strode confidently through the front door. He was stopped by a porter standing in the hallway.

"Can I help you, guv'nor?"

Adam put on an exaggerated military accent and explained that he was looking for a young man called Hans Kramer.

"Never 'eard of 'im, sir," said the porter, almost standing to attention when he recognised the regimental tie. He turned to a book that lay open on the desk. "'E isn't registered," he added, a Woodbine-stained thumb running down the list of names in front of him. "Why don't you try the lounge or the games room?" he suggested, gesturing with the thumb to a door on the right.

"Thank you," said Adam, not dropping the plummy tones. He walked smartly across the hall and through the swing doors – which, judging from the lack of paint on the base, looked as if they had been kicked open more often than they had been pushed. He glanced around the room. Several students were lounging about reading German papers and magazines. He wasn't sure where to start, until he spotted a studious-looking girl on her own in a corner, poring over a copy of *Time* magazine. Brezhnev's face stared out from the cover. Adam strolled over and took the empty seat beside her. She glanced sideways at him and couldn't hide her surprise at his formal dress. He waited for her to put the paper down before asking, "I wonder if you could assist me?"

"How?" enquired the girl, sounding a little apprehensive.

"I just need something translated."

She looked relieved. "I will see if I can help. Have you brought something with you?"

"Yes I have, I hope it isn't too difficult," Adam said. He took the envelope from his inside pocket and extracted the first paragraph of Goering's letter.

Then he put the envelope back in his pocket, took out a little notebook and waited expectantly. He felt like a cub reporter.

She read the paragraph over two or three times, then seemed to hesitate.

"Is anything wrong?"

"Not exactly," she replied, still concentrating on the words in front of her. "It's just that it's a little bit old-fashioned so that I might not be able to give you the exact sense."

Adam breathed a sigh of relief.

She repeated each sentence slowly, first in German and then in English as if wanting to feel the meaning as well as just translating the words.

"Over the last . . . past year we have come to know . . . each other somewhat . . . no, no," she said, "quite well." Adam wrote each word down as the girl translated them.

"You have never disguised – perhaps a better meaning is 'hidden' –" she added, "your distaste for the National Socialist Party."

She raised her head and stared at Adam. "It's only out of a book," he assured her. She didn't look convinced but nevertheless continued. "But you have at every time . . . no, at all times, behaved with the courtesy of an officer and a gentleman."

The girl looked up, even more puzzled, as she had now reached the last word.

"Is that all?" she asked. "It doesn't make sense. There has to be more."

"No, that's it," said Adam, quickly taking back the sheet of paper. "Thank you," he added. "It was most kind of you to help."

He left the girl and was relieved to see her shrug resignedly and return to her copy of *Time*. Adam went in search of the games room.

When he swung the door open he found a young man in a World Cup T-shirt and brown suede shorts. He was tapping a table tennis ball up and down listlessly.

"Care for a game?" said the boy, not looking at all hopeful.

"Sure," said Adam, removing his jacket and picking up the table tennis bat at his end of the table. For twenty minutes Adam had to play flat out to make sure he lost 18–21, 21–12, 17–21. As he replaced his jacket and congratulated his opponent he felt sure he had gained the young man's confidence.

"You put up good fight," said the German. "Give me good game."

Adam joined him at his end of the table. "I wonder if you could help me with something?" he said.

"Your backhand?" said the young man.

"No, thank you," said Adam, "I just need a paragraph of German translated." He handed over the middle paragraph of the letter. Once again, the would-be translator looked puzzled.

"It's from a book, so it may seem a little out of context," Adam said, unconvincingly.

"Okay, I try." As the boy began to study the paragraph, the girl who had already translated the first section came into the games room. She made her way towards them.

"This hard to make out, I am not good translation for," the young man said. "My girlfriend better, I think. I ask her. *Liebling, kannst Du dies für den Herrn ins Englische?*" Without looking at Adam he passed the second paragraph over to the girl who immediately said, "I knew there was more."

"No, no, don't bother," said Adam, and grabbed the piece of paper away from the girl. He turned back to the boy and said, "Thank you for the game. Sorry to have bothered you," and walked hurriedly out into the corridor, heading for the front door.

"Did you find 'im, sir?"

"Find him?" said Adam.

"Hans Kramer," said the porter.

"Oh, yes, thank you," said Adam. As he turned to leave he saw the young boy and his girlfriend were following close behind.

Adam ran down the drive and hailed a passing taxi.

"Where to?" said the cabbie.

"The Royal Cleveland Hotel."

"But that's only just round the corner."

"I know," said Adam, "but I'm already late."

"Suit yourself, guv," said the cabbie, "it's your money."

As the cab moved off Adam peered out of the back window to see his table-tennis opponent in conversation with the porter. The girl stood alongside them, pointing to the taxi.

Adam only relaxed when the cab turned the corner and they were out of sight.

In less than a minute the taxi had drawn up outside the Royal Cleveland. Adam handed the cabbie half a crown and waited for the change. Then he pushed through the revolving doors of the hotel and hung around in the foyer for a few moments before returning to the pavement again. He checked his watch: twelve thirty. Easily enough time for lunch, he thought, before going on to his interview with the Foreign Office. He headed across the Bayswater Road into the park at a brisk pace, knowing he couldn't hope to find a pub until he reached Knightsbridge.

Adam recalled the table tennis match. Damn, he thought. I should have thrashed him. At least that would have given him something else to think about.

Romanov's eye ran down the list of the fourteen banks. There was still an outside chance that one of them might be in possession of the Tsar's icon, but the names meant nothing to him. It was another world, and he knew he would now have to seek advice from an expert.

He unlocked the top drawer of his desk and flicked through the red book held only by the most senior ranking officers in the KGB. Many names had been scratched out or overwritten as regimes came and went but Aleksei Andreovich Poskonov had remained in his present position as Chairman of the National Bank for nearly a decade, and only Gromyko the Foreign Secretary had served in any office longer. Romanov dialled a number on his private line and asked to be put through to the Chairman of Gosbank. It was some considerable time before another voice came on the line.

"Comrade Romanov, what can I do for you?"

"I urgently need to see you," said Romanov.

"Really." The gravelly tones that came from the other end of the line sounded distinctly unimpressed. Romanov could hear pages being flicked over. "I could manage Tuesday, say eleven thirty?"

"I said it was urgent," repeated Romanov. "It concerns a State matter that can't wait."

"We are the nation's bankers and do have one or two problems of our own, you might be surprised to hear," came back the unrepentant voice. Romanov checked himself and waited. There was more flicking of pages. "Well, I suppose I could fit you in at three forty-five today, for fifteen minutes," said the banker. "But I must warn you that I have a long-standing engagement at four."

"Three forty-five it is then," said Romanov.

"In my office," said Poskonov. The phone went dead.

Romanov cursed out loud. Why did everyone feel obliged to prove their manhood with the KGB? He began to write down the questions he needed answered in order to put his plan into operation. He couldn't afford to waste even a minute of his allocated fifteen. An hour later he asked to see the Chairman of the KGB. This time he was not kept waiting.

"Trying to play the capitalists at their own game, are we?" said Zaborski, once Romanov had outlined his intentions. "Be careful. They've been at it a lot longer than we have."

"I realise that," said Romanov. "But if the icon is in the West I'm left with little choice but to use their methods to get my hands on it."

"Perhaps," said the Chairman. "But with your name such an approach could be misunderstood."

Romanov knew better than to interrupt the brief silence that ensued. "Don't worry, I'll give you all the backing you need – although I've never had a request quite like this one before."

"Am I allowed to know why the icon is so important?" Romanov enquired.

The Chairman of the KGB frowned. "I do not have the authority to answer that question, but as Comrade Brezhnev's enthusiasm for the arts is well known you must have been able to work out that it is not the painting itself that we are after."

What secret can the painting hold? thought Romanov, and decided to press on. "I wondered if . . ."

The Chairman of the KGB shook his head firmly.

Bugs don't have eyes, thought Romanov, but you know what that something is, don't you?

The Chairman rose from his desk and walked over to the wall and tore another page from the calendar. "Only ten days left to find the damn thing," he said. "The General Secretary has taken to phoning me at one o'clock every morning."

"One o'clock in the morning?" said Romanov joining in the game.

"Yes, the poor man can't sleep, they tell me," said the Chairman, returning to his desk. "It comes to all of us in time – perhaps even you, Romanov, and maybe earlier than you expect if you don't stop asking questions." He gave his young colleague a wry smile.

Romanov left the Chairman a few minutes later and returned to his office to go over the questions that did need to be answered by the Chairman of Gosbank. He couldn't help becoming distracted by thoughts of what could possibly be the significance of such a small painting, but accepted that he must concentrate his efforts on finding it and then perhaps the secret it contained would become obvious.

Romanov reached the steps of Neglinnaya 12 at three thirty because he knew he needed more than the fifteen minutes he had been allocated if he was to get all his questions answered. He only hoped Poskonov would agree to see him immediately.

After announcing himself at the reception desk he was accompanied by a uniformed guard up the wide marble staircase to the first floor, where Poskonov's secretary was waiting to greet him. Romanov was led to an anteroom. "I will inform the Chairman of the bank that you have arrived, Comrade Romanov," the secretary said, and then disappeared back into his own office. Romanov paced up and down the small anteroom impatiently, but the secretary did not return until the hands on the clock were in a straight line. At three fifty, Romanov was ushered into the Chairman's room.

The young major was momentarily taken aback by the sheer opulence of the room. The long red velvet curtains, the marble floor and the delicate French furniture wouldn't, he imagined, have been out of place in the Governor's rooms at the Bank of England. Romanov was reminded not for the first time that money still remained the most important commodity in the world – even in the Communist world. He stared at the old stooped man with the thinning grey hair and bushy walrus moustache who controlled the nation's money. The man of whom it was said that he knew of one skeleton in everyone's cupboard. Everyone's except mine, thought Romanov. His check suit might have been made before the Revolution and would once again be considered 'with it' in London's King's Road.

"What can I do for you, Comrade Romanov?" enquired the banker with a sigh, as if addressing a tiresome customer who was seeking a small loan.

"I require one hundred million American dollars' worth of gold bullion immediately," he announced evenly.

The chairman's bored expression suddenly changed. He went scarlet and fell back into his chair. He took several short, sharp breaths before pulling open a drawer, taking out a square box and extracting a large white pill from it. It took fully a minute before he seemed calm again.

"Have you gone out of your mind, Comrade?" the old man enquired. "You ask for an appointment without giving a reason, you then charge into my office and demand that I hand over one hundred million American dollars in gold without any explanation. For what reason do you make such a preposterous suggestion?"

"That is the business of the State," said Romanov. "But, since you have enquired, I intend to deposit equal amounts in a series of numbered accounts across Switzerland."

"And on whose authority do you make such a request?" the banker asked in a level tone.

"The General Secretary of the Party."

"Strange," said Poskonov. "I see Leonid Ilyich at least once a week and he has not mentioned this to me," the chairman looked down at the pad in the middle of his desk, "that a Major Romanov, a middle-ranking" – he stressed the words – "officer from the KGB would be making such an exorbitant demand."

Romanov stepped forward, picked up the phone by Poskonov's side and held it out to him. "Why don't you ask Leonid Ilyich yourself and save us all a lot of time?" He pushed the phone defiantly towards the banker. Poskonov stared back at him, took the phone and placed it to his ear. Romanov sensed the sort of tension he only felt in the field.

A voice came on the line. "You called, Comrade Chairman?"

"Yes," replied the old man. "Cancel my four o'clock appointment, and see that I am not disturbed until Major Romanov leaves."

"Yes, Comrade Chairman."

Poskonov replaced the phone and, without another word, rose from behind his desk and walked around to Romanov's side. He ushered the young man into a comfortable chair on the far side of the room below a bay window and took the seat opposite him.

"I knew your grandfather," he said in a calm, matter-of-fact tone. "I was a junior commodity clerk when I first met him. I had just left school and he was very kind to me but he was just as impatient as you are. Which was why he was the best fur trader in Russia and thought to be the worst poker player."

Romanov laughed. He had never known his grandfather and the few books that referred to him had long ago been destroyed. His father talked openly of his wealth and position which had only given the authorities ammunition finally to destroy him.

"You'll forgive my curiosity, Major, but if I am to hand over one hundred million dollars in gold I should like to know what it is to be spent on. I thought only the CIA put in chits for those sort of expenses without explanation."

Romanov laughed again and explained to the Chairman how they had discovered the Tsar's icon was a fake and he had been set the task of recovering the original. When he had completed his story he handed over the names of the fourteen banks. The banker studied the list closely while Romanov outlined the course of action he proposed to take, showing how the money would be returned intact as soon as he had located the missing icon.

"But how can one small icon possibly be that important to the State?" Poskonov asked out loud, almost as if Romanov were no longer in the room.

"I have no idea," replied Romanov truthfully and then briefed him on the results of his research.

There was an exasperated grunt from the other chair when Romanov had finished. "May I be permitted to suggest an alternative to your plan?"

"Please do," said Romanov, relieved to be gaining the older man's co-operation.

"Do you smoke?" asked the banker, taking a packet of Dunhill cigarettes from his coat pocket.

"No," said Romanov, his eyebrows lifting slightly at the sight of the red box.

The old man paused as he lit a cigarette. "That suit was not tailored in Moscow either, Major," the banker said, pointing at Romanov with his cigarette. "Now, to business – and do not hesitate to correct me if I have misunderstood any of your requirements. You suspect that lodged in one of these fourteen Swiss banks" – the Chairman tapped the list with his index finger – "is the original Tsar's icon. You therefore want me to deposit large amounts of gold with each bank in the hope that it will give you immediate access to the head of the family, or chairman. You will then offer the chairman the chance to control the entire hundred million if they promise to co-operate with you?"

"Yes," said Romanov. "Bribery is surely something the West has always understood."

"I would have said 'naïve' if I hadn't known your grandfather, though to be fair it was he who ended up making millions of roubles, not me. Nevertheless, how much do you imagine is a lot of money to a major Swiss bank?"

Romanov considered the question. "Ten million, twenty million?"

"To the Moscow Narodny Bank perhaps," said Poskonov. "But every one of the banks you hope to deal with will have several customers with deposits of over a hundred million each."

Romanov was unable to hide his disbelief.

"I confess," continued the chairman, "that our revered General Secretary showed no less incredulity when I informed him of these facts some years ago."

"Then I will need a thousand million?" asked Romanov.

"No, no, no. We must approach the problem from a different standpoint. You do not catch a poacher by offering him rabbit stew."

"But if the Swiss are not moved by the offer of vast amounts of money, what *will* move them?"

"The simple suggestion that their bank has been used for criminal activity," said the chairman.

"But how . . ." began Romanov.

"Let me explain. You say that the Tsar's icon hanging in the Winter Palace is not the original but a copy. A good copy, painted by a twentieth-century court painter, but nevertheless a copy. Therefore why not explain to each of the fourteen banks privately that, after extensive research, we have reason to believe that one of the nation's most valuable treasures has been substituted with a copy and the original is thought to have been deposited in their bank? And rather than cause a diplomatic incident – the one thing every Swiss banker wishes to avoid at any cost – perhaps they would, in the interests of good relationships, consider checking in their vaults items that have not been claimed for over twenty years."

Romanov looked straight at the old man, realising why he had survived several purges. "I owe you an apology, Comrade Poskonov."

"No, no, we each have our own little skills. I am sure I would be as lost in your world as you appear to be in mine. Now, if you will allow me to contact each of the chairmen on this list and tell them no more than the truth – a commodity I am always obliged to trade in although I imagine your counterparts are not so familiar with – namely that I suspect the Tsar's icon is in *their* bank, most of them will be disinclined to hold on to the masterpiece if they believe in so doing a crime has been perpetrated against a sovereign state."

"I cannot overstress the urgency," said Romanov.

"Just like your grandfather," Poskonov repeated. "So be it. If they can be tracked down, I shall speak to every one of them today. At least that's one of the advantages of the rest of the world waking up after us. Be assured I shall be in touch with you the moment I have any news."

"Thank you," said Romanov, rising to leave. "You have been most helpful." He was about to add, as he normally did in such circumstances, I shall so inform my Chairman, but he checked himself, realising the old man wouldn't have given a damn.

The chairman of Gosbank closed the door behind him and walked over to the bay window and watched Romanov run down the steps of the bank to a waiting car. I couldn't have supplied you with the one hundred million in gold bullion at this particular time, even if the General Secretary had ordered me to, he thought to himself. I doubt if I have ten million dollars' worth of gold left in the vaults at this moment. The General Secretary has already ordered me to fly every available ounce to the Bank of New York – so cleverly was his ploy disguised that the CIA had been informed about the deposit within an hour of its arrival. It's hard to hide over 700 million dollars in gold, even in America. I tried to tell him. The chairman watched Romanov's car drive away. Of course if, like your grandfather, you read the *Washington Post* as well as *Pravda*, you would already have known this. He returned to his desk and checked the names of the fourteen banks.

He knew instantly which of the fourteen had to be phoned.

Adam stepped out of Tattersalls Tavern on the corner of Knightsbridge Green and headed past the Hyde Park Hotel towards the Royal Thames Yacht Club. It seemed a strange place for the Foreign Office to hold an interview, but so far everything connected with the application had been somewhat mysterious.

He arrived a few minutes early and asked the ex-Royal Marines sergeant on the door where the interviews were taking place.

"Sixth floor, sir. Take the lift in the corner," he pointed ahead of him, "and announce yourself at reception."

Adam pressed a button and waited for the lift. The doors opened immediately and he stepped in. A rather overweight, bespectacled man of roughly his own age who looked as if he never turned down the third course of any meal followed him at a more leisurely pace. Adam touched the sixth button, but neither man spoke on their journey up to the sixth floor. The large man stepped out of the lift in front of Adam.

"Wainwright's the name," he informed the girl on the reception desk.

"Yes, sir," said the girl, "you're a little early, but do have a seat over there." She gestured towards a chair in the corner, then her eyes moved on to Adam and she smiled.

"Scott," he informed her.

"Yes, sir," she repeated. "Could you join the other gentleman? They will be seeing you next." Adam went over and picked up a copy of *Punch* before settling down next to Wainwright, who was already filling in the *Telegraph* crossword.

Adam soon became bored with flicking through endless issues of *Punch* and took a more careful look at Wainwright. "Do you by any chance speak German?" Adam asked suddenly, turning to face the other interviewee.

"German, French, Italian and Spanish," Wainwright replied, looking up. "I assumed that was how I managed to get this far," he added somewhat smugly.

"Then perhaps you could translate a paragraph from a German letter for me?"

"Delighted, old fellow," said Adam's companion, who proceeded to remove the pair of thick-lensed glasses from his nose, and waited for Adam to extract the middle paragraph of the letter from his envelope.

"Now, let me see," Wainwright said, taking the little slip of paper and replacing the glasses. "Quite a challenge. I say, old fellow, you're not part of the interviewing team by any chance?"

"No, no," said Adam, smiling. "I'm in exactly the same position as you – except I don't speak German, French, Italian or Spanish."

Wainwright seemed to relax. "Now let me see," he repeated, as Adam took out the small notebook from his inside pocket.

"'During the past year you cannot have failed to . . . notice that I have been receiving from one of the guards a regular, regular . . . regular supply',' he said suddenly, "yes, 'supply of Havana cigars. One of the few pleasures I have been allocated' – no, 'allowed', better still 'permitted' – 'despite my . . . incarceration'. That's the nearest I can get," Wainwright added. "'The cigars themselves have also served another purpose'," Wainwright continued, obviously enjoying himself, "'as they contained tiny capsules . . .'"

"Mr Scott."

"Yes," said Adam, jumping up obediently.

"The Board will see you now," said the receptionist.

"Do you want me to finish it off while they're finishing you off, old chap?" said Wainwright.

"Thank you," Adam replied, "if it's not too much trouble."

"Far easier than the crossword," Wainwright added, leaving on one side the little unfilled half-matrix of squares.

Alex Romanov was not a patient man at the best of times, and with the General Secretary now ringing up his chief twice a day, these were not the best of times.

While he waited for results of the chairman of Gosbank's enquiries he re-read the research papers that had been left on his desk, and checked any new intelligence that had been sent back by his agents in the field. Romanov resented the scraps of information the chairman of Gosbank must have been receiving by the hour, but he made no attempt to pester the old man despite his time problem.

Then the chairman of the bank called.

On this occasion Romanov was driven straight over to the State Bank at Neglinnaya 12 and ushered up to the finely furnished room without a moment's delay. Poskonov, dressed in another of those suits with an even larger check, was standing to greet him at the door.

"You must have wondered if I had forgotten you," were Poskonov's opening words as he ushered Romanov to the comfortable chair. "But I wanted to have some positive news to give you rather than waste your time. You don't smoke, if I remember correctly," he added, taking out his packet of Dunhill cigarettes.

"No, thank you," Romanov said, wondering if the chairman's doctor realised how much the old man smoked.

The chairman's secretary entered the room and placed two empty glasses, a frosted flask and a plate of caviar in front of them.

Romanov waited in silence.

"I have, over the past two days, managed to talk to the chairmen of twelve of the banks on your original list," Poskonov began, as he poured two vodkas, "but I have avoided making contact with the remaining two."

"Avoided?" repeated Romanov.

"Patience, Comrade," said Poskonov, sounding like a benevolent uncle. "You have longer to live than I so if there is any time to be wasted it must be yours."

Romanov lowered his eyes.

"I avoided one of the chairmen," Poskonov continued, "because he is in Mexico showing President Ordaz how not to repay their loan to Chase Manhattan while at the same time borrowing even more dollars from the Bank of America. If he pulls that off I shall have to recommend to the General Secretary of the Party that he is offered my job when I retire. The second gentleman I have avoided because he is officially in Chicago, closing a major Eurobond deal with Continental Illinois, while in fact he is booked in at the St Francis Hotel in San Francisco with his mistress. I feel certain you would agree, Comrade Major, that it would not advance our cause to disturb either of these gentlemen at this precise moment. The first has enough problems to be going on with for the rest of the week, while the second may well have his phone tapped – and we wouldn't want the Americans to discover what we are searching for, would we?"

"Agreed, Comrade," said Romanov.

"Good. Anyway as they both return to Switzerland early next week we have quite enough to be going on with for now."

"Yes, but what –" Romanov began.

"It will please you to know," continued Poskonov, "that of the twelve remaining chairmen all have agreed to co-operate with us and five have already phoned back. Four to say they have run a thorough check on the possessions of customers who have been out of contact with the bank for over twenty years, but have come up with nothing that remotely resembles an icon. In fact, one of them opened a deposit box in the presence of three other directors that had not been touched since 1931 only to discover it contained nothing but a cork from a 1929 bottle of Taylor's port."

"Only a cork?" said Romanov.

"Well, 1929 was a vintage year," admitted the chairman.

"And the fifth?" enquired Romanov.

"Now that, I suspect, may be our first breakthrough," continued Poskonov, referring to the file in front of him. He adjusted his spectacles with the forefinger of his right hand before continuing. "Herr Dieter Bischoff of Bischoff et Cie" – he looked up at his guest, as if Romanov might have recognised the name – "an honourable man with whom I have dealt many times in the past – honourable, that is, by Western standards of course, Comrade," added the chairman, obviously enjoying himself. "Bischoff has come up with something that was left with the bank in 1938. It is unquestionably an icon, but he has no way of knowing if it is the one we are looking for."

Romanov leapt up from his seat in excitement. "Then I had better go and see for myself," said Romanov. "I could fly out today," he added. The chairman waved him back into his chair.

"The plane you require does not leave Sheremtyevo airport until four thirty-five. In any case, I have already booked two seats on it for you."

"Two?" enquired Romanov.

"You will obviously need an expert to accompany you, unless you know considerably more about icons than you do about banking," Poskonov added. "I also took the liberty of booking you on the Swissair flight. One should never fly Aeroflot if it can be avoided. It has managed only one aviation record consistently every year since its inception, namely that of losing the most passengers per miles flown, and a banker never believes in going against known odds. I have fixed an appointment for you to see Herr Bischoff at ten o'clock tomorrow morning – unless, of course, you have something more pressing to keep you in Moscow, Comrade?"

Romanov smiled.

"I note from your file that you have never served in Switzerland," said the old man, showing off. "So may

I also recommend that you stay at the St Gothard while you are in Zurich. Jacques Pontin will take excellent care of you. Nationality has never been a problem for the Swiss, only currency. And so that brings my little investigation up to date, and I shall be in touch again as soon as the two itinerant chairmen return to Switzerland next Monday. All I can do for the moment however, is wish you luck in Zurich."

"Thank you," said Romanov. "May I be permitted to add how much I appreciate your thoroughness."

"My pleasure, Comrade, let's just say that I still owe your grandfather a favour, and perhaps one day you will find you owe me one, and leave it at that."

Romanov tried to fathom the meaning of the old man's words. There was no clue to be found in Poskonov's expression and so he left without another word. But as Romanov walked down the wide marble staircase, he considered the banker's sentiment again and again because throw-away lines were never delivered to an officer of the KGB.

By the time Romanov had returned to Dzerzhinsky Square, his secretary informed him that Herr Bischoff's assistant had telephoned from Zurich to confirm his appointment with the chairman at ten o'clock the following morning. Romanov asked him to call the manager at the St Gothard Hotel and book two rooms. "Oh, and confirm my flight with Swissair," he added before walking up two floors to see the Chairman and brief him on the meeting he had had with the head of the National Bank.

"Thank God for that," were Zaborski's first words. "With only nine days left at least you've given me something to discuss with the General Secretary when he calls at one tomorrow morning."

Romanov smiled.

"Good luck, Comrade. Our Embassy will be alerted to your every need. Let us fervently hope that you will be able to return the masterpiece to the walls of the Winter Palace."

"If it is in that bank, it will be in your hands by tomorrow night," said Romanov, and left the Chairman smiling.

When he walked into his own office he found Petrova waiting for him.

"You called for me, Comrade?"

"Yes, we're going to Zurich." Romanov looked at his watch. "In three hours' time. The flight and the rooms are already booked."

"In the names of Herr and Frau Schmidt, no doubt," said his lover.

CHAPTER SIX

When Adam emerged from the interview he felt quietly confident. The chairman's final words had been to ask him if he would be available for a thorough medical in a week's time. Adam had told them he could think of nothing that would stop him attending. He looked forward to the opportunity of serving in the British Foreign Service.

Back in the waiting room Wainwright looked up and handed him back his piece of paper.

"Thank you very much," said Adam, trying to look casual by slipping it into his inside pocket without looking at the results.

"What was it like, old chap?" his companion asked cautiously.

"No trouble for a man who has German, French, Spanish and Italian as part of his armoury," Adam assured him. "Best of luck, anyway."

"Mr Wainwright," said the secretary, "the Board will see you now."

Adam took the lift to the ground floor and decided to walk home, stopping on the corner of Wilton Place to buy a bag of apples from a barrow boy who seemed to spend most of his time on the lookout for the police. Adam moved on, going over in his mind the Board's questions and his answers – a pointless exercise he decided, although he still felt confident the interview had gone well. He came to such a sudden halt that the pedestrian behind only just stopped himself bumping into Adam. What had attracted his attention was a sign which read: 'The German Food Centre'. An attractive girl with a cheerful smile and laughing eyes was sitting at the cash register by the doorway. Adam strode into the shop and went straight over to her without attempting to purchase a single item.

"You have not bought anything?" she enquired with a slight accent.

"No, I'm just about to," Adam assured her, "but I wondered, do you speak German?"

"Most girls from Mainz do," she replied, grinning.

"Yes, I suppose they would," said Adam, looking at the girl more carefully. She must have been in her early twenties, Adam decided, and he was immediately attracted by her friendly smile and manner. Her shiny, dark hair was done up in a pony tail with a big red bow. Her white sweater and neat pleated skirt would have made any man take a second look. Her slim legs were tucked under the chair. "I wonder if you would be kind enough to translate a short paragraph for me?"

"I try," she said, still smiling.

Adam took the envelope containing the final section of the letter out of his pocket and handed it over to her.

"The style is a bit old-fashioned," she said, looking serious. "It may take a little time."

"I'll go and do some shopping," he told her, and started walking slowly round the long stacked shelves. He selected a little salami, frankfurters, bacon, and some German mustard, looking up now and then to see how the girl was progressing. From what he could make out, she was only able to translate a few words at a time, as she was continually interrupted by customers. Nearly twenty minutes passed before he saw her put the piece of paper on one side. Adam immediately went over to the cash register and placed his purchases on the counter.

"One pound two shillings and sixpence," she said. Adam handed over two pounds and she returned his change and the little piece of paper.

"This I consider a rough translation, but I think the meaning is clear."

"I don't know how to thank you," said Adam, as an elderly woman joined him in the queue.

"You could invite me to share with you your frankfurters," she laughed.

"What a nice idea," said Adam. "Why don't you join me for dinner tonight?"

"I was not serious," she said.

"I was," smiled Adam. Another person joined the queue and the old lady immediately behind him began to look restive.

Adam grabbed a leaflet from the counter, retreated towards the back of the store, and began to scribble down his name, address and phone number. He waited for the two customers in front of him to pay, then handed over to her a 'once in a lifetime' Persil offer.

"What's this?" the girl asked innocently.

"I've put my name and address on the centre page," Adam said. "I will expect you for dinner at about eight this evening. At least you know what's on the menu."

She looked uncertain. "I really was only joking."

"I won't eat you," said Adam. "Only the sausages."

She looked at the leaflet in her hand and laughed. "I'll think about it."

Adam strolled out on to the road whistling. A bad

morning, a good afternoon and – perhaps – an even better evening.

He was back at the flat in time to watch the five forty-five news. Mrs Gandhi, the new Prime Minister of India, was facing open revolt in her cabinet and Adam wondered if Britain could ever have a woman Prime Minister. England were 117 for seven in their first innings, with the West Indies still well on top. He groaned and turned off the television. Once he had put the food in the fridge he went into his bedroom to assemble the full text of the Goering letter. After he had read through all the little slips of paper he took out his notepad and began to copy out the translations in order: first, the paragraph supplied by the girl from the YMCA, then Wainwright's handwritten words from the notepad, and finally the section of the letter translated by the lovely girl from Mainz. He read the completed draft through slowly a second time.

Nuremberg
October 15, 1946

Dear Colonel,

Over the past year, we have come to know each other quite well. You have never disguised your distaste for the National Socialist party, but you have at all times behaved with the courtesy of an officer and a gentleman.

During the year you cannot have failed to notice that I have been receiving from one of the guards a regular supply of Havana cigars – one of the few pleasures I have been permitted, despite my incarceration. The cigars themselves have also served another purpose, as each one contained a capsule with a small amount of poison. Enough to allow me to survive my trial, while ensuring that I shall cheat the executioner.

My only regret is that you, as the officer in charge of the watch during the period when I am most likely to die, may be held responsible for something to which you were never a party. To make amends for this I enclose a document in the name of one Emmanuel Rosenbaum which should help with any financial difficulties you face in the near future.

All that will be required of you –

"Anyone at home?" shouted Lawrence. Adam folded up the pieces of paper, walked quickly over to the bookcase and inserted them alongside the original letter in the Bible seconds before Lawrence put his head round the door.

"Bloody traffic," said Lawrence cheerfully. "I can't wait to be appointed chairman of the bank and be given that luxury flat on the top floor, not to mention the chauffeur and the company car."

Adam laughed. "Had another hard day at the office, darling?" he mimicked, before joining him in the kitchen. Adam started removing food from the fridge.

"Guess who's coming to dinner," said Lawrence as each new delicacy appeared.

"A rather attractive German girl, I hope," said Adam.

"What do you mean, 'hope'?"

"Well, it could hardly have been described as a formal invitation so I'm not even certain she'll turn up."

"If that's the situation I may as well hang around in case she gives you the elbow and you need someone to help you eat that lot."

"Thanks for the vote of confidence, but I think you'll

find it's your turn to be missing, presumed dead. Anyway, what about Carolyn?" said Adam.

"Carolyn was yesterday's girl, to quote the esteemed Harold Wilson. How did you come across your *gnädiges Fräulein?*"

"She was serving at a food store in Knightsbridge."

"I see. We're down to shop assistants now."

"I have no idea what she is or even what her name is, come to that," said Adam. "But I am hoping to find out tonight. As I said, your turn to disappear."

"*Natürlich.* As you see, you can rely on me to provide a helping hand if you need anything translated."

"Just put the wine in the fridge and lay the table."

"Are there no serious jobs for a man of my accomplishments to be entrusted with?" chuckled Lawrence.

When eight o'clock chimed, the table was set and Adam had everything ready on the boil. By eight thirty both of them stopped pretending and Adam served up two plates of frankfurters, salami and lettuce with a baked potato and sauerkraut sauce. He then hung up his Goons apron behind the kitchen door and took the chair opposite Lawrence, who had begun pouring the wine.

"Oh, *mein liebes Mädchen*, you look ravishing in that Harris tweed jacket," said Lawrence, raising his glass.

Adam was just about to retaliate with the vegetable spoon when there was a loud knock on the front door. The two men stared at each other before Adam leaped to open it. Standing in the doorway was a man well over six foot with shoulders like a professional bouncer. By his side, dwarfed by him, was the girl that Adam had invited to dinner.

"This is my brother, Jochen," she explained. Adam was immediately struck by how beautiful she looked in a dark blue patterned blouse and pleated blue skirt that fell just below the knee. Her long dark hair, now hanging loose, looked as if it had just been washed and shone even under the forty watt light bulb that hung in the hall.

"Welcome," said Adam, more than a little taken aback.

"Jochen is just dropping me off."

"Yes, of course," said Adam. "Do come in and have a drink, Jochen."

"No, I thank you. I have a date as well, but I will pick up Heidi at eleven o'clock, if all right by you?"

"Fine by me," said Adam, at last learning her name.

The giant bent down and kissed his sister on both cheeks. He then shook hands with Adam before leaving them both on the doorstep.

"I am sorry to be late," said Heidi. "My brother did not get back from work until after seven."

"It was no problem," said Adam, leading her into the flat. "If you had come any earlier I wouldn't have been ready for you. By the way, this is my flatmate, Lawrence Pemberton."

"In England the men also need a chaperone?" said Heidi.

Both men laughed. "No, no," said Lawrence. "I was just on my way out. Like your brother, I already have a date. As you can see the table is only laid for two. I'll be back around eleven, Adam, just to make sure you're safe." He smiled at Heidi, put on his coat and closed the door behind him before either could object.

"I hope I don't drive him away," said Heidi.

"No, no," said Adam, as she took Lawrence's place at the table. "He's already late for his girlfriend. Charming girl called Carolyn, a social worker." He quickly topped up her wine, pretending it hadn't already been poured.

"So I am going to eat my own sausages, after all," she said, laughing. And the laughter didn't stop for the rest of the evening, as Adam learned about Heidi's life in Germany, her family and the holiday job she had taken while on vacation from Mainz University.

"My parents only allow me to come to England because my brother is already in London; it is to help my languages course. But now, Adam, I would like to know what you are doing when you are not picking up girls in food stores."

"I was in the army for nine years and I'm now hoping to join the Foreign Office."

"In what capacity, if that is the right expression?" Heidi asked.

"It's the right expression, but I'm not sure I know the right answer," said Adam.

"When someone says that about the Foreign Service it usually means they are a spy."

"I don't know what it means, to be honest, but they're going to tell me next week. In any case, I don't think I'd make a very good spy. But what are you going to do when you return to Germany?"

"Complete my final year at Mainz and then I hope to find a job as a television researcher."

"What about Jochen?" asked Adam.

"He will join my father's law practice as soon as he is arriving home."

"So how long will you be in London?" he found himself asking.

"Another two months," she said. "If I can stand the job."

"Why do you carry on with it if it's that bad?"

"There is no better way to test your English than

impatient shoppers who speak all different accents."

"I hope you stay the full two months," said Adam.

"So do I," she replied, smiling.

When Jochen arrived back punctually at eleven o'clock, he found Adam and Heidi washing the dishes.

"Thank you for a most interesting evening," she said, wiping her hands.

"Not a good word," reprimanded Jochen. "Not interesting, I think. Lovely, happy, delightful, enjoyable perhaps, but not interesting."

"It was all those things," said Adam, "but it was also interesting."

She smiled.

"May I come and buy some more sausages tomorrow?"

"I would like that," said Heidi, "but don't hold up any sour old women this time with translation demands. By the way, you never tell me why you needed the strange paragraph translated. I have been wondering who is this Rosenbaum and what it is he left to someone."

"Next time perhaps," said Adam, looking a little embarrassed.

"And next time you can bring my sister home yourself," said Jochen, as he shook Adam's hand firmly.

After Heidi had left, Adam sat down and finished off the last glass of wine, aware that he hadn't spent such a lovely, happy, delightful, enjoyable and interesting evening for a long time.

A black limousine with dark windows and unlit number plates remained parked in the VIP area of Zurich Kloten. Fastidious Swiss policemen had twice gone up to the car and checked the driver's credentials before Major Romanov and Anna Petrova emerged from the customs hall and took their places in the back of the car.

It was already dark as the driver moved off towards the neon glow of the city. When the car drew up outside the St Gothard Hotel the only words that passed between Romanov and the driver were, "I shall return to Moscow on the Tuesday morning flight."

Jacques Pontin, the manager of the hotel, was stationed at the door waiting to greet the new arrivals; he introduced himself immediately, and as soon as he had checked them both in he banged a little bell with the palm of his hand to summon a porter to assist the guests with their bags. A moment later a young man in his early twenties, dressed in green livery, appeared.

"Suite seventy-three and room seventy-four," Jacques instructed before turning back to Romanov. "I do hope your stay will prove to be worthwhile, Herr Romanov," he said. "Please do not hesitate to call upon me if there is anything you need."

"Thank you," said Romanov as he turned to join the porter who stood sentinel-like by the door of an open lift. Romanov stood to one side to allow Anna to go in first. The lift stopped at the seventh floor and the porter led the way down a long corridor to a corner suite. He turned the key in the lock and invited the two guests to go in ahead of him. The suite was as Romanov had expected, in a different league from the finest hotels he ever experienced in either Moscow or Leningrad. When he saw the array of gadgets in the marble bathroom he reflected that even prosperous travellers to Russia, if seasoned visitors, brought their own bath plugs with them.

"Your room is through there, madam," the porter informed the researcher, and unlocked an adjoining door. Although smaller in size, the room maintained the same unassuming elegance. The porter returned to Romanov, handed him his key and asked if there would be anything else he would require. Romanov assured him there was nothing and passed over a five-franc note.

Once again the porter gave a slight bow, and closing the door behind him, left Romanov to unpack while Anna Petrova went to her own room.

Romanov started to undress and then disappeared into the bathroom. He studied himself in the mirror. Although he was vain about his looks, he was even more vain about the state of his physique. At twenty-nine, despite being six feet, he still only weighed 165 pounds on Western scales, and his muscles remained hard and taut.

By the time Romanov had returned to the bedroom, he could hear the shower beating down in the adjoining bathroom. He crept over to the door and edged it open. He could see quite clearly the outline of Anna standing in the steaming shower. He smiled and noiselessly moved back across the thick carpet, slipped under the sheets and into the researcher's bed. He waited for her to turn off the steaming shower.

Adam stepped out of the freezing shower. Within minutes he was dressed and joined Lawrence in the kitchen for breakfast.

"Still unable to charge you for hot water, am I?" Lawrence said as Adam peered over his flatmate's shoulder, trying to take in the latest Test score.

"Why can't we produce any really fast fast bowlers?" he asked rhetorically.

"Can't stay and chatter to the unemployed," said Lawrence, picking up his briefcase. "Shah of Iran wants to discuss his financial problems with me. Sorry to rush off before you've had your cornflakes but I can't afford to keep His Imperial Majesty waiting."

Left on his own, Adam boiled himself an egg and burned some toast before he turned to the newspaper to learn of the latest casualties in Vietnam and President Johnson's proposed tour of the Far East. At this rate he decided he wasn't going to win the *Daily Mail*'s 'Housewife of the Year' competition. He eventually cleared away in the kitchen, made his bed and tidied up behind Lawrence – nine years of self-discipline wasn't going to change old habits that quickly – then he settled down to plan another day.

He realised he could no longer avoid making a decision. He sat once again at his desk and began to consider how to get the official document translated without arousing further suspicion.

Almost absent-mindedly he removed the Bible from the bookshelf and extracted the letter he had read the night before. The final paragraph still puzzled him. He considered Heidi's translation once again:

All that will be required of you is to present yourself at the address printed on the top right-hand corner of the enclosed document, with some proof that you are Colonel Gerald Scott. A passport should prove sufficient. You will then be given a bequest that I have left to you in the name of Emmanuel Rosenbaum.

I hope it will bring you good fortune.

Adam turned his attention to the document. He was still quite unable to discern what the bequest could possibly be, let alone whether it was of any value. Adam mused over the fact that such an evil man could involve himself in an act of kindness hours before he knew he was going to die – an act that now left him with no choice about his own involvement.

Romanov gathered the blankets together and in one movement hurled them on to the floor to expose Anna curled up like a child, knees almost touching her exposed breasts. Anna's hand groped for a corner of the sheet to cover her naked body.

"Breakfast in bed?" she murmured hopefully.

"Dressed in ten minutes, or no breakfast at all," came back the reply. Anna lowered her feet gingerly on to the thick carpet and waited for the room to stop going round in circles before heading off towards the bathroom. Romanov heard the shower burst forth its jets. "Ahhh," came the pitiful cry. Romanov smiled when he remembered that he had left the indicator locked on dark blue.

During breakfast in the dining room they mulled over the approach he intended to take with the bank if Petrova were able to confirm that the icon was in fact Rublev's original masterpiece. He kept looking up from the table and then suddenly, without warning, said, "Let's go."

"Why?" Anna asked, as she bit into another slice of toast. Romanov rose from the table and without bothering to offer an explanation strode out of the room and headed straight for the lift. Petrova caught up with her master only moments before the lift gate closed. "Why?" she asked again, but Romanov did not speak until they were both back in his suite. He then threw open the large window that overlooked the railway station.

"Ah, it's outside your room," he said, looking to his right, and quickly walked through to the adjoining bedroom. He marched past the dishevelled double bed, jerked open the nearest window, and climbed outside. Petrova stared down from the seventh floor and felt giddy. Once Romanov had reached the bottom rung of the fire escape, he ran to a passing tram. Petrova would never have made it if she hadn't been lifted bodily on to the tram by Romanov's sheer strength.

"What's going on?" she asked, still puzzled.

"I can't be sure," said Romanov, looking out of the back of the tram. "All I do know for certain is what the local CIA agent looks like."

The researcher looked back in the direction of the hotel, but all she could see was a mass of anonymous people walking up and down the pavement.

Romanov remained on the tram for about a mile before he jumped off and hailed a passing taxi going in the opposite direction.

"Bischoff et Cie," he said as he waited for his puffing assistant to join him.

The cab headed back in the direction of the hotel, winding in and out of the morning traffic, until it came to a halt in front of a large brown granite building that filled the entire block. Romanov paid off the driver and stood in front of imposing doors made of thick glass and covered in wrought iron welded to look like the branches of a tree. By the side of the doors, carved inconspicuously into the stone and inlaid with gilt, were the words 'Bischoff et Cie'. There was no other clue as to what kind of establishment lay within.

Romanov turned the heavy wrought-iron knob and the two Russians stepped into a spacious hall. On the left-hand side of the hall stood a solitary desk behind which a smartly dressed young man was seated.

"*Guten Morgen, mein Herr*", he said.

"Good morning," said Romanov. "We have an appointment with Herr Dieter Bischoff."

"Yes, Herr Romanov," said the receptionist, checking the list of names in front of him. "Will you please take the lift to the fifth floor where you will be met by Herr Bischoff's secretary." When the two of them stepped out of the lift they were greeted by a lady in a neat plain suit. "Will you please follow me," she said, without any trace of accent. The two Russians were escorted along a picture-lined corridor to a comfortable room which more resembled the reception room of a country house than a bank.

"Herr Bischoff will be with you in a moment," the lady said, withdrawing. Romanov remained standing while he took in the room. Three black-and-white framed photographs of sombre old men in grey suits, trying to look like sombre old men in grey suits, took up most of the far wall, while on the other walls were discreet but pleasant oils of town and country scenes of nineteenth-century Switzerland. A magnificent oval Louis XIV table with eight carved mahogany chairs surrounding it dominated the centre of the room. Romanov felt a twinge of envy at the thought that he could never hope to live in such style.

The door opened and a man in his mid-sixties, followed by three other men in dark grey suits, entered the room. One look at Herr Bischoff and Romanov knew whose photograph would eventually join that of the other three grey, sombre men.

"What an honour for our little bank, Mr Romanov," were Bischoff's first words as he bowed and shook the Russian by the hand. Romanov nodded and introduced his assistant, who received the same courteous bow and handshake. "May I in turn present my son and two of my partners, Herr Muller and Herr Weizkopf." The three men bowed in unison, but remained standing while Bischoff took his seat at the head of the table.

At his gesture both Romanov and Anna sat down beside him.

"I wonder if I might be permitted to check your passport?" asked Bischoff, as if to show that the formal business had begun. Romanov took out the little blue passport with a soft cover from his inside pocket and handed it over. Bischoff studied it closely, as a philatelist might check an old stamp, and decided it was mint. "Thank you," he said, as he returned it to its owner

Bischoff then raised his hand and one of the partners immediately left them. "It will only take a moment for my son to fetch the icon we have in safe-keeping," he confided. "Meanwhile perhaps a little coffee – Russian," he added.

Coffee appeared within moments borne by yet another smartly dressed lady.

"Thank you," said Petrova, clearly a little overawed, but Romanov didn't speak again until Herr Bischoff's son reappeared with a small box and handed it over to his father.

"You will understand that I have to treat this matter with the utmost delicacy," the old man confided. "The icon may not turn out to be the one your Government is searching for."

"I understand," said Romanov.

"This magnificent example of Russian art has been in our possession since 1938, and was deposited with the bank on behalf of a Mr Emmanuel Rosenbaum."

Both visitors looked shocked.

"Nevozmozhno," said Anna, turning to her master. "He would never . . ."

"I suspect that's exactly why the name was chosen in the first place," Romanov said curtly to Anna, annoyed at her indiscretion. "Can't you see? It makes perfect sense. May I see the icon now?" said Romanov, turning back to the bank's Chairman.

Herr Bischoff placed the box in the centre of the table. The three men in grey suits each took a pace forward. Romanov looked up. "Under Swiss law we must have three witnesses when opening a box in someone else's name," explained the old man.

Romanov nodded curtly.

Herr Bischoff proceeded to unlock the metal box with a key he produced from his pocket, while his son leaned over and undid a second lock with a different key. The little ceremony completed, Herr Bischoff pushed up the lid of the box and turned it round to face his guests. Romanov placed his hands into the box like an expectant child does with a Christmas stocking, and drew out the icon. He stared at the beautiful painting. A small wooden rectangle that was covered in tiny pieces of red, gold and blue making up the mosaic of a man who looked as if he had all the worries of the world on his shoulders. The face, although sad, still evoked a feeling of serenity. The painting Romanov held in his hand was quite magnificent, as fine as any he had seen at the Winter Palace. No one in the room was quite sure what would happen next as Romanov offered no opinion.

It was Anna who finally spoke.

"A masterpiece it is," she said, "and undoubtedly fifteenth century but as you can see it's not St George and the Dragon."

Romanov nodded his agreement, still unable to let go of the little painting. "But do you know the origin of this particular icon?" Romanov asked.

"Yes," Anna replied, glad to be appreciated for the first time. "It is the Icon of St Peter, you see he holds the keys . . . painted by Dionisiy in 1471, and although it is undoubtedly one of the finest examples of his work, it is not the Tsar's icon."

"But does it belong to the Russian people?" asked Romanov, still hopeful of some reward for all his trouble.

"No, Comrade Major," said the researcher emphatically. "It belongs to the Munich Gallery, from where it has been missing since the day Hitler was appointed Reichs Chancellor."

Herr Bischoff scribbled a note on a piece of paper in front of him. At least one bank in Munich was going to be happy to do business with him in the future.

Romanov reluctantly handed back the icon to Herr Bischoff, only just managing to say, "Thank you."

"Not at all," said Herr Bischoff imperturbably, replacing the icon in the box and turning his key in his lock. His son completed the same routine with his own key and then departed with the unclaimed treasure. Romanov rose, as he considered nothing more could be gained from the meeting – although he believed he had discovered Goering's alias, or one of them.

"I wonder if I might be permitted to have a word with you in private, Herr Romanov," asked the elderly banker.

"Of course."

"It is rather a delicate matter I wish to put to you," said Herr Bischoff, "so I thought you might prefer your associate to leave us."

"That won't be necessary," said Romanov, unable to think of anything Bischoff might have to say that he wouldn't later need to discuss with Petrova.

"As you wish," said Bischoff. "I am curious to discover if there was any other reason behind your request to see me."

"I don't understand what you mean," said Romanov.

"I felt perhaps I knew the real reason you had selected this bank in particular to start your enquiry."

"I didn't select you," said Romanov. "You were only one of –" he stopped himself.

"I see," said Bischoff, himself now looking somewhat bemused. "Then may I be permitted to ask you a few questions?"

"Yes, if you must," said Romanov, now impatient to get away.

"You are Alexander Petrovich Romanov?"

"You must already believe that or we would not have proceeded this far."

"The only son of Peter Nicholevich Romanov?"

"Yes."

"And grandson of Count Nicholai Alexandrovich Romanov?"

"Is this to be a history lesson on my family tree?" asked Romanov, visibly irritated.

"No, I just wanted to be sure of my facts as I am even more convinced it would be wise for your associate to leave us for a moment," the old man suggested diffidently.

"Certainly not," said Romanov. "In the Soviet Union we are all equal," he added pompously.

"Yes, of course," said Bischoff, glancing quickly at Anna before continuing. "Did your father die in 1946?"

"Yes. He did," said Romanov, beginning to feel distinctly uncomfortable.

"And you are the only surviving child?"

"I am," confirmed Romanov proudly.

"In which case this bank is in possession . . ." Bischoff hesitated as a file was put in front of him by one of the men in grey. He placed a pair of gold, half-moon spectacles on his nose, taking as long as he could over the little exercise.

"Don't say anything more," said Romanov quietly.

Bischoff looked up. "I'm sorry, but I was given every reason to believe your visit had been planned."

Petrova was now sitting on the edge of her seat, enjoying every moment of the unfolding drama. She had already anticipated exactly what was going to happen and was disappointed when Romanov turned to speak to her.

"You will wait outside," was all he said. Petrova pouted and rose reluctantly to leave them, closing the door behind her.

Bischoff waited until he was certain the door was closed, then slid the file across the table. Romanov opened it gingerly. On the top of the first page was his grandfather's name underlined three times. Below the name were printed row upon row of incomprehensible figures.

"I think you will find that we have carried out your grandfather's instructions in maintaining a conservative portfolio of investments with his funds." Bischoff leaned across and pointed to a figure showing that the bank had achieved an average increase of 6·7 per cent per annum over the previous forty-nine years.

"What does this figure at the foot of the page represent?" asked Romanov.

"The total value of your stocks, bonds and cash at nine o'clock this morning. It has been updated every Monday since your grandfather opened an account with this bank in 1916." The old man looked up proudly at the three pictures on the wall.

"Bozhe Moi," said Romanov, as he took in the final figure. "But what currency is it in?"

"Your grandfather only showed faith in the English pound," said Herr Bischoff.

"Bozhe Moi," Romanov repeated.

"May I presume from your comment that you are not displeased with our stewardship?"

Romanov was speechless.

"It may also interest you to know that we are in possession of several boxes, the contents of which we have no knowledge. Your father also visited us on one occasion soon after the war. He appeared satisfied and assured me that he would return, but we never heard from him again. We were saddened to learn of his death. You might also prefer in the circumstances to return and investigate the boxes at another time," the banker continued.

"Yes," said Romanov quietly. "Perhaps I could come back this afternoon?"

"The bank will always be at your service, Your Excellency," replied Herr Bischoff.

No one had addressed a Romanov by his title since the Revolution. He sat in silence for some time.

Eventually he rose and shook hands with Herr Bischoff. "I will return this afternoon," he repeated before joining his companion in the corridor.

Neither uttered a word until they were back on the street outside the bank. Romanov was still so overcome by what he had learned that he failed to notice that the man he had so deftly avoided at the hotel was now standing in a tram queue on the far side of the road.

CHAPTER SEVEN

The pastor sat at the table studying the document but didn't offer an opinion for some considerable time. When he had heard Adam's request he had invited the young man into the privacy of his little office at the back of the German Lutheran Church.

It turned out to be a stark room dominated by a wooden table and several wooden chairs that didn't match. A small black crucifix was the only ornament on the blank whitewashed walls. Two of the unmatching chairs were now occupied by Adam and the pastor. Adam sat bolt upright while the man of God, clad from head to toe in a black cassock, elbows on the table and head in hands, stared down at the copy of the document.

After some considerable time, without raising his eyes, he offered, "This is a receipt, if I am not mistaken. Although I have little knowledge of such things, I am fairly confident that Roget et Cie, who must be Swiss bankers based in Geneva, have in their possession an object described herein as 'The Tsar's Icon'. If I remember my history correctly, the original can be viewed somewhere in Moscow. It appears," he continued, his eyes still fixed on the document, "that if the holder of this receipt presents himself in Geneva he will be able to claim the aforementioned icon of St George and the Dragon, deposited there by a Mr Emmanuel Rosenbaum. I confess," said the pastor, looking up for the first time, "that I've never seen anything like it before." He folded up the copy of the document and handed it back to Adam.

"Thank you," said Adam. "That has been most helpful."

"I am only sorry that my superior the Bishop is away on his annual retreat because I feel sure he would have been able to throw more light on the matter than I have."

"You have told me everything I need to know," said Adam, but couldn't resist asking, "Are icons at all valuable?"

"Once again, I must confess that I am not the best man from whom to seek such an opinion. All I can tell you is that, as with all art, the value of any object can vary from one extreme to the other without any satisfactory explanation to us normal mortals."

"Then there is no way of knowing the value of this particular icon?" asked Adam.

"I wouldn't venture an opinion, but no doubt the art auctioneers Sotheby's or Christie's might be willing to do so. After all, they claim in their advertisements that they have an expert in every field waiting to advise you."

"Then I shall put their claim to the test," said Adam, "and pay them a visit." He rose from his chair, shook hands with the pastor and said, "You have been most kind."

"Not at all," said the pastor. "I was only too pleased to assist you. It makes a change from Frau Gerber's marital problems and the size of the churchwarden's marrows."

* * *

Adam took a bus up to Hyde Park Corner and jumped off as it turned left into Knightsbridge. He walked through the subway and continued briskly down Piccadilly towards the Ritz. He had read somewhere that Sotheby's was in Bond Street, although he couldn't remember having ever seen it.

He walked another hundred yards before turning left, where he shortened his stride to check all the signs on both sides of the road. He passed Gucci's, Cartier's, Asprey's and was beginning to wonder if his memory had failed him and whether he should check in the telephone directory. He continued on past the Irish Tourist Board and Celines before he finally spotted the gold lettering above a little newspaper kiosk on the far side of the road.

He crossed the one-way street and entered the front door by the side of the kiosk. He felt like a boy on his first day at a new school, unsure of his surroundings and not certain to whom he should turn for advice. Most of the people who passed him went straight up the stairs and he was just about to follow them when he heard a voice say, "Up the stairs and straight through, madam. The auction is due to start in a few minutes."

Adam turned and saw a man in a long, green coat. The name 'Sotheby' was embroidered over his left-hand pocket.

"Where do I go if I want something valued?" Adam asked.

"Straight along the passage, sir, as far as you can go and you'll see a girl on the left-hand side in reception," barked his informant. Adam thanked him, presuming that the guide's former place of work could only have been on an Aldershot drill square . . . He walked along

103

to the reception area. An old lady was explaining to one of the girls behind the counter that her grandmother had left the vase to her several years before and she wondered what it might be worth.

The girl only glanced at the heirloom before asking, "Can you come back in about fifteen minutes? By then our Mr Makepeace will have had time to look at it and will be able to give you an estimate."

"Thank you, my dear," said the old lady expectantly. The girl picked up the large ornate vase and carried it to a room in the back. She returned a few moments later to be faced with Adam.

"May I help you, sir?"

"I'm not sure," began Adam. "I need some advice concerning an icon."

"Have you brought the piece with you, sir?"

"No, it's still abroad at the moment."

"Do you have any details?"

"Details?"

"Artist's name, date, size. Or better still do you have a photograph of the piece?"

"No," said Adam sheepishly. "I only know its title but I do have some documentation," he added, handing over the receipt he had shown the pastor.

"Not a lot to go on," said the girl, studying the German transcript. "But I'll ask Mr Sedgwick, the head of our Russian and Greek Icon department, if he can help you."

"Thank you," said Adam, as the girl picked up the phone.

"Is Mr Sedgwick able to advise a customer?" the girl enquired. She listened for a moment then replaced the phone.

"Mr Sedgwick will be down in a few moments, if you would care to wait."

"Certainly," said Adam, feeling something of a fraud. While the girl attended to the next customer Adam waited for Mr Sedgwick and studied the pictures on the wall. There were several photos of items that had come under the auctioneer's hammer in recent sales. A large painting by Picasso called 'Trois Baigneuses' had been sold for fourteen thousand pounds. As far as Adam could make out the brightly coloured oil was of three women on a beach dancing. He felt confident they were women because they had breasts even if they weren't in the middle of their chests. Next to the Picasso was a Degas of a girl at a ballet lesson; this time there was no doubt it was a girl. But the painting that most caught Adam's eye was a large oil by an artist he had never heard of called Jackson Pollock that had come under the hammer for eleven thousand pounds. Adam wondered what sort of people could afford to spend such sums on works of art.

"Wonderful example of the artist's brushwork," said a voice behind him. Adam turned to face a tall, cadaverous figure with a ginger moustache and thinning red hair. His suit hung on him as if from a coathanger. "My name is Sedgwick," he announced in a donnish voice.

"Scott," said Adam, offering his hand.

"Well, Mr Scott, why don't we sit over here and then you can let me know how I can help you."

"I'm not sure you can," admitted Adam, taking the seat opposite him. "It's just that I have been left an icon in a will and I was hoping it might turn out to be valuable."

"A good start," said Sedgwick, unfolding a pair of spectacles which he had removed from his top pocket.

"It may not be," said Adam, "because I know

105

nothing about paintings and I wouldn't want to waste your time."

"You won't be wasting my time," Sedgwick assured Adam. "We sell many items for less than ten pounds, you know." Adam hadn't known and Sedgwick's gentle voice made him feel less apprehensive. "Now am I to understand you do not have a photograph of this particular icon?"

"That's right," said Adam. "The icon is still abroad, and to be honest I've never laid eyes on it."

"I see," said Sedgwick, folding up his glasses. "But can you tell me anything of its provenance?"

"A little. It is known as 'The Tsar's Icon' and the subject is St George and the Dragon."

"How strange," said Sedgwick. "Someone else was enquiring after that particular painting only last week but he wouldn't leave his name."

"Someone else wanted to know about the Tsar's icon?" said Adam.

"Yes, a Russian gentleman, if I wasn't mistaken." Sedgwick tapped his glasses on his knee. "I checked on it extensively for him but found little that wasn't already well documented. The man wondered if it had ever passed through our hands, or even if we had heard of it. I was able to explain to him that the great work by Rublev remains in the Winter Palace for all to see. One can always be certain that it's an original from the Winter Palace because the Tsar's silver crown will be embedded in the back of the frame. Since the fourteenth century many copies of Rublev's master-piece have been made and they vary greatly in quality and value; but the one he seemed interested in was a copy made for Tsar Nicholas by a court painter circa 1914. I was unable to find any trace of such an icon in any of the standard works on the subject. Do you have any documentation on your icon?" Sedgwick enquired.

"Not a lot," said Adam. "Although I do have a copy of the receipt that was left to me in the will," he added, and handed it over.

Mr Sedgwick once again unfolded his glasses before studying the paper for several moments. "Excellent, quite excellent," he said eventually. "It seems to me that, as long as Roget et Cie will release it, a copy of the Tsar's icon painted by the court painter of the time, belongs to you. But you will have to go and pick it up yourself, that's for certain."

"But is it worth all that trouble?" asked Adam. "Can you give me any idea of its value?"

"Hard to be precise without actually seeing it," Sedgwick said, returning the document.

"So what is the lowest figure I might expect to get for it?"

The older man frowned. "Ten," he said, after considerable thought. "Perhaps fifteen, but with an absolute top of twenty."

"Twenty pounds," said Adam, unable to hide his disappointment. "I'm sorry to have wasted your time, Mr Sedgwick."

"No, no, no, Mr Scott, you misunderstand me. I meant twenty *thousand* pounds."

CHAPTER EIGHT

"A little more caviar, Comrade?" enquired Petrova across the lunch table.

Romanov frowned. His pretence at 'strictly confidential information' only to be passed on at the highest level had merely elicited a knowing smile from his companion who was also not inclined to believe that her boss had a pressing appointment at the Consulate that afternoon, an appointment that he had forgotten to mention to her before.

Anna held out a spoon brimming with caviar and pushed it towards Romanov as if she was trying to feed a reluctant baby.

"Thank you – *no*," said Romanov firmly.

"Suit yourself," said the young woman before it disappeared down her own throat. Romanov called for the bill. When he was presented with the slip of paper he couldn't help thinking that for that price he could have fed a Russian family for a month. He paid without comment.

"I'll see you back in the hotel later," he said curtly.

"Of course," said Petrova, still lingering over her coffee. "What time shall I expect you?"

Romanov frowned again. "Not before seven," he replied.

"And do you have any plans for me this afternoon, Comrade Major?"

"You may do as you please," said Romanov, and left the table without further word. Once on the street, he set off in the opposite direction to the bank, but he doubted if he had fooled the researcher, who was still eyeing him suspiciously through the restaurant window; or the agent, who had waited patiently on the far side of the road for nearly two hours.

By three o'clock Romanov was once again seated in the private room on the fifth floor looked down on by the three photographs of the Herr Bischoffs, and with the fourth Herr Bischoff sitting opposite him and the fifth Herr Bischoff standing behind him.

"We are in possession of . . ." began Herr Bischoff, in the same deliberate, formal way that had dictated the pace of the morning session, ". . . five boxes which have remained unopened since your father visited us in 1945. Should it be your desire to inspect the contents . . ."

"Why else would I have returned?" asked Romanov, already made impatient by the measured voice and studied ritual.

"Indeed," said Herr Bischoff, seemingly unaware of any discourtesy. "Then all we now require is that you sign a disclaimer in order to legalise the situation under Swiss law." Romanov looked apprehensive. "It is only a formality." The Russian still didn't speak. "You can rest assured, Your Excellency, that you are not the only one of your countrymen who from time to time sits in that chair."

Herr Bischoff slid a sheet of paper across the table. There were over twenty clauses of German, all in small print. Romanov scrawled his signature between the two X's with the proffered gold pen. He made no attempt to discover what he was signing. If they hadn't stolen his grandfather's heritage already, why should they be bothering to try now, he considered.

"Perhaps you will be kind enough to accompany me," said Herr Bischoff, quickly passing the sheet of paper to his son who left immediately. He rose and led Romanov silently back to the corridor. But on this occasion they travelled down in the chairman's private lift all the way to the basement.

When the doors opened Romanov might have thought they had entered a jail had the bars not been made of highly polished steel. A man who was seated behind a desk on the far side of the bars jumped up the moment he saw the chairman and turned the lock on the steel door with a long-shafted key. Romanov followed Herr Bischoff through the open door then waited until they were both locked inside. The guard preceded them down a corridor, not unlike that of a wine cellar with temperature and humidity gauges every few yards. The light was barely bright enough to ensure that they did not lose their footing. At the end of the corridor, they found Herr Bischoff's son waiting in front of a vast circular steel door. The old man nodded and the younger Herr Bischoff placed a key in a lock and turned it. Then the chairman stepped forward and undid a second lock. Father and son pushed open the nine inch thick door but neither made any attempt to enter the vault.

"You are in possession of five boxes. Numbers 1721, 1722, 1723, 1724 . . ."

"And 1725, no doubt," interrupted Romanov.

"Precisely," said Herr Bischoff, as he removed a small package from his pocket and added, "This is your envelope and the key inside it will open all five boxes." Romanov took the envelope and turned towards the open cavern. "But we must open the bank's lock first before you proceed," said Herr Bischoff. "Will you be kind enough to follow us?" Romanov nodded and both Herr Bischoffs proceeded into the vault. Romanov ducked his head and stepped in after them. Young Mr Bischoff opened the upper lock of the five boxes, three small ones above two large ones, making a perfect cube. "Once we have left, Your Excellency," said the old man, "we shall pull the door closed, and when you require it to be opened you have only to press the red button on the side wall to alert us. But I must warn you that at six o'clock the vault locks itself automatically and it cannot be reopened until nine the following morning. However, a warning alarm will sound at five forty-five." Romanov checked the clock on the wall: three seventeen. He couldn't believe he would need over two hours to find out what was in the five boxes. The two Herr Bischoffs bowed and left.

Romanov waited impatiently for the vast door to close behind him. Once alone in the Aladdin's cave he looked around the room and estimated there must have been two or three thousand boxes filling the four walls, giving them the appearance of a library of safes. He suspected there was more private wealth in that one vault than most countries on earth could call on. He checked the numbers of his own boxes and stood waiting like an orphan who has been told there will be second helpings.

He decided to start with one of the small boxes. He turned the key and heard the lock click before pulling out the stiff drawer to discover it was full of papers. He flicked through them to find they were title deeds to many large tracts of land in Bohemia and Bulgaria – once worth millions, now controlled by the Socialist State. As he checked each document, the old saying 'not worth the paper they were written on' sprang to mind. Romanov moved to the second box which he discovered contained the bond certificates of companies once managed by His Excellency Count Nicholai Alexandrovich Romanov. The last time they had declared a profit was in 1914. He cursed the system he had been born under as he moved on to the third box which contained only one document, his grandfather's will. It took only moments to discover that it had all been left to his father and therefore he was the lawful owner of everything – and nothing.

Dismayed, Romanov knelt down to study the two larger boxes, both of which looked big enough to hold a cello. He hesitated before placing his key in the lock of the first, turning it and pulling out the vast container.

He stared down in anticipation.

It was empty. He could only presume that it had been that way for over fifty years unless his father had removed everything and there was no reason to believe that. He quickly unlocked the fifth box and in desperation pulled it open.

The box was split into twelve equal compartments. He raised the lid of the first compartment and stared down in disbelief. Before him lay precious stones of such size, variety and colour that would have made anyone who was not royal gasp. Gingerly he lifted the lid off the second compartment, to find it contained pearls of such quality that one single string of them would have transformed a plain girl into a society beauty. As he opened the third box his amazement did not lessen and he understood for the first time why his grandfather had been considered one of the most enterprising merchants of the century. And now it all belonged to Alex Romanov, an impecunious Government official who was already wondering how he could possibly enjoy such riches.

It took Romanov a further hour to go through the contents of the remaining nine compartments. When he reached the last one – almost an anti-climax, in that it contained nothing but gold coins – he felt thoroughly exhausted. He checked the clock on the wall: five thirty. He began to replace the lids on each of the compartments, but during the treasure hunt he had come across one object of such magnificence that he could not resist removing it. He paused as he held up the long heavy gold chain weighted by a medallion, also made of solid gold, that hung from it. On one side was an engraved picture of his grandfather – Count Nicholai Alexandrovich Romanov, a proud, handsome man – while on the other was a profile of his grandmother, so beautiful that she surely could have worn any of the jewellery in that treasure trove with distinction.

For some time, Romanov held the chain in his hand before finally placing it over his head and letting the medallion fall from his neck. He gave the piece one last look before tucking it under his shirt. When he had replaced the lid on the last compartment he slid the box back into place and locked it.

For the second time that day Romanov's thoughts returned to his father and the decision he must have made when faced with such a fortune. He had gone back to Russia with his secret. Had he planned to rescue Alex from the life of drudgery that was all he could look forward to? His father had always assured him that he had an exciting future but there were secrets he was too young to share and he, in turn, had passed that information on to the authorities. His reward a place at the Komsomol. But his father must have taken that secret to the grave because Alex would never have learned of the fortune if it had not been for Poskonov.

His mind turned to the old banker. Had he known all along or was it just a coincidence that he had been sent by Poskonov to this bank first? Members of his chosen profession didn't survive if they believed in coincidence.

A false move and the State would not hesitate to send him to the same grave as his father and grandfather. He would have to be at his most skilful when he next came into contact with the old banker, otherwise he might not live to choose between power in his homeland or wealth in the West.

"After I have found the Tsar's icon I will make my decision," he said, quite audibly. He turned suddenly as the alarm bell's piercing sound rang out. He checked the clock and was surprised by how much time he had spent in the locked room. He walked towards the vault door and on reaching it pressed the red button without looking back. The great door swung open to reveal two anxious-looking Herr Bischoffs. The son stepped quickly into the vault, walked over to the five boxes and made safe the bank's locks.

"We were beginning to get quite worried about the time," said the old man. "I do hope you found everything to your satisfaction."

"Entirely," said Romanov. "But what happens if I am unable to return for some considerable time?"

"It's of no importance," Herr Bischoff replied. "The boxes will not be touched again until you come back, and as they are all hermetically sealed your possessions will remain in perfect condition."

"What temperature are the boxes kept at?"

"Ten degrees Celsius," said Herr Bischoff, somewhat puzzled by the question.

"Are they airtight?"

"Certainly," replied the banker. "And watertight, not that the basement has ever been flooded," he added quite seriously.

"So anything left in them is totally safe from any investigation?"

"You are only the third person to look inside those boxes in fifty years," came back the firm response.

"Excellent," said Romanov, looking down at Herr Bischoff. "Because there is just a possibility that I shall want to return tomorrow morning, with a package of my own to deposit."

"Can you put me through to Mr Pemberton, please?" said Adam.

There was a long pause. "We don't have a Mr Pemberton working here, sir."

"That is Barclays International in the City, isn't it?"

"Yes, sir."

"Mr Lawrence Pemberton. I feel certain I've got the right branch."

The silence was even longer this time. "Ah, yes," came back the eventual reply. "Now I see which department he works in. I'll find out if he's in." Adam heard the phone ringing in the background.

"He doesn't seem to be at his desk at the moment, sir, would you like to leave a message?"

"No thank you," said Adam, and replaced the receiver. He sat alone thinking, not bothering to switch on the light as it grew darker. If he was to carry through the idea he still needed some information which Lawrence as a banker should find easy to supply.

A key turned in the door and Adam watched Lawrence enter and switch the light on. He looked startled when he saw Adam seated in front of him.

"How does one open a Swiss bank account?" were Adam's first words.

"I can't imagine one would find it that easy if all you have to offer is next week's unemployment cheque," said Lawrence. "Mind you, they usually keep a code name for English customers," he added, as he put his copy of the *Evening News* on the table. "Yours could be 'pauper'."

"It may surprise you to learn that it was a serious question," said Adam.

"Well," said Lawrence, taking the question seriously, "in truth, anyone can open a Swiss bank account as long as they have a worthwhile sum to deposit. And by worthwhile I mean at least ten thousand pounds."

"Yes, but how would you go about getting the money out?"

"That can be done over the phone or in person, and in that way Swiss banks don't differ greatly from any bank in England. Few customers, however, would risk the phone, unless they're resident in a country where there are no tax laws to break. In which case why would they need the gnomes of Zurich in the first place?"

"What happens when a customer dies and the bank can't be sure who the rightful owner of the assets is?"

"They would do nothing but a claimant would have to prove that they were the person entitled to inherit any deposits the bank held. That's not a problem if you're in possession of the correct documentation such

117

as a will and proof of identity. We deal with such matters every day."

"But you just admitted that it's illegal!"

"Not for those clients resident overseas, or when it becomes necessary to balance our gold deposits, not to mention the bank's books. But the Bank of England keeps a strict watch over every penny that goes in and out of the country."

"So, if I were entitled to a million pounds' worth of gold left to me by an Argentinian uncle deposited in a Swiss bank, and I was in possession of the right legal documents to prove I was the beneficiary, all I would have to do is go and claim it?"

"Nothing to stop you," said Lawrence. "Although under the law as it currently stands, you would have to bring it back to this country, and sell the gold to the Bank of England for the sum they deemed correct, and then pay death duty on that sum." Adam remained silent. "If you do have an Argentinian uncle who has left you all that gold in Switzerland, your best bet would be to leave it where it is. Under this Government, if you fulfilled the letter of the law, you would end up with about seven and a half per cent of its true value."

"Pity I haven't got an Argentinian uncle," said Adam.

"He doesn't have to be Argentinian," said Lawrence, watching his friend's every reaction closely.

"Thanks for the information," said Adam and disappeared into the bedroom.

The last pieces of the jigsaw were beginning to fit into place. He was in possession of Roget's receipt of the icon originally meant for his father; all he needed now was a copy of the will to show that the document had been left to him. He could then prove that he was the owner of a worthless or priceless – he still had no way of being sure which – copy of the Tsar's icon. He lay awake that night recalling the words in his father's letter. "If there is anything to be gained from the contents of this envelope I make only one request of you, namely that your mother should be the first to benefit from it without ever being told how such good fortune came about."

When Romanov returned to the hotel, via the Russian Consulate, he found Petrova in her room dressed in jeans and a bright pink jersey, sitting in a corner reading, her legs dangling over the side of the chair.

"I hope you had a fruitful afternoon?" he enquired, politely.

"I certainly did," Anna replied. "The galleries in Zurich are well worthy of a visit. But tell me about *your* afternoon. Did it also turn out to be fruitful?"

"It was a revelation, my little one, nothing less. Why don't we have a quiet supper in my room so I can tell you all about it while we celebrate in style?"

"What a magnificent idea," said the researcher. "And may I be responsible for ordering dinner?"

"Certainly," said Romanov.

Petrova dropped her book on the floor and began to concentrate on the extensive *à la carte* menu that had been left by Romanov's bedside table. She spent a considerable time selecting each dish for their banquet and even Romanov was impressed when it finally appeared.

Anna had chosen as an entrée gravad lax edged with dill sauce. Accompanying it was a half-bottle of Premier Cru Chablis 1958. Between mouthfuls Romanov told her of the contents of his family inheritance and as he described each new treasure the researcher's eyes grew larger and larger.

Romanov's monologue was only once interrupted, by a waiter who wheeled in a trolley on which sat a silver salver. The waiter lifted the salver to reveal a rack of lamb surrounded by courgettes and tiny new potatoes. To accompany this particular dish, the hotel had provided a Gevrey Chambertin.

The final course, a fluffy raspberry soufflé, required in the researcher's view only the finest Château Yquem. She had selected the 'forty-nine, which only made her lapse into singing Russian folk songs which Romanov felt, given the circumstances, was somewhat inappropriate.

As she drained the last drop of wine in her glass Petrova rose and, slightly unsteady, said, "To Alex, the man I love."

Romanov nodded his acknowledgment and suggested it might be time for them to go to bed, as they had to catch the first flight back to Moscow the following morning. He wheeled the trolley out into the corridor and placed a 'Do not disturb' sign over the door knob.

"A memorable evening," smiled the researcher, as she flicked off her shoes. Romanov stopped to admire her as she began to remove her clothes, but when he unbuttoned his shirt, the researcher stopped undressing and let out a gasp of surprise.

"It's magnificent," she said in awe. Romanov held up the gold medallion. "A bauble compared with the treasures I left behind," he assured her.

"Comrade lover," Anna said in a childlike voice, pulling him towards the bed, "you realise how much I adore, admire and respect you?"

"Um," said Romanov.

"And you also know," she continued, "that I have never asked you for any favour in the past."

"But I have a feeling you are about to now," said Romanov as she lifted back the sheet.

"Only that if the gold chain is nothing more than a mere bauble, perhaps you might allow me to wear it occasionally?"

"Occasionally?" said Romanov, staring into Anna's eyes. "Why occasionally? Why not permanently, my darling?" and without another word he removed the gold chain from around his neck and placed it over the young girl's head. Anna sighed as she fingered the thick gold rings that made up the chain that Romanov didn't let go of.

"You're hurting me, Alex," she said with a little laugh. "Please let go." But Romanov only pulled the chain a little tighter. Tears began to run down her cheeks as the metal began to bite into her skin.

"I can't breathe properly," gasped the researcher. "Please stop teasing." But Romanov only continued to tighten the chain around her throat until Anna's face began to turn red as it filled with blood.

"You wouldn't tell anyone about my windfall, would you, my little one?"

"No, never, Alex. No one. You can rely on me," she choked out desperately.

"Can I feel absolutely certain?" he asked with an edge of menace now in his voice.

"Yes, yes of course, but please stop now," she piped, her delicate hands clutching desperately at her master's blond hair, but Romanov only continued to squeeze and squeeze the heavy gold chain around her neck like a rack and pinion, tighter and tighter. Romanov was not aware of the girl's hands clinging desperately to his hair, as he twisted the chain a final time. "I'm sure you understand that I must feel absolutely certain that you wouldn't share our secret – with anyone," he explained to her. But she did not hear his plea because the vertebrae in her neck had already snapped.

On his morning run along the Embankment, Adam mulled over the tasks that still needed to be carried out next.

If he took the morning flight out of Heathrow on Wednesday, he could be back in London by the same evening, or Thursday at the latest. But there were still several things that had to be organised before he could leave for Geneva.

He came to a halt on the pavement outside his block and checked his pulse, before climbing the stairs to the flat.

"Three letters for you," said Lawrence. "None for me. Mind you," he added as his flatmate joined him in the kitchen, "two of them are in buff envelopes." Adam picked up the letters and left them on the end of his bed en route to the shower. He survived five minutes of ice-cold water before towelling down. Once he was dressed he opened the letters. He began with the white one, which turned out to be a note from Heidi thanking him for dinner, and hoping she would be seeing him again some time. He smiled and tore open the first of the buff envelopes, which was yet another missive from the Foreign Office Co-ordination Staff.

Captain Scott – the rank already seemed out of place – was requested to attend a medical at 122 Harley Street at three o'clock on the following Monday, to be conducted by Dr John Vance.

Finally he opened the other brown envelope and

pulled out a letter from Lloyds, Cox and King's branch in Pall Mall, informing Dear Sir/Madam that they had been in receipt of a cheque for five hundred pounds from Holbrooke, Holbrooke and Gascoigne, and that his current account at the close of business the previous day was in credit to the sum of £272.18s.4d. When Adam checked through the account it showed that at one point he had, for the first time in his life, run up an overdraft – a situation that he knew would have been frowned upon had he still been in the army, for as little as twenty years before it was in some regiments a court-martial offence for an officer to be overdrawn.

What would his brother officers have said if he told them he was about to remove two hundred pounds from the account with no real guarantee of a return?

Once Adam had finished dressing, he rejoined Lawrence in the kitchen.

"How was the Shah of Iran?" he asked.

"Oh, very reasonable really," said Lawrence, turning a page of the *Daily Telegraph*, "considering the circumstances. Promised he would do what he could about his current financial embarrassment, but he was a bit pushed until the West allowed him to raise the price of oil."

"Where did you eventually take him to lunch?" asked Adam enjoying the game.

"I offered him a shepherd's pie at the Green Man, but the bloody fellow became quite snotty. It seems he and the Empress had to pop along to Harrods to be measured up for a new throne. Would have gone along with him, of course, but my boss wanted his wastepaper basket emptied, so I missed out on the Harrods deal as well."

"So what are you up to today?"

"I shouldn't let you in on this," said Lawrence,

peering at the photograph of Ted Dexter, the defeated English cricket captain, "but the Governor of the Bank of England wants my views on whether we should devalue the pound from $2.80 to $2.40."

"And what are your views?"

"I've already explained to the fellow that the only 240 I know is the bus that runs between Golders Green and Edgware, and if I don't get a move on I'll miss my beloved 14," said Lawrence, checking his watch. Adam laughed as he watched his friend slam his briefcase shut and disappear out of the door.

Lawrence had changed considerably over the years since he had left Wellington. Perhaps it was that Adam could only remember him as school captain and then leaving with the top classics scholarship to Balliol. He had seemed so serious in those days and certainly destined for greater things. No one would have thought it possible that he would end up as an investment analyst at Barclays DCO. At Oxford contemporaries half joked about him being a cabinet minister. Was it possible that one always expected too much of those idols who were only a couple of years older than oneself? On leaving school their friendship had grown. And when Adam was posted to Malaya, Lawrence never accepted the army report that posted his friend as missing presumed dead. And when Adam announced that he was leaving the army, Lawrence asked for no explanation and couldn't have been kinder about his unemployment problem. Adam hoped that he would be given the chance to repay such friendship.

Adam fried himself an egg and a couple of rashers of bacon. There wasn't much more he could do before nine thirty, although he did find time to scribble a note to his sister, enclosing a cheque for fifty pounds.

At nine thirty he made a phone call. Mr Holbrooke

– Adam wondered if he actually had a Christian name
– couldn't hide his surprise at receiving a call from
young Mr Scott. Now that my father is dead, *I* must be
old Mr Scott, Adam wanted to tell him. And Holbrooke
sounded even more surprised by his request. "No
doubt connected in some way with that envelope," he
muttered, but agreed to put a copy of his father's will
in the post that afternoon.

Adam's other requirements could not be carried out
over the phone, so he locked up the flat and jumped
on a bus heading up the King's Road. He left the
double-decker at Hyde Park Corner and made his way
to Lloyds Bank in Pall Mall, where he joined a queue
at the Foreign Exchange counter.

"May I help you?" asked a polite assistant when he
finally reached the front.

"Yes," said Adam. "I would like fifty pounds in
Swiss francs, fifty pounds in cash and a hundred
pounds in traveller's cheques."

"What is your name?" she enquired.

"Adam Scott."

The girl entered some calculations on a large desk-
top machine before cranking the handle round several
times. She looked at the result, then disappeared for a
few moments to return with a copy of the bank statement Adam had received in the morning post.

"The total cost, including our charges, will be
£202.1s.8d. That would leave your account in credit
with £70.16s.4d.," she informed him.

"Yes," said Adam, but didn't add that in truth
it would only be £20.16s.4d. the moment his sister
presented her cheque. He began to hope that the
Foreign Office paid by the week, otherwise it would
have to be another frugal month. Unless of course . . .

Adam signed the tops of the ten traveller's cheques

in the cashier's presence and she then handed over five hundred and ninety-four Swiss francs and fifty pounds in cash. It was the largest sum of money Adam had ever taken out at one time.

Another bus journey took him to the British European Airways terminal in Cromwell Road where he asked the girl to book him on a return flight to Geneva.

"First class or economy?" she asked.

"Economy," said Adam, amused by the thought that anyone might think he would want to go first class.

"That will be thirty-one pounds please, sir." Adam paid in cash and placed the ticket in his inside pocket, before returning to the flat for a light lunch. During the afternoon he called Heidi who agreed to join him for dinner at the Chelsea Kitchen at eight o'clock. There was one more thing Adam needed to be certain about before he joined Heidi for dinner.

Romanov was woken by the ringing of the phone.

"Yes," he said.

"Good morning, Comrade Romanov, it's Melinski, the Second Secretary at the Embassy."

"Good morning, Comrade, what can I do for you?"

"It's about Comrade Petrova," Romanov smiled at the thought of her now lying in the bath. "Have you come across the girl since you reported her missing?"

"No," replied Romanov. "And she didn't sleep in her bed last night."

"I see," said the Second Secretary. "Then your suspicions that she might have defected are beginning to look a serious possibility."

"I fear so," said Romanov, "and I shall have to make a full report of the situation to my superiors the moment I get back to Moscow."

"Yes, of course, Comrade Major."

"I shall also point out that you have done everything possible to assist me with this problem, Comrade Second Secretary."

"Thank you, Comrade Major."

"And brief me the moment you come up with any information that might lead us to where she is."

"Of course, Comrade Major." Romanov replaced the phone and walked across to the bathroom in the adjoining room. He stared down at the body hunched up in the bath. Anna's eyes were bulging in their sockets, her face contorted and the skin already grey. After throwing a towel over the dead researcher's head and locking the door, he went into his own bathroom for an unusually long shower.

He returned and sat on his side of the bed, only a towel around his waist, and picked up the phone. He ordered breakfast which arrived fifteen minutes later, by which time he had dressed. Once he had finished orange juice and croissants he returned to the phone trying to recall the name of the hotel's manager. It came back to him just as the receptionist said, "*Guten Morgen, mein Herr.*"

"Jacques, please," was all Romanov said. A moment later he heard the manager's voice, "Good morning, Herr Romanov."

"I have a delicate problem that I was hoping you might be able to help me with."

"I shall certainly try, sir," came back the reply.

"I am in possession of a rather valuable object that I wish to deposit with my bank and I wouldn't want . . ."

"I understand your dilemma entirely," said the manager. "And how can I be of assistance?"

"I require a large container in which to place the object."

"Would a laundry basket be large enough?"

"Ideal, but does it have a secure lid?"

"Oh, yes," replied Jacques. "We often have to drop them off down lift shafts."

"Perfect," said Romanov.

"Then it will be with you in a matter of moments," said Jacques. "I shall send a porter to assist you. May I also suggest that it is taken down in the freight elevator at the rear of the hotel, thus ensuring that no one will see you leaving?"

"Very considerate," said Romanov.

"Will a car be calling to collect you?"

"No," said Romanov. "I –"

"Then I shall arrange for a taxi to be waiting. When will you require it?"

"In no more than half an hour."

"You will find it parked outside the freight entrance in twenty minutes' time."

"You have been most helpful," said Romanov, before adding, "the Chairman of the State Bank did not exaggerate his praise of you."

"You are too kind, Herr Romanov," said Jacques. "Will there be anything else?"

"Perhaps you would be good enough to have my account prepared so that there will be no delay."

"Certainly."

Romanov put the phone down wishing he could export such service to Moscow. He only waited a moment before he dialled the first of two local numbers. On both occasions his wishes were immediately granted. As he replaced the phone for the third time there was a gentle tap on the door. Romanov went quickly over to answer it. A young porter stood in the corridor, a large laundry basket by his side. He smiled politely. Romanov merely nodded and pulled in the basket. "Please return as soon as the taxi has arrived," said Romanov. The porter bowed slightly, but said nothing.

As soon as the porter had left, Romanov locked the door and put the chain in place before wheeling the laundry basket into the main bedroom and leaving it by the side of the bed. He undid the tough leather straps and threw open the lid.

Next, he unlocked the bathroom door and lifted Petrova's stiff body in his arms before trying to cram it into the basket. Rigor mortis had already gripped the body; the legs refused to bend and the researcher didn't quite fit in. Romanov placed the naked Petrova on the floor. He held his fingers out straight and suddenly brought them down with such force on the right leg that it broke like a branch in a storm. He repeated the action on her left leg. Like the guillotine, it didn't require a second attempt. He then tucked the legs under her body. It amused Romanov to consider that, had it been he who had been murdered, Anna Petrova would never have been able to get him in the basket whatever she had tried to break. Romanov then wheeled the trolley into the researcher's bedroom and, after emptying all her drawers, including Anna's clothes, clean and dirty, her shoes, her toilet bag, toothbrush and even an old photograph of himself he hadn't realised she possessed he threw them in the basket on top of her. Once he had removed the gold medallion from around her neck and was certain that there was nothing of the researcher's personal belongings left, he covered up the body with a hotel bath towel, and sprayed it with a liberal amount of Chanel No. 5 that had been left courtesy of the hotel.

Finally he strapped the lid down securely and

wheeled the creaking basket out and left it by the outer door.

Romanov began to pack his own case but there was a knock on the door before he had finished.

"Wait," he said firmly. There was a muffled reply of "*Ja, mein Herr*." A few moments later Romanov opened the door. The porter entered, nodded to him and began to tug at the laundry basket, but it took a firm shove from Romanov's foot before it got moving. The porter sweated his way down the corridor as Romanov walked by the side of the basket, carrying his suitcase. When they reached the rear of the hotel Romanov watched as the basket was wheeled safely into the freight elevator before he stepped in himself.

When the ground floor doors opened Romanov was relieved to be greeted by Jacques who was standing by a large Mercedes waiting for him with the boot already open. The taxi driver and the porter lifted up the laundry basket and wedged it into the boot, but Romanov's suitcase could not be fitted in as well so it had to be put in the front of the car alongside the driver's seat.

"Shall we forward your bill to the Consulate, *mein Herr*?" asked Jacques.

"Yes, that would be helpful . . ."

"I do hope everything has worked out to your satisfaction," said Jacques, as he held open the back door of the Mercedes for his departing guest.

"Entirely," said Romanov.

"Good, good. And will your young colleague be joining you?" asked the manager, looking back over his shoulder towards the hotel.

"No, she won't," said Romanov. "She has already gone on to the airport ahead of me."

"Of course," said Jacques, "but I am sorry to have missed her. Do please pass on my best wishes."

"I certainly will," said Romanov, "and I look forward to returning to your hotel in the near future."

"Thank you sir," the manager said as Romanov slipped into the back seat leaving Jacques to close the door behind him.

When Romanov arrived at the Swissair office his suitcase was checked in and he waited only moments before continuing on to the bank. Herr Bischoff's son, accompanied by another man, also clad in a grey suit, was waiting in the hall to greet him.

"How pleasant to see you again so soon," volunteered the young Herr Bischoff. His deep voice took Romanov by surprise. The taxi driver waited by the open boot while Herr Bischoff's companion, a man of at least six foot four and heavily built, lifted out the laundry basket as if it were a sponge cake. Romanov paid the fare and followed Herr Bischoff into the far lift.

"We are fully prepared for your deposition following your phone call," said Herr Bischoff. "My father was only sorry not to be present personally. He had a long-standing engagement with another customer and only hopes that you will understand." Romanov waved his hand.

The lift travelled straight to the ground floor where the guard, on seeing young Herr Bischoff, unlocked the great steel cage. Romanov and the two bankers proceeded at a leisurely pace down the corridor, while the giant carried the basket in their wake.

Standing with folded arms by the vault door was another of the partners Romanov recognised from the previous day. Herr Bischoff nodded and the partner placed his key in the top lock of the vault door without

131

a word. Herr Bischoff then turned the second lock and together they pushed open the massive steel door. Herr Bischoff and his partner walked in ahead of Romanov and opened the top lock of all five of his boxes, while the guard placed the laundry basket on the floor beside them.

"Will you require any assistance?" asked Herr Bischoff as he handed his Russian client a personal sealed envelope.

"No thank you," Romanov assured him, but did not relax until he had seen the vast door close behind him and all four of his Swiss helpers left invisibly on the other side.

Once he felt certain he was alone, he stared down at the one large box he knew to be empty: it was smaller than he had recalled. Beads of sweat appeared on his forehead as he unlocked it, pulled it out and raised the airtight lid. It was going to be a tight fit. Romanov unstrapped the laundry basket and removed everything except the body. He stared down at the contorted face, the deep marks in the skin around the neck had turned to a dark blue. He bent over and lifted the researcher up by her waist, but as no part of the body moved other than her broken legs he had to drop her into the box head first. Even then he had to adjust her various limbs in order that the box could be shut: had Anna been even an inch taller the exercise would have proved pointless. He then stuffed the girl's belongings down at the sides of her body, leaving only the Chanel-covered towel behind in the laundry basket.

Romanov proceeded to replace the lid on the airtight box, before pushing it back securely in place and locking it. He then double-checked it could not be opened without his own personal key. He was relieved to find he could not budge it. He hesitated for a moment glancing at the second large box, but accepted that this was not the time to indulge himself: that would have to wait for another occasion. Satisfied that everything was back in place, he closed and strapped down the lid of the laundry basket and wheeled it back to the entrance of the vault. He pressed the little red button.

"I do hope you found everything in order," said the young Herr Bischoff once he had returned from locking the five boxes.

"Yes, thank you," said Romanov. "But would it be possible for someone to return the laundry basket to the St Gothard Hotel?"

"Of course," said the banker, who nodded towards the large man.

"And I can be assured that the boxes will not be touched in my absence?" he asked as they walked down the corridor.

"Naturally, Your Excellency," said Herr Bischoff, looking somewhat aggrieved at such a suggestion. "When you return," he continued, "you will find everything exactly as you left it."

Well, not exactly, Romanov thought to himself.

When they stepped out of the lift on the ground floor, Romanov spotted Herr Bischoff's father with another customer.

A Rolls-Royce accompanied by a police motorcycle whisked the Shah of Iran quickly away, and the chairman discreetly waved his farewell.

When they reached the entrance to the bank, the young Herr Bischoff bowed. "We shall look forward to seeing you again when you are next in Zurich, Your Excellency," he said.

"Thank you," said Romanov, who shook hands with the young man and walked out on to the pavement to find the anonymous black car waiting to take him to the airport.

He cursed. This time he *did* spot the agent he had seen earlier in the hotel.

CHAPTER NINE

"Kill him, sir," the corporal whispered in Adam's ear.

"Not much hope of that," muttered Adam as he bounced into the centre of the ring.

The lean, muscle-bound instructor stood waiting for him. "Let's have a few rounds and see how you make out, sir." Adam bobbed and weaved around the Physical Training Instructor looking for an opening.

Adam led with a left and received a tap on the nose for his trouble. "Keep your guard up," said the sergeant major. Adam led again, catching the instructor a full blow on the chest, but was punished with a sharp left jab into the side of his head. He wobbled and his ear tingled but this time he managed to keep his guard up when a right and left followed. "You're feeble, sir, that's your problem. You couldn't knock the skin off a rice pudding." Adam feinted with his right and then swung a left with such force that when it caught the sergeant major full on the chin he staggered and fell.

The corporal standing by the side of the ring smirked as the instructor remained on the floor. Eventually he managed to get back on his feet.

"I'm sorry," said Adam, his guard up and ready.

"Don't be sorry, you bloody fool . . . sir. You landed

a bloody good punch. A technical knockout, to be accurate, so I'll have to wait for a day or two to seek my revenge." Adam breathed a sigh of relief and lowered his guard. "But that doesn't mean you're off the hook. It's weight training for you now, sir. Beam work and floor exercises."

For the next hour the sergeant major chased, kicked, harried and badgered Adam until he finally collapsed in a heap on the floor, incapable of lifting an evening paper.

"Not bad, sir. I feel sure the Foreign Office will be able to find some niche for you. Mind you," he added, "as most of that lot are about as wet as a dishcloth even *you*'ll have a chance to shine."

"You are most flattering, Sergeant Major," said Adam from a supine position.

"Up, sir," the instructor bellowed. Adam unwillingly got to his feet as quickly as his tired body would allow.

"Don't tell me, Sergeant Major."

"It's the recovery that proves fitness, not the speed," they said in unison.

"Sad day when you left the army," said the instructor to Adam once they were back in the Queen's Club changing room. "Can't name a lot of officers who have put me on the floor." The instructor touched his chin tenderly. "That will teach me to underestimate a man who survived nine months of Chink food. So let's hope the Foreign Office doesn't underestimate you as well."

The sergeant major rose from the bench by his locker. "Same time Wednesday?"

"Can't make it Wednesday, Sergeant Major. I may not be back from a trip to Geneva."

"Swanning around Europe nowadays, are we?"

"I could manage Thursday morning if that suits you," Adam said, ignoring the jibe.

"Your check-up with the quack is next Monday, if I remember correctly."

"Right."

"Thursday at ten then, it will give you a little longer to think about my right-hook."

The Chairman of the KGB studied the report on the desk in front of him: something didn't ring true. He looked up at Romanov. "Your reason for visiting Bischoff et Cie was because they claimed to be in possession of a fifteenth-century icon that might have fitted the description of the one we are searching for?"

"That is correct, Comrade, and the chairman of Gosbank will confirm that he personally arranged the meeting."

"But the icon turned out to be of St Peter and not of St George and the Dragon."

"Also confirmed by Comrade Petrova in her report."

"Ah, yes, Comrade Petrova," said Zaborski, his eyes returning to the sheet of paper in front of him.

"Yes, Comrade."

"And later that evening Comrade Petrova mysteriously failed to keep an appointment with you?"

"Inexplicably," said Romanov.

"But which you reported to Comrade Melinski at the Embassy." He paused. "You were responsible for selecting Petrova yourself, were you not?"

"That is correct, Comrade Chairman."

"Does that not reveal a certain lack of judgment on your part?"

Romanov made no attempt to reply.

The Chairman's eyes returned to the file. "When

you awoke the next morning, there was still no sign of the girl?"

"She also failed to turn up to breakfast as arranged," said Romanov, "and when I went to her room all her personal belongings had gone."

"Which convinced you she had defected."

"Yes, sir," said Romanov.

"But the Swiss police," said Zaborski, "can find no trace of her. So I keep asking myself why would she want to defect? Her husband and her immediate family live in Moscow. They are all employed by the State, and it is not as if this was her first visit to the West."

Romanov didn't offer an opinion.

"Perhaps Petrova disappeared because she might have been able to tell us something you didn't want us to hear."

Still Romanov said nothing.

The Chairman's gaze once again returned to the file. "I wonder what it was that young Petrova wanted to tell us? Who else you were sleeping with that night, perhaps?" Romanov felt a shiver of fear as he wondered how much Zaborski really knew. Zaborski paused and pretended to be checking something else in the report. "Perhaps she could tell us why you felt it necessary to return to Bischoff et Cie a second time." Once again, Zaborski paused. "I think I may have to open an enquiry into the disappearance of Comrade Petrova. Because, Comrade Romanov, by the time you returned to the bank a third time," said the Chairman, his voice rising with each word, "every second-rate spy from here to Istanbul knew that we were searching for something." The Chairman paused. Romanov was still desperate to find out if Zaborski had any real evidence. Neither man spoke for some time. "You have always been a loner, Major Romanov, and I do not deny that at times your results have allowed me to overlook certain indiscretions. But I am not a loner, Comrade. I am a desk man, no longer allowed your freedom of action." He fiddled with the paperweight of Luna 9 on the desk in front of him.

"I am a file man, a paper man. I make reports in triplicate, I answer queries in quadruplicate, explain decisions in quintuplicate. Now I will have to explain the circumstances of Petrova's strange disappearance to the Politburo in multiplicate."

Romanov remained silent, something the KGB had taken several years to instil into him. He began to feel confident that Zaborski was only guessing. If he had suspected the truth the interview would have taken place in the basement where a less intellectual approach to questioning was carried out.

"In the USSR," continued Zaborski, now rising from his chair, "despite our image in the Western world, we investigate a suspicious death," he paused, "or defection more scrupulously than any other nation on earth. You, Comrade Romanov, would have found your chosen profession easier to follow had you been born in Africa, South America or even Los Angeles."

Still Romanov did not venture an opinion.

"The General Secretary informed me at one o'clock this morning that he is not impressed by your latest efforts, distinctly unimpressed were the exact words he used, especially after your excellent start. All he is interested in, however, is finding the Tsar's icon, and so, for the time being, Comrade, he has decided there will be no investigation. But if you ever act in such an irresponsible way again it will not be an enquiry you are facing, but a tribunal, and we all know what happened to the last Romanov that faced a tribunal."

He closed the file. "Against my better judgment and

because we are left with less than a week, the General Secretary has allowed you a second chance in the belief that you will indeed come up with the Tsar's icon. Do I make myself clear, Comrade?" he barked.

"Very clear, Comrade Chairman," said Romanov, and turning smartly on his heel quickly left the room.

The Chairman of the KGB waited for the door to close before his eyes settled back on the file. What was Romanov up to, Zaborski needed to know, suddenly realising that his own career might now be on the line. He flicked down a switch on the little console by his side. "Find Major Valchek," he ordered.

"I've never actually had champagne and caviar," admitted Adam, as he looked up at the beautiful girl who sat opposite him across the table. He loved the way she tied her hair, and the way she dressed, the way she laughed, but most of all the way she smiled.

"Well, don't get frightened, because I can't imagine caviar will ever find its place on this particular menu," teased Heidi. "But perhaps soon when you are the proud owner of the Tsar's icon, that is if Mr Rosenbau . . ."

Adam put a finger to his lips. "No one else knows about that, not even Lawrence."

"That may be wise," Heidi whispered. "He will only expect you to invest all the money you make from the sale in his boring bank."

"What makes you think I'd sell it?" asked Adam, trying to discover how much she had worked out.

"If you own a Rolls-Royce and you are out of work you do not then go and hire a chauffeur."

"But I've only got a motorbike."

"And you'll have to sell that as well if the icon turns out to be worthless," she said, laughing.

"Would you like a coffee to follow?" asked the waiter, who was already clearing their table in the hope of fitting in two more customers before the night was out.

"Yes, please. Two cappuccinos," said Adam. He turned his gaze back to Heidi. "Funnily enough," he continued as the waiter retreated, "the only time I've ever rung Lawrence at the bank the telephonist couldn't immediately locate him."

"What's so surprising about that?" asked Heidi.

"It was as if they had never heard of him," said Adam, "but perhaps I was imagining it."

"A bank that size must have over a thousand employees. You could go years without knowing everyone who worked there."

"I suppose you're right," Adam said, as two coffees were placed in front of them.

"When do you plan on going to Geneva?" Heidi asked, after she had tried a sip of the coffee and found it too hot.

"First thing Wednesday morning. I hope to be back the same evening."

"Considerate."

"What do you mean?" asked Adam.

"To choose my one day off to fly away," she said. "Not very romantic."

"Then why not come with me?" he asked, leaning across the table to take her hand.

"That might turn out to be more significant than sharing your sausages."

"I would hope so and in any case, you could be most useful."

"You do have a way with words," said Heidi.

"You know I didn't mean it that way. It's simply that I don't speak German or French and I've never been to Switzerland other than on a school skiing trip – and then I kept falling over." Heidi tried her coffee again.

"Well?" said Adam, not letting go of her hand.

"The Swiss speak perfect English," she said eventually, "and should you have any problem with the bank, you can always get in touch with Lawrence."

"It would only be for the day," said Adam.

"And a waste of your money."

"Not very romantic," said Adam.

"Touché."

"Think about it," said Adam. "After the cost of your return flight I will be left with only £19,969. I don't know how I'll get by."

"You really mean it, don't you?" said Heidi, sounding serious for the first time. "But women are not impulsive creatures."

"You could always bring Jochen along with you."

Heidi laughed. "He wouldn't fit on the plane."

"Do say you'll come," said Adam.

"On one condition," said Heidi thoughtfully.

"Separate planes?" said Adam grinning.

"No, but if the icon turns out to be worthless you will let me refund the price of my ticket."

"It couldn't be worth less than thirty-one pounds, so I agree to your terms," said Adam. He leaned over and kissed Heidi on the lips. "Perhaps it will take more than one day," he said. "Then what would you say?"

"I would demand separate hotels," replied Heidi, "if it wasn't for the high cost of the Swiss franc," she added.

"You are always so reliable, Comrade Romanov. You fulfil the primary qualification for a successful banker." Romanov studied the old man carefully, looking for some sign that he knew exactly what had been awaiting him at the bank.

"And you are always so efficient, Comrade Poskonov," he paused, "the only qualification necessary in my chosen profession."

"Good heavens, we are beginning to sound like a couple of ageing commissars at an annual reunion. How was Zurich?" he asked, as he lit a cigarette.

"Like a Polish tractor. The bits that worked were fine."

"From that I assume the bits that didn't work failed to produce the Tsar's icon," the chairman said.

"Correct, but Bischoff turned out to be most helpful, as was Jacques. My every need was catered for."

"Your every need?"

"Yes," replied Romanov.

"Good man, Bischoff," said the banker. "That's why I sent you to him first." The old man slumped down into his chair.

"Was there any other reason you sent me to him first?" asked Romanov.

"Five other reasons," said Poskonov, "but we'll not bother with any of them until you have found your icon."

"Perhaps I'd like to bother now," said Romanov firmly.

"I've outlived two generations of Romanovs," said the old man raising his eyes. "I wouldn't want to outlive a third. Let's leave it at that for now, I'm sure we can come to an understanding when the spotlight is no longer on you."

Romanov nodded.

"Well, you will be pleased to learn that I have not been idle in your absence. But I fear my results also resemble a Polish tractor."

The banker waved Romanov to a seat before he reopened his file which had grown in size since he had last seen it. "Originally," the chairman began, "you presented me with a list of fourteen banks, eleven of which have now confirmed that they are not in possession of the Tsar's icon."

"I have been wondering about that – is their word to be taken at face value?" asked Romanov.

"Not necessarily," said the banker. "But on balance the Swiss prefer not to become involved rather than tell a deliberate lie. In time the liar is always found out, and I still, from this office, control the cash flow of eight nations. I may not wield what they would call financial clout but I can still put the odd spanner in the works of the capitalist monetary system."

"That still leaves us with three banks?" said Romanov.

"Correct, Comrade. The first is Bischoff et Cie, whom you have already visited. But the other two have refused to co-operate in any way."

"Why is it your influence does not extend to them?"

"The most obvious of reasons," replied Poskonov. "Other interests exert a stronger influence. If, for example, your major source of income emanates from the leading Jewish families, or alternatively the Americans, no amount of pressure will ever allow you to deal with the Soviet Union." Romanov nodded his understanding. "That being the case," continued Poskonov, "there still has to be an outside chance that one of these two banks is in possession of the Tsar's icon, and as they are never going to admit as much to Mother Russia I am not sure what I can recommend you do next."

The banker sat back and waited for Romanov to take in his news.

"You are unusually silent," Poskonov ventured, after he had lit another cigarette.

"You have given me an idea," said Romanov. "I think the Americans would describe it as a 'long shot'. But if I'm right, it will be the Russians who will get the home run."

"Baseball is a game that I've never understood but I am, however, glad to have been of some use today. Although I suspect you will still need this, whatever your long shot." Poskonov removed a single piece of paper from his file and handed it over to Romanov. On it were the words: Simon et Cie, Zurich (refused), Roget et Cie, Geneva (refused).

"No doubt you will be returning to Switzerland very soon."

Romanov stared directly at the banker.

"I wouldn't recommend you visit Bischoff et Cie on this trip, Alex. There will be time enough for that in the future."

Romanov straightened his fingers.

The old man returned his stare. "You won't find me as easy to get rid of as Anna Petrova," he added.

CHAPTER TEN

The elderly-looking man took his place at the back of the taxi queue. It was hard to estimate his height because he looked so bent and frail. A large overcoat that might have been even older than its wearer reached almost to the ground and the fingers that could only just be seen peeping through the sleeves were covered in grey woollen mittens. One hand clung on to a little leather suitcase, with the initials E.R. in black looking so worn that it might have belonged to his grandfather.

One would have had to bend down or be very short to see the old man's face – a face that was dominated by a nose that would have flattered Cyrano de Bergerac. He shuffled forward slowly until it was his turn to climb into a taxi. The operation was a slow one, and the driver was already drumming his fingers against the wheel when his passenger told him in guttural tones that he wanted to be taken to the bankers, Simon et Cie. The driver moved off without asking for further directions. Swiss taxi-drivers know the way to the banks in the same way as London cabbies can always find a theatre and New York's yellow cabs a westside bar.

When the old man arrived at his destination he took

some time sorting out which coins to pay with. He then pushed himself slowly out on to the pavement and stood gazing at the marble building. Its solidity made him feel safe. He was about to touch the door when a man in a smart blue uniform opened it.

"I have come to see –" he began in stilted German, but the doorman only pointed to the girl behind the reception desk. He shuffled over to her and then repeated, "I have come to see Herr Daumier. My name is Emmanuel Rosenbaum."

"Do you have an appointment?" she asked.

"I fear not."

"Herr Daumier is in conference at the moment," said the girl, "but I will find out if there is another partner available to see you." After a phone conversation in German she said, "Can you take the lift to the third floor?" Mr Rosenbaum nodded with obvious signs of reluctance, but did as he was bid. When he stepped out of the lift, only just before the door closed on him, another young woman was standing there ready to greet him. She asked him if he would be kind enough to wait in what he would have described as a cloakroom with two chairs. Some time passed before anyone came to see him, and the old man was unable to hide his surprise at the age of the boy who eventually appeared.

"I am Welfherd Praeger," said the young man, "a partner of the bank."

"Sit down, sit down," said Mr Rosenbaum. "I cannot stare up at you for so long." The young partner complied.

"My name is Emmanuel Rosenbaum. I left a package with you in 1938, and I have returned to collect it."

"Yes, of course," said the junior partner, the tone of his voice changing. "Do you have any proof of your identity, or any documentation from the bank?"

"Oh, yes," came back the reply, and the old man handed over his passport and a receipt that had been folded and unfolded so many times it was now almost in pieces.

The young man studied both documents carefully. He recognised the Israeli passport immediately. Everything seemed to be in order. The bank's receipt, too, although issued in the year of his birth, appeared authentic.

"May I leave you for a moment, sir?"

"Of course," said the old man, "after twenty-eight years I think I can wait for a few more minutes."

Shortly after the young man had left, the woman returned and invited Mr Rosenbaum to move to another room. This time it was larger and comfortably furnished. Within minutes the junior partner returned with another man, whom he introduced as Herr Daumier.

"I don't think we have ever met, Herr Rosenbaum," said the chairman courteously. "You must have dealt with my father."

"No, no," said Mr Rosenbaum. "I dealt with your grandfather, Helmut."

A look of respect came into Herr Daumier's eyes.

"I saw your father only on the one occasion, and was sad to learn of his premature death," added Rosenbaum. "He was always so considerate. You do not wear a rose in your lapel as he did."

"No, sir, a tiny rebellion."

Rosenbaum tried to laugh but only coughed.

"I wonder if you have any further proof of identity

other than your passport?" Herr Daumier asked politely.

Emmanuel Rosenbaum raised his head and, giving Herr Daumier a tired look, turned his wrist so that it faced upwards. The number 712910 was tattooed along the inside.

"I apologise," said Daumier, visibly embarrassed. "It will take me only a few minutes to bring your box up, if you will be kind enough to wait."

Mr Rosenbaum's eyes blinked as if he were too tired even to nod his agreement. The two men left him alone. They returned a few minutes later with a flat box about two feet square and placed it on the table in the centre of the room. Herr Daumier unlocked the top lock while the other partner acted as a witness. He then handed over a key to Rosenbaum saying, "We will now leave you, sir. Just press the button underneath the table when you wish us to return."

"Thank you," said Rosenbaum, and waited for the door to close behind them. He turned the key in the lock and pushed up the lid. Inside the box was a package in the shape of a picture, about eighteen by twelve inches, covered in muslin and tied securely. Rosenbaum placed the package carefully in his old suitcase. He then shut the box and locked it. He pressed the button under the table and within seconds Herr Daumier and the junior partner returned.

"I do hope everything was as you left it, Herr Rosenbaum," said the chairman, "it has been some considerable time."

"Yes, thank you." This time the old gentleman did manage a nod.

"May I mention a matter of no great consequence?" asked Herr Daumier.

"Pray do so," said the old man.

"Is it your intention to continue with the use of the

box? The funds you left to cover the cost have recently run out."

"No, I have no need for it any longer."

"It's just that there was a small charge outstanding. But in the circumstances we are happy to waive it."

"You are most kind." Herr Daumier bowed and the junior partner accompanied their client to the front door, helped him into a taxi and instructed the driver to take Mr Rosenbaum to Zurich airport.

At the airport, the old man took his time reaching the check-in desk, because he appeared to be frightened of the escalator, and with the suitcase now quite heavy the flight of steps was difficult to negotiate.

At the desk he produced his ticket for the girl to check and was pleased to find that the passenger lounge was almost empty. He shuffled over towards the corner and collapsed on to a comfortable sofa. He checked to be sure he was out of sight of the other passengers in the lounge.

He flicked back the little knobs on the old suitcase and the springs rose reluctantly. He pushed up the lid, pulled out the parcel and held it to his chest. His fingers wrestled with the knots for some time before they became loose. He then removed the muslin to check his prize. Mr Rosenbaum stared down at the masterpiece. 'The Cornfields' by Van Gogh – which he had no way of knowing had been missing from the Vienna National Gallery since 1938.

Emmanuel Rosenbaum swore, which was out of character. He packed the picture safely up and re-turned it to his case. He then shuffled over to the girl at the Swissair sales desk and asked her to book him on the first available flight to Geneva. With luck he could still reach Roget et Cie before they closed.

*　　*　　*

The BEA Viscount landed at Geneva airport at eleven twenty-five local time that morning, a few minutes later than scheduled. The stewardess advised passengers to put their watches forward one hour to Central European Time.

"Perfect," said Adam. "We shall be in Geneva well in time for lunch, a visit to the bank and then back to the airport for the five past five flight home."

"You're treating the whole thing like a military exercise," said Heidi, laughing.

"All except the last part," said Adam.

"The last part?" she queried.

"Our celebration dinner."

"At the Chelsea Kitchen again, no doubt."

"Wrong," said Adam. "I've booked a table for two at eight o'clock at the Coq d'Or just off Piccadilly."

"Counting your chickens before they're hatched, aren't we?" said Heidi.

"Oh, very droll," said Adam.

"Droll? I do not understand."

"I'll explain it to you when we have that dinner tonight."

"I was hoping we wouldn't make it," said Heidi.

"Why?" asked Adam.

"All I have to look forward to tomorrow is the check-out counter at the German Food Centre."

"That's not as bad as a work out with the sergeant major at ten," groaned Adam. "And by ten past I shall be flat on my back regretting I ever left Geneva."

"That will teach you to knock him out," said Heidi. "So perhaps we ought to stay put after all," she added, taking him by the arm. Adam leant down and kissed her gently on the cheek as they stood in the gangway waiting to be let off the plane. A light drizzle was falling out on the aircraft steps. Adam unbuttoned his raincoat and attempted to shelter Heidi beneath it as they ran across the tarmac to the Immigration Hall.

"Good thing I remembered this," he said.

"Not so much a raincoat, more a tent," said Heidi.

"It's my old army trenchcoat," he assured her, opening it up again. "It can hold maps, compasses, even an overnight kit."

"Adam, we're just going to be strolling around Geneva in the middle of summer, not lost in the Black Forest in the middle of winter."

He laughed. "I'll remember your sarcasm whenever it pours."

The airport bus that travelled to and from the city took only twenty minutes to reach the centre of Geneva.

The short journey took them through the outskirts of the city until they reached the magnificent still lake nestled in the hills. The bus continued alongside the lake until it came to a halt opposite the massive single-spouting fountain that shot over four hundred feet into the air.

"I'm beginning to feel like a day tripper," said Heidi, as they stepped out of the bus, pleased to find the light rain had stopped.

Both of them were immediately struck by how clean the city was as they walked along the wide litter-free pavement that ran alongside the lake. On the other side of the road neat hotels, shops and banks seemed in equal preponderance.

"First we must find out where our bank is so that we can have lunch nearby before going to pick up the booty."

"How does a military man go about such a demanding exercise?" asked Heidi.

"Simple. We drop in at the first bank we see and ask them to direct us to Roget et Cie."

"I'll bet your little arm must have been covered in initiative badges when you were a Boy Scout."

Adam burst out laughing. "Am I that bad?"

"Worse," said Heidi. "But you personify every German's image of the perfect English gentleman." Adam turned, touched her hair gently and leaning down, kissed her on the lips.

Heidi was suddenly conscious of the stares from passing strangers. "I don't think the Swiss approve of that sort of thing in public," she said. "In fact, I'm told some of them don't approve of it in private."

"Shall I go and kiss that old prune over there who is still glaring at us?" said Adam.

"Don't do that, Adam, you might turn into a frog. No, let's put your plan of campaign into action," she said, pointing to the Banque Populaire on the far side of the avenue.

When they had crossed the road Heidi enquired of the doorman the way to Roget et Cie. They followed his directions, once again admiring the great single-spouted fountain as they continued on towards the centre of the city.

Roget et Cie was not that easy to pinpoint, and they walked past it twice before Heidi spotted the discreet sign chiselled in stone by the side of a high wrought-iron and plate-glass door.

"Looks impressive," said Adam, "even when it's closed for lunch."

"What were you expecting – a small branch in the country? I know you English don't like to admit it but this is the centre of the banking world."

"Let's find that restaurant before our entente cordiale breaks down," said Adam. They retraced their steps towards the fountain and, as the sun was trying to find gaps between the clouds, they chose a pavement café overlooking the lake. Both selected a cheese salad and shared a half bottle of white wine. Adam was enjoying Heidi's company so much that he began to tell her stories of his army days. She had to stop him and point out that it was nearly two. He reluctantly called for the bill. "The time has now come to discover if the Tsar's icon really exists," he said.

When they had returned to the entrance of the bank Adam pushed open the heavy door, took a step inside and stared around the gloomy hall.

"Over there," said Heidi, pointing to a woman who was seated behind a desk.

"Good morning. My name is Adam Scott. I have come to collect something that has been left to me in a will."

The woman smiled. "Have you made an appointment with anyone in particular?" she asked, with only the slightest trace of accent.

"No," said Adam. "I didn't realise that I had to."

"I'm sure it will be all right," said the lady. She picked up a phone, dialled a single number and held a short conversation in French. Replacing the phone she asked them both to go to the fourth floor.

As Adam walked out of the lift, he was surprised to be met by someone of his own age.

"Good afternoon, my name is Pierre Neffe and I am a partner of the bank," said the young man in perfect English.

"I did warn you that I would be redundant," whispered Heidi.

"Don't speak too soon," replied Adam. "We haven't even begun to explain our problem yet."

M. Neffe led them to a small, exquisitely furnished room.

"I could settle down here," said Adam, taking off his coat, "without any trouble."

"We do like to make our customers feel at home," said M. Neffe condescendingly.

"You obviously haven't seen my home," said Adam. M. Neffe did not laugh.

"How can I help you?" was all the young partner offered by way of reply.

"My father," began Adam, "died last month and left me in his will a receipt for something I think you have had in your safe-keeping since 1938. It was a gift given to him by one of your customers." Adam hesitated. "A Mr Emmanuel Rosenbaum."

"Do you have any documentation relating to this gift?" enquired M. Neffe.

"Oh, yes," said Adam, digging into the map pocket of his trenchcoat. He passed over the Roget et Cie receipt to the young banker. M. Neffe studied it and nodded. "May I be permitted to see your passport, Mr Scott?"

"Certainly," said Adam, delving back into his trenchcoat and passing it to M. Neffe.

"If you will excuse me for one moment." M. Neffe rose, and left them on their own.

"What do you imagine they are up to now?" said Heidi.

"Checking first if they still have the icon, and second if my receipt is authentic. 1938 was rather a long time ago."

As the minutes ticked by, Adam started to feel disappointed, then depressed, and finally began to believe it was all going to turn out to be a complete waste of time.

"You could always take one of the pictures off the wall and put it in your trenchcoat," teased Heidi. "I'm sure it would fetch a good price in London. Perhaps even more than your beloved icon."

"Too late," said Adam as M. Neffe reappeared with another banker whom he introduced as M. Roget.

"Good morning," said M. Roget. "I am sorry that my father is not here to meet you, Mr Scott, but he has been held up in Chicago on business." He shook hands with both Adam and Heidi. "We have on file a letter from Mr Rosenbaum giving clear instructions to the bank that the box is not to be opened by any other than" – he looked at the piece of paper he had brought with him – "Colonel Gerald Scott, DSO, OBE, MC."

"My father," said Adam. "But as I explained to M. Neffe, he died last month and left me the gift in his will."

"I would be happy to accept what you say," said M. Roget, "if I might be allowed sight of a copy of the death certificate and of the will itself."

Adam smiled at his own foresight and once more searched in his trenchcoat before removing a large brown envelope with the words 'Holbrooke, Holbrooke and Gascoigne' printed in heavy black letters across the top. He took out copies of his father's death certificate, the will and a letter marked 'To Whom It May Concern' and passed them to M. Roget, who read all three documents slowly, then handed them to his senior partner, who after he had read them whispered in his chairman's ear.

"Would you object to us phoning Mr Holbrooke in your presence?" asked M. Roget.

"No," said Adam simply. "But I must warn you that he is rather curmudgeonly."

"Curmudgeonly?" said the banker. "A word I am not familiar with, but I think I can sense its meaning." He turned and spoke to M. Neffe, who swiftly left the room, only to return a minute later with a copy of the English Law Society Register, 1966.

Adam was impressed by the bank's thoroughness as M. Roget checked that the number and address on the letterhead corresponded with the number and address in the Year Book. "I don't think it will be necessary to call Mr Holbrooke," said M. Roget, "but we have encountered one small problem, Mr Scott."

"And what is that?" asked Adam, nervously.

"Mr Rosenbaum's position is somewhat overdrawn, and the bank's rule is that an account must be cleared before any box can be opened."

Adam's pulse raced as he assumed that he hadn't brought enough money to cover this eventuality.

"The account is only 120 francs in debit," continued M. Roget, "which is the charge for housing the box over the past two years since Mr Rosenbaum's deposit ran out."

Adam breathed a sigh of relief. He took out his wallet and signed a traveller's cheque and handed it over.

"And finally," said M. Roget, "we will need you to sign a form of indemnity for the bank."

M. Roget passed over a long form containing clause after clause in tightly printed French at which Adam only glanced before passing it over to Heidi. She studied each clause carefully. M. Roget used the time to explain to Adam that it was a standard disclaimer clearing the bank of any liability concerning what might be in the box and Adam's legal claim to it.

Heidi looked up and nodded her agreement.

Adam signed on the dotted line with a flourish.

"Excellent," said the banker. "All we have to do now is go and retrieve your box."

"I suppose it could be empty," said Adam once the two of them were left alone again.

"And it could be jam-packed with gold doubloons, you old pessimist," said Heidi.

When both men returned a few minutes later, M. Neffe was carrying a flat metal box about twelve by nine inches, and some three inches deep.

Adam was disappointed by its modest size, but didn't show his feelings. M. Roget proceeded to undo the top lock with the bank's key and then handed Adam a small faded envelope with signatures scrawled across the waxed seal. "Whatever is in the box belongs to you, Mr Scott. When you have finished, perhaps you would be kind enough to let us know. Until then we shall remain outside in the corridor."

Both men left the room.

"Come on," said Heidi, "I can't wait." Adam opened the envelope and a key fell out. He fumbled with the lock which clicked and then he pushed up the lid. Inside the box was a small flat package wrapped in muslin and tied tightly with string. The knots took some undoing and then finally an impatient Adam tore off the string before slowly removing the muslin. They both stared at the masterpiece in disbelief.

The simple beauty of the golds, reds and blues left them both speechless. Neither of them had expected the icon to be so breathtaking. St George towering over the dragon, a massive sword in hand on the point of plunging it into the heart of the beast. The fire that belched from the dragon's jaw was a deep red and made a startling contrast to the gold cloak that seemed to envelop the saint.

"It's magnificent," said Heidi, eventually finding her voice.

Adam continued to hold the tiny painting in his hand.

"Say something," said Heidi.

"I wish my father had seen it, perhaps it would have changed his whole life."

"Don't forget he wanted it to change yours," said Heidi.

Adam finally turned the icon over and found on the back a small silver crown inlaid in the wood. He stared at it, trying to recall what Mr Sedgwick of Sotheby's had said that proved.

"I wish my father had opened the letter," said Adam, turning the icon back over and once again admiring St George's triumph. "Because it was his by right."

Heidi checked there was nothing else left inside the box. She then flicked down the lid and Adam locked it again with his key. He tucked the muslin round the masterpiece, tied it up firmly and slipped the little painting into the map pocket of his trenchcoat.

Heidi smiled. "I knew you'd be able to prove that you needed that coat even if it didn't rain."

Adam walked over to the door and opened it. The two bankers immediately returned.

"I hope you found what you had been promised," said M. Roget.

"Yes, indeed," said Adam. "But I shall have no further need of the box," he added, returning the key.

"As you wish," said M. Roget, bowing, "and here is the change from your traveller's cheque, sir," he said, passing over some Swiss notes to Adam. "If you will excuse me I will now take my leave of you. Monsieur Neffe will show you out." He shook hands with Adam, bowed slightly to Heidi and added with a

faint smile, "I do hope you didn't find us too cur –
mud – geonly." They both laughed.

"I also hope that you will enjoy a pleasant stay in
our city," said M. Neffe as the lift took its leisurely
pace down.

"It will have to be very quick," said Adam. "We
have to be back at the airport in just over an
hour."

The lift stopped at the ground floor and M. Neffe
accompanied Adam and Heidi across the hall. The
door was held open for them but they both stood aside
to allow an old man to shuffle past. Although most
people would have stared at his nose Adam was more
struck by his penetrating eyes.

When the old man eventually reached the woman
at the reception desk, he announced, "I have come to
see Monsieur Roget."

"I'm afraid he's in Chicago at the moment, sir, but
I'll see if his son is available. What name shall I tell
him?"

"Emmanuel Rosenbaum." The woman picked up
the phone and held another conversation in French.
When she had replaced it she asked, "Would you go
to the fourth floor, Mr Rosenbaum?"

Once again he had to take the fearsome lift, and
once again he only just got out before its great teeth
sprang back on him. Another middle-aged woman
accompanied him to the waiting room. He politely
declined her offer of coffee, thumping his heart with
his right hand.

"Monsieur Roget will be with you shortly," she
reassured the old gentleman.

He did not have to wait long before a smiling M.
Roget appeared.

"How nice to make your acquaintance, Monsieur

161

Rosenbaum, but I'm afraid you have just missed Mr Scott."

"Mr Scott?" the old man uttered in surprise.

"Yes. He left only a few minutes ago, but we carried out the instructions as per your letter."

"My letter?" said Mr Rosenbaum.

"Yes," said the banker, opening for the second time that morning a file which had remained untouched for over twenty years.

He handed a letter to the old man.

Emmanuel Rosenbaum removed a pair of glasses from his inside pocket, unfolded them slowly and proceeded to read a hand that he recognised. It was a bold script written in thick black ink.

> Forsthaus Haarhot
> Amsberg 14
> Vosswinnel
> Sachsen
> Germany
> September 12, 1946
>
> Dear M. Roget,
> I have left in your safe-keeping a small icon of St George and the Dragon in my box 718. I am transferring the ownership of that painting to a British army officer, Colonel Gerald Scott, DSO, OBE, MC. If Colonel Scott should come to claim the icon at any time please ensure that he receives my key without delay.
>
> My thanks to you for your help in this matter, and I am only sorry we have never met in person.
>
> Yours sincerely,
> Emmanuel Rosenbaum

"And you say that Colonel Scott came to collect the contents of the box earlier today?"

"No, no, Monsieur Rosenbaum. The colonel died quite recently and left the contents of the box to his son, Adam Scott. Monsieur Neffe and I checked all the documents including the death eertificate and the will, and we were left in no doubt that they were both authentic and that everything was in order. He was also in possession of your receipt." The young banker hesitated. "I do hope we did the right thing, Monsieur Rosenbaum?"

"You certainly did," said the old man. "I came only to check that my wishes had been carried out."

M. Roget smiled in relief. "I feel I ought also to mention that your account had run into a small deficit."

"How much do I owe you?" asked the old man, fumbling in his breast pocket.

"Nothing," said M. Roget. "Nothing at all. Monsieur Scott dealt with it."

"I am in debt to Mr Scott. Are you able to tell me the amount?"

"One hundred and twenty francs," said M. Roget.

"Then I must repay the sum immediately," said the old man. "Do you by any chance have an address at which I can contact him?"

"No, I'm sorry I am unable to help you there," said M. Roget. "I have no idea where he is staying in Geneva." A hand touched M. Roget's elbow, and M. Neffe bent down and whispered in his ear.

"It appears," said M. Roget, "that Mr Scott was planning to return to England shortly because he had to check in at Geneva airport by five."

The old man lifted himself up. "You have been most helpful, gentlemen, and I will not take up any more of your time."

*   *   *

"It's flight BE 171 and your seats are 14A and B," the man behind the check-in counter told them. "The plane's on time so you should be boarding at gate Number Nine in about twenty minutes."

"Thank you," said Adam.

"Do you have any luggage that needs checking in?"

"No," said Adam. "We only spent the day in Geneva."

"Then have a good flight, sir," said the man, handing over their boarding passes. Adam and Heidi started walking towards the escalator that would take them to the departure lounge.

"I have seven hundred and seventy Swiss francs left," said Adam, thumbing through some notes, "and while we're here I must get my mother a box of decent liqueur chocolates. When I was a boy I used to give her a minute box every Christmas. I swore when I grew up if I ever got to Switzerland I would find her the finest box available." Heidi pointed to a counter that displayed row upon row of ornate boxes. Adam walked over and selected a large, gold-wrapped box of Lindt chocolates which the girl behind the counter gift-wrapped and placed in a carrier bag.

"Why are you frowning?" asked Adam after collecting his change.

"She's just reminded me that I have to be back behind a till tomorrow morning," said Heidi.

"Well, at least we've got the Coq d'Or to look forward to tonight," said Adam. He checked his watch. "Not much else we can do now except perhaps pick up some wine in the duty free."

"I'd like to find a copy of *Der Spiegel* before we go through customs."

"Fine," said Adam. "Why don't we try the paper shop over in the corner?"

"A call for Mr Adam Scott. Will Adam Scott please return to the BEA desk on the ground floor," came booming out over the public address system.

Adam and Heidi stared at each other. "Must have given us the wrong seat allocation, I suppose," said Adam, shrugging. "Let's go back and find out."

They returned downstairs and walked over to the man who had handed them their boarding passes. "I think you put a call out for me," said Adam. "My name is Scott."

"Oh, yes," said the man. "There's an urgent message for you," he said, reading from a pad in front of him. "Please call Monsieur Roget at Roget et Cie on Geneva 271279." He ripped off the piece of paper and handed it over. "The phones are over there in the far corner behind the KLM desk, and you'll need twenty centimes."

"Thank you," said Adam, studying the message, but it gave no clue as to why M. Roget should need to speak to him.

"I wonder what he can want," said Heidi. "It's a bit late to ask for the icon back."

"Well, there's only one way I'm going to find out," said Adam, passing over the bag to her. "Hang on to that and I'll be back in a moment."

"I'll try and pick up my magazine at the same time, if I can find a newspaper shop on this floor," said Heidi as she gripped the brightly coloured bag which contained the chocolates.

"Right," said Adam. "Meet you here in a couple of minutes."

"Roget et Cie. Est-ce-que je peux vous aider?"

"I am returning Monsieur Roget's call," said Adam, making no attempt to answer in French.

"Yes, sir. Whom shall I say is calling?" asked the telephonist, immediately switching to English.

"Adam Scott."

"I'll find out if he's available, sir."

Adam swung round to see if Heidi had returned to the BEA counter, but as there was no sign of her he assumed she must still be looking for a newspaper. Then he noticed an old man shuffling across the hall. He could have sworn he had seen him somewhere before.

"Mr Scott?" Adam leaned back into the box.

"Yes, Monsieur Roget, I am returning your call."

"Returning my call?" said the banker, sounding puzzled. "I don't understand."

"There was a message left at the BEA counter asking me to phone you. Urgent."

"There must be some mistake, I didn't leave any message. But now that you have rung, it might interest you to know that just as you were leaving Mr Emmanuel Rosenbaum paid us a visit."

"Emmanuel Rosenbaum?" said Adam, "but I assumed he was . . ."

"Could you assist me, please, young lady?" Heidi looked up at the old man who had addressed her in English, but with such a strong mid-European accent. She wondered why he had taken for granted that she spoke English but decided it must be the only language he felt confident conversing in.

"I am trying to find a taxi and I am already late, but I fear my eyesight is not what it used to be."

Heidi replaced the copy of *Der Spiegel* on the shelf and said, "They're just through the double doors in the centre. Let me show you."

"How kind," he said. "But I do hope I am not putting you to too much trouble."

"Not at all," said Heidi, taking the old man by the arm and guiding him back towards the door marked 'Taxi et Autobus'.

"Are you sure it was Rosenbaum?" said Adam anxiously.

"I'm certain," replied the banker.

"And he seemed happy about me keeping the icon?"

"Oh, yes. That was not the problem. His only concern was to return your 120 francs. I think he may try and get in touch with you."

"BEA announce the departure of their flight BE 171 to London Heathrow from gate Number Nine."

"I must leave," said Adam. "My plane takes off in a few minutes."

"Have a good flight," said the banker.

"Thank you, Monsieur Roget," said Adam and replaced the receiver. He turned towards the BEA counter and was surprised to find that Heidi had not yet returned. His eyes began to search the ground floor for a paper shop as he feared she might well not have heard the departure announcement. Then he spotted her walking out through the double door, helping the old man he had noticed earlier.

Adam called out and quickened his pace. Something didn't feel quite right. When he reached the automatic door he had to check his stride to allow it to slide back. He could now see Heidi standing on the pavement in front of him, opening a taxi door for the old man.

"Heidi," he shouted. The old gentleman suddenly turned and once again Adam found himself staring at the man he could have sworn he had seen at the bank. "Mr Rosenbaum?" he questioned. Then with a movement of his arm that was so fast and powerful it took Adam by surprise, the old man threw Heidi into the back of the taxi, jumped in beside her, and pulling the taxi door closed, hollered at the top of his voice, "*Allez vite.*"

For a moment Adam was stunned but then he dashed to the side of the taxi and only just managed to touch the handle as it accelerated away from the kerb. The car's sudden momentum knocked Adam backwards on the pavement, but not before he saw the petrified look on Heidi's face. He stared at the number plate of the departing car: GE-7-1-2 – was all he could catch, but at least he recognised it was a blue Mercedes. Desperately he looked around for another taxi but the only one in sight was already being filled up with luggage.

A Volkswagen Beetle drew up on the far side of the concourse. A woman stepped out of the driver's seat and walked to the front to open the boot. A man joined her from the passenger's side and lifted out a suitcase, before she slammed the boot lid back into place.

On the kerb, the two of them embraced. As they did so, Adam sprinted across the road and opening the passenger door of the Volkswagen, leapt inside and slid into the driver's seat. The key was still in the ignition. He turned it on, threw the car into gear, slammed his foot on the accelerator and shot backwards. The embracing couple stared at him in disbelief. Adam jerked the gear lever out of reverse into what he hoped was first. The engine turned over slowly, but just fast enough for him to escape the pursuing man. It must be third, he thought, and changed down as he began to follow the signs to the centre of Geneva.

By the time he reached the first junction he had mastered the gears, but had to concentrate hard on remaining on the right-hand side of the road. "GE712 . . . GE712," he repeated to himself again and again, to be sure it was fixed in his memory. He checked the number plate and the passengers of every blue taxi he passed. After a dozen or so, he began to wonder if Heidi's taxi might have left the motorway for a minor road. He pressed the accelerator even harder – 90, 100, 110, 120 kilometres an hour. He passed three more taxis but there was still no sign of Heidi.

Then he saw a Mercedes in the outside lane some considerable distance ahead of him, its lights full on and travelling well above the speed limit. He felt confident that the Volkswagen was powerful enough to catch the Mercedes, especially if it had a diesel engine. Metre by metre he began to narrow the gap as he tried to fathom out why the old man would want to kidnap Heidi in the first place. Could it be Rosenbaum? But he had wanted him to keep the icon, or so the banker had assured him. None of it made sense, and he drove on wondering if at any moment he was going to wake up.

When they reached the outskirts of the city Adam hadn't woken up as he followed carefully the taxi's chosen route. By the next intersection only three cars divided them. "A red light, I need a red light," Adam shouted, but the first three traffic lights into the city remained stubbornly green. And when one finally turned red, a van suddenly pulled in front of him, lengthening the gap between them. Adam cursed as he leaped out of the car and started running towards the taxi, but the light changed back to green just before he could reach it and the Mercedes sped away. Adam sprinted back to the Volkswagen and only just managed to drive the car across the junction as the light turned red. His decision to get out of the car had lost him several crucial seconds and when he looked anxiously ahead he could only just spot the taxi in the distance.

When they reached the Avenue de France, running parallel with the west side of the lake, both cars weaved in and out of the traffic, until the Mercedes suddenly turned left and climbed up a slight hill. Adam threw his steering wheel over to follow it, and for several yards careered up the wrong side of the road, narrowly missing a post van meandering down towards him. He watched carefully as the taxi turned left again, and in order to keep in contact he veered in front of a bus so sharply that it was forced to slam on its brakes. Several passengers, thrown from their seats, waved their fists at him as the bus's horn blared.

The taxi was now only a couple of hundred yards ahead. Once again Adam began to pick up some ground when suddenly it swerved into the kerbside and screeched to a halt. Nothing seemed to happen for the next few seconds as Adam weaved his way towards the stationary taxi, skidding to a halt directly behind the Mercedes. He then leaped out of the car and ran towards the parked vehicle. But, without warning, the old man jumped out of the taxi on the far side of the car and sprinted off up a side-street carrying with him Heidi's airport shopping bag and a small suitcase.

Adam pulled the back door open and stared at the beautiful girl who sat motionless. "Are you all right, are you all right?" he shouted, suddenly realising how much she meant to him. Heidi did not move a muscle and made no reply. Adam put his arms on her shoulders and looked into her eyes but they showed no response. He began to stroke her hair and then without warning her head fell limply on to his shoulder like a rag doll and a small trickle of blood started to run from the corner of her mouth. Adam felt cold and sick and began to tremble uncontrollably. He looked up at the taxi-driver. His arms were loose by his side and his body slumped over the wheel. There was no sign of life in the middle-aged man.

He refused to accept that they were dead.

Adam kept holding on to Heidi as he stared beyond her: the old man had reached the top of the hill.

Why did he still think of him as an old man? He was obviously not old at all, but young and very fit. Suddenly Adam's fear turned to anger. He had a split second to make a decision. He let go of Heidi, jumped out of the car and started to sprint up the hill after her killer. Two or three onlookers had already gathered on the kerbside and were now staring at Adam and the two cars. He had to catch the man who was still running. Adam moved as fast as he could but the trenchcoat he was wearing slowed him down, and by the time he too had reached the top of the hill the killer was a clear hundred yards ahead of him, weaving his way through the main thoroughfare. Adam tried to lengthen his stride as he watched the man leap on to a passing tram, but he was too far behind to make any impression on him and could only watch the tram moving inexorably into the distance.

The man stood on the tram steps and stared back at Adam. He held up the shopping bag defiantly with one hand. The back was no longer hunched, the figure no longer frail, and even at that distance, Adam could sense the triumph in the man's stance. Adam stood for several seconds in the middle of the road helplessly watching the tram as it disappeared out of sight.

He tried to gather his thoughts. He realised that there was little hope of picking up a taxi during the rush hour. Behind him he could hear sirens of what he presumed were ambulances trying to rush to the scene of the accident. "Accident," said Adam. "They will soon discover it was murder." He tried to start sorting out in his mind the madness of the last half hour. None of it made sense. He would surely find it was all a mistake ... Then he touched the side of his coat, touched the package that held the Tsar's icon. The killer hadn't gone to all that trouble for £20,000 – murdering two innocent people who happened to have got in his way – why, why, *why*, was the icon that important? What had the Sotheby's expert said? "A Russian gentleman had enquired after the piece." Adam's mind began to whirl. If it was Emmanuel Rosenbaum and that was what he had killed for, all he had ended up with was a large box of Swiss liqueur chocolates.

When Adam heard the whistle behind him he felt relieved that help was at hand but as he turned he saw two officers with guns out of their holsters pointing towards him. He instinctively turned his jog into a run, and looking over his shoulder he saw that several police were now giving chase. He lengthened his stride again and, despite the trenchcoat, doubted if there were a member of the Swiss force who could hope to keep up the pace he set for more than a quarter of a mile. He turned into the first alley he came to and speeded up. It was narrow – not wide enough for even two bicycles to pass. Once he was beyond the alley he selected a one-way street. It was crammed with cars, and he was able swiftly and safely to move in and out of the slow-moving oncoming traffic.

In a matter of minutes he had lost the pursuing police, but he still ran on, continually switching direction until he felt he had covered at least two miles. He finally turned into a quiet street and halfway down saw a fluorescent sign advertising the Hotel Monarque. It didn't look much more than a guest house, and certainly wouldn't have qualified under the description of an hotel. He stopped in the shadows and waited, taking in great gulps of air. After about three minutes his breathing was back to normal and he marched straight into the hotel.

CHAPTER ELEVEN

He stood naked, staring at the image of Emmanuel Rosenbaum in the hotel mirror. He didn't like what he saw. First he removed the teeth, then began to click his own up and down: he had been warned that the gums would ache for days. Then painstakingly he shed each layer of his bulbous nose, admiring the skill and artistry that had gone into creating such a monstrosity. It will be too conspicuous, he had told them. They will remember nothing else, had come back the experts' reply.

When the last layer had been removed, the aristocratic one that took its place looked ridiculous in the centre of such a face. Next he began on the lined forehead that even moved when he frowned. As the lines disappeared, so the years receded. Next the flaccid red cheeks, and finally, the two chins. The Swiss bankers would have been amazed at how easily the sharp rubbing of a pumice stone removed the indelible number on the inside of his arm. Once more he studied himself in the mirror. The hair, short and greying, would take nature longer. When they had cut his hair and smeared that thick, mud-like concoction all over his scalp he realised how an Irishman must feel to be tarred and feathered. Moments later he stood under a warm shower, his fingers massaging deep into the roots of his hair. Black treacly water started to run down his face and body before finally disappearing down the plug hole. It took half a bottle of shampoo before his hair had returned to its normal colour, but he realised that it would take considerably longer before he stopped looking like a staff sergeant in the United States Marines.

In a corner of the room lay the long baggy coat, the shiny shapeless suit, the black tie, the off-white shirt, woollen mittens and the Israeli passport. Hours of preparation discarded in a matter of minutes. He longed to burn them all, but instead left them in a heap. He returned to the main room and stretched himself out on the bed like a yawning cat. His back still ached from all the bending and crouching. He stood up, then touched his toes and threw his arms high above his head fifty times. He rested for one minute before completing fifty press-ups.

He returned to the bathroom and had a second shower – cold. He was beginning to feel like a human being again. He then changed into a freshly ironed cream silk shirt and a new double-breasted suit.

Before making one phone call to London and two more to Moscow he ordered dinner in his room so that no one would see him – he had no desire to explain how the man who checked in was thirty years younger than the man eating alone in his room. Like a hungry animal he tore at the steak and gulped the wine.

He stared at the colourful carrier bag but felt no desire to finish off the meal with one of Scott's liqueur chocolates. Once again he felt anger at the thought of the Englishman getting the better of him.

His eyes then rested on the little leather suitcase that lay on the floor by the side of his bed. He opened it and took out the copy of the icon that Zaborski had ordered he should always have with him so that there could be no doubt when he came across the original of St George and the Dragon.

At a little after eleven he switched on the late-night news. They had no photograph of the suspect, only one of that stupid taxi-driver who had driven so slowly it had cost the fool his life, and the pretty German girl who had tried to fight back. It had been pathetic, one firm clean strike and her neck was broken. The television announcer said the police were searching for an unnamed Englishman. Romanov smiled at the thought of police searching for Scott while he was eating steak in a luxury hotel. Although the Swiss police had no photograph of the murderer, Romanov didn't need one. It was a face he would never forget. In any case, his contact in England had already told him a lot more about Captain Scott in one phone call than the Swiss police could hope to discover for another week.

When Romanov was told the details of Scott's military career and decorations for bravery he considered it would be a pleasure to kill such a man.

Lying motionless on a mean little bed, Adam tried to make sense of all the pieces that made up a black jigsaw. If Goering had left the icon to his father, and his alias had been Emmanuel Rosenbaum, then a real-life Emmanuel Rosenbaum didn't exist. But he *did* exist: he had even killed twice in his attempt to get his hands on the Tsar's icon. Adam leaned over, switched on the bedside light, then pulled the small package out of the pocket of his trenchcoat. He unwrapped it carefully before holding the icon under the light. St George stared back at him – no longer looking magnificent, it seemed to Adam, more accusing. Adam would have handed the icon over to Rosenbaum without a second thought if it would have stopped Heidi from sacrificing her life.

By midnight Adam had decided what had to be done, but he didn't stir from that tiny room until a few minutes after three. He lifted himself quietly off the bed, opened the door, checked the corridor, and then locked the door noiselessly behind him before creeping down the stairs. When he reached the bottom step he waited and listened. The night porter had nodded off in front of a television that now let out a dim, monotonous hum. A silver dot remained in the centre of the screen. Adam took nearly two minutes to reach the front door, stepping on a noisy floorboard just once: but the porter's snores had been enough to cover that. Once outside, Adam checked up and down the street but there was no sign of any movement. He didn't want to go far, so he stayed in the shadows by the side of the road, moving at a pace unfamiliar to him. When he reached the corner he saw what he was searching for and it was still about a hundred yards away.

There was still no one to be seen, so he quickly made his way to the phone box. He pressed a twenty centime coin into the box and waited. A voice said, "*Est-ce-que je peux vous aider?*" Adam uttered only one word, "International." A moment later another voice asked the same question.

"I want to make a reverse charge call to London," said Adam firmly. He had no desire to repeat himself.

"Yes," said the voice. "And what is your name?"

"George Cromer," replied Adam.

"And the number you are speaking from?"

"Geneva 271982." He reversed the last three digits:

he felt the police could well be listening in on all calls to England that night. He then told the girl the number in London he required.

"Can you wait for a moment, please?"

"Yes," said Adam as his eyes checked up and down the street once again, still looking for any unfamiliar movement. Only the occasional early morning car sped by. He remained absolutely motionless in the corner of the box.

He could hear the connection being put through. "Please wake up," his lips mouthed. At last the ringing stopped and Adam recognised the familiar voice which answered.

"Who is this?" Lawrence asked, sounding irritated but perfectly awake.

"Will you accept a reverse charge call from a Mr George Cromer in Geneva?"

"George Cromer, Lord Cromer, the Governor of the Bank of Eng –? Yes, I will," he said.

"It's me, Lawrence," said Adam.

"Thank God. Where are you?"

"I'm still in Geneva but I'm not sure you're going to believe what I'm about to tell you. While we were waiting to board our plane home a man pulled Heidi into a taxi and later murdered her before I could catch up with them. And the trouble is that the Swiss police think I'm the killer."

"Now just relax, Adam. I know that much. It's been on the evening news and the police have already been around to interview me. It seems Heidi's brother identified you."

"What do you mean *identified* me? I didn't do it. You know I couldn't do it. It was a man called Rosenbaum, not me, Lawrence."

"Rosenbaum? Adam, who is Rosenbaum?"

179

Adam tried to sound calm. "Heidi and I came to Geneva this morning to pick up a gift from a Swiss bank that Pa had left me in his will. It turned out to be a painting. Then when we returned to the airport, this Rosenbaum grabbed Heidi thinking she had got the painting which didn't make any sense because the damned icon's only worth £20,000."

"Icon?" said Lawrence.

"Yes, an icon of St George and the Dragon," said Adam. "That's not important. What's important is that . . ."

"Now listen and listen carefully," interrupted Lawrence, "because I'm not going to repeat myself. Keep out of sight until the morning and then give yourself up at our Consulate. Just see you get there in one piece and I'll make sure that the Consul will be expecting you. Don't arrive until eleven because London is an hour behind Geneva and I'll need every minute to arrange matters and see that the consul staff is properly organised."

Adam found himself smiling for the first time in twelve hours.

"Did the killer get what he was after?" Lawrence asked.

"No, he didn't get the icon," said Adam, "he only got my mother's chocolates . . ."

"Thank God for that and keep out of sight of the Swiss police because they are convinced it was you who killed Heidi."

"But . . ." began Adam.

"No explanations. Just be at the Consulate at eleven. Now you'd better get off the line," said Lawrence. "Eleven, and don't be late."

"Right," said Adam, "and . . ." but the phone was only giving out a long burr. Thank God for Lawrence, he thought: the Lawrence of old who didn't need to ask any questions because he already knew the answers. Christ, what had he got himself involved in? Adam checked the street once again. Still no one in sight. He quickly stole the two hundred yards back to the hotel. The front door remained unlocked, the porter asleep, the television screen still faintly humming, the silver dot in place. Adam was back on his bed by five minutes past four. He didn't sleep. Rosenbaum, Heidi, the taxi driver, the Russian gentleman at Sotheby's. So many pieces of a jigsaw, none of them fitting into place.

But the one thing that worried him most was the conversation with Lawrence – the Lawrence of old?

The two policemen arrived at the Hotel Monarque at twenty past seven that Thursday morning. They were tired, discontented and hungry. Since midnight they had visited forty-three hotels on the west side of the city, on each occasion with no success. They had checked over a thousand registration cards and woken seven innocent Englishmen who had not come anywhere near fitting the description of Adam Scott.

At eight they would be off duty and could go home to their wives and breakfasts; but they still had three more hotels to check before then. When the landlady saw them coming into the hall she waddled as quickly as possible from the inner office towards them. She loathed the police and was willing to believe anyone who told her that the Swiss pigs were even worse than the Germans. Twice in the last year she had been fined and once even threatened with jail over her failure to register every guest. If they caught her once more she knew they would take her licence away and with it her living. Her slow mind tried to recall who had booked in the previous evening. Eight people had registered but only two had paid cash – the Englishman who hardly opened his mouth, Mr Pemberton was the name he had filled in on the missing card, and Maurice who always turned up with a different girl whenever he was in Geneva. She had destroyed both their cards and pocketed the money. Maurice and the girl had left by seven and she had already made up their bed, but the Englishman was still asleep in his room.

"We need to check your registration cards for last night, madame."

"Certainly, monsieur," she replied with a warm smile, and gathered together the six remaining cards: two Frenchmen, one Italian, two nationals from Zurich and one from Basle.

"Did an Englishman stay here last night?"

"No," said the landlady firmly. "I haven't had an Englishman," she added helpfully, "for at least a month. Would you like to see the cards for last week?"

"No, that won't be necessary," said the policeman. The landlady grunted with satisfaction. "But we will still need to check your unoccupied rooms. I see from the certificate that there are twelve guest bedrooms in the hotel," the policeman continued. "So there must be six that should be empty."

"There's no one in them," said the landlady. "I've already checked them once this morning."

"We still need to see for ourselves," the other officer insisted.

The landlady picked up her pass key and waddled towards the stairs, which she proceeded to climb as if they were the final summit of Everest. She opened bedrooms five, seven, nine, ten, eleven. Maurice's room had been remade within minutes of his leaving but the old lady knew she would lose her licence the moment they entered twelve. She just stopped herself from knocking on the door before she turned the key in the lock. The two policemen walked in ahead of her while she remained in the corridor, just in case there was any trouble. Not for the first time that day she cursed the efficiency of Swiss police.

"Thank you, madame," said the first policeman as he stepped back into the corridor. "We are sorry to have troubled you," he added. He put a tick on his list next to the Hotel Monarque.

As the two policemen made their way downstairs the landlady walked into room number twelve, mystified. The bed was undisturbed, as if it had not been slept in, and there was no sign of anyone having spent the night there. She called on her tired memory. She hadn't drunk that much the previous night – she touched the fifty francs in her pocket as if to prove the point. "I wonder where he is," she muttered.

For the past hour Adam had been crouching behind a derelict coach in a railway goods yard less than half a mile from the hotel. He had a clear view for a hundred yards in every direction. He had watched the early morning commuters flooding in on every train. By twenty past eight Adam judged they were at their peak. He checked that the icon was in place and left his hideout to join the flood as they headed to work. He stopped at the kiosk to purchase a newspaper. The only English paper on sale at that time in the morning was the *Herald-Tribune*: the London papers didn't arrive until the first plane could land, but Adam had seen the *Herald-Tribune* come in on the train from Paris. He made two other purchases at the station kiosk before rejoining the scurrying crowds: a city map of Geneva and a large bar of Nestlé's chocolate.

There was still plenty of time to kill before he could present himself at the Consulate. A glance at the map confirmed that he could already see the building he had marked out as his next place of sanctuary. He steered a route towards it that allowed him to stay in contact with the largest number of people. When he arrived in the square he continued under the shop awnings round the longest route, clinging to the wall, always avoiding the open spaces. It took a considerable time but his judgment was perfect. He reached the front door as hundreds of worshippers were leaving from the early morning Communion service.

Once inside, he felt safe. Notre Dame was the main Catholic Church in the city and Adam found his bearings in a matter of moments. He made his way slowly down the side aisle towards the Lady Chapel, dropped some coins in one of the collection boxes, lit a candle and placed it in a vacant holder below a statue of the Virgin Mother. He then fell on his knees, but his eyes never closed. A lapsed Catholic, he found he no longer believed in God – except when he was ill, frightened or in an aeroplane. After about twenty minutes had passed Adam was distressed to see that there was now only a handful of people left in the cathedral. Some old ladies dressed in black filled a front pew, moving their rosary beads methodically and chanting, "*Ave Maria, gratia plena, Domine teum, Benedicta . . .*" A few tourists were craning their necks to admire the fine roof, their eyes only looking upwards.

Adam rose slowly, his eyes darting from side to side. He stretched his legs and walked over to a confessional box partly hidden behind a pillar. A small sign on the wooden support showed that the box was not in use. Adam slipped in, sat down and pulled the curtain closed.

First he took out the *Herald-Tribune* from his trench-coat pocket, and then the bar of chocolate. He tore the silver paper from the chocolate and began to munch greedily. Next he searched for the story. Only one or two items of English news were on the front page, as most of the articles were devoted to what was happening in America. "The pound still too high at $2.80?" one headline suggested. Adam's eyes passed over the smaller headlines until he saw the paragraph he was looking for. It was in the bottom left-hand corner: "Englishman sought after German girl and Swiss taxi-driver murdered." Adam read the story, and only began to tremble when he discovered they knew his name:

"Captain Adam Scott, who recently resigned his commission from the Royal Wessex Regiment, is wanted . . . please turn to page fifteen." Adam began to turn the large pages. It was not easy in the restricted space of a confessional box. ". . . for questioning by the Geneva police in connection with . . ."

"Au nom du Père, du Fils et du Saint Esprit."

Adam looked up from the paper startled and considered making a dash for it. But he allowed his long-ago training to take hold as he found himself saying automatically, "Father, bless me, for I have sinned and wish to confess."

"Good, my son, and what form has this sin taken?" asked the priest in accented but clear English.

Adam thought quickly, I must give him no clue as to who I am. He looked out through the gap in the curtain and was alarmed to see two policemen questioning another priest by the west door. He drew the curtains tight and turned to the only accent he could ever imitate with any conviction.

"I'm over from Dublin, Father, and last night I

picked up this local girl in a bar and took her back to my hotel."

"Yes, my son."

"Well, one thing led to another, Father."

"Another what, my son?"

"Well, I took her up to my room."

"Yes, my son?"

"And she started to undress."

"And then what happened?"

"She started to undress me."

"Did you try to resist, my son?"

"Yes, Father, but it got harder."

"And did intercourse take place?" asked the priest.

"I'm afraid so, Father. I couldn't stop myself. She was very beautiful," Adam added.

"And is it your intention to marry this girl, my son?"

"Oh, no, Father, I'm already married and have two lovely children, Seamus and Maureen."

"It is a night you must for ever put behind you."

"I'd like to, Father."

"Has this happened before?"

"No, Father, it's the first time I've been abroad on my own. I swear to it."

"Then let it be a lesson to you, my son, and may the Lord find it in his mercy to forgive you this abominable sin and now you must make your act of contrition."

"Oh my God . . ."

When Adam had completed the act of contrition the priest pronounced absolution and told him he must as penance say three decades of the Rosary.

"And one more thing."

"Yes, Father?"

"You will tell your wife everything the moment you return to Ireland or you cannot hope for atonement. You must promise me that, my son."

"When I see my wife, I will tell her everything that happened last night, Father," Adam promised, as he once again checked through the curtains. The police were no longer anywhere to be seen.

"Good, and continue to pray to our Blessed Lady to keep you from the evils of temptation."

Adam folded up his paper, pushed it in the trench-coat and bolted from the little box and took a seat on the end of a pew. He lowered his head and began to whisper the Lord's Prayer as he opened the map of Geneva and began to study the road plan. He had located the British Consulate on the far side of a large garden square by the time he reached 'Deliver us from evil.' He estimated that it was just over a mile away from the cathedral, but seven streets and a bridge had to be negotiated before he would be safe. He returned to the Lady Chapel and his knees. Adam checked his watch. It was too early to leave St Peter's so he remained head in hands for another thirty minutes, going over the route again and again. He watched a party of tourists as they were conducted through the cathedral. His eyes never left them as they began to move nearer and nearer to the great door at the west end of the aisle. He needed to time it to perfection.

Suddenly Adam rose and walked quickly down the side aisle reaching the porch only a yard behind the party of tourists. They shielded him out on to the square. Adam ducked under a shop awning at the side of the road, then walked round three sides of the square to avoid the one policeman on duty by the north corner. He crossed the first road as the light turned red and headed up a one-way street. He kept on the inside of the pavement, knowing he had to turn left at the end of the road. Two uniformed policemen came round the corner and walked straight towards him. He jumped into the first shop without looking and turned his back on the pavement.

"Bonjour, monsieur," said a young lady to Adam. *"Vous désirez quelque chose?"* Adam looked around him. Lissome mannequins in knickers and bras with suspenders and long black nylon stockings stood all around him.

"I'm looking for a present for my wife."

The girl smiled. "Perhaps a slip?" she suggested.

"Yes," said Adam, "definitely a slip. Do you have one in burgundy?" he asked, as he half turned to watch the policemen stroll past.

"Yes, I think so, but I'll have to check in the stockroom."

Adam had reached the next street corner long before she had returned with 'just the thing'.

He managed the next few minutes walk without incident and with only two hundred yards to go could already feel his heart thumping as if it was trying to escape from his body. On the final corner there was only one policeman in sight, and he seemed intent on directing traffic. Adam kept his back to the officer as he could now see the garden square that had only shown up on the map as a tiny green blob. On the far side of the road he spotted a Union Jack hanging above a blue door.

Never run the last few yards, especially when it's open ground, his sergeant had told him many times when on patrol in the Malayan jungle. He crossed the road and stood on the edge of the small park, only fifty yards away from safety. A policeman was patrolling aimlessly up the road but Adam suspected that was only because there were several consulates standing adjacent to one another. He watched the officer carefully. It took the man two minutes to reach the end before he turned and continued his leisurely walk back. Adam ducked behind a tree in the corner of the little park and selected another tree on the far side of the road only yards from the Consulate front door that would shield him from the oncoming policeman. He estimated that by walking at a speed that wouldn't attract attention he could cover the last thirty yards in under ten seconds. He waited for the policeman to reach his farthest point.

He checked the Consulate door again, relieved to see a girl go in and a man carrying a briefcase come out on to the street. There seemed to be no guard in sight as the door remained half open. He looked up at the bay window on the first floor. He could see two men staring out at the park as if waiting expectantly for someone to arrive. Lawrence had succeeded. In moments he would be safe. Adam pulled up the collar of his trenchcoat and set off as the cathedral clock behind him struck eleven. The policeman was now a few paces from reaching his farthest point but still walking in the opposite direction. Adam crossed the road at a measured stride. When he reached the centre of the row he had to stop suddenly to let a car pass by. The policeman turned to start his journey back.

For several seconds Adam remained motionless in the broad street as he stared at the tree he had selected to shield him if the policeman turned before he could reach the front door. He took a confident pace towards the British Consulate. A tall man of athletic build, his head covered in a stubble of short fair hair, stepped out to greet him.

Adam would not have recognised him but for the eyes.

PART TWO

10 DOWNING STREET
LONDON SW1

June 17, 1966

CHAPTER TWELVE

10 DOWNING STREET, LONDON SW1 *June 17, 1966*

When Sir Morris Youngfield left the Prime Minister he still was unable to work out why the possession of any icon could be that important.

Leaving Number 10 behind him, Sir Morris marched quickly into the Foreign Office courtyard and within moments was stepping out of the lift on the seventh floor. When he walked into his office, Tessa, his secretary, was laying out some papers for him.

"I want a D4 assembled immediately," he said to the woman who had served him so loyally for fourteen years. "And ask Commander Busch to join the team."

Tessa raised her eyebrows but Sir Morris ignored her silent comment as he knew he couldn't hope to get to the bottom of this one without the co-operation of the Americans. Once more Sir Morris considered the Prime Minister's instructions. Harold Wilson hadn't needed to explain that he didn't get that many transatlantic calls from Lyndon Johnson seeking his help.

But why a Russian icon of an English saint?

* * *

As Romanov moved towards him, Adam took a pace backwards from the tramlines to allow the tramcar to pass between them. When the tram had passed Adam was no longer to be seen. Romanov snarled at such an amateur trick, sprinted the twenty yards necessary to catch up with the tram and to the astonishment of the passengers, leapt on. He began checking over the faces row by row.

Adam waited for the tramcar to travel another twenty yards before he emerged from behind a tree on the far side of the road. He felt confident he could reach the safety of the Consulate door long before Heidi's killer could hope to return. He checked the other side of the road and swore under his breath. The policeman patrolling was now only a few paces from the Consulate and heading relentlessly towards it. Adam looked back at the tram which had just been passed by another heading towards him. To his dismay, he saw his adversary leap from one platform to the other with the agility of a top-class gymnast. With the policeman now only yards from the Consulate door Adam was left with no choice but to retreat and sprint back up the one-way street. After fifty yards he glanced over his shoulder. The man he knew only as Rosenbaum couldn't have looked less like a helpless old man as he started running towards him.

Adam jumped between the cars and buses and dodged around the milling pedestrians as he tried to lengthen the fifty yards' distance between them. At the first crossroad he saw a plump lady coming out of a phone box a few yards away. He changed direction quickly and leapt into the empty box, crouching into the far corner. The door slowly squelched shut. Rosenbaum came hurtling round the corner and was twenty yards past the box before he realised that Adam had shot back out and down the road in the opposite direction. Adam knew he had at least five seconds before Rosenbaum could hope to see which direction he had chosen. One and two and three and four and five, he counted as he ran along the road. He then checked right, before mounting three steps and pushing through some swing doors. He found himself in front of a small counter, behind which sat a young woman holding a small wad of tickets.

"Deux francs, monsieur," said the girl. Adam looked at the little box, quickly took out two francs and made his way down the long dark passage and through another set of swing doors. He stood at the back waiting for his eyes to become accustomed to the dark. It was the first performance of the day and the cinema was nearly empty. Adam chose a seat on the end of a row that was an equal distance from both exits.

He stared at the screen, thankful that the movie had just begun, because he needed some time to formulate a plan. Whenever the screen was bright enough he checked the little red road on the map, and then using the top of his thumb as a one-inch ruler, he was able to estimate that the nearest border into France was only eight miles away at Ferney-Voltaire. From there he could travel to Paris via Dijon and be back home almost as quickly as it would take him to sit through *Exodus* a second time. Having decided on his route, the next problem for Adam was how to travel. He dismissed all forms of public transport and settled on hiring a car. He remained in his seat during the interval to double-check the routes. The moment Paul Newman reappeared on the screen, he folded up the map and left the cinema by the exit which had been least used during the past four hours.

*   *   *

When Sir Morris entered the room for the meeting of the 'Northern Department', he found the rest of the D4 were already assembled, and familiarising themselves with the files that had been presented to them only an hour before.

He glanced round the table at the specially selected D4, all hand-picked men but only one of them did he consider his equal. And it wasn't the old war-horse Alec Snell who had served at the Foreign Office longer than any of them and was touching his moustache nervously as he waited for Sir Morris to take his seat. Next to him sat Brian Matthews, known in the Department as the 'well-balanced man': a grammar school boy with a double first and a chip on both shoulders. Opposite him was Commander Ralph Busch, the CIA representative with a short fuse, who after five years attached to the Embassy in Grosvenor Square considered himself more British than the British, and even imitated the Foreign Office style of dress to prove it. At the far end of the table, Sir Morris's second in command, who some said was a little too young, although everyone except Tessa had forgotten that Sir Morris had held his job at the same age.

The four members of the committee stopped talking once Sir Morris had settled in his seat at the head of the table.

"Gentlemen," he began – the only lady present being Tessa, whose existence he rarely acknowledged – "the Prime Minister has given this D4 his full blessing. And he requires detailed reports to be sent to him every twelve hours, wherever he is, and at any time of the night or day if there should be any unexpected development. So, as you can see, there is no time to waste. This particular D4 has co-opted as part of its team a liaison officer from the CIA, Commander Ralph

Busch. I have worked with Commander Busch several times over the past five years and I am delighted that the American Embassy has chosen him to represent them."

The man seated on Sir Morris's right bowed slightly. At five feet nine inches, with broad, muscular shoulders and a neat black beard, he looked every inch the sailor whom Player's cigarettes were always trying to please. Indeed, a sailor wouldn't have been a bad guess because Busch had been a commander in PT boats during the Second World War.

"From the latest reports I have received," Sir Morris continued, opening the file in front of him, "it appears that Scott never reached the Consulate this morning, despite our request for the police to have no more than a token force on duty within two hundred yards of the park.

"Since our sketchy information yesterday, BEA have confirmed," said Sir Morris consulting a note in front of him, "that Scott received a call from Roget et Cie while he was at the airport. After considerable pressure from our Ambassador and Interpol we have learned from Mr Roget that the purpose of Scott's visit to the bank was to pick up an unknown bequest from a Mr Emmanuel Rosenbaum. Further checking shows that a Mr Rosenbaum arrived in Zurich yesterday morning and travelled on to Geneva in the afternoon. He left his hotel first thing this morning and has subsequently vanished from the face of the earth. None of this would be of any great significance if Mr Rosenbaum had not boarded the aeroplane to Zurich from –" Sir Morris couldn't resist a short dramatic pause "– Moscow. I think it is not unreasonable therefore to assume that Mr Rosenbaum, whoever he is, works directly or indirectly for the KGB.

"The KGB, as we know to our cost, is well serviced in Geneva, by a large number of East Europeans working under the guise of the United Nations for ILO and WHO, all with the necessary diplomatic status they need to carry out undercover work. What still remains a mystery to me is why Mr Rosenbaum should be willing to kill two innocent people for a relatively obscure icon. That brings my report up to date. But perhaps you have come up with something new," said Sir Morris turning to his Number Two.

Lawrence Pemberton looked up from his end of the table. "Since our meeting this morning, Sir Morris," he began, "I have spoken to Scott's sister, his mother and a firm of solicitors in Appleshaw who administered his father's will. It transpires that Scott was left with nothing of any real importance in the will apart from an envelope which his mother says contained a letter from Reichsmarshal Hermann Goering." There was an immediate buzz around the table until Sir Morris tapped his knuckle on the desk.

"Do we have any idea of the contents of Goering's letter?" asked Sir Morris.

"The whole letter, no, sir. But one of our examination entrants, a Mr Nicholas Wainwright, was asked by Scott to translate what we now believe was a paragraph from the letter because later Wainwright asked the examination board if it was part of his test." Lawrence extracted a piece of paper from the file in front of him and read out the paragraph:

During the year you cannot have failed to notice that I have been receiving from one of the guards a regular supply of Havana cigars – one of the few pleasures I have been permitted, despite my incarceration. The cigars themselves have also served another purpose, as each one contained a capsule with a small amount of poison. Enough to allow me to survive my trial, while ensuring that I shall cheat the executioner.

"That's all?" said Sir Morris.

"I'm afraid so," said Lawrence, "although I believe it confirms what Scott told me last night was his reason for travelling to Geneva. There is no doubt in my mind that the package he went to pick up contained the icon of St George and the Dragon left to his father by Goering."

"St George and the Dragon," said Matthews interrupting, "but that's the icon that half of the KGB have been searching for during the past two weeks and my Department has been trying to find out why."

"And what have you come up with?" asked Sir Morris.

"Very little," admitted Matthews. "But we began to assume that it must be a decoy because the Tsar's icon of St George and the Dragon hangs in the Winter Palace at Leningrad and has done so for three hundred years."

"Anything else?" asked Sir Morris.

"Only that the section leader in search of the icon is Alex Romanov," said Matthews.

Snell gave out a low whistle. "Well, at least we know we're dealing with the First Division," he said.

There was a long silence before Sir Morris offered, "One thing is clear. We have to get to Scott first and must assume that it's Romanov we're up against. So what are we doing about it?"

"As much as we can get away with," said Lawrence. "Along with the Americans we have seventeen men operatives in Geneva, all of them trying to find Scott."

"The Swiss police have a thousand doing the same job, though heaven knows whose side they imagine they're on," added Snell.

Lawrence chipped back in. "And it's been almost impossible to convince them that Scott is not in any way responsible for the two murders. So we may have to get him out without relying on their co-operation."

"But what do you imagine would be the outcome if Romanov or this Rosenbaum, who must also be part of the KGB, manages to get to Scott before we do?" asked Matthews.

"A civilian up against one of the Russians' most ruthless agents. That's all we need," said Commander Busch.

Lawrence inclined his head towards the American. "I've known Adam for most of my life. The irony of his particular predicament is that it was I who, without his knowledge, recommended that he should be interviewed for a place in the Northern Department. It was my intention that he should join us as soon as he had completed his course as a trainee. If Romanov or any of his cohorts come face to face with Scott they'd better remember that he was awarded a Military Cross when faced with a thousand Chinese."

"But if it turned out to be Romanov," asked Snell, "would Scott be able to kill him?"

"I would have said no before Rosenbaum murdered his girlfriend," said Lawrence.

"I wouldn't be confident of his chances even then," said Busch.

"Neither would I," added Matthews.

"That's because you don't know Adam Scott," said Lawrence.

Matthews lowered his eyes in order to avoid a clash with his boss. His boss. Ten years his junior. A shortlist of two and they had chosen another Oxbridge man to be Under-Secretary. Matthews knew that as far as the Foreign Office was concerned, he had gone to the wrong school and the wrong university. He should have taken his father's advice and joined the police force. There were no class barriers there, and he would probably have been a chief superintendent by now.

Sir Morris ignored the little outburst which had become fairly common since he had selected Pemberton to leapfrog the older man.

"Are we allowed to know," interrupted Snell, looking straight at Busch, "why a relatively obscure icon is of such disproportionate importance to both Russia and the United States?"

"We are as mystified as you," said the American. "All we can add to your current information, is that two weeks ago the Russians deposited gold bullion in New York to the value of over seven hundred million dollars without any explanation. We are, of course, not certain at the moment there is any connection."

"Seven hundred million dollars?" said Sir Morris. "You could buy half the countries in the United Nations for that."

"And every icon that has ever been painted," said Matthews.

"Let's get down to what we actually know, and stop guessing at what might be," said Sir Morris turning back to his Number Two. "What's the exact IA position?"

Lawrence undid a folder with a red band around it, the words 'Immediate Action' printed across the top in black. He did not need to refer to it, but still glanced down from time to time to check he had not forgotten anything. "As I have already briefed you, we have seventeen agents in the field and the Americans are flying a further twelve into Geneva today. With the Russians and the Swiss roaming the city like knights of the round table in search of the Holy Grail, I can only believe that someone will come across Scott fairly soon. One of our biggest problems, as I explained, is that the Swiss are unwilling to co-operate. As far as they are concerned, Scott is a common criminal on the run and should they get to him first they have made it clear they will not allow him diplomatic immunity.

"We, as well as the Swiss police, and undoubtedly the Russians," continued Lawrence, "have started checking out all the obvious places: hotels, guest houses, restaurants, airports, car hire companies, even lavatories, and we remain in constant touch with every one of our agents on the ground. So if Scott suddenly appears out of nowhere we should be able to go to his aid at a moment's notice." Lawrence looked up to observe that one of the team was taking down all the details. "Added to that, the Post Office are intercepting every call made to Barclays DCO from Geneva. If Scott does try to get in contact with me again at the bank or at my flat it will be put through to this office automatically," he said.

"Is he aware that you work for the Service?" asked Snell, putting a hand through his dark hair.

"No. He, like my dear mother, still thinks I'm a bank official in the International Department of Barclays DCO. But it won't be long before he works out that that's only a front. Unlike my mother, he doesn't always believe everything I tell him and after our conversation last night he is bound to have become suspicious."

"Do we have anything else to go on?" Sir Morris asked, looking up at Lawrence.

"Not a lot more at the moment, sir. We are doing

everything possible, remembering this is not a home match; but I still anticipate that the exercise will be over one way or another within twenty-four hours. Because of that I have requested overnight facilities to be set up in the building should you feel we need them. When you return after dinner you will find beds already made up in your offices."

"No one will be going out to dinner tonight," said Sir Morris.

The cinema door opened on to the busy pavement and Adam slipped into the main stream of commuters who were now returning home for dinner. As he kept walking he made certain of as little head movement as possible but his eyes never stayed still, checking everything within 180 degrees. After he had covered three blocks, he spotted a red Avis sign swinging in the afternoon breeze on the far side of the road. He safely reconnoitred the crowded crossing, but once his foot touched the far pavement he froze on the spot. Just ahead of him in the fast, jostling crowd stood a man in a raincoat. He was continually looking around, while making no attempt to walk in either direction. Was he one of Rosenbaum's men, the police, or even British? There was no way of telling whose side he was on. Adam's eyes didn't leave the man as he took out an intercom and, putting it to his mouth, whispered into it. "Nothing to report, sir. Still no sign of our man, and I haven't seen any of the KGB either."

Adam, unable to hear the words, switched into a side road and almost knocked over a boy selling papers. '*Le soldat anglais toujours à Genève*' the headline blared. Quickly he crossed another road, where he came to a stop again, this time behind a marble statue in the centre of a small patch of grass. He stared at the building in front of him but he knew there would be no point in his trying to hide there. He started to move away as a large, empty touring coach drew up and parked in front of the block. Smart blue lettering along the side of the coach proclaimed 'The Royal Philharmonic Orchestra'. Adam watched as some musicians walked out of the front door and climbed on to the coach carrying their instrument cases of assorted lengths and widths. One was even lugging a large kettle drum which he deposited in the boot of the coach. As the musicians continued to stream out of the hotel Adam decided he wouldn't get a better opportunity. When the next group came through the double doors he walked quickly forward and stepped into the middle of them before anyone could have spotted him. He then continued on past them through the open hotel door. The first thing he spotted in the crowded lobby was a double bass leaning against the wall. He glanced at the label around the neck of the unwieldy case. 'Robin Beresford.'

Adam walked over to the counter and gestured to the clerk. "I need my room key quickly – I've left my bow upstairs and now I'm holding everyone up."

"Yes, sir. What room number?" asked the clerk.

"I think it's 312, or was that yesterday?" said Adam.

"What name, sir?"

"Beresford – Robin Beresford."

The clerk handed him key 612. His only comment was: "You were three floors out."

"Thank you," said Adam. As he left the counter, he turned to check that the receptionist was already dealing with another customer. He walked smartly over to the lift which was disgorging still more musicians. Once it had emptied he stepped in, pressed the button for the sixth floor, and waited. He felt exhilarated as the lift doors eventually slid across and he was alone for the first time in several hours. When the doors opened again he was relieved to find there was no one standing in the corridor. He made his way quickly along the passage to room 612.

As he turned the key and opened the door he said firmly in as good a French accent as he could manage, "Room service", but as no one responded, he stepped in and locked the door behind him. An unopened suitcase had been left in one corner. Adam checked the label. Obviously Mr Beresford hadn't even had time to unpack. Adam checked the room, but there was no other sign of the hotel guest apart from a piece of paper on the side table. It was a typed itinerary:

'European Tour: Geneva, Frankfurt, Berlin, Amsterdam, London.

'Geneva, Bus 5.00 to Concert Hall rehearsal 6.00, Concert performance 7.30, encores 10.00.

'Programme: Mozart's Third Horn Concerto, First Movement, Brahms's Second Symphony, Schubert's Unfinished Symphony.'

Adam looked at his watch: by the time Robin Beresford had completed the 'Unfinished Symphony' he would be over the border; but he still felt safe to remain in Room 612 until it was dark.

He picked up the phone by the bed and dialled room service. "Beresford, 612," he announced, and ordered himself some dinner before going into the bathroom. On the side of the basin was propped a little plastic bag with the words 'Compliments of the Management' printed across it. Inside Adam found soap, a tiny toothbrush, toothpaste and a plastic razor.

He had just finished shaving when he heard a knock on the door and someone calling "Room service". Adam quickly covered his face with lather again and put on a hotel dressing gown before he opened the door. The waiter set up a table without giving Adam a second look. When he had finished his task he enquired, "Will you sign the bill, please, sir?"

He handed Adam a slip of paper. He signed it 'Robin Beresford' and added a fifteen per cent tip.

"Thank you," said the waiter and left. As soon as the door closed behind him Adam's eyes settled on the feast of onion soup, rump steak with green beans and potatoes, and finally a raspberry sorbet. A bottle of house wine had been uncorked and needed only to be poured. He suddenly didn't feel that hungry.

He still couldn't accept what he had gone through. If only he hadn't pressed Heidi into joining him on this unnecessary journey. A week before she hadn't even known him and now he was responsible for her death. He would have to explain to her parents what had happened to their only daughter. But before Adam could face them he still had to come up with some explanation for the things he hadn't yet begun to understand. Not least the unimportant icon. Unimportant?

After he had half finished the meal he wheeled the trolley out into the corridor and placed the 'Do not disturb' sign on the door. Once back in the bedroom he stared out of the window over the city. The sun looked as if it had another hour allocated for Geneva. Adam lay down on the bed and began to consider what had happened in the last twenty-four hours of his life.

"Antarctic is in possession of an icon of St George and the Dragon. But we know from our files of that period that that particular icon was destroyed when the Grand Duke of Hesse's plane crashed over Belgium in 1937."

"That may well be what is written in your files," said the man on the other end of the phone. "But what if your information at Langley turns out to be wrong and the icon was found by Goering but not returned to the Grand Duke?"

"But Stalin confirmed at Yalta that the icon and its contents had been destroyed in the plane crash. He agreed to make no protest while he was not in possession of the original document. After all, that was the reason Roosevelt appeared to be gaining so little at the time while Stalin was getting so much in return. Can't you remember the fuss Churchill made?"

"I certainly can because he had worked out that it wasn't Britain who was going to benefit from such a decision."

"But if the Russians have now discovered the existence of the original icon?"

"You are suggesting they might also get their hands on the original document?"

"Precisely. So you must be sure to get to Antarctic before the Russians do, or for that matter, the Foreign Office."

"But I'm part of the Foreign Office team."

"And that's precisely what we want the Foreign Office to go on believing."

"And who's been sleeping in my bed, said Mother Bear."

Adam woke with a start. Looking down at him was a girl who held a double bass firmly by the neck with one hand and a bow in the other. She was nearly six foot and certainly weighed considerably more than Adam. She had long, gleaming red hair that was in such contrast to the rest of her that it was as if the Maker had started at the top and quickly lost interest.

She wore a white blouse and a black flowing skirt that stopped an inch above the ground.

"Who are you?" asked Adam, startled.

"I'm not Goldilocks, that's for sure," parried the girl. "More to the point, who are you?"

Adam hesitated. "If I told you, you wouldn't believe me."

"I can't imagine why not," she said. "You don't look like Prince Charles or Elvis Presley to me, so go on, try me."

"I'm Adam Scott."

"Am I meant to swoon and run to your side, or scream and run away?" she enquired.

Adam suddenly realised that the girl couldn't have watched television or read a paper for at least two days. He switched tactics. "I thought my friend Robin Beresford was meant to be booked into this room," he said confidently.

"And so did I until I saw you on my bed."

"You're Robin Beresford?"

"You're quite sharp for someone who has just woken up."

"But Robin?"

"It's not my fault my father wanted a boy," she said. "And you still haven't explained what you're doing on my bed."

"Is there any hope of you listening to me for five minutes without continually interrupting?" asked Adam.

"Yes, but don't bother with any more fairy stories," said Robin. "My father was a born liar, and by the time I was twelve I could see through him like a pane of glass."

"I should have a seat if I were you," said Adam. "This may take longer than the average double bass accompaniment."

"I'll remain on my feet, if you don't mind," said Robin. "At least until the first lie."

"Suit yourself. What would you like first? The good news or the bad news?"

"Try me on the bad news," said Robin.

"The Swiss police want to arrest me and . . ."

"What for?" interrupted Robin.

"Murder," said Scott.

"What's the good news?" she asked.

"I'm innocent."

Romanov stood in the Ambassador's office and rested his fingers on the table. "I blame myself," he said very quietly, "even more than I blame any of you. I underestimated the Englishman. He's good, and if any of you are hoping to kill him before I get to him you'll have to be *very* good." No one assembled in the Ambassador's office that night was disposed to disagree with the Comrade Major. Romanov paused to study the group of men who had been flown in from several Eastern satellites at short notice. All with long records of service to the State but only one of them, Valchek, was known to Romanov personally and he worked too closely with Zaborski to be trusted. Romanov had already faced the fact that only a few of them were acquainted with Geneva. He could only pray that the British and Americans were suffering from the same problem.

His eyes swept around the room. The Swiss police had the best chance of finding Scott and they weren't being at all helpful, he thought ruefully. However, Romanov had been pleased to learn from their head man stationed in Geneva that the Swiss had also refused to co-operate with the British or the Americans.

"Comrades," he said, the moment they had all

settled, "there is no need to remind you that we have been entrusted with a vital assignment for the Motherland." He paused to check if any of the faces registered the slightest suggestion of cynicism. Satisfied, he continued, "We will therefore maintain a tight surveillance over Geneva in case Scott is still holed up somewhere in the city. My own guess is that, like all amateurs, he is, and will wait until it's dark, perhaps even first light, before he makes a run for the nearest border. The French border will be his most obvious choice. Despite going to war against the Germans twice in the past fifty years, the English have never bothered to master the German language, although a few of them can manage to speak passable French. So he's more likely to feel safe in that country. It also offers him the opportunity to cross only one border before reaching the coast.

"If he's stupid enough to try and leave by plane he will find we have the airports covered; if by train, we have the stations manned. But my guess is still that he will try to escape by motor vehicle.

"I shall therefore take five men to the French border with me while Major Valchek will take another five to Basle to cover the German crossing point. The rest of you will remain on surveillance in Geneva. Those of you who have just arrived will relieve those agents who are in the field already. And don't expect Scott to be roaming around looking like a tourist on holiday. Study your picture of the Englishman carefully and even be prepared for him to try and get away with some amateur disguise."

Romanov paused for effect. "The man who brings me the Tsar's icon need have no fear for his future prosperity when we return home." Hopeful expressions appeared on their faces for the first time as Romanov pulled out the duplicate icon from his coat pocket and held it high above his head for all to see.

"When you find the original of this your task will be completed. Study it carefully, Comrades, because no photographs are being issued. And remember," Romanov added, "the only difference between this and Scott's icon is that his has a small silver crown embedded in the back of the frame. Once you see the crown you will know that you have found the missing masterpiece."

Romanov put the icon back in his pocket and looked down at the silent men.

"Remember that Scott is good but he's not that good."

CHAPTER THIRTEEN

"You're not bad, Scott, not bad at all," said Robin, who had remained standing by the double bass throughout Adam's story. "Either you're one hell of a liar, or I've lost my touch." Adam smiled up at the massive girl, who made the bow she was holding in her right hand look like a toothpick.

"Am I permitted to see this icon, or am I just supposed to take your word for it?"

Adam jumped off the bed and pulled out the package containing the Tsar's icon from the map pocket of his trenchcoat. Robin put her double bass up against the wall and leaving the bow propped against it, lowered herself into the only chair in the room.

Adam handed the icon over to her. For some time, she stared at the face of St George without making any comment. "It's magnificent," she said at last. "And I can understand anyone wanting to possess it. But no painting could be worth the tragedy and trouble you've had to go through."

"I agree it's inexplicable," said Adam. "But Rosenbaum or whatever his real name is has been willing to kill twice to get his hands on the piece, and he's already convinced me that as long as I am in possession of the icon then I'll be the next in line."

Robin continued to stare at the tiny pieces of gold, red, blue and yellow that made up St George and the Dragon.

"No other clues?" she asked, looking up.

"Only the letter given to my father by Goering."

Robin turned the painting over. "What does that mean?" she asked, pointing to the tiny silver crown embedded in the wood.

"That proves it was once owned by a Tsar, according to the man from Sotheby's. And greatly enhances its value, he assured me."

"Still couldn't be worth killing for," said Robin. She handed the icon back to Adam. "So what other secret is St George keeping to himself?"

Adam shrugged and frowned, having asked himself the same question again and again since Heidi's death. He returned the silent saint to his trenchcoat.

"What was to have been your plan if you had stayed awake?" asked Robin. "Other than making the bed?"

Adam smiled. "I hoped to call Lawrence again once I could be sure he had returned home and check if he had any more news for me. If he wasn't back, or couldn't help, I was going to hire a car and try to get across the Swiss border to France and then on to England. I felt sure that between Rosenbaum and his men and the Swiss police they would have had all the airports and stations fully covered."

"No doubt Rosenbaum will have also thought that much out as well, if he's half as good as you claim," said Robin. "So we'd better try and get in touch with your friend Lawrence and see if he's come up with any bright ideas." She pushed herself up out of the chair and walked across to the phone.

"You don't have to get yourself involved," said Adam hesitantly.

"I am involved," said Robin. "And I can tell you it's far more exciting than Schubert's Unfinished. Once I've got your friend on the line I'll pass him over to you and then no one will realise who's phoning." Adam told her the number of the flat and she asked the girl on the switchboard to connect her.

Adam checked his watch: eleven forty. Surely Lawrence would be home by now? The phone didn't complete its first two rings before Robin heard a man's voice on the line. She immediately handed the receiver over.

"Hello, who is that?" asked the voice. Adam was reminded how strange he always found it that Lawrence never announced his name.

"Lawrence, it's me."

"Where are you?"

"I'm still in Geneva."

"My clients were waiting for you at eleven o'clock this morning."

"So was Rosenbaum."

"Who is Rosenbaum?"

"A six-foot, fair-haired, blue-eyed monster, who seems determined to kill me."

Lawrence did not speak for some time. "And are you still in possession of our patron saint?"

"Yes, I am," said Adam. "But what can be so important about . . ."

"Put the phone down and ring me back again in three minutes."

The line went dead. Adam couldn't fathom the sudden change in his old friend's manner. What had he missed during those months he had lodged with him? He tried to recall details that he had previously considered unimportant and that Lawrence had so skilfully disguised.

"Is everything all right?" asked Robin, breaking into his thoughts.

"I think so," said Adam, a little mystified. "He wants me to ring back in three minutes. Will that be all right with you?"

"This tour's already lost eight thousand pounds of the taxpayers' money, so what difference can a few international calls make?" she said.

Three minutes later, Robin picked up the receiver and repeated the number. In one ring Lawrence was back on the line.

"Only answer my questions," said Lawrence.

"No, I will not answer your questions," said Adam, becoming increasingly annoyed with Lawrence's manner. "I want one or two of my own answered before you get anything more out of me. Do I make myself clear?"

"Yes," said a more gentle sounding Lawrence.

"Who is Rosenbaum?"

Lawrence didn't immediately reply.

"You'll get nothing further from me until you start telling the truth," said Adam.

"From your description I have every reason to believe Rosenbaum is a Russian agent whose real name is Alex Romanov."

"A Russian agent? But why should a Russian agent want to get his hands on my icon?"

"I don't know," said Lawrence. "We were rather hoping you might be able to tell us."

"Who's we?"

Another long silence.

"Who's we?" repeated Adam. "You can't really expect me to go on believing you work for Barclays DCO."

"I work at the Foreign Office," said Lawrence.

"In what capacity?"

"I am not at liberty . . ."

"Stop being so pompous, Lawrence. In what capacity?"

"I'm the Number Two in a small section that deals in . . ." Lawrence hesitated.

"Espionage I think is the current jargon we laymen are using," said Adam, "and if you want my icon that badly you had better get me out of this mess alive because Romanov is willing to kill for it as I am sure you are aware."

"Where are you?"

"The Richemond Hotel."

"In a public phone box?" asked Lawrence, sounding incredulous.

"No, in a private room."

"But not registered in your name?"

"No, in the name of a friend. A girlfriend."

"Is she with you now?" asked Lawrence.

"Yes," said Adam.

"Damn," said Lawrence. "Right. Don't leave that room until seven a.m., then phone on this number again. That will give me enough time to get everything in place."

"Is that the best you can do?" said Adam, but the phone had already gone dead. "It looks as if I'm stuck with you for the night," he told Robin as he replaced the phone.

"On the contrary, it is I who am stuck with you," said Robin, and disappeared into the bathroom. Adam paced around the room several times before he tested the sofa. Either he had to rest his head on a cushion, balanced on the thin wooden arm, or he had to let his legs dangle over the far end. By the time Robin had come back out clad in a pair of sky-blue pyjamas he had selected the floor as his resting place.

"Not much of a chair, is it?" said Robin. "But then British Intelligence didn't warn me to book a double room." She climbed into the bed and turned out the light. "Very comfortable," were the last words she uttered.

Adam lay down flat on the bedroom floor, using the cushion from the chair as a pillow and a hotel dressing gown as a blanket. He slept intermittently, his mind switching between why the icon could be that important, how Lawrence knew so much about it, and, most immediate, how the hell were they going to get him out of the hotel alive?

Romanov waited patiently for the phone to be picked up.

"Yes," said a voice that he recognised immediately.

"Where is he?" were the only words Romanov uttered. Four words were all he received from Mentor in reply before the phone went dead.

Adam woke with a start an hour before he was due to phone Lawrence back. For nearly forty minutes he lay on the floor with only Robin's steady breathing to remind him he was not alone. Suddenly he became aware of a strange sound coming from the corridor outside – two or three steps, a pause, then whoosh, two or three steps, a pause, another whoosh. Adam raised himself up silently from the floor and crept to the door. The rhythm of Robin's breathing never faltered. Whoosh: it now sounded closer. He picked up a heavy wooden coathanger from the table by the door. He gripped it firmly in his right hand, raised it above his head and waited. Whoosh – and a newspaper shot under the door and the steps moved on. He didn't have to bend down to see that it was his photograph that dominated the front page of the international edition of the *Herald Tribune*.

Adam took the paper into the bathroom, closed the door silently, switched on the light and read the lead article. It was yesterday's story with guarded comments from his old commanding officer and embarrassed silence from his mother. He felt helpless.

He crept up to Robin hoping she wouldn't wake. He stood over her but she didn't stir. He silently picked up the phone and dragged it to the bathroom. He could only just manage to close the door behind him. He dialled the operator and repeated the number.

When the ringing stopped, he immediately said, "Is that you, Lawrence?"

"Yes," came back the reply.

"Things have become much worse now. I'm still holed up in the hotel but my picture is on the front page of every paper."

"I know," said Lawrence. "We tried to prevent it, but yet again the Swiss wouldn't co-operate."

"Then I may as well give myself up to the Swiss," said Adam. "Damn it all, I am innocent."

"No, Adam, in Switzerland you're guilty until proven innocent and you must have worked out by now that you're involved in something far more important than a double murder."

"What could be more important than a double murder when the rest of the world thinks you're the murderer?" asked Adam angrily.

"I can understand exactly how you feel, but your only chance now is to carry out my instructions to the letter and treat with suspicion every other person with whom you come in contact."

"I'm listening," said Adam.

"Just remember everything I say because I am only going to tell you once. The Royal Philharmonic Orchestra are staying in the same hotel as you. They are going on to Frankfurt at ten o'clock this morning. Leave your room at five to ten, join the orchestra in the lobby and then make your way to the front door where you'll find their coach parked. We will have a car waiting for you on the far side of the road. The car is a black Mercedes and you will see a man in grey chauffeur's uniform holding the door open for you. We have already arranged that no other car will be able to park on that side of the road between nine thirty and ten thirty, so you can't mistake it. Just get into the back and wait. There will be another man in the back with you and you will then be driven to the safety of our Consulate. Do you need me to repeat any of that?"

"No," said Adam, "but . . ."

"Good luck," said Lawrence, and the phone went dead.

By seven-thirty he had showered, while Robin remained unrepentant in a deep sleep. Adam envied her; only a twig had to break outside and he was wide awake. Two years of living in the Malayan jungle, never knowing when the Chinese would strike, never being able to sleep for more than two or three hours at a time if one wanted to stay alive, still kept its hold on him.

Robin did not stir for another thirty minutes, during which time Adam sat on the sofa and went over Lawrence's plan in his mind. At ten to eight she finally woke, even then taking several minutes before she was fully conscious. Robin blinked at Adam and a large grin appeared on her face.

"So you didn't murder me while I slept," she said.

"I don't think you'd have noticed if I had," said Adam.

"When your father is an habitual drunk and comes home at all hours of the night, you learn to sleep through anything," she explained, placing both feet firmly on the carpet. "Aren't you meant to have phoned London by now?"

"I already have."

"And what is the master plan to be?" she asked, rubbing her eyes on her way to the bathroom.

"I will be leaving with you," said Adam.

"Most of my one-night stands don't bother to stay that long," she remarked as she closed the bathroom door behind her. He tried to read the paper while the bath was filling up.

"Does that mean we're sharing a room in Frankfurt as well?" she asked a few minutes later when the bathroom door reopened, as if the conversation had never been interrupted.

"No, as soon as we're clear of the hotel I leave you at the coach and make my own way to a car on the far side of the road."

"That sounds more like the men in my life," she said. "But at least we can have a farewell breakfast," she added, picking up the phone. "I'm nuts about kippers. How about you?"

Adam didn't answer. He had begun looking at his watch every few moments. The waiter arrived with breakfast about fifteen minutes later: Adam waited in the bathroom. When he reappeared he showed no interest in the food, so Robin ate four kippers and most of the toast. Nine o'clock passed; a porter took away the breakfast trolley and Robin began to pack. The phone rang and Adam jumped nervously as Robin picked it up.

"Yes, Stephen," she said. "No, I won't need any help with my luggage. Not this time." She put the phone down. "We depart for Frankfurt at ten."

"I know," said Adam.

"We ought to make Lawrence the orchestra manager. He seems to know everything even before it's been decided." Adam had been thinking the same thing. "Well, at least I've found someone to help with my luggage for a change," added Robin.

"I'll carry the double bass for you if you like," offered Adam.

"I'd like to see you try," said Robin. Adam walked over to the large instrument that was propped up in its case against the wall. He tried the double bass from all angles but couldn't manage to do better than hold it off the floor for a few moments. Robin joined him and with one flick she had the stem on her shoulder and the instrument balanced perfectly. She walked up and down the bedroom demonstrating her prowess.

"It's a matter of skill, my puny friend," she said. "And to think I believed all those stories last night about your outrunning half the Swiss police force to spend a night with me."

Adam tried to laugh. He picked up his trenchcoat, checking the icon was zipped up. But he couldn't stop himself shaking from a combination of fear and anticipation.

Robin looked at him. "Don't worry," she said gently. "It will all be over in a few minutes' time." Then she saw the paper on the floor. "I should sue them if I were you."

"Why?" asked Adam.

"You're a lot better looking than that." Adam smiled and walked across, and just managed to get his arms round her to give her a hug.

"Thanks for everything," he said. "But now we have to go."

"You're sounding more like one of my lovers all the time," said Robin, mournfully.

Adam picked up her suitcase while Robin jerked up the stem of the double bass onto her shoulder. She opened the door and checked the corridor: two of her colleagues from the RPO were waiting by the lift, otherwise there was nobody else in sight. Robin and Adam joined the two musicians and after "Good mornings" no one spoke until the lift doors slid open. Once the doors were closed Robin's colleagues couldn't resist taking a closer look at Adam. At first Adam was anxious they had recognised him from the newspaper. Then he realised that it was who Robin had spent the night with that fascinated them. Robin gave him a lewd wink, as if she fully intended to live off this one for a long time. For his part Adam ducked behind the double bass and remained in the corner breathing deeply in and out as the lift trundled down towards the ground floor. The doors sprang open and Robin waited for her two colleagues to leave before she shielded Adam as best she could all the way across the foyer. His eyes were now fixed on the front door. He could see the bus taking up most of the road and several members of the orchestra were already clambering on. One more minute and he should be safely away. He watched as the drums were packed carefully in the large boot.

"Oh, God, I forgot," said Robin. "I'm meant to put this in the boot at the back of the bus."

"Do it later," said Adam sharply. "Just keep going until you reach the coach door." Then he saw the car on the far side of the road. He felt light with relief, almost dizzy. The car door was being held open for him. Another man was seated in the back just as Lawrence had promised. Ten o'clock struck somewhere in the distance. The man dressed in chauffeur's uniform, hat pulled down over his forehead, stood by the open door. He turned towards the hotel in anticipation. Adam stared towards him as the man's eyes scanned the hotel entrance. The uniform wasn't a good fit.

"Into the bus," hissed Adam.

"With this thing? They'll kill me," said Robin.

"If you don't, he'll kill me."

Robin obeyed, despite the adverse comments as she lumbered down the aisle with her double bass screening Adam from the gaze of anyone on the far side of the road. He wanted to be sick.

Adam slumped into a seat next to Robin with the double bass between them.

"Which one?" she whispered.

"In the chauffeur's uniform."

Robin glanced out of the window. "He may be evil, but he's damned good looking," she said, inconsequentially.

Adam looked disbelieving. Robin smiled apologetically.

"Everybody's in," called a man from the front of the bus, "and I've double-checked and we seem to have one extra."

Oh, my God, thought Adam, he's going to throw me off the bus.

"My brother," shouted Robin from the back. "He's only travelling with us for part of the journey."

"Oh, that's okay then," said the manager. "Well, let's be on our way." He turned to the driver.

"He's started looking at the bus," said Robin.

"But I don't think he can see you. No, you're all right, he's now turned his gaze back to the hotel entrance."

"I didn't realise you had a brother," said the manager, who was suddenly standing beside them. The coach moved slowly out of the square.

"Neither did I until this morning," mumbled Robin, still looking out of the window. She turned and faced her boss. "Yes, I forgot to mention to you that he might be in Switzerland at the same time as the orchestra. I do hope it's not going to cause a problem."

"Not at all," said the manager.

"Adam, this is Stephen Grieg who, as you will already have gathered, is the orchestra's manager."

"Are you a musician as well?" asked Stephen as he shook Adam's hand.

"No, I can truthfully say that I have never been able to master any instrument," said Adam.

"He's tone deaf," butted in Robin. "Takes after my father. He's in tyres, actually," she continued, enjoying herself.

"Oh, really. Which company are you with?" enquired Stephen.

"I'm with Pirelli," said Adam, mentioning the first tyre company that came into his head.

"Pirelli, the company that produces those fabulous calendars?"

"What's so special about their calendars?" asked Robin innocently. "If you want one I'm sure Adam can get you one."

"Oh, that would be great," said Stephen. "I hope it won't put you to too much trouble."

"No trouble at all," said Robin, leaning over Adam conspiratorially. "Actually, to let you in on a little family secret there is a rumour at HQ that Adam will soon be joining the main board. The youngest member in the company's history, you know."

"How impressive," said the manager, taking a closer look at the orchestra's latest recruit.

"Where shall I send the calendar?" bleated out Adam.

"Oh, direct to the RPO. No need to tell you the address, is there?"

"In a brown envelope, no doubt," said Robin. "And don't worry about the year. It's not the dates that he gets worked up about."

"What time are we expecting to reach Frankfurt, Stephen?" shouted a voice from the front. "Must leave you now," said the manager. "Thanks for the promise of a calendar. Robin's right, of course – any year will do."

"Who taught you to spin a yarn like that?" asked Adam, as soon as he was out of earshot.

"My father," said Robin. "You should have heard him at his best. In a class of his own. The problem was my mother still believed every word."

"He would have been proud of you today."

"Now we've found out what you do for a living," said Robin, "may we learn what's next on the agenda for the youngest director of Pirelli?"

Adam smiled. "I've started trying to reason like Rosenbaum, and I think he'll stay in Geneva for at least an hour, two at the most, so with luck I'll get a fifty-mile start on him." He unfolded the map across the two seats.

His finger ran along the road the bus was travelling on, and it was Robin who spoke first.

"That means you could make Zurich airport before he has any chance of catching up with you."

"Perhaps," said Adam, "but that would be too much

of a risk. Whoever Rosenbaum is," he went on, abiding by Lawrence's request to be cautious by not letting Robin into his secret, "we now know for certain that he has a professional organisation behind him so I must expect the airports to be the first place he will have covered. And don't forget the Swiss police are still on the lookout for me as well."

"So why don't you come on to Frankfurt with us?" asked Robin. "I can't believe you'll have any trouble from Stephen."

"I've thought about that already but discounted it also as too great a risk," said Adam.

"Why?"

"Because, when Rosenbaum has had time to think about it," said Adam, "the one thing he'll remember is this bus. Once he's found out the direction we're heading in he's sure to come after us."

Robin's eyes returned to the map. "So you'll need to decide where and when to get off."

"Exactly," whispered Adam. "I can risk sixty to seventy miles, but not a lot further."

Robin's finger ran along the little road. "About here," she said, her finger stopping on a little town called Solothurn.

"Looks about the right distance."

"But once you're off the bus what will you do for transport?"

"I've little choice but to walk or thumb lifts – unless I pinch another car."

"With your luck, Rosenbaum will be the one person who stops to pick you up."

"Yes, I've thought about that as well," said Adam. "I would have to find a long stretch of road where I can see without being seen for about one hundred yards, and then thumb lifts only from British cars or cars with British number plates."

"They taught you a trick or two in the army, didn't they?" said Robin. "But how do you intend to cross the frontier with your passport?"

"That's one of the many problems I haven't yet come up with a solution for."

"If you decide to stay with us," said Robin, "it wouldn't be a problem."

"Why?" asked Adam.

"Because whenever we cross a border they only count the number of people on the bus and the number of passports, and as long as they tally the customs officials don't bother to check everyone individually. After all, why should they? The RPO is not exactly an unknown quantity. All I would have to do is add your passport to the bundle and mention it to the manager."

"It's a clever idea but it's not on. If Rosenbaum caught up with me while I'm still on this bus then I would be left with no escape route."

Robin was silent for a moment. "Once you're on your own will you contact Lawrence again?"

"Yes. I've got to let him know what happened this morning, because whoever he's dealing with must have a direct line to Rosenbaum."

"Could it be Lawrence himself?"

"Never," said Adam.

"Your loyalty is touching," said Robin, turning to look at him, "but what you actually mean is you don't want to believe it could be Lawrence."

"What are you getting at?"

"Like my mother didn't want to believe that my father was a liar and a drunk. So she turned a blind eye to his little foibles. You know even when he dropped dead of cirrhosis of the liver, her only words were, 'strange for a man who never drank'."

Adam thought about his relationship with Lawrence and wondered if you could know someone for twenty years and really not know them at all.

"Just be wary how much you let him know," advised Robin.

They sat in silence as Adam checked the map and went over all the different possible routes he could take once he had left the bus. He decided to aim for the German border and take the long route back to England, from Hamburg or Bremerhaven, rather than the shorter, more obvious route via Calais or Ostend.

"Got it," said Robin suddenly.

"Got what?" said Adam, looking up from the map.

"How we solve your passport problem," she murmured.

Adam glanced at her hopefully. "If you let me have your passport," she explained, "I'll substitute it for the member of the orchestra who most resembles you. No one will notice anything strange at our end until we're back home in Britain on Sunday night."

"Not a bad idea, if there is anyone who remotely resembles me."

"We'll have to see what we can do," said Robin. She sat bolt upright, her eyes moving slowly from person to person. By the time she had scanned all those in the bus from front to back, a small smile appeared on her face. "There are two of our lot who bear a passable resemblance to you. One is about five years older and the other is four inches shorter, but you go on working out the safest way of escape while I carry out some research. Let me have your passport," she said. Adam handed it over and then watched Robin walk up to the front and sit next to the manager. He was chatting to the driver about the most convenient place to stop for lunch.

"I need to check something in my passport," Robin broke in. "Sorry to bother you."

"No bother. You'll find them all under my seat in a plastic bag," he said, and continued his conversation with the driver.

Robin bent down and started to shuffle through the passports as if searching for her own. She picked out the two she had considered as possible substitutes and compared the photographs. The shorter man's photo looked nothing like Adam. The older man's was at least five years out of date but could have passed for Adam as long as the officials didn't study the date of birth too carefully. She bundled up the passports, placing Adam's in the middle. She then put them back in the plastic bag and returned the bag under the manager's seat.

Robin made her way back to her seat. "Take a look at yourself," she said, slipping the passport over to Adam. He studied the photo.

"Other than the moustache, not a bad likeness, and it's certainly my best chance in the circumstances. But what will happen when you return to London and they find out my passport has been substituted?"

"You'll be back in England long before us," said Robin. "So put this one in an envelope with the calendar and send it direct to the RPO in Wigmore Street, W1, and I'll see that they return yours." Adam vowed to himself that if he ever got back to London, he would become a life subscriber to the Friends of the Royal Philharmonic.

"That seems to have solved one of your problems."

"For the moment at least," said Adam. "I only wish I could take you with me for the rest of the trip."

Robin smiled. "Frankfurt, Berlin, Amsterdam – just in case you get bored. I wouldn't mind meeting up with Rosenbaum. But this time face to face."

"He might just have met his match," said Adam.

"Can I have a last look at the icon?" Robin asked, ignoring the comment.

Adam bent down to retrieve his trenchcoat and slipped the painting out of his map pocket, careful to shield it from anyone else's view. Robin stared into the eyes of St George before she spoke again. "When I lay awake last night waiting for you to ravish me, I passed the time trying to fathom out what secret the icon held."

"I thought you were asleep," said Adam smiling. "When all along we were both doing the same thing. Anyway, did you come up with any worthwhile conclusions?"

"First, I decided your taste was for male double bass players," said Robin, "or how else could you have resisted me?"

"But what about St George and the Dragon?" asked Adam, grinning.

"To begin with I wondered if the little pieces of mosaic made up a code. But the picture is so magnificently executed that the code would have to have been worked out afterwards. And that didn't seem credible."

"Good thinking, Batman."

"No, you're Batman. So I wondered if there was another painting underneath. I remembered from my schooldays that Rembrandt and Constable often painted on the top of their paintings, either because they didn't care for their original effort or because, in the case of Rembrandt, he couldn't afford another canvas."

"If that were the answer only an expert could have

carried out the task of removing every piece of paint."

"Agreed," said Robin. "So I dismissed that as well. My third idea was that the crown on the back" – she turned the icon over and stared at the little piece of silver embedded in the wood – "indicates as your expert suggested that this is the original by Rublev and not a copy as you have been led to believe."

"I had already considered that," said Adam, "during my sleepless night and although it would place a far higher value on the work, it is still not enough to explain why Rosenbaum would kill indiscriminately for it."

"Perhaps someone else needs St George every bit as much as Rosenbaum does," said Robin.

"But who and why?"

"Because it's not the icon they're after, but something else. Something hidden in or behind the painting."

"That was the first thing I checked," said Adam smugly. "And I'm convinced that it's a solid piece of wood."

"I don't agree with you," said Robin as she began tapping the wood all over like a doctor examining someone's chest. "I've worked with instruments all my life, watched them being made, played with them, even slept with them, and this icon is not solid right through, though God knows how I can prove it. If something is hidden inside it was never intended to be discovered by laymen like ourselves."

"Quite an imaginative little thing, aren't you?" said Adam.

"Comes naturally," she said as she handed the icon back to Adam. "Do let me know if you ever discover what is inside," she added.

"When I get five minutes to myself I might even

spend some time on one or two of my own theories," said Adam, returning the icon to his trenchcoat pocket.

"Two more kilometres to Solothurn," said Robin, pointing out of the window at a signpost.

Adam buttoned up his coat. "I'll see you off," she said, and they both made their way up the aisle. When Adam reached the front of the coach he asked the driver if he could drop him off just before they reached the next village.

"Sure thing," said the driver without looking back.

"Leaving us so soon?" said Stephen.

"Afraid so," said Adam. "But thanks for the lift. And I won't forget the calendar." The driver pulled into a lay-by, pressed a knob and the hydraulic doors swung back.

"Bye, Robin," said Adam, giving her a brotherly kiss on the cheek.

"Goodbye, baby brother," said Robin. "Give my love to mother if you see her before I do." She smiled and waved at him as the door swung closed and the coach returned to the highway to continue its journey on to Frankfurt.

Adam was on his own again.

CHAPTER FOURTEEN

Professor Brunweld was rarely treated with any respect. It was the fate of academics, he had long ago concluded. The 'President' was all they had said and he had wondered if he should believe it. Certainly they had got him out of bed in the middle of the night and escorted him silently to the Pentagon. They wanted Brunweld's expert opinion, they had assured him. Could it be possible? After Cuba and Dallas he'd begun to believe anything was possible.

He had once read that the Pentagon had as many floors below the ground as there were above it. He could now confirm that as an established fact.

Once they had handed him the document they left him alone. They only wanted one question answered. He studied the clauses for over an hour and then called them back. It was, he told them, in his opinion, authentic and if the Russians were still in possession of their copy, also signed in 1867, then his adopted country was – what was that awful American expression? Ah, yes – in all sorts of trouble.

He began to realise how serious it was when they told him that he would not be allowed to leave the Pentagon until Monday. That didn't surprise him once he'd seen the date on the bottom of the treaty. So it was to be three days of solitude away from his demanding students and chattering wife. He would never have a better opportunity to settle down and read the collected works of Proust.

Romanov knew he couldn't risk standing by the side of the car for much longer. He was too conspicuously dressed not to be noticed by everyone who came out of the hotel. Three minutes later he thew his grey cap on the back seat and instructed Valchek to get rid of the car and then return to the Consulate.

Valchek nodded. He had already carried out Romanov's orders to kill the two British agents as if he had been asked to fix a burst water pipe. The only thing that hadn't run to plan was when Valchek tried to button up the dead chauffeur's uniform. Romanov thought he detected the suggestion of a smirk on Valchek's face when he realised who would have to be the chauffeur.

Romanov slipped into the shadows and waited for another half hour, by which time he was sure the plan must have been aborted from the London end. He hailed a taxi and asked the driver to take him to the Soviet Consulate. He didn't notice the taxi-driver's look of disbelief at his passenger's chauffeur-clad vision.

Could he really have lost Scott twice? Had he also underestimated him? Once more and Zaborski was going to require a very convincing explanation.

On his way back to the Consulate an image kept flashing across Romanov's mind, but he couldn't make any sense of it. Something had happened outside the hotel that didn't quite fit. If he could only think clearly for a moment he felt certain it would become clear to him. He kept playing the last thirty minutes over in his mind, as if rewinding the reel of an old film; but some of the frames still remained blurred.

Once Romanov was back in the Consulate Valchek handed him a large envelope which he was informed had just arrived in the diplomatic pouch from Moscow.

Romanov read over the decoded telex a second time, still unable to fathom its possible significance.

"Information has come to light concerning the late Colonel Gerald Scott, DSO, OBE, MC, that may prove useful when you make contact with your quarry. Full documentation will be with you by morning, latest, A1."

Romanov wondered what headquarters had discovered about Scott's father that could possibly prove of interest to him. It was still his avowed intention that the son would be despatched to join the father long before any further missive from Moscow had arrived.

Romanov thought of his own father and the escape route he had made possible by leaving such a fortune, and how for the sake of advancement he had betrayed him to the State. Now, for the sake of further advancement he had to kill Scott and bring home the icon. If he failed . . . He dismissed both fathers.

"Either he's very clever or he's living on an amateur's luck," Romanov said, moving into the small office that had been made available for his use. Valchek who followed him did not comment other than to ask what he should do next.

"Tell me what you saw when we were at the hotel."

"What do you mean?" asked Valchek.

"Don't ask questions," said Romanov, changing back into his own clothes, "answer them. Tell me everything you remember seeing, from the moment we drew up outside the hotel."

"We arrived at the Richmond a few minutes before ten," began Valchek, "parked the Mercedes on the far side of the road, and waited for Scott to show up. We stayed put for a few minutes after ten but Scott never materialised."

"No, no, no. Be more specific. Don't just generalise. For instance, do you remember anything unusual taking place while we were waiting?"

"Nothing in particular," said Valchek. "People continually entering and leaving the hotel – but I'm sure Scott wasn't among them."

"You are fortunate to be so certain. What happened next?" asked Romanov.

"Next? You instructed me to go back to the Consulate and wait for you to return."

"What time was that?"

"It must have been about seven minutes past ten. I remember because I checked my watch when that coach left."

"The coach?" said Romanov.

"Yes, the one that was being loaded up with musical instruments. It left about . . ."

"Instruments, that's it," said Romanov. "Now I remember what was worrying me. Cellos, violins, and a double bass that didn't go into the boot." Valchek looked puzzled but said nothing. "Ring the hotel immediately and find out who was on that bus and where they are heading." Valchek scurried away.

Romanov checked his watch: ten fifty-five. We are going to have to move, and move quickly. He pressed the intercom by the side of the phone. "I want a fast car, and more important, a superb driver." Valchek returned as Romanov replaced the receiver. "The bus was hired by the Royal Philharmonic Orchestra, who are on a European tour . . ."

"Where are they heading next?" asked Romanov.
"Frankfurt."

He strolled away from the village, having checked everything with a professional soldier's eye. The main street was deserted but for a little boy who relentlessly kicked a plastic football into a gap in the hillside which he was using as a goal. The boy turned when he saw Adam and kicked the ball towards him. Adam kicked it back and the boy took it in his arms, a wide smile appearing on his face. The smile disappeared as he watched Adam continue quickly up the hill. There were only a few old houses on the main road. On one side was a dangerous ravine with tree-covered hills rising in the distance, while on the other side stretched green fields in which cows, bells round their necks, munched happily away. It made Adam feel hungry.

He went further up the road until he came to a sharp bend in the hill. Standing on the corner he could see down the hill for about half a mile without being seen. He tested the feasibility of his plan for several minutes and soon became expert at picking out British cars or cars with British number plates as far as two or three hundred yards away. It didn't take long to work out how few foreigners bought British.

During the next twenty minutes he thumbed optimistically at seven cars with English number plates heading towards Lausanne, but they all ignored him. He had forgotten just how easy it had been for him when he was a cadet in uniform. In those days almost everyone would stop. He checked his watch: he could only risk it for a few more minutes. Three more cars refused to pull up and when a fourth slowed down it only sped away again as Adam ran towards it.

By eleven twenty Adam decided he could no longer

chance being seen on the road. He stared down the ravine, realising there was no alternative left open to him now but to travel by foot. He shrugged and began to climb down one of the steep trails that led into the valley, in the hope of meeting up with the other road that was marked clearly on the map.

He cursed when he looked at the open ground between him and safety. If only he'd started an hour earlier.

"I fear Antarctic has become expendable."

"Why?"

"Because we now know his father was involved in helping Goering to an easy death."

"I don't understand."

"No reason why you should although it's quite simple. That patriotic stiff-upper-lipped Englishman of yours is the son of the bastard who smuggled a cyanide capsule into Goering's cell at Nuremberg. His reward for services rendered turns out to be the Tsar's icon."

"But all the members of D4 are convinced that he's our only hope."

"I don't give a damn what your D4 thinks. If the father would side with the Germans during a war, why shouldn't the son side with the Russians in peace?"

"Like father, like son."

"Precisely."

"So what am I expected to do?"

"Just keep us briefed as to what the Foreign Office is up to. Our agents in Switzerland will do the rest."

"Faster!" said Romanov, aware that it was not possible as the Ambassador's driver was proving to be a consummate professional. Not once did Romanov feel that he had missed a gap, a light, a chance to overtake. In fact another five kilometres an hour on the speedometer might well have seen them over the precipice. The moment they were on the highway, with full lights blazing and the driver's hand almost lodged on the horn, the speedometer rarely fell below 130 kilometres an hour. "We must beat them to the border," he kept repeating as he thumped his fist on the leather dashboard. After they had covered one hundred kilometres in fifty-five minutes, the three men began watching ahead of them for the coach, but it was another thirty kilometres before Valchek was able to point ahead and shout, "That must be them, about a kilometre up the hill."

"Force them off the road," said Romanov, his eyes never leaving the bus. The Embassy driver swung out to overtake and once he was in front immediately cut across, forcing the coach driver to throw on his brakes and swerve into the side. Valchek waved dictatorially at the coach driver to slow down and the man stopped the vehicle just off the road on the edge of the mountain.

"Don't either of you speak. Just leave everything to me," said Romanov, "and remain near the driver in case there's trouble." Romanov jumped out of the car and ran towards the coach, his eyes already searching for anyone who might be attempting to leave it. He banged on the door impatiently until the driver pressed a knob and the big doors swung open. Romanov leapt on, with the other two following only paces behind. He took out his passport from an inside pocket, flashed it in the frightened driver's face and shouted, "Who's in charge here?"

Stephen Grieg stood up. "I am the manager of the company, and I can . . ."

"Swiss police," said Romanov. Grieg was about to ask a question when Romanov said, "When you left

241

your hotel in Geneva this morning, did you take on any extra passengers?"

"No," said Grieg. Romanov scowled. "Unless you count Robin Beresford's brother."

"Robin Beresford's brother?" enquired Romanov, his eyebrows raising interrogatively.

"Yes," said the manager. "Adam Beresford. But he only travelled with us as far as Solothurn. Then he got off."

"Which one of you is Robin?" said Romanov, staring around a sea of men's faces.

"I am," piped up a voice from the back. Romanov marched down the bus and saw the double bass case and then everything fitted into place. It always worried him when something was out of context. Yes, that was what hadn't rung true. Why hadn't she put the double bass in the boot with all the other large instruments? He stared down at the heavy-framed woman who now sat behind the monstrous instrument.

"Your brother is the one called Adam?"

"Yes," said Robin.

"Quite a coincidence."

"I don't understand what you mean," she said, trying not to sound nervous.

"The man I am looking for just happens to be called Adam as well."

"Common enough name," said Robin. "Perhaps you've never read the first chapter of the Bible?"

"Six foot one inch, perhaps two inches, dark hair, dark eyes, slim and fit. Not a convincing brother for you," added Romanov studying her frame.

Robin pushed back her red hair but didn't rise. Romanov could sense from the nervous expressions on the faces around him that it was Scott who had been on the bus.

"Where was your *brother*," he emphasised the word, "intending to go once he had left the coach?" Romanov asked, tapping his passport against his other hand, like a baton.

"I have no idea," said Robin, still not changing her expression from one of uninterested politeness.

"I will give you one more chance to co-operate with me. Where was your brother heading?"

"And I'll tell you once more, I don't know."

"If you refuse to answer my questions," said Romanov, "I shall have to arrest you."

"On whose authority?" asked Robin calmly.

Romanov considered showing her his passport but realised that this girl was sharper than either the driver or the manager.

"With the authority of the Swiss police," Romanov said confidently.

"Then no doubt you'll be happy to show me proof of your identity."

"Don't be insolent," Romanov said sharply. He towered over her.

"It is you who are insolent," said Robin, standing up. "You drive in front of our coach like a lunatic, nearly sending us down the mountain, then the three of you burst in like a bunch of Chicago mobsters, claiming to be Swiss police. I have no idea who you are or what you are, but I'll let you into two secrets. You touch me and there are forty men on this coach who will beat you and your two cronies to pulp. And even if you managed to get off this bus alive, we are members of the Royal Philharmonic Orchestra of Great Britain, and as such are guests of the Swiss Government. In a few moments when we cross the border, we will become guests of the West German Government, so you're about to get yourself on to every front page in the world. Single-handedly, you will bring a totally new meaning to the words 'diplomatic incident'." She leaned forward and pointing a finger at him said, "So I'm telling you, whoever you are, in as ladylike fashion as I can, 'piss off'."

Romanov stood staring at her for some moments and then backed away as Robin's eyes remained glued on him. When he reached the front he waved at Valchek and the chauffeur, indicating that they should leave the coach. Reluctantly they obeyed him. The coach driver closed the door the moment Romanov's foot touched the ground and he quickly moved into first gear and drove back on to the highway.

The entire orchestra turned round and gave Robin the kind of ovation normally reserved for the entrance of the leader of the orchestra.

It went unappreciated. Robin had collapsed back into her seat, shaking uncontrollably, only too aware that not one of the forty men on that coach would have lifted a finger against Rosenbaum.

Sir Morris Youngfield glanced round the table: everyone was in place despite the few minutes' notice the head of D4 had given them.

"Let's hear the latest report," said Sir Morris, looking up at his Number Two, who was once again seated at the far end of the table.

"Not clever, sir, I'm afraid," began Lawrence. "Two of our most experienced agents were selected to pick up Scott at the Richmond Hotel as planned and then take him to the safety of the British Consulate."

"So what happened?" asked Sir Morris.

"No one at our Geneva office can be certain. Our men certainly never turned up at the hotel and they haven't been seen since."

"What are the Swiss police saying?" asked Busch.

"They are not being very helpful," said Lawrence, turning to the American. "They are aware that we are not the only foreign power involved and as is their custom in such circumstances, they have no intention of being seen to favour either side."

"Bloody Swiss," said Snell with feeling.

"And where do we imagine Scott is now?" asked Matthews.

"We've also drawn a blank on that," said Lawrence. Matthews smiled at Lawrence's embarrassment. "We feel certain he must have got on the coach with the girl –" he looked down at the sheet of paper on the table in front of him "– Robin Beresford. But he wasn't on it when we were waiting for them at the border. The orchestra is due at their Frankfurt hotel in about one hour so we will be able to find out more then. The German police are being far more co-operative," Lawrence added.

"Meanwhile what else are *we* doing?" asked Sir Morris.

"Checking all the usual places as well as keeping a close eye on Romanov who, incidentally, turned up on the French border last night. One of our old hands recognised him despite the fact that he's cut his hair very short; doesn't suit him, apparently."

"So Scott could be anywhere by now?" said Matthews. "Do you think he's still in Switzerland, or managed to cross one of the borders?"

Lawrence hesitated. "I have no idea," he said without expression.

Sir Morris stared at him from the far end of the table but didn't comment.

"Do you think he'll contact you again?" asked Snell.

"Almost certainly, if he's still alive."

"If Romanov is still in Switzerland, Scott *must* still be alive," said Busch. "Because the moment he gets his hands on the icon he will head east."

"Agreed," said Lawrence, "and we have men stationed at the airport checking every flight out to the East. I therefore suggest we follow up any further leads and assemble again tomorrow at seven a.m. unless Scott contacts me before then."

Sir Morris nodded and rose to leave. Everyone stood.

"Thank you, gentlemen," he said, and walked towards the far end of the room. As he passed Lawrence, he murmured, "Perhaps you could come to my office when you have a moment."

Adam slipped and stumbled the last few yards down the ravine before finally landing with a bump on his backside. His hands were cut and bleeding in several places, his trousers torn and smeared with clay and earth. He sat still for about two minutes trying to get his breath back as he looked back up towards the road. He had taken just under an hour to cover what a stone could have managed in three seconds. Still, there had been one advantage: no one could have seen him from the road. He gazed across the valley ahead. Anyone would be able to see him now, but he had left himself with no alternative.

Judge by eye, check by map. The map wasn't much help but he estimated the distance to the far ridge to be about two more miles. At least the map had promised him there was a road, hidden from sight on the other side of the ridge. He studied the terrain – rolling green fields, no hedgerows to shield him, and then one wide, shallow river. He reckoned he could cover the ground to the road in about twenty minutes. He checked that the icon was securely in place and then set off at an even pace.

Romanov had hardly uttered a word since the three men had been unceremoniously removed from the coach, and Valchek and the driver certainly hadn't ventured any opinions. Romanov knew the girl had called his bluff, and he couldn't afford a further diplomatic incident which would undoubtedly be reported back to his Chairman in Moscow. But Romanov would never forget the girl with the man's name.

Solothurn was about forty kilometres back in the direction they had already travelled, and the driver could have completed the journey in about twenty minutes had Romanov not insisted on slowing down as they passed every vehicle that travelled towards them. They checked the occupants of each vehicle on the other side of the road, just in case Scott had managed to thumb a lift. It was a necessary precaution in Romanov's judgment, but it meant a total time of thirty-one minutes before they arrived back in Solothurn. At least Romanov felt confident Scott wasn't heading for the German border – unless he had been very well disguised or travelled in the boot of a car.

As soon as they reached Solothurn Romanov instructed the driver to leave the car in the middle of the town while they split up to see if they could discover any clues as to the route Scott might have taken. None of the locals whom they questioned had seen anyone resembling Scott that morning, and Romanov was beginning to wonder which border he should now head for when he saw the driver kicking a football back to a little boy. Romanov ran down the hill and was about to remonstrate with him when the boy turned and kicked the ball hard at the Russian. Romanov trapped the ball automatically and kicked it firmly past the boy and into the goal. Romanov turned towards the driver and was about to shout at him when the ball reappeared at his feet. He picked it up in anger and was going to throw it back at the boy when he saw his hopeful smile. Romanov held the ball high above his head. The boy ran up and jumped towards the ball but however hard he tried he couldn't reach it.

"Have you seen any strangers this morning?" he asked in slow deliberate German.

"Yes, yes," said the boy. "But he didn't score a goal."

"Where did he go?" asked Romanov.

"Up the hill," said the boy. To the child's dismay, Romanov dropped the ball and began to run. Valchek and the driver followed after him.

"*Nein, nein,*" cried the little boy who followed after them. Romanov looked back to see the boy was standing on the spot where Adam had been thumbing lifts, pointing out over the ravine.

Romanov quickly turned to the driver. "Get the car, I need the glasses and the map." The driver ran back down the hill once again followed by the boy. A few minutes later the Mercedes drew up by Romanov's side. The driver jumped out and handed the glasses over to Romanov, while Valchek spread a map out on the car bonnet.

Romanov focused the binoculars and began to sweep the hills in the distance. It was several minutes before the glasses stopped and settled upon a brown speck climbing up the farthest hill.

"The rifle," were Romanov's only words.

Valchek ran to the boot of the car and took out a Dragunov sniper's rifle with telescopic sights. He assembled the long, slim weapon with its distinctive wooden skeleton stock and checked that it was loaded. He then raised it, moved it around until it felt comfortable nestled in his shoulder and swept the ground in front of him until he too focused on Scott. Romanov followed Adam's relentless stride with the binoculars. Valchek's arm moved with him, keeping the same pace. "Kill him," said Romanov. Valchek was grateful for the clear windless day as he kept the rifle sight in the middle of the Englishman's back, waited for three more strides, then slowly squeezed the trigger. Adam had almost reached the top of the ridge when the bullet tore through him. He fell to the ground with a thud. Romanov smiled and lowered the glasses.

Adam knew exactly what had ripped through his shoulder and where the shot must have come from. He instinctively rolled over until he reached the nearest tree. And then the pain began. Although the bullet had lost a lot of its power at such a distance, it still stung like an adder's bite, and blood was already beginning to seep through his trenchcoat from the torn muscle. He turned his head and gazed back behind him. He could see no one but he knew Romanov must be standing there waiting to take a second shot.

Turning with difficulty, he looked back up towards the edge of the hill. Only thirty yards to the safety of the ridge, but he would have to run over the top, remaining exposed for several vital seconds. Even if he made it Romanov would still be able to reach him by car within thirty minutes.

Nevertheless, that was his one chance. Slowly, very slowly, he crawled inch by inch up the ridge, thankful for the tree that he could still use as protection. One arm followed one leg, like a beached crab. Once he had covered ten yards he knew the angle would be against him and Romanov would have a flat, slow-moving target to aim at. He moved four more lengths of his body and stopped.

You can't hold a rifle up on your shoulder for ever, Adam thought. He counted to two hundred slowly.

"I suspect he's going to make a run for it," Romanov told Valchek as he raised the glasses, "which will give you about three seconds. I'll shout the moment he moves." Romanov kept the glasses trained on the tree. Suddenly Adam jumped up and sprinted as though it were the last twenty metres of an Olympic final. Romanov shouted "Now" and Valchek pulled the rifle up into his shoulder, focused on the moving man and squeezed the trigger as Adam threw himself over the ridge. The second bullet whistled by the side of Adam's head.

Romanov cursed, as he stared through the binoculars, knowing that Valchek had missed. He turned to the open map. The others joined him around the car as he began to consider the alternatives. "He should reach that road in about ten minutes," he said, putting his finger in the middle of a small red line that ran between Neuchâtel and the French border. "Unless the first bullet hit him, in which case it could take him longer. So how long will it take you to get to that border?" Romanov asked the driver.

The chauffeur studied the map. "About twenty-five, at most thirty minutes, Comrade Major," came back the reply.

Romanov turned and looked back towards the hills. "Thirty minutes, Scott, that's how long you've got to live."

When the car sped away, the little boy ran home as fast as he could. He quickly told his mother everything he had seen. She smiled understandingly. Only children always had such vivid imaginations.

* * *

When Adam looked up, he was relieved to see the road was only about a mile away. He jogged towards it at a steady pace, but found that the running caused him even more discomfort. He was anxious to stop and check the wound but waited till he reached the road. The bullet had torn through the outer flesh of his shoulder muscle leaving him in considerable pain. An inch lower and he would have been unable to move. He was relieved to see that the blood had only made a small stain on his trenchcoat. He folded a handkerchief in four and placed it between his shirt and the wound. He knew he daren't risk a hospital. As long as he could get to a pharmacy by nightfall, he felt he could take care of the problem himself.

Adam checked the map. He was now only a few kilometres from the French border, and decided, because of the wound, to cross into France as quickly as possible rather than keep to his original plan of going up through Basle and on to Bremerhaven.

Desperately he began to thumb at any car that passed, no longer bothering with the nationality of the number plates. He felt he was safe for about twenty minutes but after that he would have to disappear back into the hills. Unfortunately there were far fewer cars driving towards the French border than there had been on the Basle road, and they all ignored his plea. He feared that the time was fast approaching for him to return to the hills when a yellow Citroën drew into the side of the road a few yards ahead of him.

By the time Adam had reached the car the woman in the passenger seat had already wound down the window.

"Where – are – you – going?" asked Adam, pronouncing each word slowly and carefully.

The driver leant across, took a lengthy look at Adam and said in a broad Yorkshire accent, "We're on our way to Dijon. Any use to you, lad?"

"Yes, please," said Adam, relieved that his scruffy appearance had not put them off.

"Then jump in the back with my daughter."

Adam obeyed. The Citroën moved off, as Adam checked out of the back window; he was relieved to see an empty road stretching out behind him.

"Jim Hardcastle's the name," said the man, as he moved the car into third gear. Jim appeared to have a large, warm smile perpetually imprinted on his chubby red face. His dark ginger hair went straight back and was plastered down with Brylcreem. He wore a Harris tweed jacket and an open-necked shirt that revealed a little red triangle of hair. It looked to Adam as if he had given up attempts to do anything about his waistline. "And this is the wife, Betty," he said, gesturing with his elbow towards the woman in the front seat. She turned towards Adam, revealing the same ruddy cheeks and warm smile. Her hair was dyed blonde but the roots remained an obstinate black. "And sitting next to you is our Linda," Jim Hardcastle added, almost as an afterthought. "Just left school and going to work for the local council, aren't you, Linda?" Linda nodded sulkily. Adam stared at the young girl whose first experiment with make-up hadn't worked that well. The dark over-lined eye shadow and the pink lipstick did not help what Adam considered was an attractive girl probably in her late teens. "And what's your name, lad?"

"Dudley Hulme," said Adam, recalling the name on his new passport. "And are you on holiday?" he asked, trying to keep his mind off the throbbing shoulder.

"Mixing business with pleasure," said Jim. "But this part of the trip is rather special for Betty and myself. We flew to Genoa on Saturday and hired the car to tour Italy. First we travelled up through the Simplon Pass. It's a bit breathtaking after our home town of Hull."

Adam would have asked for details, but Jim didn't reckon on any interruptions. "I'm in mustard, you see. Export director for Colman's, and we're on our way to the annual conference of the IMF. You may have heard of us." Adam nodded knowingly. "International Mustard Federation," Jim added. Adam wanted to laugh, but because of the pain in his shoulder, managed to keep a straight face.

"This year they've elected me President of the IMF, the high point of my career in mustard, you might say. And, if I may be so bold as to suggest, an honour for Colman's as well, the finest mustard in the world," he added, as if he said it at least a hundred times a day. "As President I have to preside over the conference meetings and chair the annual dinner. Tonight I shall be making a speech of welcome to delegates from all over the world."

"How fascinating," winced Adam, as the car went over a pothole.

"It certainly is," said Jim. "People have no idea how many makes of mustards there are." He paused for a second and then said, "One hundred and forty-three. There's no doubt the Frogs make one or two good attempts and even the Krauts don't do too badly, but there's still nothing to beat Colman's. British is best after all, I always say. Probably the same in your line of country," said Jim. "By the way, what is your line of country?"

"I'm in the army," said Adam.

"What's a soldier doing thumbing a lift on the borders of Switzerland?"

"Can I speak to you in confidence?" asked Adam.

"Mum's the word," said Jim. "We Hardcastles know how to keep our traps shut."

In the case of Jim's wife and daughter, Adam had no proof to the contrary.

"I'm a captain in the Royal Wessex, at present on a NATO exercise," began Adam. "I was dumped off the coast at Brindisi in Italy last Sunday with a false passport and ten English pounds. I have to be back in barracks at Aldershot by midnight Saturday." When he saw the look of approbation appear on Jim's face, he felt even Robin would have been proud of him. Mrs Hardcastle turned around to take a more careful look at him.

"I knew you were an officer the moment you opened your mouth," said Jim. "You couldn't have fooled me. I was a sergeant in the Royal Army Service Corps in the last war myself. Doesn't sound much, but I did my bit for the old country." The acronym for the Corps – 'Rob All Serving Comrades' – flashed through Adam's mind. "Have you seen any action yourself, Dudley?" Jim was asking.

"A little in Malaya," said Adam.

"I missed that one," said Jim. "After the big one was over, I went back into mustard. So where's the problem in getting you back to England?"

"There are about eight of us trying to reach Aldershot, and a thousand Americans trying to stop us."

"Yanks," said Jim with disdain. "They only join wars just as we're about to win them. All medals and glory, that lot. No, I mean is there any real problem?"

"Yes, the border officials have been briefed that eight British officers are attempting to get over into

France and the Swiss love to be the ones to pull us in. Only two officers out of twelve made it back to barracks last year," said Adam, warming to his own theme. "Both were promoted within weeks."

"The Swiss," said Jim. "They're even worse than the Americans. They don't even join in a war – happy to fleece both sides at the same time. They won't pick you up, lad, believe me. I'll see to that."

"If you can get me across the border, Mr Hardcastle, I'm confident I will be able to make it all the way back to Aldershot."

"Consider it done, lad."

The fuel indicator was flashing red. "How many kilometres left when that happens?" demanded Romanov.

"About twenty, Comrade Major," said the driver.

"Then we should still make the French border?"

"Perhaps it might be safer to stop and fill up," suggested the driver.

"There is no time for safety," said Romanov. "Go faster."

"Yes, Comrade Major," said the driver, who decided it was not the occasion to point out they would run out of petrol even more quickly if he was made to push the car to its limits.

"Why didn't you fill the tank up this morning, you fool?" said Romanov.

"I thought I was only taking the Consul to lunch at the town hall today, and I had intended to fill the tank up during my lunch hour."

"Just pray for your sake that we reach the border," said Romanov. "Faster."

The Mercedes touched 140 kilometres per hour and Romanov relaxed only when he saw a sign saying they were only ten kilometres from the border. A few minutes later a smile grew on his face as they passed the five-kilometre sign, and then suddenly the engine spluttered as it tried helplessly to continue turning over at the speed the pressed-down accelerator was demanding. The indicator on the speedometer started to drop steadily as the engine continued to chug. The driver turned off the ignition and threw the gear lever into neutral. The sheer momentum of the heavy Mercedes took them another kilometre before the car slowed to a complete stop.

Romanov did not even look at the driver as he jumped out of the car and began running the last three kilometres towards the border.

"I've come up with an idea," said Jim, as they passed a signpost warning drivers that the border was only two kilometres away.

"What's that, sir?" asked Adam, who could now feel his shoulder beating like a steady tune hammered out by a child on a tin drum.

"When it comes to the time for us to present our passports, you put your arm round Linda and start cuddling her. Leave the rest to me."

Mrs Hardcastle turned round and gave Adam a much closer look as Linda went scarlet. Adam looked across at the mini-skirted pink-lipped Linda and felt embarrassed by the predicament her father had placed his daughter in. "Don't argue with me, Dudley," continued Jim confidently. "I promise you what I have in mind will work." Adam made no comment and neither did Linda. When they reached the Swiss border a few moments later, Adam could see that there were two checkpoints about one hundred yards apart. Drivers were avoiding one line of traffic in which a row was going on between a customs official and an irate lorry driver. Jim drove up straight behind the gesticulating Frenchman. "Give me your passport, Dudley," he said. Adam handed over the violinist's passport.

Why did you choose this line? Adam wanted to ask.

"I chose this line," continued Jim, "because by the time it comes for our passports to be inspected I reckon the customs officer will be only too happy to allow us through without much fuss." As if in reaction to his logic, a long queue started to form behind Jim, but still the argument raged in front of them. Adam remained alert, continually looking out of the back window, waiting for the moment when Romanov would appear. When he turned back, he was relieved to find that the lorry in front of them was being told to pull over into the side and wait.

Jim drove quickly up to the customs post. "Get necking, you two," he said.

Up until that point Adam had kept his hands hidden in his trenchcoat pocket because they were so scratched and bruised. But he obeyed Jim and took Linda in his arms and kissed her perfunctorily, one eye still open watching for Romanov. To his surprise she parted his lips and began exploring inside his mouth with her tongue. Adam thought about protesting but realised there was no way he could make it sound gallant or credible.

"The wife, the daughter and the future son-in-law," said Jim, handing over the four passports.

The customs man started to check.

"What was all the trouble about, officer?"

"Nothing for you to worry about," said the official, flicking through the passports. "I hope it hasn't inconvenienced you."

"No, no," said Jim. "They didn't even notice," he said, pointing over his shoulder and laughing.

The policeman shrugged and, handing the passports back, he said, "*Allez*," waving them on.

"Sharp as mustard Jim, that's what they call me back in Hull." He looked over his shoulder towards Adam. "You can stop that now, Dudley, thank you." Adam felt Linda release him with some reluctance.

She glanced at him shyly, then turned towards her father. "But we still have to go over the French border, don't we?"

"We have already been alerted to look out for him and I can assure you he hasn't been through this post," said the senior customs officer. "Otherwise one of my men would have spotted him. But if you want to double-check, be my guest."

Romanov went quickly from officer to officer showing them the blown-up photograph of Adam, but none of them could recall anyone resembling him. Valchek joined him a few minutes later and confirmed that Scott was not in any of the cars still waiting to be allowed over the border and that the Mercedes was being pushed into the border garage.

"Is it back to the hills, Comrade Major?" asked Valchek.

"Not yet. I want to be absolutely certain he hasn't managed to cross the border."

The senior official emerged from his post in the centre of the road. "Any luck?" he asked.

"No," said Romanov glumly. "You seem to be right."

"I thought as much. If any of my men had let the Englishman through they would have been looking for a new job by now."

Romanov nodded in acknowledgment. "Could I have missed any of your staff?"

"Doubt it – unless there's a couple of them taking a break. If so you'll find them in the bar about a hundred metres up towards the French border point."

Four customs officers and a French waitress were the only people to be found in the bar. Two of the officers were playing pool while the other two sat at a corner table, drinking coffee. Romanov took the photo out once more and showed it to the two men at the pool table. They both shook their heads in an uninterested fashion and returned to potting the multi-coloured balls.

The two Russians made their way to the bar. Valchek passed Romanov a cup of coffee and a sandwich, which he took over to the table where the other two border guards sat. One of them was telling his colleague the trouble he had had with a French lorry driver who was trying to smuggle Swiss watches over the border. Romanov pushed the photograph of Scott across the table.

"Have you seen this man today?"

Neither showed any sign of recognition and the younger one quickly returned to his story. Romanov sipped his coffee, and began to consider whether he should make a run for Basle or call for reinforcements to sweep the hills. Then he noticed that the young man's eyes kept returning to the photo. He asked once again if he had seen Scott.

"No, no," said the young officer, a little too quickly. In Moscow Romanov would have had a 'yes' out of him within minutes, but he would have to follow a more gentle approach here.

"How long ago?" Romanov asked quietly.

"What do you mean?" asked the policeman.

"How long ago?" repeated Romanov in a firmer voice.

"It wasn't him," said the officer, sweat now appearing on his forehead.

"If it wasn't him, how long ago wasn't it him?"

The officer hesitated. "Twenty minutes, maybe thirty."

"What make of vehicle?"

The young officer hesitated. "A Citroën, I think."

"Colour?"

"Yellow."

"Other passengers?"

"Three. Looked like a family. Mother, father, daughter. He was in the back with the daughter. The father said they were engaged."

Romanov had no more questions.

Jim Hardcastle managed to keep a one-sided conversation going for over an hour.

"Naturally," he said, "the IMF holds its annual conference in a different city every year. Last year it was in Denver in Colorado, and next year it'll be at Perth in Australia, so I manage to get around a bit. But as the export man you have to get used to a lot of travel."

"I'm sure you do," said Adam, trying to concentrate on his benefactor's words while his shoulder throbbed on.

"I'm only President for a year, of course," continued Jim. "But I have plans to ensure that my fellow delegates won't forget 1966 in a hurry."

"I'm sure they won't," said Adam.

"I shall point out to them that Colman's has had another record year on the export side."

"How impressive."

"Yes, but I must admit that most of our profits are left on the side of the plate," he said, laughing.

Adam laughed as well but sensed that Mrs Hardcastle and Linda might have heard the line before.

"I've been thinking, Dudley, and I'm sure the wife would agree with me, that it would be most acceptable to us if you felt able to join the presidential table for dinner tonight – as my guest, of course." Mrs Hardcastle nodded, as did Linda with enthusiasm.

"I can think of nothing that would give me greater pleasure," said Adam. "But I fear my commanding officer might not be quite as delighted to hear I had stopped on the way back to England to take in a party. I do hope you'll understand."

"If he is anything like my old CO I certainly do," said Jim. "Still, if you should ever be Hull way, look us up." He took a card out of his top pocket and passed it over his shoulder.

Adam studied the embossed letters and wondered what 'MIFT' stood for. He didn't ask.

"Where in Dijon would you like to be dropped off?" asked Jim as he drove into the outskirts of the town.

"Anywhere near the centre that's convenient for you," replied Adam.

"Just holler when it suits you then," said Jim. "Of course, I always maintain that a meal without mustard . . ."

"Can you drop me on the next corner?" said Adam suddenly.

"Oh," said Jim, sad to be losing such a good listener. And he reluctantly drew the car up alongside the kerb.

Adam kissed Linda on the cheek before getting out of the back. He then shook hands with Mr and Mrs Hardcastle.

"Nice to have made your acquaintance," said Jim. "If you change your mind you'll find us at the hotel . . . Is that blood on your shoulder, lad?"

"Just a graze from a fall – nothing to worry about. Wouldn't want the Americans to think they'd got the better of me."

"No, no, of course not," said Jim. "Well, good luck."

As the car moved off Adam stood on the pavement watching them disappear. He smiled and tried to wave, then turning, he walked quickly down a side street looking for a shopping precinct. Within moments he was in the centre of town, relieved to find that all the shops were still open. He began to search up and down the street for a green cross above a door. Adam had to walk only fifty yards before he spotted one. He entered the shop tentatively and checked the shelves.

A tall man with short fair hair, wearing a long leather coat, stood in the corner with his back to the entrance. Adam froze. Then the man turned round, frowning at the packet of tablets he wanted to purchase, while at the same time rubbing his thick Gallic moustache.

Adam walked up to the counter.

"Do you speak English, by any chance?" he asked the dispenser, trying to sound confident.

"Passable, I hope," came back the reply.

"I need some iodine, cotton wool, a bandage and heavy Elastoplast. I fell and bruised my shoulder on a rock," Adam explained.

The dispenser quickly put the order together without showing much interest.

"This is what you require but you will find that the trade names are different," explained the dispenser. "That will be twenty-three francs," he added.

"Will Swiss do?"

"Certainly."

"Is there a hotel anywhere nearby?" asked Adam.

"Around the next corner, on the other side of the square."

Adam thanked him, handed over the Swiss notes, and then left the pharmacy in search of the hotel. The Hotel Frantel was, as promised, only a short distance away. He walked across the square and up the steps into the hotel to find several people were waiting at reception to be booked in. Adam swung his trenchcoat over his blood-stained shoulder and walked past them as he checked the signs on the wall. He then strode across the entrance hall as though he were a guest of several days' standing. He followed the sign he had been looking for which took him down a flight of stairs, to come head on with three further signs. The first had the silhouette of a man on the door, the second a woman, the third a wheelchair.

He opened the third tentatively and was surprised to find behind it nothing more than a sizeable square room with a high-seated lavatory against the wall. Adam locked himself in and let his trenchcoat fall to the ground.

He rested for a few minutes before slowly stripping to the waist. He then ran a basinful of warm water.

Adam was thankful for the endless first-aid seminars every officer had to go through, never believing they would serve any purpose. Twenty minutes later the pain had subsided and he even felt comfortable.

He picked up his coat with his right hand and tried to throw it back over his shoulder. The very movement caused the icon to fall out of the map pocket and onto the tiled floor. As it hit the ground, the sound made Adam fear that it might have broken in half. He stared down anxiously and then fell to his knees.

The icon had split open like a book.

CHAPTER FIFTEEN

When Adam returned to the Hotel Frantel an hour later few guests would have recognised the man who had crept in earlier that afternoon.

He wore a new shirt, trousers, tie and a double-breasted blazer that wouldn't be fashionable in Britain for at least another year. Even the raincoat had been ditched because the icon fitted snugly into the blazer pocket. He considered the shop had probably given him a poor exchange rate for his traveller's cheques but that was not what had been occupying his mind for the past hour.

He booked himself into a single room in the name of Dudley Hulme and a few minutes later took the lift to the third floor.

Lawrence picked the phone up even before Adam heard the second ring.

"It's me," said Adam.

"Where are you?" were Lawrence's first words.

"I'll ask the questions," said Adam.

"I can understand how you feel," said Lawrence, "but . . ."

"No buts. You must be aware by now that someone on your so-called team has a direct line to the Russians because it was Romanov and his friends who were waiting for me outside the hotel in Geneva, not your lot."

"We realise that now," said Lawrence.

"We?" said Adam. "Who are we? Because I'm finding it rather hard to work out who's on my side."

"You don't believe that . . ."

"When you get your girlfriend murdered, chased across Europe by professional killers, shot at and . . ."

"Shot at?" said Lawrence.

"Yes, your friend Romanov took a shot at me today, hit me in the shoulder. Next time we meet I intend it to be the other way round and it won't be the shoulder."

"There won't be a next time," said Lawrence, "because we'll get you out safely if you'll only let me know where you are."

The memory of Robin's words, "Just be wary of how much you let him know," stopped Adam from telling Lawrence his exact location.

"Adam, for God's sake, you're on your own; if you don't trust me who can you trust? I admit it looks as if we let you down. But it won't happen again."

There was another long silence before Adam said, "I'm in Dijon."

"Why Dijon?"

"Because the only person who would give me a lift was going to a mustard conference in Dijon."

Lawrence couldn't stop himself smiling. "Give me your number and I'll phone you back within the hour."

"No," said Adam, "I'll phone *you* back in one hour."

"Adam, you've got to show some trust in me."

"Not now that I know what it is you're all after, I can't afford to trust anybody."

Adam replaced the phone and stared down at the icon which lay open on the bed. It wasn't the signature of Stoeckle or Seward that worried him. It was the date – June 20, 1966 – that read like a death warrant.

"Goodnight, sir," said the doorkeeper as the senior civil servant left Century House that evening. "Another late night for you," he added sympathetically. He acknowledged the doorman by raising his rolled umbrella a few inches. It *had* been another late night, but at least they had caught up with Scott again. He was beginning to develop quite a respect for the man. But how they failed to pick him up in Geneva still required a fuller explanation than the one Lawrence Pemberton had supplied the D4 with that afternoon.

He set off at a brisk pace towards the Old Kent Road, conspicuous in his black coat and pin-striped trousers. He tapped his umbrella nervously before hailing a passing taxi.

"Dillon's bookshop, Malet Street," he told the driver, before getting in the back. Already seven thirty, but he still wouldn't be too late and a few minutes either way wasn't going to make that much difference. Pemberton had agreed to remain at his desk until all the loose ends were tied up and he was sure that nothing could go wrong this time. He allowed himself a wry smile as he thought how they had all accepted his plan. It had the double advantage of ensuring enough time for them to get their best men into position, while keeping Scott well out of sight in a deserted hideaway. He hoped that this was the last time they would expect him to come up with an original proposal.

"Eight shillings, guv'nor," said the taxi-driver, as he drew up outside Dillon's. He handed over the money and added a sixpenny tip. He stood staring at the window of the university bookshop, watching the reflection of the taxi as it moved off. The moment the taxi had turned the corner into Gower Street he began walking away. In moments he had reached a side road into which he turned. Ridgmount Gardens was one of those streets which even London cabbies had to think about for a few moments. He had walked only a matter of yards before he disappeared down some stone steps to a basement flat. He inserted a Yale key in the front door lock, turned it quickly, stepped inside and closed the door behind him.

During the next twenty minutes he made two telephone calls – one international, one local – and then had a bath. He emerged back on Ridgmount Gardens less than an hour later dressed in a casual brown suit, pink floral open shirt and brown brogue shoes. The parting in his hair had changed sides. He returned to Dillon's on foot and hailed another taxi.

"The British Museum," he instructed the driver, as he stepped into the back. He checked his watch: nearly ten past eight. Scott would be fully briefed by now, he thought, although his associates would be already on the way back to Dijon, as his plan had allowed for a two-hour delay.

The taxi drew up outside the British Museum. He paid and walked up the twelve steps in front of the museum, admiring the Byzantine architecture as he regularly did each week, before walking back down again to hail another taxi.

"Middlesex Hospital, please," was all he said. The taxi executed a U-turn and headed west.

Poor bastard. If Scott hadn't opened that envelope in the first place the icon would have ended up with its rightful owner.

"Shall I drive up to the entrance?" asked the cabbie.

"Yes, please."

A moment later he strolled into the hospital, checked

the board on the wall as if he were looking for a certain ward, then walked back out on to the street. From the Middlesex Hospital it always took him about three minutes at a steady pace to reach Charlotte Street, where he stopped outside a house and pressed a buzzer attached to a little intercom.

"Are you a member?" enquired a voice suspiciously.

"Yes."

On the hour Adam phoned and listened carefully to all Lawrence had to say.

"I'll take one more risk," said Adam, "but if Romanov turns up this time I'll hand over the icon to him personally and with it a piece of property so valuable that no amount of money the Americans could offer would be sufficient to purchase it back."

When Adam put the phone down Lawrence and Sir Morris played the conversation back over again and again.

"I think *property*'s the key word," said Sir Morris.

"Agreed," said Lawrence, "but what piece of property could be that valuable to both the Russians and the Americans?"

Sir Morris began slowly rotating the globe that stood by the side of his desk.

"What does that buzz mean?" asked Romanov. "We are not running out of petrol again, are we?"

"No, sir," said the chauffeur. "It's the new calling device now fixed to all ambassadorial cars. It means they expect me to check in."

"Turn round and go back to that petrol station we passed a couple of miles ago," Romanov said quietly.

Romanov started tapping the dashboard impatiently as he waited for the petrol station to reappear on the horizon. The sun was going down quickly and he feared it would be dark within the hour. They had travelled about ninety kilometres beyond Dijon and neither he nor Valchek had even seen a yellow Citroën going either way.

"Fill up again while I phone Geneva," Romanov said the moment he saw the petrol station. He ran to the phone box while Valchek still kept a watchful eye on the passing traffic.

"I am answering your signal," said Romanov when he was put through to the euphemistically titled Second Secretary.

"We've had another call from Mentor," said the Second Secretary. "How far are you from Dijon?"

The member stumbled about the dimly lit room until he came across an unoccupied table wedged up against a pillar in one corner. He sat down on a little leather stool by its side. He swivelled around nervously, as he always did when waiting for someone to bring him his usual malt whisky on the rocks. When the drink was placed on the table in front of him he sipped at it, in between trying to discover if there were any new faces spread around the dark room. Not an easy task, as he refused to put on his glasses. His eyes eventually became accustomed to the dim light thrown out by the long red fluorescent bulb that stretched above the bar. All he could make out were the same old faces staring at him hopefully; but he wanted something new.

The proprietor, noticing that a regular customer had remained on his own, came out and sat opposite him on the other little stool. The member never could get himself to look the man in the eyes.

"I've got someone who's very keen to meet you," whispered the proprietor.

"Which one?" he asked, looking up once more to check the faces at the bar.

"Leaning on the juke box in the corner. The tall, slim one. And he's young," added the proprietor. He looked towards the blaring machine. A pleasing new face smiled at him. He smiled nervously back.

"Was I right?" asked the proprietor.

"Is he safe?" was all he asked.

"No trouble with this one. Upper-class lad, right out of a top-drawer public school. Just wants to earn a bit of pocket money on the side."

"Fine." The member took a sip of whisky.

The proprietor walked over to the juke box. The member watched him talking to the young man. The boy downed his drink, hesitated for a moment, then strolled across the crowded floor to take the empty stool.

"My name is Piers," the young man said.

"Mine's Jeremy," the member said.

"A gentle name," said Piers. "I've always liked the name Jeremy."

"Would you care for a drink?"

"A dry Martini, please," said Piers.

The member ordered a dry Martini and another malt whisky. The waiter hurried away. "I haven't seen you here before."

"No, it's only my second time," said Piers. "I used to work in Soho, but it's got to be so rough lately, you never know who you might end up with."

The drinks arrived and the member took a quick gulp.

"Would you like to dance?" asked Piers.

"It's an emergency," the voice said. "Is the tape on?"

"I'm listening."

"Antarctic is in Dijon and he's discovered what's in the icon."

"And did he give them any clue?"

"No, all he told Pemberton was that he was in possession of a piece of property so valuable that no amount of money we could offer would be sufficient to purchase it back."

"Indeed," said the voice.

"The British think the important word is property," said the caller.

"They're wrong," said the voice on the other end of the line. "It's purchase."

"How can you be so sure?"

"Because the Russian Ambassador in Washington has requested a meeting with the Secretary of State on June 20 and he's bringing with him a bullion order to the value of 712 million dollars in gold."

"So where does that leave us?"

"On our way to Dijon so that we can be sure to lay our hands on that icon before the British or the Russians. The Russians obviously feel confident that it will soon be in their possession, so my bet is that they must already be on the way."

"But I've already agreed to go along with the British plan."

"Try not to forget which side you're on, Commander."

"Yes, sir. But what are we going to do about Antarctic if we get our hands on the icon?"

"It's only the icon we're after. Once that's in our possession, Antarctic is expendable."

Adam checked his watch: a few minutes after seven.

It was time for him to leave because he had decided not to carry out Lawrence's instructions to the letter.

He intended to be waiting for *them*, and not as Lawrence had planned. He locked the bedroom door and returned to reception where he paid for the use of the room and the telephone calls he had made.

"Thank you," he said to the receptionist, and turned to leave.

"Dudley." Adam froze on the spot.

"Dudley," the voice boomed again. "I almost didn't recognise you. Did you change your mind?" A hand thumped him on the shoulder – at least it wasn't the left shoulder, he thought – as he stared down at Jim Hardcastle.

"No," said Adam, wishing he possessed the guile of Robin's father. "I think I was spotted in town so I had to get a change of clothes and keep out of sight for a few hours."

"Then why don't you come to the mustard dinner?" said Jim. "No one will see you there."

"Wish I were able to," said Adam, "but I can't afford to lose any more time."

"Anything I can do to help?" said Jim conspiratorially.

"No, I've got to get to . . . I have a rendezvous just outside the town in less than an hour."

"Wish I could take you there myself," said Jim. "Do anything to help an old soldier, but I'm a bit stuck tonight – of all nights."

"Don't give it a second thought, Jim, I'll be all right."

"I could always take him, Dad," said Linda, who had slipped up by her father's side and was listening intently.

They both turned towards Linda who was wearing a tight-fitting black crêpe dress that started as low and ended as high as it dared while her freshly washed hair

273

now fell to her shoulders. She looked up hopefully.

"You've only just got your licence, lass. Don't be daft."

"You always treat me like a child when there's something worthwhile to do," came back her immediate response.

Jim hesitated. "How far is this rendezvous?" he asked apprehensively.

"About five, maybe six miles," said Adam, "but I'll be fine. I can get a taxi easily."

"The lass is right," said Jim, and taking his car keys out of his pocket, he turned to her and added, "but if you ever let on to your mother I'll kill you." Jim took Adam by the hand and shook it furiously.

"But I'll be just fine . . ."

"I won't hear of it, lad. Never forget, that in the end we're both on the same side, and good luck."

"Thank you, sir," said Adam reluctantly.

Jim beamed. "You'd better be getting along, lass, before your mother shows up."

Linda happily took Adam by the hand and led him away to the car park.

"Which direction?" she asked, once they were seated in the car.

"The Auxerre road," said Adam, looking down at the piece of paper on which he had written the directions Lawrence had read over the phone to him.

Linda set off at a slow pace, seeming at first to be unsure of the car, but once they had reached the outskirts of the town Adam suggested that she might go a little faster.

"I'm very nervous," she said, as she put her hand on Adam's knee.

"Yes, I can tell you are," said Adam, crossing his

legs quickly. "Don't miss the turning," he added when he noticed a signpost pointing to the left.

Linda swung down off the main road on to a country lane while Adam kept his eyes peeled for the building Lawrence had described. It was another two miles before it came into sight.

"Draw into the side," said Adam, "and turn the lights off."

"At last," said Linda, sounding more hopeful, as she brought the car to a halt.

"Thank you very much," said Adam, as he touched the door handle.

"Is that all I get for risking life and limb?" asked Linda.

"I wouldn't want you to be late for the dinner."

"That dinner will be about as exciting as a dance at the Barnsley Young Conservatives."

"But your mother will be worried about you."

"Dudley, you're so up-tight."

"I wouldn't be in normal circumstances but if you stay much longer your life could be in danger," Adam said quietly.

Linda turned ashen. "You're not joking, are you?"

"I wish I was," said Adam. "Now, when I get out of this car you must turn round and go back to the hotel and never mention this conversation to anyone, especially your mother."

"I will," Linda said, sounding nervous for the first time.

"You're a fantastic girl," said Adam, and took her in his arms and gave her the longest, warmest kiss she had ever experienced. Adam then got out of the car and watched her do a five-point turn before she headed off back in the direction of Dijon.

He checked his watch: an hour and a half still to go

before they were due, and by then it would be pitch dark. He jogged over to the airfield and studied the burnt-out buildings that ran alongside the road. It was exactly as Lawrence had described it. It was like a ghost town and Adam was confident that no one else could be there yet as they still wouldn't have had enough time to carry out Lawrence's plan.

Looking across the runway, Adam spotted the ideal place to hide while he waited to see which of the two plans he had prepared would prove necessary.

Flight Lieutenant Alan Banks was thankful that the moon shone so brightly that night. He had landed the little Beaver full of combat men in far worse conditions when a runway had been lit up like the Blackpool seafront.

Banks circled the perimeter of the airfield once and studied the two runways carefully. The airport had been out of action for such a long time that none of the aircraft manuals included a detailed ground plan.

The flight lieutenant was breaking every rule in the book, including piloting an unmarked aircraft informing the French that they would be landing in Paris; not easy to explain overshooting an airport by over a hundred miles.

"I can make a landing on the north–south runway more easily," Banks said, turning to the SAS captain, who sat crouched in the back with his five men. "How near to that hangar do you want me to go?" he said, pointing out of the window.

"Stay well clear, at least a couple of hundred yards," came back the reply. "We still don't know what to expect."

The six SAS men continued to stare cautiously out of the side windows. They had been briefed to pick up a lone Englishman called Scott who would be waiting for them, and then get out fast. It sounded easy enough but it couldn't be that easy otherwise they wouldn't have been called in.

The pilot swung the Beaver round to the south and put the nose down. He smiled when he spotted the burnt-out Spitfire that had been left derelict on the corner of the runway. Just like the ones his father used to fly during the Second World War. But this one had obviously never made it home. He descended confidently and as the little plane touched down it bounced along not because the pilot lacked experience but because the surface of the runway was so badly pitted.

Flight Lieutenant Banks brought the plane to a halt about two hundred yards from the hangar and swung the fuselage round a full circle ready for that quick getaway the captain seemed so keen to execute. He pressed the button that cut the propellers' engines and turned the lights out. The whirring slowed to an eerie whisper. They were forty-three minutes early.

Adam watched the new arrivals suspiciously from the cockpit of the Spitfire some four hundred yards away. He wasn't going to make a run for it across that open ground while the moon shone so brightly. His eyes never left the little unmarked plane as he waited for some clue as to who the occupants might be. He estimated it would be another fifteen minutes before the moon would be shielded by clouds. A few minutes more passed before Adam watched six men drop out of the blind side of the aircraft and lie flat on the tarmac on their stomachs. They were correctly dressed in SAS battle kit but Adam remained unconvinced while he still recalled Romanov's chauffeur's uniform. The six soldiers made no attempt to move. Neither did

Adam as he was still uncertain which side they were on.

All six men on the ground hated the moon and even more the open space. The captain checked his watch: thirty-six minutes to go. He raised his hand and they began to crawl towards the hangar where Pemberton had said Scott would be waiting, a journey which took them nearly twenty minutes, and with each movement they made they became more confident that Pemberton's warning of an enemy waiting for them was unjustified.

At last a mass of clouds reached the moon and a shadow was thrown across the whole airfield. The SAS captain quickly checked his watch. Five minutes to go before the rendezvous was due. He was the first to reach the door of the hangar and he pushed it open with the palm of his hand. He wriggled in through the gap. The bullet hit him in the forehead even before he had found time to raise his gun.

"Move, laddies," shouted the second in command, and the other four were up in a flash, firing in an arc in front of them and running for the protection of the building.

As soon as Adam heard the Scottish brogue, he jumped out of the cockpit and sprinted across the tarmac towards the little plane whose propellers were already beginning to turn. He jumped on the wing and climbed in by the side of the surprised pilot.

"I'm Adam Scott, the man you've come to pick up," he shouted.

"I'm Flight Lieutenant Alan Banks, old chap," said the pilot, thrusting out his hand. Only a British officer could shake hands in such a situation, thought Adam, relieved if still terrified.

They both turned and watched the battle.

"We ought to get going," said the pilot. "My orders are to see you are brought back to England in one piece."

"Not before we are certain none of your men can make it back to the plane."

"Sorry, mate. My instructions are to get you out. Their orders are to take care of themselves."

"Let's at least give them another minute," Adam said.

They waited until the propellers were rotating at full speed. Suddenly the firing stopped and Adam could hear his heart thumping in his body.

"We ought to get moving," said the pilot.

"I know," replied Adam, "but keep your eyes skinned. There's something I still need to know."

Years of night marches made it possible for Adam to see him long before the pilot.

"Get going," said Adam.

"What?" said the pilot.

"Get going."

The pilot moved the joystick forward and the plane started moving slowly down the crumbling runway.

Suddenly a dark figure was running towards them firing long bursts straight at them. The pilot looked back to see a tall man whose fair hair shone in the moonlight.

"Faster, man, faster," said Adam.

"The throttle's full out," said the pilot, as the firing began again, but this time the bullets were ripping into the fuselage. A third burst came but by then the plane was going faster than the man and Adam let out a scream of delight when it left the ground.

He looked back to see that Romanov had turned around and was now firing at someone who was not wearing an SAS uniform.

"They couldn't hope to hit us now unless they've got a bazooka," said Flight Lieutenant Banks.

"Well done, well done," said Adam turning back to the pilot.

"And to think my wife had wanted me to go to the cinema tonight," said the pilot laughing.

"And what were you hoping to see?" asked Adam.

"My Fair Lady."

"Isn't it time for us to be going home?" asked Piers, removing his hand from the member's leg.

"Good idea," he said. "Just let me settle the bill."

"And I'll pick up my coat and scarf," said Piers. "Join you upstairs in a few moments?"

"Fine," he said. Catching the eye of the proprietor the member scribbled his signature in the air. When the 'account' appeared – a bare figure written out on a slip of paper without explanation – it was, as always, extortionate. As always, the member paid without comment. He thanked the proprietor as he left and walked up the dusty, creaky stairs to find his companion already waiting for him on the pavement. He hailed a taxi and while Piers climbed in the back he directed the cabbie to Dillon's bookshop.

"Not in the cab," he said, as his new friend's hand began to creep up his leg.

"I can't wait," said Piers. "It's way past my bedtime."

"Way past my bedtime," his companion repeated involuntarily, and checked his watch. The die must have been cast. They would have moved in by now: surely they had caught Scott this time and, more important, the . . . ?

"Four bob," said the cabbie, flicking back the glass.

He handed over five shillings and didn't wait for any change.

"Just around the corner," he said, guiding Piers past the bookshop and into the little side street. They crept down the stone steps and Piers waited as he unlocked the door, switched on the lights, and led the young man in.

"Oh, very cosy," said Piers. "Very cosy indeed."

Flight Lieutenant Alan Banks stared out of his tiny window as the plane climbed steadily.

"Where to now?" said Adam, relief flooding through his body.

"I had hoped England but I'm afraid the answer is as far as I can manage."

"What do you mean?" said Adam anxiously.

"Look at the fuel gauge," said Alan Banks, putting his forefinger on a little white indicator that was pointing halfway between a quarter full and empty. "We had enough to get us back to Northolt in Middlesex until those bullets ripped into my fuel tank."

The little white stick kept moving towards the red patch even as Adam watched it and within moments the propellers on the left side of the aircraft spun to a halt.

"I am going to have to put her down in a field. I can't risk going on as there are no other airports anywhere nearby. Just be thankful it's a clear moonlit night."

Without warning the plane began to descend sharply. "I shall try for that field over there," said the flight lieutenant, sounding remarkably blasé as he pointed to a large expanse of land to the west of the aircraft. "Hold on tight," he said as the plane spiralled inevitably down. The large expanse of land suddenly looked very small as the plane began to approach it.

Adam found himself gripping the side of his seat and gritting his teeth.

"Relax," said the pilot. "These Beavers have landed on far worse places than this," he went on, as the wheels touched the brown earth. "Damn mud. I hadn't anticipated that," he cursed as the wheels lost their grip in the soft earth and the plane suddenly nosedived forward. A few seconds passed before Adam realised he was still alive but upside down swinging from his seat belt.

"What do I do next?" he asked the pilot but there was no reply.

Adam tried to get his bearings and began to rock his body backwards and forwards until he could touch the side of the plane with one hand while gripping the joystick with his feet. Once he was able to grab the side of the fuselage he undid the belt and collapsed onto the roof of the plane.

He picked himself up, relieved to find nothing was broken. He quickly looked around but there was still no sign of the pilot. Adam clambered out of the plane, glad to feel the safety of the ground. He scrambled around for a considerable time before he found Alan Banks some thirty yards in front of the aircraft motionless on his back.

"Are you all right?" asked the pilot before Adam could ask the same question.

"I'm fine, but how about you, Alan?"

"I'm OK. I must have been thrown clear of the aircraft. Just sorry about the landing, old chap, have to admit it wasn't up to scratch. We must try it again some time."

Adam burst out laughing as the pilot slowly sat up.

"What next?" Banks asked.

"Can you walk?"

"Yes, I think so," said Alan, gingerly lifting himself up. "Damn," he said, "it's only my ankle but it's sure going to slow me down. You'd better get going without me. That bunch back there with the arsenal can only be about thirty minutes behind us."

"But what will you do?"

"My father landed in one of these bloody fields during the Second World War and still managed to get himself back to England without being caught by the Germans. I owe you a great debt of gratitude, Adam, because if I can get back I'll be able to shut him up once and for all. Which lot are chasing us this time, by the way?"

"The Russians," said Adam who was beginning to wonder if perhaps there was a second enemy.

"The Russians – couldn't be better. Anything less and Dad wouldn't have accepted it as a fair comparison."

Adam smiled as he thought of his own father and how much he would have liked Alan Banks. He touched the icon instinctively and was relieved to find it was still in place. The pilot's words had only made him more determined to get back to England.

"Which way?" asked Adam.

The pilot looked up at the Great Bear. "I'll head east, seems appropriate, so you'd better go west, old fellow. Nice to have made your acquaintance," and with that he limped off.

"I'm not sure how much longer I can last, Comrade Major."

"You must try to hold on, Valchek. It's imperative that you try. We cannot afford to stop now," said

Romanov. "I know that plane isn't far. I saw it falling out of the sky."

"I believe you, Comrade, but at least let me die a peaceful death on the side of the road, rather than endure the agony of this car."

Romanov glanced across at his colleague who had been shot in the abdomen. Valchek's hands were covered in blood, and his shirt and trousers were already drenched as he tried helplessly to hold himself in. He continued to clutch on to his stomach like a child who is about to be sick. The driver had also been shot, but in the back while attempting to run away. If he hadn't died instantly, Romanov would have put the next bullet into the coward himself. But Valchek was a different matter. No one could have questioned his courage. He had first taken on the British flat on their stomachs and then the Americans charging in like the seventh cavalry. Romanov had Mentor to thank for ensuring that they had been there first. But he must now quickly warn him that someone else was also briefing the Americans. Romanov, however, felt some satisfaction in having tricked the Americans into turning their fire on the British while he and Valchek waited to pick off the survivors. The last survivor was an American who fired at Valchek continually as they were making their getaway.

Romanov reckoned he had a clear hour before the French, British and Americans would be explaining away several bodies on a disused airfield. Romanov's thoughts returned to Valchek when he heard his comrade groan.

"Let's turn off into this forest," he begged. "I cannot hope to last much longer now."

"Hold on, Comrade, hold on," repeated Romanov.

"We can't be far away from Scott. Think of the Motherland."

"To hell with the Motherland," said Valchek. "Just let me die in peace." Romanov looked across again and realised that he could be stuck with a dead body within a few minutes. Despite Valchek's efforts the blood was now seeping on to the floor like a tap that wouldn't stop dripping.

Romanov noticed a gap in the trees ahead of him. He switched his lights on to full beam and swung off the road on to a dirt track and drove as far as he could until the thicket became too dense. He switched off the headlights and ran round the car to open the door.

Valchek could only manage two or three steps before he slumped to the ground, still holding on to his intestines. Romanov bent down and helped him ease himself up against the trunk of a large tree.

"Leave me to die, Comrade Major. Do not waste any more of your time on me."

Romanov frowned.

"How do you wish to die, Comrade?" he asked. "Slowly and in agony, or quickly and peacefully?"

"Leave me, Comrade. Let me die slowly, but you should go while you still have Scott in your sights."

"But if the Americans were to find you, they might force you to talk."

"You know better than that, Comrade." Romanov accepted the rebuke, then rose and after a moment's thought, ran back to the car.

Valchek began to pray that once the bastard had left someone might find him. He'd never wanted this assignment in the first place, but Zaborski needed two extra eyes on Romanov and Zaborski was not a man to cross. Valchek wouldn't talk, but he still wanted to live.

The bullet from the 9mm Makarov went straight through the back of Valchek's temple and blew away one side of his head. Valchek slumped to the ground and for several seconds his body trembled and spasmed, subsiding into twitches as he emptied his bowels and bladder on to the brown earth.

Romanov stood over him until he was certain he was dead. Valchek would probably not have talked, but this was not a time for taking unnecessary risks.

When he woke the next morning he felt the same familiar guilt. Once again he swore it would be the last time. It was never as good as he had anticipated, and the regret always lingered on for several hours.

The expense of keeping up an extra flat, the taxi fares and the club bills nearly made it prohibitive. But he always returned, like a salmon to its breeding ground. "A queer fish," he murmured out loud, and then groaned at his own pun.

Piers began to wake, and for the next twenty minutes he made his companion forget those regrets. After a moment of lying in exhausted silence the older man slipped out of bed, took ten pounds out of his wallet and left it on the dresser before going to run himself a bath. He anticipated that by the time he returned the boy and the money would have gone.

He soaked himself in the bath wondering about Scott. He knew he should feel guilty about his death. A death that, like so many others before him, had been caused by his picking up a young Pole who he had thought was safe. It was now so many years ago that he couldn't even remember his name.

But Mentor had never been allowed to forget the

name of the young aristocratic KGB officer he had found sitting on the end of their bed when he woke the next morning, or the look of disgust he showed for them both.

CHAPTER SIXTEEN

Adam lay flat on his stomach in the bottom of the empty barge. His head propped on one side, he remained alert to the slightest unfamiliar sound.

The bargee stood behind the wheel counting the three hundred Swiss francs for a second time. It was more than he could normally hope to earn in a month. A woman standing on tiptoes was eyeing the notes happily over his shoulder.

The barge progressed at a stately pace down the canal and Adam could no longer see the crashed plane.

Suddenly, far off in the distance, he heard distinctly the report of what sounded like a gunshot. Even as he listened the woman turned and scuttled down the hatch like a frightened rat. The barge ploughed its course on slowly through the night while Adam listened anxiously for any other unnatural noises, but all he could hear was the gentle splash of the water against the barge's hull. The clouds had moved on and full moon once again lit up the bank on both sides of the river. It became abundantly clear to Adam as he watched the towpath that they were not moving very fast. He could have run quicker. But even if it had cost him the remainder of his money, he was grateful to be escaping. He lowered himself again and curled up in the bow of the boat. He touched the icon, something he found himself doing every few minutes since he had discovered its secret. He did not move for another half hour, although he doubted that the barge had covered more than five miles.

Although everything appeared absolutely serene, he still remained alert. The river was far wider now than when he had first leapt on the barge.

The bargee's eyes never left him for long. He stood gripping the wheel, his oil-covered face not much cleaner than the old dungarees he wore – which looked as if they were never taken off. Occasionally he took a hand from the wheel, but only to remove the smokeless pipe from his mouth, cough, spit and put it back again.

The man smiled, took both hands off the wheel and placed them by the side of his head to indicate that Adam should sleep. But Adam shook his head. He checked his watch. Midnight had passed and he wanted to be off the barge and away long before first light.

He stood up, stretched, and wobbled a little. His shoulder, although healing slowly, still ached relentlessly. He walked up the centre of the barge and took his place next to the wheel.

"La Seine?" he asked, pointing at the water.

The bargee shook his head, no. "Canal de Bourgogne," he grunted.

Adam then pointed in the direction they were moving. "*Quelle ville?*"

The bargee removed his pipe. "*Ville? Ce n'est pas une ville, c'est Sombernon,*" he said, and put the stem back between his teeth.

Adam returned to his place in the bow. He tried to find a more comfortable position to relax and, curling up against the side of the boat, rested his head on some old rope and allowed his eyes to close.

"You know Scott better than any of us," said Sir Morris, "and you still have no feel as to where he might be now, or what he might do next, do you?"

"No, sir," admitted Lawrence. "The only thing we know for certain is that he has an appointment for a medical on Monday afternoon, but somehow I don't think he'll make it."

Sir Morris ignored the comment. "But someone was able to get to Scott, even though we didn't call D4," he continued. "That icon must hold a secret that we haven't begun to appreciate."

"And if Scott is still alive," said Lawrence, "nothing is going to convince him now that we're not to blame."

"And if we're not, who is?" asked Sir Morris. "Because someone was so desperate to discover our next move that they must have taken one hell of a risk during the last twenty-four hours. Unless, of course, it was you," said Sir Morris. The Permanent Secretary rose from his desk and turned around to look out of his window on to Horse Guards Parade.

"Even if it was me," said Lawrence, his eyes resting on a picture of the young Queen which stood on the corner of his master's desk, "it doesn't explain how the Americans got there as well."

"Oh, that's simple," said Sir Morris. "Busch has been briefing them direct. I never doubted he would from the moment he joined us. What I hadn't anticipated was how far the Americans would go without keeping us informed."

"So it was you who told Busch," said Lawrence.

"No," said Sir Morris. "You don't end up sitting behind this desk risking your own skin. I told the Prime

Minister, and politicians can always be relied on to pass on your information if they consider it will score them a point. To be fair, I knew the Prime Minister would tell the President. Otherwise I wouldn't have told him in the first place. More important: do you think Scott can still be alive?"

"Yes, I do," said Lawrence. "I have every reason to believe that the man who ran across the tarmac to our waiting plane was Scott. The French police, who incidentally have been far more co-operative than the Swiss, have informed us that our plane crashed in a field twelve miles north of Dijon but neither Scott nor the pilot were to be found at the scene of the crash."

"And if the French reports on what took place at the airport are accurate," said Sir Morris, "Romanov escaped and they must have had a couple of hours' start on us."

"Possibly," said Lawrence.

"And do you think it equally possible," asked Sir Morris, "that they have caught up with Scott and are now in possession of the icon?"

"Yes, sir, I fear that is quite possible," Lawrence said. "But I can't pretend it's conclusive. However, the BBC monitoring service at Caversham Park picked up extra signals traffic to all Soviet embassies during the night."

"That could mean anything," said Sir Morris, removing his spectacles.

"I agree, sir. But NATO reports that Russian strategic forces have been placed at a state of readiness and several Soviet Ambassadors across Europe have requested formal audiences with their Foreign Secretaries, ours included."

"That *is* more worrying," said Sir Morris. "They don't do that unless they are hoping for our support."

"Agreed, sir. But most revealing of all is that the Active Measures section of the KGB, First Chief Directorate, has booked pages of advertising space in newspapers right across Europe and, I suspect, America."

"Next you'll be telling me they hired J. Walter Thompson to write the copy," growled Sir Morris.

"They won't need them," said Lawrence. "I suspect it's a story that will make every front page."

If it hadn't been for the ceaseless throbbing in his shoulder, Adam might not have woken so quickly. The barge had suddenly swung at 90° and started heading east when Adam woke up with a start. He looked at the bargee and indicated that as the river was far wider now could he ease them nearer to the bank so he could jump off. The old man shrugged his shoulders pretending not to understand as the barge drifted aimlessly on.

Adam looked over the side and despite the lateness of the hour could see the bed of the river quite clearly. He tossed a stone over the side and watched it drop quickly to the bottom. It looked almost as if he could reach down and touch it. He looked up helplessly at the bargee who continued to stare over his head into the distance.

"Damn," said Adam, and taking the icon out of his blazer pocket held it high above his head. He stood on the edge of the barge feeling like a football manager asking the referee for permission to substitute a player. Permission was granted and Adam leaped into the water. His feet hit the canal bed with a thud and knocked the breath out of his body despite the fact that the water only came up to his waist.

Adam stood in the canal, the icon still held high above his head as the barge sailed past him. He waded to the nearest bank and clambered up on to the tow-path, turning slowly round as he tried to get some feel for direction. He was soon able to distinguish the Plough again and plot a course due west. After an hour of soggy jogging he began to make out a light in the distance which he estimated to be under a mile away. His legs were soaking and cold as he started to squelch his way across a field towards the first rays of the morning sun.

Whenever he came to a hedge or gate he climbed over or under like a Roman centurion determined to hold a straight line with his final destination. He could now see the outline of a house, which as he got nearer he realised was no more than a large cottage. He remembered the expression 'peasant farmer' from his school geography lessons. A little cobbled path led up to a half-open wooden door that looked as if it didn't need a lock. Adam tapped gently on the knocker and stood directly below the light above the doorway so that whoever answered would see him immediately.

The door was pulled back by a woman of perhaps thirty, who wore a plain black dress and a spotless white apron. Her rosy cheeks and ample waist confirmed her husband's profession.

When she saw Adam standing under the light she couldn't mask her surprise – she had been expecting the postman, but he didn't often appear in a neat navy blue blazer and soaking grey trousers.

Adam smiled. "*Anglais*," he told her, and added, "I fell in the canal."

The lady burst out laughing and beckoned Adam into her kitchen. He walked in to find a man evidently dressed for milking. The farmer looked up and when he saw Adam he joined in the laughter – a warm, friendly laugh more with Adam than against him.

When the woman saw that Adam was dripping all over her spotless floor she quickly pulled down a towel from the rack above the fire and said, "*Enlevez-moi ça*," pointing to Adam's trousers.

Adam turned towards the farmer for guidance but his host only nodded his agreement and added with a mime of pulling down his own trousers.

"*Enlevez les, enlevez les*," the woman repeated, pointing at him, and handed him the towel.

Adam removed his shoes and socks but the farmer's wife went on pointing until he took off his trousers, and she didn't budge before he had finally removed his shirt and underclothes and wrapped the towel around his waist. She stared at the large bandage on his shoulder but then quickly picked up everything except his blazer and took them over to the sink while he stood by the fire and dried himself.

Adam hitched up the towel around his waist, as the farmer beckoned him to join him at the table, pouring a large glass of milk for his guest and another for himself. Adam sat down next to the farmer, hanging his fashionable new blazer over the back of the chair near the fire. A delicious aroma arose from the pan where the farmer's wife was frying a thick slice of bacon which she had cut from the joint hanging in the smoky recess of the chimney.

The farmer raised his glass of milk high in the air.

"Winston Churchill," he toasted. Adam took a long gulp from his own glass and then raised it dramatically.

"Charles de Gaulle," he said, and finished off the warm milk as if it had been his first pint at the local pub.

The farmer picked up the jug once more and refilled their glasses. "*Merci*," said Adam, turning to the farmer's wife as she placed in front of him a large plate sizzling with eggs and bacon. She nodded and handed Adam a knife and fork before saying, "*Mangez.*"

"*Merci, merci,*" Adam repeated, as she cut him a thick oval slice from the huge loaf in front of im.

Adam began to devour the freshly cooked food which was the first meal he'd managed since the dinner he'd ordered at Robin's expense.

Without warning the farmer suddenly rose from his place and thrust out his hand. Adam also got up and shook it gratefully, only to be reminded how sore his shoulder still was.

"*Je dois travailler à la laiterie,*" he explained.

Adam nodded, and remained standing as his host left the room, but the farmer waved him down with a further, "*Mangez.*"

When Adam had finished the last scrap of food – he did everything except lick the plate – he took it over to the farmer's wife who was busy removing a pot from the stove in order to pour him a large, steaming cup of hot coffee. He sat back down and began to sip at it.

Adam tapped the jacket pocket almost automatically to make sure the icon was still safely in place. He pulled it out and studied St George and the Dragon. He turned it over, hesitated and then pressed the silver crown hard. The icon split in half like a book revealing two tiny hinges on the inside.

He glanced up at the farmer's wife, who was now wringing out his socks. Adam noticed his pants had already joined the trousers on the rack above the fire. She removed an ironing board from a little alcove by the side of the stove and began to set it up, showing no interest in Adam's discovery.

Once again he stared down at the inside of the open icon which was now laid flat on the table in front of him. The true irony was that the woman pressing his trousers was able to understand every word on the parchment while at the same time unable to explain the full significance to him. The complete surface of the inside of the icon was covered by a parchment which was glued to the wood and fell only a centimetre short of the four edges. Adam swivelled it round so that he could study it more clearly. The scrawled signatures in black ink at the bottom and the seals gave it the look of a legal document. On each reading he learned something new. Adam had been surprised originally to discover it was written in French until he came to the date on the bottom – June 20, 1867 – and then he remembered from his military history lectures at Sandhurst that long after Napoleonic times most international agreements remained conducted in French. Adam began to reread the script again slowly.

His French was not good enough to translate more than a few odd words from the finely handwritten scroll. Under *Etas Unis* William Seward's bold hand was scrawled across a crest of a two-headed eagle. Next to it was the signature of Edward de Stoeckle below a crown that mirrored the silver ornament embedded in the back of the icon. Adam double-checked. It had to be some form of agreement executed between the Russians and the Americans in 1867.

He then searched for other words that would help to explain the significance of the document. On one line he identified: '*Sept millions deux cent mille dollars d'or (7.2 million)*' and on another '*Sept cent douze millions huit cent mille dollars d'or (712.8 million) le 20 juin 1966*.

His eyes rested on a calendar hanging by a nail from the wall. It was Friday, June 17, 1966. If the date in the agreement were to be believed, then in only three days the document would no longer have any legal validity. No wonder the two most powerful nations on earth seemed desperate to get their hands on it, thought Adam.

Adam read through the document line by line searching for any further clues, pondering over each word slowly.

His eyes came to a halt on the one word that would remain the same in both languages.

The one word he had not told Lawrence.

Adam wondered how the icon had ever fallen into the hands of Goering in the first place. He must have bequeathed it to his father unknowingly – for had he realised the true importance of what was hidden inside it, he would surely have been able to bargain for his own freedom with either side.

"Voilà, voilà," said the farmer's wife, waving her hands as she placed warm socks, pants and trousers in front of Adam. How long had he spent engrossed in his fateful discovery? She looked down at the upside down parchment and smiled. Adam quickly snapped the icon closed and then studied the masterpiece carefully. So skilfully had the wood been cut that he could no longer see the join. He thought of the words of the letter left to him in his father's will: "But if you open it only to discover its purpose is to involve you in some dishonourable enterprise, be rid of it without a second thought." He did not need to give a second thought to how his father would have reacted in the same circumstances. The farmer's wife was now standing hands on hips, staring at him with a puzzled look.

Adam quickly replaced the icon in his jacket pocket and pulled back on his trousers.

He could think of no adequate way of thanking the farmer's wife for her hospitality, her lack of suspicion or inquisitiveness, so he simply walked over to her, took her gently by the shoulders, and kissed her on the cheek. She blushed and handed him a small plastic bag. He looked inside to find three apples, some bread and a large piece of cheese. She removed a crumb from his lip with the edge of her apron and led him to the open door.

Adam thanked her and then walked outside into his other world.

PART THREE

THE WHITE HOUSE
WASHINGTON DC

June 17, 1966

CHAPTER SEVENTEEN

THE WHITE HOUSE
WASHINGTON DC *June 17, 1966*

"I don't want to be the first god-damn President in the history of the United States to hand back an American state rather than be founding one."

"I appreciate that, Mr President," said the Secretary of State. "But . . ."

"Where do we stand on this legally, Dean?"

"We don't, Mr President. Abraham Brunweld, the leading authority on documents of this period, confirms that the terms of the ninety-nine year lease are binding on both sides. The lease was signed on behalf of Russia by Edward de Stoeckle and for the US by the then Secretary of State, William Seward."

"Can this agreement still be valid today?" asked the President, turning to his chief legal officer, Nicholas Katzenbach.

"It certainly can, sir," said the Attorney General. "But only if they can produce their original. If they do, the UN and the international court at The Hague would have no choice but to support the Russian claim. Otherwise no international agreement signed by us in the past or in the future would carry any credibility."

"What you're asking me to do is lie down and wag my tail like a prize labrador while the Russians shit all over us," said the President.

"I understand how you feel, Mr President," said the Attorney General, "but it remains my responsibility to make you aware of the legal position."

"God dammit, is there a precedent for this kind of stupidity by a Head of State?"

"The British," chipped in Dean Rusk, "will be facing a similar problem with the Chinese in 1999 over the New Territories of Hong Kong. They have already accepted the reality of the situation and indeed have made it clear to the Chinese Government that they are willing to come to an agreement with them."

"That's just one example," said the President, "and we all know about the British and their 'fair play' diplomacy."

"Also, in 1898," continued Rusk, "the Russians obtained a ninety-nine-year lease on Port Arthur in Northern China. The port was vital to them because, unlike Vladivostok, it is ice-free all year round."

"I had no idea the Russians *had* a port in China."

"They don't any longer, Mr President. They returned it to Mao in 1955, as an act of goodwill between fellow Communists."

"You can be damn sure the Russians won't return this piece of land to *us* as an act of goodwill," said the President. "Am I left with any alternative?"

"Short of military action to prevent the Soviets claiming what they will rightfully see as theirs, no sir," replied the Secretary of State.

"So one Johnson buys the land from the Russians in 1867 and another has to sell it back in 1966. Why did Seward and the President ever agree to such a damn cockamaney idea in the first place?"

"At the time," said the Attorney General, removing his spectacles, "the purchase price of the land in question was seven point two million dollars and inflation was then virtually unheard of. Andrew Johnson could never have imagined the Russians wanting to purchase it back at ninety-nine times its original value, or in real terms, seven hundred and twelve point eight million dollars in gold bullion. In reality, years of inflation have made the asking price cheap. And the Russians have already lodged the full amount in a New York bank to prove it."

"So we can't even hope that they won't stump up in time," said the President.

"It would seem not, sir."

"But why did Tsar Alexander want to lease the damn land in the first place? That's what beats me."

"He was having trouble with some of his senior ministers at the time over the selling off of land belonging to Russia in Eastern Asia. The Tsar thought this transaction would be more palatable to his inner circle if he presented it as nothing more than a long lease, with a buy-back clause, rather than an outright sale."

"Why didn't Congress object?"

"After Congress ratified the main treaty, the amendment was not strictly subject to approval by the House, because no further expenditure by the United States government was involved," Rusk explained. "Ironically, Seward was proud of the fact he had demanded such a high premium in the repayment clause. At the time he had every reason to believe it would be impossible to repay."

"Now it's worth that in annual oil revenue alone," said the President, looking out of the Oval Office window towards the Washington Monument. "Not to mention the military chaos it's going to create in this country if they've got their hands on their copy of the treaty. Don't ever forget that I was the President who asked Congress to spend billions of dollars putting the early warning system right across that border so the American people could sleep easy."

Neither adviser felt able to contradict their elected leader.

"So what are the British doing about all this?"

"Playing it close to the chest, as usual, Mr President. It's an English national who is thought to be in possession of the treaty at the moment and they still seem quietly confident that they will get their hands on him and the icon before the Russians, so they may yet turn out to be our saviours."

"Nice to have the British coming to *our* rescue for a change," said the President. "But have we meanwhile been sitting on our asses while they try to solve our problems for us?"

"No, sir. The CIA have been on it for over a month."

"Then it's only surprising that the Russians haven't got their hands on the icon already."

Nobody laughed.

"So what am I expected to do next? Sit and wait for the Soviets to move 712 million dollars of gold from their New York bank to the US Treasury before midnight on Monday?"

"They must also deliver their original copy of the agreement to me at the same time," said Rusk. "And they have only sixty hours left to do that."

"Where's our copy, at this moment?" asked the President.

"Somewhere deep in the vaults of the Pentagon. Only two people know the exact location. Since the

Yalta conference, our copy of the treaty has never seen the light of day."

"Why have I never been told about it before today?" asked the President. "At least I could have put a stop to so much expenditure."

"For over fifty years, we've believed the Russians' copy was destroyed at the time of the Revolution. As the years passed it became clear that the Soviets accepted this as a *fait accompli* with the final acknowledgment of this fact coming from Stalin at Yalta. Brezhnev must have come across something within the last month that convinced him that their copy had only been mislaid."

"Christ, another month and we would have had a home run."

"That is correct, sir," said the Secretary of State.

"Do you realise, Dean, that if the Russians turn up at your office before midnight on Monday with their copy, all I'll be able to do will be so much piss in a thunderstorm?"

CHAPTER EIGHTEEN

When the cottage door closed behind Adam, all he could make out was the outskirts of a small town. While it was still so early he felt safe to jog towards the '*centre ville*', but as soon as the early-morning workers began to appear on the streets, he slowed to a walk. Adam opted not to go straight into the centre of the town but to look for somewhere to hide while he considered his next move. He came to a halt outside a multi-storey car park and decided he was unlikely to find a better place to formulate a plan.

Adam walked through an exit door at ground level and came to a lift that indicated that the car park was on four floors. He ran down the steps to the lowest level, tentatively pulled back the door to the basement, and found it was badly lit and almost empty. Adam had chosen the basement as he assumed that it would be the last floor to fill up with customers. He walked around the perimeter of the floor and studied the layout. Two cars were parked in the far corner, and a thick layer of dust suggested that they had been there for some time. He crouched down behind one of them and found that he was safely out of sight to all but the most inquisitive.

He began to fantasise that someone might park a

car on that floor and leave the keys in the ignition. He checked the doors of the two cars already parked but both were securely locked. He settled back to work out a more serious plan of how he could reach the coast by nightfall.

He was deep in thought when he heard a scraping noise that made him jump. He peered round the gloomy basement, and out of the darkness a man appeared pulling behind him a plastic dustbin half full of rubbish. Adam could barely see the old man dressed in a dirty brown coat that stretched nearly to the ground and left little doubt about the height of the previous employee. He wasn't sure what he would do if the man continued to walk towards him. But as he came nearer Adam could see that he was stooped and old; the stub of a cigarette protruded from his lips. The cleaner stopped in front of him, spotted a cigarette packet, picked it up and checked to be sure it was empty before dropping it in the dustbin. After that, a sweet paper, a Pepsi-Cola can and an old copy of *Le Figaro* all found their way into the dustbin. His eyes searched slowly round the room for more rubbish, but still he didn't notice Adam tucked away behind the farthest car. Satisfied that his task was completed, he dragged the dustbin across the floor and pushed it outside the door. Adam began to relax again but after about two minutes, the old man returned, walked over to a wall and pulled open a door that Adam hadn't previously noticed. He took off the long brown coat and replaced it with a grey one that didn't look in a much better state but at least it made a more convincing fit. He then disappeared through the exit. Moments later Adam heard a door close with a bang.

The cleaner had ended his day.

Adam waited for some time before he stood up and stretched. He crept around the edge of the wall until he reached the little door. He pulled it open quietly and removed the long brown coat from its nail, then headed back to his place in the corner. He ducked down as the first of the morning cars arrived. The driver swung into the far corner in such a fluent circle that Adam felt sure it must have been a daily routine. A short dapper man with a pencil moustache, dressed in a smart pin-stripe suit, jumped out of the car carrying a briefcase. Once he had locked the car door he proceeded with fast mincing strides towards the exit. Adam waited until the heavy door swung back into place before he stood up and tried on the brown coat over his blazer. It was tight on the shoulders and a little short in the arm, but at least it made him look as if he might have worked there.

For the next hour he watched the cars as they continued to arrive at irregular intervals. Tiresomely, all the owners carefully locked their doors and checked them before disappearing through the exit with their keys.

When he heard ten o'clock strike in the distance Adam decided that there was nothing to be gained by hanging around any longer. He had crept out from behind the car that was shielding him and began to make his way across the floor towards the exit when a Rover with English registration plates swung round the corner and nearly blinded him. He jumped to one side to let the car pass but it screeched to a halt beside him and the driver wound down his window.

"All – right – park – here?" the driver asked, emphasising each word in an English accent.

"Oui, monsieur," said Adam.

"Other – floors – marked – *privé*," the man continued, as if addressing a complete moron. "Anywhere?" His arm swept round the floor.

"*Oui*," repeated Adam, "bert ay merst paak you," he added, fearing he sounded too much like Peter Sellers.

Balls, was what Adam expected to hear him reply. "Fine," was what the man actually said. He got out of the car, and handed Adam his keys and a ten franc note.

"*Merci*," said Adam, pocketing the note and touching his forehead with his hand. "*Quelle – heure – vous – retournez?*" he asked, playing the man at his own game.

"One hour at most," said the man as he reached the door. Adam waited by the car for a few minutes but the man did not come back. He opened the passenger door and dropped the food bag on the front seat. He then walked round to the other side and climbed in the driver's seat, switched on the ignition and checked the fuel gauge: a little over half full. He revved the engine and drove the car up the ramp until he reached the first floor, where he came to a halt unable to escape. He needed a two-franc piece to make the arm swing up and let him out. The lady in the car behind him reluctantly changed his ten-franc note once she realised there was no other way of getting out.

Adam drove quickly out on to the road looking for the sign 'Toutes Directions'. Once he had found one, it was only minutes before he was clear of the town and travelling up the N6 to Paris.

Adam estimated that he had two hours at best. By then the police would surely have been informed of the theft of the car. He felt confident he had enough petrol to reach Paris; but he certainly couldn't hope to make Calais.

He remained in the centre lane of the N6 for most

of the journey, always keeping the speedometer five kilometres below the limit. By the end of the first hour Adam had covered nearly ninety kilometres. He opened the bag the farmer's wife had given him and took out an apple and a piece of cheese. His mind began to drift to Heidi, as it had so often in the past two days.

If only he had never opened the letter.

Another hour passed before he spotted him limping up a hill only a few hundred yards from the main road. A broad smile came over Romanov's face when he realised he could get to Scott long before he could hope to reach the road. When Romanov was within a few yards of him the flight lieutenant turned round and smiled at the stranger.

When Romanov left Banks thirty minutes later hidden behind a tree with a broken neck he reluctantly admitted that the young pilot officer had been as brave as Valchek – but he couldn't waste any more time trying to discover in which direction Scott was heading.

Romanov headed west.

The moment Adam heard the siren he came out of his reverie. He checked the little clock on the dashboard. He had only been driving for about an hour and a half. Could the French police be that efficient? The police car was now approaching him fast on his left but Adam maintained the same speed – except for his heartbeat, which climbed well above the approved limit – until the police car shot past him.

As the kilometres sped by, he began to wonder if it might be wiser to turn off on to a quieter road, but decided, on balance, to risk pushing on to Paris as quickly as possible.

He remained alert for further sirens as he continued to follow the signs to Paris. When he finally reached the outskirts of the city, he proceeded to the Boulevard de l'Hôpital and even felt relaxed enough to bite into another apple. In normal circumstances he would have appreciated the magnificent architecture along the banks of the Seine, but today his eyes kept returning to the rear view mirror.

Adam decided he would abandon the vehicle in a large public car park: with any luck it could be days before anyone came across it.

He turned down the Rue de Rivoli and took in at once the long colourful banners looming up in front of him. He could hardly have picked a better place, as he felt sure it would be packed with foreign cars.

Adam backed the Rover in the farthest corner of the square. He then wolfed down the last piece of cheese, and locked the car. He started walking towards the exit, but had only gone a few yards when he realised that the strolling holidàymakers were amused by his ill-fitting brown jacket which he had completely forgotten. He decided to turn back and throw the coat in the boot. He quickly took it off and folded it in a small square.

He was only a few yards away from the car when he saw the young policeman. He was checking the Rover's number plate and repeating the letters and numbers into an intercom. Adam inched slowly back, never taking his eyes from the officer. He only needed to manage another six or seven paces before he would be lost in the throng of the crowd.

Five, four, three, two, he backed, as the man continued speaking into the intercom. Just one more pace . . . *"Alors!"* hollered the lady on whose foot Adam stepped.

"I'm so sorry," said Adam, instinctively in his native

language. The policeman immediately looked up and stared at Adam, then shouted something into the intercom and began running towards him.

Adam dropped the brown coat and swung round quickly, nearly knocking the stooping lady over before sprinting off towards the exit. The car park was full of tourists who had come to enjoy the pleasures of the Louvre, and Adam found it hard to pick up any real speed through the dense crowd. By the time he reached the entrance to the car park he could hear the policeman's whistle a few paces behind him. He ran across the Rue de Rivoli, through an archway and into a large square.

By then another policeman was coming from his right, leaving him with no choice but to run up the steps in front of him. When he reached the top he turned to see at least three other policemen in close pursuit. He threw himself through the swing door and past a group of Japanese tourists who were surrounding the Rodin statue that stood in the hallway. He charged on past a startled ticket collector, and on up the long marble staircase. "*Monsieur, monsieur, votre billet?*" he heard shouted in his wake.

At the top of the staircase he turned right and ran through *The Special '66' Centuries Exhibition*, Modern – Pollock, Bacon, Hockney – into the Impressionist room – Monet, Manet, Courbet – desperately looking for any way out. On into Eighteenth Century – Fragonard, Goya, Watteau – but still no sign of an exit. Through the great arch into Seventeenth Century – Murillo, Van Dyck, Poussin – as people stopped looking at the pictures and turned their attention to what was causing such a commotion. Adam ran on into Sixteenth Century – Raphael, Caravaggio, Michelangelo – suddenly aware that there were only two centuries of paintings to go.

Right or left? He chose right, and entered a huge square room. There were three exits. He slowed momentarily to decide which would be his best bet when he became aware that the room was full of Russian icons. He came to a halt at an empty display case. '*Nous regrettons que ce tableau soit soumis à la restauration.*'

The first policeman had already entered the large room and was only a few paces behind as Adam dashed on towards the farthest exit. There were now only two exits left open for him from which to choose. He swung right, only to see another policeman bearing straight down on him. Left: two more. Ahead, yet another.

Adam came to a halt in the middle of the Icon Room at the Louvre, his hands raised above his head. He was surrounded by policemen, their guns drawn.

CHAPTER NINETEEN

Sir Morris picked up the phone on his desk.

"An urgent call from Paris, sir," said his secretary.

"Thank you, Tessa." He listened carefully as his brain quickly translated the exciting news.

"Merci, merci," said Sir Morris to his opposite number at the French Foreign Ministry. "We will be back in touch with you as soon as we have made all the necessary arrangements to collect him. But for now, please don't let him out of your sight." Sir Morris listened for a few moments before he said: "And if he has any possessions on him, please keep them guarded under lock and key. Thank you once again." His secretary took down every word of the conversation in shorthand – as she had done for the past seventeen years.

Once the police had snapped the handcuffs on Adam and marched him off to a waiting car, he was surprised how relaxed, almost friendly, they became. He was yanked into the back of the car by the policeman to whom he was attached. He noticed that there was a police car in front of him and yet another behind. Two motorcycle outriders led the little motorcade away. Adam felt more like visiting royalty than a criminal who was wanted for questioning for two murders, two car thefts and travelling under false identification. Was it possible at last that someone had worked out he was innocent?

When Adam arrived at the Sûreté on the Ile de la Cité, he was immediately ordered to empty all his pockets. One wristwatch, one apple, forty pounds in traveller's cheques, eight francs, and one British passport in the name of Dudley Hulme. The station inspector asked him politely to strip to his vest and pants. It was the second time that day. Once Adam had done so, the inspector carefully checked every pocket of the blazer, even the lining. His expression left Adam in no doubt he hadn't found what he was looking for.

"Do you have anything else in your possession?" the officer asked in slow, precise English.

Damn silly question, thought Adam. You can see for yourself. "No," was all he replied. The inspector checked the blazer once again but came across nothing new. "You must be dressed," he said abruptly.

Adam put back on his shirt, jacket and trousers but the inspector kept his tie and shoelaces.

"All your things will be returned to you when you leave," the inspector explained. Adam nodded as he slipped on his shoes, which flapped uncomfortably when he walked. He was then accompanied to a small cell on the same floor, locked in and left alone. He looked around the sparsely furnished room. A small wooden table was placed in its centre, with two wooden chairs on either side. His eyes checked over a single bed in the corner which had on it an ancient horse-hair mattress. He could not have described the room properly as a cell because there were no bars, even across the one small window. He took off his jacket, hung it over the chair and lay down on the bed. At least it was an improvement over anything he had slept on for the past two nights, he reflected. Could it have only been two nights since he had slept on the floor of Robin's hotel room in Geneva?

As the minutes ticked by, he made only one decision. That when the inspector returned, he would demand to see a lawyer. "What the hell's the French for lawyer?" he asked out loud.

When an officer eventually appeared, in what Adam estimated must have been about half an hour, he was carrying a tray laden with hot soup, a roll, and what looked to Adam like a steak with all the trimmings and a plastic cup filled to the brim with red wine. He wondered if they had got the wrong man, or if this was simply his last meal before the guillotine. He followed the officer to the door.

"I demand to speak to a lawyer," he said emphatically, but the policeman only shrugged.

"Je ne comprends pas l'anglais," he said, and slammed the door behind him.

Adam settled down to eat the meal that had been set before him, thankful that the French assumed good food should be served whatever the circumstances.

Sir Morris told them his news an hour later and then studied each of them round the table carefully. He would never have called the D4 if he hadn't felt sure that Adam was at last secure. Matthews continued to show no emotion. Busch was unusually silent while Snell looked almost relaxed for a change. Lawrence was the only one who seemed genuinely pleased.

"Scott is locked up in the Ministry of the Interior off the Place Beauvais," continued Sir Morris, "and I have already contacted our military attaché at the Embassy . . ."

"Colonel Pollard," interrupted Lawrence.

"Colonel Pollard," said Sir Morris, "who has been sent over in the Ambassador's car and will bring Scott back to be debriefed at our Embassy in Faubourg St Honoré. Sûreté rang a few moments ago to confirm that Colonel Pollard had arrived." Sir Morris turned towards his Number Two. "You will fly over to Paris tonight and conduct the debriefing yourself."

"Yes, sir," said Lawrence, looking up at his boss, a smile appearing on his face.

Sir Morris nodded. A cool lot, he considered, as he stared round that table, but the next half hour would surely find out which one of them it was who served two masters.

"Good. I don't think I shall need any of you again today," said Sir Morris as he rose from his chair.

Mentor smiled as Sir Morris left the room; his task had already been completed. So simple when you can read upside-down shorthand.

A black Jaguar bearing CD plates had arrived at police headquarters a few minutes earlier than expected. The traffic had not been as heavy as the colonel had anticipated. The inspector was standing on the steps as Pollard jumped out of the car. The policeman looked at the flapping Union Jack on the bonnet and considered the whole exercise was becoming rather melodramatic.

Pollard, a short, thickset man, dressed in a dark suit, regimental tie and carrying a rolled umbrella, looked like so many of those Englishmen who refuse to acknowledge that they could possibly be abroad.

The inspector took Pollard directly through to the little room where Adam had been incarcerated.

"Pollard's the name, Colonel Pollard. British Military Attaché stationed here in Paris. Sorry you've been put through this ordeal, old fellow, but a lot of paperwork had to be completed to get you out. Bloody red tape."

"I understand," said Adam, jumping off the bed and shaking the colonel by the hand. "I was in the army myself."

"I know. Royal Wessex, wasn't it?"

Adam nodded, feeling a little more confident.

"Still, the problem's been sorted out now," continued the colonel. "The French police have been most co-operative and have agreed to let you accompany me to our Embassy."

Adam looked at the colonel's tie. "Duke of York's?"

"What? Certainly not," said Pollard, his hand fingering his shirt front. "Green Jackets."

"Yes, of course," said Adam, pleased to have his mistake picked up.

"Now I think we ought to be cutting along, old fellow, I know you'll be relieved to hear that they won't be laying any charges."

The colonel didn't know just how relieved Adam did feel.

The inspector led them both back out into the hall where Adam had only to identify and sign for his personal belongings. He put them all in his pocket, except for the watch, which he slipped over his wrist, and his shoelaces, which he quickly inserted and tied. He wasn't surprised they didn't return Dudley Hulme's passport.

"Don't let's hang around too long, old fellow," said the colonel, beginning to sound a little anxious.

"I won't be a moment," said Adam. "I'm just as keen to get out of this place as you are." He checked his laces before following Colonel Pollard and the inspector out to the waiting Jaguar. He noticed for the first time that the colonel had a slight limp. A chauffeur held the door open for him; Adam laughed.

"Something funny, old fellow?" asked the colonel.

"No. It's just that the last chauffeur who offered to do that for me didn't look quite as friendly."

Adam climbed into the back of the Jaguar and the colonel slipped in beside him.

"Back to the Embassy," said Pollard, and the car moved off briskly.

Adam stared in horror at the flapping Union Jack.

CHAPTER TWENTY

When Adam awoke he was naked.

He looked around the sparse room but this time, unlike the French jail, he was unable to see what was behind him: his arms, legs and body were bound tightly by a nylon cord to a chair that had been placed in the middle of the room, and which made him all but immobile.

When he looked up from the chair all he could see was Colonel Pollard standing over him. The moment the colonel was satisfied that Adam had regained consciousness he quickly left the room.

Adam turned his head to see all his clothes laid out neatly on a bed at the far side of the cell. He tried to manoeuvre the chair, but he could barely manage to make it wobble from side to side, and after several minutes had advanced only a few inches towards the door. He switched his energies to trying to loosen the cords around his wrists, rubbing them up and down against the wood of the slats, but his arms were bound so tightly that he could only manage the slightest friction.

After struggling ineffectively for several minutes he was interrupted by the sound of the door swinging open. Adam looked up as Romanov strode through.

323

He decided he was no less terrifying at close quarters. He was followed by another man whom Adam didn't recognise. The second man was clutching what looked like a cigar box as he took his place somewhere behind Adam. Pollard followed him, carrying a large plastic sheet.

Romanov looked at Adam's naked body and smiled; enjoying his humiliation he came to a halt directly in front of the chair.

"My name is Alexander Petrovich Romanov," he announced with only a slight accent.

"Or Emmanuel Rosenbaum," said Adam, staring at his adversary closely.

"I am only sorry that we are unable to shake hands," he added, as he began circling the chair. "But I felt in the circumstances certain precautions were necessary. First I should like to congratulate you on having eluded me for so long, but as you will now realise my source in London can place a call every bit as quickly as yours."

"Your source?" said Adam.

"Don't be naïve, Captain. You must be painfully aware by now that you're in no position to be asking questions, only answering them."

Adam fixed his gaze on a brick in the wall in front of him, making no attempt to follow Romanov's circum-navigations.

"Pollard," said Romanov sharply, "put Captain Scott back in the centre of the room. He seems to have managed to move at least a foot in his getaway attempt."

Pollard did as he was bid, first spreading the plastic sheet on the floor, then manoeuvring Adam till the chair was on the centre of the sheet.

"Thank you," said Romanov. "I think you have

already met our Colonel Pollard," he continued. "That's not his real name, of course, and indeed he's not a real colonel either, but that's what he always wanted to be in life, so when the opportunity arose, we happily obliged.

"In fact the good colonel did serve in the British Army, but I fear he entered the service of King and country as a private soldier and eighteen years later left, still as a private soldier. And despite an injury to his leg – unfortunately not received from any known enemy of the Crown – he was unable to claim a disability pension. Which left him fairly destitute. But, as I explained, he always wanted to be a colonel," continued Romanov. "It was a good attempt of yours – 'The Duke of York's?' – but as the colonel had genuinely served with the Green Jackets it was the one tie he felt safe wearing."

Adam's eyes remained fixed on the wall. "Now I confess, our mistake over the Union Jack was lax but as it is impossible to fly the Russian flag upside down without everyone noticing, it was perhaps understandable. Although, in truth, Pollard should have spotted it immediately, we must be thankful that you did not until the car doors were safely locked."

Romanov stopped his endless circling and stared down at the nude body.

"Now I think the time has come for you to be introduced to our Dr Stavinsky who has so been looking forward to making your acquaintance because he hasn't had a lot of work to do lately and he fears he might be becoming a little rusty."

Romanov took a pace backward allowing Stavinsky to come and take his place immediately in front of Adam. The cigar box was still tucked under his arm. Adam stared at the diminutive figure who seemed to be sizing him up. Stavinsky must have been no taller than five feet and wore an open-necked grey shirt and a badly creased grey suit that made him resemble a junior clerk in a not very successful solicitor's office. A one-day bristle covered his face, leaving the impression that he hadn't expected to be working that day. His thin lips suddenly parted in a grin as if he had come to some conclusion.

"It is a pleasure to make your acquaintance, Captain Scott," began Stavinsky. "Although you are an unexpected guest of the Embassy you are most welcome. You could of course make our association very short by simply letting me have one piece of information. In truth" – he let out a small sigh – "I only require to know the whereabouts of the Tsar's icon." He paused. "Although I have a feeling it's not going to be that easy. Am I correct?"

Adam didn't reply.

"It doesn't come as a great surprise. I warned Comrade Romanov that after his laudatory description of you a simple series of questions and answers would be unlikely to suffice. However, I must follow the normal procedure in such circumstances. As you will find, the Russians go by the book every bit as much as the British. Now you may have wondered," added Stavinsky as if it were an afterthought, "why a man who never smokes should be seen carrying a Cuban cigar box."

Stavinsky waited for Adam's reply but none was forthcoming.

"Ah, no attempt at conversation. I see you have been through such an experience before. Well, then I must continue talking to myself for the moment. When I was a student at the University of Moscow my subject was chemistry, but I specialised in one particular aspect of the science."

Adam feigned no interest as he tried not to recall his worst days in the hands of the Chinese.

"What few people in the West realise is that we Russians were the first to pioneer, at university level, a Department of Scientific Interrogation with a full professorial chair and several research assistants. They are still without one at either Oxford or Cambridge I am told. But then the West continues to preserve a quixotic view of the value of life and the right of the individual. Now, as you can imagine, only certain members of the university were aware of the existence of such a department, let alone able to enrol as a student – especially as it was not on the curriculum. But as I had already been a member of the Perviyotdel it was common sense that I should add the craft of torture to my trade. Now I am basically a simple man," continued Stavinsky, "who had previously shown little interest in research but once I had been introduced to the 'cigar box' I became, overnight, an enthralled and retentive pupil. I could not wait to be let loose to experiment." He paused to see what effect he was having on Scott, and was disappointed to be met by the same impassive stare.

"Torture, of course, is an old and honourable profession," continued Stavinsky. "The Chinese have been at it for nearly three thousand years as I think you have already experienced, Captain Scott, and even you British have come a long way since the rack. But that particular instrument has proved to be rather cumbersome for carrying around in a modern world. With this in mind, my tutor at Moscow, Professor Metz, has developed something small and simple that even a man of average intelligence can master after a few lessons."

Adam was desperate to know what was in the box but his look remained impassive.

"With torture, as with making love, Captain Scott, foreplay is the all-important factor. Are you following me, Captain?" asked Stavinsky.

Adam tried to remain relaxed and calm.

"Still no response, Captain Scott, but as I explained I am in no hurry. Especially, as I suspect in your case, the whole operation may take a little longer than usual, which I confess will only add to my enjoyment. And although we are not yet in possession of the Tsar's icon I *am* at least in control of the one person who knows where it is."

Adam still made no comment.

"So I will ask you once and once only before I open the box. Where is the Tsar's icon?"

Adam spat at Stavinsky.

"Not only ill-mannered," remarked Stavinsky, "but also stupid. Because in a very short time you will be desperate for any liquid we might be kind enough to allow you. But, to be fair, you had no way of knowing that."

Stavinsky placed the box on the floor and opened it slowly.

"First, I offer you," he said, like a conjurer in front of a child, "a six-volt nickel-cadmium battery, made by EverReady." He paused. "I thought you would appreciate that touch. Second," he continued, putting his hand back in the box, "a small pulse generator." He placed the rectangular metal box next to the battery. "Third, two lengths of wire with electrodes attached to their ends. Fourth, two syringes, fifth, a tube of collodion glue and finally, a phial, of which more later. When I say 'finally', there are still two items left in the box which I shall not require unless it becomes necessary for us to progress to Stage Two in our little experiment, or even Stage Three."

Stavinsky placed everything in a straight line on the floor in front of Adam.

"Doesn't look a lot, I confess," said Stavinsky. "But with a little imagination I'm sure you will be able to work out its potential. Now. In order that Comrade Romanov and the colonel can enjoy the spectacle I am about to offer it is necessary to add a few details about the nervous system itself. I do hope you are following my every word, Captain Scott, because it is the victim's knowledge which allows him to appreciate the true genius of what is about to follow."

It didn't please Adam that Stavinsky spoke English so well. He could still vividly remember how the Chinese had told Adam what they were going to do to him in a language that he couldn't understand. With them, he had found it easier to allow his mind to drift during their diatribe but he still ended up in a fridge for four hours.

"Now to the practical," continued the grey figure. "By sending a small electrical impulse to the end of the synapse, it is possible to pass on a large electric message to thousands of other nerves within a fraction of a second. This causes a nasty sensation not unlike touching a live wire when the electrical power has been left on in one's home, more commonly known as an electric shock. Not deadly, but distinctly unpleasant. In the Moscow school this is known as Stage One and there is no necessity for you to experience this if you are now willing to tell me where I can find the Tsar's icon."

Adam remained impassive.

"I see you have not paid attention during my little

lecture so I fear we will have to move from the theoretical to the practical."

Adam began reciting to himself the thirty-seven plays of Shakespeare. How his old English master would have been delighted to know that after all those years of drumming the complete Shakespearean canon into a reluctant student, Adam could still recall them at a moment's notice.

Henry VI part one, Henry VI part two, Henry VI part three, Richard II . . .

Stavinsky picked up the tube of collodion glue, removed the cap and smeared two lumps of it on Adam's chest.

. . . *Comedy of Errors, Titus Andronicus, The Taming of the Shrew* . . .

The Russian attached the two electrodes to the glue, taking the wires back and screwing them to the six-volt battery, which in turn was connected to the tiny pulse generator.

. . . *Two Gentlemen of Verona, Love's Labour's Lost, Romeo and Juliet* . . .

Without warning, Stavinsky pressed down the handle of the generator for two seconds during which time Adam received a two-hundred-volt shock. For those seconds Adam screamed as he experienced excruciating pain as the volts forced their way to every part of his body. But the sensation was over in a moment.

"Do feel free to let us know how exactly you feel. You are in a soundproof room, and therefore you won't be disturbing anyone else in the building."

Adam ignored the comment and gripping the side of the chair, mumbled . . . *Richard III, Midsummer Night's Dream, King John* . . .

Stavinsky pressed the plunger down for another two

seconds. Adam felt the pain instantly the second time. The moment it was over he felt violently nauseated, but he managed to remain conscious.

Stavinsky waited for some time before he volunteered an opinion. "Impressive. You have definitely qualified to enter Stage Two, from which you can be released immediately by answering one simple question. Where is the Tsar's icon?"

Adam's mouth had become so dry that he couldn't speak, let alone spit.

"I did try to warn you, Captain Scott." Stavinsky turned towards the door. "Do go and fetch the captain some water, Colonel."

. . . *The Merchant of Venice, Henry IV part one, Henry IV part two* . . .

A moment later Pollard was back, and a bottle was thrust into Adam's mouth. He gulped half the contents down until it was pulled away.

"Mustn't overdo it. You might need some more later. But that won't be necessary if you let me know where the icon is."

Adam spat what was left of the water towards where his adversary was standing.

Stavinsky leapt forward and slapped Adam hard across the face with the back of his hand. Adam's head slumped.

"You give me no choice but to advance to Stage Two," said Stavinsky. He looked towards Romanov who nodded. Stavinsky's thin lips parted in another smile. "You may have wondered," he continued, "how much more harm I can do with a simple six-volt battery, and indeed having seen in numerous American gangster movies an execution by the electric chair you will know a large generator is needed to kill a man. But first it is important to remember that I don't want to kill you. Second, my science lessons didn't end at Stage One. Professor Metz's mind was also exercised by the feebleness of this stage and after a lifetime of dedicated research he came up with an ingenious solution known as 'M', which the Academy of Science named after him in his honour. If you inject 'M' into the nervous system, messages can be transmitted to all your nerves many times more efficiently, thus allowing the pain to multiply without actually proving fatal.

"I only need to multiply a few milli-amps by a suitable factor to create a far more interesting effect – so I must ask you once again, where is the Tsar's icon?"

. . . *Much Ado About Nothing, Henry V, Julius Caesar* . . .

"I see you are determined that I should proceed," said Stavinsky, removing a syringe from the floor and jabbing the long thin needle into a phial before withdrawing the plunger until the barrel of the syringe was half full. Stavinsky held the needle in the air, pressed the knob and watched a little spray flow out like a tiny fountain. He moved behind Adam.

"I am now going to give you a lumbar puncture which if you attempt to move will paralyse you from the neck down for life. By nature I am not an honest man but on this occasion I must recommend you to trust me. I assure you that the injection will not kill you because, as you already know, that is not in our best interest."

Adam didn't move a muscle as he felt the syringe go into his back. *As You Like* . . . he began. Then excruciating pain swept his body, and suddenly, blessedly, he felt nothing.

When he came round there was no way of telling how much time had passed. His eyes slowly focused on his tormentor pacing up and down the room impatiently. Seeing Adam's eyes open, the unshaven man stopped pacing, smiled, walked over to the chair and ran his fingers slowly over the large piece of sticking plaster that covered Adam's two-day-old shoulder wound. The touch appeared gentle, but to Adam it felt like a hot iron being forced across his shoulder.

"As I promised," said Stavinsky. "A far more interesting sensation is awaiting you. And now I think I'll rip the plaster off." He waited for a moment while Adam pursed his lips. Then, in one movement, he tore the plaster back. Adam screamed as if the bullet had hit him again. Romanov came forward, leaned over and studied the wound.

"I'm relieved to see my colleague didn't miss you completely," Romanov said before adding, "can you imagine what it will be like when I allow Mr Stavinsky to wire you up again and then press the little generator?"

"... *Twelfth Night, Hamlet, The Merry Wives of Windsor* ..." Adam said aloud for the first time.

"I see you wish to leave nothing to the imagination," said Romanov and disappeared behind him. Stavinsky checked that the wires were attached to the collodion glue on Adam's chest and then he returned to the generator. "I shall press down the handle in three seconds' time. You know what you have to do to stop me."

"... *Troilus and Cressida, All's Well That Ends Well* ..."

As the handle plunged down the volts seemed to find their way to every nerve-ending in his body. Adam let out such a scream that if they had not been in a soundproofed room anyone within a mile would have heard him. When the initial effect was over he was left shaking and retching uncontrollably. Stavinsky and Pollard rushed forward to the chair and quickly undid the nylon cords. Adam fell on his hands and knees, still vomiting.

"Couldn't afford to let you choke to death, could we?" said Stavinsky. "We lost one or two that way in the early days but we know better now."

As soon as the sickness subsided, Stavinsky threw Adam back up on to the chair and Pollard tied him up again.

"Where is the Tsar's icon?" shouted Stavinsky.

"... *Measure for Measure, Othello, King Lear* ..." Adam said, his voice now trembling.

Pollard picked up another bottle of water and thrust it at Adam's lips. Adam gulped it down but it was as a tiny oasis in a vast desert. Romanov came forward and Stavinsky took his place beside the plunger.

"You are a brave man, Scott," said Romanov, "with nothing left to prove, but this is madness. Just tell me where the icon is and I will send Stavinsky away and order the colonel to leave you on the steps of the British Embassy."

"... *Macbeth, Antony and Cleopatra* ..."

Romanov let out a sigh and nodded. Stavinsky pushed the plunger down once again. Even the colonel turned white as he watched Adam's reaction. The pitch of the scream was even higher and the muscles contorted visibly as Adam felt the volts reach the millions of little nerve-ends in his body. When once more he had been released, Adam lay on the floor on his hands and knees. Was there anything left in his stomach that could still possibly come up? He raised his head, only to be hurled back on to the chair and bound up again. Stavinsky stared down at him.

"Most impressive, Captain Scott, you have qualified for Stage Three."

When Lawrence arrived at Orly Airport that evening he was looking forward to a quiet dinner with his old friend at the Ambassador's residence. He was met at the barrier by Colonel Pollard.

"How is he?" were Lawrence's first words.

"I hoped you were going to tell us," said Pollard, as he took Lawrence's overnight suitcase. Lawrence stopped in his tracks and stared at the tall, thin soldier who was in the full dress uniform of the Royal Dragoon Guards.

"What do you mean?" said Lawrence.

"Simply that," said Pollard. "I followed your instructions to the letter and went to pick up Scott at the Ile de la Cité but when I arrived I was informed that he had been taken away twenty minutes earlier by someone else using my name. We contacted your office immediately but as you were already en route the Ambassador ordered me straight to the airport while he phoned Sir Morris."

Lawrence staggered and nearly fell. The colonel came quickly to his side. He didn't understand what Lawrence meant when he said, "He's bound to believe it's me."

When Adam regained consciousness, Romanov stood alone.

"Sometimes," said the Russian, continuing as if Adam had never passed out, "a man is too proud to show lack of resolution in front of the torturer or indeed one of his own countrymen, especially a traitor. That is why I have removed Stavinsky and the colonel from our presence. Now I have no desire to see Stavinsky continue his experiment to Stage Three, but I can stop him only if you will tell me where you have put the icon."

"Why should I?" said Adam belligerently. "It's legally mine."

"Not so, Captain Scott. What you picked up from the bank in Geneva is the priceless original painted by Rublev which belongs to the Union of Soviet Socialist Republics. And if that icon were to appear in any auction house or gallery in the world, we would immediately claim it as a national treasure stolen by the seller."

"But how could that be . . .?" began Adam.

"Because," said Romanov, "it is you who are now in possession of the original that the Tsar left in the safe-keeping of the Grand Duke of Hesse and for over fifty years the Soviet Union has only had a copy." Adam's eyes opened wide in disbelief as Romanov removed from the inside pocket of his overcoat an icon of St George and the Dragon. Romanov paused and then turned it over; a smile of satisfaction crossed his face as Adam's eyes registered the significance of the missing crown.

"Like you," continued Romanov, "I only have this one on loan — but you tell me where the original is and I will release you and exchange the copy for the original. No one will be any the wiser and you'll still be able to make yourself a worthwhile profit."

"Old lamps for new," said Adam with a sneer.

Romanov's eyes narrowed menacingly. "Surely you realise, Scott, that you are in possession of a priceless masterpiece that belongs to the Soviet Union. Unless you return the icon you are going to cause considerable embarrassment for your country and you will probably

336

end up in jail. All you have to do is tell me where the icon is and you can go free."

Adam didn't even bother to shake his head.

"Then the time has obviously come to let you into some information you will be more interested in," Romanov said, extracting a single sheet of paper from an envelope he removed from his inside pocket. Adam was genuinely puzzled, quite unable to think what it could be. Romanov opened it slowly and held it up so that Adam could only see the back.

"This single sheet of paper reveals a sentence carried out in Moscow in 1946 by Judge I. T. Nikitchenko – the death sentence," continued Romanov, "pronounced on a certain Major Vladimir Kosky, the Russian guard in charge of the Soviet watch the night Reichsmarshal Hermann Goering died." He turned the paper round so Adam could see it. "As you can see, Major Kosky was found guilty of collaboration with the enemy for financial gain. It was proved he was directly responsible for smuggling cyanide into the Reichsmarshal's cell on the night he died." Adam's eyes widened. "Ah, I see I have dealt the ace of spades," said Romanov. "Now I think you will finally tell me where the icon actually is because you have an expression in England, if I recall correctly: fair exchange is no robbery. Your icon for my icon, plus the legal judgment that will finally vindicate your father's honour."

Adam closed his eyes, painfully aware for the first time that Romanov had no idea what was inside the icon.

Romanov was unable to hide his anger. He walked to the door and flung it open. "He's yours," he said.

Dr Stavinsky re-entered the room and, smiling, continued as if nothing had interrupted him. "Professor

Metz was never really satisfied with Stage Two because he found the recovery time even for an extremely brave and fit man like yourself could sometimes hold him up for hours, even days. So during his final years at the university he devoted his time to finding how he could possibly speed the whole process up. As for all geniuses the final solution was staggering in its simplicity. All he had to produce was a chemical formula that when injected into the nervous system caused an immediate recovery – a rapid analgesic. It took him twelve years and several deaths before he came up with the final solution," said Stavinsky, removing another phial from the cigar box and plunging the needle of a second syringe into the seal on the top of the phial.

"This," Stavinsky said, holding up the little phial in triumph, "when injected into your blood stream, will aid recovery so quickly that you may even wonder if you ever went through any pain in the first place. For this piece of genius Metz should have been awarded the Nobel Prize, but it was not something we felt he could share with the rest of the scientific world. But because of him I can repeat the process you have just experienced again and again, never permitting you to die. You see, I can keep this generator pumping up and down every thirty minutes for the next week if that is your desire," said Stavinsky, as he stared down at Adam's white, disbelieving face flecked with yellow specks of his vomit.

"Or I can stop immediately after I have administered the antidote the moment you let me know where the Tsar's icon is."

Stavinsky stood in front of Adam and half filled the syringe. Adam felt intensely cold, yet the shock of his torture had caused him to sweat profusely. "Sit still, Captain Scott, I have no desire to do you any permanent injury." Adam felt the needle go deep in and moments later the fluid entered his blood stream.

He could not believe how quickly he felt himself recovering. Within minutes he no longer felt sick or disorientated. The sensation in his arms and legs returned to normal while the wish never to experience Stage Two again became acute.

"Brilliant man, Professor Metz, on that I'm sure we can both agree," said Stavinsky, "and if he were still alive I feel certain he would have written a paper on your case." Slowly and carefully Stavinsky began to smear more lumps of jelly on Adam's chest. When he was satisfied with his handiwork he once again attached the electrodes to the jelly.

"Coriolanus, Timon of Athens, Pericles." Stavinsky thrust his palm down and Adam hoped that he would die. He found a new level to scream at, as his body shook and shook. Seconds later he felt ice cold and, shivering uncontrollably, he started to retch.

Stavinsky was quickly by his side to release him. Adam fell to the ground and coughed up what was left in his body. When he was only spitting, Pollard placed him back in the chair.

"You must understand I can't let you die, Captain. Now where is the icon?" Stavinsky shouted.

In the Louvre, Adam wanted to scream, but his words barely came out as a whisper, the inside of his mouth feeling like sandpaper. Stavinsky proceeded to fill the second syringe again and injected Adam with the fluid. Once again it was only moments before the agony subsided and he felt completely recovered.

"Ten seconds, we go again. Nine, eight, seven . . ."
"Cymbeline."
". . . six, five, four . . ."
"The Winter's Tale."

". . . three, two, one."

"*The Tempest*. Aahhhh," he screamed and immediately fainted. The next thing Adam remembered was the cold water being poured over him by the colonel before he began to retch again. Once tied back in the chair Stavinsky thrust the syringe into him once more, but Adam couldn't believe he would ever recover again. He must surely die, because he wanted to die. He felt the syringe jab into his flesh again.

Romanov stepped forward and looking straight at Adam, said, "I feel Dr Stavinsky and I have earned a little supper. We did consider inviting you but felt your stomach wouldn't be up to it, but when we return fully refreshed Dr Stavinsky will repeat the entire exercise again and again until you let me know where you have hidden the icon."

Romanov and Stavinsky left as Colonel Pollard came back in. Romanov and the colonel exchanged a few sentences which Adam could not make out. Then Romanov left the room, closing the door quietly behind him.

Pollard came over to Adam and offered him the water bottle. Adam gulped it down and was genuinely surprised how quickly he was recovering. Yet although his senses were returning to normal Adam still doubted he could survive one more time.

"I'm going to throw up again," said Adam and suddenly thrust his head forward. Pollard quickly undid the knots and watched Adam slump to his hands and knees. He threw up some spit and rested before the colonel helped him gently back into the chair. As he sat down Adam gripped both sides of the chair legs firmly, then with all the strength he could muster jack-knifed forward, swung the chair over his head, and brought it crashing down on top of the unsuspecting colonel. Pollard collapsed in a heap, unconscious, on the floor in front of Adam and never heard him utter the words, "*Henry VIII* and *Two Noble Kinsmen* – I'll bet that's one you've never heard of, Colonel. Mind you, to be fair, not everyone thinks Shakespeare wrote it."

Adam remained on his knees over the colonel's body, wondering what his next move should be. He was grateful that the soundproofed room was now working in his favour. He waited for a few more seconds as he tried to measure what was left of his strength. He picked up the water bottle that had been knocked over and drained it of its last drops. He then crawled across to the bed and pulled on his pants and socks, shoes, and his not so white shirt, followed by his trousers. He was about to put on the blazer, but found the lining had been ripped to shreds. He changed his mind and stumbled like an old man back towards the colonel, removed his Harris tweed coat and slipped it on. It was large round the shoulders but short at the hips.

Adam made his way to the door, feeling almost exhilarated. He turned the handle and pulled. The door came open an inch – nothing happened – two inches – still nothing. He stared through the crack but all he could see was a dark corridor. As he pulled the door wide open the hinges sounded to Adam like racing tyres screeching. Once he was certain that no one was going to return, he ventured into the corridor.

Standing against the wall he stared up and down the thin windowless passage, waiting for his eyes to adjust to the dark. He could make out a light shining through a pebbled pane in a door at the far end of the corridor, and began to take short steps towards it. He continued on, as if he were a blind man, creeping slowly forward until he saw another beam of light coming from under a door to his right about ten yards away from the one he needed to reach. He edged cautiously on and was only a pace away from the first door when it opened abruptly and out stepped a small man in a white tunic and blue kitchen overalls. Adam froze against the wall as the kitchen hand removed a packet of cigarettes and a box of matches from his pocket and headed away in the opposite direction. When the man reached the glazed door he opened it and walked out. Adam watched the silhouette outlined against the pebbled window, a match being struck, a cigarette being lit, the first puff of smoke; he even heard a sigh.

Adam crept past what he now assumed was a kitchen and on towards the outer door. He turned the knob slowly, waiting for the silhouette to move. The outer door also possessed hinges which no one had bothered to oil for months. The smoker turned round and smiled as Adam's left hand landed firmly in his stomach. As the smoker bent over, Adam's right fist came up to the man's chin with all the force he could muster. The smoker sank in a heap on the ground, and Adam stood over him thankful that he didn't move.

He dragged the limp body across the grass, dumped it behind a bush and remained kneeling by it while he tried to work out his bearings. Adam could just make out a high wall ahead of him with a gravelled courtyard in front of it. The wall threw out a long shadow from the moon across the tiny stones. About twenty yards . . . Summoning up every ounce of energy, he ran to the wall and then clung to it like a limpet, remaining motionless in its shadow. Slowly and silently he moved round the wall, yard by yard, until he reached the front of what he now felt sure was the Russian Embassy. The great green wooden gates at the front entrance were open, and every few seconds limousines swept past him. Adam looked back up towards the front door of the Embassy and at the top of the steps he saw a massive man, medals stretching across his formal dress jacket, shaking hands with each of his departing guests. Adam assumed he was the Ambassador.

One or two of the guests were leaving by foot. There were two armed gendarmes on the gate who stood rigidly to attention and saluted as each car or guest passed by.

Adam waited until a vast BMW, the West German flag fluttering on its bonnet, slowed as it passed through the gates. Using the car to shield him, Adam walked out into the centre of the drive, then, following closely behind, walked straight between the guards towards the road.

"Bonsoir," he said lightly to the guards as the car moved forward: he was only a yard from the road. "Walk," he told himself, "don't run. Walk, walk until you are out of their sight." They saluted deferentially. "Don't look back." Another car followed him out, but he kept his eyes firmly to the front.

"Tu cherches une femme?" a voice repeated from the shadows of a recessed doorway. Adam had ended up in a badly lit one-way street. Several men of indeterminate age seemed to be walking aimlessly up and down the kerbside. He eyed them with suspicion as he moved on through the darkness.

"Wha –?" said Adam, stepping sharply into the road, his senses heightened by the unexpected sound.

"From Britain, eh? Do you search for a girl?" The voice held an unmistakable French accent.

"You speak English," said Adam, still unable to see the woman clearly.

"You have to know a lot of languages in my profession, *chéri*, or you'd starve."

Adam tried to think coherently. "How much for the night?"

"*Eh bien*, but it's not yet midnight," said the girl. "So I would have to charge two hundred francs."

Although he had no money Adam hoped the girl might at least lead him to safety.

"Two hundred is fine."

"*D'accord*," said the girl, at last stepping out of the shadows. Adam was surprised by how attractive she turned out to be. "Take my arm and if you pass a gendarme say only, '*Ma femme*'."

Adam stumbled forward.

"Ah, I think you drink too much, *chéri*. Never mind, you can lean on me, yes."

"No, I'm just tired," said Adam, trying hard to keep up with her pace.

"You have been to party at Embassy, *n'est-ce pas?*"

Adam was startled.

"Don't be surprised, *chéri*. I find most of my regulars from the Embassies. They can't risk to be involved in casual affairs, *tu comprends?*"

"I believe you," said Adam.

"My apartment is just round the corner," she assured him. Adam was confident he could get that far but he took a deep breath when they arrived at a block of flats and first saw the steps. He just managed to reach the front door.

"I live on the top of the house, *chéri*. Very nice view," she said matter-of-factly, "but I'm afraid – how you say – no lift."

Adam said nothing, but leaned against the outside wall, breathing deeply.

"You are *fatigué*," she said. By the time they had

reached the second floor she almost had to drag Adam up the last few steps.

"I don't see you getting it up tonight, *chéri*," she said, opening her front door and turning on the light. "Still, it's your party." She strode in, turning on other lights as she went.

Adam staggered across the floor towards the only chair in sight and collapsed into it. The girl had by this time disappeared into another room and he had to make a supreme effort not to fall asleep before she returned.

As she stood in the light of the doorway Adam was able to see her properly for the first time. Her blonde hair was short and curly and she wore a red blouse and a knee-length skin-tight black skirt. A wide white plastic belt emphasised her small waist. She wore black mesh stockings and what he could see of her legs would have normally aroused him had he been in any other condition.

She walked over to Adam with a slight swing of the hips, and knelt down in front of him. Her eyes were a surprisingly luminous green.

"Would you please give me the two hundred now?" she asked, without harshness. She ran her hand along his thigh.

"I don't have any money," said Adam quite simply.

"What?" she said, sounding angry for the first time. Placing her hand in his inside pocket she removed a wallet and asked, "Then what's this? I don't play the games," handing the thick wallet over to Adam. He opened the flap to find it was jammed full of French francs and a few English notes. Adam concluded that the colonel was obviously paid in cash for his services.

Adam extracted two one-hundred francs and dutifully handed them over.

"That's better," she said, and disappeared into the other room.

Adam checked quickly through the wallet to discover a driving licence and a couple of credit cards in the colonel's real name of Albert Tomkins. He quickly looked around: a double bed that was wedged up against the far wall took up most of the floor space. Apart from the chair he was settled in, the only other pieces of furniture were a dressing table and a tiny stool with a red velvet cushion on it. A stained l lue carpet covered most of the wooden floor.

To his left was a small fireplace with logs stacked neatly in one corner. All Adam wished to do was fall asleep but with what strength was left in his body, he pushed himself up, wobbled over to the fireplace and hid the wallet between the logs. He lurched back towards the chair and fell into it as the door reopened.

Again the girl stood in the light of the doorway but this time she wore only a pink negligée, which even in his present state Adam could see right through whenever she made the slightest movement. She walked slowly across the room and once more knelt down beside him.

"How you like it, *mon cher*? Straight or the French way?"

"I need to rest," said Adam.

"For two hundred francs you sleep in any 'otel," she said in disbelief.

"I only want to be allowed to rest a few minutes," he assured her.

"L'Anglais," she said, and began to try to lift Adam out of the chair and towards the bed. He stumbled and fell, landing half on and half off the corner of the mattress. She undressed him as deftly as any nurse could have done before lifting his legs up on to the

bed. Adam made no effort to help or hinder her. She hesitated for a moment when she saw the shoulder wound, bewildered as to what kind of accident could have caused such a gash. She rolled him over to the far side and pulled back the top sheet and blanket. Then she walked round to the other side of the bed and rolled him back again. Finally she pushed him flat on his back and covered him with the sheet and blankets.

"I could still give you French if you like," she said. But Adam was already asleep.

CHAPTER TWENTY-ONE

When Adam eventually awoke the sun was already shining through the small window of the bedroom. He blinked as he took in his surroundings and tried to recall what had happened the night before. Then it all came back to him and suddenly he felt sick again at the memory. He sat on the edge of the bed but the moment he tried to stand he felt giddy and weak, and fell back down. At least he had escaped. He looked around the room but the girl was nowhere to be seen or heard. Then he remembered the wallet.

He sat bolt upright, gathering himself for a few moments before standing up again and trying to walk. Although he was still unsteady it was better than he had expected. It's only the recovery that counts, not the speed, he thought ironically. When he reached the fireplace he fell on his knees and searched among the logs, but the colonel's wallet was no longer there. As quickly as he could he went to the jacket hanging over the back of the chair. He checked in the inside pocket: a pen, a half-toothless comb, a passport, a driving licence, some other papers, but no wallet. He searched the outside pockets: a bunch of keys, a penknife, a few assorted coins, English and French, but that was all that was left. With a string of oaths he collapsed on to the floor. He sat there for some time and didn't move until he heard a key in the lock.

The front door of the flat swung open and the girl sauntered in carrying a shopping basket. She was dressed in a pretty floral skirt and white blouse that would have been suitable for any churchgoer on a Sunday morning. The basket was crammed with food.

"Woken up, 'ave we, *chéri*? *Est-ce-que tu prends le petit déjeuner?*"

Adam looked a little taken aback.

She returned his stare. "Even working girls need their breakfast, *n'est-ce pas*? Sometimes is the only meal I manage all day."

"Where's my wallet?" asked Adam coldly.

"On the table," said the girl, pointing.

Adam glanced across the room, to see that she had left the wallet in the most obvious place.

"It not necessary of you to 'ide it," she reprimanded him. "Because I'm a whore don't think I'm a thief." With this she strode off into the kitchen, leaving the door open.

Adam suddenly knew how big Tom Thumb felt.

"Coffee and croissants?" she shouted.

"Fantastic," said Adam. He paused. "I'm sorry. I was stupid."

"Not to think about it," she said. "*Ça n'est rien.*"

"I still don't know your name," said Adam.

"My working name is Brigitte, but as you 'ave not use my services last night or this morning you can call me by my real name – Jeanne."

"Can I have a bath, Jeanne?"

"The door in the corner, but don't take too long, unless you like croissants cold." Adam made his way to the bathroom and found Jeanne had provided for everything a man might need: a razor, shaving cream, soap, flannel, clean towels – and a gross box of Durex.

After a warm bath and a shave – delights Adam had nearly forgotten – he felt almost back to normal again, if still somewhat fragile. He tucked a pink towel around his waist before joining Jeanne in the kitchen. The table was already laid and she was removing a warm croissant from the oven.

"Good body," she said, turning round and scrutinising him carefully. "Much better than I usually 'ave." She put the plate down in front of him.

"You're not so bad yourself," said Adam grinning, taking the seat opposite her.

"I am 'appy you notice," said Jeanne. "I was beginning to think about you." Adam spread the roll liberally with jam and didn't speak again for several seconds.

"When 'ave you last eat?" asked Jeanne as he devoured the final scrap left on the plate.

"Yesterday lunch. But I emptied my stomach in between."

"Sick, eh? You mustn't drink so much."

"I think 'drained' might be a better word. Tell me, Jeanne," said Adam, looking up at her, "are you still available for work?"

She checked her watch. "One of my regulars is at two this afternoon, and I must be back on the streets by five. So it would 'ave to be this morning," she said matter-of-factly.

"No, no, that's not what I meant," said Adam.

"You could quickly give a girl, how do you say in England? – a complex," said Jeanne. "You not one of those weird ones, are you?"

"No, nothing like that," said Adam, laughing. "But I would be willing to pay you another two hundred francs for your services."

"Is it legal?"

"Absolutely."

"*Alors,* that makes a change. 'Ow long you need me?"

"An hour, two at the most."

"It's better than the rate for my present job. What am I expected to do?"

"For one hour I want every man in Paris to fancy you. Only this time you won't be available – at any price."

"Scott has just contacted me a few minutes ago," said Lawrence to the assembled D4.

"What did he have to say?" asked an anxious Sir Morris.

"Only that he was turning back the clock."

"What do you think he meant by that?" asked Snell.

"Geneva would be my guess," said Lawrence.

"Why Geneva?" said Matthews.

"I'm not certain," said Lawrence, "but he said it had something to do with the German girl, or the bank, but I can't be sure which."

No one spoke for some time.

"Did you trace the call?" asked Busch.

"Only the area," said Lawrence, "Neuchâtel on the German–Swiss border."

"Good. Then we're in business again," said Sir Morris. "Have you informed Interpol?"

"Yes sir, and I've personally briefed the German, French and Swiss police," added Lawrence, which was the only true word he had spoken since the meeting had begun.

Jeanne took forty minutes to get herself ready and when Adam saw the result he let out a long whistle.

"No one is going to give me a second look, even if I were to empty the till in front of them," he told her.

"That is the idea, *n'est-ce pas?*" Jeanne said, grinning.

"Now, are you sure you know exactly what you have to do?"

"I know well." Jeanne checked herself once more in the long mirror. "We 'ave rehearse like military exercise four times already."

"Good," said Adam. "You sound as if you're ready to face the enemy. So let's begin with what in the army they call 'advance to contact'."

Jeanne took out a plastic bag from a drawer in the kitchen. The single word 'Céline' was printed across it. She handed it over to Adam. He folded the bag in four, and stuffed it into his jacket pocket before walking into the corridor. She then locked the flat door behind them, and they walked down the stairs together and out on to the pavement.

Adam hailed a taxi and Jeanne told the driver "Tuileries gardens". Once they had arrived, Adam paid the fare and joined Jeanne on the pavement.

"Bonne chance," said Adam as he remained on the corner, allowing Jeanne to walk twenty yards ahead of him. Although he still felt unsteady he was able to keep up at her pace. The sun beat down on his face as he watched her walk in and out of the ornate flower beds. Her pink leather skirt and tight white sweater made almost every man she passed turn and take a second look. Some even stopped in their tracks and continued watching until she was out of sight.

The comments she could hear and Adam, twenty yards behind, couldn't, ranged from "*Je payerais n'importe quoi,*" which she reluctantly had to pass up, to just plain "*Putain*", which Adam had told her to ignore. Her part had to be acted out, and for two hundred francs she would just have to suffer the odd insult.

Jeanne reached the far side of the gardens and did not look back: she had been instructed not to turn around in any circumstances. Keep going forwards, Adam had told her. He was still twenty yards behind her when she reached the Quai des Tuileries. She waited for the lights to turn green before she crossed the wide road, keeping in the centre of a throng of people.

At the end of the quai she turned sharp right, and for the first time could see the Louvre straight in front of her. She had been too embarrassed to admit to him that she had never been inside the building before.

Jeanne climbed the steps to the entrance hall. By the time she had reached the swing doors, Adam was approaching the bottom step. She continued on up the marble staircase with Adam still following discreetly behind.

When Jeanne reached the top of the stairs she passed the statue of the Winged Victory of Samothrace. She proceeded into the first of the large crowded rooms and began counting to herself, noting as she passed through each gallery that there was at least one attendant on duty in each, usually standing around aimlessly near one of the exits. A group of schoolchildren were studying 'The Last Supper' by Giovanni but Jeanne ignored the masterpiece and marched straight on. After passing six attendants she arrived in the room Adam had described to her so vividly. She strode purposefully into the centre and paused for a few seconds. Some of the men began to lose interest in the paintings. Satisfied by the impact she was making, she flounced over to the guard, who straightened up his jacket and smiled at her.

"Dans quelle direction se trouve la peinture du seizième siècle?" Jeanne asked innocently. The guard turned to point in the direction of the relevant room. The moment he turned back, Jeanne slapped him hard across the face and shouted at him at the top of her voice: *"Quelle horreur! Pour qui est-ce que vous me prenez?"*

Only one person in the Icon Room didn't stop to stare at the spectacle. *"Je vais parler à la Direction,"* she screamed, and flounced off towards the main exit. The entire charade was over in less than thirty seconds. The bemused guard remained transfixed, staring after his assailant in bewilderment.

Jeanne continued on through three centuries more quickly than H. G. Wells. She took a left turn into the sixteenth-century room as instructed and then another left brought her back into the long corridor. A few moments later, she joined Adam at the top of the marble staircase leading down to the front entrance.

As they walked back down the steps together, Adam handed her the Céline bag and was about to set off again, when two attendants waiting on the bottom step threw out their arms indicating they should halt.

"Do you wish a run for it?" she whispered.

"Certainly not," said Adam very firmly. "Just don't say anything."

"Madame, excusez-moi, mais je dois fouiller votre sac."

"Allez-y pour tout ce que vous y trouvez!" said Jeanne.

"Certainly you can search her bag," said Adam, returning to her side before Jeanne could say anything more. "It's an icon, quite a good one, I think. I purchased it in a shop near the Champs-Elysées only this morning."

"Vous me permettez, monsieur?" the senior attendant asked suspiciously.

"Why not?" said Adam. He removed the Tsar's icon

355

from the bag and handed it over to the attendant, who seemed surprised by the way things were turning out. Two more attendants rushed over and stood on each side of Adam.

The senior attendant asked in broken English if Adam would mind if one of the gallery's experts were to look at the painting.

"Only too delighted," said Adam. "It would be fascinating to have a second opinion."

The senior attendant was beginning to look unsure of himself. "*Je dois vous demander de me suivre,*" he suggested in a tone that was suddenly less hostile. He ushered them quickly through to a little room at the side of the gallery. The attendant put the Tsar's icon in the middle of a table that dominated the room. Adam sat down and Jeanne, still bemused, took the seat beside him.

"I'll only be a moment, sir." The senior attendant almost ran out while the two other attendants remained stationed near the door. Adam still did not attempt to speak to Jeanne although he could see that she was becoming more and more apprehensive. He shot her a little smile as they sat waiting.

When the door eventually opened, an elderly man with a scholarly face preceded the senior attendant.

"*Bonjour, monsieur,*" the man began, looking at Adam, the first man who did not show an overt interest in Jeanne. "I understand that you are English," and without giving either of them more than a glance, he picked up the icon.

He studied the painting carefully for some time before he spoke. Adam felt just a moment's apprehension. "Most interesting. Yes, yes." One of the attendants put a hand on his truncheon.

"Interesting," he repeated. "I would be so bold as

to suggest," he hesitated, "late nineteenth century, eighteen seventy, possibly eighty. Fascinating. Not that we have ever had anything quite like it at the Louvre," he added. "You do realise it's an inferior copy," he said as he handed the icon back to Adam. "The original Tsar's icon of St George and the Dragon hangs in the Winter Palace in Leningrad. I've seen it, you know," he added, sounding rather pleased with himself.

"You certainly have," said Adam under his breath as he placed the icon back in its plastic bag. The old man bowed low to Jeanne and said as he shuffled away, "Funnily enough, someone else was making enquiries about the Tsar's icon only a few weeks ago." Adam was the only person who didn't seem surprised.

"I was only –" began the senior attendant.

"Doing your duty," completed Adam. "A natural precaution, if I may say so," he added a little pompously. "I can only admire the way you carried out the entire exercise."

Jeanne stared at them both, quite unable to comprehend what was happening.

"You are kind, *monsieur*," said the attendant, sounding relieved. "Hope you come again," he added, smiling at Jeanne.

The attendant accompanied the two of them to the entrance of the Louvre, and when they pushed through the door he stood smartly to attention and saluted.

Adam and Jeanne walked down the steps and into the Paris sun.

"Well, now can I know what that's all about?" asked Jeanne.

"You were *magnifique*," said Adam, not attempting to explain.

"I know, I know," said Jeanne. "But why you need

357

Oscar-winning show by me when the picture was always yours?"

"True," agreed Adam. "But I had left it in their safe-keeping overnight. And without your bravura performance it might have taken considerably longer to convince the authorities that it belonged to me in the first place."

Adam realised from the look on her face that Jeanne had no idea what he was talking about.

"You know, that my first time in the Louvre?" said Jeanne linking her arm in Adam's.

"You're priceless," said Adam, laughing.

"That I'm not," she said, turning to face him. "Two hundred francs was our bargain even if it belongs to you or not."

"Correct," said Adam, taking out the colonel's wallet and extracting two hundred francs, to which he added another hundred. "A well-earned bonus," said Adam.

She pocketed the money gratefully. "I think I'll take an evening off," she said.

Adam held her in his arms and kissed her on both cheeks as if she was a French general.

She kissed him on the lips and smiled. "When you next in Paris, *chéri*, look me up. I owe you one – on the house."

"How can you be so sure?"

"Because Antarctic was willing to give Pemberton too many facts."

"What do you mean?"

"You told me that Pemberton said he would never phone back if you let him down again. Not only did he phone back but he peppered you with facts. Which way did he say he was going?"

"Back to Geneva. Something to do with the German girl and the bank."

"The girl's dead and the bank's closed for the weekend. He must be on his way to England."

"I would like to rent a car which I will be dropping off at the coast. I haven't decided which port yet," he told the girl behind the counter.

"Bien sûr, monsieur," said the girl. "Would you be kind enough to fill in the form, and we will also need your driving licence." Adam removed all the papers from his inside pocket and passed over the colonel's driving licence. He filled in the forms slowly, copying the signature off the back of the colonel's Playboy Club card. He handed over the full amount required in cash hoping it would speed up the transaction.

The girl picked up the cash and counted the notes carefully before checking the back of the licence against the signature on the form. Adam was relieved that she hadn't spotted the disparity in the dates of birth. He replaced all Albert Tomkins's documents and the wallet in his inside jacket pocket, as the girl turned round and removed an ignition key from a hook on a board behind her.

"It's a red Citroën, parked on the first floor," she told him. "The registration number is stamped on the key ring."

Adam thanked her and walked quickly up to the first floor where he handed the key over to an attendant, who drove the car out of its parking space for him.

When the attendant returned the key, Adam handed him a ten-franc note. Exactly the same sum as the other man had given him to let him know if an Englishman who fitted Adam's description tried to hire a car. What had he promised? Another hundred francs if he phoned within five minutes of seeing him.

PART FOUR

THE KREMLIN
MOSCOW

June 19, 1966

CHAPTER TWENTY-TWO

THE KREMLIN, MOSCOW
June 19, 1966

Leonid Ilyich Brezhnev entered the room, hardly allowing the other four members of the inner quorum of the Defence Council enough time to stand. Their faces were grim, resolute, no different from their public image – unlike Western politicians.

The General Secretary took his place at the head of the table and nodded to his colleagues to sit.

The last time the inner quorum of the Defence Council had been summoned to a meeting at an hour's notice had been at the request of Khrushchev, who was hoping to enlist support for his Cuban adventure. Brezhnev would never forget the moment when his predecessor had uncontrollably burst into tears because they forced him to order the Soviet ships to return home. From that moment, Brezhnev knew it could only be a matter of time before he would succeed Khrushchev as the leader of the Communist world. On this occasion he had no intention of bursting into tears.

On his right sat Marshal Malinovsky, Minister of Defence: on his left Andrei Gromyko, the young

363

Foreign Minister. Beside him sat the Chief of the General Staff, Marshal Zakharov, and, on his left, Zaborski. Even the seating plan confirmed Brezhnev's obvious displeasure with the Chairman of the KGB.

He raised his eyes and stared up at the massive oil painting of Lenin reviewing an early military parade in Red Square: a picture no one other than members of the Politburo had seen since it disappeared from the Tretyakov in 1950.

If only Lenin had realised the icon was a fake in the first place, Brezhnev reflected ... Yet, despite the traditional Russian pastime of blaming the dead for everything that goes wrong, he knew that Vladimir Ilyich Lenin was beyond criticism. He would have to find a living scapegoat.

His eyes rested on Zaborski. "Your report, Comrade Chairman."

Zaborski fingered a file in front of him although he knew the contents almost off by heart. "The plan to locate the Tsar's icon was carried out in an exemplary fashion," he began. "When the Englishman, Adam Scott, was caught and later ... questioned" – they all accepted the euphemism – "by Comrade Dr Stavinsky in the privacy of our Embassy in Paris, the Englishman gave no clue as to where we would find the icon. It became obvious he was a professional agent of the West. After three hours, interrogation was momentarily suspended. It was during this period that the prisoner managed to escape."

"Managed," interjected Brezhnev.

Just as he had taught his subordinates over the years, the Chairman of the KGB made no attempt to reply.

"Don't you realise," continued the General Secretary, "that we had within our grasp the opportunity to turn the very land the Americans use for their early warning system into a base for our short range missiles? If it had proved possible to retrieve our icon it would also have been possible to site those very missiles along a border less than a thousand eight hundred kilometres from Seattle – two thousand kilometres from Chicago. Not only could we have made the Americans' early warning system redundant, we could have greatly improved our ability to detect any enemy missiles while they were still thousands of kilometres from our nearest border."

The General Secretary paused to see if the Chairman of the KGB had any further explanation to offer but Zaborski kept his eyes fixed on the table in front of him. When Brezhnev began again it was almost in a whisper:

"And for such a prize we would not have had to sacrifice one life, one rocket, one tank or even one bullet – because all this was ours by right. But if we fail to locate the Tsar's icon in the next thirty-six hours we will never be given such a chance again. We will have lost our one opportunity to remove a star from the American flag."

Foreign Secretary Gromyko waited until he was certain Brezhnev had completed his statement before he enquired:

"If I may ask, Comrade Chairman, why was Major Romanov allowed to continue being involved in such a sensitive operation after it was suspected he had killed" – with this he glanced down at the papers in front of him – "Researcher Petrova?"

"Because when that situation was drawn to my attention," replied Zaborski, at last looking up, "I had only seven days left to tomorrow's deadline, and in my judgment there was *no one* who could have taken over Romanov's place at such short notice –"

There was a timid knock on the door. All the faces round the table showed surprise. The Minister of Defence had given specific orders that no one was to interrupt them.

"Come," shouted Brezhnev.

The great door inched open and a secretary appeared in the gap; the thin piece of paper in his hand shook, betraying his nervousness. The Minister of Defence waved him in as Brezhnev had no intention of turning around to see who it was. The secretary walked quickly towards them. As soon as he had deposited the telex on the table he turned, and almost ran from the room.

Brezhnev slowly unfolded his tortoise-shell glasses before picking up the missive. Once he had read through the cable, he looked up at the expectant faces in front of him. "It seems an Englishman left an icon in the Louvre and picked it back up this morning."

The blood quickly drained from Zaborski's face.

The four ministers round the table all began talking together, until Brezhnev raised the vast palm of his right hand. There was immediate silence. "I intend to continue my plans on the assumption that it will still be us who get to the Englishman first."

Brezhnev turned towards his Foreign Minister. "Alert all our Western Ambassadors to be prepared to brief the Foreign Ministers of the country in which they reside on the full implications of honouring the amendment to the treaty. Then instruct Anatoly Dobrynin in Washington to demand an official meeting with the Secretary of State to be fixed for late Monday. At the same time I want a further meeting arranged between our Ambassador at the United Nations and U Thant."

Gromyko nodded as Brezhnev turned his attention to the Chief of the General Staff. "See that our strategic forces in all zones are put at a state of readiness to coincide with the timing of the announcement of our diplomatic initiative." Malinovsky smiled. The General Secretary finally turned to the Chairman of the KGB. "Do we still have advertising space booked in every major newspaper in the West?"

"Yes, Comrade General Secretary," replied Zaborski. "But I cannot be certain they will be willing to print the statement as you have prepared it."

"Then pay every one of them in advance," said Brezhnev. "Few Western editors will withdraw a full page advertisement when they already have the money in the bank."

"But if we then don't find the icon . . ." began the Chairman of the KGB.

"Then your last duty as Chairman of State Security will be to withdraw all the advertisements," said the General Secretary of the Communist Party.

CHAPTER TWENTY-THREE

Adam wound down the car window and immediately the warm summer air flooded in. He had decided to avoid the main road to Calais in favour of the N1 to Boulogne. He still considered it possible that Romanov would have men watching at every port on the Channel coast although he doubted if Lawrence or the Americans were aware he had escaped.

Once he had cleared the outskirts of the French capital, he was confident that he could average seventy kilometres an hour the rest of the way. But what he hadn't anticipated was running into a hundred or more cyclists, daubed in their various stripes of reds, greens, blues, blacks and golds, bobbing along ahead of him. As he drifted past them Adam was able accurately to check that they were averaging 40 miles an hour.

Having followed the build-up for the forthcoming World Cup in Britain, he was also able to make out the national colours of France, Germany, Italy and even Portugal. He honked his horn loudly as he passed a group of four men quite near the front, clad in red, white and blue T-shirts with the British team van driving just ahead of them. A few moments later he had overtaken the leaders, and was able to put the car back into fourth gear.

He switched on the car radio and fiddled around for some time before he tuned in to the Home Service of the BBC. He settled back to listen to the news in English for the first time in days. The usual reports of long strikes, high inflation, and of England's chances when the second Test Match at Lord's resumed after the rest day almost made him feel he was already back home, and then he nearly swerved off the road and into a tree.

The news reader reported matter-of-factly that a young RAF pilot had been found dead in a field off the Auxerre/Dijon road after his plane had crashed in mysterious circumstances. No more details were available at the present time. Adam cursed and slammed his fist on the steering wheel at the thought of Alan Banks becoming another victim of Romanov. He tapped the icon and cursed again.

"It was foolish of you to contact me, young man," said the old banker. "You're not exactly a hero of the Soviet Union at the present time."

"Listen, old man, I don't have to be a hero any longer because I may never come back to the Soviet Union."

"Be warned: Mother Russia has extremely long finger nails."

"And because of my grandfather's foresight, I can afford to cut them off," the caller said, touching the gold medallion he wore beneath his shirt. "I just need to be sure you don't let them know where I keep the scissors."

"Why should I remain silent?" asked Poskonov.

"Because if I haven't got my hands on St George within the next twenty-four hours, I'll phone again with the details of how you can hope to collect a larger golden handshake than you could have expected from your present employers." The banker offered no comment.

The Ambassador's secretary rushed into the room without knocking. "I told you no interruptions," shouted Romanov, covering the mouthpiece with his hand.

"But we've located Scott."

Romanov slammed the phone down. In Moscow, the old Russian banker wound the tape back. Poskonov smiled and listened to Romanov's words a second time and came to the conclusion that Romanov had left him with only one choice. He booked a flight to Geneva.

"Robin?"

"Batman. Where have you got to?"

"I'm just outside Paris on my way back home," Adam said. "Are you sticking to the schedule you outlined on the bus?"

"Sure am. Why, are you still desperate to spend the night with me?"

"Sure am," said Adam, mimicking her. "But when do you get back home?"

"The orchestra is taking the ferry from Dunkerque at six thirty tonight. Can you join us?"

"No," said Adam. "I have to return by another route. But, Robin, when I reach London can you put me up for the night?"

"Sounds like an offer I can't refuse," she said, and then repeated her address to be sure he had time to write it down. "When shall I expect you?" she asked.

"Around midnight tonight."

"Do you always give a girl so much notice?"

The young KGB officer standing in the adjoining box had caught most of the conversation. He smiled when he recalled Major Romanov's words: "The man who brings me the Tsar's icon need have no fear for his future in the KGB."

Adam jumped back in the car and drove on until he reached the outskirts of Beauvais, where he decided to stop at a wayside *routier* for a quick lunch.

According to the timetable he had picked up from the Hertz counter, the ferry he wanted to catch was due to leave Boulogne at three o'clock, so he felt confident he would still make it with about an hour to spare.

He sat hidden in an alcove by the window enjoying what might have been described in any English pub as a ploughman's lunch. With each mouthful he became aware that the French ploughmen demanded far higher standards of their innkeepers than any English farmworker was happy to settle for.

As he waited for his coffee he took out Albert Tomkins's papers from his inside pocket and began to scrutinise them carefully. He was interested to discover exactly how many weeks he had been claiming unemployment benefit.

Through the window of the inn he watched the first of the cyclists as they pedalled by. The athletes' muscles strained in their determination to remain among the leading group. As they shot through Beauvais, Adam was amused by the fact that they were all breaking the speed limit. The sight of the competitors reminded him that he was expected to attend the final part of his medical for the Foreign Office tomorrow afternoon.

Romanov read the decoded message a second time. "Scott returning Geneva. Check German girl and bank." He looked up at the senior KGB officer who had handed him the missive.

"Does Mentor think I'm that naïve?" said Romanov to his Parisian colleague. "We already know from our agent in Amsterdam that he's now on his way towards the French coast."

"Then why should Mentor want to send you in the opposite direction?"

"Because it must be him who's been briefing the Americans," said Romanov coldly.

Romanov turned to the colonel who was standing by his side. "We know it can't be Dunkerque, so how many other possibilities are we left with?"

"Cherbourg, Le Havre, Dieppe, Boulogne, or Calais," replied the colonel, looking down at the map laid out on the table in front of him. "My bet would be Calais," he added.

"Unfortunately," said Romanov, "Captain Scott is not quite *that* simple. And as the motorway takes you direct to Calais, the captain will expect us to have that part of his route well covered. I think our friend will try Boulogne or Dieppe first."

He checked the timetable the Second Secretary had supplied him with. "The first boat he could hope to catch leaves Boulogne for Dover at three, and then there's one from Dieppe to Newhaven at five."

Romanov also checked Calais and Le Havre. "Good. Calais left at twelve this morning, and as he phoned the girl after twelve he had no hope of catching that one. And Le Havre doesn't leave until seven fifteen tonight, and he won't risk leaving it that late. Assuming we can beat him to the coast, Colonel, I think Captain Scott is once again within our grasp."

*   *   *

Once Adam had left the *relais routier* it was only minutes before he began to catch up with the straggling cyclists as they pedalled on towards Abbeville. His thoughts reverted to Romanov. Adam suspected that his agents would have the airports, stations, autoroute and ports well covered. But even the KGB could not be in fifty places at once.

Adam took the Boulogne route out of Abbeville but had to remain in the centre of the road to avoid the bobbing cyclists. He even had to slam his brakes on once when an Italian and a British rider collided in front of him. The two men, both travelling at some speed, were thrown unceremoniously to the ground. The British rider remained ominously still on the side of the road.

Adam felt guilty about not stopping to help his fellow countryman but feared that any hold-up might prevent him catching his boat. He spotted the British team van ahead of him and speeded up until he was alongside. Adam waved at the driver to pull over.

The man behind the steering wheel looked surprised but stopped and wound down the window. Adam pulled up in front of him, leaped out of his car and ran to the van.

"One of your chaps has had an accident about a mile back," shouted Adam, pointing towards Paris.

"Thanks, mate," said the driver who turned round and sped quickly back down the road.

Adam continued to drive on at a sedate speed until he had passed all the leaders. Then, once again, he put the car into top gear. A signpost informed him that it was now only thirty-two kilometres to Boulogne: he would still make the three o'clock sailing comfortably.

He began to imagine what it might be like if he could survive beyond Monday. Would his life ever be routine again? Jogs in the park, Foreign Office interviews, workouts with the sergeant major and even the acknowledgment of the part he had played in delivering the icon into safe hands. The problem was that he hadn't yet decided who had safe hands.

A helicopter looking like a squat green bullfrog swept over him; now that would be the ideal way to get back to England, Adam considered. With help like that he could even make it to Harley Street in time for his medical for the Foreign Office.

He watched as the helicopter turned and swung back towards him. He assumed that there must be a military airport somewhere nearby, but couldn't remember one from his days in the army. A few moments later he heard the whirl of the blades as the helicopter flew across his path at a considerably lower level. Adam gripped the wheel of the car until his knuckles went white as an impossible thought crossed his mind. As he did so the helicopter swung back again, and this time flew straight towards him.

Adam wound the window up and crouching over the top of the steering wheel, stared into the sky. He could see the silhouetted outline of three figures sitting in the helicopter cockpit. He banged his fist on the steering wheel in anger as he realised how easy it must have been for them to trace a car signed for in the one name they would immediately recognise. He could sense Romanov's smile of triumph as the chopper hovered above him.

Adam saw a signpost looming up ahead of him and swung off the main road towards a village called Fleureville. He pushed the speedometer well over ninety causing the little car to skid along country lanes.

The helicopter likewise swung to the right, and dog-like followed his path.

Adam took a hard left and only just avoided colliding with a tractor coming out of a newly ploughed field. He took the next right and headed back towards the Boulogne road, desperately trying to think what he could do next. Every time he looked up the helicopter was there above him: he felt like a puppet dancing on the end of Romanov's string.

A road sign depicting a low tunnel ahead flashed past them and Adam dismissed the melodramatic idea of trying to make them crash; he didn't need reminding that it was he who was proving to be the novice.

When he first saw the tunnel he estimated it to be sixty or seventy yards in length. Although it was quite wide, a double-decker bus could not have entered it without the upstairs passengers ending up walking on the bridge.

For a brief moment Adam actually felt safe. He slammed on the little Citroën's brakes and skidded to a halt about thirty yards from the end of the tunnel. The car ended up almost scraping the side of the wall. He switched on his side lights and they flashed brightly in the darkness. For several seconds he watched as approaching cars slowed down before safely overtaking him.

At last he jumped out of the car and ran to the end of the tunnel where he pinned himself against the wall. The helicopter had travelled on some way, but was already turning back, and heading straight towards the tunnel. Adam watched it fly over his head, and moments later heard it turn again. As he waited, two hitch-hikers passed by on the other side, chatting away to themselves, oblivious to Adam's predicament.

He looked across desperately at the two young men

and shouted, "Were you hoping to thumb a lift?"

"Yes," they called back in unison. Adam staggered across the road to join them.

"Are you all right?" Adam heard one of them ask but he could hardly make out which one as his eyes had not yet become accustomed to the darkness.

"No, I'm not," Adam explained simply. "I drank too much wine at lunch and because of a cycle race the road is just crawling with police. I'm sure to be picked up if I go much further. Can either of you drive?"

"I only have my Canadian licence," said the taller of the two youths. "And in any case we are heading for Paris and your car is facing the opposite direction."

"It's a Hertz Rent-a-Car," Adam explained. "I picked it up on the Rue St Ferdinand this morning, and I have to return it by seven tonight. I don't think I can make it in my present state."

The two young men looked at him apprehensively. "I will give you both one hundred francs if you will return it safely for me. You see I can't afford to lose my licence, I'm a commercial traveller," Adam explained. Neither of them spoke. "My papers are all in order, I can assure you." Adam handed them over to the taller man who crossed back over the road and used the car lights to study Albert Tomkins's licence and insurance before carying on a conversation with his friend.

Adam could hear the helicopter blades whirling above the tunnel entrance.

"We don't need the hundred francs," the taller one said eventually. "But we will need a note from you explaining why we are returning the car to Hertz in Paris on your behalf." Adam pulled out the colonel's pen and, feeling remarkably sober, he bent over the hood of the car and scribbled on the back of the Hertz agreement.

"Do you want to come back to Paris with us?"

Adam hesitated fractionally. Couldn't they hear the noise too? "No. I have to get to Boulogne."

"We could drive you to Boulogne and still have enough time to take the car to Paris."

"No, no. That's very considerate. I can take care of myself as long as I feel confident that the car will be delivered back as soon as possible."

The taller one shrugged while his companion opened a rear door and threw their rucksacks on the back seat. Adam remained in the tunnel while they started up the engine. He could hear the purr of the helicopter blades change cadence: it had to be descending to land in a nearby field.

Go, go, for God's sake go, he wanted to shout as the car shot forward towards Boulogne. He watched them travel down the road for about a hundred yards before turning in at a farm entrance, reversing, and heading back towards the tunnel. They tooted as they passed him in the dark, disappearing in the direction of Paris. Adam sank down on to his knees with relief and was about to pick himself up and start walking towards Boulogne when he saw two figures silhouetted at the far entrance of the tunnel. Against the clear blue sky he could make out the outline of two tall, thin men. They stood peering into the tunnel. Adam didn't move a muscle, praying they hadn't spotted him.

And then suddenly one of them started walking towards him, while the other remained motionless. Adam knew he could not hope to escape again. He knelt there cursing his own stupidity. In seconds they would be able to see him clearly.

"Don't let's waste any more valuable time, Marvin, we already know that the limey bastard's heading back to Paris."

"I just thought perhaps . . ." began the one called Marvin in a Southern drawl.

"Leave the thinking to me. Now let's get back to the chopper before we lose him."

When Marvin was only twenty yards away from Adam he suddenly stopped, turned around and began running back.

Adam remained rooted to the spot for several minutes. A cold, clammy sweat had enveloped his body the moment he realised his latest pursuer was not Romanov. If one of them hadn't referred to him as a 'limey bastard', Adam would have happily given himself up. Suddenly he had become painfully aware of the difference between fact and fiction: he had been left with no friends.

Adam did not move again until he heard the helicopter rise above him. Peering out, he could see outlined against the arc of the tunnel the Americans heading back in the direction of Paris.

He staggered outside and put a hand across his eyes. The sunlight seemed much fiercer than a few minutes before. What next? He had less than an hour to catch the boat but no longer had any transport. He wasn't sure whether to thumb lifts, search for a bus stop, or simply get as far away from the main road as possible. His eyes were continually looking up into the sky. How long before they reached the car, and realised it was not him inside?

Cyclists began to pass him again as he jogged slowly towards Boulogne. He kept on moving, and even found enough strength to cheer the British competitors as they pedalled by. The British team van followed close behind and Adam gave it the thumbs-up sign. To his surprise the van came to a halt in front of him.

The driver wound down the window. "Weren't you the fellow who stopped me back in Abbeville?"

"That's right," said Adam. "Has your man recovered?"

"No, he's resting in the back – pulled ligament. What happened to your car?"

"Broke down about a mile back," said Adam, shrugging philosophically.

"Bad luck. Can I give you a lift?" the man asked. "We're only going as far as Boulogne on this stage, but jump in if it will help."

"Thank you," said Adam, with the relief of a bearded beatnik who has found the one person willing to stop to pick him up. The driver leaned across and pushed open the door for him.

Before climbing in, Adam shielded his eyes and once more looked up into the sky. The helicopter was nowhere to be seen – although he knew it couldn't be long before it returned. They would quickly work out that there was only one place where the switch could possibly have been made.

"My name's Bob," said the track-suited driver, thrusting out his free hand. "I'm the British team manager."

"Mine's Adam." He shook the other's hand warmly.

"Where are you heading?"

"Boulogne," said Adam, "and with luck I could still make my crossing by three."

"We should be there about two thirty," said Bob. "We have to be: the afternoon stage starts at three."

"Will your man be able to ride?" asked Adam, pointing over his shoulder.

"No, he won't be competing in this race again," said

the team manager. "He's pulled a ligament in the back
of his leg, and they always take a couple of weeks to
heal properly. I shall have to leave him in Boulogne
and complete the last leg myself. You don't ride by
any chance, do you?" Bob asked.

"No," said Adam. "Run a little, but haven't done
a lot on wheels since my sister crashed the family
tricycle."

"We're still in with a chance for the bronze," Bob
said, as they overtook the British riders once more.

Adam gave them the thumbs-up sign and then
looked over his shoulder through the back window. He
was thankful to see that there was still no sign of the
helicopter as they drove into the outskirts of Boulogne.
Bob took him all the way up to the dockside. "Hope
you get that bronze medal," said Adam as he jumped
out of the van. "And thanks again. Good luck with the
next stage."

Adam checked his watch: twenty minutes before the
boat was due to sail. He wondered if it was too much
time. He walked over to the booking office and waited
in a short line before buying a passenger ticket. He
kept looking round to check if anyone was watching
him, but no one seemed to be showing the slightest
interest. Once he had purchased his ticket he headed
towards the ship and had just begun to start whistling
a tuneless version of 'Yesterday' when a black speck
appeared in the distance. There was no mistaking it –
the sound was enough.

Adam looked up at the gangway which led to the
deck of the ship now only yards away from him, and
then back to the speck as it grew larger and larger in
the sky. He checked his watch: the ship was due to
leave in twelve minutes – still time enough for his
pursuers to land the helicopter and get on board. If he

climbed on and the Americans followed, they were
bound to discover him. But if the Americans got on
and he stayed off that would still give him enough time
to reach Dieppe before the next sailing . . .

Adam jogged quickly back towards the large crowd
that was hanging about waiting for the start of the next
stage of the road race. As he did so the helicopter swept
overhead and started hovering, like a kestrel that is
looking for a mouse.

"I thought you said you were desperate to be on
that ship."

Adam swung round, his fist clenched, only to face
the British team manager now dressed in riding gear.

"Changed my mind," said Adam.

"Wouldn't care to drive the van for us on the next
stage?" said Bob hopefully.

"Where does the next stage go?" Adam asked.

"Dunkerque," said the team manager.

Adam tried to remember what time Robin had said
her boat left from Dunkerque.

"Six minutes," a voice said over the loudspeaker.

"Okay," said Adam.

"Good," said the team manager. "Then follow me."

Adam ran behind the team manager as he headed
towards the van.

"Quatre minutes," Adam heard clearly as Bob unlocked the van and handed him the keys. He stared
towards the ship. The two Americans were emerging
from the ticket office.

"Deux minutes."

Adam jumped up into the driver's seat, looked over
towards the boat and watched Marvin and his colleague stride up the gangplank.

"Une minute."

"Just get the van to Dunkerque and leave the keys

at the British checkpoint. We'll see you when we get there."

"Good luck," said Adam.

"Thank you," said Bob, and ran to the starting line to join his team mates who were anxiously holding his bike.

"Trente secondes."

Adam watched the gangplank being hoisted up as the starter raised his gun.

"On your marks, set . . ."

The ship's fog horn belched out a droning note and the two Americans started their journey to Dover. A second later, the gun went off as Adam put the van into second gear and headed towards Dunkerque.

CHAPTER TWENTY-FOUR

Adam sat in the little dockside café waiting for the coach to appear. The team van had been left at the checkpoint and he was now ready to board the ship but he still needed to be sure Robin was on it. The coach trundled in with only ten minutes to spare and Adam greeted her as she stepped off.

"Just couldn't keep away from me, could you?" said Robin.

Adam burst out laughing and threw his arms almost round her.

"It's good to see you," he said.

"I thought you were going back to England by some mysterious route, you know, spy rocket or something even more exotic."

"I wanted to," said Adam, "but the Americans were sitting at the controls just as I decided to climb aboard."

"The Americans?" she said.

"I'll explain everything once we're on board," said Adam. Neither of them noticed the young agent who had trailed Robin from Berlin. He sat in a phone booth on the far side of the dock and dialled an overseas number.

"I wouldn't have believed a word of it a week ago," she said, "but for two things."

"Namely?"

"First, a senior official of the Foreign Office returned Dudley Hulme's passport to him in Amsterdam. Which reminds me to give you yours back." She rummaged around in her bag for a few moments before taking out a dark blue passport and handing it to him.

"And what's the second thing?" said Adam, taking the passport gratefully.

"I had the doubtful pleasure of coming face to face with Comrade Romanov, and I have no desire to do so again."

"I intend to meet him again," said Adam.

"Why?" asked Robin.

"Because I'm going to kill him."

Romanov and Pollard arrived in Dover a few minutes before the ferry was due to dock. They waited expectantly. Romanov stationed himself so that he could look through the customs hall window and watch the ferry as it sailed into Dover harbour. He had found the perfect spot behind a coffee-vending machine from which he could observe everyone who entered or left the customs hall, while at the same time remaining hidden from view.

"Just in case he should act out of character for a change," said Romanov, "and fails to go in a straight line, you will cover the car exit and report back to me if you notice anything unusual."

The colonel left Romanov secreted behind the coffee machine while he selected a place for himself on the dockside where he could watch the cars as they entered the customs area some fifty yards from the exit gate. If Scott did leave the ferry in a car Pollard would easily have enough time to run back and warn Romanov before Scott could hope to clear customs and reach the main gate. At least this would be the one place Scott couldn't risk hiding in the trunk. Both men waited.

The captain switched on his ship-to-shore radio to channel nine and spoke clearly into the small microphone. "This is the MV *Chantilly* calling the Dover Harbour Master. Are you receiving me?" He waited for a moment, flicked up the switch in front of him and then heard: "Harbour Master to MV *Chantilly*. Receiving you loud and clear, over."

"This is the captain speaking. We have an emergency. A male passenger has fallen out of a lifeboat on to the deck and contracted multiple injuries to his arms and legs." Adam groaned as the captain continued. "I shall need an ambulance to be standing by at the quayside to take him to the nearest hospital once we have docked. Over."

"Message received and understood, Captain. An ambulance will be waiting for you when the ship docks. Over and out."

"Everything will be all right, my dear," said Robin in a gentle voice that Adam had not heard before. "As soon as we arrive, they are going to see you are taken straight to a hospital."

"I must get back to the bridge," said the captain gruffly. "I shall instruct two stewards to bring a stretcher down for your brother."

"Thank you, Captain," said Robin. "You have been most helpful."

"It's quite all right, miss. You did say your brother?"

"Yes, Captain," said Robin.

"Well, you might advise him in future that it's in

his best interests to drink less before he comes on board."

"I've tried," said Robin, sighing. "You couldn't believe how many times I've tried, Captain, but I'm afraid he takes after my father." Adam held on to his leg and groaned again.

"Um," said the captain, looking down at the gash across Adam's shoulder. "Let's hope it turns out not to be serious. Good luck," he added.

"Thank you again, Captain," said Robin as she watched the cabin door close behind them.

"So far, so good," said Robin. "Now let's hope the second part of the plan works. By the way, your breath smells foul."

"What do you expect after making me swirl whisky round in my mouth for twenty minutes and then forcing me to spit it out all over my own clothes?"

Adam was lifted carefully on to the stretcher, then carried out on to the deck by two stewards. They waited at the head of the gangplank and placed Adam gently on the deck while a customs officer, accompanied by an immigration officer, ran up to join them. Robin handed over his passport. The immigration officer flicked through the pages and checked the photograph.

"Quite a good likeness for a change," said Robin, "but I'm afraid they may have to include this under 'unusual scars' in the next edition." She threw back the blanket dramatically and revealed the deep gash on Adam's shoulder. Adam looked suitably crestfallen.

"Is he bringing anything in with him that needs to be declared?" asked the customs official. Adam couldn't stop himself from touching the icon.

"No, I wouldn't let him buy any more booze on this

trip. And I'll be responsible for checking his personal belongings through with mine when I leave the ship."

"Right. Thank you, miss. Better see he gets off to the hospital then," said the officer, suddenly aware that a restless mob of people were waiting at the top of the gangplank to disembark.

The two stewards carried Adam down the gangplank. An attendant was on hand to check his wound. Adam waved gamely at Robin as they placed him in the ambulance.

Romanov spotted her as she came through customs. "Now I know exactly how Captain Scott hopes to get off the ship, and we will be waiting for him when he least expects it. Go and hire a car to take us to London," he barked at the colonel.

The ambulance shot out through the customs gates with its lights full on and bells ringing. By the time they had arrived at The Royal Victoria Hospital the attendant had watched his patient's remarkable recovery en route with disbelief. He was beginning to feel that the captain might have exaggerated the scale of the emergency.

Romanov stood by the gate and smiled as he watched the coach carrying the musicians emerge from the deep black hole of the ship and take its turn in the queue for customs.

As Romanov's eyes ranged up and down the coach he quickly picked out Robin Beresford. Just as he had anticipated, the double bass was propped up by her side, making it impossible to see who was seated next to her.

"You won't pull that one on me a second time," Romanov muttered, just as the colonel appeared by his side, red in the face.

"Where's the car?" the Russian demanded, not taking his eye from the coach.

"I've booked one provisionally," said the colonel, "but they'll need your international licence. I forgot Scott has got mine, along with all my other papers."

"You stay put," said Romanov, "and make sure Scott doesn't try to get off that coach." Romanov ran to the Avis desk at the same time as Adam was being wheeled into a little cubicle to be examined by the duty registrar.

The young doctor leant over his patient for several minutes. He had never seen a wound quite like it before. He examined him carefully, before making any comment. "Nasty lacerations," he said finally, cleaning Adam's shoulder wound. "Can you circle your arm?" Adam turned the arm in a full circle and straightened it again. "Good. No break, at least." He continued to clean the wound.

"I'm going to put some iodine on the open cut and it may sting a little," said the doctor. He cleaned up both elbows before placing a plaster on them.

"That didn't happen today, did it?" he asked, staring at Adam's half-healed shoulder.

"No," said Adam, without offering any explanations.

"You have been in the wars lately. I'm going to give you an anti-tetanus injection." Adam turned white. "Funny how many grown men don't care for the sight of a needle," said the doctor. Adam groaned.

"Now that wasn't so bad, was it?" he coaxed as he placed a large bandage over the top of the shoulder. "Do you have someone to collect you?" the doctor asked finally.

"Yes, thank you," said Adam. "My wife is waiting for me."

"Good, then you can go now, but please report to your GP the moment you get back home."

Romanov sat in the driver's seat and watched the coach clear customs. He followed it out of the main gate and on to the A2 in the direction of London.

"Are we going to intercept them on the way?" asked Pollard nervously.

"Not this time," said Romanov without explanation. He never once allowed the coach out of his sight all the way into the capital.

Adam walked out of the hospital and checked to see that no one was following him. The only people in sight were a man in a blue duffle coat walking in the opposite direction, and a nurse scurrying past him, looking anxiously at her watch. Satisfied, he took a taxi to Dover Priory station and purchased a single ticket to London.

"When's the next train?" he asked.

"Should be in any moment," said the ticket collector, checking his watch. "The ship docked about forty minutes ago, but it always takes a bit of time to unload all the passengers." Adam walked on to the platform, keeping a wary eye out for anyone acting suspiciously. He didn't notice the dark-haired man in a blue duffle coat leaning against the shutters of the W. H. Smith's stall reading the *Evening Standard*.

Adam's thoughts returned to Robin getting safely home. The London train drew in, packed with passengers who had been on the boat. Adam moved out of the shadows and jumped on, selecting a carriage full of teddy-boys who were apparently returning from a day at the seaside. He thought it would be unlikely anyone else would wish to join them. He took the only seat left in the far corner and sat silently but not in silence looking out of the window.

By the time the train had pulled into Canterbury no one had entered the carriage other than the ticket collector, who discreetly ignored the fact that one of the youths only presented him with a platform ticket for his inspection. Adam felt strangely safe in the corner of that particular compartment even when he noticed a dark-haired man in a blue duffle coat pass by the compartment door and look in carefully.

Adam was jolted out of his thoughts by a noisy claim made by one of the gang who during the journey had given every appearance of being its leader.

"There's a foul smell in this compartment," he declared, sniffing loudly.

"I agree, Terry," said his mate who was sitting next to Adam and also began imitating the sniff. "And I think it's quite close to me." Adam glanced towards the young man whose black leather jacket was covered in small shiny studs. The words 'Heil Hitler' were printed right across his back. He got up and pulled open the window. "Perhaps some fresh air will help," he said as he sat back down. In moments all four of them were sniffing. "Sniff, sniff, sniff, sniff, I think the smell's getting worse," their leader concluded.

"It must be me," said Adam.

The sniffing stopped and the youths stared towards the corner in disbelief – momentarily silenced by Adam's offensive.

"I didn't have time to take a shower after my judo lesson," Adam added before any of them had found time to recover their speech.

"Any good at judo, are you?" asked the one sitting next to him.

"Passable," said Adam.

"What belt are you?" demanded Terry belligerently. "Go on, tell me, a black belt, I knew it," he added, sniggering.

"I haven't been a black belt for nearly eight years," said Adam casually, "but I've been recently awarded my second Dan."

A look of apprehension came over three of the four faces.

"I was thinkin' about taking up judo myself," continued the leader, straightening his arm. "How long does it take to get any good at it?"

"I've been working at it three hours a day for nearly twelve years and I'm still not up to Olympic standard," replied Adam as he watched the dark-haired man in the duffle coat pass by the compartment again. This time he stared directly at Adam before quickly moving on.

"Of course," continued Adam, "the only quality you really need if you are thinking of taking up judo seriously is nerve, and no one can teach you that. You've either got it or you haven't."

"I've got nerve," said Terry belligerently. "I'm not frightened of nothin'. Or nobody," he added, staring straight at Adam.

"Good," said Adam. "Because you may be given the chance to prove your claim before this journey is over."

"What're you getting at?" said the 'Heil Hitler'-clad youth. "You trying to pick a fight or somethin'?"

"No," said Adam calmly. "It's just that at this moment I'm being followed by a private detective who is hoping to catch me spending the night with his client's wife."

The four of them sat still for the first time during

393

the journey and stared at Adam with something approaching respect.

"And are you?" asked the leader.

Adam nodded conspiratorially.

"Nice bit of skirt when you've got it in the hay?" Terry asked, leering.

"Not bad," said Adam, "not bad at all."

"Then just point out this detective git and we'll sew him up for the night," said the leader, thrusting his left hand on his right bicep while pulling up his clenched fist with gusto.

"That might turn out to be overkill," said Adam. "But if you could delay him for a little when I get off at Waterloo East, that should at least give me enough time to warn the lady."

"Say no more, squire," said the leader. "Your friend the Peeping Tom will be delivered to Charing Cross all trussed up like a British Rail parcel."

The other three youths burst out laughing and Adam was beginning to realise that it had taken Romanov only one week to turn him into a storyteller almost in the class of Robin's late father.

"That's him," whispered Adam as the duffle-coated man passed by a third time. They all looked out into the corridor but only saw his retreating back.

"The train is due to arrive at Waterloo East in eleven minutes' time," said Adam, checking his watch. "So what I suggest we do is . . . if you still think you're up to it, that is." All four of his new-found team leaned forward in eager anticipation.

A few minutes later Adam slipped out of the compartment, leaving the door wide open. He started to walk slowly in the direction opposite to that in which the man in the blue duffle coat had last been seen going. When Adam reached the end of the carriage, he turned to find the man was now following quickly behind. As he passed the open compartment the man smiled and raised a hand to attract Adam's attention but two leather-clad arms shot out and the man disappeared inside the compartment with a muffled cry. The door was slammed and the blinds pulled quickly down.

The train drew slowly into Waterloo East station.

Robin remained tense as the bus drew into Wigmore Street and came to a halt outside the RPO headquarters. A dark green Ford had been following them for at least thirty miles, and once she had become aware of it she had not dared to move from her seat.

As she dragged her double bass off the bus she looked back to see that the Ford had stopped about fifty yards down the road and turned off its headlights. Romanov was standing on the pavement looking like a caged animal that wanted to spring. Another man that Robin did not recognise remained seated behind the wheel. Adam had warned her not to turn around at any time but to walk straight into the RPO headquarters without stopping. Even so, she couldn't resist looking Romanov in the eye and shaking her head. Romanov continued to stare impassively ahead of him.

When the last musician had left the bus Romanov and 'the Colonel' searched up and down the inside of the vehicle and then finally the trunk, despite noisy protests from the driver. Robin eyed them nervously from an upstairs window, as the two of them jumped back into the green Ford and drove off. She continued watching the car until the back lights had faded away in the darkness.

* * *

The colonel swung out of Wigmore Street towards Baker Street, bringing the car to a halt opposite Baker Street station. Romanov jumped out, walked into a vacant telephone booth and started thumbing through the A–D directory. Only one Robin Beresford was listed and it was the same address as the young agent had read over to him. He dialled the number and after ten unanswered rings smiled at the realisation that she lived alone. He was not surprised.

"What now?" asked the colonel, once Romanov was back at the car.

"Where's Argyle Crescent, NW3?"

"Must be out towards Hampstead," said the colonel. "But I'll first check in the London A to Z roadmap. What's the plan?"

"Rather than waiting for Miss Beresford to come out we will be waiting for her to come in," said Romanov.

Robin slipped out of the back of the RPO headquarters about thirty minutes later. She zig-zagged around Portman Square then walked as quickly as she knew how up to the corner. She kept telling herself that Romanov was not coming back, but she found it impossible to stop herself from shaking all the same. She hailed a taxi and was relieved to see one draw up to her side almost immediately. She checked the driver and the back seat, as Adam had advised her, then climbed in.

Romanov arrived at Robin's front door a few moments after she had hailed the taxi. The name holder on the side wall indicated that Miss Beresford resided on the fourth floor.

The door itself would have proved no problem to any self-respecting petty thief in Moscow and

Romanov had secured entry within moments. The colonel quickly joined him before they proceeded silently up the dark staircase to the fourth floor.

Romanov slipped the Yale lock faster than Robin could have opened it with her own key. Once inside he quickly checked the layout of the room and assured himself no one else was in the flat.

The colonel stood around fidgeting. "Settle down, Colonel. I don't expect the lady will keep us waiting too long." The colonel laughed nervously.

The taxi drew up outside the house that Robin pointed to. She then jumped out and tipped the cabbie extra because the bewitching hour had long passed and at last she felt safe. It seemed ages since she had been home. All she was looking forward to now was a hot bath and a good night's sleep.

Adam stepped off the train at Waterloo East a little after midnight and was pleased to find the underground was still running. He had avoided going on to Charing Cross, as he couldn't be sure which side would have a reception committee waiting for him. He produced a season ticket for the West Indian on the ticket barrier and waited around on the underground platform for some time before the train eventually drew in.

There were several stations between Waterloo and his destination, and even at this time of night there seemed to be a prolonged stop at every one. Several late-night revellers got in at the Embankment, more still at Leicester Square. Adam waited nervously at each station, now aware that he must have caught the last train. He only hoped Robin had carried out his instructions faithfully. He looked around the carriage he was sitting in. It was full of night people, waiters, nurses, party returners, drunks – even a traffic warden. The train eventually pulled into his station, at twelve forty.

The ticket collector was able to give him the directions he needed. It was a relief to reach his final destination so quickly because there was no one else around to ask the way at that time of night. He moved slowly towards number twenty-three. There were no lights on in the house. He opened the swinging gate and walked straight up the path, removed the bunch of keys from his pocket, putting the Chubb one in the lock. Adam pushed open the door cautiously and then closed it noiselessly behind him.

A little after twelve ten the last train from Dover pulled into Charing Cross station. As Adam was nowhere to be seen, Lawrence instructed his driver to take him back to Cheyne Walk. He couldn't understand why the agent whom he had hand-picked hadn't reported in. When Lawrence arrived back at the flat he put the key in his lock, hoping to find Adam was already waiting for him.

CHAPTER TWENTY-FIVE

He pushed open the swinging gate and made his way slowly up the path in the pitch darkness. Once he reached the corner of the house he searched for the third stone on the left. When he located the correct stone where he always left his spare key, he pulled it up with his fingers and felt around in the dirt. To his relief the key was still in place. Like a burglar he pushed it into the lock quietly.

He crept into the hall and closed the door behind him, switched on the light and began to climb the stairs. Once he had reached the landing he switched off the hall light, turned the knob of his bedroom door and pushed.

As he stepped in an arm circled his throat like a whiplash and he was thrown to the ground with tremendous force. He felt a knee pressed hard against his spine and his arm was jerked up behind his back into a half nelson. He lay on the floor, flat on his face, hardly able to move or even breathe. The light switch flashed on and the first thing Adam saw was the colonel.

"Don't kill me, Captain Scott sir, don't kill me," he implored.

"I have no intention of doing so, Mr Tomkins,"

said Adam calmly. "But first, where is your esteemed employer at this moment?"

Adam kept his knee firmly in the middle of the colonel's back and pressed his arm a few inches higher before the colonel bleated out, "He went back to the Embassy once he realised the girl wasn't going to return to the flat."

"Just as I planned," said Adam, but he didn't lessen the pressure on the colonel's arm as he described in vivid detail everything that would now be expected of him.

The colonel's face showed disbelief. "But that will be impossible," he said. "I mean, he's bound to noti – Ahhh."

The colonel felt his arm forced higher up his back. "You could carry out the whole exercise in less than ten minutes and he need never be any the wiser," said Adam. "However, I feel that it's only fair that you should be rewarded for your effort."

"Thank you, sir," said the fawning colonel.

"If you succeed in delivering the one item I require and carry out my instructions to the letter you will be given in exchange your passport, driving licence, papers, wallet and a guarantee of no prosecution for your past treachery. But if, on the other hand, you fail to turn up by nine thirty tomorrow morning with the object of my desire," said Adam, "all those documents will be placed thirty minutes later on the desk of a Mr Lawrence Pemberton of the FO, along with my report on your other sources of income which you have failed to declare on your tax return."

"You wouldn't do that to me, would you, Captain Scott?"

"As ten o'clock chimes," said Adam.

"But think what would then happen to me, Captain

Scott, sir, if you carried out such a threat," moaned the colonel.

"I have already considered that," said Adam, "and I have come to two conclusions."

"And what are they, Captain Scott?"

"Spies," continued Adam, not loosening his grip, "at the present time seem to be getting anything from eighteen to forty-two years at Her Majesty's pleasure, so you might, with good behaviour, be out before the turn of the century, just in time to collect your telegram from the Queen."

The colonel looked visibly impressed. "And the other conclusion?" he blurted out.

"Oh, simply that you could inform Romanov of my nocturnal visit and he in return would arrange for you to spend the rest of your days in a very small dacha in a suitably undesirable suburb of Moscow. Because, you see, my dear Tomkins, you are a very small spy. I personally am not sure when left with such an alternative which I would view with more horror."

"I'll get it for you, Captain Scott, you can rely on me."

"I'm sure I can, Tomkins. Because if you were to let Romanov into our little secret, you would be arrested within minutes. So at best, you could try to escape on the Aeroflot plane to Moscow. And I've checked, there isn't one until the early evening."

"I'll bring it to you by nine thirty on the dot, sir. You can be sure of that. But for God's sake have yours ready to exchange."

"I will," said Adam, "as well as all your documents, Tomkins."

Adam lifted the colonel slowly off the ground and then shoved him towards the landing. He switched on the light and then pushed the colonel on down the stairs until they reached the front door.

"The keys," said Adam.

"But you've already got my keys, Captain Scott, sir."

"The car keys, you fool."

"But it's a hire car, sir," said the colonel.

"And I'm about to hire it," said Adam.

"But how will I get myself back to London in time, sir?"

"I have no idea, but you still have the rest of the night to come up with something. You could even walk it by then. The keys," Adam repeated, jerking the colonel's arm to shoulder-blade level.

"In my left hand pocket," said the colonel, almost an octave higher.

Adam put his hand into the colonel's new jacket and pulled out the car keys.

He opened the front door, shoved the colonel on to the path, and then escorted him to the pavement.

"You will go and stand on the far side of the road," said Adam, "and you will not return to the house until I have reached the end of the road. Do I make myself clear, Tomkins?"

"Abundantly clear, Captain Scott, sir."

"Good," said Adam releasing him for the first time, "and just one more thing, Tomkins. In case you think of double-crossing me, I have already instructed the Foreign Office to place Romanov under surveillance and put two extra lookouts near the Soviet Embassy with instructions to report the moment anyone suspicious turns up or leaves before nine tomorrow morning." Adam hoped he sounded convincing.

"Thought of everything, haven't you, sir?" said the colonel mournfully.

"Yes, I think so," said Adam. "I even found time to disconnect your phone while I was waiting for you to return." Adam pushed the colonel across the road before getting into the hire car. He wound the window down. "See you at nine thirty tomorrow morning. Prompt," he added, as he put the Ford into first gear.

The colonel stood shivering on the far pavement, nursing his right shoulder, as Adam drove to the end of the road. He was still standing there when Adam took a left turn back towards the centre of London.

For the first time since Heidi's death, Adam felt it was Romanov who was on the run.

"What a great honour for our little establishment," said Herr Bischoff, delighted to see the most important banker in the East sitting in his boardroom sharing afternoon tea.

"Not at all, my dear Bischoff," said Poskonov. "After all these years the honour is entirely mine. And kind of you to be so understanding about opening the bank on a Sunday. But now to business. Did you manage to get Romanov to sign the release form?"

"Oh, yes," said Bischoff, matter-of-factly. "He did it without even reading the standard clauses, let alone the extra three you asked us to put in."

"So his inheritance automatically returns to the Russian state?"

"That is so, Mr Poskonov, and we in return . . ."

". . . will represent us in all the currency exchange transactions we carry out in the West."

"Thank you," said Herr Bischoff. "And we shall be delighted to assist you in your slightest requirement, but what happens when Romanov returns to the bank and demands to know what has become of his inheritance?" asked the chairman of the bank anxiously.

"He will not return," the Russian banker said emphatically. "You can have my word on it. Now, I would like to see what is in those boxes."

"Yes, of course," said Herr Bischoff. "Will you please accompany me?"

The two banking chairmen took the private lift to the basement and Herr Bischoff accompanied his guest to the underground vault.

"I will unlock the five boxes now in your name with the bank's key but only you can open them with your key."

"Thank you," said Poskonov, and left Herr Bischoff to open the five locks and return to the entrance of the vault.

"Do take as long as you like," said Herr Bischoff, "but at six o'clock the great door is automatically locked until nine o'clock tomorrow morning, and nothing less than a nuclear weapon would prise it open. At five forty-five, an alarm goes off to warn you that you only have fifteen minutes left."

"Excellent," said the man who through his entire banking career had never been given a fifteen-minute warning of anything.

Herr Bischoff handed Comrade Poskonov the envelope with Romanov's key inside it.

As soon as the massive steel door had been swung closed behind him the Russian checked the clock on the wall. They had left him with over two hours to sort out what could be transported to Brazil and what would have to be left behind. A state pension and the Order of Lenin (second class) hadn't seemed much of an alternative to Poskonov.

He turned the key and opened the first of the small boxes and found the deeds to lands the State had owned for decades. He growled. The second box contained the shares of companies once brilliantly successful, now shells in every sense of the word. And to Poskonov's disappointment the third of the small boxes only held a will proving everything belonged to Romanov's father and his immediate heirs. Had he waited all these years to discover the stories the old man had told him of gold, jewels and pearls were nothing but a fantasy? Or had Romanov already removed them?

Poskonov opened the first of the large boxes and stared down at the twelve little compartments. He removed the lid of the first one tentatively, and when he saw the array of gems and stones that shone in front of him his legs felt weak. He put both hands into the box and let the gems slip through his fingers like a child playing with pebbles on a beach.

The second box produced pearls and the third gold coins and medallions that could make even an old man's eyes sparkle. He hadn't realised how long it had taken him to go through the remaining boxes but when the alarm went off he was five thousand miles away already enjoying his new-found wealth. He glanced at the clock. He had easily enough time to get everything back into the compartments and then he would return the following day and remove once and for all what he had earned from fifty years of serving the State.

When the last lid had been placed back on he checked the clock on the wall: six minutes to six. Just enough time to glance in the other box and see if he could expect the same again.

He turned the key and licked his lips in anticipation as he pulled the large box out. Just a quick look, he promised himself, as he lifted the lid. When he saw the decaying body with its grey skin and eyes hanging in their sockets he reeled backwards from the sight and, falling to the floor, clutched his heart.

Both bodies were discovered at nine the next morning.

The phone rang and Adam grabbed at it before the shrill tone could deafen him a second time.

"Your alarm call, sir," said a girl's voice gently. "It's eight o'clock."

"Thank you," Adam replied and replaced the receiver. The call had proved unnecessary because he had been sitting up in bed considering the implications of his plan for nearly an hour. Adam had finally worked out exactly how he was going to finish Romanov.

He jumped out of bed, threw back the curtains and stared down at the Soviet Embassy. He wondered how long the Russian had been awake.

He returned to the side of the bed and picked up the phone to dial the number Robin had given him. The phone rang several times before it was answered by an elderly voice saying, "Mrs Beresford."

"Good morning, Mrs Beresford. My name is Adam Scott, I'm a friend of Robin's. I was just phoning to check that she reached home safely last night."

"Oh, yes, thank you," said Robin's mother. "It was a pleasant surprise to see her before the weekend. She usually spends the night in the flat when she gets back that late. I'm afraid she's still asleep. Would you like me to wake her?"

"No, no, don't disturb her," said Adam. "I only rang to fix up a lunch date. Can you tell her I'll call back later?"

"I certainly will," she replied. "Thank you for phoning, Mr Scott."

Adam replaced the receiver and smiled. Each piece of the jigsaw was fitting neatly into place but without the colonel's help he still lacked the vital corner-piece.

Adam began to put everything Tomkins needed, including his passport, personal papers and wallet into a large envelope. He removed the icon from his jacket pocket, turned it over and carefully examined the little silver crest of the Tsar. He then flicked open the colonel's penknife and began the slow and delicate task of removing the crown.

Thirty minutes later, Adam was in the lift on the way to the hotel basement. When he stepped out, he walked across to the space where he had parked the green Cortina earlier that morning. He unlocked the door and threw the colonel's old jacket on to the seat, then locked the car, checking all the doors before taking the lift back up to the ground floor.

The manager of the men's shop in the arcade had just flicked over the 'closed' sign and Adam took his time selecting a white shirt, grey flannels and a blue blazer, trying them on in their little changing room.

At nine twenty-three he settled his bill with the Royal Garden Hotel and asked the doorman to bring the green Ford up from the parking lot. He waited by the hotel entrance.

As the minutes passed, he began to fear that the colonel wouldn't turn up. If he failed to, Adam knew that the next call would have to be to Lawrence and not Romanov.

His reverie was disturbed by a honk on a car horn; the colonel's rented car had been left by the entrance.

"Your car is waiting on the ramp," said the doorman, as he returned the keys to Adam.

"Thank you," said Adam and handed over the last of the colonel's pound notes. He dropped the wallet into the large envelope, which he sealed, before checking his watch again.

He stood waiting anxiously for another two minutes

before he spotted the colonel puffing up the slope leading to the hotel entrance.

He was clinging on to a small carrier bag.

"I've done it, Captain Scott, sir, I've done it," said the colonel, before he had reached Adam's side. "But I must return immediately or he's bound to notice it's gone."

He passed the carrier bag quickly to Adam who opened the top and stared down at the object inside.

"You're a man of your word," said Adam, "and as promised you'll find everything you need in there." He passed over his own package along with the car keys without speaking. He pointed to the hire car.

The colonel ran to it, jumped in and drove quickly down the ramp of the Royal Garden Hotel before turning left into Kensington Palace Gardens.

Adam checked his watch: nine thirty-five.

"Could you call me a taxi?" he asked the doorman.

The driver pulled the window down and gave Adam an enquiring look.

"Chesham Place, SW1. A carpenter's shop."

Adam spent twenty minutes looking around the shop while the craftsman carried out his unusual request. Adam studied the result with satisfaction, paid him two half-crowns and then walked back on to King's Road, to hail another taxi.

"Where to, guv'nor?"

"The Tower of London."

Everyone was in their place for the D4 meeting at nine thirty and Busch had gone on the attack even before Lawrence had had the chance to sit down.

"How in hell did you manage to lose him this time?"

"I must take the blame myself," said Lawrence. "We had every port from Newhaven to Harwich covered, but the moment my man saw Romanov and his henchman leave the quayside at Dover and chase off down the motorway after the coach he assumed he must have seen Scott. I had already instructed the senior immigration officer at the port," he continued, "to allow Scott to disembark without a fuss. It had been my intention to take over once he passed through customs. There seemed no reason to change that plan while we had Romanov under close surveillance. Scott then proceeded to fool both Romanov and our man at Dover."

"But we were given a second chance when Scott got on the train," persisted Busch. Lawrence stared at the American, waiting to see if he would admit that his two CIA agents had also lost Scott at Dover.

"My man was on the train," said Lawrence emphatically, "but had only the one opportunity to make contact with Scott while he was on his own, and at just that moment he was grabbed and badly beaten up by a bunch of drunken louts – teenagers, apparently – who were on their way back from a day trip to the seaside."

"Perhaps we're recruiting our agents from the wrong class of person," said Matthews, staring down at his briefing papers.

Lawrence made no attempt to reply.

"So, as far as we can tell, Scott, the Tsar's icon and Romanov are still holed up somewhere in London?" said Snell.

"It looks that way," admitted Lawrence.

"Perhaps all is not lost then," suggested Snell. "Scott may still try and get in touch with you again."

"I think not," said Lawrence quietly.

"How can you be so sure?" asked Busch.

"Because Scott knows that one of us in this room is a traitor and he thinks it's me."

"Good morning. Soviet Embassy."

"My name is Adam Scott and I need to get in contact with a Major Romanov."

"Good morning, Mr Scott. We do not have a Major Romanov working at the Embassy," came back the polite reply.

"I'm sure you don't."

"But if you would like to leave your number, I will make further enquiries."

"I'll wait. Wouldn't surprise me if you find him very quickly once he knows who it is calling."

There was a long silence at the other end, and Adam only hoped the shilling he had pressed into the call box would prove to be enough. At last there was a click, and then Adam heard a voice.

"Who is this?" said the voice, unable to mask its incredulity.

"You know very well who it is," said Adam curtly. "I want to make a deal."

"A deal?" Romanov repeated, his voice changing from one of disbelief to surprise.

"I'll swap you my icon – which as you so vividly pointed out is worthless to me – in exchange for your copy, which is not. But I also require the papers that prove my father's innocence."

"How do I know you're not setting me up?"

"You don't," said Adam. "But you're the one with nothing to lose."

The pips began to sound across the line.

"Tell me your number," said Romanov.

"738–9121," said Adam.

"I'll phone you back," said Romanov as the line went dead.

"How quickly can we find out where 738–9121 is located?" Romanov asked the local KGB operative who sat opposite him.

"About ten minutes," the aide replied. "But it could be a trap."

"True, but with nineteen hours to go before the icon has to be in America I don't have a lot of choice."

Romanov turned back to the KGB agent. "What's the traffic like in London on a Friday morning?"

"One of the busiest times in the week. Why do you ask?"

"Because I'll need a motorbike and a superb driver," was all Romanov said.

Adam could do nothing about the middle-aged lady who was now occupying his phone booth. He had nervously walked out to check the bridge when she slipped in. She must have been puzzled as to why the young man didn't use the empty box that stood next to it.

He checked his watch anxiously: ten forty-five. He knew he couldn't risk waiting a minute after eleven but was confident that Romanov would have traced where he'd made the call from long before then.

The talkative woman was another twelve minutes before she eventually put the phone down. When she stepped out of the box she gave Adam a warm smile.

Three more minutes and he would have to phone Lawrence and abort his original plan. He began to watch the Beefeaters as they patrolled under Traitors' Gate. Traitors' Gate – how appropriate, Adam thought. He had chosen the spot because he could see clearly up and down the path leading to the drawbridge and felt he could not be taken by surprise. And in desperation there was always the moat that surrounded them on all sides.

For the first time in his life, Adam discovered exactly how long five minutes could be. When the phone rang, it sounded like an alarm bell. He picked it up nervously, his eyes never leaving the main road.

"Scott?"

"Yes."

"I can now see you clearly as I am less than one minute away. I will be standing at the end of Tower Bridge until the end of that minute. Be sure you're there with the icon. If you're not, I shall burn the papers that prove your father's innocence in front of you."

The phone went dead.

Adam was delighted that another piece of the jigsaw had fallen into place. He stepped out of the phone booth and checked up and down the road. A BMW motorcycle swerved to a halt at the end of the bridge. A rider dressed in a leather jacket sat astride the bike but only seemed interested in watching the flow of traffic as it passed by the Tower. It was the man seated behind him who stared directly at Adam.

Adam began to walk slowly towards the end of the bridge. He put a hand in his pocket to be sure the icon was still in its place.

He was about thirty yards from the end of the bridge when the second figure got off the bike and started walking towards him. When their eyes met, Romanov stopped in his tracks and held up a small, square frame. Adam did not respond in kind, but simply tapped the side of his pocket and continued walking. Both men advanced towards each other like knights of old until they were only a few paces apart. Almost simultaneously they stopped and faced one another.

"Let me see it," said Romanov.

Adam paused, then slowly removed the icon from his pocket and held it to his chest for his adversary to see St George stared at him.

"Turn it over," said Romanov.

Adam obeyed, and the Russian could not hide his delight when he saw the little silver crown of the Tsar embedded in the back.

"Now you," said Adam. Romanov held his icon away from his body, as if brandishing a sword. The masterpiece shone in the summer sun.

"And the documents," said Adam, forcing himself to speak calmly.

The Russian pulled out a package from within his jacket and slowly unfolded them. Adam stared at the official court verdict for a second time.

"Go to the wall," said Adam, pointing with his left hand to the side of the bridge, "and leave the icon and the documents on it."

It was Romanov who now obeyed as Adam proceeded to the wall on the other side of the bridge and placed his icon in the middle of it.

"Cross slowly," called Adam. The two men moved sideways back across the bridge, never getting closer than a couple of yards from each other until they had come to a halt at each other's icon. The moment the painting was within his reach, Romanov grabbed it, ran and jumped on to the motorcycle without looking back. Within seconds the BMW had disappeared into the dense traffic.

Adam did not move. Although it had only been out of his sight for just over an hour, he was relieved to have the original back. Adam checked the papers that would establish his father's innocence and placed them in his inside pocket. Ignoring the tourists, some of whom had stopped to stare at him, Adam began to relax when suddenly he felt a sharp prod in the middle of his back. He jumped round in fright.

A little girl was staring up at him.

"Will you and your friend be performing again this morning?"

When the BMW motorcycle drew up outside the Soviet Embassy in Kensington Palace Gardens, Romanov leapt off and ran up the steps and straight into the Ambassador's office without knocking. The Ambassador didn't need to ask if he had been successful.

"It worked out just as I planned. He was taken completely by surprise," said Romanov, as he handed the icon over to the Ambassador.

The Ambassador turned the painting over and saw the little silver crown of the Tsar. Any doubts that he might have had were also dispelled.

"I have orders to send the icon to Washington in the diplomatic pouch immediately. There is no time to be lost."

"I wish I could deliver it in person," said Romanov.

"Be satisfied, Comrade Major, that you have carried out your part of the operation in an exemplary fashion."

The Ambassador pressed a button on the side of his desk. Two men appeared immediately. One held open the diplomatic pouch while the other stood motionless by his side. The Ambassador handed over the icon and watched it being placed into the pouch. The two couriers looked as if they would have had no trouble in carrying out the Ambassador's desk as well, thought Romanov.

"There is a plane standing by at Heathrow to take

you both direct to Washington," said the Ambassador. "All the necessary documentation for customs has already been dealt with. You should touch down at National airport around five o'clock Washington time, easily giving our comrades in America enough time to fulfil their part of the contract."

The two men nodded, sealed the diplomatic pouch in the Ambassador's presence and left. Romanov walked over to the window and watched the official car drive the two men out into Kensington High Street and off in the direction of Heathrow.

"Vodka, Comrade Major?"

"Thank you," Romanov replied, not moving from the window until the car was out of sight.

The Ambassador went over to a side cabinet and took out two glasses and a bottle from the fridge before pouring Romanov a large vodka.

"It would not be exaggerating to say that you have played your part in establishing the Soviet Union as the most powerful nation on earth," he said as he handed over the drink. "Let us therefore drink to the repatriation of the people of Aleuts as full citizens of the Union of Soviet Socialist Republics."

"How is that possible?" asked Romanov.

"I think the time has come to let you know," said the Ambassador, "the significance of your achievement." He then went on to tell Romanov of the briefing he had received from Moscow that morning.

Romanov was thankful he had never known how much was at stake.

"I have made an appointment to see the Foreign Secretary at three o'clock this afternoon in order to brief him. We can be sure the British will only be interested in fair play," the Ambassador continued. "I am told he is not at all pleased as he had hoped to be in his constituency to open some fete; the British have some strange ideas about how to keep their party system going."

Romanov laughed. "To Aleuts," he said, raising his glass. "But what is happening in Washington at this moment?"

"Our Ambassador has already requested a meeting with the American Secretary of State to be scheduled for eight this evening. He is also setting up a press conference at the Embassy to follow that meeting. It may amuse you to know that President Johnson had to cancel his visit to Texas this weekend and has requested that the networks should allow him to address 'his fellow Americans' at peak time on Monday as a matter of national importance."

"And we achieved it with only hours to spare," said Romanov, pouring himself another vodka.

"Touch and go, as the English would say. Let us also be thankful for the time difference between here and the United States because without that we would never have been able to beat the deadline."

Romanov shuddered at the thought of how close it had been and downed his second vodka in one gulp.

"You must join me for lunch, Comrade. Although your orders are to return to Moscow immediately my secretary assures me that the first plane leaving Heathrow for Moscow does not depart until eight this evening. I envy you the reception you will receive when you arrive back in the Kremlin tomorrow."

"I still need the £1000 for . . ."

"Ah, yes," said the Ambassador, "I have it ready for you." He unlocked the little drawer of his desk and passed over a slim wad of notes in a small cellophane wrapper.

Romanov slipped the tiny packet in his pocket and joined the Ambassador for lunch.

Busch barged into Lawrence's office.

"Romanov's got the icon," he shouted.

Lawrence's jaw dropped. A look of desperation appeared on his face. "How can you be so sure?" he demanded.

"I've just had a message from Washington. The Russians have requested an official meeting with the Secretary of State to be arranged for eight this evening."

"I don't believe it," said Lawrence.

"I do," said Busch. "We've always known that God-damned friend of yours, like his father, was a lousy traitor. There's no other explanation."

"He could be dead," said Lawrence quietly.

"I hope he is, for his sake," said Busch.

The phone on Lawrence's desk rang. He grabbed it as if it were a lifeline. "A Dr John Vance wants a word with you, sir," said his secretary. "He said you had asked him to call."

Vance? Vance? Lawrence recalled the name but couldn't quite place it. "Put him on," he said.

"Good morning, Mr Pemberton," said a voice.

"Good morning, Dr Vance. What can I do for you?"

"You asked me to call you after I had examined Scott."

"Scott?" repeated Lawrence, not believing what he was hearing.

"Yes, Adam Scott. Surely you remember? You wanted him to complete a medical for your department."

Lawrence was speechless.

"I've given him a clean bill of health," continued

417

the doctor. "Some cuts and a nasty bruise, but nothing that won't heal in a few days."

"Cuts and bruises?" said Lawrence.

"That's what I said, old chap. But don't worry about Scott. He's fit enough to start work whenever you want him. That's if you still want him."

"If I still want him," repeated Lawrence. "Mr Scott isn't there with you at this moment, by any chance?"

"No," said Vance. "Left my surgery about ten minutes ago."

"He didn't happen to tell you where he was going?" asked Lawrence.

"No, he wasn't specific. Just said something about having to see a friend off at the airport."

Once the coffee had been cleared away, Romanov checked his watch. He had left easily enough time to keep the appointment and still catch his plane. He thanked the Ambassador for all his help, left him, ran down the Embassy steps and climbed into the back of the anonymous black car.

The driver moved off without speaking as he had already been briefed as to where the major wanted to go.

Neither of them spoke on the short journey, and when the driver drew into Charlotte Street he parked the car in a lay-by. Romanov stepped out, walked quickly across the road to the door he was looking for and pressed the buzzer.

"Are you a member?" said a voice through the intercom.

"Yes," said Romanov, who heard a metallic click as he pushed the door open and walked down the dark staircase. Once he had entered the club it took a few seconds for his eyes to become accustomed to the light.

But then he spotted Mentor seated on his own at a little table near a pillar in the far corner of the room.

Romanov nodded and the man got up and walked across the dance floor and straight past him. Romanov followed as the member entered the only lavatory. Once inside, Romanov checked that they were alone. Satisfied, he led them both into a little cubicle and slipped the lock to engaged. Romanov removed the thousand pounds from his pocket and handed it over to the man who sat down on the lavatory seat. Mentor greedily ripped open the packet, leaned forward and began to count. He never even saw Romanov straighten his fingers; and when the hand came down with a crushing blow on the back of Mentor's neck he slumped forward and fell to the ground in a heap.

Romanov yanked him up; it took several seconds to gather the ten-pound notes that had fallen to the floor. Once he had all hundred, he stuffed them into the member's pocket. Romanov then undid the member's fly buttons one by one and pulled down his trousers until they fell around his ankles. He lifted the lid and placed the man on the lavatory seat. The final touch was to pull his legs as wide open as the fallen trousers would allow, the feet splayed apart. Romanov then slipped under the large gap at the bottom of the door leaving the cubicle locked from the inside. He quickly checked his handiwork. All that could be seen from the outside was the splayed legs and fallen trousers.

Sixty seconds later, Romanov was back in the car on his way to Heathrow.

Adam arrived at Heathrow two hours before the Aeroflot flight was due to depart. He stationed himself with a perfect view of the forty-yard stretch Romanov

419

would have to walk to board the Russian aircraft. He felt confident he would never reach the Aeroflot steps.

Romanov checked in at the BEA desk a little after six. He couldn't resist taking the BEA flight rather than Aeroflot even though he knew Zaborski would frown at such arrogance; he doubted if anyone would comment on this of all days.

Once he had been given his boarding card, he took the escalator to the executive lounge and sat around waiting to be called. It was always the same – the moment any operation had been completed, all he wanted to do was get home. He left his seat to pour himself some coffee and, passing a table in the centre of the room, caught the headline on the London *Evening Standard*. Exclusive. 'Johnson Texas Weekend Cancelled – Mystery.' Romanov grabbed the paper from the table and read the first paragraph but it contained no information he couldn't have already told them. None of the speculation in the paragraphs that followed even began to get near the truth.

Romanov couldn't wait to see the front page of *Pravda* the next day in which he knew the true story would be emblazoned. By Western standards it would be an exclusive.

"BEA announce the departure of their flight 117 to Moscow. Would all first class passengers now board through gate No. 23." Romanov left the lounge and walked the half mile long corridor to the plane. Romanov strolled across the tarmac to the waiting plane a few minutes after six fifty. The plane carrying the icon would be touching down in Washington in about two hours. Romanov would arrive back in Moscow well in time to see Dynamo play Spartak at the Lenin Stadium on Tuesday. He wondered if they would announce his arrival to the crowd over the loudspeakers as they always did when a member of the Politburo attended a match. Romanov walked up the steps and on board, stepping over the feet of the passenger placed next to him, thankful that he had been given the window seat.

"Would you care for a drink before take-off?" the stewardess asked.

"Just a black coffee for me," said his neighbour. Romanov nodded his agreement.

The stewardess arrived back a few minutes later with the two coffees and helped the man next to Romanov pull out his table from the armrest. Romanov flicked his over as the stewardess passed him his coffee.

He took a sip but it was too hot so he placed it on the table in front of him. He watched his neighbour take out a packet of saccharines from his pocket and flick two pellets into the steaming coffee.

Why did he bother, thought Romanov. Life was too short.

Romanov stared out of the window and watched the Aeroflot plane start to taxi out on to the runway. He smiled at the thought of how much more comfortable his own flight would be. He tried his coffee a second time: just as he liked it. He took a long gulp and began to feel a little drowsy which he didn't find that strange as he had hardly slept for the last week.

He leaned back in his seat and closed his eyes. He would now take every honour the State could offer him. With Valchek conveniently out of the way, he could even position himself to take over from Zaborski. If that failed, his grandfather had left him another alternative.

He was leaving London with only one regret: he had failed to kill Scott. But then he suspected that the

421

Americans would take care of that. For the first time in a week he didn't have to stop himself falling asleep . . .

A few moments later the passenger seated next to Romanov picked up the Russian's coffee cup and put it next to his own. He then flicked Romanov's table back into the armrest and placed a woollen blanket over Romanov's legs. He quickly slipped the BEA eye shades over the Russian's head, covering his open eyes. He looked up to find that the stewardess was standing by his side.

"Can I help?" she asked, smiling.

"No, thank you. All he said was that he did not want to be disturbed during the flight as he has had a very hard week."

"Of course, sir," said the stewardess. "We'll be taking off in a few minutes," she added, and picked up the two coffee cups and whisked them away.

The man tapped his fingers impatiently on the little table. At last the chief steward appeared at his side.

"There's been an urgent call from your office, sir. You're to return to Whitehall immediately."

"I had been half expecting it," he admitted.

Adam stared up at the Russian plane as it climbed steeply and swung in a semi-circle towards the East. He couldn't understand why Romanov hadn't boarded it. Surely he wouldn't have taken the BEA flight. Adam slipped back into the shadows the moment he saw him. He stared in disbelief. Lawrence was striding back across the tarmac, a smile of satisfaction on his face.

EPILOGUE

SOTHEBY'S
FOUNDED 1744

SOTHEBY'S
NEW BOND STREET,
LONDON W1

October 18, 1966

EPILOGUE

"Sold to the gentleman in the centre of the room for five thousand pounds.

"We now move on to Lot no. 32," said the auctioneer, looking down from the raised platform at the front of the crowded room. "An icon of St George and the Dragon," he declared as an attendant placed a little painting on the easel next to him. The auctioneer stared down at the faces of experts, amateurs and curious onlookers. "What am I bid for this magnificent example of Russian art?" he asked, expectantly.

Robin gripped Adam's hand. "I haven't felt this nervous since I came face to face with Romanov."

"Don't remind me," said Adam.

"It is, of course, not the original that hangs in the Winter Palace," continued the auctioneer, "but it is nevertheless a fine copy, probably executed by a court painter circa 1914," he added, giving the little painting an approving smile. "Do I have an opening bid? Shall I say eight thousand?" The next few seconds seemed interminable to Robin and Adam. "Thank you, sir," said the auctioneer, eventually looking towards an anonymous sign that had been given somewhere at the front of the room.

Neither Adam nor Robin were able to make out

where the bid had come from. They had spent the last hour seated at the back of the room watching the previous items coming under the hammer and had rarely been able to work out whose hands they had ended up in.

"How much did the expert say it might go for?" Robin asked again.

"Anywhere between ten and twenty thousand," Adam reminded her.

"Nine thousand," said the auctioneer, his eyes moving to a bid that appeared to come from the right-hand side of the room.

"I still think it's amazing," said Robin, "that the Russians ever agreed to the exchange in the first place."

"Why?" asked Adam. "Once the Americans had extracted the treaty, there was no harm in allowing the Russians to have their original back in exchange for the copy which rightly belonged to me. As an example of diplomatic ingenuity it was Lawrence at his most brilliant."

"Ten thousand from the front of the room. Thank you, sir," said the auctioneer.

"What are you going to do with all that money?"

"Buy a new double bass, get a wedding present for my sister and hand over the rest to my mother."

"Eleven thousand, a new bid on the centre aisle," said the auctioneer. "Thank you, madam."

"No amount of money can bring back Heidi," said Robin quietly.

Adam nodded thoughtfully.

"How did the meeting with Heidi's parents turn out?"

"The Foreign Secretary saw them personally last week. It couldn't help, but at least he was able to confirm that I had only been telling them the truth."

"Twelve thousand." The auctioneer's eye returned to the front of the room.

"Did you see the Foreign Secretary yourself?"

"Good heavens, no, I'm far too junior for that," said Adam. "I'm lucky if I get to see Lawrence, let alone the Foreign Secretary."

Robin laughed. "I consider you were *lucky* to have been offered a place at the Foreign Office at all."

"Agreed," said Adam chuckling to himself, "but a vacancy arose unexpectedly."

"What do you mean, 'unexpectedly'?" asked Robin, frustrated by how few of her questions had been answered directly in the past half hour.

"All I can tell you is that one of Lawrence's old team was 'retired early'," said Adam.

"Was that also true of Romanov?" asked Robin, still desperately trying to discover all that had taken place since they had last met.

"Thirteen thousand," said the auctioneer, his eyes returning to the lady on the centre aisle.

"After all he can't have survived for long once they discovered you had done a switch on Tower Bridge that gave the Russians back the copy while Romanov ended up presenting you with the original," said Robin.

"He's never been heard of since," admitted Adam innocently.

"And all our information leads us to believe that his boss Zaborski is soon to be replaced by someone called Yuri Andropov."

"Fourteen thousand," said the auctioneer, his eye settling on the gentleman at the front once again.

"What happened when you produced the papers proving that it was not your father who had smuggled the poison into Goering's cell?"

"Once they had been authenticated by the Russians," Adam said, "Lawrence paid an official visit to the Colonel of the Regiment and furnished him with the conclusive evidence."

"Any reaction?" probed Robin.

"They're going to hold a memorial service in Pa's memory and have commissioned some fellow called Ward to paint his portrait for the regimental mess. Mother has been invited to unveil it in the presence of all those officers who served with my father."

"Fourteen thousand for the first time then," said the auctioneer raising the little gavel a few inches in the air.

"She must have been over the moon," said Robin.

"Burst into tears," said Adam. "All she could say was 'I wish Pa could have lived to see it.' Ironic, really. If only he had opened that letter."

"Fourteen thousand for the second time," said the auctioneer, the gavel now hovering.

"How do you fancy a celebration lunch at the Ritz?" said Adam, delighted with how well the sale was turning out.

"No thank you," said Robin.

Adam looked across at his companion in surprise.

"It won't be much fun if every time I ask you a question I only get the official Foreign Office briefing."

Adam looked sheepish. "I'm sorry," he said.

"No, that wasn't fair," said Robin. "Now you're on the inside it can't be easy, so I suppose I will have to go to my grave wondering what treaty was inside that icon."

Adam looked away from the girl who had saved his life.

"Or perhaps I'll find out the truth in 1996 when the cabinet papers are released."

He turned slowly to face her.

"Alas . . ." he began as the auctioneer's hammer came down with a thud. They both looked up.

"Sold to the gentleman at the front for fourteen thousand pounds."

"Not a bad price," said Adam, smiling.

"A bargain in my opinion," replied Robin quietly.

Adam turned to her, a quizzical look on his face.

"After all," she said in a whisper, "imagine what the forty-ninth state would have fetched if it had come up for auction."

THE END

FALSE
IMPRESSION

TO TARA

9/10

1

VICTORIA WENTWORTH sat alone at the table where Wellington had dined with sixteen of his field officers the night before he set out for Waterloo.

General Sir Harry Wentworth sat at the right hand of the Iron Duke that night, and was commanding his left flank when a defeated Napoleon rode off the battlefield and into exile. A grateful monarch bestowed on the general the title Earl of Wentworth, which the family had borne proudly since 1815.

These thoughts were running through Victoria's mind as she read Dr Petrescu's report for a second time. When she turned the last page, she let out a sigh of relief. A solution to all her problems had been found, quite literally at the eleventh hour.

The dining-room door opened noiselessly and Andrews, who from second footman to butler had served three generations of Wentworths, deftly removed her ladyship's dessert plate.

'Thank you,' Victoria said, and waited until he had reached the door before she added, 'and has everything been arranged for the removal of the painting?' She couldn't bring herself to mention the artist's name.

'Yes, m'lady,' Andrews replied, turning back to face his mistress. 'The picture will have been dispatched before you come down for breakfast.'

'And has everything been prepared for Dr Petrescu's visit?'

'Yes, m'lady,' repeated Andrews. 'Dr Petrescu is expected around midday on Wednesday, and I have already informed cook that she will be joining you for lunch in the conservatory.'

'Thank you, Andrews,' said Victoria. The butler gave a slight bow and quietly closed the heavy oak door behind him.

By the time Dr Petrescu arrived, one of the family's most treasured heirlooms would be on its way to America, and although the masterpiece would never be seen at Wentworth Hall again, no one outside the immediate family need be any the wiser.

Victoria folded her napkin and rose from the table. She picked up Dr Petrescu's report and walked out of the dining room and into the hall. The sound of her shoes echoed in the marble hallway. She paused at the foot of the staircase to admire Gainsborough's full-length portrait of Catherine, Lady Wentworth, who was dressed in a magnificent long silk and taffeta gown, set off by a diamond necklace and matching earrings. Victoria touched her ear and smiled at the thought that such an extravagant bauble must have been considered quite risqué at the time.

Victoria looked steadfastly ahead as she climbed the wide marble staircase to her bedroom on the first floor. She felt unable to look into the eyes of her ancestors, brought to life by Romney, Lawrence, Reynolds, Lely and Kneller, conscious of having let them all down. Victoria accepted that before she retired to bed she must finally write to her sister and let her know the decision she had come to.

Arabella was so wise and sensible. If only her beloved twin had been born a few minutes earlier rather than a few minutes later, then *she* would have inherited the estate, and undoubtedly handled the problem with considerably more panache. And worse, when Arabella learned the news, she would neither complain nor remonstrate, just continue to display the family's stiff upper lip.

Victoria closed the bedroom door, walked across the room and placed Dr Petrescu's report on her desk. She undid her bun, allowing the hair to cascade onto her shoulders. She spent the next few minutes brushing her hair, before taking off her clothes and slipping on a silk nightgown, which a maid had laid out on the end of the bed. Finally she stepped into her bedroom slippers. Unable to avoid the responsibility any longer, she sat down at her writing desk and picked up her fountain pen.

WENTWORTH HALL

September 10th, 2001

My dearest Arabella,

 I have put off writing this letter for far too long, as you are the last person who deserves to learn such distressing news.

 When dear Papa died and I inherited the estate, it was some time before I appreciated the full extent of the debts he had run up. I fear my lack of business experience, coupled with crippling death duties, only exacerbated the problem.

 I thought the answer was to borrow even more, but that has simply made matters worse. At one point I feared that because of my naivety we might even end up having to sell our family's estate. But I am pleased to tell you that a solution has been found.

 On Wednesday, I will be seeing—

Victoria thought she heard the bedroom door open. She wondered which of her servants would have considered entering the room without knocking.

By the time Victoria had turned to find out who it was, she was already standing by her side.

Victoria stared up at a woman she had never seen before. She was young, slim, and even shorter than Victoria. She smiled sweetly, which made her appear vulnerable. Victoria returned her smile, and then noticed she was carrying a kitchen knife in her right hand.

'Who—' began Victoria as a hand shot out, grabbed her by the hair and snapped her head back against the chair. Victoria felt the thin, razor-sharp blade as it touched the skin of her neck. In one swift movement the knife sliced open her throat as if she were a lamb being sent to slaughter.

Moments before Victoria died, the young woman cut off her left ear.

9/11

2

ANNA PETRESCU touched the button on the top of her bedside clock. It glowed 5.56am. Another four minutes and it would have woken her with the early morning news. But not today. Her mind had been racing all through the night, only allowing her intermittent patches of sleep. By the time she finally woke, Anna had decided exactly what she must do if the chairman was unwilling to go along with her recommendations. She switched off the automatic alarm, avoiding any news that might distract her, jumped out of bed and headed straight for the bathroom. Anna remained under the cold shower a little longer than usual, hoping it would fully wake her. Her last lover – heaven knows how long ago that must have been – thought it amusing that she always showered *before* going out for her morning run.

Once she had dried herself, Anna slipped on a white T-shirt and blue running shorts. Although the sun had not yet risen, she didn't need to open the bedroom curtains of her little room to know that it was going to be another clear, sunny day. She zipped up her tracksuit top, which still displayed a faded 'P' where the bold blue letter had been unstitched. Anna didn't want to advertise the fact that she had once been a member of the University of Pennsylvania track team. After all, that was nine years ago. Anna finally pulled on her Nike training shoes and tied the laces very tight. Nothing annoyed her more than having to stop in the middle of her morning run to retie her laces. The only other thing she wore that morning was her front-door key, attached to a thin silver chain that hung around her neck.

Anna double-locked the front door of her four-room apartment, walked across the corridor and pressed the elevator button. While she waited for the little cubicle to travel grudgingly up to the tenth floor, she began a series of stretching exercises that would be completed before the elevator returned to the ground floor.

Anna stepped out into the lobby and smiled at her favourite doorman, who quickly opened the front door so that she didn't have to stop in her tracks.

'Morning, Sam,' Anna said, as she jogged out of Thornton House onto East 54th Street and headed towards Central Park.

Every weekday she ran the Southern Loop. On the weekends she would tackle the longer six-mile loop, when it didn't matter if she was a few minutes late. It mattered today.

◄◦►

Bryce Fenston also rose before six o'clock that morning, as he too had an early appointment. While he showered, Fenston listened to the morning news: a suicide bomber who had blown himself up on the West Bank – an event that had become as commonplace as the weather forecast, or the latest currency fluctuation – didn't cause him to raise the volume.

'Another clear, sunny day, with a gentle breeze heading south-east, highs of 77, lows of 65,' announced a chirpy weather girl as Fenston stepped out of the shower. A more serious voice replaced hers, to inform him that the Nikkei in Tokyo was up fourteen points, and Hong Kong's Hang Seng down one. London's FTSE hadn't yet made up its mind in which direction to go.

He considered that Fenston Finance shares were unlikely to move dramatically either way, as only two other people were aware of his little coup. Fenston was having breakfast with one of them at seven, and he would fire the other at eight.

By 6.40am, Fenston had showered and dressed. He glanced at his reflection in the mirror; he would like to have been a couple of inches taller, and a couple of inches thinner. Nothing that a good tailor and a pair of Cuban shoes with specially designed insoles couldn't rectify. He would also like to have grown his hair again, but not while there were so many exiles from his country who might still recognize him.

Although his father had been a tram conductor in Bucharest, anyone who gave the immaculately dressed man a second glance as he stepped out of his brownstone on East 79th Street and into his chauffeur-driven limousine would have assumed that he had been born into the upper eastside establishment. Only those who looked more closely would have spotted the small diamond in his left ear – an affectation that he believed singled him out from his more conservative colleagues. None of his staff dared to tell him otherwise.

Fenston settled down in the back of his limousine. 'The office,' he barked before touching a button in the armrest. A smoked grey screen purred up, cutting off any unnecessary conversation between him and the driver. Fenston picked up a copy of the *New York Times* from the seat beside him. He flicked through the pages to see if any particular headline grabbed his attention. Mayor Giuliani seemed to have lost the plot. Having installed his mistress in Gracie Mansion, he'd left the first lady only too happy to voice her opinion on the subject to anyone who cared to listen. This morning it was the *New York Times*. Fenston was poring over the financial pages when his driver swung onto FDR Drive, and he had reached the obituaries by the time the limousine came to a halt outside the North Tower. No one would be printing the only obituary he was interested in until tomorrow, but, to be fair, no one in America realized she was dead.

'I have an appointment on Wall Street at eight thirty,' Fenston informed his driver as he opened the back door for him. 'So pick me up at eight fifteen.' The driver nodded, as Fenston marched off in the direction of the lobby. Although there were ninety-nine elevators in the building, only one went directly to the restaurant on the 107th floor.

As Fenston stepped out of the elevator a minute later – he had once calculated that he would spend a week of his life in elevators – the maître d' spotted his regular customer, bowed his head slightly and escorted him to a table in the corner, overlooking the Statue of Liberty. On the one occasion Fenston had turned up to find his usual table occupied, he'd turned round and stepped straight back into the elevator. Since then, the corner table had remained empty every morning – just in case.

Fenston was not surprised to find Karl Leapman waiting for him. Leapman had never once been late in the ten years he had worked for Fenston Finance. Fenston wondered how long he had been sitting there, just to be certain that the chairman didn't turn up before him. Fenston looked down at a man who had proved, time and time again, that there was no sewer he wasn't willing to swim in for his master. But then Fenston was the only person who had been willing to offer Leapman a job after he'd been released from jail. Disbarred lawyers with a prison sentence for fraud don't expect to make partner.

Even before he took his seat, Fenston began speaking. 'Now we are in possession of the Van Gogh,' he said, 'we only have one matter to discuss this morning. How do we rid ourselves of Anna Petrescu without her becoming suspicious?'

Leapman opened a file in front of him, and smiled.

3

NOTHING HAD gone to plan that morning.

Andrews had instructed cook that he would be taking up her ladyship's breakfast tray just as soon as the painting had been dispatched. Cook had developed a migraine, so her number two, not a reliable girl, had been put in charge of her ladyship's breakfast. The security van turned up forty minutes late, with a cheeky young driver who refused to leave until he'd been given coffee and biscuits. Cook would never have stood for such nonsense, but her number two caved in. Half an hour later, Andrews found them sitting at the kitchen table, chatting.

Andrews was only relieved that her ladyship hadn't stirred before the driver finally departed. He checked the tray, refolded the napkin and left the kitchen to take breakfast up to his mistress.

Andrews held the tray on the palm of one hand and knocked quietly on the bedroom door before opening it with the other. When he saw her ladyship lying on the floor in a pool of blood, he let out a gasp, dropped the tray and rushed over to the body.

Although it was clear Lady Victoria had been dead for several hours, Andrews did not consider contacting the police until the next in line to the Wentworth estate had been informed of the tragedy. He quickly left the bedroom, locked the door and ran downstairs for the first time in his life.

—◦—

Arabella Wentworth was serving someone when Andrews called.

She put the phone down and apologized to her customer, explaining that she had to leave immediately. She switched the OPEN sign to CLOSED and locked the door of her little antiques shop only moments after Andrews had uttered the word *emergency*, not an opinion she'd heard him express in the past forty-nine years.

Fifteen minutes later, Arabella brought her mini to a halt on the gravel outside Wentworth Hall. Andrews was standing on the top step, waiting for her.

'I'm so very sorry, m'lady,' was all he said, before he led his new mistress into the house and up the wide marble staircase. When Andrews touched the banister to steady himself, Arabella knew her sister was dead.

Arabella had often wondered how she would react in a crisis. She was relieved to find that, although she was violently sick when she first saw her sister's body, she didn't faint. However, it was a close thing. After a second glance, she grabbed the bedpost to help steady herself before turning away.

Blood had spurted everywhere, congealing on the carpet, the walls, the writing desk and even the ceiling. With a Herculean effort, Arabella let go of the bedpost and staggered towards the phone on the bedside table. She collapsed onto the bed, picked up the receiver and dialled 999. When the phone was answered with the words, 'Emergency, which service?' she replied, 'Police.'

Arabella replaced the receiver. She was determined to reach the bedroom door without looking back at her sister's body. She failed. Only a glance, and this time her eyes settled on the letter addressed 'My dearest Arabella'. She grabbed the sheet of paper, unwilling to share her sister's last thoughts with the local constabulary, stuffed it into her pocket and walked unsteadily out of the room.

4

ANNA JOGGED WEST along East 54th Street, past the Museum of Modern Art, crossing 6th Avenue before taking a right on 7th. She barely glanced at the familiar landmarks of the massive 𝐋𝐎𝐕𝐄 sculpture that dominated the corner of East 55th Street, or Carnegie Hall as she crossed 57th. Most of her energy and concentration was taken up with trying to avoid the early morning commuters as they hurried towards her or blocked her progress. Anna considered the jog to Central Park nothing more than a warm-up and didn't start the stopwatch on her left wrist until she passed through Artisans' Gate and ran into the park.

Once Anna had settled into her regular rhythm, she tried to focus on the meeting scheduled with the chairman for eight o'clock that morning.

Anna had been both surprised and somewhat relieved when Bryce Fenston had offered her a job at Fenston Finance only days after she'd left her position as the number two in Sotheby's Impressionist department.

Her immediate boss had made it only too clear that any thought of progress would be blocked for some time after she'd admitted to being responsible for losing the sale of a major collection to their main rival, Christie's. Anna had spent months nurturing, flattering and cajoling this particular customer into selecting Sotheby's for the disposal of their family's estate, and had naively assumed when she shared the secret with her lover that he would be discreet. After all, he was a lawyer.

When the name of the client was revealed in the arts section of the *New York Times*, Anna lost both her lover and her job. It didn't help when, a few days later, the same paper reported that Dr Anna Petrescu had left Sotheby's 'under a cloud' – a euphemism for fired – and the columnist helpfully added that she needn't bother to apply for a job at Christie's.

Bryce Fenston was a regular attendee at all the major Impressionist sales, and he couldn't have missed Anna standing by the side of the auctioneer's podium, taking notes and acting as a spotter. She resented any suggestion that her striking good looks and athletic figure were the reason Sotheby's regularly placed her in so prominent a position, rather than at the side of the auction room along with the other spotters.

Anna checked her watch as she ran across Playmates Arch: 2 minutes 18 seconds. She always aimed to complete the loop in twelve minutes. She knew that wasn't fast, but it still annoyed her whenever she was overtaken, and it made her particularly mad if it was by a woman. Anna had come ninety-seventh in last year's New York marathon, so on her morning jog in Central Park she was rarely passed by anything on two legs.

Her thoughts returned to Bryce Fenston. It had been known for some time by those closely involved in the art world – auction houses, leading galleries and private dealers – that Fenston was amassing one of the great Impressionist collections. He, along with Steve Wynn, Leonard Lauder, Anne Dias and Takashi Nakamura, was regularly among the final bidders for any major new acquisition. For such collectors, what often begins as an innocent hobby can quickly become an addiction, every bit as demanding as any drug. For Fenston, who owned an example of all the major Impressionists and post-Impressionists except Van Gogh, even the thought of possessing a work by the Dutch master was an injection of pure heroin, and once purchased he quickly craved another fix, like a shaking addict in search of a dealer. His dealer was Anna Petrescu.

When Fenston read in the *New York Times* that Anna was leaving Sotheby's, he immediately offered her a place on his board with a salary that reflected how serious he was about continuing to build his collection. What tipped the balance for Anna was the discovery that Fenston also originated from Romania. He continually reminded Anna that, like her, he had escaped the oppressive Ceauşescu regime to find refuge in America.

Within days of her joining the bank, Fenston quickly put Anna's expertise to the test. Most of the questions he asked her at their first meeting, over lunch, concerned Anna's knowledge of any large collections still in the hands of second- or third-generation families. After six years at Sotheby's, there was barely a major Impressionist work that came under the hammer that hadn't passed through Anna's hands, or at least been viewed by her and then added to her database.

One of the first lessons Anna learned after joining Sotheby's was that old money was more likely to be the seller and new money the buyer, which was how she originally came into contact with Lady Victoria Wentworth, elder daughter of the seventh earl of Wentworth – old, old money – on behalf of Bryce Fenston – nouveau, nouveau riche.

Anna was puzzled by Fenston's obsession with other people's collections, until she discovered that it was company policy to advance large loans against works of art. Few banks are willing to consider 'art', no matter what form, as collateral. Property, shares, bonds, land, even jewellery, but rarely art. Bankers do not understand the market, and are reluctant to reclaim the assets from their customers, not least because storing the works, insuring them and often ending up having to sell them is not only time-consuming but impractical. Fenston Finance was the rare exception. It didn't take Anna long to discover that Fenston had no real love, or particular knowledge, of art. He fulfilled Oscar Wilde's dictum: *A man who knows the price of everything and the value of nothing.* But it was some time before Anna discovered his real motive.

–◦–

One of Anna's first assignments was to take a trip to England and value the estate of Lady Victoria Went-worth, a potential customer, who had applied for a large loan from Fenston Finance. The Wentworth collection turned out to be a typically English one, built up by the second earl, an eccentric aristocrat with a great deal of money, considerable taste and a good enough eye for later generations to describe him as a gifted amateur. From his own countrymen he acquired Romney, West, Constable, Stubbs and Morland, as well as a magnificent example of a Turner, *Sunset over Plymouth.*

The third earl showed no interest in anything artistic, so the collection gathered dust until his son, the fourth earl, inherited the estate, and with it his grandfather's discriminating eye.

Jamie Wentworth spent nearly a year exiled from his native land taking what used to be known as the Grand Tour. He visited Paris, Amsterdam, Rome, Florence, Venice and St Petersburg before returning to Wentworth Hall in possession of a Raphael, Tintoretto, Titian, Rubens, Holbein and Van Dyck, not to mention an

Italian wife. However, it was Charles, the fifth earl, who, for all the wrong reasons, trumped his ancestors. Charlie was also a collector, not of paintings, but of mistresses. After an energetic weekend spent in Paris – mainly on the racecourse at Longchamp, but partly in a bedroom at the Crillon – his latest filly convinced him to purchase from her doctor a painting by an unknown artist. Charlie Wentworth returned to England having discarded his paramour but stuck with a painting that he relegated to a guest bedroom, although many aficionados now consider *Self-portrait with Bandaged Ear* to be among Van Gogh's finest works.

Anna had already warned Fenston to be wary when it came to purchasing a Van Gogh, because attributions were often more dubious than Wall Street bankers – a simile Fenston didn't care for. She told him that there were several fakes hanging in private collections, and even one or two in major museums, including the national museum of Oslo. However, after Anna had studied the paperwork that accompanied the Van Gogh *Self-portrait*, which included a reference to Charles Wentworth in one of Dr Gachet's letters, a receipt for eight hundred francs from the original sale and a certificate of authentication from Louis van Tilborgh, Curator of Paintings at the Van Gogh Museum in Amsterdam, she felt confident enough to advise the chairman that the magnificent portrait was indeed by the hand of the master.

For Van Gogh addicts, *Self-portrait with Bandaged Ear* was the ultimate high. Although the maestro painted thirty-five self-portraits during his lifetime, he attempted only two after cutting off his left ear. What made this particular work so desirable for any serious collector was that the other one was on display at the Courtauld

Institute in London. Anna was becoming more and more anxious about just how far Fenston would be willing to go in order to possess the only other example.

Anna spent a pleasant ten days at Wentworth Hall cataloguing and valuing the family's collection. When she returned to New York, she advised the board – mainly made up of Fenston's cronies or politicians who were only too happy to accept a handout – that should a sale ever prove necessary, the assets would more than cover the bank's loan of thirty million dollars.

Although Anna had no interest in Victoria Wentworth's reasons for needing such a large sum of money, she often heard Victoria speak of the sadness of 'dear Papa's' premature death, the retirement of their trusted estates manager and the iniquity of 40 per cent death duties during her stay at Wentworth Hall. 'If only Arabella had been born a few moments earlier . . .' was one of Victoria's favourite mantras.

Once she was back in New York, Anna could recall every painting and sculpture in Victoria's collection without having to refer to any paperwork. The one gift that set her apart from her contemporaries at Penn, and her colleagues at Sotheby's, was a photographic memory. Once Anna had seen a painting, she would never forget the image, its provenance or its location. Every Sunday she would idly put her skill to the test, by visiting a new gallery, a room at the Met, or simply studying the latest catalogue raisonné. On returning to her apartment, she would write down the name of every painting she had seen, before checking it against the different catalogues. Since leaving university, Anna had added the Louvre, the Prado and the Uffizi, as well as the National Gallery of Washington, the Phillips Collection and the Getty Museum, to her memory bank. Thirty-seven private collections and countless catalogues were also stored in the database of her brain, an asset Fenston had proved willing to pay over the odds for.

Anna's responsibility did not go beyond valuing the collections of potential clients and then submitting written reports for the board's consideration. She never became involved in the drawing up of any contract. That was exclusively in the hands of the bank's in-house lawyer, Karl Leapman. However, Victoria did let slip on one occasion that the bank was charging her 16 per cent compound interest. Anna had quickly become aware that debt, naivety and a lack of any financial expertise were the ingredients on which Fenston Finance thrived. This was a bank that seemed to relish its customers' inability to repay their debts.

Anna lengthened her stride as she passed by the carousel. She checked her watch – off twelve seconds. She frowned, but at least no one had overtaken her. Her thoughts returned to the Wentworth collection, and the recommendation she would be making to Fenston that morning. Anna had decided she would have to resign if the chairman felt unable to accept her advice, despite the fact that she had worked for the company for less than a year and was painfully aware that she still couldn't hope to get a job at Sotheby's or Christie's.

During the past year, she had learnt to live with Fenston's vanity, and even tolerate the occasional out-burst when he didn't get his own way, but she could not condone misleading a client, especially one as naive as Victoria Wentworth. Leaving Fenston Finance after such a short time might not look good on her résumé, but an ongoing fraud investigation would look a lot worse.

5

'WHEN WILL we find out if she's dead?' asked Leapman, as he sipped his coffee.

'I'm expecting confirmation this morning,' Fenston replied.

'Good, because I'll need to be in touch with her lawyer to remind him – ' he paused – 'that in the case of a suspicious death – ' he paused a second time – 'any settlement reverts to the jurisdiction of the New York State Bar.'

'Strange that none of them ever query that clause in the contract,' said Fenston, buttering another muffin.

'Why should they?' asked Leapman. 'After all, they have no way of knowing that they're about to die.'

'And is there any reason for the police to become suspicious about our involvement?'

'No,' replied Leapman. 'You've never met Victoria Wentworth, you didn't sign the original contract, and you haven't even seen the painting.'

'No one has outside the Wentworth family and Petrescu,' Fenston reminded him. 'But what I still need to know is how much time before I can safely—'

'Hard to say, but it could be years before the police are willing to admit they don't even have a suspect, especially in such a high-profile case.'

'A couple of years will be quite enough,' said Fenston. 'By then, the interest on the loan will be more than enough to ensure that I can hold on to the Van Gogh and sell off the rest of the collection without losing any of my original investment.'

'Then it's a good thing that I read Petrescu's report when I did,' said Leapman, 'because if she'd gone along with Petrescu's recommendation, there would have been nothing we could do about it.'

'Agreed,' said Fenston, 'but now we have to find some way of losing Petrescu.'

A thin smile appeared on Leapman's lips. 'That's easy enough,' he said, 'we play on her one weakness.'

'And that is?' asked Fenston.

'Her honesty.'

—◦—

Arabella sat alone in the drawing room, unable to take in what was happening all around her. A cup of Earl Grey tea on the table beside her had gone cold, but she hadn't noticed. The loudest noise in the room was the tick of the clock on the mantelpiece. Time had stopped for Arabella.

Several police cars and an ambulance were parked on the gravel outside. People going about their business, dressed in uniforms, white coats, dark suits and even face masks, came and went without bothering her.

There was a gentle tap on the door. Arabella looked up to see an old friend standing in the doorway. The chief superintendent removed a peaked cap covered in silver braid as he entered the room. Arabella rose from the sofa, her face ashen, her eyes red from crying. The tall man bent down and kissed her gently on both cheeks, and then waited for her to sit back down before he took his place in the leather wing chair opposite her. Stephen Renton offered his condolences, which were genuine; he'd known Victoria for many years.

Arabella thanked him, sat up straight and asked

quietly, 'Who could have done such a terrible thing, especially to someone as innocent as Victoria?'

'There doesn't seem to be a simple or logical answer to that question,' the chief superintendent replied. 'And it doesn't help that it was several hours before her body was discovered, allowing the assailant more than enough time to get clean away.' He paused. 'Do you feel up to answering some questions, my dear?'

Arabella gave a nod. 'I'll do anything I can to help you track down the *assailant*.' She repeated the word with venom.

'Normally, the first question I would ask in any murder enquiry is do you know if your sister had any enemies, but I confess that knowing her as I did that doesn't seem possible. However, I must ask if you were aware of any problems Victoria might have been facing, because – ' he hesitated – 'there have been rumours in the village for some time that, following your father's death, your sister was left with considerable debts.'

'I don't know, is the truth,' Arabella admitted. 'After I married Angus, we only came down from Scotland for a couple of weeks in the summer, and every other Christmas. It wasn't until my husband died that I returned to live in Surrey' – the chief superintendent nodded, but didn't interrupt – 'and heard the same rumours. Local gossips were even letting it be known that some of the furniture in my shop had come from the estate, in order that Victoria could still pay the staff.'

'And was there any truth in those rumours?' asked Stephen.

'None at all,' replied Arabella. 'When Angus died and I sold our farm in Perthshire, there was more than enough to allow me to return to Wentworth, open my little shop and turn a life-long hobby into a worthwhile enterprise. But I did ask my sister on several occasions if the rumours of Father's financial position were true. Victoria denied there was any problem, always claiming that everything was under control. But then she adored Father, and in her eyes he could do no wrong.'

'Can you think of anything that might give some clue as to why . . .'

Arabella rose from the sofa and, without explanation, walked across to a writing desk on the far side of the room. She picked up the blood-spattered letter that she had found on her sister's table, walked back and handed it across to him.

Stephen read the unfinished missive twice before asking, 'Do you have any idea what Victoria could have meant by "a solution has been found"?'

'No,' admitted Arabella, 'but it's possible that I'll be able to answer that question once I've had a word with Arnold Simpson.'

'That doesn't fill me with confidence,' said Stephen.

Arabella noted his comment, but didn't respond. She knew that the chief superintendent's natural instinct was to mistrust all solicitors, who appeared unable to disguise a belief that they were superior to any police officer.

The chief superintendent rose from his place, walked across and sat next to Arabella. He took her hand. 'Call me whenever you want to,' he said gently, 'and try not to keep too many secrets from me, Arabella, because I'll need to know everything, and I mean everything, if we're to find who murdered your sister.'

Arabella didn't reply.

—◦—

'Damn,' muttered Anna to herself when an athletic, dark-haired man jogged casually past her, just as he'd done several times during the last few weeks. He didn't glance back – serious runners never did. Anna knew that it would be pointless to try and keep up with him, as she would be 'legless' within a hundred yards. She had once caught a sideways glimpse of the mystery man, but he then strode away and all she had seen was the back of his emerald-green T-shirt as he continued towards Strawberry Fields. Anna tried to put him out of her mind and focus once again on her meeting with Fenston.

Anna had already sent a copy of her report to the chairman's office, recommending that the bank sell the self-portrait as quickly as possible. She knew a collector in Tokyo who was obsessed with Van Gogh and still had the yen to prove it. And with this particular painting there was another weakness she would be able to play on, which she had highlighted in her report. Van Gogh had always admired Japanese art, and on the wall behind the self-portrait he had reproduced a print of *Geishas in a Landscape*, which Anna felt would make the painting even more irresistible to Takashi Nakamura.

Nakamura was chairman of the largest steel company in Japan, but lately he'd been spending more and more time building up his art collection, which he'd let it be known was to form part of a foundation that would eventually be left to the nation. Anna also considered it an advantage that Nakamura was an intensely secretive individual, who guarded the details of his private collection with typical Japanese inscrutability. Such a sale would allow Victoria Wentworth to save face – something the Japanese fully understood. Anna had once acquired a Degas for Nakamura, *Dancing Class with Mme Minette*, which the seller had wished to dispose of privately, a service the great auction houses offer to those who want to avoid the prying eyes of journalists who hang around the sale rooms. She was confident that Nakamura would offer at least sixty million dollars for the rare Dutch masterpiece. So if Fenston accepted her proposal – and why shouldn't he? – everyone would be satisfied with the outcome.

When Anna passed the Tavern on the Green, she once again checked her watch. She would need to pick up her pace if she still hoped to be back at Artisans' Gate in under twelve minutes. As she sprinted down the hill, she reflected on the fact that she shouldn't allow her personal feelings for a client to cloud her judgement, but frankly Victoria needed all the help she could get. When Anna passed through Artisans' Gate, she pressed the stop button on her watch: twelve minutes and four seconds. *Damn.*

Anna jogged slowly off in the direction of her apartment, unaware that she was being closely watched by the man in the emerald-green T-shirt.

6

JACK DELANEY still wasn't sure if Anna Petrescu was a criminal.

The FBI agent watched her as she disappeared into the crowd on her way back to Thornton House. Once she was out of sight, Jack resumed jogging through Sheep Meadow towards the lake. He thought about the woman he'd been investigating for the past six weeks. An enquiry that was hampered by the fact that he didn't need Anna to find out that the bureau were also investigating her boss, who Jack had no doubt *was* a criminal.

It was nearly a year since Richard W. Macy, Jack's Supervising Special Agent, had called him into his office and allocated him a team of eight agents to cover a new assignment. Jack was to investigate three vicious murders on three different continents which had one thing in common: each of the victims had been killed at a time when they also had large outstanding loans with Fenston Finance. Jack quickly concluded that the murders had been planned and were the work of a professional killer.

Jack cut through Shakespeare Garden as he headed back towards his small apartment on the West Side. He had just about completed his file on Fenston's most recent recruit, although he still couldn't make up his mind if she was a willing accomplice or a naive innocent.

Jack had begun with Anna's upbringing and discovered that her uncle, George Petrescu, had emigrated from Romania in 1968, to settle in Danville, Illinois.

Within weeks of Ceauşescu appointing himself president, George had written to his brother imploring him to come to America. When Ceauşescu declared Romania a socialist republic and made his wife Elena his deputy, George wrote to his brother renewing his invitation, which included his young niece, Anna.

Although Anna's parents refused to leave their homeland, they did allow their seventeen-year-old daughter to be smuggled out of Bucharest in 1987 and shipped off to America to stay with her uncle, promising her that she could return the moment Ceauşescu had been overthrown. Anna never returned. She wrote home regularly, begging her parents to join them in the States, but she rarely received a response. Two years later she learned that her father had been killed in a border skirmish while attempting to oust the dictator. Her mother repeated that she would never leave her native land, her excuse now being, 'Who would tend to your father's grave?'

That much, one of Jack's squad members had been able to discover from an essay Anna had written for her high school magazine. One of her classmates had also written about the gentle girl with long fair plaits and blue eyes, who came from somewhere called Bucharest and knew so few words of English that she couldn't even recite the Pledge of Allegiance at morning assembly. By the end of her second year, Anna was editing the magazine, from where Jack had gathered so much of his information.

From high school, Anna won a scholarship to Williams University in Massachusetts to study art history. A local newspaper recorded that she also won the intervarsity mile against Cornell in a time of 4 minutes 48 seconds. Jack followed Anna's progress to the University of Pennsylvania, where she continued her studies for a

PhD, her chosen thesis subject the Fauve Movement. Jack had to look up the word in Webster's. It referred to a group of artists led by Matisse, Derain and Vlaminck who wished to break away from the influence of Impressionism and move towards the use of bright and dissonant colour. He also learned how the young Picasso had left Spain to join the group in Paris, where he shocked the public with paintings that *Paris Match* described as 'of no lasting importance'; 'sanity will return,' they assured their readers. It only made Jack want to read more about Vuillard, Luce and Camoin – artists he'd never heard of. But that would have to wait for an off-duty moment, unless it became evidence that would nail Fenston.

After Penn, Dr Petrescu joined Sotheby's as a graduate trainee. Here Jack's information became somewhat sketchy as he could allow his agents only limited contact with her former colleagues. However, he did learn of her photographic memory, her rigorous scholarship and the fact that she was liked by everyone from the porters to the chairman. But no one would discuss in detail what 'under a cloud' meant, although he did discover that she would not be welcome back at Sotheby's under the present management. And Jack couldn't fathom out why, despite her dismissal, she considered joining Fenston Finance. For that part of his enquiry he had to rely on speculation, because he couldn't risk approaching anyone she worked with at the bank, although it was clear that Tina Forster, the chairman's secretary, had become a close friend.

In the short time Anna had worked at Fenston Finance, she had visited several new clients who had recently taken out large loans, all of whom were in possession of major art collections. Jack feared that it could only be a matter of time before one of them suffered the same fate as Fenston's three previous victims.

Jack ran onto West 86th Street. Three questions still needed answering. One, how long had Fenston known Petrescu before she joined the bank? Two, had they, or their families, known each other in Romania? And three, was she the hired assassin?

◄○►

Fenston scrawled his signature across the breakfast bill, rose from his place and, without waiting for Leapman to finish his coffee, marched out of the restaurant. He stepped into an open elevator, but waited for Leapman to press the button for the eighty-third floor. A group of Japanese men in dark blue suits and plain silk ties joined them, having also had breakfast at Windows on the World. Fenston never discussed business matters while in an elevator, well aware that several of his rivals occupied the floors above and below him.

When the elevator opened on the eighty-third floor, Leapman followed his master out, but then turned the other way and headed straight for Petrescu's office. He opened her door without knocking to find Anna's assistant, Rebecca, preparing the files Anna would need for her meeting with the chairman. Leapman barked out a set of instructions that didn't invite questions. Rebecca immediately placed the files on Anna's desk and went in search of a large cardboard box.

Leapman walked back down the corridor and joined the chairman in his office. They began to go over tactics for their showdown with Petrescu. Although they had been through the same procedure three times in the past eight years, Leapman warned the chairman that it could be different this time.

'What do you mean?' demanded Fenston.

'I don't think Petrescu will leave without putting up a fight,' he said. 'After all, she isn't going to find it easy to get another job.'

'She certainly won't if I have anything to do with it,' said Fenston, rubbing his hands.

'But perhaps in the circumstances, chairman, it might be wise if I—'

A knock on the door interrupted their exchange. Fenston looked up to see Barry Steadman, the bank's head of security, standing in the doorway.

'Sorry to bother you, chairman, but there's a FedEx courier out here, says he has a package for you and no one else can sign for it.'

Fenston waved the courier in and, without a word, penned his signature in the little oblong box opposite his name. Leapman looked on, but neither of them spoke until the courier had departed and Barry had closed the door behind him.

'Is that what I think it is?' asked Leapman quietly.

'We're about to find out,' said Fenston as he ripped open the package and emptied its contents onto the desk.

They both stared down at Victoria Wentworth's left ear.

'See that Krantz is paid the other half million,' said Fenston. Leapman nodded. 'And she's even sent a bonus,' said Fenston, staring down at the antique diamond earring.

--◇--

Anna finished packing just after seven. She left her suitcase in the hall, intending to return and pick it up on the way to the airport straight after work. Her flight to London was scheduled for 5.40pm that afternoon, touching down at Heathrow just before sunrise the following day. Anna much preferred taking the overnight flight, when she could sleep and still have enough time to prepare herself before joining Victoria for lunch at Wentworth Hall. She only hoped that Victoria had read her report and would agree that selling the Van Gogh privately was a simple solution to all her problems.

Anna left her apartment building for the second time that morning, just after 7.20am. She hailed a taxi – an extravagance, but one she justified by wanting to look her best for her meeting with the chairman. She sat in the back of the cab and checked her appearance in her compact mirror. Her recently acquired Anand Jon suit and white silk blouse would surely make heads turn. Although some might be puzzled by her black sneakers.

The cab took a right on FDR Drive and speeded up a little as Anna checked her cellphone. There were three messages, all of which she would deal with after the meeting: one from her secretary, Rebecca, needing to speak to her urgently, which was surprising given they were going to see each other in a few minutes' time; confirmation of her flight from BA, and an invitation to dinner with Robert Brooks, the new chairman of Bonhams.

Her cab drew up outside the entrance to the North Tower twenty minutes later. She paid the driver and jumped out to join a sea of workers as they filed towards the entrance and through the bank of turnstiles. She took the shuttle express elevator, and less than a minute later stepped out onto the dark green carpet of the executive floor. Anna had once overheard in the elevator that each floor was an acre in size, and some fifty thousand people worked in a building that never closed – more than double the population of her adopted home town of Danville, Illinois.

Anna went straight to her office and was surprised to

find that Rebecca wasn't waiting for her, especially as she knew how important her eight o'clock meeting was. But she was relieved to see that all the relevant files had been piled neatly on her desk. She double-checked that they were in the order she had requested. Anna still had a few minutes to spare, so she once again turned to the Wentworth file and began reading her report. 'The value of the Wentworth Estate falls into several categories. My department's only interest is in . . .'

⊷◦⊶

Tina Forster didn't rise until just after seven. Her appointment with the dentist wasn't until eight thirty and Fenston had made it clear that she needn't be on time this morning. That usually meant he had an out-of-town appointment, or was going to fire someone. If it was the latter, he wouldn't want her hanging around the office, sympathizing with the person who had just lost their job. Tina knew that it couldn't be Leapman, because Fenston wouldn't be able to survive without the man, and although she would have liked it to be Barry Steadman, she could dream on, because he never missed an opportunity to praise the chairman, who absorbed flattery like a beached sea sponge waiting for the next wave.

Tina lay soaking in the bath – a luxury she usually only allowed herself at weekends – wondering when it would be her turn to be fired. She'd been Fenston's personal assistant for over a year, and although she despised the man and all he stood for, she'd still tried to make herself indispensable. Tina knew that she couldn't consider resigning until . . .

The phone rang in her bedroom, but she made no attempt to answer it. She assumed it would be Fenston demanding to know where a particular file was, a phone number, even his diary. 'On the desk in front of you' was usually the answer. She wondered for a moment if it might be Anna, the only real friend she'd made since moving from the West Coast. Unlikely, she concluded, as Anna would be presenting her report to the chairman at eight o'clock, and was probably, even now, going over the finer details for the twentieth time.

Tina smiled as she climbed out of the bath and wrapped a towel round her body. She strolled across the corridor and into her bedroom. Whenever a guest spent the night in her cramped apartment they had to share her bed or sleep on the sofa. They had little choice, as she only had one bedroom. Not many takers lately, and not because of any shortage of offers. But after what she'd been through with Fenston, Tina no longer trusted anyone. Recently she'd wanted to confide in Anna, but this remained the one secret she couldn't risk sharing.

Tina pulled open the curtains and, despite its being September, the clear, sparkling morning convinced her that she should wear a summer dress. It might even make her relax when she stared up at the dentist's drill.

Once she was dressed and had checked her appearance in the mirror, Tina went off to the kitchen and made herself a cup of coffee. She wasn't allowed to have anything else for breakfast, not even toast – instructions from the ferocious dental assistant – so she flicked on the television to catch the early morning news. There wasn't any. A suicide bomber on the West Bank was followed by a 320-pound woman who was suing McDonald's for ruining her sex life. Tina was just about to turn off *Good Morning America* when the quarterback for the 49ers appeared on the screen.

It made Tina think of her father.

7

JACK DELANEY arrived at his office at 26 Federal Plaza just after seven that morning. He felt depressed as he stared down at the countless files that littered his desk. Every one of them connected with his investigation of Bryce Fenston, and a year later he was no nearer to presenting his boss with enough evidence to ask a judge to issue an arrest warrant.

Jack opened Fenston's personal file in the vain hope that he might stumble across some tiny clue, some personal trait, or just a mistake that would finally link Fenston directly to the three vicious murders that had taken place in Marseille, Los Angeles and Rio de Janeiro.

In 1984, the 32-year-old Nicu Munteanu had presented himself at the American Embassy in Bucharest, claiming that he could identify two spies working in the heart of Washington, information he was willing to trade in exchange for an American passport. A dozen such claims were handled by the embassy every week and almost all proved groundless, but in Munteanu's case the information stood up. Within a month, two well-placed officials found themselves on a flight back to Moscow, and Munteanu was issued with an American passport.

Nicu Munteanu landed in New York on February 17, 1985. Jack had been able to find little intelligence on Munteanu's activities during the following year, but he suddenly re-emerged with enough money to take over Fenston Finance, a small, ailing bank in Manhattan.

Nicu Munteanu changed his name to Bryce Fenston – not a crime in itself – but no one could identify his backers, despite the fact that during the next few years the bank began to accept large deposits from unlisted companies across Eastern Europe. Then in 1989 the cash flow suddenly dried up, the same year as Ceauşescu and his wife Elena fled from Bucharest following the uprising. Within days they were captured, tried and executed.

Jack looked out of his window over lower Manhattan, and recalled the FBI maxim: never believe in coincidences, but never dismiss them.

Following Ceauşescu's death, the bank appeared to go through a couple of lean years until Fenston met up with Karl Leapman, a disbarred lawyer, who had recently been released from prison for fraud. It was not too long before the bank resumed its profitable ways.

Jack stared down at several photographs of Bryce Fenston, who regularly appeared in the gossip columns with one of New York's most fashionable women on his arm. He was variously described as a brilliant banker, a leading financier, even a generous benefactor, and with almost every mention of his name there was a reference to his magnificent art collection. Jack pushed the photographs to one side. He hadn't yet come to terms with a man who wore an earring, and he was even more puzzled why someone who had a full head of hair when he first came to America would choose to shave himself bald. Who was he hiding from?

Jack closed the Munteanu/Fenston personal file, and turned his attention to Pierre de Rochelle, the first of the victims.

Rochelle required seventy million francs to pay for his share in a vineyard. His only previous experience of the wine industry seemed to have come from draining

39

the bottles on a regular basis. Even a cursory inspection would have revealed that his investment plan didn't appear to fulfil the banking maxim of being 'sound'. However, what caught Fenston's attention when he perused the application was that the young man had recently inherited a chateau in the Dordogne, in which every wall was graced with fine Impressionist paintings, including a Degas, two Pissarros and a Monet of Argenteuil.

The vineyard failed to show a return for four fruitless years, during which time the chateau began to render up its assets, leaving only outline shapes where the pictures had once hung. By the time Fenston had shipped the last painting back to New York to join his private collection, Pierre's original loan had, with accumulated interest, more than doubled. When his chateau was finally placed on the market, Pierre took up residence in a small flat in Marseille, where each night he would drink himself into a senseless stupor. That was until a bright young lady, just out of law school, suggested to Pierre, in one of his sober moments, that were Fenston Finance to sell his Degas, the Monet and the two Pissarros, he could not only pay off his debt, but take the chateau off the market and reclaim the rest of his collection. This suggestion did not fit in with Fenston's long-term plans.

A week later, the drunken body of Pierre de Rochelle was found slumped in a Marseille alley, his throat sliced open.

Four years later, the Marseille police closed the file, with the words 'NON RESOLU' stamped on the cover.

When the estate was finally settled, Fenston had sold off all the works, with the exception of the Degas, the Monet and the two Pissarros, and after compound interest, bank charges and lawyers' fees, Pierre's younger brother, Simon de Rochelle, inherited the flat in Marseille.

Jack rose from behind his desk, stretched his cramped limbs and yawned wearily, before he considered tackling Chris Adams Jr. Although he knew Adams's case history almost by heart.

Chris Adams Senior had operated a highly successful fine art gallery on Melrose Avenue in Los Angeles. He specialized in the American School, so admired by the Hollywood glitterati. His untimely death in a car crash left his son Chris Jr with a collection of Rothkos, Pollocks, Jasper Johnses, Rauschenbergs and several Warhol acrylics, including a *Black Marilyn*.

An old school friend advised Chris that the way to double his money would be to invest in the dot.com revolution. Chris Jr pointed out that he didn't have any ready cash, just the gallery, the paintings and *Christina*, his father's old yacht – and even that was half owned by his younger sister. Fenston Finance stepped in and advanced him a loan of twelve million dollars, on their usual terms. As in so many revolutions, several bodies ended up on the battlefield: among them, Chris Jr's.

Fenston Finance allowed the debt to continue mounting without ever troubling their client. That was until Chris Jr read in the *Los Angeles Times* that Warhol's *Shot Red Marilyn* had recently sold for over four million dollars. He immediately contacted Christie's in LA, who assured him that he could expect an equally good return for his Rothkos, Pollocks and Jasper Johnses. Three months later, Leapman rushed into the chairman's office bearing the latest copy of a Christie's sale catalogue. He had placed yellow Post-it notes against seven different lots that were due to come under the hammer. Fenston made one phone call, then booked himself on the next flight to Rome.

Three days later, Chris Jr was discovered in the lavatory of a gay bar with his throat cut.

Fenston was on holiday in Italy at the time, and Jack had a copy of his hotel bill, plane tickets, and even his credit-card purchases from several shops and restaurants.

The paintings were immediately withdrawn from the Christie's sale while the LA police carried out their investigations. After eighteen months of no new evidence and dead ends, the file joined the other LAPD cold cases stored in the basement. All Chris's sister ended up with was a model of *Christina*, her father's much-loved yacht.

Jack tossed Chris Jr's file to one side, and stared down at the name of Maria Vasconcellos, a Brazilian widow who had inherited a house and a lawn full of statues – and not of the garden-centre variety. Moore, Giacometti, Remington, Botero and Calder were among Señora Vasconcellos's husband's bequest. Unfortunately, she fell in love with a gigolo, and when he suggested—
The phone rang on Jack's desk.

'Our London embassy is on line two,' his secretary informed him.

'Thanks, Sally,' said Jack, knowing it could only be his friend Tom Crasanti, who had joined the FBI on the same day as he had.

'Hi, Tom, how are you?' he asked even before he heard a voice.

'In good shape,' Tom replied. 'Still running every day, even if I'm not as fit as you.'

'And my godson?'

'He's learning to play cricket.'

'The traitor. Got any *good* news?'

'No,' said Tom, 'that's why I'm calling. You're going to have to open another file.'

Jack felt a cold shiver run through his body. 'Who is it this time?' he asked quietly.

'The lady's name, and Lady she was, is Victoria Wentworth.'

'How did she die?'

'In exactly the same manner as the other three, throat cut, almost certainly with a kitchen knife.'

'What makes you think Fenston was involved?'

'She owed the bank over thirty million.'

'And what was he after this time?'

'A Van Gogh self-portrait.'

'Value?'

'Sixty, possibly seventy million dollars.'

'I'll be on the next plane to London.'

8

At 7.56, Anna closed the Wentworth file and bent down to open the bottom drawer of her desk. She slipped off her sneakers and replaced them with a pair of black high-heeled shoes. She rose from her chair, gathered up the files and glanced in the mirror – not a hair out of place.

Anna stepped out of her office and walked down the corridor towards the large corner suite. Two or three members of staff greeted her with 'Good morning, Anna', which she acknowledged with a smile. A gentle knock on the chairman's door – she knew Fenston would already be seated at his desk. Had she been even a minute late, he would have pointedly stared at his watch. Anna waited for an invitation to enter, and was surprised when the door was immediately pulled open and she came face to face with Karl Leapman. He was wearing an almost identical suit to the one Fenston had on, even if it wasn't of the same vintage.

'Good morning, Karl,' she said brightly, but didn't receive a response.

The chairman looked up from behind his desk and motioned Anna to take the seat opposite him. He also didn't offer any salutation, but then he rarely did. Leapman took his place on the right of the chairman and slightly behind him, like a cardinal in attendance on the Pope. Status clearly defined. Anna assumed that Tina would appear at any moment with a cup of black coffee, but the secretary's door remained resolutely shut.

Anna glanced up at the Monet of Argenteuil that hung on the wall behind the chairman's desk. Although Monet had painted the peaceful riverbank scene on several occasions, this was one of the finest examples. Anna had once asked Fenston where he'd acquired the painting, but he'd been evasive, and she couldn't find any reference to the sale among past transactions.

She looked across at Leapman, whose lean and hungry look reminded her of Cassius. It didn't seem to matter what time of day it was, he always looked as if he needed a shave. She turned her attention to Fenston, who was certainly no Brutus, and shifted uneasily in her chair, trying not to appear fazed by the silence, which was suddenly broken, on Fenston's nod.

'Dr Petrescu, some distressing information has been brought to the attention of the chairman,' Leapman began. 'It would appear,' he continued, 'that you sent one of the bank's private and confidential documents to a client, before the chairman had been given the chance to consider its implications.'

For a moment Anna was taken by surprise, but she quickly recovered and decided to respond in kind. 'If, Mr Leapman, you are referring to my report concerning the loan to the Wentworth Estate, you are correct. I did send a copy to Lady Victoria Wentworth.'

'But the chairman was not given enough time to read that report and make a considered judgement before you forwarded it to the client,' said Leapman, looking down at some notes.

'That is not the case, Mr Leapman. Both you and the chairman were sent copies of my report on September first, with a recommendation that Lady Victoria should be advised of her position before the next quarterly payment was due.'

'I never received the report,' said Fenston brusquely.

'And indeed,' said Anna, still looking at Leapman, 'the chairman acknowledged such, when his office returned the form I attached to that report.'

'I never saw it,' repeated Fenston.

'Which he initialled,' said Anna, who opened her file, extracted the relevant form and placed it on the desk in front of Fenston. He ignored it.

'The least you should have done was wait for my opinion,' said Fenston, 'before allowing a copy of a report on such a sensitive subject to leave this office.'

Anna still couldn't work out why they were spoiling for a fight. They weren't even playing good cop, bad cop.

'I waited for a week, chairman,' she replied, 'during which time you made no comment on my recommendations, despite the fact that I will be flying to London this evening to keep an appointment with Lady Victoria tomorrow afternoon. However,' Anna continued before the chairman could respond, 'I sent you a reminder two days later.' She opened her file again, and placed a second sheet of paper on the chairman's desk. Once again he ignored it.

'But I hadn't read your report,' Fenston said repeating himself, clearly unable to depart from his script.

Stay calm, girl, stay calm, Anna could hear her father whispering in her ear.

She took a deep breath before continuing. 'My report does no more, and certainly no less, than advise the board, of which I am a member, that if we were to sell the Van Gogh, either privately or through one of the recognized auction houses, the amount raised would more than cover the bank's original loan, plus interest.'

'But it might not have been my intention to sell the Van Gogh,' said Fenston, now clearly straying from his script.

'You would have been left with no choice, chairman, had that been the wish of our client.'

'But I may have come up with a better solution for dealing with the Wentworth problem.'

'If that was the case, chairman,' said Anna evenly, 'I'm only surprised you didn't consult the head of the department concerned, so that, at least as colleagues, we could have discussed any difference of opinion before I left for England tonight.'

'That is an impertinent suggestion,' said Fenston, raising his voice to a new level. 'I report to no one.'

'I don't consider it is impertinent, chairman, to abide by the law,' said Anna calmly. 'It's no more than the bank's legal requirement to report any alternative recommendations to their clients. As I feel sure you realize, under the new banking regulations, as proposed by the IRS and recently passed by Congress—'

'And I feel sure you realize,' said Fenston, 'that your first responsibility is to me.'

'Not if I believe that an officer of the bank is breaking the law,' Anna replied, 'because that's something I am not willing to be a party to.'

'Are you trying to goad me into firing you?' shouted Fenston.

'No, but I have a feeling that you are trying to goad me into resigning,' said Anna quietly.

'Either way,' said Fenston, swivelling round in his chair and staring out of the window, 'it is clear you no longer have a role to play in this bank, as you are simply not a team player – something they warned me about when you were dismissed from Sotheby's.'

Don't rise, thought Anna. She pursed her lips and stared at Fenston's profile. She was about to reply when she noticed there was something different about him, and then she spotted the new earring. Vanity will surely be his downfall, she thought as he swivelled back round and glared at her. She didn't react.

'Chairman, as I suspect this conversation is being recorded, I would like to make one thing absolutely clear. You don't appear to know a great deal about banking law, and you clearly know nothing about employment law, because enticing a colleague to swindle a naive woman out of her inheritance is a criminal offence, as I feel sure Mr Leapman, with all his experience, of both sides of the law, will be happy to explain to you.'

'Get out, before I throw you out,' screamed Fenston, jumping up from his chair and towering over Anna. She rose slowly, turned her back on Fenston and walked towards the door.

'And the first thing you can do is clear your desk because I want you out of your office in ten minutes. If you are still on the premises after that, I will instruct security to escort you from the building.'

Anna didn't hear Fenston's last remark as she had already closed the door quietly behind her.

The first person Anna saw as she stepped into the corridor was Barry, who had clearly been tipped off. The whole episode was beginning to look as if it had been choreographed long before she'd entered the building.

Anna walked back down the corridor with as much dignity as she could muster, despite Barry matching her stride for stride and occasionally touching her elbow. She passed an elevator that was being held open for someone and wondered who. Surely it couldn't be for her. Anna was back in her office less than fifteen minutes after she'd left it. This time Rebecca was waiting for her. She was standing behind her desk clutching a large brown cardboard box. Anna walked across to her desk, and was just about to turn on her computer when a voice behind her said, 'Don't touch anything. Your personal belongings have already been packed, so let's go.' Anna turned round to see Barry still hovering in the doorway.

'I'm so sorry,' said Rebecca. 'I tried to phone and warn you, but—'

'Don't speak to her,' barked Barry, 'just hand over the box. She's outta here.' Barry rested the palm of his hand on the knuckle of his truncheon. Anna wondered if he realized just how stupid he looked. She turned back to Rebecca and smiled.

'It's not your fault,' she said as her secretary handed over the cardboard box.

Anna placed the box on the desk, sat down and pulled open the bottom drawer.

'You can't remove anything that belongs to the company,' said Barry.

'I feel confident that Mr Fenston won't be wanting my sneakers,' said Anna, as she removed her high-heeled shoes and placed them in the box. Anna pulled on her sneakers, tied the laces, picked up the box and headed back into the corridor. Any attempt at dignity was no longer possible. Every employee knew that raised voices in the chairman's office followed by Barry escorting you from the premises meant only one thing: you were about to be handed your pink slip. This time passers-by quickly retreated into their offices, making no attempt to engage Anna in conversation.

The head of security accompanied his charge to an office at the far end of the corridor that Anna had never entered before. When she walked in, Barry once again positioned himself in the doorway. It was clear that they'd also been fully briefed, because she was met by another employee who didn't even venture 'good morning' for fear it would be reported to the chairman. He swivelled a piece of paper around that displayed the figures $9,116 in bold type. Anna's monthly salary. She signed on the dotted line without comment.

'The money will be wired through to your account later today,' he said without raising his eyes.

Anna turned to find her watchdog still prowling around outside, trying hard to look menacing. When she left the accounts office, Barry accompanied her on the long walk back down an empty corridor.

When they reached the elevator, Barry pressed the down arrow, while Anna continued to cling onto her cardboard box.

They were both waiting for the elevator doors to open when American Airlines Flight 11 out of Boston crashed into the ninety-fourth floor of the North Tower.

9

RUTH PARISH looked up at the departure monitor on the wall above her desk. She was relieved to see that United's flight 107 bound for JFK had finally taken off at 1.40pm. Forty minutes behind schedule.

Ruth and her partner Sam had founded Art Locations nearly a decade before, and when he left her for a younger woman Ruth ended up with the company – by far the better part of the bargain. Ruth was married to the job, despite its long hours, demanding customers and planes, trains and cargo vessels that never arrived on time. Moving great, and not so great, works of art from one corner of the globe to the other allowed her to combine a natural flair for organization with a love of beautiful objects – if sometimes she saw the objects only for a fleeting moment.

Ruth travelled around the world accepting commissions from governments who were planning national exhibitions, while also dealing with gallery owners, dealers and several private collectors, who often wanted nothing more than to move a favourite painting from one home to another. Over the years, many of her customers had become personal friends. But not Bryce Fenston. Ruth had long ago concluded that the words 'please' and 'thank you' were not in this man's vocabulary, and she certainly wasn't on his Christmas card list. Fenston's latest demand had been to collect a Van Gogh from Wentworth Hall and transport it, without delay, to his office in New York.

Obtaining an export licence for the masterpiece had not proved difficult, as few institutions or museums could raise the sixty million dollars necessary to stop the painting leaving the country. Especially after the National Galleries of Scotland had recently failed to raise the required £7.5 million to ensure that Michelangelo's *Study of a Mourning Woman* didn't leave these shores to become part of a private collection in the States.

When a Mr Andrews, the butler at Wentworth Hall, had rung the previous day to say that the painting would be ready for collection in the morning, Ruth had scheduled one of her high-security air-ride trucks to be at the hall by eight o'clock. Ruth was pacing up and down the tarmac long before the truck turned up at her office, just after ten.

Once the painting was unloaded, Ruth supervised every aspect of its packing and safe dispatch to New York, a task she would normally have left to one of her managers. She stood over her senior packer as he wrapped the painting in acid-free glassine paper and then placed it into the foam-lined case he'd been working on throughout the night so it would be ready in time. The captive bolts were tightened on the case, preventing anyone breaking into it without a sophisticated socket set. Special indicators were attached to the outside of the case that would turn red if anyone attempted to open it during its journey. The senior packer stencilled the word 'FRAGILE' on both sides of the box and the number '47' in all four corners. The customs officer had raised an eyebrow when he checked the shipping papers, but as an export licence had been granted, the eyebrow returned to its natural position.

Ruth drove across to the waiting 747 and watched as the red box disappeared into the vast hold. She didn't return to her office until the heavy door was secured in place. She checked her watch and smiled. The plane had taken off at 1.40pm.

Ruth began to think about the painting that would be arriving from the Rijksmuseum in Amsterdam later that evening to form part of the Rembrandt's Women exhibition at the Royal Academy. But not before she had put a call through to Fenston Finance to inform them that the Van Gogh was on its way.

She dialled Anna's number in New York, and waited for her to pick up the phone.

10

THERE WAS a loud explosion, and the building began to sway from side to side.

Anna was hurled across the corridor, ending up flat on the canvas as if she'd been floored by a heavyweight boxer. The elevator doors opened and she watched as a fireball of fuel shot through the shaft, searching for oxygen. The hot blast slapped her in the face as if the door of an oven had been thrown open. Anna lay on the ground, dazed.

Her first thought was that the building must have been struck by lightning, but she quickly dismissed that idea as there wasn't a cloud in the sky. An eerie silence followed and Anna wondered if she had gone deaf, but this was soon replaced by screams of 'Oh, my God!' as huge shards of jagged glass, twisted metal and office furniture flew past the windows in front of her.

It must be another bomb, was Anna's second thought. Everyone who had been in the building in 1993 retold stories of what had happened to them on that bitterly cold February afternoon. Some of them were apocryphal, others pure invention, but the facts were simple. A truck filled with explosives had been driven into the underground garage beneath the building. When it exploded, six people were killed and over a thousand injured. Five underground floors were wiped out, and it took several hours for the emergency services to evacuate the building. Since then, everyone who worked in the World Trade Center had been required to participate in regular fire drills. Anna tried to remember what she was supposed to do in such an emergency.

She recalled the clear instructions printed in red on the exit door to the stairwell on every floor: 'In case of emergency, do not return to your desk, do not use the elevator, exit by the nearest stairwell.' But first Anna needed to find out if she could even stand up, aware that part of the ceiling had collapsed on her and the building was still swaying. She tried tentatively to push herself up, and although she was bruised and cut in several places, nothing seemed to be broken. She stretched for a moment, as she always did before starting out on a long run.

Anna abandoned what was left of the contents of the cardboard box and stumbled towards stairwell C in the centre of the building. Some of her colleagues were also beginning to recover from the initial shock, and one or two even returned to their desks to pick up personal belongings.

As Anna made her way along the corridor, she was greeted with a series of questions to which she had no answers.

'What are we supposed to do?' asked a secretary.

'Should we go up or down?' said a cleaner.

'Do we wait to be rescued?' asked a bond dealer.

These were all questions for the security officer, but Barry was nowhere to be seen.

Once Anna reached the stairwell, she joined a group of dazed people, some silent, some crying, who weren't quite sure what to do next. No one seemed to have the slightest idea what had caused the explosion or why the building was still swaying. Although several of the lights on the stairwell had been snuffed out like candles, the photoluminescent strip that ran along the edge of each step shone brightly up at her.

Some of those around her were trying to contact the outside world on their cellphones, but few were succeeding. One who did get through was chatting to her boyfriend. She was telling him that her boss had told her she could go home, take the rest of the day off. Another began to relay to those around him the conversation he was having with his wife: 'A plane has hit the North Tower,' he announced.

'But where, where?' shouted several voices at once. He asked his wife the same question. 'Above us, some-where in the nineties,' he said, passing on her reply.

'But what are we meant to do?' asked the chief accountant, who hadn't moved from the top step. The younger man repeated the question to his wife, and waited for her reply. 'The mayor is advising everyone to get out of the building as quickly as possible.'

On hearing this news, all those in the stairwell began their descent to the eighty-second floor. Anna looked back through the glass window and was surprised to see how many people had remained at their desks, as if they were in a theatre after the curtain had come down and had decided to wait until the initial rush had dispersed.

Anna took the mayor's advice. She began to count the steps as she walked down each flight – eighteen to each floor, which she calculated meant at least another fifteen hundred before she would reach the lobby. The stairwell became more and more crowded as countless people swarmed out of their offices to join them on each floor, making it feel like a crowded subway during rush hour. Anna was surprised by how calm the descending line was.

The stairwell quickly separated into two lanes, with the slowest on the inside while the latest models were able to pass on the outside. But just like any highway, not everyone kept to the code, so regularly everything came to a complete standstill before moving off unsteadily again. Whenever they reached a new stairwell, some pulled into the hard shoulder, while others motored on.

Anna passed an old man who was wearing a black felt hat. She recalled seeing him several times during the past year, always wearing the same hat. She turned to smile at him and he raised his hat.

On, on, on she trudged, sometimes reaching the next floor in less than a minute, but more often being held up by those who had become exhausted after descending only a few floors. The outside lane was becoming more and more crowded, making it impossible for her to break the speed limit.

Anna heard the first clear order when she reached the sixty-eighth floor.

'Get to the right, and keep moving,' said an authoritative voice from somewhere below her. Although the instruction became louder with each step she took, it was still several more floors before she spotted the first fireman heading slowly towards her. He was wearing a baggy fireproof suit and sweating profusely under his black helmet emblazoned with the number 28. Anna could only wonder what state he'd be in after he'd climbed another thirty floors. He also appeared to be overloaded with equipment: coiled ropes over one shoulder and two oxygen tanks on his back, like a mountaineer trying to conquer Everest. Another fireman followed closely behind, carrying a vast length of hose, six pole arms and a large bottle of drinking water. He was dripping so much sweat that from time to time he removed his helmet and poured some of the drinking water over his head.

Those who continued to leave their offices and join

Anna in her downward migration were mostly silent, until an old man in front of her tripped and fell on a woman. The woman cut her leg on the sharp edge of the step and began to scream at the old man.

'Get on with it,' said a voice behind her. 'I made this journey after the '93 bombing, and I can tell you, lady, you ain't seen nothin' yet.'

Anna leant forward to help the old man to his feet, hindering her own progress, while allowing others to scramble past her.

Whenever she reached a new stairwell, Anna stared through the vast panes of glass at workers who remained at their desks, apparently oblivious of those fleeing in front of their eyes. She even overheard snatches of conversation through the open doors. One of them, a broker on the sixty-second floor, was trying to close a deal before the markets opened at nine o'clock. Another was staring out at her, as if the pane of glass was a television screen and he was reporting on a football game. He was giving a running commentary over the phone to a friend in the South Tower.

More and more firemen were now climbing towards her, turning the highway into two-way traffic, their constant cry: 'Get to the right, keep moving.' Anna kept moving, her speed often dictated by the slowest participant. Although the building had stopped swaying, tension and fear could still be seen on the faces of all those around her. They didn't know what had happened above them, and had no idea what awaited them below. Anna felt guilty as she passed an old woman who was being carried down in a large leather chair by two young men, her legs swollen, her breathing uneven.

On, on, on, Anna went, floor after floor, until even she began to feel tired.

She thought about Rebecca and Tina, and prayed

they were both safe. She even wondered if Fenston and Leapman were still sitting in the chairman's office, believing themselves impervious to any danger.

Anna began to feel confident that she was now safe and would eventually wake up from this nightmare. She even smiled at some of the New York humour that was bouncing around her, until she heard a voice behind her scream.

'A second plane has hit the South Tower.'

11

JACK WAS APPALLED by his first reaction when he heard what sounded like a bomb exploding on the other side of the road. Sally had rushed in to tell him that a plane had crashed into the North Tower of the World Trade Center.

'Let's hope it scored a direct hit on Fenston's office,' he said.

His second thoughts were a little more professional, as expressed when he joined Dick Macy, the Supervising Special Agent, along with the rest of the senior agents in the command centre. While other agents hit the phones in an attempt to make some sense of what was happening less than a mile away, Jack told the SSA that he was in no doubt that it was a well-planned act of terrorism. When a second plane crashed into the South Tower at 9.03am, all Macy said was, 'Yes, but *which* terrorist organization?'

Jack's third reaction was delayed, and it took him by surprise. He hoped that Anna Petrescu had managed to escape, but when the South Tower came crashing down fifty-six minutes later, he assumed it would not be long before the North Tower followed suit.

He returned to his desk and switched on his computer. Information was flooding in from their Massachusetts field office, reporting that the two attack flights had originated out of Boston and two more were in the air. Calls from passengers in those planes that had taken off from the same airport suggested they were also under the terrorists' control. One was heading for Washington.

The President, George W. Bush, was visiting a school in Florida when the first plane struck, and he was quickly whisked off to Barksdale Air Force Base in Louisiana. Vice-president Dick Cheney was in Washington. He'd already given clear instructions to shoot down the other two planes. The order was not carried out. Cheney also wanted to know which terrorist organization was responsible, as the President planned to address the nation later that evening and he was demanding answers. Jack remained at his desk, taking calls from his agents on the ground, frequently reporting back to Macy. One of those agents, Joe Corrigan, reported that Fenston and Leapman had been seen entering a building on Wall Street just before the first plane crashed into the North Tower. Jack looked down at the many files strewn across his desk and dismissed as wishful thinking, 'Case Closed'.

'And Petrescu?' he asked.

'No idea,' Joe replied. 'All I can tell you is that she was seen entering the building at seven forty-six, and hasn't been seen since.'

Jack looked up at the TV screen. A third plane had crashed into the Pentagon. The White House must be next, was his only thought.

◆

'A second plane's hit the South Tower,' a lady on the step above Anna repeated. Anna refused to believe that kind of freak accident could happen twice on the same day.

'It's no accident,' said another voice from behind, as if reading her thoughts. 'The only plane to crash into a building in New York was in '45. Flew into the seventy-ninth floor of the Empire State Building. But that was on a foggy day, without any of the sophisticated tracking devices they've got now. And don't forget, the air space above the city is a no-fly zone, so it must have been well planned. My bet is we're not the only folks in trouble.'

Within minutes, conspiracy theories, terrorist attacks and stories of freak accidents were being bandied about by people who had no idea what they were talking about. There would have been a stampede if they could have moved any faster. Anna quickly became aware that several people on the staircase were now masking their worst fears by all talking at once.

'Keep to the right, and keep moving,' was the constant cry emanating from whatever uniform trudged past them. Some of the migrants on the downward journey began to tire, allowing Anna to overtake them. She was thankful for all those hours spent running around Central Park and the shot after shot of adrenalin that kept her going.

It was somewhere in the lower forties that Anna first smelled smoke, and she could hear some of those on the floors below her coughing loudly. When she reached the next stairwell, the smoke became denser and quickly filled her lungs. She covered her eyes and began coughing uncontrollably. Anna recalled reading somewhere that 90 per cent of deaths in a fire are caused by smoke inhalation. Her fears were only exacerbated when those ahead of her slowed to a crawl and finally came to a halt. The coughing had turned into an epidemic. Had they all become trapped, with no escape route up or down?

'Keep moving,' came the clear order from a fireman heading towards them. 'It gets worse for a couple of floors but then you'll be through it,' he assured those who were still hesitating. Anna stared into the face of the man who had given the order with such authority.

She obeyed him, confident that the worst must surely be behind her. She kept her eyes covered and continued coughing for another three floors, but the fireman turned out to be right, because the smoke was already beginning to disperse. Anna decided to listen only to the professionals coming up the stairwell and to dismiss the opinions of any amateurs going down.

A sudden feeling of relief swept through those emerging from the smoke, and they immediately tried to speed up their descent. But sheer numbers prevented swift progress in the one-way traffic lane. Anna tried to remain calm as she slipped in behind a blind man, who was being led down the stairs by his guide dog. 'Don't be frightened by the smoke, Rosie,' said the man. The dog wagged its tail.

Down, down, down, the pace always dictated by the person in front. By the time Anna reached the deserted cafeteria on the thirty-ninth floor, the overloaded firemen had been joined by Port Authority officers and policemen from the Emergency Service Unit – the most popular of all New York's cops because they deal only in safety and rescue, no parking tickets, no arrests. Anna felt guilty about passing those who were willing to continue going up while she went in the opposite direction.

By the time Anna reached the twenty-fourth floor, several bedraggled stragglers were stopping to take a rest, a few even congregating to exchange anecdotes, while others were still refusing to leave their offices, unable to believe that a problem on the ninety-fourth floor could possibly affect them. Anna looked around, desperately hoping to see a familiar face, perhaps Rebecca or Tina, even Barry, but she could have been in a foreign land.

'We've got a level three up here, possibly level four,' a battalion commander was saying over his radio, 'so I'm sweeping every floor.'

Anna watched the commander as he systematically cleared every office. It took him some time because each floor was the size of a football field.

On the twenty-first floor, one individual remained resolutely at his desk; he'd just settled a currency deal for a billion dollars and he was awaiting confirmation of the transaction.

'OUT,' shouted the battalion commander, but the smartly dressed man ignored the order and continued tapping away on his keyboard. 'I said OUT,' repeated the senior fire officer, as two of his younger officers lifted the man out of his chair and deposited him in the stairwell. The unfulfilled broker reluctantly joined the exodus.

When Anna reached the twentieth floor, she encountered a new problem. She had to wade through water that was now pouring in on them from the sprinklers and leaking pipes on every floor. She stepped tentatively over fragments of broken glass and flaming debris that littered the stairwell and were beginning to slow everyone down. She felt like a football fan trying to get out of a crowded stadium that had only one turnstile. When she finally reached the teens, her progress became dramatically faster. All the floors below her had been cleared, and fewer and fewer office staff were joining them on the stairs.

On the tenth floor, Anna stared through an open door into a deserted office. Computer screens were still flickering and chairs had been pushed aside as if their occupants had gone to the washroom and would be back at any moment. Plastic cups of cold coffee and half-drunk cans of Coke littered almost every surface. Papers were scattered everywhere, even on the floor, while silver-framed family photographs remained in place. Someone following closely behind Anna bumped into her, so she quickly moved on.

By the time Anna reached the seventh floor, it was no longer her fellow workers, but the water and flotsam that were holding her up. She was picking her way tentatively through the debris when she first heard the voice. To begin with, it was faint, and then it became a little louder. The sound of a megaphone was coming from somewhere below them, urging her on. 'Keep moving, don't look back, don't use your cellphones – it slows up those behind you.'

Three more floors had to be negotiated before she found herself back in the lobby, paddling through inches of water, and on past the express shuttle elevator that had whisked her up to her office only a couple of hours before. Suddenly even more sprinklers jetted down from the ceiling above, but Anna was already drenched to the skin.

The orders bellowing from the megaphones were becoming louder and louder by the moment, and their demands even more strident. 'Keep moving, get out of the building, get as far away as you possibly can.' Not that easy, Anna wanted to tell them. When she reached the turnstiles she'd passed through earlier that morning, she found them battered and twisted. They must have been brushed aside by wave after wave of firemen when they transported their heavy equipment into the building.

Anna felt disorientated and unsure what to do next. Should she wait for her colleagues to join her? She stood still, but only for a moment, before she heard another insistent command that she felt was being addressed directly at her. 'Keep moving, lady, don't use your cellphone, and don't look back.'

'But where do we go?' someone shouted.

'Down the escalator, through the mall, and then get as far away from the building as possible.'

Anna joined the horde of tired savages as they stepped onto an overcrowded escalator. She allowed it to carry her down to the concourse before taking another escalator up to the open promenade, where she often joined Tina and Rebecca for an al fresco lunch while they enjoyed an open-air concert. No open air now, and certainly no calming sound of a violin – just another voice bellowing, 'Don't look back, don't look back.' An order Anna disobeyed, which not only slowed her down, but also caused her to fall on her knees retching. She watched in disbelief as first one person then another, who must have been trapped above the ninetieth floor, jumped out of their office windows to a certain death rather than face the slow agony of burning. 'Get back on your feet, lady, and keep movin'.'

Anna picked herself up and stumbled forward, suddenly aware that none of the officers in charge of the evacuation was making eye contact with those fleeing from the building or even attempting to answer any of their individual questions. She assumed this must be because it would only slow things down and impede the progress of those still trying to get out of the building.

When Anna passed Borders bookshop, she glanced in the window displaying the number-one bestseller, *Valhalla Rising*.

'Keep movin', lady,' a voice repeated, even louder.

'Where to?' she asked desperately.

'Anywhere, but just keep goin'.'

'In which direction?'

'I don't care, as long as it's as far away from the tower as possible.'

Anna spat out the last bits of vomit as she continued to move away from the building.

When she reached the entrance to the plaza, she came across firetrucks and ambulances that were tending to the walking wounded and those who just simply couldn't manage another step. Anna didn't waste their time. When she finally reached the road, she looked up to see a sign with an arrow covered in black grime. She could just make out the words 'City Hall'. Anna began jogging for the first time. Her jog turned into a run and she started to overtake some of those who had departed earlier from the lower floors. And then she heard another unfamiliar noise behind her. It sounded like a clap of thunder that seemed to grow louder and louder by the second. She didn't want to look back, but she did.

Anna stood transfixed as she watched the South Tower collapse in front of her eyes, as if it had been constructed of bamboo. In a matter of seconds, the remnants of the building came crashing to the ground, throwing up dust and debris that mushroomed into the sky, causing a dense mountain of flames and fumes that hovered for a moment, then began to advance indiscriminately through the crowded streets, engulfing anyone and everyone who stood in its way.

Anna ran as she had never run before, but she knew it was hopeless. It could only be a matter of seconds before the grey ruthless snake was upon her, suffocating all in its progress. Anna wasn't in any doubt that she was about to die. She only hoped it would be quick.

◄○►

Fenston stared across at the World Trade Center from the safety of an office on Wall Street.

He watched in disbelief as a second plane flew directly into the South Tower.

While most New Yorkers worried about how they could assist their friends, relations and colleagues at this tragic time, and others what it meant for America, Fenston had only one thought on his mind.

He and Leapman had arrived on Wall Street for their meeting with a prospective client only moments before the first plane crashed into the North Tower. Fenston abandoned his appointment and spent the next hour on a public telephone in the corridor trying to contact someone, anyone, in his office, but no one responded to his calls. Others would have liked to use the phone, but Fenston didn't budge. Leapman was carrying out the same exercise on his cellphone.

When Fenston heard a second volcanic eruption, he left the phone dangling and rushed to the window. Leapman walked quickly across to join him. They both stood in silence as they watched the South Tower collapse.

'It can't be long before the North Tower goes the same way,' said Fenston.

'Then I think we can assume that Petrescu will not survive,' said Leapman, matter-of-factly.

'I don't give a damn about Petrescu,' said Fenston. 'If the North Tower goes, then I've lost my Monet, and it isn't insured.'

12

ANNA BEGAN RUNNING flat out, more and more aware, with each step she took, that everything around her was becoming quieter. One by one the screams were dying, and she knew she had to be next. There no longer seemed to be anyone behind her, and for the first time in her life Anna wanted someone to overtake her, anyone, just so she didn't feel like the last person on earth. She now understood what it must be like to be pursued by an avalanche at a speed ten times faster than any human could achieve. This particular avalanche was black.

Anna took deep breaths as she forced her body to achieve speeds that she had never experienced before. She lifted her white silk blouse – now black, sodden and crumpled – and placed it over her mouth, just moments before she was overtaken by the relentless, all-enveloping grey cloud.

A whoosh of uncontrolled air hurled her forward and threw her onto the ground, but she still tried desperately to keep moving. She hadn't managed more than a few feet before she began choking uncontrollably. She pushed forward for another yard, and then another, until her head suddenly bumped into something solid. Anna placed a hand on the surface of a wall and tried to feel her way along. *But was she walking away from, or back into, the grey cloud?* Ash, dirt, dust were in her mouth, eyes, ears, nose and hair and clinging to her skin. It felt as if she was about to be burned alive. Anna thought about the people she had seen jumping because they felt that must be an easier way to die. She now understood their feelings, but she had no building to jump from and could only wonder how much longer it would be before she suffocated. She took her last step, knelt down on the ground and began to pray.

Our Father . . . She felt peaceful, and was about to close her eyes and give way to deep sleep when out of nowhere she saw a flashing police light. *Who art in Heaven* . . . She made one last effort to get back on her feet and move towards the blue light. *Hallowed be thy name* . . . but the car drifted past, unaware of her plaintive cry for help. *Thy Kingdom come* . . . Anna fell once again and cut her knee on the edge of the sidewalk, *Thy will be done* . . . but felt nothing. *On earth, as it is in Heaven.* She clung onto the edge of the sidewalk with her right hand and somehow managed a few more inches. She was about to stop breathing when she thought she touched something warm. Was it alive? 'Help,' she murmured feebly, expecting no response.

'Give me your hand,' came back the immediate reply. His grip was firm. 'Try and stand.'

With his help, Anna somehow pushed herself up. 'Can you see that triangle of light coming from over there?' the voice said, but she couldn't even see where he was pointing. Anna turned a complete circle, and stared into 360 degrees of black night. Suddenly she let out a muffled yelp of joy when she spotted a ray of sunlight trying to break through the heavy overcoat of gloom. She took the stranger's hand and they began inching towards a light that grew brighter and brighter with every step, until she finally walked out of hell and back into New York.

Anna turned to the grey ash-coated figure who had

saved her life. His uniform was so covered in dirt and dust that if he hadn't been wearing the familiar peaked cap and badge she wouldn't have known that he was a cop. He smiled and cracks appeared on his face as if he was daubed in heavy makeup. 'Keep heading towards the light,' he said, and disappeared back into the murky cloud before she could thank him. *Amen.*

—◇—

Fenston gave up trying to contact his office only when he saw the North Tower collapse in front of his eyes. He replaced the receiver and rushed back down the unfamiliar corridor to find Leapman scrawling SOLD on a 'To Rent' board that was attached to the door of an empty office.

'Tomorrow there will be ten thousand people after this space,' he explained, 'so at least that's one problem solved.'

'You may be able to replace an office, but what you can't replace is my Monet,' Fenston said ungraciously. He paused. 'And if I don't get my hands on the Van Gogh . . .'

Leapman checked his watch. 'It should be halfway across the Atlantic by now.'

'Let's hope so, because we no longer have any documentation to prove we even own the painting,' said Fenston as he looked out of the window and stared at a grey cloud that hung above the ground where the Twin Towers had once proudly stood.

—◇—

Anna joined a group of fellow stragglers as they emerged out of the gloom. Her compatriots looked as if they'd already completed a marathon, but hadn't yet reached the finish line. Coming out of such darkness, Anna found

71

she couldn't bear to look up at the glaring sun; even opening her dust-covered eyelids demanded effort. On, on, she stumbled, inch by inch, foot by foot, coughing up dirt and dust with every step, wondering how much more black liquid there could possibly be left in her body. After a few more paces she collapsed onto her knees, convinced the grey cloud could no longer overtake her. She continued coughing, spitting. When Anna looked up, she became aware of a group of startled onlookers, who were staring at her as if she'd just landed from another planet.

'Were you in one of the towers?' asked one of them. She didn't have the strength to answer, and decided to get as far away from their gawping eyes as possible. Anna had only covered a few more paces before she bumped into a Japanese tourist who was bending down trying to take a photograph of her. She angrily waved him away. He immediately bowed even lower, and apologized.

When Anna reached the next intersection, she collapsed on the sidewalk and stared up at the street sign – she was on the corner of Franklin and Church. I'm only a few blocks from Tina's apartment, was her first thought. But as Tina was still somewhere behind her, how could she possibly have survived? Without warning, a bus came to a halt by her side. Although it was as full as a San Francisco tram car during rush hour, people edged back to allow her to clamber on. The bus stopped on the corner of every block, allowing some to jump off while others got on, with no suggestion of anyone paying a fare. It seemed that all New Yorkers were united in wanting to play some part in the unfolding drama.

'Oh my God,' whispered Anna as she sat on the bus, and buried her head in her hands. For the first time she thought about the firemen who had passed her on the stairwell, and of Tina and Rebecca, who must be dead.

It's only when you know someone that a tragedy becomes more than a news item.

When the bus came to a halt in the village near Washington Square Park, Anna almost fell off. She stumbled over to the sidewalk, coughing up several more mouthfuls of grey dust that she'd avoided bringing up while she was on the bus. A woman sat down on the kerb beside her and offered her a bottle of water. Anna filled her mouth several times before spitting out dollops of black liquid. She emptied the bottle without swallowing a drop. The woman then pointed in the direction of a small hotel where escapees were trooping in and out in a steady stream. She bent down and took Anna by the arm, guiding her gently towards the ladies' room on the ground floor. The room was full of men and women oblivious of their sex. Anna looked at herself in the mirror and understood why onlookers had stared at her so curiously. It was as if someone had poured several bags of grey ash all over her. She left her hands under a flowing tap until only her nails remained black. She then tried to remove a layer of the caked dust from her face – an almost pointless exercise. She turned to thank the stranger, but she, like the cop, had already disappeared to assist someone else.

Anna limped back onto the road, her throat dry, her knees cut, her feet blistered and aching. As she stumbled slowly up Waverly Place, she tried to remember the number of Tina's apartment. She continued on past an uninhabited Waverly Diner before pausing outside number 273.

Anna grabbed at the familiar wrought-iron balustrade like a lifeline and yanked herself up the steps to the front door. She ran her finger down the list of names by the side of the buzzers: Amato, Kravits, Gambino, O'Rourke, Forster ... Forster, Forster, she repeated joyfully, before pressing the little bell. But how could Tina answer her call, when she must be dead, was Anna's only thought. She left her finger on the buzzer as if it would bring Tina to life, but it didn't. She finally gave up and turned to leave, tears streaming down her dust-caked face, when out of nowhere an irate voice demanded, 'Who is it?'

Anna collapsed onto the top step.

'Oh thank God,' she cried, 'you're alive, you're alive.'

'But you can't be,' said a disbelieving voice.

'Open the door,' pleaded Anna, 'and you can see for yourself.'

The click of the entry button was the best sound Anna had heard that day.

13

'YOU'RE ALIVE,' repeated Tina as she flung open the front door and threw her arms around her friend. Anna might resemble a street urchin who had just climbed out of a Victorian chimney, but it didn't prevent Tina from clinging to her.

'I was thinking about how you could always make me laugh, and wondering if I'd ever laugh again, when the buzzer sounded.'

'And I was convinced that even if you'd somehow managed to get out of the building, you still couldn't have survived once the tower collapsed.'

'If I had a bottle of champagne, I'd open it so that we could celebrate,' said Tina, finally letting go of her friend.

'I'll settle for a coffee, and then another coffee, followed by a bath.'

'I do have coffee,' said Tina, who took Anna by the hand and led her through to the small kitchen at the end of the corridor. She left a set of grey footprints on the carpet behind her.

Anna sat down at a small round wooden table and kept her hands in her lap while a soundless television was showing images of the other side of the story. She tried to stay still, aware that anything she touched was immediately smeared with ash and dirt. Tina didn't seem to notice.

'I know this may sound a little strange,' said Anna, 'but I haven't a clue what's going on.'

Tina turned up the sound on the television.

'Fifteen minutes of that,' Tina said as she filled the coffee pot, 'and you'll know everything.'

Anna watched the endless replays of a plane flying into the South Tower, people throwing themselves from the higher floors to a certain death, and the collapse of first the South and then the North Tower.

'And another plane hit the Pentagon?' she asked. 'So how many more are out there?'

'There was a fourth,' said Tina, as she placed two mugs on the table, 'but no one seems certain where it was heading.'

'The White House, possibly,' suggested Anna, as she looked up at the screen to see President Bush speaking from Barksdale Air Force Base in Louisiana: 'Make no mistake, the United States will hunt down and punish those responsible for these cowardly acts.'

The images flashed back to the second plane flying into the South Tower.

'Oh my God,' said Anna. 'I hadn't even thought about the innocent passengers on board those planes. Who's responsible for all this?' she demanded, as Tina filled her mug with black coffee.

'The State Department is being fairly cautious,' said Tina, 'and all the usual suspects – Russia, North Korea, Iran and Iraq – have all been quick to scream, "Not me," swearing they will do everything they can to track down those responsible.'

'But what are the anchormen saying, because there's no reason for them to be cautious.'

'CNN is pointing a finger at Afghanistan, and in particular at a terrorist group called Al-Qaeda – I think that's how you pronounce it, but I'm not sure as I've never heard of them,' Tina said as she sat down opposite Anna.

'I think they're a bunch of religious fanatics, who I thought were only interested in taking over Saudi Arabia so they could get hold of its oil.' Anna glanced back up at the television and listened to the commentator, who was trying to imagine what it must have been like to be in the North Tower when the first plane struck. How could you possibly know, Anna wanted to ask him. A hundred minutes telescoped into a few seconds, and then repeated again and again like a familiar advertisement. When the South Tower collapsed and smoke billowed up into the sky, Anna started coughing loudly, shaking ash onto everything around her.

'Are you OK?' asked Tina, jumping up from her chair.

'Yes, I'll be fine,' said Anna, draining her coffee. 'Would you mind if I turned the TV off ? I don't think I can face continually being reminded what it was like to be there.'

'Of course not,' said Tina, who picked up the remote and touched the off button. The images melted from the screen.

'I can't stop thinking about all our friends who were in the building,' said Anna, as Tina refilled her mug with coffee. 'I wonder if Rebecca . . .'

'No word from her,' said Tina. 'Barry is the only person who's reported in so far.'

'Yeah, I can believe Barry was the first down the stairs, trampling over anyone who got in his way. But who did Barry call?' asked Anna.

'Fenston. On his mobile.'

'Fenston?' said Anna. 'How did he manage to escape when I left his office only a few minutes before the first plane hit the building?'

'He'd arrived on Wall Street by then – he had an appointment with a potential client, whose only asset was a Gauguin. So there was no way he was going to be late for that.'

'And Leapman?' asked Anna as she took another sip of coffee.

'One step behind him as usual,' said Tina.

'So that's why the elevator door was being held open.'

'The elevator door?' repeated Tina.

'It's not important,' said Anna. 'But why weren't you at work this morning?'

'I had a dental appointment,' said Tina. 'It had been in my diary for weeks.' She paused and looked across the table. 'The moment I heard the news I never stopped trying to call you on your cell, but all I got was a ringing tone. So where were you?'

'Being escorted off the premises,' said Anna.

'By a firefighter?' asked Tina.

'No,' replied Anna, 'by that ape, Barry.'

'But why?' demanded Tina.

'Because Fenston had just fired me,' said Anna.

'Fired you?' said Tina in disbelief. 'Why would he fire you, of all people?'

'Because in my report to the board, I recommended that Victoria Wentworth should sell the Van Gogh, which would allow her not only to clear her overdraft with the bank, but hold on to the rest of the estate.'

'But the Van Gogh was the only reason Fenston ever agreed to that deal,' said Tina. 'I thought you realized that. He's been after one for years. The last thing he would have wanted was to sell the painting and get Victoria off the hook. But that's hardly a reason to fire you. What excuse—'

'I also sent a copy of my recommendations to the client, which I considered to be no more than ethical banking practice.'

'I don't think it's ethical banking practice that keeps

Fenston awake at night. But that still doesn't explain why he got rid of you so quickly.'

'Because I was just about to fly to England and let Victoria Wentworth know that I'd even lined up a prospective buyer. A well-known Japanese collector, Takashi Nakamura, who I felt sure would be happy to close the deal quickly, if we were sensible about the asking price.'

'You picked the wrong man in Nakamura,' said Tina. 'Whatever the asking price, he's the last person on earth Fenston would be willing to do business with. They've both been after a Van Gogh for years, and are regularly the last two bidders for any major Impressionists.'

'Why didn't he tell me that?' said Anna.

'Because it doesn't always suit him to let you know what he's up to,' said Tina.

'But we were both on the same team.'

'You're so naive, Anna. Haven't you worked out that there's only one person on Fenston's team?'

'But he can't make Victoria hand over the Van Gogh unless—'

'I wouldn't be so sure about that,' said Tina.

'Why not?'

'Fenston put a call through to Ruth Parish yesterday and ordered her to pick up the painting immediately. I heard him repeat the word "immediately".'

'Before Victoria was given the chance to act on my recommendations.'

'Which would also explain why he had to fire you before you could get on that plane and upset his plans. Mind you,' added Tina, 'you're not the first person to have ventured down that well-trodden path.'

'What do you mean?' said Anna.

'Once anyone works out what Fenston is really up to, they're quickly shown the door.'

'Then why hasn't he fired you?'

'Because I don't make any recommendations he isn't willing to go along with,' said Tina. 'That way, I'm not considered a threat.' She paused. 'Well, not for the moment.'

Anna thumped the table in anger, sending up a small cloud of dust. 'I'm so dumb,' she said. 'I should have seen it coming, and now there's nothing I can do about it.'

'I'm not so sure about that,' said Tina. 'We don't know for certain that Ruth Parish has picked up the painting from Wentworth Hall. If she hasn't, you'll still have enough time to call Victoria and advise her to hold on to the picture until you've had a chance to get in touch with Mr Nakamura – that way she could still clear her debt with Fenston and he couldn't do anything about it,' added Tina, as her cellphone began ringing, 'California Here I Come'. She checked its caller ID: BOSS flashed up. She put a finger to her lips. 'It's Fenston,' she warned. 'He probably wants to find out if you've been in touch with me,' she added, flipping open the phone.

'Do you realize who got left behind in the rubble?' Fenston asked before Tina could speak.

'Anna?'

'No,' said Fenston. 'Petrescu is dead.'

'Dead?' repeated Tina as she stared across the table at her friend. 'But—'

'Yes. When Barry reported in, he confirmed that the last time he saw her she was lying on the floor, so she can't possibly have survived.'

'I think you'll find—'

'Don't worry about Petrescu,' said Fenston. 'I already had plans to replace her, but what I can't replace is my Monet.'

Tina was shocked into a moment's silence, and was about to tell him just how wrong he was, when she suddenly realized that she just might be able to turn Fenston's crassness to Anna's advantage.

'Does that also mean we've lost the Van Gogh?'

'No,' said Fenston. 'Ruth Parish has already confirmed that the painting is on its way from London. It should arrive at JFK this evening, when Leapman is going to pick it up.'

Tina sank down into the chair, feeling deflated.

'And make sure you're in by six tomorrow morning.'

'Six am?'

'Yes,' said Fenston. 'And don't complain. After all, you've had the whole of today off.'

'So where do I report?' asked Tina, not bothering to argue.

'I've taken over offices on the thirty-second floor of the Trump Building at 40 Wall Street, so at least for us it will be business as usual.' The line went dead.

'He thinks you're dead,' said Tina, 'but he's more fussed about losing his Monet,' she added as she snapped her cellphone shut.

'He'll find out soon enough that I'm not,' said Anna.

'Only if you want him to,' said Tina. 'Has anyone else seen you since you got out of the tower?'

'Only looking like this,' said Anna.

'Then let's keep it that way, while we try and work out what needs to be done. Fenston says the Van Gogh is already on its way to New York and Leapman will pick it up as soon as it lands.'

'Then what can we do?'

'I could try and delay Leapman somehow, while you pick up the painting.'

'But what would I do with it,' asked Anna, 'when Fenston would be certain to come looking for me?'

'You could get yourself on the first plane back to London, and return the picture to Wentworth Hall.'

'I couldn't do that without Victoria's permission,' said Anna.

'Good God, Anna, when will you grow up? You've got to stop thinking like a school prefect, and start imagining what Fenston would do if he were in your position.'

'He'd find out what time the plane was landing,' said Anna. 'So the first thing I need to do—'

'The first thing you need to do is have a shower, while I find out what time the plane lands, and also what Leapman's up to,' said Tina as she stood up. 'Because one thing's for sure, they won't let you pick up anything from the airport looking like that.'

Anna drained her coffee and followed Tina out into the corridor. Tina opened the bathroom door and looked closely at her friend. 'See you in about –' she hesitated – 'an hour.'

Anna laughed for the first time that day.

◄○►

Anna slowly peeled off her clothes and dropped them in a heap on the floor. She glanced in the mirror, to see a reflection of someone she had never met before. She removed the silver chain from round her neck and placed it on the side of the bath, next to the model of a yacht. She finally took off her watch. It had stopped at eight forty-six. A few seconds later, and she would have been in the elevator.

As Anna stepped into the shower, she began to consider Tina's audacious plan. She turned on both taps and allowed the water to cascade down on her for some time before she even thought about washing. She watched the water turn from black to grey, but however hard she scrubbed, the water still remained grey. Anna continued scrubbing until her skin was red and sore, before turning her attention to a bottle of shampoo. She didn't emerge from the shower until she'd washed her hair three times, but it was going to be days before anyone realized that she was a natural blonde. Anna didn't bother to dry herself; she bent down, put the plug in the bath and turned on the taps. As she lay soaking, her mind revisited all that had taken place that day.

She thought about how many friends and colleagues she must have lost, and realized just how lucky she was to be alive. But mourning would have to wait, if she was to have any chance of rescuing Victoria from a slower death.

Anna's thoughts were interrupted by Tina knocking on the door. She walked in and sat on the end of the bath. 'A definite improvement,' she said with a smile, as she looked at Anna's newly scrubbed body.

'I've been thinking about your idea,' said Anna, 'and if I could—'

'Change of plan,' said Tina. 'It's just been announced by the FAA that all aircraft across America have been grounded until further notice and no incoming flights will be allowed to land, so by now the Van Gogh will be on its way back to Heathrow.'

'Then I'll need to call Victoria immediately,' said Anna, 'and tell her to instruct Ruth Parish to return the painting to Wentworth Hall.'

'Agreed,' said Tina, 'but I've just realized that Fenston has lost something even more important than the Monet.'

'What could be more important to him than the Monet?' asked Anna.

'His contract with Victoria, and all the other paperwork that proves he owns the Van Gogh, along with the rest of the Wentworth estate should she fail to clear the debt.'

'But didn't you keep back-ups?' asked Anna.

Tina hesitated. 'Yes,' she said, 'in a safe in Fenston's office.'

'But don't forget that Victoria will also be in possession of all the relevant documents.'

Tina paused again. 'Not if she was willing to destroy them.'

'Victoria would never agree to that,' said Anna.

'Why don't you phone her and find out? If she did feel able to, it would give you more than enough time to sell the Van Gogh and clear the debt with Fenston, before he could do anything about it.'

'There's only one problem.'

'What's that?' asked Tina.

'I don't have her number. Her file is in my office, and I've lost everything, including my cellphone and palm pilot, even my wallet.'

'I'm sure international directories can solve that problem,' suggested Tina. 'Why don't you dry yourself and put on a bathrobe? We can sort out some clothes later.'

'Thank you,' said Anna, gripping her by the hand.

'You might not thank me when you find out what you're having for lunch. Mind you, I wasn't expecting a guest, so you'll have to make do with leftover Chinese.'

'Sounds great,' said Anna, as she stepped out of the bath and grabbed a towel, wrapping it tightly round her.

'See you in a couple of minutes,' said Tina, 'by which time the microwave should have completely finished off my gourmet offering.' She turned to leave.

'Tina, can I ask you something?'

'Anything.'

'Why do you continue to work for Fenston, when you obviously detest the man as much as I do?'

Tina hesitated. 'Anything but that,' she eventually replied. She closed the door quietly behind her.

14

RUTH PARISH picked up her outside line.

'Hi, Ruth,' said a familiar voice, about to deliver an unfamiliar message. 'It's Ken Lane over at United, just to let you know that our flight 107, bound for New York, has been ordered to turn back, and we're expecting it to touch down at Heathrow in about an hour.'

'But why?' asked Ruth.

'Details are a bit sketchy at the moment,' Ken admitted, 'but reports coming out of JFK suggest there's been a terrorist attack on the Twin Towers. All US airports have been ordered to ground their planes, and won't be allowing any incoming flights until further notice.'

'When did all this happen?'

'Around one thirty our time, you must have been at lunch. You can get an update on any news station. They're all carrying it.'

Ruth picked up the remote control from her desk and pointed it towards the TV screen.

'Will you be putting the Van Gogh in storage?' asked Ken, 'or do you want us to return it to Wentworth Hall?'

'It certainly won't be going back to Wentworth,' said Ruth. 'I'll lock the painting up in one of our customs-free zones overnight, and then put it on the first available flight to New York once JFK lifts the restrictions.' Ruth paused. 'Will you confirm an ETA about thirty minutes before your plane is due to touch down, so I can have one of my trucks standing by?'

'Will do,' said Ken.

Ruth replaced the receiver and glanced up at the TV. She tapped out the number 501 on her remote control. The first image she saw was a plane flying into the South Tower.

Now she understood why Anna hadn't returned her call.

—◦—

As Anna dried herself, she began to speculate on what possible reason Tina could have to go on working for Fenston. She found herself shaking her head. After all, Tina was bright enough to pick up a far better job.

She pulled on her friend's bathrobe and slippers, placed the key on its chain back round her neck and put on her one-time watch. She looked at herself in the mirror; the outward façade had considerably improved, but Anna still felt queasy whenever she thought about what she had been through only a few hours before. She wondered for how many days, months, years it would be a recurring nightmare.

She opened the bathroom door and manoeuvred her way down the corridor, avoiding the ashy footprints she'd left on the carpet. When she walked into the kitchen, Tina stopped laying the table and handed over her cellphone.

'Time to call Victoria and warn her what you're up to.'

'What am I up to?' asked Anna.

'For starters, ask her if she knows where the Van Gogh is.'

'Locked up in a customs-free zone at Heathrow would be my bet, but there's only one way to find out.' Anna dialled 00.

'International operator.'

'I need a number in England,' said Anna.

'Business or residential?'

'Residential.'

'Name?'

'Wentworth, Victoria.'

'Address?'

'Wentworth Hall, Wentworth, Surrey.'

There was a long silence before Anna was informed, 'I'm sorry, ma'am, that number is ex-directory.'

'What does that mean?' asked Anna.

'I can't give out the number.'

'But this is an emergency,' insisted Anna.

'I'm sorry, ma'am, but I still can't release that number.'

'But I'm a close personal friend.'

'I don't care if you're the Queen of England, I repeat, I'm unable to give out that number.' The line went dead. Anna frowned.

'So what's plan B?' asked Tina.

'No choice but to get myself to England somehow and try to see Victoria so I can warn her what Fenston's up to.'

'Good. Then the next thing to decide is which border you're going to cross.'

'What chance have I got of crossing any border, when I can't even go back to my apartment and pick up my things – unless I want the whole world to know I'm alive and kicking?'

'There's nothing to stop me going to your place,' said Tina. 'Tell me what you want and I can pack a bag and—'

'No need to pack,' said Anna. 'Everything I want is ready and waiting in the hallway – don't forget I was expecting to fly to London this evening.'

'Then all I need is the key to your apartment,' said Tina.

Anna unclasped the chain round her neck and handed over her key.

'How do I get past the doorman?' asked Tina. 'He's bound to ask who I've come to see.'

'That won't be a problem,' said Anna. 'His name is Sam. Tell him you're visiting David Sullivan and he'll just smile and call for the elevator.'

'Who's David Sullivan?' asked Tina.

'He's got an apartment on the fourth floor, and rarely entertains the same girl twice. He pays Sam a few dollars every week to keep them all blissfully unaware that they are not the only woman in his life.'

'But that doesn't solve the cash problem,' said Tina. 'Don't forget you lost your wallet and credit card in the crash, and all I have to my name is about seventy dollars.'

'I took three thousand dollars out of my account yesterday,' said Anna. 'Whenever you're moving a valuable painting, you can't risk any hold-ups, so you have to be prepared to take care of the odd baggage handler along the way. I've also got another five hundred in the drawer by the side of my bed.'

'And you'll need to take my watch,' said Tina.

Anna took off her watch and swapped it with Tina's.

Tina studied Anna's watch more closely. 'You're never going to be allowed to forget what time it was when that plane flew into the building,' she said as the microwave beeped.

'This may well be inedible,' Tina warned her, as she served up a dish of yesterday's chicken chow mein and egg fried rice. Between mouthfuls, the two of them considered the alternatives for getting out of the city, and which border would be safest to cross.

By the time they had devoured every last scrap of leftovers along with another pot of coffee, they had gone over all the possible routes out of Manhattan, although Anna still hadn't settled on whether she should head north or south. Tina placed the plates in the sink and said, 'Why don't you decide on which direction you think would be quickest, while I try to get myself uptown and in and out of your apartment without Sam becoming suspicious?'

Anna hugged her friend again. 'Be warned,' she said, 'it's hell on earth out there.'

◄○►

Tina stood on the top step of her apartment building and waited for a few moments. Something felt wrong. And then she realized what it was. New York had changed over day.

The streets were no longer full of bustling, haven't-the-time-to-stop-and-chat people, who made up the most energetic mass on earth. It felt more like a Sunday to Tina. But not even Sunday. People stood and stared in the direction of the World Trade Center. The only background music was the noise of perpetual sirens, which continually reminded the indigenous population – if they needed reminding – that what they had been watching on television in their homes, clubs, bars, even shop windows, was taking place just a few blocks away.

Tina walked down the road in search of a taxi, but the familiar yellow cabs had been replaced by the red, white and blue of fire engines, ambulances and police cars, all heading in one direction. Little clusters of citizens gathered on street corners to applaud the three different services as they raced by, as if they were young recruits leaving their homeland to fight a foreign foe. You no longer have to travel abroad to do that, thought Tina.

Tina walked on and on, block after block, aware that just like the weekend, commuters had fled to the hills, leaving the locals to man the pumps. But now there was another unfamiliar group roaming around the city in a daze. New York had, over the past century, absorbed citizens from every nation on earth, and now they were adding another race to their number. This most recent group of immigrants looked as if they had arrived from the bowels of the earth, and like any new race could be distinguished by their colour – ash grey. They roamed around Manhattan, like marathon runners limping home hours after the more serious competitors had departed from the scene. But there was an even more visual reminder for anyone who looked up that autumn evening. The New York skyline was no longer dominated by its proud, gleaming skyscrapers because they were overshadowed by a dense grey haze that hung above the city like an unwelcome visitor. Occasionally there were breaks in the ungodly cloud, when Tina noticed for the first time shards of jagged metal sticking out of the ground – all that was left of one of the tallest buildings in the world. The dentist had saved her life.

Tina walked past empty shops and restaurants in a city that never closed. New York would recover, but would never be the same again. Terrorists were people who lived in far-off lands: the Middle East, Palestine, Israel, even Spain, Germany and Northern Ireland. She looked back at the cloud. They had taken up residence in Manhattan, and left their calling card.

Tina once again waved unhopefully at the rare sight of a passing taxi. It screeched to a halt.

15

ANNA STROLLED BACK into the kitchen and began
washing the dishes. She was keeping herself occupied
in the hope that her mind wouldn't continually return
to those faces coming up the stairs, faces she feared
would remain etched on her memory for the rest of
her life. She had discovered a downside to her unusual
gift.

She tried to think about Victoria Wentworth instead,
and how she might stop Fenston from ruining someone
else's life. Would Victoria believe that Anna hadn't
known Fenston always planned to steal the Van Gogh
and bleed her dry? Why should she, when Anna was a
member of the board and had been fooled so easily
herself?

Anna left the kitchen in search of a map. She found
a couple on a bookshelf in the front room above Tina's
desk: a copy of *Streetwise Manhattan*, and *The Columbia
Gazetteer of North America*, propped up against the
recent bestseller on John Adams, second president of
the US. She paused to admire the Rothko poster on the
wall opposite the bookshelf – not her period, but she
knew he must be one of Tina's favourite artists, because
she also had another in her office. No longer, thought
Anna, her mind switching back to the present. She
returned to the kitchen and laid the map of New York
out on the table.

Once she'd decided on a route out of Manhattan,

Anna folded up the map and turned her attention to the larger volume. She hoped that it would help her make up her mind which border to cross.

Anna looked up Mexico and Canada in the index, and then began making copious notes as if she was preparing a report for the board to consider; she usually suggested two alternatives, but always ended her reports with a firm recommendation. When she finally closed the cover on the thick blue book, Anna wasn't in any doubt in which direction she had to go if she hoped to reach England in time.

◄○►

Tina spent the cab journey to Thornton House considering how she would get into Anna's apartment and leave with her luggage without the doorman becoming suspicious. As the cab drew up outside the building, Tina moved a hand to her jacket pocket. She wasn't wearing a jacket. She turned scarlet. She'd left the apartment without any money. Tina stared through the plastic window at the driver's identity disc: Abdul Affridi – worry beads dangling from the rear-view mirror. He glanced around, but didn't smile. No one was smiling today.

'I've come out without any money,' Tina blurted, and then waited for a string of expletives to follow.

'No problem,' muttered the driver, who jumped out of his cab to open the door for her. Everything had changed in New York.

Tina thanked him and walked nervously towards the entrance door, her opening line well prepared. The script changed the moment she saw Sam seated behind the counter, head in hands, sobbing.

'What's the matter?' Tina asked. 'Did you know someone in the World Trade Center?'

Sam looked up. On the desk in front of him was a photo of Anna running in the marathon. 'She hasn't come home,' he said. 'All my others who worked at the WTC returned hours ago.'

Tina put her arms round the old man. Yet another victim. How much she wanted to tell him Anna was alive and well. But not today.

◄○►

Anna took a break just after eight and began flicking through the TV channels. There was only one story. She found that she couldn't go on watching endless reports without continually being reminded of her own small walk-off part in this two-act drama. She was about to turn off the television when it was announced that President Bush would address the nation. 'Good evening. Today, our fellow citizens . . .' Anna listened intently, and nodded when the President continued: 'The victims were in airplanes, or in their offices; secretaries, businessmen and women . . .' Anna once again thought about Rebecca. 'None of us will ever forget this day . . .' the President concluded, and Anna felt able to agree with him. She switched off the television as the South Tower came crashing down again, like the climax of a disaster movie.

Anna sat back and stared down at the map on the kitchen table. She double-checked, or was it triple, her route out of New York. She was writing detailed notes of everything that needed to be done before she left in the morning when the front door burst open and Tina staggered in – a laptop over one shoulder, dragging a bulky case behind her. Anna ran out into the corridor to welcome her back. She looked exhausted.

'Sorry to have taken so long, honey,' said Tina as she dumped the luggage in the hallway, and walked down the freshly vacuumed corridor and into the kitchen. 'Not many buses going in my direction,' she added, 'especially when you've left your money behind,' she added as she collapsed into a kitchen chair. 'I'm afraid I had to break into your five hundred dollars, otherwise I wouldn't have been back until after midnight.'

Anna laughed. 'My turn to make you coffee,' she suggested.

'I was only stopped once,' continued Tina, 'by a very friendly policeman who checked through your luggage, and accepted that I'd been sent back from the airport after being unable to board a flight. I was even able to produce your ticket.'

'Any trouble at the apartment?' asked Anna, as she filled the coffee pot for a third time.

'Only having to comfort Sam, who obviously adores you. He looked as if he'd been crying for hours. I didn't even have to mention David Sullivan, because all Sam wanted to do was talk about you. By the time I got into the elevator, he didn't seem to care where I was going.' Tina stared around the kitchen. She hadn't seen it so clean since she'd moved in. 'So have you come up with a plan?' she asked, looking down at the map that was spread across the kitchen table.

'Yes,' said Anna. 'It seems my best bet will be the ferry to New Jersey and then to rent a car, because according to the latest news all the tunnels and bridges are closed. Although it's over four hundred miles to the Canadian border, I can't see why I shouldn't make Toronto airport by tomorrow night, in which case I could be in London the following morning.'

'Do you know what time the first ferry sails in the morning?' asked Tina.

'In theory, it's a non-stop service,' said Anna, 'but in practice, every fifteen minutes after five o'clock. But who

95

knows if they'll be running at all tomorrow, let alone keeping to a schedule.'

'Either way,' said Tina, 'I suggest you have an early night, and try to snatch some sleep. I'll set my alarm for four thirty.'

'Four,' said Anna. 'If the ferry is ready to depart at five, I want to be first in line. I suspect getting out of New York may well prove the most difficult part of the journey.'

'Then you'd better have the bedroom,' said Tina with a smile, 'and I'll sleep on the couch.'

'No way,' said Anna, as she poured her friend a fresh mug of coffee. 'You've done more than enough already.'

'Not nearly enough,' said Tina.

'If Fenston ever found out what you were up to,' said Anna quietly, 'he'd fire you on the spot.'

'That would be the least of my problems,' Tina responded without explanation.

◄○►

Jack yawned involuntarily. It had been a long day, and he had a feeling that it was going to be an even longer night.

No one on his team had considered going home, and they were all beginning to look, and sound, exhausted. The telephone on his desk rang.

'Just thought I ought to let you know, boss,' said Joe, 'that Tina Forster, Fenston's secretary, turned up at Thornton House a couple of hours ago. Forty minutes later she came out carrying a suitcase and a laptop, which she took back to her place.'

Jack sat bolt upright. 'Then Petrescu must be alive,' he said.

'Although she obviously doesn't want us to think so,' said Joe.

'But why?'

'Perhaps she wants us to believe she's missing, presumed dead,' suggested Joe.

'Not us,' said Jack.

'Then who?'

'Fenston, would be my bet.'

'Why?'

'I have no idea,' said Jack, 'but I have every intention of finding out.'

'And how do you propose to do that, boss?'

'By putting an OPS team on Tina Forster's apartment until Petrescu leaves the building.'

'But we don't even know if she's in there,' said Joe.

'She's in there,' said Jack, and put the phone down.

9/12

16

DURING THE NIGHT, Anna managed to catch only a few minutes of sleep as she considered her future. She came to the conclusion that she might as well return to Danville and open a gallery for local artists while any potential employers could get in touch with Fenston and be told his side of the story. She was beginning to feel that her only hope of survival was to prove what Fenston was really up to, and she accepted that she couldn't do that without Victoria's full cooperation, which might include destroying all the relevant documentation, even her report.

Anna was surprised how energized she felt when Tina knocked on the door just after four.

Another shower, followed by another shampoo, and she felt almost human.

Over a breakfast of black coffee and bagels, Anna went over her plan with Tina. They decided on some ground rules they should follow while she was away. Anna no longer had a credit card or a cellphone, so she agreed to call Tina only on her home number, and always from a public phone booth – never the same one twice. Anna would announce herself as 'Vincent', and no other name would be used. The call would never last for more than one minute.

Anna left the apartment at 4.52am, dressed in jeans, a blue T-shirt, a linen jacket and a baseball cap. She wasn't sure what to expect as she stepped out onto the sidewalk that cool, dark morning. Few people were out on the streets, and those that were had their heads bowed – their downcast faces revealed a city in mourning. No one gave Anna a second glance as she strode purposefully along the sidewalk pulling her suitcase, the laptop bag slung over her shoulder. It didn't matter in which direction she looked, a foggy grey haze still hung over the city. The dense cloud had dispersed, but like a disease it had spread to other parts of the body. For some reason, Anna had assumed when she woke it would have gone, but, like an unwelcome guest at a party, it would surely be the last to leave.

Anna passed a line of people who were already queuing to give blood in the hope that more survivors would be found. She was a survivor, but she didn't want to be found.

◄o►

Fenston was seated behind his desk in his new Wall Street office by six o'clock that morning. After all, it was already eleven in London. The first call he made was to Ruth Parish.

'Where's my Van Gogh?' he demanded, without bothering to announce who it was.

'Good morning, Mr Fenston,' said Ruth, but she received no reply in kind. 'As I feel sure you know, the aircraft carrying your painting was turned back, following yesterday's tragedy.'

'So where's my Van Gogh?' repeated Fenston.

'Safely locked up in one of our secure vaults in the restricted customs area. Of course, we will have to reapply for customs clearance and renew the export licence. But there's no need to do that before—'

'Do it today,' said Fenston.

'This morning I had planned to move four Vermeers from—'

'Fuck Vermeer. Your first priority is to make sure my painting is packed and ready to be collected.'

'But the paperwork might take a few days,' said Ruth. 'I'm sure you appreciate that there's now a backlog following—'

'And fuck any backlog,' said Fenston. 'The moment the FAA lift their restrictions, I'm sending Karl Leapman over to pick up the painting.'

'But my staff are already working round the clock to clear the extra work caused by—'

'I'll only say this once,' said Fenston. 'If the painting is ready for loading by the time my plane touches down at Heathrow, I will triple, I repeat triple, your fee.'

Fenston put the phone down, confident that the only word she'd remember would be 'triple'. He was wrong. Ruth was puzzled by the fact that he hadn't mentioned the attacks on the Twin Towers, or made any reference to Anna. Had she survived, and if so, why wasn't *she* travelling over to pick up the painting?

Tina had overheard every word of Fenston's conversation with Ruth Parish on the extension in her office – without the chairman being aware. Tina vainly wished that she could contact Anna and quickly pass on the information – an eventuality neither of them had considered. Perhaps Anna would call this evening.

Tina flicked off the phone switch, but left on the screen that was fixed to the corner of her desk. This allowed her to watch everything and, more important, everybody who came in contact with the chairman, something else that Fenston wasn't aware of, but then he hadn't asked. Fenston would never have considered entering her office when the press of a button would summon her, and if Leapman walked into the room – without knocking, as was his habit – she would quickly flick the screen off.

When Leapman took over the short lease on the thirty-second floor, he hadn't shown any interest in the secretary's office. His only concern seemed to be settling the chairman into the largest space available, while he took over an office at the other end of the corridor. Tina had said nothing about her IT extras, aware that in time someone was bound to find out, but perhaps by then she would have gathered all the information she needed to ensure that Fenston would suffer an even worse fate than he had inflicted on her.

When Fenston put the phone down on Ruth Parish, he pressed the button on the side of his desk. Tina grabbed a notepad and pencil and made her way through to the chairman's office.

'The first thing I need you to do,' Fenston began, even before Tina had closed the door, 'is find out how many staff I still have. Make sure they know where we are relocated, so they can report for work without delay.'

'I see that the head of security was among the first to check in this morning,' said Tina.

'Yes, he was,' Fenston replied, 'and he's already confirmed that he gave the order for all staff to evacuate the building within minutes of the first plane crashing into the North Tower.'

'And then led by example, I'm told,' said Tina tartly.

'Who told you that?' barked Fenston, looking up.

Tina regretted the words immediately, and quickly turned to leave, adding, 'I'll have those names on your desk by midday.'

She spent the rest of the morning trying to contact the forty-three employees who worked in the North Tower. Tina was able to account for thirty-four of them by twelve o'clock. She placed a provisional list of nine names who were still missing, presumed dead, on Fenston's desk before he went to lunch.

Anna Petrescu was the sixth name on that list.

◄○►

By the time Tina had placed the list on Fenston's desk, Anna had finally made it to Pier 11, by cab, bus, foot and then cab again, only to find a long queue waiting patiently to board a ferry to New Jersey. She took her place at the back of the line, put on a pair of sunglasses and pulled down the peak of her baseball cap so it nearly covered her eyes. She stood with her arms tightly folded, the collar of her jacket turned up and her head bowed, so that only the most insensitive individual would have considered embarking on a conversation with her.

The police were checking the IDs of everyone leaving Manhattan. She looked on as a dark-haired, swarthy young man was taken to one side. The poor man looked bemused when three police-men surrounded him. One fired questions, while another searched him.

It was almost an hour before Anna finally reached the front of the queue. She took off her baseball cap to reveal her long fair hair and cream skin.

'Why are you going to New Jersey?' enquired the policeman as he checked her ID.

'A friend of mine was working in the North Tower, and she's still missing.' Anna paused. 'And I thought I'd spend the day with her parents.'

'I'm sorry, ma'am,' said the policeman. 'I hope they find her.'

'Thank you,' said Anna, and quickly carried her bags up the gangway and onto the ferry. She felt so guilty about lying that she couldn't look back at the policeman. She leaned on the railing and stared across at the grey cloud that still enveloped the site of the World Trade Center and several blocks either side. She wondered how many days, weeks or even months it would be before that dense blanket of smoke dispersed. What would they finally do with the desolate site, and how would they honour the dead? She raised her eyes and stared up at the clear blue sky above her. Something was missing. Although they were only a few miles from JFK and La Guardia, there wasn't a plane in the sky, as if they had all, without warning, migrated to another part of the world.

The old engine juddered into action and the ferry began to drift slowly away from the pier on its short journey across the Hudson to New Jersey.

One o'clock struck on the pier tower. Half a day had gone.

—◦—

'The first flights out of JFK won't be taking off for another couple of days,' said Tina.

'Does that include private aircraft?' asked Fenston.

'There are no exceptions,' Tina assured him.

'The Saudi royal family are being allowed to fly out tomorrow,' interjected Leapman, who was standing by the chairman's side, 'but they seem to be the only exception.'

'Meanwhile, I'm trying to get you on what the press are describing as the priority list,' said Tina, who decided not to mention that the port authorities didn't consider his desire to pick up a Van Gogh from Heathrow quite fell into the category of emergency.

'Do we have any friends at JFK?' asked Fenston.

'Several,' said Leapman, 'but they've all suddenly acquired a whole lot of rich relations.'

'Any other ideas?' asked Fenston, looking up at both of them.

'You might consider driving across the border into Mexico or Canada,' suggested Tina, 'and taking a commercial flight from there,' knowing only too well that he wouldn't consider it.

Fenston shook his head and, turning to Leapman, said, 'Try and turn one of our friends into a relation – someone will want something,' he added. 'They always do.'

17

'I'LL TAKE ANY CAR you've got,' said Anna.

'I have nothing available at the moment,' said the weary-looking young man behind the Happy Hire Company desk, whose plastic badge displayed the name Hank. 'And I don't anticipate anything being returned until tomorrow morning,' he added, failing to fulfil the company's motto displayed on the counter top, *No one leaves Happy Hire without a smile on their face.* Anna couldn't mask her disappointment.

'I don't suppose you'd consider a van?' Hank ventured. 'It's not exactly the latest model, but if you're desperate.'

'I'll take it,' said Anna, well aware of the long queue of customers waiting in line behind her, all no doubt willing her to say no. Hank placed a form in triplicate on the counter top and began filling in the little boxes. Anna pushed across her driver's licence, which she had packed along with her passport, enabling him to complete even more boxes. 'How long do you require the vehicle?' Hank asked.

'A day, possibly two – I'll be dropping it off at Toronto airport.'

Once Hank had completed all the little boxes, he swivelled the form round for her signature.

'That'll be sixty dollars, and I'll need a two-hundred-dollar deposit.'

Anna frowned, and handed over two hundred and sixty dollars.

'And I'll also need your credit card.'

Anna slipped another hundred-dollar bill across the counter. The first time she'd ever attempted to bribe someone.

Hank pocketed the money. 'It's the white van in bay thirty-eight,' he told her, handing over a key.

When Anna located bay thirty-eight, she could see why the little two-seater white van was the last vehicle on offer. She unlocked the back door and placed her case and laptop inside. She then went to the front and squeezed herself into the plastic-covered driver's seat. She checked the dashboard. The milometer read 98,617, and the speedometer suggested a maximum of 90, which she doubted. It was clearly coming to the end of its rental life, and another 400 miles might well finish it off. She wondered if the vehicle was even worth three hundred and sixty dollars.

Anna started the engine and tentatively reversed out of the parking lot. She saw a man in her wing mirror, who quickly stepped out of the way. It was less than a mile before she discovered the vehicle was built for neither speed nor comfort. She glanced down at the route map she'd placed on the passenger seat beside her, then began to look for signs to the Jersey Turnpike and Del Water Gap. Although she hadn't eaten since breakfast, Anna decided she needed to put a few miles on the clock before she started thinking about food.

—◇—

'You were right, boss,' said Joe, 'she's not going to Danville.'

'So where *is* she headed?'

'Toronto airport.'

'Car or train?' he asked.

'Van,' replied Joe.

Jack tried to calculate how long the journey would take, and concluded that Petrescu ought to reach Toronto by late the next afternoon.

'I've already fixed a GPS on her rear bumper,' Joe added, 'so we'll be able to track her night and day.'

'And be sure you have an agent waiting for her at the airport.'

'He's already been detailed,' said Joe, 'with instructions to let me know where she intends to fly.'

'She'll be flying to London,' said Jack.

—◦—

By three that afternoon, Tina had been able to remove four more names from the missing list. Three of them had been voting in the primary elections for mayor, while the fourth had missed her train.

Fenston studied the list, as Leapman placed a finger on the only name he was interested in. Fenston nodded when his eyes settled on the Ps. He smiled.

'Saved having to do it ourselves,' was Leapman's only comment.

'What's the latest from JFK?' Fenston asked.

'They're allowing a few flights out tomorrow,' said Leapman, 'visiting diplomats, hospital emergencies and some senior politicians vetted by the State Department. But I've managed to secure us an early slot for Friday morning.' He paused. 'Someone wanted a new car.'

'Which model?' asked Fenston.

'A Ford Mustang,' replied Leapman.

'I would have agreed to a Cadillac.'

—◦—

Anna had reached the outskirts of Scranton by three thirty that afternoon, but decided to press on for a couple more hours. The weather was clear and crisp, and the three-lane highway crowded with cars heading north, almost all of them overtaking her. Anna relaxed a little once tall trees replaced skyscrapers on both sides. Most of the highways had a fifty-five-mile speed limit, which suited her particular mode of transport. But she still had to hold on to the steering wheel firmly to make sure the van didn't drift into another lane. Anna glanced down at the tiny clock on the dashboard. She would try and make Buffalo by seven, and then perhaps take a break.

She checked her rear-view mirror, suddenly aware what it must feel like to be a criminal on the run. You couldn't use a credit card or a cellphone, and the sound of a distant siren doubled your heart beat. A life spent wary of strangers, as you looked over your shoulder every few minutes. Anna longed to be back in New York, among her friends, doing the job she loved. Her father once said – 'Oh God,' said Anna out loud. Did her mother think she was dead? What about Uncle George and the rest of the family in Danville? Could she risk a phone call? Hell, she wasn't very good at thinking like a criminal.

--◦--

Leapman walked into Tina's office unannounced. She quickly flicked off the screen on the side of her desk.

'Wasn't Anna Petrescu a friend of yours?' Leapman asked without explanation.

'Yes, she is,' said Tina looking up from her desk.

'Is?' said Leapman.

'Was,' said Tina, quickly correcting herself.

'So you haven't heard from her?'

'If I had, I wouldn't have left her name on the missing list, would I?'

'Wouldn't you?' said Leapman.

'No, I wouldn't,' said Tina, looking directly at him. 'So perhaps you'll let me know if she gets in touch with you,' she added.

Leapman frowned and left the room.

◄○►

Anna pulled off the road and swung into the forecourt of an uninviting-looking diner. She was pleased to see there were only two other vehicles in the parking lot, and when she entered the building just three customers were seated at the counter. Anna took a seat in a booth with her back to the counter, pulled down her baseball cap and studied the one-sided greasy plastic menu. She ordered a tomato soup and the chef's special, grilled chicken.

Ten dollars and thirty minutes later, she was back on the road. Although she'd drunk nothing but coffee since breakfast, it wasn't long before she began to feel sleepy. She'd covered three hundred and ten miles in just over eight hours before stopping to eat, and now she was having to make an effort to keep her eyes open.

Feel Tired? Take A Break advised a bold sign on the side of the highway, which only caused her to yawn again. Ahead of her, she spotted a twelve-wheeler truck turning off the road into a rest stop. Anna glanced at the clock on the dashboard – just after eleven. She'd been on the road for nearly nine hours. She decided to catch a couple of hours' rest before tackling the rest of the journey. After all, she could always sleep on the plane.

Anna followed the articulated truck into the rest stop, and then drove across to the farthest corner. She parked behind a large stationary vehicle. She jumped out of the van and made sure all the doors were locked before climbing into the back, relieved that there was no other vehicle nearby. Anna tried to make herself comfortable, using her laptop bag as a pillow. She couldn't have been more uncomfortable, but fell asleep within minutes.

—◦—

'Petrescu still worries me,' said Leapman.

'Why should a dead woman worry you?' asked Fenston.

'Because I'm not convinced she's dead.'

'How could she have survived that?' asked Fenston, looking out of the window at the black shroud that refused to lift its veil from the face of the World Trade Center.

'We did.'

'But we left the building early,' said Fenston.

'Perhaps *she* did. After all, you ordered her off the premises within ten minutes.'

'Barry thinks otherwise.'

'Barry's alive,' Leapman reminded him.

'Even if Petrescu did escape, she still can't do anything,' said Fenston.

'She could get to London before I do,' said Leapman.

'But the painting is safely under lock and key at Heathrow.'

'But all the documentation to prove you own it was in your safe in the North Tower, and if Petrescu was able to convince—'

'Convince who? Victoria Wentworth is dead, and try not to forget that Petrescu is also missing, presumed dead.'

'But that might prove to be just as convenient for her as it is for us.'

'Then we'll have to make it less convenient.'

9/13

18

A LOUD, REPEATED banging jolted Anna out of a deep sleep. She rubbed her eyes and looked through the windscreen. A man with a pot belly hanging out of his jeans was thumping on the bonnet of the van with a clenched fist. In his other hand he was carrying a can of beer that was frothing at the mouth. Anna was about to scream at him when she realized that someone else was at the same time trying to wrench open the back door. An ice-cold shower couldn't have woken her any quicker.

Anna scrambled into the driver's seat and quickly turned the key in the ignition. She looked in her wing mirror and was horrified to see that another forty-ton truck was now stationed directly behind her, leaving her with almost no room for manoeuvre. She pressed the palm of her hand on the horn, which only encouraged the man holding the beer can to clamber up onto the bonnet and advance towards her. Anna saw his face clearly for the first time, as he leered at her through the windscreen. She felt cold and sick. He leant forward, opened his toothless mouth and began licking the glass, while his friend continued trying to force open the back door. The engine finally spluttered into life.

Anna yanked the steering wheel round to give her the tightest possible lock, but the space between the two trucks only allowed her to advance a few feet before she had to reverse. Power steering was not one of the van's extras. When she shot back, Anna heard a yell from behind as the second man threw himself to one side. Anna crashed into first gear and pressed her foot back down on the accelerator. As the van leapt forward, the pot-bellied man slid off the bonnet, and onto the ground with a thud. Anna thrust the gearstick back into reverse, praying this time there would be enough room to escape. But before she had pulled the steering wheel fully round, she glanced to the side to see that the second man was now staring at her through the passenger window. He clamped both of his massive hands on the roof and began rocking the van slowly backwards and forwards. She slammed her foot on the pedal and the van dragged him slowly forward, but she still failed to make it through the gap, if only by inches. Anna rammed the gear into reverse for a third time and was horrified to see the first man's hands reappear on the front of the bonnet, as he pulled himself back up onto his feet. He lurched forward, stuck his nose flat against the windscreen, and gave her a thumbs-down sign. He then shouted to his buddy, 'I get to go first this week.' His buddy stopped rocking the car and burst out laughing.

Anna broke out into a cold sweat when her eyes settled on the pot-bellied man, walking unsteadily towards his truck. A quick glance in her wing mirror and she could see his mate climbing up into his cab.

It didn't take Anna more than a split second to work out exactly what they had in mind. She was about to become the meat in their next sandwich. Anna hit the accelerator so hard that she careered into the truck behind her just as he turned on his full headlights. She crashed the gears back into first as the engine of the front truck roared into life, belching a cloud of black smoke all over the windscreen. Anna yanked the steering wheel over with a jerk and once again thrust her foot hard down on the accelerator. The van jumped forward, just as the truck in front of her began to reverse. She collided with the corner of the front truck's massive mudguard, which tore off her bumper followed by her offside mudguard. She then felt herself being shunted from behind as the rear truck ploughed into her, ripping off her rear bumper. The little van came hurtling out of the gap with inches to spare and spun around a full three hundred and sixty degrees before it came to a halt. Anna looked across to see the two trucks, unable to react in time, crash into each other.

She accelerated across the parking lot, raced past several stationary trucks and out onto the highway. She continued to look in her rear-view mirror as the two trucks disentangled themselves. A loud screeching of brakes and a cacophony of horns followed as she narrowly missed colliding with a stream of vehicles coming down the highway, several of which had to career across two lanes to avoid her. The first driver left his hand on the horn for some time, leaving Anna in no doubt of his feelings. Anna waved an apologetic hand to the overtaking vehicle as it shot past her, while she continued to glance into her wing mirror, dreading seeing either of the trucks pursuing her. She jammed her foot down on the accelerator until it touched the floor, determined to find out the maximum speed the van could manage: 68mph was the answer.

Anna checked her wing mirror once again. A vast eighteen-wheeler was coming up behind her on the inside lane. She gripped the steering wheel firmly and jammed her foot back down on the accelerator, but the van had no more to offer. The truck was now eating up the ground, yard by yard, and in moments she knew it would convert itself into a bulldozer. Anna thrust the palm of her left hand down on the horn, and it let out a bleat that wouldn't have disturbed a flock of starlings from their nests. A large green sign appeared on the side of the road, indicating the turn-off for the I-90, one mile.

Anna moved into the middle lane and the massive truck followed her like a magnet hoping to sweep up any loose filings. The truck driver was now so close that Anna could see him in her wing mirror. He gave her another toothless grin and then honked his horn. It let forth a sound that would have drowned out the last bars of a Wagner opera.

Half a mile to the exit, the new sign promised. She moved across to the fast lane, causing a line of advancing cars to throw on their brakes and slow down. Several pressed their horns this time. She ignored them and slowed down to fifty, when they became an orchestra.

The eighteen-wheeler drew up beside her. She slowed down, he slowed down; quarter of a mile to the turn-off, the next sign declared. She saw the exit in the distance, grateful for the first shafts of the morning sun appearing through the clouds, as none of her lights were now working.

Anna knew that she would only have one chance and her timing had to be perfect. She gripped the steering wheel firmly as she reached the exit for the I-90 and drove on past the green triangle of grass that divided the two highways. She suddenly jammed her foot back down on the accelerator, and although the van didn't leap forward, it spurted and managed to gain a few yards. Was it enough? The truck driver responded immediately and also began to accelerate. He was only a car's length away when Anna suddenly swung the steering wheel to the right and carried on across the middle and inside lanes, before mounting the grass verge. The van bounced across the uneven triangle of grass and onto the far exit lane. A car travelling down the inside lane had to swerve onto the hard shoulder to avoid hitting her, while another shot past on the outside. As Anna steadied the van on the inside lane, she looked across to see the eighteen-wheeler heading on down the highway and out of sight.

She slowed down to fifty, although her heart was still beating at three times that speed. She tried to relax. As with all athletes, it is speed of recovery that matters. As she swung onto the I-90, she glanced in her wing mirror. Her heartbeat immediately returned to 150 when she saw a second eighteen-wheeler bearing down on her.

Pot-belly's buddy hadn't made the same mistake.

19

As THE STRANGER entered the lobby, Sam looked up from behind his desk. When you're a doorman, you have to make instant decisions about people. Do they fall in the category of 'Good morning, sir' or 'Can I help you?' or simply 'Hi'? Sam studied the tall, middle-aged man who had just walked in. He was wearing a smart but well-worn suit, the cloth a little shiny at the elbows, and his shirt cuffs were slightly frayed. He wore a tie that Sam reckoned had been tied a thousand times.

'Good morning,' Sam settled on.

'Good morning,' replied the man. 'I'm from the Department of Immigration.'

That only made Sam nervous. Although he'd been born in Harlem, he'd heard stories of people being deported by mistake.

'How can I help you, sir?' he asked.

'I'm checking up on those people who are still missing, presumed dead, following the terrorist attack on Tuesday.'

'Anyone in particular?' asked Sam, cautiously.

'Yes,' said the man. He placed his briefcase on the counter, opened it and extracted a list of names. He ran a finger down the list and came to a halt at the Ps. 'Anna Petrescu,' he said. 'This is the last known address we have for her.'

'I haven't seen Anna since she left for work on Tuesday morning,' said Sam, 'though several people have asked after her, and one of her friends came round that night and took away some of her personal things.'

'What did she take?'

'I don't know,' said Sam. 'I just recognized the suit-case.'

'Do you know the girl's name?'

'Why do you want to know?'

'It might help if we could get in touch with her. Anna's mother is quite anxious.'

'No, I don't know her name,' admitted Sam.

'Would you recognize her, if I showed you a photograph?'

'Might,' said Sam.

Once again, the man opened his briefcase. This time he extracted a photo and passed it across to Sam. He studied it for a moment.

'Yes, that's her. Pretty girl,' he paused, 'but not as pretty as Anna. She was beautiful.'

—◦—

As she swung onto the I-90, Anna noticed that the speed limit was seventy. She would have been happy to break it, but however hard she pressed down on the accelerator she could still only manage 68mph.

Although the second truck was still some way behind, it was closing on her rapidly, and this time she didn't have an exit strategy. She prayed for a sign. The truck must have been only fifty yards behind her, and closing by the second, when she heard the siren.

She was delighted at the thought of being pulled over, and didn't care whether she would be believed when she explained why she had careered across two lanes of the highway and onto the exit ramp, not to mention why her van was missing both bumpers and a mudguard and that none of its lights were working. She began to slow down as the patrol car sped past the truck and slipped in behind her. The officer looked back and indicated that the truck driver should pull over. Anna watched in her offside mirror as both vehicles came to a halt on the hard shoulder.

It was over an hour before she was calm enough to stop looking in her wing mirror every few minutes.

After another hour she even began to feel hungry, and decided to pull into a roadside cafe for breakfast. She parked the van, strolled in and took a seat at the far end of the counter. She perused the menu before ordering 'the big one' – eggs, bacon, sausage, hash browns, pancakes and coffee. Not her usual fare, but then not much had been usual about the past forty-eight hours.

Between mouthfuls, Anna checked her route map. The two drunken men who'd pursued her had helped her keep to her schedule. Anna calculated that she had already covered around three hundred and eighty miles, but there were still at least another fifty to go to reach the Canadian border. She studied the map more closely. Next stop, Niagara Falls, which she estimated would take her another hour.

The television behind the counter was reporting the early morning news. The hope of finding any more survivors was fading. New York had begun mourning its dead and setting about the long and arduous task of clearing up. A memorial service, attended by the President, was to be held in Washington DC, as part of a national day of remembrance. The President then intended to fly on to New York and visit Ground Zero. Mayor Giuliani was next to appear on the screen. He was wearing a T-shirt proudly emblazoned with the letters NYPD, and a cap with NYFD printed across the peak. He praised the spirit of New Yorkers, and pledged his determination to put the city back on its feet as quickly as possible.

The news camera cut to JFK, where an airport spokesman confirmed that the first commercial flights would resume their normal schedule the following morning. That one sentence determined Anna's timetable. She knew she had to touch down in London before Leapman took off from New York if she was to have any chance of convincing Victoria ... Anna glanced out of the window. Two trucks were pulling into the parking lot. She froze, unable to watch as the drivers climbed out of their cabs. She was checking the fire exit as they entered the cafe. They both took seats at the counter, smiled at the waitress and didn't give her a second look. She had never previously understood why people suffered from paranoia.

Anna checked her watch: 7.55am. She drained her coffee, left six dollars on the table and walked across to the phone booth on the far side of the diner. She dialled a 212 number.

—◇—

'Good morning, sir, my name is Agent Roberts.'

'Morning, Agent Roberts,' replied Jack, leaning back in his chair, 'have you anything to report?'

'I'm standing in a vehicle rest stop, somewhere between New York and the Canadian border.'

'And what are you doing there, Agent Roberts?'

'I'm holding a bumper.'

'Let me guess,' said Jack, 'the bumper was at one time attached to a white van, driven by the suspect.'

'Yes, sir.'

'So where is the van now?' asked Jack, trying not to sound exasperated.

'I don't know, sir. When the suspect drove into the

rest stop to take a break, I must admit, sir, I also fell asleep. When I woke, the suspect's van had left, leaving the bumper with the GPS still attached.'

'Then she's either very clever,' said Jack, 'or she's been involved in an accident.'

'I agree.' He paused, and then added, 'What do you think I should do next, sir?'

'Join the CIA,' said Jack.

-<o>-

'Hi, it's Vincent, any news?'

'Yep, just as you thought, Ruth Parish has the painting locked up in the secure customs area at Heathrow.'

'Then I'll have to unlock it,' said Anna.

'That might not prove quite that easy,' said Tina, 'because Leapman flies out of JFK first thing tomorrow morning to pick up the painting, so you've only got another twenty-four hours before he joins you.' She hesitated. 'And you have another problem.'

'Another problem?' said Anna.

'Leapman isn't convinced you're dead.'

'What makes him think that?'

'He keeps asking about you, so be especially careful. Never forget Fenston's reaction when the North Tower collapsed. He may have lost half a dozen staff, but his only interest was the Monet in his office. Heaven knows what he'd do if he lost the Van Gogh as well. Dead artists are more important to him than living people.'

Anna could feel the beads of sweat breaking out on her forehead as the line went dead. She checked her watch: 32 seconds.

-<o>-

'Our "friend" at JFK has confirmed we've been allocated a slot at seven twenty tomorrow morning,' Leapman said. 'But I haven't informed Tina.'

'Why not?' asked Fenston.

'Because the doorman at Petrescu's apartment block told me that someone looking like Tina was seen leaving the building on Tuesday evening.'

'Tuesday evening?' repeated Fenston. 'But that would mean—'

'And she was carrying a suitcase.'

Fenston frowned, but said nothing.

'Do you want me to do anything about it?'

'What do you have in mind?' asked Fenston.

'Bug the phone in her apartment for a start. Then if Petrescu is in contact with her, we'll know exactly where she is and what she's up to.'

Fenston didn't reply, which Leapman always took to mean yes.

—◦—

Canadian Border 4 miles declared a sign on the side of the road. Anna smiled – a smile that was quickly removed when she swung round the next corner and came to a halt behind a long line of vehicles that stretched as far as the eye could see.

She stepped out onto the road and began to stretch her tired limbs. Anna grimaced as she looked across at what was left of her battered transport. How would she explain that to the Happy Hire Company? She certainly didn't need to part with any more cash – the first $500 of any damage, if she remembered correctly. While continuing to stretch, she couldn't help noticing that the other side of the road was empty; no one seemed to be in a rush to enter the United States.

Anna progressed only another hundred yards during the next twenty minutes, ending up opposite a gas station. She made an instant decision – breaking another habit of a lifetime. She swung the van across the road and onto the forecourt, drove past the pumps and parked the van next to a tree – just behind a large sign declaring *Superior Car Wash*. Anna retrieved her two bags from the back of the van and started out on the four-mile trek to the border.

20

'I'M SO SORRY, my dear,' said Arnold Simpson as he
looked across his desk at Arabella Wentworth. 'Dreadful
business,' he added, dropping another sugar lump into
his tea. Arabella didn't comment as Simpson leant forward and placed his hands on the partners' desk, as if
about to offer up a prayer. He smiled benignly at his
client and was about to offer an opinion when Arabella
opened the file on her lap and said, 'As our family's
solicitor, perhaps you can explain how my father and
Victoria managed to run up such massive debts, and in
so short a period of time?'

Simpson leaned back and peered over his half-moon
spectacles. 'Your dear father and I,' he began, 'had been
close friends for over forty years. We were, as I feel sure
you are aware, at Eton together.' Simpson paused to
touch his dark blue tie with the light blue stripe, which
looked as if he'd worn it every day since he'd left school.

'My father always described it as "at the same time",
rather than "together",' retorted Arabella. 'So perhaps
you could now answer my question.'

'I was just coming to that,' said Simpson, momentarily lost for words as he searched round the scattered
files that littered his desk. 'Ah, yes,' he declared eventually, picking up one marked 'Lloyd's of London'.
He opened the cover and adjusted his spectacles.
'When your father became a name at Lloyd's in 1971, he
signed up for several syndicates, putting up the estate as

collateral. For many years, the insurance industry showed handsome returns and your father received a large annual income.' Simpson ran his finger down a long list of figures.

'But did you point out to him at the time,' asked Arabella, 'the meaning of unlimited liability?'

'I confess,' said Simpson, ignoring the question, 'that like so many others, I did not anticipate such an unprecedented run of bad years.'

'It was no different from being a gambler hoping to make a profit from a spin of the roulette wheel,' said Arabella. 'So why didn't you advise him to cut his losses and leave the table?'

'Your father was an obstinate man,' said Simpson, 'and having ridden out some bad years, remained convinced that the good times would return.'

'But that didn't prove to be the case,' said Arabella, turning to another of the numerous papers in her one file.

'Sadly not,' confirmed Simpson, who seemed to have sunk lower in his chair so that he nearly disappeared behind the partners' desk.

'And what happened to the large portfolio of stocks and shares that the family had accumulated over the years?'

'They were among the first assets your father had to liquidate to keep his current account in surplus. In fact,' continued the solicitor, turning over another page, 'at the time of your father's death, I fear he had run up an overdraft of something over ten million pounds.'

'But not with Coutts,' Arabella said, 'as it appears some three years ago he transferred his account to a small bank in New York called Fenston Finance.'

'That is correct, dear lady,' said Simpson. 'Indeed, it

has always been a bit of a mystery to me how that particular establishment came across—'

'It's no mystery to me,' retorted Arabella, as she extracted a letter from her file. 'It's clear that they singled him out as an obvious target.'

'But I still can't work out how they knew—'

'They only had to read the financial pages of any broadsheet. They were reporting the problems faced by Lloyd's on a daily basis, and my father's name appeared regularly, along with several others, as being placed with unfortunate, if not crooked, syndicates.'

'That is pure speculation on your part,' said Simpson, his voice rising.

'Just because you didn't consider it at the time,' replied Arabella, 'doesn't mean it's speculation. In fact, I'm only surprised that you allowed your *close friend* to leave Coutts, who had served the family for over two hundred years, to join such a bunch of shysters.'

Simpson turned scarlet. 'Perhaps you are falling into the politician's habit of relying on hindsight, madam.'

'No, sir,' replied Arabella. 'My late husband was also offered the opportunity to join Lloyd's. The broker assured him that the farm would be quite enough to cover the necessary deposit, whereupon Angus showed him the door.'

Simpson was speechless.

'And how, may I ask, with you as her principal adviser, did Victoria manage to double that debt in less than a year?'

'I am not to blame for that,' snapped Simpson. 'You can direct your anger at the tax man, who always demands his pound of flesh,' he added as he searched for a file marked 'Death Duties'. 'Ah, yes, here it is. The Exchequer is entitled to 40 per cent of any assets on death, unless the assets are directly passed on to a spouse, as I feel sure your late husband would have explained to you. However, I managed, with some considerable skill, even if I do say so myself, to reach a settlement of eleven million pounds with the inspectors, which Lady Victoria seemed well satisfied with at the time.'

'My sister was a naive spinster who never left home without her father and didn't have her own bank account until she was thirty,' said Arabella, 'but still you allowed her to sign a further contract with Fenston Finance, which was bound to land her in even more debt.'

'It was that, or putting the estate on the market.'

'No, it wasn't,' replied Arabella. 'It only took me one phone call to Lord Hindlip, the chairman of Christie's, to be told that he would expect the family's Van Gogh to make in excess of thirty million pounds were it to come up for auction.'

'But your father would never have agreed to sell the Van Gogh.'

'My father wasn't alive when you approved the second loan,' countered Arabella. 'It was a decision *you* should have advised her on.'

'I had no choice, dear lady, under the terms of the original contract.'

'Which you witnessed, but obviously didn't read. Because not only did my sister agree to go on paying 16 per cent compound interest on the loan, but you even allowed her to hand over the Van Gogh as collateral.'

'But you can still demand that they sell the painting, and then the problem will be solved.'

'Wrong again, Mr Simpson,' said Arabella. 'If you had read beyond page one of the original contract, you would have discovered that should there be a dispute, any decision will revert to a New York court's jurisdiction, and I certainly don't have the wherewithal to take on Bryce Fenston in his own backyard.'

'You don't have the authority to do so, either,' retorted Simpson, 'because I—'

'I am next of kin,' said Arabella firmly.

'But there is no will to indicate to whom Victoria intended to leave the estate,' shouted Simpson.

'Another duty you managed to execute with your usual prescience and skill.'

'Your sister and I were at the time in the process of discussing—'

'It's a bit late for that,' said Arabella. 'I am facing a battle here and now with an unscrupulous man, who seems to have the law on his side thanks to you.'

'I feel confident,' said Simpson, once again placing his hands on the desk in a prayer-like position as if ready to give the final blessing, 'that I can wrap this whole problem up in—'

'I'll tell you exactly what you can wrap up,' said Arabella rising from her place, 'all those files concerning the Wentworth estate, and send them to Wentworth Hall.' She stared down at the solicitor. 'And at the same time, enclose your final account –' she checked her watch – 'for one hour of your invaluable advice.'

21

ANNA WALKED DOWN the middle of the road, pulling her suitcase behind her, with the laptop hanging over her left shoulder. With each stride she took, Anna became more and more aware of passengers sitting in their stationary cars, staring at the strange lone figure as she passed them.

The first mile took fifteen minutes, and one of the families who had settled down for a picnic on the grass verge by the side of the road offered her a glass of wine. The second mile took eighteen minutes, but she still couldn't see the border post. It was another twenty minutes before she passed a *1 mile to the border* sign, when she tried to speed up.

The last mile reminded her which muscles ached after a long, tiring run, and then she saw the finish line. An injection of adrenalin caused her to step up a gear.

When Anna was about a hundred yards from the barrier, the staring looks made her feel like a queue jumper. She averted her eyes and walked a little more slowly. When she came to a halt on the white line, where each car is asked to turn off its engine and wait, she stood to one side.

There were two customs officials on duty that day, having to deal with an unusually long queue for a Thursday morning. They were sitting in their little boxes, checking everyone's documents much more assiduously than usual. Anna tried to make eye contact with the younger of the two officers in the hope that he would take pity on her, but she didn't need a mirror to know that after what she'd been through during the past twenty-four hours, she couldn't have looked a lot better than when she staggered out of the North Tower.

Eventually, the younger of the two guards beckoned her over. He checked her travel documents and stared at her quizzically. Just how far had she trudged with those bags? He checked her passport carefully. Everything seemed to be in order.

'What is your reason for visiting Canada?' he asked.

'I'm attending an art seminar at McGill University. It's part of my PhD thesis on the pre-Raphaelite movement,' she said, staring directly at him.

'Which artists in particular?' asked the guard, casually.

A smart ass or a fan. Anna decided to play along. 'Rossetti, Holman Hunt and Morris, among others.'

'What about the other Hunt?'

'Alfred? Not a true pre-Raphaelite, but—'

'But just as good an artist.'

'I agree,' said Anna.

'Who's giving the seminar?'

'Er, Vern Swanson,' said Anna, hoping the guard would not have heard of the most eminent expert in the field.

'Good, then I'll get a chance to meet him.'

'What do you mean?'

'Well, if he's still the Professor of Art History at Yale he'll be coming from New Haven, won't he, and as there are no flights in and out of the US, this is the only way he can cross the border.'

Anna couldn't think of a suitable response and was grateful to be rescued by the woman behind her, who began commenting to her husband in a loud voice about how long she'd been waiting in line.

'I was at McGill,' said the young officer with a smile, as he handed Anna back her passport. Anna wondered if the colour of her cheeks betrayed her embarrassment. 'We're all sorry about what happened in New York,' he added.

'Thank you,' said Anna, and walked across the border. *Welcome to Canada*.

'Who is it?' demanded an anonymous voice.

'You've got an electrical fault on the tenth floor,' said a man standing outside the front door, dressed in green overalls, wearing a Yankee baseball cap and carrying a tool box. He closed his eyes and smiled into the security camera. When he heard the buzzer, the man pushed open the door and slipped in without any further questions.

He walked past the elevator and began to climb the stairs. That way there was less chance of anyone remembering him. He stopped when he reached the tenth floor, glancing quickly up and down the corridor. No one in sight; 3.30pm was always a quiet time. Not that he could tell you why, it was simply based on experience. When he reached her door, he pressed the buzzer. No reply. But then he had been assured that she would still be at work for at least another couple of hours. The man placed his bag on the floor and examined the two locks on the door. Hardly Fort Knox. With the precision of a surgeon about to perform an operation, he opened his bag and selected several delicate instruments.

Two minutes and forty seconds later, he was inside the apartment. He quickly located all three telephones. The first was in the front room on a desk, below a

Warhol print of Marilyn Monroe. The second was by her bed, next to a photograph. The intruder glanced at the woman in the centre of the picture. She was standing between two men who looked so alike they had to be her father and brother.

The third phone was in the kitchen. He looked at the fridge door and grinned; they were both fans of the 49ers.

Six minutes and nine seconds later he was back in the corridor. Down the stairs and out of the front door.

Job completed in less than ten minutes. Fee $1,000. Not unlike a surgeon.

‑<o>‑

Anna was among the last to step onto the Greyhound bus that was due to leave Niagara Falls at three o'clock.

Two hours later, the bus came to a halt on the western shore of Lake Ontario. Anna was first down the steps, and without stopping to admire the Mies van der Rohe buildings that dominate the Toronto skyline, she hailed the first available cab.

'The airport please, and as fast as possible.'

'Which terminal?' asked the driver.

Anna hesitated. 'Europe.'

'Terminal three,' he said as he moved off, adding, 'Where you from?'

'Boston,' Anna replied. She didn't want to talk about New York.

'Terrible, what happened in New York,' he said. 'One of those moments in history when everyone remembers exactly where they were. I was in the cab, heard it on the radio. How about you?'

'I was in the North Tower,' said Anna.

He knew a smart ass when he saw one.

It took just over twenty-five minutes to drive the seventeen miles from Bay Street to Lester B. Pearson International Airport, and during that time the driver never uttered another word. When he finally pulled up outside the entrance to terminal three, Anna paid the fare and walked quickly into the airport. She stared up at the departure board, as the digital clock flicked over to twenty-eight minutes past five.

The last flight to Heathrow had just closed its gates. Anna cursed. Her eyes scanned the list of cities for any remaining flights that evening: Tel Aviv, Bangkok, Hong Kong, Sydney, Amsterdam. *Amsterdam.* How appropriate, she thought. Flight KL692 departs 18.00 hours, gate C31, now boarding.

Anna ran to the KLM desk and asked the man behind the counter, even before he'd looked up, 'Can I still get on your flight to Amsterdam?'

He stopped counting the tickets. 'Yes, but you'll have to hurry as they're just about to close the gate.'

'Do you have a window seat available?'

'Window, aisle, centre, anything you like.'

'Why's that?'

'Not many people seem to want to fly today, and it's not just because it's the thirteenth.'

—◇—

'JFK have reconfirmed our slot at seven twenty tomorrow morning,' said Leapman.

'Good,' said Fenston. 'Phone me the moment the plane takes off. What time do you touch down at Heathrow?'

'Around seven,' replied Leapman. 'Art Locations will be waiting on the runway to load the painting on board. Three times the usual fee seems to have concentrated their minds.'

'And when do you expect to be back?'

'In time for breakfast the following morning.'

'Any news on Petrescu?'

'No,' Leapman said. 'Tina's only had one call so far, a man.'

'Nothing from—'

Tina entered the room.

—◇—

'She's on her way to Amsterdam,' said Joe.

'Amsterdam?' repeated Jack, tapping his fingers on the desk.

'Yes, she missed the last flight to Heathrow.'

'Then she'll be on the first flight into London tomorrow morning.'

'We already have an agent at Heathrow,' said Joe. 'Do you want agents anywhere else?'

'Yes, Gatwick and Stansted,' said Jack.

'If you're right, she'll be in London only hours before Karl Leapman.'

'What do you mean?' asked Jack.

'Fenston's private jet has a slot booked out of JFK at seven twenty tomorrow morning, and the only passenger is Leapman.'

'Then they probably plan to meet up,' said Jack. 'Call Agent Crasanti at our London embassy and ask him to put extra agents at all three airports. I want to know what exactly those two are up to.'

'We won't be on our own territory,' Joe reminded him. 'If the British were to find out, not to mention the CIA—'

'At all three airports,' Jack repeated, before putting the phone down.

—◇—

Moments after Anna stepped onto the plane, the door was locked into place. She was guided to her seat and asked to fasten her seatbelt, as they were expecting to take off almost immediately. Anna was pleased to find the other seats in her row were unoccupied, and as soon as the seatbelt sign had been turned off, she pulled up the armrests in her row and lay down, covering herself with two blankets before resting her head on a real pillow. She had dozed off even before the plane had reached its cruising height.

Someone was gently touching her shoulder. Anna cursed under her breath. She'd forgotten to mention that she didn't want a meal. Anna looked up at the stewardess and blinked sleepily. 'No thank you,' she said firmly, and closed her eyes again.

'I'm sorry, but I have to ask you to sit up and fasten your seatbelt,' said the stewardess politely. 'We're expecting to land in about twenty minutes. If you would like to alter your watch, the local time in Amsterdam is 6.55am.'

9/14

22

LEAPMAN WAS AWAKE long before the limousine was due to pick him up. This was not a day for oversleeping.

He climbed out of bed and headed straight for the bathroom. However closely he shaved, Leapman knew he would still have stubble on his chin long before he went to bed. He could grow a beard over a long weekend. Once he'd showered and shaved, he didn't bother with making himself breakfast. He'd be served coffee and croissants later by the company stewardess on the bank's private jet. Who, in this rundown apartment block in such an unfashionable neighbourhood, would believe that in a couple of hours Leapman would be the only passenger on a Gulfstream V on its way to London?

He walked across to his half-empty closet and selected his most recently acquired suit, his favourite shirt and a tie that he would be wearing for the first time. He didn't need the pilot to look smarter than he was.

Leapman stood by the window, waiting for the limousine to appear, aware that his little apartment was not much of an improvement on the prison cell where he'd spent four years. He looked down on 43rd Street as the incongruous limousine drew up outside the front door.

Leapman climbed into the back of the car, not speaking to the driver as the door was opened for him. Like Fenston, he pushed the button in the armrest and watched as the smoke-grey window slid up, cutting him off from the driver. For the next twenty-four hours, he would live in a different world.

Forty-five minutes later the limousine turned off the Van Wyck Expressway and took the exit to JFK. The driver swept through an entrance that few passengers ever discover and drew up outside a small terminal building that served only those privileged enough to fly in their own aircraft. Leapman stepped out of the car and was escorted to a private lounge, where the captain of the company's Gulfstream V jet was waiting for him.

'Any hope of taking off earlier than planned?' Leapman asked, as he sank into a comfortable leather armchair.

'No, sir,' the captain replied, 'planes are taking off every forty-five seconds, and our slot is confirmed for seven twenty.'

Leapman grunted, and turned his attention to the morning papers.

The *New York Times* was leading on the news that President Bush was offering a $50-million-dollar reward for the capture of Osama Bin Laden, which Leapman considered to be no more than the usual Texan approach to law and order over the past hundred years. The *Wall Street Journal* listed Fenston Finance off another twelve cents, a fate suffered by several companies whose headquarters had been based in the World Trade Center. Once he'd got his hands on the Van Gogh, the company could ride out a period of weak share prices while he concentrated on consolidating the bottom line. Leapman's thoughts were interrupted by a member of the cabin crew.

'You can board now, sir, we'll be taking off in around fifteen minutes.'

Another car drove Leapman to the steps of the aircraft, and the plane began to taxi even before he'd finished his orange juice, but he didn't relax until the jet reached its cruising altitude of 30,000 feet and the *Fasten seatbelt* sign had been turned off. He leant forward, picked up the phone and dialled Fenston's private line.

'I'm on my way,' he said, 'and I can't see any reason why I shouldn't be back by this time tomorrow –' he paused – 'with a Dutchman sitting in the seat next to me.'

'Call me the moment you land,' was the chairman's response.

–◦–

Tina flicked off the extension to the chairman's phone.

Leapman had been dropping into her office more and more recently – always without knocking. He made no secret of the fact that he believed Anna was still alive, and in touch with her.

The chairman's jet had taken off from JFK on time that morning, and Tina had listened in on his conversation with Leapman. She realized that Anna only had a few hours' start on him, and that was assuming she was even in London.

Tina thought about Leapman returning to New York the following day, that sickly grin plastered on his face as he handed over the Van Gogh to the chairman. Tina continued to download the latest contracts, having earlier emailed them to her private address – something she only did when Leapman was out of the office and Fenston was fully occupied.

–◦–

The first available flight to London Gatwick that morning was due out of Schiphol at ten o'clock. Anna purchased a ticket from British Airways, who warned her that the flight was running twenty minutes late as the incoming plane had not yet landed. She took advantage of the delay to have a shower and change her clothes. Schiphol was accustomed to overnight travellers. Anna selected the most conservative outfit from her small wardrobe for her meeting with Victoria.

As she sat in Caffè Nero sipping coffee, Anna turned the pages of the *Herald Tribune*: '$50-million-dollar reward', read a headline on the second page – less of a bounty than the Van Gogh would fetch at any auction house. Anna didn't waste any time reading the article as she needed to concentrate on her priorities once she came face to face with Victoria.

First she had to find out where the Van Gogh was. If Ruth Parish had the picture in storage, then she would advise Victoria to call Ruth and insist that it was returned to Wentworth Hall without delay, and add that she'd be quite happy to advise Ruth that Fenston Finance couldn't hold on to the painting against Victoria's wishes, especially if the only contract in existence were to disappear. She had a feeling Victoria would not agree to that, but if she did, Anna would get in touch with Mr Nakamura in Tokyo and try to find out if— 'British Airways flight 8112 to London Gatwick is now ready for boarding at Gate D14,' announced a voice over the public-address system.

As they crossed the English Channel, Anna went over her plan again and again, trying to find some fault with her logic, but she could think of only two people who would consider it anything other than common sense. The plane touched down at Gatwick thirty-five minutes late.

Anna checked her watch as she stepped onto English soil, aware that it would only be another nine hours before Leapman landed at Heathrow. Once she was through passport control and had retrieved her baggage, Anna went in search of a rental car. She avoided the Happy Hire Company desk, and stood in line at the Avis counter.

Anna didn't see the smartly dressed young man who was standing in the duty-free shop whispering into a cellphone, 'She's landed. I'm on her tail.'

—◦—

Leapman settled back in the wide leather chair, far more comfortable than anything in his apartment on 43rd Street. The stewardess served him a black coffee in a gold-rimmed china cup on a silver tray. He leant back and thought about the task ahead of him. He knew he was nothing more than a bagman, even if the bag today contained one of the most valuable paintings on earth. He despised Fenston, who never treated him as an equal. If Fenston just once acknowledged his contribution to the company's success, and responded to his ideas as if he was a respected colleague, rather than a paid lackey – not that he was paid that much. If he just occasionally said thank you – it would be enough. True, Fenston had picked him up out of the gutter, but only to drop him into another.

He had served Fenston for a decade, and watched as the unsophisticated immigrant from Bucharest climbed up the ladder of wealth and status – a ladder he had held in place, while remaining nothing more than a sidekick. But that could change overnight. She only needed to make one mistake, and their roles would be reversed. Fenston would end up in prison, and he would have a fortune at his disposal that no one could ever trace.

'Would you care for some more coffee, Mr Leap-man?' asked the stewardess.

—◦—

Anna didn't need a map to find her way to Wentworth Hall, although she did have to remember not to go the wrong way round the numerous traffic islands en route.

Forty minutes later, she drove through the gates of the Hall. Anna had no special knowledge of the Baroque architecture that dominated the late seventeenth- and early eighteenth-century homes of aristocratic England before she stayed at Wentworth Hall. The pile – Victoria's description of her home – had been built in 1697 by Sir John Vanbrugh. It was his first commission before he moved on to create Castle Howard and, later, Blenheim Palace, for another triumphant soldier – after which he became the most sought-after architect of the age.

The long drive up to the house was shaded by fine oaks of the same vintage as the hall itself, although gaps were now visible where trees had succumbed to the violent storms of 1987. Anna drove by an ornate lake full of Magoi Koi carp – immigrants from Japan – and on past two tennis courts and a croquet lawn, sprinkled with the first leaves of autumn. As she rounded the bend, the great hall, surrounded by a thousand green English acres, loomed up to dominate the skyline.

Victoria had once told Anna that the house had sixty-seven rooms, fourteen of them guest bedrooms. The bedroom she had stayed in on the first floor, the Van Gogh room, was about the same size as her apartment in New York.

As she approached the hall, Anna noticed that the crested family flag on the east tower was fluttering at half mast. As she brought the car to a halt, she wondered which of Victoria's many elderly relatives had died.

The massive oak door was pulled open even before Anna reached the top step. She prayed that Victoria was at home, and that Fenston still had no idea she was in England.

'Good morning, madam,' the butler intoned. 'How may I help you?'

It's me, Andrews, Anna wanted to say, surprised by his formal tone. He had been so friendly when she stayed at the hall. She echoed his formal approach. 'I need to speak to Lady Victoria, urgently.'

'I'm afraid that will not be possible,' replied Andrews, 'but I will find out if her ladyship is free. Perhaps you would be kind enough to wait here while I enquire.'

What did he mean, *that will not be possible, but I will find out if her ladyship* . . .

As Anna waited in the hall, she glanced up at Gainsborough's portrait of Catherine, Lady Wentworth. She recalled every picture in the house, but her eye moved to her favourite at the top of the staircase, a Romney of *Mrs Siddons as Portia*. She turned to face the entrance to the morning room, to be greeted with a painting by Stubbs of *Actaeon, Winner of the Derby*, Sir Harry Wentworth's favourite horse – still safely in his paddock. If Victoria took her advice, at least she could still save the rest of the collection.

The butler returned at the same even pace.

'Her ladyship will see you now,' he said, 'if you would care to join her in the drawing room.' He gave a slight bow, before leading her across the hall.

Anna tried to concentrate on her six-point plan, but first she would need to explain why she was forty-eight hours late for their appointment, although surely Victoria would have followed the horrors of Tuesday and might even be surprised to find that she had survived.

When Anna entered the drawing room, she saw Victoria, head bowed, dressed in mourning black, seated on the sofa, a chocolate Labrador half asleep at her feet. She couldn't remember Victoria having a dog, and was surprised when she didn't jump up and greet her in her usual warm manner. Victoria raised her head, and Anna gasped, as Arabella Wentworth stared coldly up at her. In that split second, she realized why the family's crest had been flying at half mast. Anna remained silent, as she tried to take in the fact that she would never see Victoria again, and would now need to convince her sister, whom she had never met before. Anna couldn't even remember her name. The mirror image did not rise from her place, or offer to shake her hand.

'Would you care for some tea, Dr Petrescu?' Arabella asked in a distant voice that suggested she hoped to hear her reply, No, thank you.

'No, thank you,' said Anna, who remained standing. 'May I ask how Victoria died?' she said quietly.

'I assumed you already knew,' replied Arabella drily.

'I have no idea what you mean,' said Anna.

'Then why are you here,' asked Arabella, 'if it's not to collect the rest of the family silver?'

'I came to warn Victoria not to let them take away the Van Gogh, before I had a chance to—'

'They took the painting away on Tuesday,' said Arabella, pausing. 'They didn't even have the good manners to wait until after the funeral.'

'I tried to call, but they wouldn't give me her number. If only I'd got through,' Anna mumbled incoherently, and then added, 'And now it's too late.'

'Too late for what?' asked Arabella.

'I sent Victoria a copy of my report recommending that—'

'Yes, I've read your report,' said Arabella, 'but you're right, it's too late for that now. My new lawyer has already warned me that it could be years before the estate can be settled, by which time we'll have lost everything.'

'That must have been the reason he didn't want me to travel to England and see Victoria personally,' Anna said without explanation.

'I'm not sure I understand,' said Arabella, looking more closely at her.

'I was fired by Fenston on Tuesday,' said Anna, 'for sending a copy of my report to Victoria.'

'Victoria read your report,' said Arabella quietly. 'I have a letter confirming that she was going to take your advice, but that was before her cruel death.'

'How did she die?' asked Anna gently.

'She was murdered, in a vile and cowardly fashion,' said Arabella. She paused and, looking directly at Anna, added, 'And I have no doubt that Mr Fenston will be able to fill in the details for you.' Anna bowed her head, unable to think of anything to say, her six-point plan in tatters. Fenston had beaten both of them. 'Dear Victoria was so trusting, and, I fear, so naive,' continued Arabella, 'but no human being deserved to be treated in that way, let alone someone as good-natured as my sweet sister.'

'I am so sorry,' said Anna, 'I didn't know. You have to believe me. I had no idea.'

Arabella looked out of the window across the lawn, and didn't speak for some time. She turned back to see Anna, trembling.

'I believe you,' Arabella eventually said. 'I originally assumed that it was you who was responsible for this evil charade.' She paused again. 'I see now that I was wrong. But, sadly, it's all too late. There's nothing we can do now.'

'I'm not so sure about that,' said Anna, looking at Arabella with a fierce determination in her eyes. 'But if I'm to do anything, I'll have to ask you to trust me, as much as Victoria did.'

'What do you mean, trust you?' said Arabella.

'Give me a chance,' said Anna, 'to prove that I wasn't responsible for your sister's death.'

'But how can you hope to do that?' asked Arabella.

'By retrieving your Van Gogh.'

'But as I told you, they've already taken the painting away.'

'I know,' said Anna, 'but it still has to be in England, because Fenston has sent a Mr Leapman to pick up the picture.' Anna checked her watch. 'He'll be landing at Heathrow in a few hours' time.'

'But even if you managed to get your hands on the painting, how would that solve the problem?'

Anna outlined the details of her plan, and was pleased to find Arabella nodding from time to time. Anna ended by saying, 'I'll need your backing, otherwise what I have in mind could get me arrested.'

Arabella remained silent for some time, before she said, 'You're a brave young woman, and I wonder if you even realize just how brave. But if you're willing to take such a risk, so am I, and I'll back you to the hilt,' she added.

Anna smiled at the quaint English expression, and said, 'Can you confirm who collected the Van Gogh?'

Arabella rose from the sofa and crossed the room to the writing desk, with the dog following in her wake. She picked up a business card. 'A Ms Ruth Parish,' she read, 'of Art Locations.'

'Just as I thought,' said Anna. 'Then I'll have to leave immediately, as I only have a few hours before Leapman arrives.'

Anna stepped forward and thrust out her hand, but Arabella didn't respond. She simply took her in her arms and said, 'If I can do anything to help you avenge my sister's death . . .'

'Anything?'

'Anything,' repeated Arabella.

'When the North Tower collapsed, all the documentation concerning Victoria's loan was destroyed,' said Anna, 'including the original contract. The only copy is in your possession. If—'

'You don't have to spell it out,' said Arabella.

Anna smiled. She wasn't dealing with Victoria any longer.

She turned to leave and had reached the hall long before the butler had time to open the front door.

Arabella watched from the drawing-room window as Anna's car disappeared down the drive and out of sight. She wondered if she would ever see her again.

‹○›

'Petrescu,' said a voice, 'is just leaving Wentworth Hall. She's heading back in the direction of central London. I'm following her, and will keep you briefed.'

23

ANNA DROVE OUT OF Wentworth Hall and headed back towards the M25, looking for a sign to Heathrow. She checked the clock on the dashboard. It was almost 2pm, so she had missed any chance of calling Tina, who would now be at her desk on Wall Street. But she did need to make another call if there was to be the slightest chance of her coup succeeding.

As she drove through the village of Wentworth, Anna tried to recall the pub where Victoria had taken her to dinner. Then she saw the familiar crest flapping in the wind, also at half mast.

Anna swung into the forecourt of the Wentworth Arms and parked her car near the entrance. She walked through the reception and into the bar.

'Can you change five dollars?' she asked the barmaid. 'I need to make a phone call.'

'Of course, love,' came back the immediate reply. The barmaid opened the cash register and handed Anna two pound coins. Daylight robbery, Anna wanted to tell her, but she didn't have time to argue.

'The phone's just beyond the restaurant, to your right.'

Anna dialled a number that she could never forget. The phone rang only twice before a voice announced, 'Good afternoon, Sotheby's.'

Anna fed a coin into the slot, and said, 'Mark Polti-more, please.'

'I'll put you through.'

'Mark Poltimore.'

'Mark, it's Anna, Anna Petrescu.'

'Anna, what a pleasant surprise. We've all been anxious about you. Where were you on Tuesday?'

'Amsterdam,' she replied.

'Thank God for that,' said Mark. 'Terrible business. And Fenston?'

'Not in the building at the time,' said Anna, 'and that's why I'm calling. He wants your opinion on a Van Gogh.'

'Authenticity or price?' asked Mark. 'Because when it comes to provenance, I bow to your superior judgement.'

'There's no discussion on its provenance,' said Anna, 'but I would like a second opinion on its value.'

'Is it one we would know?'

'*Self-portrait with Bandaged Ear*,' said Anna.

'The Wentworth *Self-portrait*?' queried Mark. 'I've known the family all my life and had no idea they were considering selling the painting.'

'I didn't say they were,' said Anna, without offering further explanation.

'Are you able to bring the painting in for inspection?' asked Mark.

'I'd like to, but I don't have secure enough transport. I was hoping you might be able to help.'

'Where is it now?' asked Mark.

'In a bonded warehouse at Heathrow.'

'That's easy enough,' said Mark. 'We have a daily pick-up from Heathrow. Would tomorrow afternoon be convenient?'

'Today, if possible,' said Anna, 'you know what my boss is like.'

'Hold on, I'll just need to find out if they've already

left.' The line went silent, although Anna could hear her heart thumping. She placed the second pound coin in the slot – the last thing she needed was to be cut off. Mark came back on the line. 'You're in luck. Our handler is picking up some other items for us around four. How does that suit you?'

'Fine, but could you do me another favour, and ask them to call Ruth Parish at Art Locations, just before the van is due to arrive?'

'Sure. And how long do we have to value the piece?'

'Forty-eight hours.'

'You'd come to Sotheby's first if you ever considered selling the *Self-portrait*, wouldn't you, Anna?'

'Of course.'

'I can't wait to see it,' said Mark.

Anna replaced the receiver, appalled by how easily she could now lie. She was also becoming aware just how simple it must have been for Fenston to deceive her.

She drove out of the Wentworth Arms car park, aware that everything now depended on Ruth Parish being in her office. Once she reached the orbital road, Anna remained in the slow lane as she went over all the things that could go badly wrong. Was Ruth aware that she had been fired? Had Fenston told her she was dead? Would Ruth accept her authority to make such a crucial decision? Anna knew that there was only one way she was going to find out. She even considered calling Ruth, but decided any prior warning would only give her more time to check up. If she was to have any chance at all, she needed to take Ruth by surprise.

Anna was so deep in thought as she considered every possibility that she nearly missed her exit for Heathrow. Once she had turned off the M25, she drove on past the signs for terminals one, two, three and four, and headed for the cargo depots just off the Southern Perimeter Road.

She parked her car in a visitor's space directly outside the offices of Art Locations. She sat in the car for some time, trying to compose herself. Why didn't she just drive off? She didn't need to become involved, or even consider taking such a risk. She then thought about Victoria, and the role she had unwittingly played in her death. 'Get on with it, woman,' Anna said out loud. 'They either know, or they don't, and if they've already been tipped off, you'll be back in the car in less than two minutes.' Anna looked in the mirror. Were there any giveaway signs? 'Get on with it,' she admonished herself even more firmly, and finally opened the car door. She took a deep breath as she strolled across the tarmac towards the entrance of the building.

She pushed through the swing doors and came face to face with a receptionist she'd never seen before. Not a good start.

'Is Ruth around?' Anna asked cheerily, as if she popped by the office every day.

'No, she's having lunch at the Royal Academy to discuss the upcoming Rembrandt exhibition.'

Anna's heart sank.

'But I'm expecting her back at any moment.'

'Then I'll wait,' Anna said with a smile.

She took a seat in reception. She picked up an out-of-date copy of *Newsweek*, with Al Gore on the cover, and flicked through the pages. She found herself continually looking up at the clock above the reception desk, watching the slow progress of the minute hand: 3.10, 3.15, 3.20.

Ruth finally walked through the door at 3.22pm. 'Any messages?' she asked the receptionist.

'No,' replied the girl, 'but there is a lady waiting to see you.'

Anna held her breath as Ruth swung around.

'Anna,' she exclaimed. 'It's good to see you.' First hurdle crossed. 'I wondered if you'd still be on this assignment after the tragedy in New York.' Second hurdle crossed. 'Especially when your boss told me that Mr Leapman would be coming across to collect the picture personally.' Third hurdle crossed. No one had told Ruth she was missing, presumed dead.

'You look a bit pale,' continued Ruth. 'Are you all right?'

'I'm fine,' said Anna, stumbling over the fourth hurdle, but at least she was still on her feet, even if there were another six hurdles to cross before the finishing line.

'Where were you on the eleventh?' asked Ruth with concern. 'We feared the worst. I would have asked Mr Fenston, but he never gives you a chance to ask anything.'

'Covering a sale in Amsterdam,' Anna replied, 'but Karl Leapman called me last night and asked me to fly over and double-check everything was in place, so that when he arrives all we have to do is load the picture onto the plane.'

'We're more than ready for him,' said Ruth testily, 'but I'll drive you across to the warehouse and you can see for yourself. Just hang on for a minute. I need to see if I've had any calls and let my secretary know where I'm going.'

Anna paced anxiously up and down, wondering if Ruth would call New York to check her story. But why should she? Ruth had never dealt with anyone else in the past.

Ruth was back within a couple of minutes. 'This just arrived on my desk,' she said, handing Anna an email.

Anna's heart sank. 'Confirming that Mr Leapman is scheduled to land around seven, seven thirty, this evening. He expects us to be waiting on the runway, ready to load the painting, as he's hoping to turn round in less than an hour.'

'That sounds like Leapman,' said Anna.

'Then we'd better get moving,' said Ruth, as she began walking towards the door.

Anna nodded her agreement, followed her out of the building and jumped into the passenger seat of Ruth's Range Rover.

'Terrible business, Lady Victoria,' said Ruth as she swung the car round and headed for the south end of the cargo terminal. 'The press are making a real meal of the murder – mystery killer, throat cut with a kitchen knife – but the police still haven't arrested anyone.'

Anna remained silent, the words 'throat cut' and 'mystery killer' reverberating in her mind. Was that why Arabella had told her that she was a brave woman?

Ruth pulled up outside an anonymous-looking concrete building, which Anna had visited several times in the past. She checked her watch: 3.40pm.

Ruth flashed a security pass to the guard, who immediately unlocked the three-inch steel door. He accompanied them both down a long, grey concrete corridor that always felt like a bunker to Anna. He stopped at a second security door, this time with a digital pad. Ruth waited for the guard to stand back before she entered a six-digit number. She pulled open the heavy door, allowing them to enter a square concrete room. A thermometer on the wall indicated a temperature of 20 degrees centigrade.

The room was lined with wooden shelves, which were stacked with pictures waiting to be transported to different parts of the world, all packed in Art Locations' distinctive red boxes. Ruth checked her inventory, before walking across the room and looking up at a row of shelves. She tapped a crate showing the number 47 stencilled in all four corners.

Anna strolled across to join her, playing for time. She also checked the inventory, number forty-seven, Vincent Van Gogh, *Self-portrait with Bandaged Ear*, 24 by 18 inches.

'Everything seems to be in order,' said Anna, as the guard reappeared at the door.

'Sorry to interrupt you, Ms Parish, but there are two security men from Sotheby's outside, say they've been instructed to pick up a Van Gogh for valuation.'

'Do you know anything about this?' asked Ruth, turning to face Anna.

'Oh, yes,' said Anna, not missing a beat, 'the chairman instructed me to have the Van Gogh valued for insurance purposes before it's shipped to New York. They'll only need the piece for about an hour, and then they will send it straight back.'

'Mr Leapman didn't mention anything about this,' said Ruth. 'It wasn't in his email.'

'Frankly,' said Anna, 'Leapman's such a philistine, he wouldn't know the difference between Van Gogh and Van Morrison.' Anna paused for a moment. Normally she never took risks, but she couldn't afford to let Ruth call Fenston and check. 'If you're in any doubt, why don't you call New York and have a word with Fenston?' she said. 'That should clear the matter up.'

Anna waited nervously as Ruth considered her suggestion.

'And have my head bitten off again,' said Ruth eventually. 'No, thank you, I think I'll take your word for it. That's assuming you will take responsibility for signing the release order?'

'Of course,' said Anna, adding, 'That's no more than my fiduciary duty as an officer of the bank,' hoping her reply sounded suitably pompous.

'And you'll also explain the change of plan to Mr Leapman?'

'That won't be necessary,' said Anna, 'the painting will be back long before his plane lands.'

Ruth looked relieved, and turning to the guard said, 'It's number forty-seven.'

They both accompanied the guard as he removed the red packing case from the shelf and carried it out to the Sotheby's security van.

'Sign here,' said the driver.

Anna stepped forward and signed the release document.

'When will you be bringing the picture back?' Ruth asked the driver.

'I don't know anything about—'

'I asked Mark Poltimore to return the painting within a couple of hours,' interjected Anna.

'It had better be back before Mr Leapman lands,' said Ruth, 'because I don't need to get on the wrong side of that man.'

'Would you be happier if I accompanied the painting to Sotheby's?' asked Anna innocently. 'Then perhaps I can speed up the whole process.'

'Would you be willing to do that?' asked Ruth.

'It might be wise given the circumstances,' said Anna, and she climbed up into the front of the van and took the seat between the two men.

Ruth waved as the van disappeared through the perimeter gate and joined the late-afternoon traffic on its journey into London.

24

BRYCE FENSTON'S Gulfstream V executive jet touched down at Heathrow at 7.22pm, and Ruth was standing on the tarmac waiting to greet the bank's representative. She had already alerted customs with all the relevant details so that the paperwork could be completed just as soon as Anna returned.

For the past hour, Ruth had spent more and more time looking towards the main gate, willing the security van to reappear. She had already rung Sotheby's, and was assured by the girl in their Impressionist department that the painting had arrived. But that was more than two hours ago. Perhaps she should have called the States to double-check, but why question one of your most reliable customers. Ruth turned her attention back to the jet and decided to say nothing. After all, Anna was certain to turn up in the next few minutes.

The fuselage door opened and the steps unfolded onto the ground. The stewardess stood to one side to allow her only passenger to leave the plane. Karl Leapman stepped onto the tarmac and shook hands with Ruth, before joining her in the back of an airport limousine for the short journey to the private lounge. He didn't bother to introduce himself, just assumed she would know who he was.

'Any problems?' asked Leapman.

'None that I can think of,' replied Ruth confidently, as the driver pulled up outside the executive building.

'We've carried out your instructions to the letter, despite the tragic death of Lady Victoria.'

'Yeah,' said Leapman as he stepped out of the car. 'The company will be sending a wreath to her funeral,' and without pausing, added, 'is everything ready for a quick turnaround?'

'Yes,' said Ruth. 'We'll begin loading the moment the captain has finished refuelling – shouldn't be more than an hour. Then you can be on your way.'

'I'm glad to hear it,' said Leapman, pushing through the swing doors. 'We have a slot booked for eight thirty and I don't want to miss it.'

'Then perhaps it might be more sensible if I left you, to oversee the transfer,' said Ruth, 'but I'll report back the moment the painting is safely on board.'

Leapman nodded and sank back in a leather chair. Ruth turned to leave.

'Can I get you a drink, sir?' asked the barman.

'Scotch on the rocks,' said Leapman, scanning the short dinner menu.

As Ruth reached the door, she turned and said, 'When Anna comes back, would you tell her I'll be over at customs, waiting to complete the paperwork?'

'Anna?' exclaimed Leapman, jumping out of his chair.

'Yes, she's been around for most of the afternoon.'

'Doing what?' Leapman demanded as he advanced towards Ruth.

'Just checking over the manifest,' Ruth said, trying to sound relaxed, 'and making sure that Mr Fenston's orders were carried out.'

'What orders?' barked Leapman.

'To send the Van Gogh to Sotheby's for an insurance valuation.'

'The chairman gave no such order,' said Leapman.

'But Sotheby's sent their van, and Dr Petrescu confirmed the instruction.'

'Petrescu was fired three days ago. Get me Sotheby's on the line, now.'

Ruth ran across to the phone and dialled the main number.

'Who does she deal with at Sotheby's?'

'Mark Poltimore,' Ruth said, handing the phone across to Leapman.

'Poltimore,' he barked, the moment he heard the word Sotheby's, then realized he was addressing an answering machine. Leapman slammed down the phone. 'Do you have his home number?'

'No,' said Ruth, 'but I have a mobile.'

'Then call it.'

Ruth quickly looked up the number on her palm pilot and began dialling again.

'Mark?' she said.

Leapman snatched the phone from her. 'Poltimore?'

'Speaking.'

'My name is Leapman. I'm the—'

'I know who you are, Mr Leapman,' said Mark.

'Good, because I understand you are in possession of our Van Gogh.'

'*Was*, would be more accurate,' replied Mark, 'until Dr Petrescu, your art director, informed us, even before we'd had a chance to examine the painting, that you'd had a change of heart and wanted the canvas taken straight back to Heathrow for immediate transport to New York.'

'And you went along with that?' said Leapman, his voice rising with every word.

'We had no choice, Mr Leapman. After all, it was her name on the manifest.'

25

'HI, IT'S VINCENT.'

'Hi. Is it true what I've just heard?'

'What have you heard?'

'That you've stolen the Van Gogh.'

'Have the police been informed?'

'No, he can't risk that, not least because our shares are still going south and the picture wasn't insured.'

'So what's he up to?'

'He's sending someone to London to track you down, but I can't find out who it is.'

'Maybe I won't be in London by the time they arrive.'

'Where will you be?'

'I'm going home.'

'And is the painting safe?'

'Safe as houses.'

'Good, but there's something else you ought to know.'

'What's that?'

'Fenston will be attending your funeral this afternoon.'

The phone went dead. Fifty-two seconds.

Anna replaced the receiver, even more concerned about the danger she was placing Tina in. What would Fenston do if he were to discover the reason she always managed to stay one step ahead of him?

She walked over to the departures desk.

'Do you have any bags to check in?' asked the woman

behind the counter. Anna heaved the red box off the luggage cart and onto the scales. She then placed her suitcase next to it.

'You're quite a bit over weight, madam,' the woman said. 'I'm afraid there will be an excess charge of thirty-two pounds.' Anna took the money out of her wallet while the woman attached a label to her suitcase and fixed a large 'fragile' sticker on the red box. 'Gate forty-three,' she said, handing her a ticket. 'They'll be boarding in about thirty minutes. Have a good flight.'

Anna began walking towards the departures gate.

Whoever Fenston was sending to London to track her down would be landing long after she had flown away. But Anna knew that they only had to read her report carefully to work out where the picture would be ending up. She just needed to be certain that she got there before they did. But first she had to make a phone call to someone she hadn't spoken to for over ten years, to warn him that she was on her way. Anna took the escalator to the first floor and joined a long line waiting to be checked through security.

'She's heading towards gate forty-three,' said a voice, 'and will be departing on flight BA 272 to Bucharest at eight forty-four . . .'

◄○►

Fenston squeezed himself into a line of dignitaries as President Bush and Mayor Giuliani shook hands with a selected group who were attending the latest service at Ground Zero.

He hung around until the President's helicopter had taken off and then walked across to join the other mourners. He took a place at the back of the crowd and listened as the names were read out. Each one followed by the single peal of a bell.

Greg Abbot.

He glanced around the crowd.

Kelly Gullickson.

He studied the faces of the relations and friends who had gathered in memory of their loved ones.

Anna Petrescu.

Fenston knew that Petrescu's mother lived in Bucharest and wouldn't be travelling to the service. He looked more carefully at the strangers who were huddled together, and wondered which one of them was Uncle George from Danville, Illinois.

Rebecca Rangere.

He glanced across at Tina. Tears were filling her eyes, certainly not for Petrescu.

Brulio Real Polanco.

The priest bowed his head. He delivered a prayer, then closed his Bible and made the sign of a cross. 'In the name of the Father, the Son and the Holy Ghost,' he declared.

'Amen,' came back the unison reply.

◄○►

Tina looked across at Fenston, not a tear shed, just the familiar movement from one foot to the other – the sign that he was bored. While others gathered in small groups to remember, sympathize and pay their respects, Fenston left without commiserating with anyone. No one else joined the chairman as he strode off purposefully towards his waiting car.

Tina stood among a little group of mourners, although her eyes remained fixed on Fenston. His driver was holding open the back door for him. Fenston climbed into the car and sat next to a woman Tina had never seen before. Neither spoke until the driver had returned to the front seat and touched a button on the dashboard to cause a smoked-glass screen to rise behind him. Without waiting, the car eased out into the road to join the midday traffic. Tina watched as the chairman disappeared out of sight. She hoped it wouldn't be long before Anna called again – so much to tell her, and now she had to find out who the waiting woman was. Were they discussing Anna? Had Tina put her friend in unnecessary danger? Where was the Van Gogh?

—◦—

The woman seated next to Fenston was dressed in a grey trouser suit. Anonymity was her most important asset. She had never once visited Fenston at either his office or his apartment, even though she had known him for almost twenty years. She'd first met Nicu Munteanu when he was bagman for President Nicolae Ceauşescu.

Fenston's primary responsibility during Ceauşescu's reign was to distribute vast sums of money into countless bank accounts across the world – backhanders for the dictator's loyal henchmen. When they ceased to be loyal, the woman seated next to Fenston eliminated them, and he then redistributed their frozen assets. Fenston's speciality was money laundering, to places as far afield as the Cook Islands and as close to home as Switzerland. Her speciality was to dispose of the bodies – her chosen instrument a kitchen knife, available in any hardware store in any city, and unlike a gun not requiring a licence. Both knew, literally, where the bodies were buried.

In 1985, Ceauşescu decided to send his private banker to New York to open an overseas branch for him. For the next four years, Fenston lost touch with the woman seated next to him, until in 1989 Ceauşescu was arrested by his fellow countrymen, tried and finally executed on Christmas Day. Among those who avoided the same fate was Olga Krantz, who crossed seven borders before she reached Mexico, from where she slipped into America to become one of the countless illegal immigrants who do not claim unemployment benefit and live off cash payments from an unscrupulous employer. She was sitting next to her employer.

Fenston was one of the few people alive who knew Krantz's true identity. He'd first watched her on television when she was fourteen years old and representing Romania in an international gymnastics competition against the Soviet Union.

Krantz came second to her team-mate Mara Moldoveanu, and the press were already tipping them for the gold and silver at the next Olympics. Unfortunately, neither of them made the journey to Moscow. Moldoveanu died in tragic, unforeseen circumstances, when she fell from the beam attempting a double somersault and broke her neck. Krantz was the only other person in the gymnasium at the time. She vowed to win the gold medal in her memory.

Krantz's exit was far less dramatic. She pulled a hamstring warming up for a floor exercise, only days before the Olympic team was selected. She knew she wouldn't be given a second chance. Like all athletes who don't quite make the grade, her name quickly disappeared from the headlines. Fenston assumed he would never hear of her again, until one morning he thought he saw her coming out of Ceauşescu's private office. The short, sinewy woman might have looked a little older, but she had lost none of her agile movement, and no one could forget those steel-grey eyes.

A few well-placed questions and Fenston learned that Krantz was now head of Ceauşescu's personal protection squad. Her particular responsibility: breaking selected bones of those who crossed the dictator or his wife.

Like all gymnasts, Krantz wanted to be number one

in her discipline. Having perfected all the routines in the compulsory section – broken arms, broken legs, broken necks – she moved on to her voluntary exercise, 'cut throats', a routine at which no one could challenge her for the gold medal. Hours of dedicated practice had resulted in perfection. While others attended a football match or went to the movies on a Saturday afternoon, Krantz spent her time at a slaughterhouse on the outskirts of Bucharest. She filled her weekend cutting the throats of lambs and calves. Her Olympic record was forty-two in an hour. None of the slaughtermen reached the final.

Ceauşescu had paid her well. Fenston paid her better. Krantz's terms of employment were simple. She must be available night and day, and work for no one else. In a space of twelve years, her fee had risen from $250,000 to $1 million. Not for her the hand-to-mouth existence of most illegal immigrants.

Fenston extracted a folder from his briefcase and handed it across to Krantz without comment. She turned the cover and studied five recent photographs of Anna Petrescu.

'Where is she at the moment?' asked Krantz, still unable to disguise her mid-European accent.

'London,' replied Fenston, before he passed her a second file.

Once again she opened it and this time extracted a single colour photograph. 'Who's he?' she enquired.

'He's even more important than the girl,' replied Fenston.

'How can that be possible?' Krantz asked as she studied the photo more carefully.

'Because he's irreplaceable,' Fenston explained, 'unlike Petrescu. But whatever you do, don't kill the girl until she's led you to the painting.'

'And if she doesn't?'

'She will,' said Fenston.

'And my payment for kidnapping a man who has already lost an ear?' enquired Krantz.

'One million dollars. Half in advance, the other half on the day you deliver him to me, unharmed.'

'And the girl?'

'The same tariff, but only after I have attended her funeral for the second time.' Fenston tapped the screen in front of him and the driver pulled in to the kerb. 'By the way,' said Fenston, 'I've already instructed Leapman to deposit the cash in the usual place.' Krantz nodded, opened the door, stepped out of the car and disappeared into the crowd.

9/15

26

'GOODBYE, SAM,' said Jack, as his cellphone began to play the first few bars of 'Danny Boy'. He let it go on ringing until he was back out on East 54th Street because he didn't want Sam to overhear the conversation. He pressed the green button as he continued walking towards 5th Avenue. 'What have you got for me, Joe?'

'Petrescu landed at Gatwick,' said Joe. 'She rented a car and drove straight to Wentworth Hall.'

'How long was she there?'

'Thirty minutes, no more. When she came out, she dropped into a local pub to make a phone call before travelling on to Heathrow, where she met up with Ruth Parish at the offices of Art Locations.' Jack didn't interrupt. 'Around four, a Sotheby's van turns up, picks up a red box—'

'Size?'

'About three foot by two.'

'No prizes for guessing what's inside,' said Jack. 'So where did the van go?'

'They delivered the painting to their West End office.'

'And Petrescu?'

'She goes along for the ride. When the van turned up in Bond Street, two porters unloaded the picture and she followed them in.'

'How long before she came back out?'

'Twenty minutes, and this time she was on her own, except she was carrying the red box. She hailed a taxi, put the painting in the back and disappeared.'

'Disappeared?' said Jack, his voice rising. 'What do you mean, disappeared?'

'We don't have too many spare agents at the moment,' said Joe. 'Most of our guys are working round the clock trying to identify terrorist groups that might have been involved in Tuesday's attacks.'

'Understood,' said Jack, calming down.

'But we picked her up again a few hours later.'

'Where?' asked Jack.

'Gatwick airport. Mind you,' said Joe, 'an attractive blonde carrying a red box does have a tendency to stand out in a crowd.'

'Agent Roberts would have missed her,' said Jack, as he hailed a cab.

'Agent Roberts?' queried Joe.

'Another time,' said Jack, climbing into the back of a cab. 'So where was she heading this time?'

'Bucharest.'

'Why would she want to take a priceless Van Gogh to Bucharest?' asked Jack.

'On Fenston's instructions, would be my bet,' said Joe. 'After all, it's his home town as well as hers, and I can't think of a better place to hide the picture.'

'Then why send Leapman to London if it wasn't to pick the painting up?'

'A smokescreen,' said Joe, 'which would also explain why Fenston attended her funeral when he knows only too well that she's alive and still working for him.'

'There is an alternative we have to consider,' said Jack.

'What's that, boss?'

'That she's no longer working for him, and she's stolen the Van Gogh.'

'Why would she risk that,' asked Joe, 'when he wouldn't hesitate to come after her?'

'I don't know, but there's only one way I'm going to find out.' Jack touched the red button on his phone, and gave the taxi driver an address on the West Side.

—◦—

Fenston switched off the recorder and frowned. Both of them had listened to the tape for a third time.

'When are you going to fire the bitch?' was all Leapman asked.

'Not while she's the one person who can still lead us to the painting,' Fenston replied.

Leapman scowled. 'And did you pick up the only word in their conversation that matters?' he asked. Fenston raised an eyebrow. '*Going*,' said Leapman. Fenston still didn't speak. 'If she'd used the word *coming*, "I'm coming home," it would have been New York.'

'But she used the word *going*,' said Fenston, 'so it has to be Bucharest.'

—◦—

Jack sat back in the cab seat and tried to work out what Petrescu's next move might be. He still couldn't make up his mind if she was a professional criminal or a complete amateur. And where did Tina Forster fit into the equation? Was it possible that Fenston, Leapman, Petrescu and Forster were all working together? If that was the case, why did Leapman only spend a few hours in London before returning to New York? Because he certainly didn't meet up with Petrescu, or take the painting back to New York.

But if Petrescu had branched out on her own, surely she realized that it would only be a matter of time before Fenston caught up with her. Although, Jack had to admit, Petrescu was now on her own ground, and didn't seem to have any idea how much danger she was in.

But Jack remained puzzled as to why Petrescu would steal a painting worth millions when she couldn't hope to dispose of such a well-known work without one of her former colleagues finding out. The art world was so small, and the number of people who could afford that sort of money even smaller. And even if she succeeded, what could she hope to do with the money? The FBI would trace such a large amount within hours, wherever she tried to hide it, especially after Tuesday's events. It just didn't add up.

But if she did take her audacious act to its obvious conclusion, Fenston was in for a nasty surprise, and no doubt would react in character.

As the taxi swung into Central Park, Jack tried to make some sense of all that had happened during the past few days. He had even wondered if he would be taken off the Fenston case after 9/11, but Macy insisted that not all of his agents should be following up terrorist leads while other criminals got away with murder.

Jack hadn't found it difficult to obtain a search warrant for Anna's apartment while she remained on the missing list. After all, relatives and friends needed to be contacted to find out if she had been in touch with them. And then there was the outside possibility, Jack had argued in front of a judge, that she might be locked in her apartment, recovering from the ordeal. The judge signed the order without too many questions.

'I hope you find her,' he said, a sentiment His Honour had cause to repeat several times that day.

Sam had burst into tears at just the mention of

Anna's name. He told Jack that he'd do anything to assist, and accompanied him up to her apartment and even opened the door.

Jack had walked around the small, tidy apartment, while Sam remained in the hallway. Jack hadn't learnt a great deal more than he already knew. An address book confirmed her uncle's number in Danville, Illinois, and an envelope showed her mother's address in Bucharest. Perhaps the only real surprise was a small Picasso drawing hanging in the hallway, signed in pencil by the artist. He studied the matador and the bull more closely, and it certainly wasn't a print. He couldn't believe she'd stolen it and then left the drawing in the hall for everyone to admire. Or was the drawing a bonus from Fenston for helping him to acquire the Van Gogh? If it was, it would at least explain what she was up to now. And then he walked into the bedroom and saw the one clue that confirmed that Tina had been in the apartment on the evening of 9/11. By the side of Anna's bed was a watch. Jack checked the time: 8.46.

Jack returned to the main room and glanced at a photograph on the corner of the writing desk of what must have been Anna with her parents. He opened a box file, to discover a bundle of letters that he couldn't read. Most of them were signed 'Mama' although one or two were from someone called Anton. Jack wondered if he was a relation or a friend. He looked back up at the photograph and couldn't help thinking that if his mother had seen the picture, she would have invited Anna back to sample her Irish stew.

'Damn,' said Jack, loud enough for the cab driver to ask, 'What's the problem?'

'I forgot to phone my mother.'

'Then you're in big trouble,' said the driver. 'I should know, I'm Irish too.'

Hell, is it that obvious? thought Jack. Mind you, he should have called his mother to let her know that he wouldn't be able to make 'Irish stew night', when he usually joined his parents to celebrate the natural superiority of the Gaelic race over all God's other creatures. It didn't help that he was an only child. He must try to remember to call her from London.

His father had wanted Jack to be a lawyer, and both his parents had made sacrifices to make it possible. After twenty-six years with the NYPD, Jack's father had come to the conclusion that the only people who made a profit out of crime were the lawyers and the criminals, so he felt his son ought to make up his mind which he was going to be.

Despite his father's cryptic advice, Jack signed up for the FBI, only days after he had graduated from Columbia with a law degree. His father continued to grumble every Saturday about him not being a lawyer, and his mother kept asking if he was ever going to make her a grandmother.

Jack enjoyed every aspect of the job, from the first moment he arrived at Quantico for training, to joining the New York field office, to being promoted to Senior Investigating Officer. He seemed to be the only person who was surprised when he was the first among his contemporaries to be promoted. Even his father begrudgingly congratulated him, before he added, 'Only proves what a damn good lawyer you would have made.'

Macy had also made it clear that he hoped Jack would take over from him once he was transferred back to Washington DC. But before that could happen, Jack still had to put in jail a man who was turning any such thoughts of promotion into fantasies. And so far, Jack had to admit, he hadn't so much as landed a glove on Bryce Fenston, and was now having to rely on an amateur to deliver the knock-out punch.

He stopped day-dreaming, and put a call through to his secretary.

'Sally, book me on the first available flight to London, with an onward connection to Bucharest. I'm on my way home to pack.'

'I ought to warn you, Jack,' his secretary replied, 'that JFK is stacked solid for the next week.'

'Sally, just get me on a plane to London, and I don't care if I'm sitting next to the pilot.'

◄○►

The rules were simple. Krantz stole a new cellphone every day. She'd call the chairman once, and when the conversation was finished dispose of the phone. That way, no one could ever trace her.

Fenston was sitting at his desk when the little red light flashed on his private line. Only one person had that number. He picked up the phone.

'Where is she?'

'Bucharest,' was all he said, and then replaced the receiver.

Krantz dropped today's cellphone into the Thames and hailed a cab.

'Gatwick.'

◄○►

When Jack came down the steps at Heathrow, he wasn't surprised to find Tom Crasanti standing on the runway waiting for him. A car was parked behind his old friend, engine running, the back door held open by another agent.

Neither of them spoke until the door was closed and the car was on the move.

'Where's Petrescu?' was Jack's first question.

'She's landed in Bucharest.'

'And the painting?'

'She wheeled it out of customs on a baggage trolley,' said Tom.

'That woman's got style.'

'Agreed,' said Tom, 'but then perhaps she has no idea what she's up against.'

'I suspect she's about to find out,' said Jack, 'because one thing's for sure: if she stole the painting, I won't be the only person out there looking for her.'

'Then you'll have to keep an eye out for them as well,' said Tom.

'You're right about that,' said Jack, 'and that's assuming I get to Bucharest before she's moved on to her next destination.'

'Then there's no time to waste,' said Tom, before adding, 'We've got a helicopter standing by to take you to Gatwick, and they're holding up the flight to Bucharest for thirty minutes.'

'How did you manage that?' asked Jack.

'The helicopter is ours, the hold-up is theirs. The ambassador called the Foreign Office. I don't know what he said,' admitted Tom, as they came to a halt beside the helicopter, 'but you've only got thirty minutes.'

'Thanks for everything,' said Jack, as he stepped out of the car and began to walk towards the helicopter.

'And try not to forget,' Tom shouted above the noise of the whirring blades, 'we don't have an official presence in Bucharest, so you'll be on your own.'

27

ANNA STEPPED ONTO the concourse of Otopeni, Bucharest's international airport, pushing a trolley laden with a wooden crate, a large case and a laptop. She stopped in her tracks when she saw a man rushing towards her.

Anna stared at him suspiciously. He was around five nine, balding, with a ruddy complexion and a thick black moustache. He must have been over sixty. He wore a tight-fitting suit, which suggested he'd once been slimmer. He came to a halt in front of Anna.

'I'm Sergei,' he announced in his native tongue. 'Anton told me you'd called and asked to be picked up. He has already booked you into a small hotel downtown.' Sergei took Anna's trolley and pushed it towards his waiting taxi. He opened the back door of a yellow Mercedes that already had 300,000 miles on the clock, and waited until Anna had stepped in before he loaded her luggage into the trunk and took his place behind the wheel.

Anna stared out of the taxi window and thought how the city had changed since her birth – it was now a thrusting, energetic capital, demanding its place at the European table. Modern office buildings and a fashionable shopping centre had replaced the drab Communist grey-tiled façade of only a decade before.

Sergei drew up outside a small hotel tucked away down a narrow street. He lifted the red crate out of the trunk while Anna took the rest of the luggage and headed into the hotel.

'I'd like to visit my mother first thing,' said Anna once she'd checked in.

Sergei looked at his watch. 'I'll pick you up around nine. That will give you the chance to grab a few hours' sleep.'

'Thank you,' said Anna.

He watched as she disappeared into the lift, carrying the red box.

—◦—

Jack had first spotted her when he was standing in line to board the plane. It's a basic surveillance technique: hang back, just in case you're being followed. The trick, then, is not to let the pursuer realize that you're on to them. Act normal, never look back. Not easy.

His class supervisor at Quantico would carry out a surveillance detection run every evening after class, when he would follow one of the new recruits home. If you managed to lose him, you were singled out for a commendation. Jack went one better. Having lost him, he then carried out an SDR on his supervisor and followed *him* home without being spotted.

Jack climbed the steps of the plane. He didn't look back.

—◦—

When Anna strolled out of her hotel a few minutes after nine, she found Sergei standing by his old Mercedes waiting for her.

'Good morning, Sergei,' she said as he opened the back door for her.

'Good morning, madam. Do you still wish to visit your mother?'

184

'Yes,' replied Anna. 'She lives at—'

Sergei waved a hand to make it clear that he knew exactly where to take her.

Anna smiled with pleasure as he drove through the centre of town past a magnificent fountain that would have graced a lawn at Versailles. But once Sergei had reached the outskirts of the city, the picture quickly changed from colour to black and white. By the time her driver had reached the neglected outpost of Berceni, Anna realized that the new regime still had a long way to go if they were to achieve the prosperity-for-all programme they had promised the voters following the downfall of Ceauşescu. Anna had, in the space of a few miles, returned to the more familiar scenes of her youth. She found many of her countrymen downcast, looking older than their years. Only the young kids playing football in the street seemed unaware of the degradation that surrounded them. It appalled Anna that her mother was still so adamant about remaining in her birthplace after her father had been killed in the uprising. She had tried so many times to convince her to join them in America, but she wouldn't be budged.

In 1987 Anna had been invited to visit Illinois by an uncle she had never met. He'd even sent her two hundred dollars to assist with her passage. Her father told her to leave, and leave quickly, but it was her mother who predicted that she would never come back. She purchased a one-way ticket, and her uncle promised to pay for the return journey whenever she wanted to go home.

Anna was seventeen at the time, and she had fallen in love with America even before the boat had docked. A few weeks later, Ceauşescu began his crackdown on any individual who dared to oppose his draconian regime. Her father wrote to warn Anna that it was not safe for her to come home.

That was his last letter. Three weeks later he joined the rebels, and was never seen again.

Anna missed her mother dreadfully and repeatedly begged her to join them in Illinois. But her response was always the same. 'This is my homeland, where I was born, and where I shall die. I am too old to begin a new life.' Too old, Anna had remonstrated. Her mother was only fifty-one, but they were fifty-one stubborn Romanian years, so Anna reluctantly accepted that nothing would change her mind. A month later, her uncle George enrolled Anna in a local school. While civil unrest in Romania continued unabated, Anna graduated from college and later accepted the opportunity to study for a PhD at Penn, in a discipline that had no language barriers.

Dr Petrescu still wrote to her mother every month, only too aware that most of her letters were not reaching her because the spasmodic replies often asked questions she had already answered.

The first decision Anna made after she left college and joined Sotheby's was to open a separate bank account for her mother in Bucharest, to which she transferred $400 by standing order on the first day of every month. Although she would rather have . . .

'I'll wait for you,' said Sergei, as the taxi finally came to a halt outside a dilapidated block of flats in Piazza Resitei.

'Thank you,' said Anna, as she looked out at the pre-war estate where she was born, and where her mother still lived. Anna could only wonder what Mama had spent the money on. She stepped out onto the weed-covered path that she had once thought so wide because she couldn't jump across it.

The children playing football in the road watched

suspiciously as the stranger in her smart linen jacket, jeans with fashionable tears and fancy sneakers walked up the worn, pot-holed path. They also wore jeans with tears. The elevator didn't respond to Anna's button-pressing – nothing changes – which was why, Anna recalled, the most sought-after flats were always those on the lower floors. She couldn't understand why her mother hadn't moved years ago. Anna had sent more than enough money for her to rent a comfortable apartment on the other side of town. Anna's feeling of guilt grew the higher up she climbed. She had forgotten just how dreadful it was, but like the children playing football in the street, it had once been all she knew.

When Anna eventually reached the sixteenth floor, she stopped to catch her breath. No wonder her mother so rarely left the flat. On the floors above her resided sixty-year-olds who were housebound. Anna hesitated before she knocked on a door that hadn't seen a splash of paint since she'd last stood there.

She waited for some time before a frail, white-haired lady, dressed from head to toe in black, pulled the door open, but by only a few inches. Mother and daughter stared at each other, until suddenly Elsa Petrescu flung open the door, threw her arms round her daughter and shouted in a voice as old as she looked, 'Anna, Anna, Anna.' Both mother and daughter burst into tears.

The old lady continued to cling onto Anna's hand as she led her into the flat in which she had been born. It was spotless, and Anna could still remember everything, because nothing had changed. The sofa and chairs her grandmother had left them, the family photographs, all black and white unframed, a coal scuttle with no coal, a rug that was so worn it was hard to make out the original pattern. The only new addition to the room was a magnificent painting that hung on otherwise blank walls. As Anna admired the portrait of her father, she was reminded where her love of art had begun.

'Anna, Anna, so many questions to ask,' her mother said. 'Where do I begin?' she asked, still clutching her daughter's hand.

The sun was setting before Anna had responded to every one of her mother's questions, and then she begged once again, 'Please, Mama, come back with me and live in America.'

'No,' she replied defiantly, 'all my friends and all my memories are here. I am too old to begin a new life.'

'Then why not move to another part of the city? I could find you something on a lower—'

'This is where I was married,' her mother said quietly, 'where you were born, where I lived for over thirty years with your beloved father, and where, when God decrees it is my time, I shall die.' She smiled up at her daughter. 'Who would tend your father's grave?' she asked as if she'd never asked the question before. She looked into her daughter's eyes. 'You know he was so pleased to see you settled in America with his brother –' she paused – 'and now I can see that he was right.'

Anna looked round the room. 'But why haven't you spent some of the money I've been sending to you each month?'

'I have,' she said firmly, 'but not on myself,' she admitted, 'because I want for nothing.'

'Then what have you spent it on?' Anna queried.

'Anton.'

'Anton?' repeated Anna.

'Yes, Anton,' said her mother. 'You knew that he'd been released from jail?'

'Oh yes,' said Anna, 'he wrote to me soon after Ceauşescu was arrested to ask if I had a photo of Papa that he could borrow.' Anna smiled as she looked up at the painting of her father.

'It's a good likeness,' said her mother.

'It certainly is,' said Anna.

'They gave him back his old job at the academy. He's now the Professor of Perspective. If you'd married him, you would be a professor's wife.'

'Is he still painting?' she asked, avoiding her mother's next inevitable question.

'Yes,' she replied, 'but his main responsibility is to teach the graduates at the Universitatea de Arte. You can't make a living as an artist in Romania,' she said sadly. 'You know, with his talent, Anton should also have gone to America.'

Anna looked up again at Anton's magnificent portrait of her father. Her mother was right; with such a gift, he would have flourished in New York. 'But what does he do with the money?' she asked.

'He buys canvases, paints, brushes and all those materials that his pupils can't afford, so you see, your generosity is being put to good use.' She paused. 'Anton was your first love, Anna, yes?'

Anna wouldn't have believed that her mother could still make her blush. 'Yes,' she admitted, 'and I suspect I was his.'

'He's married now, and they have a little boy called Peter.' She paused again. 'Do you have a young man?'

'No, Mama.'

'Is that what brings you back home? Are you running away from something, or someone?'

'What makes you ask that?' Anna asked defensively.

'There is a sadness in your eyes, and fear,' she said, looking up at her daughter, 'which you could never hide as a child.'

'I do have one or two problems,' admitted Anna, 'but

nothing that time won't sort out.' She smiled. 'In fact, I rather think that Anton might be able to help me with one of them, and I'm hoping to join him at the academy for a drink. Do you have any message you want passed on?' Her mother didn't reply. She had quietly dozed off. Anna rearranged the rug on her mother's lap and kissed her on the forehead. 'I'll be back again tomorrow morning, Mama,' she whispered.

She slipped silently out of the room. As she walked back down the littered staircase, she was pleased to see the old yellow Mercedes was still parked by the kerb.

28

ANNA RETURNED TO her hotel, and after a quick shower and change of clothes, her newly acquired chauffeur took her to the Academy of Art on Piata Universitatii.

The building had lost none of its elegance or charm with the passing of time, and when Anna climbed the steps towards the massive sculptured doors, memories came flooding back of her introduction to the great works of art hanging in galleries she thought she would never see. Anna reported to the front desk and asked where Professor Teodorescu's lecture was taking place.

'In the main theatre on the third floor,' said the girl behind the counter, 'but it has already started.'

Anna thanked the young student and, without asking for any directions, climbed the wide marble staircase to the third floor. She stopped to glance at a poster outside the hall:

THE INFLUENCE OF PICASSO ON TWENTIETH-CENTURY ART

Professor Anton Teodorescu

TONIGHT, 7.00PM →

She didn't require the arrow to point her in the right direction. Anna gingerly pushed open the door, pleased to find that the lecture theatre was in darkness. She walked up the steps at the side of the hall and took a seat towards the back.

A slide of *Guernica* filled the screen. Anton was explaining that the massive canvas was painted in 1937, at the time of the Spanish Civil War, when Picasso was at the height of his powers. He went on to say that the depiction of the bombing and the resulting carnage had taken Picasso three weeks, and the image was unquestionably influenced by the artist's hatred of the Spanish dictator, Franco. The students were listening attentively, several taking notes. Anton's bravura performance reminded Anna why she'd had a crush on him all those years ago, when she not only lost her virginity to an artist, but began a life-long love affair with art.

When Anton's presentation came to an end, the rapturous applause left Anna in no doubt how much the undergraduates had enjoyed his lecture. He'd lost none of his skill in motivating and nurturing the young's enthusiasm for their chosen subject.

Anna watched her first love as he collected together his slides and began to put them in an old briefcase. Tall and angular, his mop of curly dark hair, ancient brown corduroy jacket and open-neck shirt gave him the air of a perpetual student. She couldn't help noticing that he had put on a few pounds, but she didn't feel it made him any less attractive. When the last student had filed out, Anna made her way to the front of the hall.

Anton glanced up over his half-moon spectacles, apparently anticipating a question from the student who was approaching him. When he first saw Anna, he didn't speak, just stared.

'Anna,' he finally exclaimed. 'Thank God I didn't realize you were in the audience, as you probably know more about Picasso than I do.'

Anna kissed him on both cheeks and said with a laugh, 'You've lost none of your charm, or ability to flatter.'

Anton held up his hands in mock defeat, grinning widely. 'Was Sergei at the airport to pick you up?'

'Yes, thank you,' said Anna. 'Where did you meet him?'

'In jail,' admitted Anton. 'He was lucky to survive the Ceauşescu regime. And have you visited your sainted mother?'

'I have,' replied Anna, 'and she's still living in conditions not much better than a jail.'

'I agree, and don't think I haven't tried to do something about it, but at least your dollars, and her generosity, allow some of my best students to—'

'I know,' said Anna, 'she's already told me.'

'You can't begin to know,' continued Anton. 'So let me show you some of the results of your investment.'

Anton took Anna by the hand as if they were still students and guided her down the steps to the long corridor on the first floor, where the walls were crammed with paintings in every medium.

'This year's prize-winning students,' he told her, holding out his arms like a proud father. 'And every entry has been painted on a canvas supplied by you. In fact, one of the awards is in your name – the Petrescu Prize.' He paused. 'How appropriate if you were to select the winner, which would make not only me, but one of my students, very proud.'

'I'm flattered,' said Anna with a smile, as she walked towards a long row of paintings. She took her time as she strolled slowly up and down the canvas-filled corridor, pausing occasionally to study an image more closely. Anton had clearly taught them the importance of drawing before he allowed them to move on to other media. *Don't bother with the brush if you can't first handle the pencil*, he liked to repeat. But the range of subjects and bold approach showed that he had also let them express themselves. Some didn't quite come off, while others showed considerable talent. Anna finally stopped in front of an oil entitled *Freedom*, depicting the sun rising over Bucharest.

'I know a certain gentleman who'll appreciate that,' she said.

'You haven't lost your touch,' said Anton, smiling. 'Danuta Sekalska is this year's star pupil, and she's been offered a place at the Slade in London to continue her studies, if only we can raise enough money to cover her expenses.' He looked at his watch. 'Do you have time for a drink?'

'I certainly do,' replied Anna, 'because I confess there's a favour I need to ask of you – ' she paused – 'in fact, two favours.'

Anton once again took her by the hand and led her back down the corridor towards the staff refectory. When they entered the senior common room, Anna was greeted by the sound of good-humoured chatter as tutors swapped anecdotes while they sat around in groups enjoying nothing stronger than a coffee. They didn't seem to notice that the furniture, the cups, saucers and probably even the cookies would have been rejected by any self-respecting hobo visiting a Salvation Army hostel in the Bronx.

Anton poured two cups of coffee. 'Black, if I remember. Not quite Starbucks,' he mocked, 'but we're getting there slowly.' Heads turned as Anton guided his former pupil to a place by the fire. He took a seat opposite her. 'Now, what can I do for you, Anna?' he asked. 'Because I am unquestionably in your debt.'

'It's my mother,' she said quietly. 'I need your help. I can't get her to spend a cent on herself. She could do with a new carpet, sofa, a TV and even a telephone, not to mention a splash of fresh paint on that front door.'

'You think I haven't tried?' Anton repeated. 'Where do you imagine you get your stubborn streak from? I even suggested she move in with us. It's not palatial, but it's a damn sight better than that dump she's living in now.' Anton took a long draught of his coffee. 'But I promise I'll try again – ' he paused – 'even harder.'

'Thank you,' said Anna, who remained silent while Anton rolled a cigarette. 'And I see I failed to convince you to give up smoking.'

'I don't have the bright lights of New York to distract me,' he said with a laugh. He lit his hand-rolled cigarette before adding, 'And what's the second favour?'

'You'll need to think long and hard about it,' she said in an even tone.

Anton put down his coffee, inhaled deeply and listened carefully as Anna explained in detail how he could help her.

'Have you discussed the idea with your mother?'

'No,' Anna admitted. 'I think it's best she doesn't find out why I really came to Bucharest.'

'How much time have I got?'

'Three, perhaps four days. Depends how successful I am while I'm away,' she added without explanation.

'And if I'm caught?' he asked, once again dragging deeply on his cigarette.

'You'd probably go back to jail,' admitted Anna.

'And you?'

'The canvas would be shipped to New York and used as evidence against me. If you need any more money for—'

'No, I'm still holding over eight thousand dollars of your mother's money, so—'

'Eight thousand?'

'A dollar goes a long way in Romania.'

'Can I bribe you?'

'Bribe me?'

'If you'll take on the assignment, I'll pay for your pupil, Danuta Sekalska, to go to the Slade.'

Anton thought for a moment. 'And you'll be back in three days,' he said, stubbing out his cigarette.

'Four at the most,' said Anna.

'Then let's hope I'm as good as you think I am.'

—◦—

'It's Vincent.'

'Where are you?'

'Visiting my mother.'

'Then don't hang about.'

'Why?'

'The stalker knows where you are.'

'Then I'm afraid he'll miss me again.'

'I'm not even convinced the stalker's a man.'

'What makes you say that?'

'I saw Fenston talking to a woman in the back of his car while I was attending your funeral.'

'That doesn't prove—'

'I agree, but it worries me that I've never seen her before.'

'She could be one of Fenston's girlfriends.'

'That woman was nobody's girlfriend.'

'Describe her.'

'Five foot, slim, dark-haired.'

'There will be a lot of people like that where I'm going.'

'And are you taking the painting with you?'

'No, I've left it where no one can give it a second look.'

The phone went dead.

—◦—

Leapman pressed the off button. 'Where no one can give it a second look,' he repeated.

'*Can*, not will?' said Fenston. 'It must still be in the box.'

'Agreed, but where's she off to next?'

'To a country where the people are five foot, slim and dark haired.'

'Japan,' said Leapman.

'How can you be so sure?' asked Fenston.

'It's all in her report. She's going to try and sell your painting to the one person who won't be able to resist it.'

'Nakamura,' said Fenston.

9/16

29

JACK HAD CHECKED IN at what was ambitiously described on a flashing neon sign as the Bucharesti International. He spent most of the night either turning the radiator up because it was so cold, or turning it off because it was so noisy. He rose just after 6.00am and skipped breakfast, fearing it might be as unreliable as the radiator.

He hadn't spotted the woman again since he stepped onto the plane, so either he'd made a mistake, or she was a professional. But he was no longer in any doubt that Anna was working independently, which meant Fenston would soon be dispatching someone to retrieve the Van Gogh. But what did Petrescu have in mind, and didn't she realize what danger she was putting herself in? Jack had already decided the most likely place to catch up with Anna would be when she visited her mother. This time he'd be waiting for her. He wondered if the woman he'd seen when he stood in line for the plane had the same idea, and, if so, was she Fenston's retriever or did she work for someone else?

The hotel porter offered him a tourist map, which colourfully detailed the finer parts of the city centre but not the outskirts, so he walked across to the kiosk and purchased a guidebook entitled *Everything You Need to Know About Bucharest*. There wasn't a single paragraph devoted to the Berceni district where Anna's mother lived, although they were considerate enough to include

Piazza Resitei on the larger fold-out map at the back. With the aid of a matchstick placed against the scale at the bottom left-hand corner of the page, Jack worked out that Anna's birthplace must be about six miles north of the hotel.

He decided he would walk the first three miles, not least because he needed the exercise, but also because it would give him a better chance to discover if he was the target of an SDR.

Jack left the International at 7.30am, and set off at a brisk pace.

◄○►

Anna also had a restless night, finding it hard to sleep while the red box was under her bed. She was beginning to have doubts about Anton taking on such an unnecessary risk to assist her in her plan, even if it was only for a few days. They'd agreed to meet at the academy at eight o'clock, an hour no self-respecting student would admit existed.

When she stepped out of the hotel, the first thing she saw was Sergei in his old Mercedes parked by the entrance. She wondered how long he'd been waiting for her. Sergei jumped out of the car.

'Good morning, madam,' he said as he loaded the red box back into the trunk.

'Good morning, Sergei,' Anna replied. 'I would like to go back to the academy, where I'll be leaving the crate.' Sergei nodded, and opened the back door for her.

On the journey over to the Piata Universitatii, Anna learnt that Sergei had a wife, that they had been married for over thirty years and had a son who was serving in the army. Anna was about to ask if he'd ever met her father, when she spotted Anton, standing on the bottom step of the academy, looking anxious and fidgeting.

Sergei brought the car to a halt, jumped out and unloaded the crate from the trunk.

'Is that it?' asked Anton, viewing the red box suspiciously. Anna nodded. Anton joined Sergei as he carried the crate up the steps. Anton opened the front door for him and they both disappeared inside the building.

Anna kept checking her watch every few moments and looking back up the steps towards the entrance. They were only away for a few minutes, but she never felt alone. Was Fenston's stalker watching her even now? Had he worked out where the Van Gogh was? The two men finally reappeared carrying another wooden box. Although it was exactly the same size, the plain slats of timber were unmarked in any way. Sergei placed the new crate in the trunk of the Mercedes, slammed the lid down and climbed back behind the wheel.

'Thank you,' said Anna, before kissing Anton on both cheeks.

'I won't be getting much sleep while you're away,' Anton mumbled.

'I'll be back, three, four days at the most,' Anna promised, 'when I'll happily take the painting off your hands and no one will be any the wiser.' She climbed into the back of the car.

As Sergei drove away, she stared through the rear window at the forlorn figure of Anton, who was standing on the bottom step of the academy, looking worried. Was he up to the job? she wondered.

–◇–

Jack didn't look back, but once he'd covered the first mile, he slipped into a large supermarket and disappeared

peared behind a pillar. He waited for her to walk by. She didn't. An amateur would have strolled past and been unable to resist glancing in, and might even have been tempted to enter the building. He didn't hang around for too long, knowing it would make her suspicious. He bought a bacon and egg baguette and walked back onto the road. As he munched his breakfast, he tried to work out why he was being followed. Who did she represent? What was her brief? Was she hoping he would lead her to Anna, was he a selected target for counter-surveillance – the unspoken fear of every FBI agent – or was he just paranoid?

Once he was out of the city centre, Jack stopped to study the map. He decided to grab a taxi, as he doubted he'd be able to pick one up in the Berceni district, when he might need to make a speedy exit. Jumping into a taxi might also make it easier for him to lose his tail, as a yellow cab would be more conspicuous once they were no longer in the city centre. He rechecked his map, turned left at the next corner and didn't look back or even glance into the shop window with its large plate-glass pane. If she was a pro, it would be a dead giveaway. He hailed a cab.

⟨o⟩

Anna asked her driver – as she now thought of Sergei – to take her back to the same block of flats they'd visited the previous day. Anna would have liked to call and warn her mother what time to expect her, but it wasn't possible because Elsa Petrescu didn't approve of phones. They were like elevators, she'd once told her daughter: when they break down, no one comes to repair them, and in any case they create unnecessary bills. Anna knew her mother would have risen by six to be sure everything, in her already spotless flat, had been dusted and polished for a third time.

When Sergei parked at the end of the weed-strewn path of the Piazza Resitei, Anna told him that she expected to be about an hour, and then wanted to go to Otopeni airport. Sergei nodded.

◅◦▻

A taxi drew up beside him. Jack strolled round to the driver's side, and motioned for him to wind down the window.

'Do you speak English?'

'A little,' said the driver hesitantly.

Jack opened his map and pointed to Piazza Resitei, before taking a seat behind the driver. The taxi driver grimaced in disbelief, and looked up at Jack to double-check. Jack nodded. The driver shrugged his shoulders and set out on a journey no tourist had ever requested before.

The taxi slipped out into the middle lane and both of them checked the rear-view mirror. Another taxi was following them. There was no sign of any passenger, but then she wouldn't have sat in the front. Had he lost her, or was she in one of three taxis he could now see in the rear-view mirror? She was a pro, she'd be in one of those taxis, and he had the feeling she knew exactly where he was going.

Jack knew that every major city has its run-down districts, but he had never experienced anything quite like Berceni, with its grim, high-rise concrete blocks that littered every corner of what could only be described as a desolate slum. Even the graffiti would have been frowned on in Harlem.

The taxi was already slowing down when Jack spotted

205

another yellow Mercedes parked by the kerb a few yards ahead of them, in a street that hadn't seen two taxis in the same year.

'Drive on,' he said sharply, but the taxi continued to slow. Jack tapped the driver firmly on the shoulder and waved frantically forward to suggest he should keep going.

'But, this is place you ask for,' insisted the driver.

'Keep moving,' shouted Jack.

The puzzled driver shrugged his shoulders and accelerated past the stationary taxi.

'Turn at the next corner,' said Jack, pointing left. The driver nodded, now looking even more perplexed. He awaited his next instruction. 'Turn back round,' Jack said slowly, 'and stop at the end of the road.'

The driver carried out his new instruction, continually glancing back at Jack, the perplexed expression never leaving his face.

Once he'd parked, Jack got out of the car and walked slowly to the corner, cursing his unforced error. He wondered where the woman was, because she clearly hadn't made the same mistake. He should have anticipated that Anna might already be there, and her only form of transport was likely to be a taxi.

Jack stared up at the grey concrete block where Anna was visiting her mother, and swore he'd never complain about his cramped one-bedroom apartment on the West Side ever again. He had to wait another forty minutes before Anna emerged from the building. He remained still as she walked back down the path to her taxi.

Jack jumped back into his own cab and, pointing frantically, said, 'Follow them, but keep your distance until the traffic is heavier.' He wasn't even sure that the driver understood what he said. The taxi drove out of the side road, and although Jack kept tapping the driver's shoulder and repeating, 'Hold back,' the two yellow cabs must have looked like camels in a desert as they drove through the empty streets. Jack cursed again, knowing he was burnt. Even an amateur would have spotted him by now.

◆

'You do realize that someone is following you?' Sergei said, as he drove off.

'No, but I'm not surprised,' Anna replied, but she still felt cold and sick now that Sergei had confirmed her worst fear. 'Did you get a look at them?' she asked.

'Only a glimpse,' Sergei replied. 'A man, around thirty, thirty-five, slim, dark hair, not much else, I'm afraid.' So Tina was wrong when she thought the stalker was a woman, was Anna's first reaction. 'And he's a professional,' added Sergei.

'What makes you say that?' asked Anna anxiously.

'When the taxi passed me, he didn't look back,' said Sergei. 'Mind you, I can't tell you which side of the law he's on.'

Anna shivered, as Sergei checked his rear-view mirror. 'And I'm pretty sure he's following us now, but don't look round,' said Sergei sharply, 'because then he'll know you've spotted him.'

'Thank you,' said Anna.

'Do you still want me to take you to the airport?'

'I don't have any choice,' Anna replied.

'I could lose him,' said Sergei, 'but then he *would* know that you were on to him.'

'Not much point,' said Anna. 'He already knows where I'm going.'

◆

Jack always carried his passport, wallet and credit card with him in case of just such an emergency. 'Damn,' he said, when he saw the sign for the airport and remembered his unpacked suitcase sitting in the hotel room.

Three or four other taxis were also heading in the direction of Otopeni airport, and Jack wondered which one the woman was in, whether she was already at the airport and booked on the same flight as Anna Petrescu.

—◦—

Anna handed Sergei a twenty-dollar bill, long before they'd reached Otopeni, and told him which flight she was booked to return on.

'Would you be able to pick me up?' she asked.

'Of course,' promised Sergei, as he came to a halt outside the international terminal.

'Is he still following us?' Anna asked.

'Yes,' Sergei replied, as he jumped out of the car.

A porter appeared, and helped load the crate and her suitcase onto a trolley.

'I'll be here when you return,' Sergei assured Anna, before she disappeared into the terminal.

Jack's cab screeched to a halt behind the yellow Mercedes. He leapt out and ran towards the driver's window, waving a ten-dollar bill. Sergei wound the window down slowly and took the proffered money. Jack smiled.

'The lady in your cab, do you know where she's going?'

'Yes,' replied Sergei, stroking his thick moustache.

Jack peeled off another ten-dollar bill, which Sergei happily pocketed.

'Well, where?' demanded Jack.

'Abroad,' replied Sergei, put the car into first gear and drove off.

Jack cursed, ran back to his own cab, paid the fare – three dollars – and walked quickly into the airport. He stood still while checking in every direction. Moments later he spotted Anna leaving the check-in counter and heading towards the escalator. He didn't move again until she was out of sight. By the time he had reached the top of the escalator, Anna was already in the cafe. She'd taken a seat in the far corner from where she could observe everything and, more important, everybody. Not only was *he* being followed, but now the person he was following was also looking out for him. She had already mastered being a tool, so she could identify her target. Jack feared that this could end up as a case study at Quantico on how not to trail a suspect.

He retraced his steps back down to the ground floor and checked the departure board. There were only five international flights out of Bucharest that day: Moscow, Hong Kong, New Delhi, London and Berlin.

Jack dismissed Moscow, as it was due to depart in forty minutes and Anna was still in the cafe. New Delhi and Berlin weren't scheduled to leave until the early evening, and he also considered Hong Kong unlikely, although it departed in just under two hours, while the London flight was fifteen minutes later. It had to be London, he decided, but he still couldn't take the risk. He would purchase two tickets, one for Hong Kong, and a second for London. If she didn't appear at the departure gate for Hong Kong, he would board the flight to Heathrow. He wondered if her other pursuer was considering the same options, although he had a feeling she already knew which flight Anna was on.

Once Jack had purchased both tickets, and explained twice that he had no luggage, he headed straight for Gate 33 to carry out a point surveillance. When he arrived, he took a seat among those passengers who were waiting at Gate 31 for the departure of their flight to Moscow. Jack even gave a moment's thought to going back to the hotel, packing his bags, paying the bill and then returning to the airport, but only a moment's thought, because if the choice was between losing his bags or losing his quarry, it wasn't much of a choice.

Jack called the hotel manager at the Bucharesti International on his cellphone, and without going into any detail explained what he needed doing. He could imagine the puzzled expression on the manager's face when he asked for his bags to be packed and left in reception. However, his suggestion that they add twenty dollars to his bill elicited the response, 'I'll deal with it personally, sir.'

Jack began to wonder if Anna was simply using the airport as a decoy, while actually planning to return to Bucharest and pick up the red crate. He certainly couldn't have acted in a more unprofessional manner when he chased after her driver. But if she had worked out that someone was following her, as an amateur her first reaction would have been to try and lose her pursuer as quickly as possible. Only a professional would consider such a devious ploy when trying to shake someone off. Was it possible that Anna was a professional, and still working for Fenston? In which case, was he the one being pursued?

Flight 3211 to Moscow was already boarding when Anna strolled by. She looked relaxed as she took her place among those waiting to board Cathay Pacific flight 017 to Hong Kong. Once she was seated in the lounge, Jack slipped back down to the concourse and kept out of sight while he waited for the final call of flight 017. Forty minutes later, he ascended the escalator a third time.

All three of them boarded the Boeing 747 bound for Hong Kong, at different times. One in first class, one in business and one in economy.

9/17

30

'I'M SORRY to interrupt you, m'lady, but a large box of documents has been delivered by Simpson and Simpson, and I wondered where you wished me to put it.'

Arabella put down her pen and looked up from the writing desk. 'Andrews, do you remember when I was a child and you were second butler?'

'I do, m'lady,' said Andrews, sounding somewhat puzzled.

'And every Christmas we used to play a game called Hunt the Parcel?'

'We did indeed, m'lady.'

'And one Christmas you hid a box of chocolates. Victoria and I spent an entire afternoon trying to find them – but we never did.'

'Yes, m'lady. Lady Victoria accused me of eating them and burst into tears.'

'But you still refused to tell her where they were.'

'That is correct, m'lady, but I must confess your father promised me sixpence if I didn't reveal where they were hidden.'

'Why did he do that?' asked Arabella.

'His lordship hoped to spend a peaceful Christmas afternoon, enjoying a glass of port and a leisurely cigar, happy in the knowledge that you were both fully occupied.'

'But we never found them,' said Arabella.

'And I was never paid my sixpence,' said Andrews.

'Can you still recall where you hid them?'

Andrews considered the question for a few moments, before a smile appeared on his face.

'Yes, m'lady,' he said, 'and for all I know, they are still there.'

'Good, because I should like you to put the box that Simpson and Simpson have just delivered in the same place.'

'As you wish, m'lady,' said Andrews, trying to look as if he had some idea what his mistress was talking about.

'And next Christmas, Andrews, should I attempt to find them, you must be sure not to let me know where they are hidden.'

'And will I receive sixpence on this occasion, m'lady?'

'A shilling,' promised Arabella, 'but only if no one else finds out where they are.'

—◇—

Anna settled herself into a window seat at the back of economy. If the man Fenston had sent to track her down was on the plane, as she suspected he was, at least Anna now knew what she was up against. She began to think about him, and how he'd discovered that she would be in Bucharest. How did he know her mother's address, and was he already aware that her next stop was Tokyo?

The man she had watched from the check-in counter as he ran up to Sergei's taxi and tapped on the window wasn't hoping for a ride, although Sergei had clearly taken him for one. Anna wondered if it had been her phone calls to Tina that had given her away. She felt confident her close friend would never have betrayed her, so she must have become an unwitting accomplice.

Leapman was well capable of tapping her phone, and far worse.

Anna had purposely dropped clues in her last two conversations to find out if there was an eavesdropper, and they must have been picked up: *going home* and *there will be a lot of people like that where I'm going*. Next time she would plant a clue that would send Fenston's man in completely the wrong direction.

—◇—

Jack sat in business class sipping a Diet Coke and trying to make some sense of the past two days. If you're out there on your own, always prepare for the worst-case scenario, his SSA used to repeat ad nauseam to each new recruit.

He tried to think logically. He was pursuing a woman who had stolen a sixty-million-dollar painting, but had she left the picture in Bucharest, or had it been transferred into the new crate, with the intention of selling the painting to someone in Hong Kong? Then he turned his thoughts to the other person who was pursuing Anna. That was easier to explain. If Petrescu had stolen the painting, the woman was clearly employed by Fenston to follow her until she found out where the picture was. But how did she always know where Anna would be, and did she now realize that he was also following her? And what were her instructions once she'd caught up with the Van Gogh? Jack felt the only way he could redeem himself was to get a step ahead of both of them and somehow stay there.

He found himself falling into a trap that he regularly warned his junior officers to be wary of. Don't be lulled into believing that the suspect is innocent. A jury will make that decision for you. You must always assume they are guilty, and occasionally, very occasionally, be surprised. He didn't remember his instructor saying anything about what to do if you found the suspect attractive. Although there was a directive in the FBI training manual that stated: 'Under no circumstances must an agent enter into a personal relationship with any person under investigation.' In 1999 the guide had been updated following a Congressional directive, when the words 'male or female' had been added before 'person'.

But it still puzzled Jack what Anna intended to do with the Van Gogh. If she was about to try and sell the picture in Hong Kong, where would she deposit such a huge sum of money, and how could she hope to benefit from the spoils of her crime? Jack couldn't believe she was willing to live in Bucharest for the rest of her life.

And then he remembered that she had visited Wentworth Hall.

◄○►

Krantz sat alone in first class. She always flew first class, because it allowed her to be the last on, and first off, any flight, especially when she knew exactly where her victim was travelling.

But now she was aware someone else was following Petrescu, she would have to be even more cautious. After all, she couldn't afford to kill Petrescu with an audience watching, even if it was an audience of one.

Krantz was puzzled by who the tall, dark-haired man could be, and who he was reporting back to. Had Fenston sent someone else to check up on her, or was the man working for a foreign government? If so, which one? It had to be Romanian or American. He was certainly a professional because she hadn't spotted him before, or after, his crass mistake with the yellow taxis. She assumed he must be an American. She hoped so, because if she had to kill him, that would be a bonus.

Krantz didn't relax on the long flight to Hong Kong. Her instructor in Moscow was fond of repeating that concentration usually lapsed on the fourth day. Tomorrow.

9/18

31

'THOSE PASSENGERS travelling to onward destinations . . .'

'That's all I need,' muttered Jack.

'What do you need, sir?' asked an attentive stewardess.

'Transit.'

'Where is your final destination, sir?'

'I have no idea,' said Jack. 'What's the choice?'

The stewardess laughed. 'Are you still hoping to travel east?'

'That makes sense.'

'Then it has to be Tokyo, Manila, Sydney or Auckland.'

'Thank you,' said Jack, thinking, that doesn't help, but adding out loud, 'If I decided to spend the night in Hong Kong, I would have to go through passport control, whereas if I wanted transit . . .'

The stewardess continued to humour him, 'When you disembark, sir, there are clear signs directing you to baggage claim or transit. Is your luggage booked through, sir, or will you be picking it up?'

'I don't have any luggage,' Jack admitted.

The stewardess nodded, smiled and left to attend to some of her more sane passengers.

Jack realized that once he disembarked he would have to move quickly if he hoped to locate a concealed vantage point from where he could observe Anna's next move, and not be observed by her other admirer.

—◦—

Anna stared distractedly out of the cabin window as the plane descended smoothly into Chek Lap Kok airport.

She would never forget her first experience of flying into Hong Kong some years before. To begin with, it felt like a normal approach, and then at the last moment, without warning, the pilot banked steeply and headed straight for the hills. He then descended between the city high-rises, bringing gasps from first-timers, before finally bumping down the short runway into Kowloon, as if he were auditioning for a part in a 1944 war movie. When the plane came to a halt, several of the passengers applauded. Anna was glad that the new airport meant she would not have to experience a repeat performance.

She checked her watch. Although the flight was running twenty minutes late, her onward connection wasn't scheduled for another couple of hours. She would use any spare time to pick up a guide to Tokyo, a city she had never visited before.

Once they'd come to a halt at the terminal gate, Anna progressed slowly down the aisle, waiting for other passengers to rescue their bags from the overhead lockers. She looked around, wondering if Fenston's man was watching her every move. She tried to remain calm, though in truth her heartbeat must have shot above a hundred every time a man even glanced in her direction. She felt sure he must have already disembarked and would now be lying in wait. Perhaps he even knew her final destination. Anna had already decided on the false piece of information she would drop, when she next phoned Tina, that would send Fenston's man flying in the wrong direction.

Anna stepped off the aircraft and looked around her for the sign. At the end of a long corridor, an arrow directed transit passengers to the left. She joined a handful of travellers heading for other destinations, while the majority of passengers turned right.

When she walked into the transit area, she was greeted by a neon-lit city, half as old as Swatch, lurking in wait for its imprisoned customers to part with their foreign currency. Anna strolled from shop to shop, admiring the latest fashions, electrical equipment, cell-phones and jewellery. Although she saw several items she would have considered in normal circumstances, because of her pecuniary predicament the only shop she thought about entering was a bookmart, displaying for-eign newspapers and all the latest bestsellers – in several languages. She strolled across to the travel section, to be faced with row upon row of gazetteers of countries as far afield as Azerbaijan and Zanzibar.

Her eyes settled on the section on Japan, which included a shelf devoted to Tokyo. She picked up the Lonely Planet guide to Japan, along with a Berlitz mini guide to the capital. She began to flick through them.

◄○►

Jack slipped into an electrical shop on the other side of the mall from where he had a clear sightline of his quarry. All he could make out was that she was standing below a large, multicoloured *Travel* sign. Jack would have liked to get close enough to discover which title was causing her to turn the pages so intently, but he knew he couldn't risk it. He began to count down the shelves in an attempt to pinpoint which country had monopolized her attention.

'Can I assist you, sir?' asked the young lady behind the counter.

'Not unless you have a pair of binoculars,' said Jack, not taking his eyes off Anna.

'Several,' replied the assistant, 'and can I recommend this particular model? They are this week's special offer, reduced from ninety dollars to sixty, while stocks last.'

Jack looked round as the young girl removed a pair of binoculars from the shelf behind her and placed them on the counter.

'Thank you,' said Jack. He picked them up and focused them on Anna.

She was still turning the pages of the same book but Jack couldn't make out the title.

'I'd like to see your latest model,' he said, placing the special offer back on the counter. 'One that could focus on a street sign at a hundred metres.'

The assistant bent down, unlocked the display cabinet and extracted another pair.

'These are Leica, top-of-the-range, 12×50,' she assured him. 'You could identify the label on the coffee they're serving in the cafe opposite.'

Jack focused on the bookshop. Anna was replacing the book she had been reading, only to extract the one next to it. He had to agree with the assistant, they were top of the range. He could make out the word *Japan* and even the letters *TOKYO* that were displayed above the shelf Anna was taking so much interest in. Anna closed the book, smiled and headed across to the counter. She also picked up a copy of the *Herald Tribune* as she waited in the queue.

'They are good, yes?' said the assistant.

'Very good,' said Jack, replacing the binoculars on the counter, 'but I'm afraid they're out of my budget. Thank you,' he added, before leaving the shop.

'Strange,' said the girl to her colleague behind the counter. 'I never even told him the price.'

Anna had reached the head of the line and was paying for her two purchases when Jack headed off in the opposite direction. He joined another queue at the far end of the concourse.

When he reached the front of the line, he asked for a ticket to Tokyo.

'Yes, sir, which flight – Cathay Pacific or Japan Airlines?'

'When do they leave?' asked Jack.

'Japan Airlines will be boarding shortly, as the flight departs in forty minutes. Cathay's flight 301 is due to take off in an hour and a half.'

'Japan Airlines please,' said Jack, 'business class.'

'How many bags will you be checking in?'

'Hand luggage only.'

The sales assistant printed the ticket, checked his passport and said, 'If you proceed to gate seventy-one, Mr Delaney, boarding is about to commence.'

Jack walked back towards the coffee shop. Anna was sitting at the counter, engrossed in the book she had just purchased. He was even more careful to avoid her gaze, as he felt sure she now realized she was being followed. Jack spent the next few minutes purchasing goods from shops he wouldn't normally have visited, all made necessary by the woman perched on the corner stool in the coffee shop. He ended up with an overnight bag, which would be allowed on board as hand luggage, a pair of jeans, four shirts, four pairs of socks, four pairs of underpants, two ties (special offer), a packet of razors, shaving cream, aftershave, soap, toothbrush and tooth-paste. He hung around inside the pharmacy waiting to see if Anna was about to move.

'Last call for passengers on Japan Airlines flight 416 to Tokyo. Please proceed immediately to Gate Seventy-one for final boarding.'

Anna turned another page of her book, which convinced Jack that she must be booked onto the Cathay Pacific flight leaving an hour later. This time he would be waiting for her. He tugged at his overnight bag and followed the signs for Gate 71. Jack was among the last to board the aircraft.

◄◦►

Anna checked her watch, ordered another coffee and turned her attention to the *Herald Tribune*. The pages were full of stories on the aftermath of 9/11, with a report on the memorial service held in Washington DC attended by the President. Did her family and friends still believe that she was dead, or just missing? Had the news that she'd been seen in London already percolated back to New York? Clearly Fenston still wanted everyone to believe she was dead, at least until he got his hands on the Van Gogh. All that would change in Tokyo, if—

Something made her look up and she spotted a young man with thick, dark hair staring at her. He quickly looked away. She jumped off her stool and walked straight across to him.

'Are you following me, by any chance?' she demanded.

The man gave Anna a startled look. 'Non, non, mademoiselle, mais peut-être voulez-vous prendre un verre avec moi?'

'This is the first call for . . .'

Two more eyes were also watching Anna as she

apologized to the Frenchman, settled her bill, and made her way slowly to Gate 69.

Krantz only let her out of her sight after she'd boarded the plane.

Krantz was among the last passengers to board flight CX 301. On entering the aircraft, she turned left and took her usual window seat in the front row. Krantz knew that Anna was seated at the back of economy, but she had no idea where the American was. Had he missed the flight, or was he roaming around Hong Kong searching for Petrescu?

32

JACK'S FLIGHT touched down at Narita international airport, Tokyo, thirty minutes late, but he wasn't anxious, because he was an hour ahead of both women, who would still be some 30,000 feet above the Pacific. Once Jack had cleared customs, his first stop was the enquiry desk, where he asked what time the Cathay flight was due to land. Just over forty minutes.

He turned and faced the arrivals gate, then tried to work out in which direction Petrescu would go once she had cleared customs. What would be her first choice of transport into the city: taxi, rail or bus? She would have to decide after she'd progressed a mere fifty yards. If she was still in possession of the crate, it would surely have to be a taxi. Having checked out every possible exit, Jack handed over five hundred dollars at a Bank of Tokyo booth in exchange for 53,868 yen. He placed the large-denomination notes in his wallet and returned to the arrivals hall, where he watched people assemble as they waited for the most recent arrivals. He looked up. Above him, to his left, was a mezzanine floor, which overlooked the hall. He walked up the stairs and inspected the space. Although the area was cramped, it was nevertheless ideal. There were two telephone booths fixed to the wall, and if he stood behind the second one, he could look down on any new arrivals without being spotted. Jack checked the board. CX 301 was due to land in twenty minutes. Easily enough time for him to carry out his final task.

He left the airport and stood in the taxi queue, which was being organized by a man in a light blue suit and white gloves, who not only controlled the taxis but directed the passengers. When he reached the front, Jack climbed into the back of the distinctive green Toyota and instructed a surprised driver to park on the other side of the road.

'Wait here until I return,' he added, leaving his new bag on the back seat. 'I should be about thirty minutes, forty at the most.' He removed a 5,000-yen note from his wallet. 'And you can keep the meter running.' The driver nodded, but looked puzzled.

Jack returned to the airport to find that flight CX 301 had just landed. He walked back up to the terrace and took his place behind the second phone booth. He waited to see who would be the first through the door with the familiar green and white Cathay Pacific label attached to their luggage. It had been a long time since Jack had waited to pick up *one* girl at an airport, let alone two. And would he even recognize his blind date?

The indicator board flicked over once again. Passengers on flight CX 301 were now in the baggage hall. Jack began to concentrate. He didn't have long to wait. Krantz was first through the door – she needed to be, she had work to do. She headed for a melee of eagerly waiting locals, who weren't much taller than her. She nestled in behind them before she risked turning around. From time to time, the patient crowd moved like a slow wave, as some people departed, while others took their place. Krantz moved with the tide so that no one would notice her. But a blonde crew cut standing among a black-haired race made Jack's task a lot easier. If she then followed Anna, Jack would know for certain who he was up against.

While Jack kept one eye on the thin, short, muscular

woman with the blonde crew cut, he repeatedly turned back to check on the new arrivals who were now swarming through the exit in little clusters, several with green and white labels attached to their luggage. Jack gingerly took a step forward, praying she wouldn't look up, but her eyes remained doggedly fixed on the new arrivals.

She must have also worked out that there were only three exit routes for Anna to consider, because she was strategically placed to pounce in whichever direction her quarry selected.

Jack slipped a hand into an inside pocket, slowly removed the latest Samsung cellphone, flicked it open and focused it directly towards the crowd below him. For a moment he couldn't see her, then an elderly man stepped forward to greet his visitor and she was exposed for a split second. Click, then once again she disappeared. Jack continually switched his attention back to the new arrivals, who were still pouring out into the hall. As he turned back, a mother bent down to pick up an errant child and she was exposed again, click, and just as suddenly disappeared from sight. Jack turned to watch as Anna came striding through the swing doors. He closed his phone, hoping that one of the two images would be enough for the tech guys to identify her.

Jack's wasn't the only head to turn when the slim, blonde American strode into the arrivals hall pushing a luggage cart with a suitcase and a wooden crate on board. He stepped back into the shadows the moment Petrescu paused to look up. She was checking the exit boards. She turned right. Taxi.

Jack knew that Petrescu would also have to join a long queue before she could hope to get a cab, so he allowed both women to leave the airport before he came down from the balcony. When he eventually descended, Jack took a circuitous route back to his taxi. He walked to the far end of the hall and then out onto the sidewalk. He ducked behind a waiting bus on his way to the underground parking lot, then continued along the second row of cars and out of the far end of the garage. He was relieved to see the green Toyota still waiting for him, engine running, meter ticking. He climbed into the back seat and said to the driver, 'See the blonde with a crew cut, seventh in the taxi line? I want you to follow her, but she mustn't know.'

Jack's eyes returned to Petrescu, who was fifth in the line. When she reached the front, she didn't climb into the waiting taxi, but turned round and walked slowly to the back of the line. Clever girl, thought Jack as he waited to see how Crew Cut would react. Jack tapped his own driver on the shoulder, and said, 'Don't move,' when Crew Cut stepped into the back of a taxi, which drove off and disappeared around the corner. Jack knew she'd be parked in a side turning only a few yards away waiting for Petrescu to reappear. Eventually, Petrescu reached the front again. Jack tapped his driver on the shoulder and said, 'Follow that woman, stay well back, but don't lose her.'

'But it isn't the same woman.' queried the taxi driver.

'I know,' said Jack. 'Change of plan.'

The driver looked perplexed. Japanese don't understand 'change of plan'.

As Petrescu's taxi drove past him and onto the freeway, Jack watched an identical vehicle come out of a side road and slip in behind her. At last it was Jack's turn to be the pursuer, and not the pursued.

For the first time, Jack was thankful for the notorious snarl-ups and never-ending traffic jams that are the accepted norm for anyone driving from Narita airport into the city centre. He was able to keep his distance while never losing sight of either of them.

It was another hour before Petrescu's taxi came to a halt outside the Hotel Seiyo in the Ginza district. A bell boy stepped forward to help with her luggage, but the moment he saw the wooden crate, he motioned for a colleague to assist him. Jack didn't consider entering the hotel until some time after Petrescu and the box had disappeared inside. But not Crew Cut. She was already secreted in the far corner of the lobby with a clear view of the staircase and elevators, out of sight of anyone working behind the reception desk.

The moment he spotted her, Jack retreated through the swing doors and back out into the courtyard. A bell boy rushed forward. 'Do you want a taxi, sir?'

'No, thank you,' he said, and, pointing to a glass door on the other side of the courtyard, enquired, 'What's that?'

'Hotel health club, sir,' replied the bell boy.

Jack nodded, walked round the perimeter of the courtyard and entered the building. He strolled up to reception.

'Room number, sir?' he was asked by a young man sporting a hotel tracksuit.

'I can't remember,' said Jack.

'Name?'

'Petrescu.'

'Ah, yes, Dr Petrescu,' said the young man looking at his screen, 'room 118. Do you need a locker, sir?'

'Later,' said Jack. 'When my wife joins me.'

He took a seat by the window overlooking the court-yard and waited for Anna to reappear. He noted that there were always two or three taxis waiting in line, so following her should not prove too much of a problem. But if she reappeared without the crate, he was in no doubt that Crew Cut, who was still sitting in the lounge, would be working on a plan to relieve his 'wife' of its contents.

While Jack sat patiently by the window, he flicked open his cellphone and dialled through to Tom in London. He tried not to think what time it was.

'Where are you?' asked Tom, when he saw the name 'Good Cop' flash up on his screen.

'Tokyo.'

'What's Petrescu doing there?'

'I can't be sure, but I wouldn't be surprised if she's trying to sell a rare painting to a well-known collector.'

'Have you found out who the other interested party is?'

'No,' said Jack, 'but I did manage to get a couple of images of her at the airport.'

'Well done,' said Tom.

'I'm sending the pictures through to you now,' said Jack. He keyed a code into his phone and the images appeared on Tom's screen moments later.

'They're a bit blurred,' was Tom's immediate response, 'but I'm sure the tech guys can clean them up enough to try and work out who she is. Any other information?'

'She's around five foot, slim, with a blonde crew cut and the shoulders of a swimmer.'

'Anything else?' asked Tom, as he made notes.

'Yes, when you've finished with the American mug shots, move on to Eastern Europe. I've got a feeling she may be Russian, or possibly Ukrainian.'

'Or even Romanian?' suggested Tom.

'Oh God, I'm so dumb,' said Jack.

'Bright enough to get two photos. No one else has managed that, and they may turn out to be the biggest break we've had in this case.'

'I'd be only too happy to bask in a little glory,' admitted Jack, 'but the truth is that both of them are well aware of my existence.'

'Then I'd better find out who she is pretty fast. I'll be back in touch as soon as the boys in the basement come up with anything.'

—◦—

Tina turned on the switch under her desk. The little screen on the corner came on. Fenston was on the phone. She flicked up the switch to his private line, and listened.

'You were right,' said a voice, 'she's in Japan.'

'Then she probably has an appointment with Nakamura. All his details are in your file. Don't forget that getting the painting is more important than removing Petrescu.'

Fenston put the phone down.

Tina was confident that the voice fitted the woman she had seen in the chairman's car. She must warn Anna.

Leapman walked into the room.

33

ANNA STEPPED OUT of the shower, grabbed a towel and began drying her hair. She glanced across at the digital clock in the corner of the TV screen. It was just after twelve, the hour when most Japanese businessmen go to their club for lunch. Not the time to disturb Mr Nakamura.

Once she was dry, Anna put on the white towelling bathrobe that hung behind the bathroom door. She sat on the end of the bed and opened her laptop. She tapped in her password, MIDAS, which accessed a file on the richest art collectors around the globe: Gates, Cohen, Lauder, Magnier, Nakamura, Rales, Wynn. She moved the cursor across to his name. *Takashi Nakamura, industrialist. Tokyo University 1966–70, BSc in engineering. UCLA 1971–73, MA Economics. Joined Maruha Steel Company 1974, Director 1989, Chief Executive Officer 1997, Chairman 2001.* Anna scrolled down to Maruha Steel. Last year's annual balance sheet showed a turnover of nearly three billion dollars, with profits of over four hundred million. Mr Nakamura owned 22 per cent of the company, and according to *Forbes* was the ninth richest man in the world. Married with three children, two girls and a boy. Under other interests, only two words appeared, golf and art. No details of his fabled high handicap or his valuable Impressionist collection, thought to be among the finest in private hands.

Nakamura had made several statements over the

years, saying that the pictures belonged to the company. Although Christie's never make such matters public, it was well known by those in the art world that Nakamura had been the under-bidder for Van Gogh's *Sunflowers* in 1987, when he was beaten by his old friend and rival Yasuo Goto, chairman of Yasuda Fire and Marine Insurance Company, whose hammer bid was $39,921,750.

Anna hadn't been able to add a great deal to Mr Nakamura's profile since leaving Sotheby's. The Degas she had purchased on his behalf, *Dancing Class with Mme Minette*, had proved a wise investment, which Anna hoped he would remember. She wasn't in any doubt that she had chosen the right man to help pull off her coup.

She unpacked her suitcase and selected a smart blue suit with a skirt that fell just below the knees, a cream shirt and low-heeled navy leather shoes; no make-up, no jewellery. While she pressed her clothes, Anna thought about a man she had met only once, and wondered if she had made any lasting impression on him. When she was dressed, Anna checked herself in the mirror. Exactly what a Japanese businessman would expect a Sotheby's executive to wear.

Anna looked up his private number on her laptop. She sat on the end of the bed, picked up the phone, took a deep breath and dialled the eight digits.

'Hai, Shacho-Shitso desu,' announced a high-pitched voice.

'Good afternoon, my name is Anna Petrescu. Mr Nakamura may remember me from Sotheby's.'

'Are you hoping to be interviewed?'

'Er, no, I simply want to speak to Mr Nakamura.'

'One moment please, I will see if he is free to take your call.'

How could she possibly expect him to remember her after only one meeting?

'Dr Petrescu, how nice to hear from you again. I hope you are well?'

'I am, thank you, Nakamura San.'

'Are you in Tokyo? Because if I am not mistaken it is after midnight in New York.'

'Yes, I am, and wondered if you would be kind enough to see me.'

'You weren't on the interview list, but you are now. I have half an hour free at four o'clock this afternoon. Would that suit you?'

'Yes, that would be just fine,' said Anna.

'Do you know where my office is?'

'I have the address.'

'Where are you staying?'

'The Seiyo.'

'Not the usual haunt for Sotheby's, who, if I remember correctly, prefer the Imperial.' Anna's mouth went dry. 'My office is about twenty minutes from the hotel. I look forward to seeing you at four o'clock. Goodbye, Dr Petrescu.'

Anna replaced the receiver and for some time didn't budge from the end of the bed. She tried to recall his exact words. What had his secretary meant when she asked, 'Are you hoping to be interviewed?' and why did Mr Nakamura say, 'You weren't on the interview list, but you are now'? Was he expecting her call?

-◦-

Jack leant forward to take a closer look. Two bell boys were coming out of the hotel carrying the same wooden crate that Anna had exchanged with Anton Teodorescu on the steps of the academy in Bucharest. One of them spoke to the driver of the front taxi, who jumped out and carefully placed the wooden crate in the trunk. Jack rose slowly from his chair and walked across to the window, making sure he remained out of sight. He waited in anticipation, realizing it could well be another false alarm. He checked the taxi rank, four cars waiting in line. He glanced towards the entrance of the health club and calculated he could reach the second taxi in about twenty seconds.

He looked back at the hotel's sliding doors, wondering if Petrescu was about to appear. But the next person who caused the doors to slide open was Crew Cut, who slipped past the doorman and out onto the main road. Jack knew she wouldn't take one of the hotel taxis and risk being remembered – a chance Jack would have to take.

Jack switched his attention back to the hotel entrance, aware that Crew Cut would now be sitting in a taxi well out of sight, waiting for both of them.

Seconds later, Petrescu appeared, dressed as if she was about to attend a board meeting. The doorman escorted her to the front taxi and opened the back door for her. The driver eased out onto the road and joined the afternoon traffic.

Jack was seated in the back of the second taxi before the doorman had a chance to open the door for him.

'Follow that cab,' said Jack pointing ahead of him, 'and if you don't lose it, you can double the fare.' The driver shot off. 'But,' continued Jack, 'don't make it too obvious,' well aware that Crew Cut would be in one of the numerous green vehicles ahead of them.

Petrescu's taxi turned left at Ginza and headed north, away from the fashionable shopping area, towards the city's prestigious business district of Marunouchi. Jack wondered if this could be the appointment with a potential buyer, and found himself sitting on the edge of his seat in anticipation.

Petrescu's green taxi turned left at the next set of

lights and Jack repeated firmly, 'Don't lose her.' The driver switched lanes, moved to within three cars' length of her car and stuck like a limpet. Both cabs came to a halt at the next red light. Petrescu's taxi was indicating right and, when the lights turned green, several other cars followed in her wake. Jack knew Crew Cut would be in one of them. As they swung into the three-lane highway, Jack could see a string of overhead lights awaiting them, all of them on green. He swore under his breath. He preferred red lights; stopping and starting was always better when you needed to remain in contact with a mark.

They all moved safely through the first green and then the second, but when the third light turned amber Jack's taxi was the last to cross the intersection. As they passed in front of the Imperial Palace gardens, he tapped the driver on the shoulder in appreciation. He leaned forward, willing the next light to remain green. It turned amber just as Petrescu's taxi crossed the inter- section. 'Go, go,' shouted Jack as two of the taxis in front of them followed Anna across, but instead of the driver pressing hard down on his accelerator and running the lights, he came meekly to a halt. Jack was about to explode, when a police patrol car drew up beside them. Jack stared ahead. The green Toyota had come to a halt at the next light. He was still in with a chance. The lights were running in a sequence and all changed within sec- onds of each other. Jack willed the patrol car to turn right so they could make up any lost ground, but it remained resolutely by their side. He watched as her green taxi swung left onto Eitai-dori Avenue. He held his breath, once again willing the green light not to change, but it turned amber and the car ahead of them came to a halt, having no doubt spotted the patrol car in its wake. When the light eventually returned to green, the longest minute Jack could remember, his driver quickly swung left, only to come face to face with a sea of green. It was bad enough that he'd lost Petrescu, but the thought that Crew Cut was probably still on her tail caused Jack to turn and curse the patrol car, just as it turned right and drifted away.

◂◦▸

Krantz watched attentively as the green taxi edged across to the inside lane and drew up outside a modern, white marble building in Otemachi. The sign above the entrance, *Maruha Steel Company*, was in Japanese and English, as is common with most international companies in Tokyo.

Krantz allowed her taxi to pass the front of the building before she asked the driver to draw into the kerb. She turned and watched through the rear-view window as Anna stepped out. Her driver walked to the back of the taxi and opened the trunk. Anna joined him, as the doorman came running down the steps to assist. Krantz continued to watch as the two men carried the wooden box up the steps and into the building.

Once they were out of sight, Krantz paid her fare, stepped out of the car and slipped into the shadows. She never kept a cab waiting unless absolutely necessary. That way, they were unlikely to remember her. She needed to think quickly, in case Petrescu suddenly reappeared. Krantz recalled her brief. Her first priority was to repossess the painting. Once she had done that, she was free to kill Petrescu, but as she had just got off a plane she didn't have a weapon to hand. She was satisfied that the American no longer posed a threat, and briefly wondered if he was still roaming around Hong Kong in search of Petrescu, or the picture, or both.

It was beginning to look as if the painting had

reached its destination; there had been a full page on Nakamura in the file Fenston had given her. If Petrescu reappeared with the crate, she must have failed, which would make it that much easier for Krantz to carry out both of her assignments. If she walked out only carrying her briefcase, Krantz would need to make an instant decision. She checked to make sure that there was a regular flow of taxis. Several passed her in the next few minutes, half of them empty.

The next person through the door was the taxi driver, who climbed back behind the wheel of his Toyota. She waited for Petrescu to follow, but the empty green cab swung onto the street, in search of its next customer. Krantz had a feeling that this was going to be a long wait.

She stood in the shadows of a department store on the opposite side of the road and waited. She looked up and down a street full of designer label shops, which she despised, until her eyes settled on an establishment that she had only read about in the past and had always wanted to visit: not Gucci, not Burberry, not Calvin Klein, but the Nozaki Cutting Tool Shop, which nestled uneasily among its more recent neighbours.

Krantz was drawn to the entrance as a filing is to a magnet. As she crossed the road, her eyes remained fixed on the front door of the Maruha Steel Company in case Petrescu made an unscheduled reappearance. She suspected that Petrescu's meeting with Mr Nakamura would last some considerable time. After all, even he wouldn't spend that amount of money without expecting several questions to be answered.

Once across the road, Krantz stared into the window, like a child for whom Christmas had come three months early. Tweezers, nail clippers, left-handed scissors, Swiss Army knives, long-bladed tailor's shears, a Victorinox machete with a fifteen-inch blade – all played second fiddle to a ceremonial samurai sword (*circa* 1783). Krantz felt that she had been born in the wrong century.

She stepped inside to be met with row upon row of kitchen knives, for which Mr Takai, a samurai's descendant, had become so famous. She spotted the proprietor standing in one corner, sharpening knives for his customers. Krantz recognized him immediately, and would have liked to shake hands with the maestro – her equivalent of Brad Pitt – but she knew she would have to forgo that particular pleasure.

While keeping a wary eye on the Maruha Company's front door, Krantz began to study the hand-forged Japanese implements – razor-sharp and deceptively light, with the name NOZAKI stamped into the shoulder of each blade, as if, like Cartier, they wished to emphasize that a counterfeit was not acceptable.

Krantz had long ago accepted that she could not risk carrying her preferred weapon of death on a plane, so she was left with no choice but to pick up a local product in whichever country Fenston needed a client account closed indefinitely.

Krantz began the slow process of selection while being serenaded by suzumushi, bell crickets, in tiny bamboo cages suspended from the ceiling. She stared back at the entrance door across the road, but there was still no sign of Petrescu. She returned to her task, first testing the different categories of knife – fruit, vegetable, bread, meat – for weight, balance and size of blade. No more than eight inches, never less than four.

In a matter of minutes, Krantz was down to a shortlist of three, before she finally settled on the award-winning Global GS5 – fourteen centimetres, which it was claimed would cut through a rump steak as easily as a ripe melon.

She handed her chosen instrument to an assistant,

who smiled – such a thin neck – and wrapped the kitchen knife in rice paper. Krantz paid in yen. Dollars would have drawn attention to her, and she didn't possess a credit card. One last look at Mr Takai before she reluctantly left the shop to return to the anonymity of the shadows on the other side of the road.

While she waited for Petrescu to reappear, Krantz removed the rice paper from her latest acquisition, desperate to try it out. She slipped the blade into a sheath that had been tailor-made to fit on the inside of her jeans. It fitted perfectly, like a gun in a holster.

34

THE RECEPTIONIST could not hide her surprise when the doorman appeared carrying a wooden crate. She placed her hands in front of her mouth – an unusually animated response for a Japanese.

Anna offered no explanation, only her name. The receptionist checked the list of applicants to be interviewed by the chairman that afternoon, and placed a tick next to 'Dr Petrescu'.

'Mr Nakamura is interviewing another candidate at the moment,' she said, 'but should be free shortly.'

'Interviewing them for what?' asked Anna.

'I have no idea,' said the receptionist, seeming equally puzzled that an interviewee needed to ask such a question.

Anna sat in reception and glanced at the crate that was propped up against the wall. She smiled at the thought of how she would go about asking someone to part with sixty million dollars.

Punctuality is an obsession with the Japanese, so Anna was not surprised when a smartly dressed lady appeared at two minutes to four, bowed and invited Anna to follow her. She too looked at the wooden box, but showed no reaction other than to ask, 'Would you like it to be taken to the chairman's office?'

'Yes, please,' said Anna, again without explanation.

The secretary led Anna down a long corridor, passing several doors that displayed no name, title or rank. When they reached the last door, the secretary knocked quietly, opened it and announced, 'Dr Petrescu.'

Mr Nakamura rose from behind his desk and came forward to greet Anna, whose mouth was wide open. A reaction not caused by the short, slim, dark-haired man who looked as if he had his suits tailored in Paris or Milan. It was Mr Nakamura's office that caused Anna to gasp. The room was a perfect square and one of the four walls was a single pane of glass. Anna stared out onto a tranquil garden, a stream winding from one corner to the other, crossed by a wooden bridge and bordered by willow trees, whose branches cascaded over the rails.

On the wall behind the chairman's desk was a magnificent painting, duplicating exactly the same scene. Anna closed her mouth and turned to face her host.

Mr Nakamura smiled, clearly delighted with the effect his Monet had created, but his first question equally shocked her.

'How did you manage to survive 9/11, when, if I recall correctly, your office was in the North Tower?'

'I was very lucky,' replied Anna, quietly, 'although I fear that some of my colleagues . . .'

Mr Nakamura raised a hand. 'I apologize,' he said, 'how tactless of me. Shall we begin the interview by testing your remarkable photographic memory, and first ask you the provenance of all three paintings in the room? Shall we begin with the Monet.'

'*Willows at Vétheuil*,' said Anna. 'Its previous owner was a Mr Clark of Sangton, Ohio. It was part of Mrs Clark's divorce settlement when her husband decided to part with her, his third wife, which meant sadly that he had to part with his third Monet. Christie's sold the oil for twenty-six million dollars, but I had no idea you were the purchaser.'

Mr Nakamura revealed the same smile of pleasure.

Anna turned her attention to the opposite wall and paused. 'I have for some time wondered where that particular painting ended up,' she said. 'It's a Renoir, of course. *Madame Duprez and Her Children*, also known as *The Reading Lesson*. It was sold in Paris by Roger Duprez, whose grandfather purchased it from the artist in 1868. I therefore have no way of knowing how much you paid for the oil,' Anna added, as she turned her attention to the final piece. 'Easy,' she declared, smiling. 'It's one of Manet's late Salon works, probably painted in 1871 –' she paused – 'entitled *Dinner at the Café Guerbois*. You will have observed that his mistress is seated in the right-hand corner, looking directly out at the artist.'

'And the previous owner?'

'Lady Charlotte Churchill, who, following the death of her husband, was forced to sell it to meet death duties.'

Nakamura bowed. 'The position is yours.'

'The position, Nakamura San?' said Anna, puzzled.

'You are not here to apply for the job as the director of my foundation?'

'No,' said Anna, suddenly realizing what the receptionist had meant when she said that the chairman was interviewing another candidate. 'Although I am flattered that you would consider me, Nakamura San, I actually came to see you on a completely different matter.'

The chairman nodded, clearly disappointed, and then his eyes settled on the wooden box.

'A small gift,' said Anna, smiling.

'If that is the case, and you will forgive the pun, I cannot open your offering until you have left, otherwise I will insult you.' Anna nodded, well aware of the custom. 'Please have a seat, young lady.'

Anna smiled.

'Now, what is your real purpose in visiting me?' he asked as he leant back in his chair and stared at her intently.

'I believe I have a painting that you will be unable to resist.'

'As good as the Degas pastel?' asked Nakamura, showing signs of enjoying himself.

'Oh yes,' she said, a little too enthusiastically.

'Artist?'

'Van Gogh.'

Nakamura smiled an inscrutable smile that gave no sign if he was or wasn't interested.

'Title?'

'*Self-portrait with Bandaged Ear.*'

'With a famous Japanese print reproduced on the wall behind the artist, if I remember correctly,' said Nakamura.

'*Geishas in a Landscape,*' said Anna, 'demonstrating Van Gogh's fascination with Japanese culture.'

'You should have been christened Eve,' said Nakamura. 'But now it's my turn.' Anna looked surprised, but didn't speak. 'I presume that it has to be the Wentworth *Self-portrait*, purchased by the fifth marquis?'

'Earl.'

'Earl. Ah, will I ever understand English titles? I always think of Earl as an American first name.'

'Original owner?' enquired Anna.

'Dr Gachet, Van Gogh's friend and admirer.'

'And the date?'

'1889,' replied Nakamura, 'when Van Gogh resided at Arles, shortly after Gauguin returned to Paris.'

'And how much did Dr Gachet pay for the piece?' asked Anna, aware that few people on earth would have considered teasing this man.

'It is always thought that Van Gogh only sold one

247

painting in his lifetime, *The Red Vineyard*. However, Dr Gachet was not only a close friend, but unquestionably his benefactor and patron. In the letter he wrote after receiving the picture, he enclosed a cheque for six hundred francs.'

'Eight hundred,' said Anna, as she opened her brief-case and handed over a copy of the letter. 'My client is in possession of the original,' she assured him.

Nakamura read the letter in French, requesting no assistance with a translation. He looked up and smiled. 'What figure do you have in mind?' he asked.

'Sixty million dollars,' said Anna without hesitation.

For a moment, the inscrutable face appeared puzzled, but he didn't speak for some time. 'Why is such an acknowledged masterpiece so underpriced?' he asked eventually. 'There must be some conditions attached.'

'The sale must not be made public,' said Anna in reply.

'That has always been my custom, as you well know,' said Nakamura.

'You will not resell the work for at least ten years.'

'I buy pictures,' said Nakamura. 'I sell steel.'

'During the same period of time, the painting must not be displayed in a public gallery.'

'Who are you protecting, young lady?' asked Naka-mura, without warning. 'Bryce Fenston, or Victoria Wentworth?'

Anna didn't reply, and now understood why the chairman of Sotheby's had once remarked that you underestimate this man at your peril.

'It was impertinent of me to ask such a question,' said Nakamura. 'I apologize,' he added as he rose from his place. 'Perhaps you would be kind enough to allow me to consider your offer overnight.' He bowed low, clearly indicating that the meeting was over.

'Of course, Nakamura San,' she said, returning the bow.

'Please drop the San, Dr Petrescu. In your chosen field, I am not your equal.'

She wanted to say, please call me Anna; in your chosen field, I know nothing – but she lost her nerve.

Nakamura walked across to join her, and glanced at the wooden box. 'I will look forward to finding out what is in the box. Perhaps we can meet again tomorrow, Dr Petrescu, after I've had a little more time to consider your proposition.'

'Thank you, Mr Nakamura.'

'Shall we say ten o'clock? I'll send my driver to pick you up at nine forty.'

Anna gave a farewell bow and Mr Nakamura returned the compliment. He walked to the door and as he opened it, added, 'I only wish you *had* applied for the job.'

—◦—

Krantz was still standing in the shadows when Petrescu came out of the building. The meeting must have gone well because a limousine was waiting for her with a chauffeur holding open the back door, and, more significantly, there was no sign of the wooden box. Krantz was left with two choices. She was confident that Petrescu would be returning to the hotel for the night, while the painting must still be in the building. She made her choice.

—◦—

Anna sat back in the chairman's car and relaxed for the first time in days, confident that even if Mr Nakamura didn't agree to sixty million, he would still make a realistic offer. Otherwise why put his car at her disposal and invite her to return the following day?

When Anna was dropped outside the Seiyo, she went straight to the reception desk and picked up her key before heading towards the elevator. If she had turned right instead of left, she would have walked straight past a frustrated American.

Jack's eyes never left her as she stepped into an empty elevator. She was on her own. No sign of the package and, perhaps more significant, no sign of Crew Cut. She must have made the decision to stay with the painting rather than with its courier. Jack had to quickly decide what he would do if Petrescu reappeared with her bags and left for the airport. At least he hadn't unpacked this time.

–◦–

Krantz had been standing in different shadows for nearly an hour, only moving with the sun, when the chairman's car returned and parked outside the entrance to Maruha Steel. A few moments later, the front doors slid open and Mr Nakamura's secretary appeared with a man in a red uniform who was carrying the wooden crate. The driver opened the trunk, while the doorman placed the painting in the back. The driver listened as the secretary passed on the chairman's instructions. The chairman needed to make several calls to America and England overnight, and would therefore be staying in the company flat. He had seen the picture and wanted it to be delivered to his home in the country.

Krantz checked the traffic. She knew she'd get one chance, and then only if the lights were red. She was thankful it was a one-way street. She already knew that the lights at the far end of the road would remain on green for forty-five seconds. During that time, Krantz calculated about thirteen cars crossed the intersection. She stepped out of the shadows and moved stealthily down the sidewalk, like a cat, aware that she was about to risk one of her nine lives.

The chairman's black limousine emerged onto the street and joined the early evening traffic. The light was green, but there were fifteen cars ahead of him. Krantz stood exactly opposite where she thought the vehicle would come to a halt. When the light turned red, she walked slowly towards the limousine; after all, she had another forty-five seconds. When she was only a pace away, Krantz fell on to her right shoulder and rolled under the car. She gripped the two sides of the outer frame firmly and, spreadeagled, pulled herself up. One of the advantages of being four foot eleven and weighing less than a hundred pounds. When the lights turned green and the chairman's car moved off, she was no-where to be seen.

Once, in the Romanian hills when escaping from the rebels, Krantz had stuck like a limpet to the bottom of a two-ton truck as it travelled for miles across rough terrain. She survived for fifty-one minutes, and when the sun finally set, she fell to the ground, exhausted. She then trekked across country to safety, jogging the last fourteen miles.

The limousine drove at an uneven pace through the city, and it was another twenty minutes before the driver turned off the highway and began to climb into the hills. A few minutes later, another turn, a much smaller road and far less traffic. Krantz wanted to fall off, but knew that every minute she could cling on would be to her advantage. The car came to a halt at a crossroads, turned sharp left and continued along what appeared to be a wide, uneven path. When they stopped at the next crossroads, Krantz listened attentively. A passing lorry was holding them up.

She slowly released her right arm, which was almost

numb, unsheathed the knife from her jeans, turned to one side and thrust the blade into the right-hand rear tyre, again and again, until she heard a loud hissing sound. As the car moved off, she fell to the ground and didn't move an inch until she could no longer hear the engine. She rolled over to the side of the road and watched the limousine as it drove higher into the hills. She didn't attempt to get up until the car was out of sight.

Once the limousine had disappeared over the hill, she pushed herself up and began to carry out a series of stretching exercises. She wasn't in a hurry. After all, it would be waiting for her on the other side of the hill. Once Krantz had recovered, she began jogging slowly towards the brow of the hill. Some miles ahead of her, she could see a magnificent mansion nestling in the hills that dominated the surrounding landscape.

When Krantz came over the rise, she saw the chauffeur in the distance, on one knee, staring at the flat tyre. She checked up and down what was clearly a private road and probably led only to the Nakamura residence. As she approached, the driver looked up and smiled. Krantz returned the smile, and jogged up to his side. He was about to speak when, with one swift movement of her left leg, Krantz kicked him in the throat, then in the groin. She watched as he collapsed on the ground, like a puppet whose strings had been cut. For a moment, she considered slitting his throat, but now she had the painting, why bother, when she would have the pleasure of cutting someone else's throat tonight. And in any case, she wasn't being paid for this one.

Once again Krantz looked up and down the road. Still clear. She ran to the front of the limousine and removed the keys from the ignition, before returning to unlock the trunk. The lid swung up and her eyes settled on the wooden crate. She would have smiled, but first she needed to make sure that she'd earned the first million dollars.

Krantz grabbed a heavy screwdriver from the toolkit in the trunk and wedged it into a crack in the top right-hand corner of the crate. It took all of her strength to wrench the lid open, only to find her prize was covered in bubble wrap. She tore at it with her bare hands. When the last remnant had been removed, she stared down at the prize-winning painting by Danuta Sekalska, entitled *Freedom*.

—◦—

Jack waited for another hour, one eye on the door for Crew Cut, the other on the elevator for Petrescu, but neither appeared. Yet another hour passed, by which time Jack was convinced Anna must be staying overnight. He walked wearily up to reception and asked if they had a vacant room.

'Name, sir,' asked the booking clerk.

'Fitzgerald,' Jack replied.

'Your passport, please?'

'Certainly,' said Jack, taking a passport out of an inside pocket and handing the document over.

'How many nights will you be staying with us, Mr Fitzgerald?'

Jack would have liked to be able to answer that question.

9/19

35

WHEN ANNA WOKE the next morning, the first thing she did was to phone Wentworth Hall.

'It's going to be a close-run thing,' warned Arabella, once Anna had imparted her news.

'What do you mean?' asked Anna.

'Fenston has issued a bankruptcy order against the estate, giving me fourteen days to clear the debt or he'll put Wentworth Hall on the market. So let's hope Nakamura doesn't find out, because if he does, it will certainly weaken your bargaining position and might even cause him to have second thoughts.'

'I'm seeing him at ten o'clock this morning,' said Anna, 'I would call you back as soon as I find out his decision, but it will be the middle of the night.'

'I don't care what time it is,' said Arabella, 'I'll be awake.'

Once Anna had put the phone down, she began to go over her tactics for the meeting with Nakamura. In truth, she'd thought of little else for the past twelve hours.

She knew that Arabella would be happy with a sum that would clear her debts with Fenston Finance and allow her to make sure that the estate was safe from prying creditors, with enough over to cover any taxes. Anna calculated that sum to be around fifty million. She had already decided she would settle for that amount and the chance to return to New York, no longer with the sobriquet 'missing' attached to her name, and be reacquainted with both loops in Central Park. She might even ask Nakamura for more details about the job she wasn't interviewed for.

Anna lingered in a bath that went from boiling to tepid – an indulgence she normally only allowed herself at weekends – as she continued to think through her approach to the meeting with Nakamura. She smiled at the thought of Nakamura opening his present. For all serious collectors, it's as much of a thrill to discover the next master as it is to pay a vast sum for an established one. When Nakamura saw the bold brush work and the sheer flair, he would surely hang *Freedom* in his private collection. Always the ultimate test.

Anna thought long and hard about what she would wear for their second meeting. She settled on a beige linen dress with a modest hemline, a wide brown leather belt and a simple gold necklace – an outfit that would be considered demure in New York, but almost brash in Tokyo. Yesterday she'd dressed for her opening move, today for closing.

She opened her bag for a third time that morning to check that she had included a copy of Dr Gachet's letter to Van Gogh, along with a simple one-page contract that was standard among recognized dealers. If she could agree a price with Nakamura, Anna was going to ask for 10 per cent down, as an act of good faith, to be returned in full if, after inspecting the masterpiece, he was not satisfied. Anna felt that once he set his eyes on the original . . .

Anna checked her watch. The meeting with the chairman was at ten, and he had promised to send his limousine to pick her up at nine forty. She would be waiting in the lobby. The Japanese quickly lose patience with people who play games.

Anna took the elevator to the lobby and walked across to reception. 'I expect to be checking out later today,' she said, 'and would like my bill prepared.'

'Certainly, Dr Petrescu,' said the receptionist. 'May I ask if you have had anything from the mini-bar?'

Anna thought for a moment. 'Two Evian waters.'

'Thank you,' said the clerk and began tapping the information into his computer as a bell boy came rushing up to her.

'Chauffeur here to collect you,' was all he said, before leading Anna out to the waiting car.

Jack was already sitting in a taxi when she appeared at the entrance. He was determined he wasn't going to lose her a second time. After all, Crew Cut would be waiting for her, and she even knew where Anna was going.

--◦--

Krantz had also spent the night in the centre of Tokyo, but unlike Petrescu, not in a hotel bed. She had slept in the cab of a crane, some one hundred and fifty feet above the city. She was confident that no one would come looking for her there. She stared down on Tokyo as the sun rose over the Imperial Palace. She checked her watch. 5.56am. Time to descend, if she were to leave unnoticed.

Once Krantz was back on the ground, she joined the office staff and early morning commuters as they disappeared underground and made their way to work.

Seven stops later, Krantz emerged in the Ginza and quickly retraced her steps to the Seiyo. She slipped back into the hotel, a regular guest who never booked in, and never stayed overnight.

Krantz positioned herself in the corner of the lounge, where she had a perfect sightline of the two elevators, while she could be seen by only the most observant of waiters. It was a long wait, but then patience was a skill developed over hours of practice – like any other skill.

–◦–

The chauffeur closed the back door behind her. Not the same driver as the night before, Anna noted – she never forgot a face. He drove off without a word, and she became more and more confident as each mile passed.

When the chauffeur opened the back door again, Anna could see Mr Nakamura's secretary waiting for her in the lobby. Sixty million dollars, Anna whispered to herself as she climbed the steps, and I won't consider a cent less. The glass doors slid open, and the secretary bowed low.

'Good morning, Dr Petrescu. Nakamura San is looking forward to seeing you.' Anna smiled and followed her down the long corridor of untitled offices. A gentle tap, and the secretary opened the door to the chairman's room and announced Dr Petrescu.

Once again, Anna was stunned by the effect the room had on her, but this time managed to keep her mouth closed. Nakamura rose from behind his desk and bowed. Anna returned the compliment before he ushered her into a chair on the opposite side of the desk. He sat down. Yesterday's smile had been replaced by a grim visage. Anna assumed this was nothing more than a bargaining ploy.

'Dr Petrescu,' he began as he opened a file on the desk in front of him, 'it seems that when we met yesterday, you were less than frank with me.'

Anna felt her mouth go dry, as Nakamura glanced down at some papers. He removed his spectacles and looked directly at Anna. She tried not to flinch.

'You did not tell me, for instance, that you no longer

work for Fenston Finance, nor did you allude to the fact that you were recently dismissed from the board for conduct unworthy of an officer of the bank.' Anna tried to breathe regularly. 'You also failed to inform me of the distressing news that Lady Victoria had been murdered, at a time when she had run up debts with your bank' – he put his glasses back on – 'of over thirty million dollars. You also forgot to mention the small matter of the New York police being under the illusion that you are currently classified as missing, presumed dead. But perhaps the most damning indictment of all was your failure to let me know that the painting you were attempting to sell is, to use police jargon, stolen goods.' Nakamura closed the file, removed his glasses once more and stared directly at her. 'Perhaps there is a simple explanation for such a sudden attack of amnesia?'

Anna wanted to jump up and run out of the room, but she couldn't move. Her father always told her when you've been found out, confess. She confessed everything. In fact, she even let him know where the painting was hidden. Once she finished, Nakamura didn't speak for some time. Anna sat and waited to be escorted unceremoniously from a building for the second time in just over a week.

'I now understand why you didn't wish the painting to be sold for at least ten years, and certainly wouldn't want it to be put on public display. But I am bound to ask how you intend to square the circle with your former boss. It is clear to me that Mr Fenston is more interested in holding on to such a valuable asset than having the debt cleared.'

'But that's the point,' said Anna. 'Once the overdraft has been cleared, the Wentworth Estate can sell the painting to whomever they wish.'

Mr Nakamura nodded. 'Assuming that I accept your

version of events, and if I was still interested in purchasing the *Self-portrait*, I would want to make some conditions of my own.'

Anna nodded.

'First, the painting would have to be purchased directly from Lady Arabella, and only after legal tenure had been properly established.'

'I can see no objection to that,' said Anna.

'Second, I would expect the work to be authenticated by the Van Gogh Museum in Amsterdam.'

'That causes me no problems,' said Anna.

'Then perhaps my third condition will cause you a problem,' said Nakamura, 'and that is the price I am willing to pay, as I do believe that I am, to use that ghastly but appropriate American expression, in the driving seat.'

Anna nodded her reluctant agreement.

'If, and I repeat if, you are able to meet my other conditions, I am happy to offer, for the Wentworth Van Gogh *Self-portrait with Bandaged Ear*, fifty million dollars, which I have worked out will not only clear Lady Arabella's debt, but leave enough over to cover any taxes.'

'But the painting is worth seventy, perhaps, eighty million on the open market,' Anna protested.

'But this is a distinctly closed market,' responded Nakamura, 'as long as Bryce Fenston is the only other bidder. I am advised that Mr Fenston has recently issued a bankruptcy order against your client, and knowing the Americans as I do, it might be years before any legal action can be settled, and my London lawyers confirm that Lady Arabella is in no position to consider the crippling legal costs such a lengthy process would undoubtedly incur.'

Anna took a deep breath. 'If, and I repeat if' – Nakamura had the grace to smile – 'I accept your terms, in return I would expect some gesture of goodwill.'

'And what do you have in mind?'

'You will place 10 per cent, five million dollars, in escrow with Lady Arabella's solicitors in London, to be returned if you do not wish to purchase the original.'

Nakamura shook his head. 'No, Dr Petrescu, I am unable to accept your gesture of goodwill.'

Anna felt deflated.

'However, I am willing to place five million in escrow with *my* London lawyers, the full amount to be paid on exchange of contracts.'

'Thank you,' said Anna, unable to disguise a sigh of relief.

But Nakamura continued. 'Having accepted your terms, I would also expect some gesture of goodwill in return,' he said as he rose from behind his desk. Anna rose nervously. 'Should the deal go through, you will give serious consideration to taking up the appointment as the CEO of my foundation.'

Anna smiled, but did not bow. She offered her hand and said, 'To use another ghastly but appropriate American expression, Mr Nakamura, we have a deal.' She turned to leave.

'And one more thing before you go,' said Nakamura, picking up an envelope from his desk. Anna turned back, hoping she didn't look apprehensive. 'Would you be kind enough to pass on this letter to Miss Danuta Sekalska, a huge talent that I can only hope will be allowed to mature.' Anna smiled as the chairman accompanied her down the corridor and back to the waiting limousine. They chatted about the tragic events in New York, and the long-term consequences for America. However,

Nakamura made no reference to why his regular driver was in hospital, recovering from serious injuries, not least to his pride.

But then the Japanese have always considered that some secrets are best kept in the family.

‑‑<o>‑‑

Whenever Jack was in a strange city, he rarely informed the embassy of his presence. They always asked too many questions he didn't want to answer. Tokyo was no exception, but he did need some of his own questions answered, and he knew exactly who to ask.

A conman, whom Jack had put behind bars for several years, once told him that whenever you're abroad and in need of information, book yourself into a good hotel. But don't seek advice from the manager, and don't bother with the receptionist, only deal with the head concierge. Information is how he makes his living; his salary is incidental.

For fifty dollars, Jack learnt everything he needed to know about Mr Nakamura, even his golf handicap – fourteen.

‑‑<o>‑‑

Krantz watched as Petrescu emerged from the building and climbed back into the chairman's limousine. She quickly hailed a taxi and asked to be dropped a hundred yards from the Seiyo hotel. If Petrescu was about to depart, she would still have to retrieve her luggage and settle the bill.

‑‑<o>‑‑

Once the temporary chauffeur had dropped Anna back at the Seiyo, she couldn't wait to check out – she picked up her key from reception and ran up the stairs to her room on the first floor. She sat on the end of the bed and called Arabella first. She sounded wide awake.

'A veritable Portia,' was Arabella's final comment after she had learned the news. Which Portia, Anna wondered. Shylock's nemesis, or Brutus's wife? She unclasped her gold chain, unfastened the leather belt, kicked off her shoes and finally slipped out of her dress. She exchanged her more formal attire for a T-shirt, jeans and sneakers. Although checkout was at noon, she still had enough time to make one more call. Anna needed to plant the clue.

The ringing tone continued for some time before a sleepy voice answered.

'Who's this?'

'Vincent.'

'Christ, what time is it? I must have fallen asleep.'

'You can go back to sleep after you've heard my news.'

'You've sold the painting?'

'How did you guess?'

'How much?'

'Enough.'

'Congratulations. So where are you going next?'

'To pick it up.'

'And where's that?'

'Where it's always been. Go back to sleep.'

The phone went dead.

◆—◇—◆

Tina smiled as she drifted back to sleep. Fenston was going to be beaten at his own game for once.

'Oh my God,' she said out loud, suddenly wide awake. 'I didn't warn her that the stalker *is* a woman, and knows she's in Tokyo.'

36

FENSTON STRETCHED an arm across the bed and fumbled for the phone as he tried to keep his eyes shut.

'Who the fuck is this?'

'Vincent's just made a call.'

'And where was she calling from this time?' asked Fenston, his eyes suddenly wide open.

'Tokyo.'

'So she must have seen Nakamura.'

'Sure has,' said Leapman, 'and claims she's sold the painting.'

'You can't sell something that you don't own,' said Fenston, as he switched on the bedside light. 'Did she say where she was going next?'

'To pick it up.'

'Did she give any clue as to where that might be?'

'Where it's always been,' replied Leapman.

'Then it has to be London,' said Fenston.

'How can you be so sure?' asked Leapman.

'Because if she had taken the painting to Bucharest, why not take it on to Tokyo? No, she left the picture in London,' said Fenston adamantly, '*where it's always been.*'

'I'm not so sure,' said Leapman.

'Then where do you think it is?'

'In Bucharest, *where it's always been*, in the red box.'

'No, the box was just a decoy.'

'Then how can we ever hope to find the painting?' asked Leapman.

'That will be simple enough,' said Fenston. 'Now that Petrescu thinks she's sold the painting to Nakamura, her next stop will be to pick it up. And this time Krantz *will* be waiting for her, and then she'll end up having something in common with Van Gogh. But before then, there's another call I have to make.' He slammed the phone down before Leapman had a chance to ask to whom.

❖

Anna checked out of the hotel just after twelve. She took a train to the airport, no longer able to afford the luxury of a cab. She assumed that once she boarded the shuttle, the same man would be following her, and she intended to make his task as easy as possible. After all, he would already have been informed of her next stop.

What she didn't know was that her pursuer was sitting eight rows behind her.

❖

Krantz opened a copy of the *Shinbui Times*, ready to raise it and cover her face should Petrescu look round. She didn't.

Time to make her call. Krantz dialled the number and waited for ten rings. On the tenth, it was picked up. She didn't speak.

'London,' was the only word Fenston uttered before the line went dead.

Krantz dropped the cellphone out of the window, and watched as it landed in front of an oncoming train.

❖

When her train came to a halt at the airport terminal, Anna jumped out and went straight to the British Airways desk. She enquired about an economy fare to London, although she had no intention of purchasing the ticket. She had only thirty-five dollars to her name, after all. But Fenston had no way of knowing that. She checked the departure board. There were ninety minutes between the two flights. Anna walked slowly towards Gate 91B, making sure that whoever was following her couldn't lose her. She window-shopped all the way to the departure gate and arrived just before they began boarding. She selected her seat in the lounge carefully, sitting next to a small child. 'Would those passengers in rows . . .' The child screamed and ran away, a harassed parent chasing after him.

◄◦►

Jack had only been distracted for a moment, but she was gone. Had she boarded the plane or turned back? Perhaps she had worked out that *two* people were following her. Jack's eyes searched the concourse below him. They were now boarding business class and she wasn't anywhere to be seen. He checked all the remaining passengers who were seated in the lounge, and he wouldn't have spotted the other woman in his life if she hadn't touched her hair, no longer a blonde crew cut, now a black wig. She also looked puzzled.

Krantz hesitated when they invited all first-class passengers to board. She walked across to the ladies' washroom, which was directly behind where Petrescu had been sitting. She emerged a few moments later and returned to her seat. When they called final boarding, she was among the last to hand over her ticket.

Jack watched as Crew Cut disappeared down the ramp. How could she be so confident that Anna was on the London flight? Had he lost both of them again?

Jack waited until the gate closed, now painfully aware

that both women were obviously on the flight to London. But there had been something about Anna's manner since she'd left the hotel – almost as if, this time, she wanted to be followed.

Jack waited until the last airline official had packed up and gone. He was about to return to the ground floor and book himself on the next plane to London, when the door of the men's washroom opened.

Anna stepped out.

◄o►

'Put me through to Mr Nakamura.'

'Who shall I say is calling?'

'Bryce Fenston, the chairman of Fenston Finance.'

'I'll just find out if he's available, Mr Fenston.'

'He'll be available,' said Fenston.

The line went silent and it was some time before another voice ventured, 'Good morning, Mr Fenston, this is Takashi Nakamura, how can I help you?'

'I just phoned to warn you—'

'Warn me?' said Nakamura.

'I'm told that Petrescu tried to sell you a Van Gogh.'

'Yes, she did,' said Nakamura.

'And how much did she ask for?' said Fenston.

'I think, to use an American expression, an arm and a leg.'

'If you were foolish enough to agree to buy the picture, Mr Nakamura, it could end up being your arm and your leg,' said Fenston, 'because that picture belongs to me.'

'I had no idea it belonged to you. I thought that it—'

'Then you thought wrong. Perhaps you were also unaware that Petrescu no longer works for this bank.'

'Dr Petrescu made that all too clear, in fact—'

'And did she tell you she was fired?'

'Yes, she did.'

'But did she tell you why?'

'In great detail.'

'And you still felt able to do business with her?'

'Yes. In fact I am trying to persuade her to join *my* board, as CEO of the company's foundation.'

'Despite the fact that I had to dismiss her for conduct unworthy of an officer of a bank.'

'Not *a* bank, Mr Fenston, *your* bank.'

'Don't bandy words with me,' said Fenston.

'So be it,' said Nakamura, 'then let me make it clear that should Dr Petrescu join this company, she will quickly discover that we do not condone a policy of swindling clients out of their inheritance, especially when they are old ladies.'

'Then how would you feel about directors who steal bank assets worth a hundred million dollars?'

'I am delighted to learn you consider the painting is worth that amount, because the owner—'

'I am the owner,' bellowed Fenston, 'under New York state law.'

'Whose jurisdiction does not stretch to Tokyo.'

'But doesn't your company also have offices in New York?'

'At last we've found something on which we can agree,' said Nakamura.

'Then there's nothing to stop me serving you with a writ in New York, were you foolish enough to attempt to buy my picture.'

'And in which name will the writ be issued?' asked Nakamura.

'What are you getting at?' shouted Fenston.

'Only that my New York lawyers will need to know

who they're up against. Will it be Bryce Fenston, the chairman of Fenston Finance, or Nicu Munteanu, money launderer to Ceauşescu, the late dictator of Romania?'

'Don't threaten me, Nakamura, or I'll—'

'Break my driver's neck?'

'It won't be your driver next time.'

There was a long pause, before Nakamura said, 'I can see that it might be sensible for me to reconsider my position.'

'I knew you'd come to your senses in the end,' said Fenston, before putting down the phone.

<o>

When Anna boarded the flight for Bucharest an hour later, she felt confident that she had shaken off Fenston's man. Following her call to Tina, they would have been convinced that she was on her way back to London to pick up the painting, *where it's always been.* The sort of clue Fenston and Leapman would undoubtedly have argued over.

She had perhaps overdone it a little by spending so much time at the British Airways desk and then heading straight for Gate 91B when she didn't even have a ticket. The little boy turned out to be a bonus, but even Anna was surprised by how much fuss he made when she'd pinched him on his calf.

Anna's only real concern was for Tina. By this time tomorrow, Fenston and Leapman would realize that Anna had fed them false information, having obviously worked out that her conversations were being bugged. Anna feared that losing her job might end up the least of Tina's problems.

As the wheels lifted off Japanese soil, Anna's mind

drifted to Anton. She only hoped that three days would have proved long enough.

Fenston's man was chasing her down an alley. At the far end was a high, jagged stone wall covered in barbed wire. Anna knew there was no way out. She turned to face her adversary as he came to a halt only a few feet in front of her. The short, ugly man drew a pistol from his holster, cocked the trigger, grinned and aimed it directly at her heart. She turned as she felt the bullet graze her shoulder . . . 'If you would like to adjust your watches, the time in Bucharest is now three twenty in the afternoon.'

Anna woke with a start. 'What day is it?' she asked the passing steward.

'Thursday the twentieth, madam.'

9/20

37

ANNA RUBBED her eyes, and set her watch to the correct time.

She had kept her agreement with Anton to be back within four days. Now her biggest problem would be to transport the painting to London, while at the same time . . . 'Ladies and gentlemen, the captain has turned on the *Fasten seatbelt* sign. We will be landing in Bucharest in approximately twenty minutes.'

She smiled at the thought that by now Fenston's man would have landed in Hong Kong, and would be puzzled why this time he couldn't spot her in duty free. Would he carry on to London, or risk switching flights for the Romanian capital? Perhaps he would arrive back in Bucharest just as she set off for London.

When Anna stepped out onto the pavement, she was delighted to see a smiling Sergei, standing by the door of his yellow Mercedes. He opened the back door for her. Her only problem was she barely had enough cash to cover his fare.

'Where to?' he asked.

'First, I need to go to the academy,' she told him.

Anna would have liked to share with Sergei all she had been through, but still didn't feel she knew him well enough to risk it. Not trusting people was another experience she didn't enjoy.

Sergei dropped her at the bottom of the steps, where she'd left Anton before going to the airport. She no longer needed to ask him to wait. The student working at the reception desk told Anna that Professor Teodorescu's lecture on 'Attribution' was just about to begin.

Anna made her way to the lecture theatre on the first floor. She followed a couple of students in just as the lights were dimmed, and slipped into a seat at the end of the second row, looking forward to a few minutes' escape from the real world.

'Attribution and provenance,' began Anton, running a hand through his hair in that familiar way the students mimicked behind his back, 'are the cause of more discussion and disagreement among art scholars than any other subject. Why? Because it's sexy, open to debate and rarely conclusive. There is no doubt that several of the world's most popular galleries currently display works that were not painted by the artists whose names are suggested on the frame. It is, of course, possible that the master painted the main figure, the Virgin or Christ for example, while leaving an assistant to fill in the background. We must consider, therefore, whether several paintings, all depicting the same subject, can have been executed by one master, or if it is more likely that one of them, possibly even more, are the works of his star pupils, which several hundred years later are mistaken for the master.' Anna smiled at the words 'star pupil', and remembered the letter she had to pass on to Danuta Sekalska.

'Now let us consider some examples,' continued Anton, 'and see if you can detect the hand of a lesser mortal. The first is of a painting currently on display at the Frick Museum in New York.' A slide was beamed up on the screen behind Anton. 'Rembrandt, I hear you cry, but the Rembrandt research project, set up in 1974, would not agree with you. They believe that *The Polish Rider* is the work of at least two hands, one of which may – I repeat, may – have been that of Rembrandt. The Metropolitan Museum, just a few blocks away from the Frick on the other side of 5th Avenue, was unable to hide its angst when the same distinguished scholars dismissed the two portraits of *The Beresteyn Family*, acquired by them in 1929, as not executed by the Dutch master.

'Don't lose too much sleep over the problems faced by these two great institutions, because, of the twelve paintings attributed to Rembrandt in London's Wallace Collection, only one, *Titus, the Artist's Son*, has been pronounced genuine.' Anna became so engrossed that she began taking notes. 'The second artist I would ask you to consider is the great Spanish maestro, Goya. Much to the embarrassment of the Prado in Madrid, Juan Jose Junquera, the world's leading authority on Goya, has suggested that the "black paintings", which include such haunting visions as *Satan Devouring His Children*, cannot have been the hand of Goya, as he points out that the room for which they were painted as murals was not completed until after his death. The distinguished Australian critic Robert Hughes, in his book on Goya, suggests they are the work of the artist's son.

'And now I turn to the Impressionists and after. Several examples of Manet, Monet, Matisse and Van Gogh currently on display in leading galleries around the world have not been authenticated by the relevant scholars. *Sunflowers*, for example, which came under the hammer at Christie's in 1987 selling for just under forty million dollars, has yet to be authenticated by Louis van Tilborgh of the Van Gogh Museum.'

As Anton turned to display the next slide, his eyes rested on Anna. She smiled, and he put up a Raphael instead of the Van Gogh, which caused a ripple of laughter among the students. 'As you can see, I am also capable of attributing the wrong painting to the wrong artist.' The laughter turned to applause. But then, to Anna's surprise, he looked back and stared at her. 'This great city,' he said, no longer referring to his notes, 'has produced its own scholar in the field of attribution, who currently works out of New York. Some years ago when we were both students, we used to have long discussions into the night about this particular painting.' The Raphael returned to the screen. 'After attending a lecture, we would meet up at our favourite rendezvous,' – once again he fixed his gaze on Anna – '*Koskies*, where I'm reliably informed many of you still congregate. We always used to meet at *nine o'clock*, following the evening lecture.' He turned his attention back to the picture on the screen. 'This is a portrait known as *The Madonna of the Pinks*, recently acquired by the National Gallery in London. Raphael experts are divided, but many are concerned by how many examples there are of the same subject, attributed to the same artist. Some argue that this painting is more likely to be "school of Raphael", or "after Raphael".'

Anton looked back into the audience, to see that the seat on the end of the second row was no longer occupied.

Anna arrived at Koskies a few minutes before the suggested hour. Only an attentive student would have noticed that the lecturer had departed from his prepared script for a few moments to let her know where they should meet. She could not mistake that look of fear in Anton's eyes, a look that is obvious only to those who've had to survive in a police state.

Anna glanced around the room. Her old student haunt hadn't changed that much. The same plastic tables, the same plastic chairs and probably the same plastic wine that couldn't find an exporter. Not a natural rendezvous for a Professor of Perspective and a New York art dealer. She ordered two glasses of the house red.

Anna could still remember when she had considered a night at Koskies so cool, where she would discuss with her friends the virtues of Constantin Brancusi and U2, Tom Cruise and John Lennon, and have to suck a peppermint on the way home so that her mother wouldn't find out that she'd been smoking and sipping alcohol. Her father always knew – he'd wink and point to whichever room her mother was in.

Anna recalled when she and Anton first made love. It was so cold they both had to keep their coats on, and when it was over, Anna even wondered if she would bother to do it again. No one seemed to have explained to Anton that it might take a woman a little longer to have an orgasm.

Anna looked up to see a tall man coming towards her. For a moment she couldn't be sure that it was Anton. The advancing man was dressed in an army greatcoat too big for him, with a woollen scarf wrapped around his neck, topped off by a fur hat with flaps that covered his ears. An ideal outfit for a New York winter, was her immediate thought.

Anton took the seat opposite her and removed his hat, but nothing else. He knew that the only heater that worked was on the other side of the room.

'Do you have the painting?' asked Anna, unable to wait a moment longer to find out.

'Yes,' said Anton. 'The canvas never left my studio the whole time you were away, as even the least observant of my students would have noticed it wasn't my usual style,' he added, before sipping his red wine. 'Though I confess I'll be glad to be rid of the damn man.

I went to jail for less, and I haven't slept for the past four days. Even my wife suspects something is wrong.'

'I'm so sorry,' said Anna, as Anton began to roll a cigarette. 'I shouldn't have placed you in such danger, and what makes it worse is I have to ask you for another favour.' Anton looked apprehensive, but waited to hear what her latest request would be. 'You told me you kept eight thousand dollars of my mother's money hidden in the house.'

'Yes, most Romanians stash the cash under their mattress, in case there's a change of government in the middle of the night,' said Anton as he lit his cigarette.

'I need to borrow some of it,' said Anna. 'I'll refund the money just as soon as I get back to New York.'

'It's your money, Anna, you can have every last cent.'

'No, it's my mother's, but don't let her know, or she'll only assume I'm in some sort of financial trouble and start selling off the furniture.'

Anton didn't laugh. 'But you are in some sort of trouble, aren't you?'

'Not as long as I have the painting.'

'Would you rather I held on to it for another day?' he asked as he took a sip of wine.

'No, that's kind of you,' said Anna, 'but that would only mean that neither of us was able to get a night's sleep. I think the time has come to take the canvas off your hands.'

Anna rose without another word, having not touched her wine.

Anton drained his glass, stubbed out his cigarette and left a few coins on the table. He pulled his hat back on and followed Anna out of the bar. She couldn't help remembering the last time they'd walked out of Koskies together.

Anna looked up and down the street before she joined Anton, who was whispering intently to Sergei.

'Will you have time to visit your mother?' asked Anton as Sergei opened the back door for her.

'Not while someone is watching my every move.'

'I didn't see anyone,' said Anton.

'You don't see him,' said Anna. 'You feel him.' She paused. 'And I was under the illusion that I'd got rid of him.'

'You haven't,' said Sergei as they drove off.

No one spoke for the rest of the short journey to Anton's home. Once Sergei had brought the car to a halt, Anna jumped out and followed Anton into the house. He led her quickly up the stairs to an attic on the top floor. Although Anna could hear the sound of Sibelius coming from a room below, it was clear that he didn't want her to meet his wife.

Anna walked into a room crowded with canvases. Her eyes were immediately drawn to the painting of Van Gogh, his left ear bandaged. She smiled. The picture was in its familiar frame, inside the open red box.

'Couldn't be better,' said Anna. 'Now all I have to do is make sure it ends up in the right hands.'

Anton didn't comment, and when Anna turned round, she found him on his knees in the far corner of the room, lifting up a floorboard. He reached inside and extracted a thick envelope, which he slipped into an inside pocket. He then returned to the red box, replaced the lid and began to hammer the nails back in place. It was only too clear that he wanted to be rid of the painting as quickly as possible. Once the final nail was secured, he lifted up the box and, without a word, led Anna out of the room and back down the stairs.

Anna opened the front door to allow Anton to step

out onto the street. She was pleased to see Sergei waiting by the back of the car, the trunk already open. Anton placed the red box in the trunk and brushed his hands together, showing how happy he was to be free of the painting. Sergei slammed the lid closed and returned to his seat behind the wheel.

Anton extracted the thick envelope from his inside pocket and handed it over to Anna.

'Thank you,' she said, before passing across another envelope in exchange, but it was not addressed to Anton.

He looked at the name, smiled and said, 'I'll see she gets it. Whatever it is you're up to,' he added, 'I hope it works out.'

He kissed her on both cheeks before disappearing back into the house.

'Where will you stay tonight?' asked Sergei as Anna joined him in the front of the car.

Anna told him.

9/21

38

WHEN ANNA WOKE, Sergei was sitting on the bonnet of the car, smoking a cigarette. Anna stretched, blinked and rubbed her eyes. It was the first time she'd slept on the back seat of a car – a definite improvement on the back of a van, somewhere on the way to the Canadian border, with no one to protect her.

She got out of the car and stretched her legs. The red box was still in place.

'Good morning,' said Sergei. 'I hope you slept well?'

She laughed. 'Better than you it seems.'

'After twenty years in the army, sleep becomes a luxury,' said Sergei. 'But please do join me for breakfast.' He returned to the car and retrieved a small tin box from under the driver's seat. He removed the lid and revealed its contents: two bread rolls, a boiled egg, a hunk of cheese, a couple of tomatoes, an orange and a thermos of coffee.

'Where did all of this come from?' asked Anna as she peeled the orange.

'Last night's supper,' explained Sergei, 'prepared by my dear wife.'

'How will you explain why you didn't go home?' Anna asked.

'I'll tell her the truth,' said Sergei. 'I spent the night with a beautiful woman.' Anna blushed. 'But I fear I am too old for her to believe me,' he added. 'So what do we do next? Rob a bank?'

'Only if you know one with fifty million dollars in loose change,' said Anna, laughing. 'Otherwise I have to get that,' she pointed to the crate, 'into the cargo hold on the next flight to London, so I'll need to find out when the freight depot opens.'

'When the first person turns up,' said Sergei as he removed the shell from the egg. 'Usually around seven,' he added before handing the egg across to Anna.

Anna took a bite. 'Then I'd like to be there by seven, when they open,' she said, 'so I can be sure the crate is definitely on board.' She looked at her watch. 'So we'd better get moving.'

'I don't think so.'

'What do you mean?' asked Anna, sounding anxious.

'When a woman like you has to spend the night in a car, not a hotel, there has to be a reason. I have a feeling *that* is the reason,' said Sergei, pointing to the crate. 'So perhaps it would be unwise for you to be seen checking in a red box this morning.' Anna continued to stare at him, but didn't speak. 'Could there possibly be something inside the box that you don't want the authorities to take an interest in?' He paused, but Anna still didn't comment. 'Just as I thought,' said Sergei. 'You know, when I was a colonel in the army, and I needed something done that I didn't want anyone else to know about, I always chose a corporal to carry out the task. That way, I found, no one took the slightest interest. I think today I will have to be your corporal.'

'But what if you're caught?'

'Then I'll have done something worthwhile for a change. Do you think it's fun being a taxi driver when you've commanded a regiment? Do not concern yourself, dear lady. One or two of my boys work in the customs shed, and if the price is right, they won't ask too many questions.'

Anna flicked open her briefcase, took out the envelope Anton had given her and passed Sergei five twenty-dollar bills.

'No, no, dear lady,' he said, throwing his hands in the air. 'We are not trying to bribe the chief of police, just a couple of local boys,' he added, taking one of the twenty-dollar notes. 'And in any case, I may be in need of their services again at some time in the future, so we don't want expectations to exceed their usefulness.'

Anna laughed. 'And when you sign the manifest, Sergei, be sure your signature is illegible.'

He looked at her closely. 'I understand, but then I do not understand,' he said, pausing. 'You stay here, and keep out of sight. All I'll need is your plane ticket.'

Anna opened her bag again, placed the eighty dollars back in the envelope and handed over her ticket to London.

Sergei climbed into the driver's seat, turned on the engine and waved goodbye.

Anna watched as the car disappeared round the corner with the painting, her luggage, her ticket to London and twenty dollars. All she had as security was a cheese and tomato roll and a thermos of cold coffee.

<o>

Fenston picked up the receiver on the tenth ring.

'I've just landed in Bucharest,' she said. 'The red crate you've been looking for was loaded onto a flight to London, which will be landing at Heathrow around four this afternoon.'

'And the girl?'

'I don't know what her plans are, but when I do—'

'Just be sure to leave the body in Bucharest.'

The phone went dead.

Krantz walked out of the airport, placed the recently

acquired cellphone under the front wheel of an articulated truck and waited for it to move off before she slipped back into the terminal.

She checked the departures board, but this time she didn't assume Petrescu would be travelling to London; after all, there was also a flight to New York that morning. If Petrescu was booked on that one, she'd have to kill her at the airport. It wouldn't be the first time – at this particular airport.

Krantz tucked herself in behind a large drinks machine and waited. She made sure she had an unimpeded view of any taxis dropping off their customers. She was only interested in one taxi, and one customer. Petrescu wouldn't fool her a second time, because on this occasion, she intended to take out some insurance.

◄○►

After thirty minutes, Anna began to feel anxious. After forty minutes, worried. After fifty, close to panic. An hour after he'd left, Anna even wondered if Sergei worked for Fenston. A few minutes later, an old yellow Mercedes, driven by an even older man, came trundling round the bend.

Sergei smiled. 'You look relieved,' he said as he opened the front door for her and handed back her ticket.

'No, no,' said Anna, feeling guilty.

Sergei smiled. 'The package is booked for London, and it's on the same flight as you,' he said once he'd climbed back behind the wheel.

'Good,' said Anna, 'then perhaps it's time for me to be on my way as well.'

'Agreed,' said Sergei, turning the key in the ignition. 'But you'll have to be careful, because the American is already there waiting for you.'

'He's not interested in me,' said Anna, 'only the package.'

'But he saw me take it into the cargo depot, and for another twenty dollars he'll know exactly where it's going.'

'I don't care any longer,' said Anna, without explanation.

Sergei looked puzzled, but didn't question her as he eased the Mercedes back onto the highway and continued to follow the signs for the airport.

'I owe you so much,' said Anna.

'Four dollars,' said Sergei, 'plus gourmet meal. I'll settle for five.'

Anna opened her bag, took out Anton's envelope, removed all but five hundred dollars and resealed it. When Sergei came to a halt at the taxi rank outside the main terminal, Anna passed him the envelope.

'Five dollars,' she said.

'Thank you, ma'am,' he replied.

'Anna,' she said, and kissed him on the cheek. She didn't look back, otherwise she would have seen an old soldier crying.

Should he have told her that Colonel Sergei Slatinaru was standing by her father's side when he was executed?

‹○›

When Tina stepped out of the elevator, she spotted Leapman leaving her office. She slipped into the washroom, her heart beating frantically as she considered the consequences. Did he now know that she could overhear every phone conversation Fenston had, while at the same time being able to watch everything that was going on in the chairman's office? But worse, had he found out that she had been emailing confidential documents to herself for the past year? Tina tried to remain calm as she stepped back into the corridor and walked slowly towards her office. One thing she was certain about, there would be no clue that Leapman had even entered the room.

She sat at her desk and flicked on the screen. She felt ill. Leapman was in the chairman's office, talking to Fenston. The chairman was listening intently.

◄◦►

Jack watched as Anna kissed the driver on the cheek, and couldn't forget that this was the same man who had extracted twenty dollars from him – a sum that wouldn't be appearing on his expense sheet. He thought about the fact that the two of them had stayed awake all night while she had slept. If he'd dozed off, even for a moment, Jack feared that Crew Cut would have moved in and stolen the crate, although he hadn't spotted her since she boarded the plane for London. He wondered where she was now. Not far away, he suspected. As each hour had passed, Jack became more aware that he wasn't just dealing with a taxi driver, but someone willing to risk his life for the girl, perhaps without even knowing the significance of what was in that crate. There had to be a reason.

Jack knew it would be a waste of time to try and bribe the taxi driver, as he had already discovered to his own cost, but the cargo manager had beckoned him into his private office and even printed out the relevant page of the manifest. The crate was booked on the next flight to London. Already loaded on board, he assured him. Not a bad investment for fifty dollars, even if he couldn't read the signature. But would she be on the same flight? Jack remained puzzled. If the Van Gogh was in the red box on its way back to London, what was in the box that Petrescu had taken to Japan and delivered to Nakamura's office? He had no choice but to wait and see if she boarded the same plane.

—◦—

Sergei watched as Anna walked towards the airport entrance, pulling her suitcase. He would call Anton later, to let him know he had delivered her safely. Anna turned to wave, so he didn't notice a customer climb into the back of the car, until he heard the door close. He glanced up at his rear-view mirror.

'Where to, madam?' he asked.

'The old airport,' she said.

'I didn't realize it was still in service,' he ventured, but she didn't reply. Some customers don't.

When they reached the second traffic island, Sergei took the next exit. He checked once again in the mirror. There was something familiar about her – had she been in the back of his cab before? At the crossroads, Sergei turned left onto the old airport road. It was deserted. He'd been right, nothing had flown out of there since Ceauşescu had attempted to escape in November 1989. He glanced up at the mirror again, while trying to maintain a steady speed, and suddenly it all came back to him. He now remembered exactly where he'd last seen her. The hair had been longer, and blonde, and although it was over a decade ago, those eyes hadn't changed – eyes that registered nothing when she killed, eyes that bored into you when you died.

His platoon had been surrounded on the border with Bulgaria. They were quickly rounded up and marched to the nearest prisoner-of-war camp. He could still hear the cries of his young volunteers, some of whom had only just left school. And then, once they had told her everything they knew, or nothing at all, she would slit their throats while staring into their eyes. Once she was certain they were dead, with one more sweeping movement of her knife she would hack off the head, then dump it in the middle of an overcrowded cell. Even the most hardened of her henchmen had to avert their eyes.

Before leaving, she would spend a little time looking around at those who had survived. Each night she left with the same parting words, 'I still haven't decided which one of you will be next.'

Three of his men had survived, and only because a new set of prisoners, with more up-to-date information, had recently been captured. But for thirty-seven sleepless nights, Colonel Sergei Slatinaru could only wonder when it would be his turn. Her last victim had been Anna's father, one of the bravest men he'd ever known, who, if he had to die, deserved to go to his grave fighting the enemy – not at the hands of a butcher.

When they were finally repatriated, one of his first duties as commanding officer was to tell Anna's mother how Captain Petrescu had been killed. He lied, assuring her that her husband died bravely on the battlefield. Why should he pass his nightmare on to her? And then Anton phoned to say he'd had a call from Captain Petrescu's daughter; she was coming to Bucharest, and would he . . . someone else he didn't pass his secret on to.

Once the hostility had ceased, rumour concerning Krantz was rife. She was in jail, she had escaped to America, she'd been killed. He prayed that she was still alive, as he wanted to be the one to kill her. But he feared that she would never show her face in Romania again, because so many former comrades would recognize her and line up for the privilege of cutting her throat. But why had she returned? What could possibly be in that crate to make her take such a risk?

Sergei slowed down when he reached a barren stretch of land, where the runway had once been but was now covered in weeds and potholes. He kept one hand on the wheel, while the other moved slowly down his left side and reached underneath the seat for a gun he hadn't used since Ceaușescu had been executed.

'Where do you want me to drop you, madam?' he asked, as if they were in the middle of a busy street. He placed his fingers round the handle of the gun. She didn't reply. His eyes glanced up into the rear-view mirror, realizing that any sudden movement would alert her. Not only did she have the advantage of being behind him, but she was now watching his every move. He knew one of them would be dead in the next sixty seconds.

Sergei placed his index finger round the trigger, eased the gun from under his seat and began to raise his arm slowly, inch by inch. He was about to throw the brakes on, when a hand grabbed his hair and jerked back his head in one sharp movement. His foot came off the accelerator and the car slowed to a halt in the middle of the runway. He raised the gun another inch.

'Where is the girl going?' she demanded, pulling his head even further back so that she could look into his eyes.

'What girl?' he managed to say as he felt the knife touch his skin just below the Adam's apple.

'Don't play games with me, old man. The girl you dropped at the airport.'

'She didn't say.' Another inch.

'She didn't say, even though you drove her everywhere? Where?' she shouted, the edge of the blade now piercing the skin.

One more inch.

'I'll give you one last chance,' she screamed as the

blade broke the skin and warm blood began to trickle down his neck. 'Where – was – she – going?' Krantz demanded.

'I don't know,' Sergei screamed, as he raised the gun, pointed it towards her head and pulled the trigger.

The bullet ripped into Krantz's shoulder and threw her backwards, but she never let go of his hair. Sergei pulled the trigger again, but there was a full second between the two shots. Just long enough for her to slit his throat in a single movement.

Sergei's last memory before he died was staring into those cold grey eyes.

39

LEAPMAN WASN'T ASLEEP when his phone rang. But then he rarely slept, although he knew there was only one person who would consider calling him at such an ungodly hour.

He picked up the phone, and said, 'Good morning, chairman,' as if he was sitting at his desk in the office.

'Krantz has located the painting.'

'Where is it?' asked Leapman.

'It was in Bucharest, but it's now on its way back to Heathrow.'

Leapman wanted to say, I told you so, but confined himself to, 'When does the plane land?'

'Just after four, London time.'

'I'll have someone standing by to pick it up.'

'And they should put it on the first available flight to New York.'

'So where's Petrescu?' asked Leapman.

'No idea,' said Fenston, 'but Krantz is at the airport waiting for her. So don't expect her to be on the same flight.'

Leapman heard the click. Fenston never said goodbye. He climbed out of bed, picked up his phonebook and thumbed through until he reached the Ps. He checked his watch and dialled her office number.

'Ruth Parish.'

'Good morning, Ms Parish. It's Karl Leapman.'

'Good morning,' replied Ruth, cautiously.

'We've found our painting.'

'You have the Van Gogh?' said Ruth.

'No, not yet, but that's why I'm calling.'

'How can I help?'

'It's in the cargo hold of a flight on its way from Bucharest, due to land outside your front door just after four o'clock this afternoon.' He paused. 'Just make sure you're there to pick it up.'

'I'll be there. But whose name is on the manifest?'

'Who gives a fuck? It's our painting and it's in your crate. Just be sure you don't mislay it a second time.' Leapman put the phone down before she had a chance to protest.

⬤

Ruth Parish and four of her carriers were already on the tarmac when flight 019 from Bucharest landed at Heathrow. Once the aircraft had been cleared for unloading, the little motorcade of a customs official's car, Ruth's Range Rover and an Art Locations security van drove up and parked within twenty metres of the cargo hold.

If Ruth had looked up, she would have seen Anna's smiling face in her tiny window at the back of the aircraft. But she didn't.

Ruth stepped out of her car and joined the customs officer. She had earlier informed him that she wished to transfer a painting from an incoming flight to an onward destination. The customs official had looked bored, and wondered why she had chosen such a senior officer to carry out such a routine task, until he was told, in confidence, the value of the painting. His promotion board was due in three weeks' time. If he screwed up this simple exercise, he could forget the extra silver stripe he'd promised his wife she would be sewing on his sleeve before the end of the month. Not to mention the pay rise.

When the hold eventually opened, they both walked forward together, but only the customs officer addressed the chief loader. 'There's a red wooden crate on board' – he checked his file – 'three foot by two, and three or four inches deep. It's stamped with an Art Locations logo on both sides, and the number forty-seven stencilled in all four corners. I want it unloaded before anything else is moved.'

The chief loader passed on the instructions to his two men in the hold, who disappeared into the darkness. By the time they reappeared, Anna was heading towards passport control.

'That's it,' said Ruth when the two loaders reappeared on the edge of the hold, carrying a red crate. The customs official nodded. A forklift truck moved forward, expertly extracted the crate from the hold and lowered it slowly to the ground. The customs man checked the manifest, followed by the logo and even the stencilled forty-sevens.

'Everything seems to be in order, Ms Parish. If you'll just sign here.'

Ruth signed the form, but couldn't make out the signature on the original manifest. The customs officer's eyes never left the forklift truck as the package was driven across to the Art Locations van, where two of Ruth's carriers loaded the crate on board.

'I'll still have to accompany you to the outgoing aircraft, Ms Parish, so I can confirm that the package has been loaded for its onward destination. Not until then can I sign a clearance certificate.'

'Of course,' said Ruth, who carried out the same procedure two or three times a day.

Anna had reached the baggage area by the time the security van began its circuitous journey from terminal three to terminal four. When the driver came to a halt, he parked beside a United Airlines plane bound for New York.

The security van waited on the tarmac for over an hour before the cargo hold was opened, by which time Ruth knew the life history of the customs official, even which school he intended to send his third child to if he was promoted. Ruth then watched the process in reverse. The back door of the security van was unlocked, the painting placed on a forklift truck, driven to the side of the hold, raised and accepted on board by two handlers before it disappeared into the bowels of the aircraft.

The customs official signed all three copies of the dispatch documents and bade farewell to Ruth before returning to his office. In normal circumstances, Ruth would also have gone back to her office, filed the relevant forms, checked her messages and then left for the day. However, these were not normal circumstances. She remained seated in her car and waited until all the passengers' bags had been loaded on board and the cargo doors had been locked. Still she didn't move, even after the aircraft began to taxi towards the north runway. She waited until the plane's wheels had left the ground before she phoned Leapman in New York. Her message was simple. 'The package is on its way.'

—◦—

Jack was puzzled. He had watched Anna stroll into the arrivals hall, exchange some dollars at Travelex and then join the long queue for a taxi. Jack's cab was already waiting on the other side of the road, two sets of luggage on board, engine running, as he waited for Anna's cab to pass him.

'Where to, guv?' asked the driver.

'I'm not sure,' admitted Jack, 'but my first bet would be cargo.'

Jack assumed that Anna would drive straight to the cargo depot and retrieve the package the taxi driver had dispatched from Bucharest.

But Jack was wrong. Instead of turning right, when the large blue sign indicating cargo loomed up in front of them, Anna's taxi swung left and continued to drive west down the M25.

'She's not going to cargo, guv, so what's your next bet – Gatwick?'

'So what's in the crate?' asked Jack.

'I've no idea, sir.'

'I'm so stupid,' Jack said.

'I wouldn't want to venture an opinion on that, sir, but it would help if I knew where we was goin'.'

Jack laughed. 'I think you'll find it's Wentworth.'

'Right, guv.'

Jack tried to relax, but every time he glanced out of the rear window he could have sworn that another black cab was following them. A shadowy figure was seated in the back. Why was she still pursuing Anna, when the painting must have been deposited in cargo?

When his driver turned off the M25 and took the road to Wentworth, the taxi Jack had imagined was following them continued on in the direction of Gatwick.

'You're not stupid, after all, guv, because it looks as if it could be Wentworth.'

'No, but I am paranoid,' admitted Jack.

'Make up your mind, sir,' the driver said, as Anna's taxi swung through the gates of Wentworth Hall and disappeared up the drive. 'Do you want me to keep followin' her, guv?'

'No,' said Jack. 'But I'll need a local hotel for the night. Do you know one by any chance?'

'When the golf tournament is on, I drop a lot of my customers off at the Wentworth Arms. They ought to be able to fix you up with a room at this time of year.'

'Then let's find out,' said Jack.

'Right you are, guv.'

Jack sat back and dialled a number on his cellphone.

'American embassy.'

'Tom Crasanti, please.'

40

WHEN KRANTZ CAME ROUND following the operation, the first thing she felt was a stabbing pain in her right shoulder. She managed to raise her head a couple of inches off the pillow as she tried to focus on the small white-walled, unadorned room: just the basic necessities – a bed, a table, a chair, one sheet, one blanket and a bed pan. It could only be a hospital, but not of the private variety. The only light came from a tiny window so high in the wall that they hadn't even bothered to put a bar across it. There were no flowers, no fruit, no get-well cards, and the one exit was a door that was not only locked and barred, but had two guards permanently stationed on the other side.

Krantz tried to piece together what had happened to her. She could recall spotting the taxi driver's gun pointing at her head, but that was where the memory faded. She'd just had enough time to turn – an inch, no more – before the bullet ripped into her shoulder. No one had been that close before. The next bullet missed completely, but by then he'd given her another second, easily enough time to cut his throat. He had to be a pro, an ex-policeman perhaps, possibly a soldier. But then she must have passed out.

❦

Jack checked himself into the Wentworth Arms for the night, and booked a table for dinner at eight. After a shower and a change of clothes, he looked forward to devouring a large juicy steak.

Even though Anna was safely ensconced at Wentworth Hall, he didn't feel he could relax while Crew Cut might well be hovering somewhere nearby. He had already asked Tom to brief the local police, while he continued to carry out his own surveillance.

He sat in the lounge enjoying a Guinness and thinking about Anna. Long before the hall clock struck eight, Tom walked in, looked around and spotted his old friend by the fire. Jack rose to greet him, and apologized for having to drag him down to Wentworth when he could have been spending the evening with Chloe and Hank.

'As long as this establishment can produce a decent Tom Collins, you'll not hear me complain,' Tom answered him.

Tom was explaining to Jack how Hank had scored a half century – whatever that was – when they were joined by the head waiter, who took their orders for dinner. They both chose steaks, but as a Texan, Tom admitted he hadn't got used to the English version that was served up looking like a lamb chop.

'I'll call you through,' said the head waiter, 'as soon as your table is ready.'

'Thank you,' said Jack, as Tom bent down to open his briefcase. He extracted a thick file and placed it on the table between them. Small talk had never been his forte.

'Let's begin with the important news,' said Tom, opening the file. 'We've identified the woman in the photograph you sent through from Tokyo.' Jack put his drink down and concentrated on the contents of the file. 'Her name is Olga Krantz, and she has one thing in common with Dr Petrescu.'

'And what's that?' asked Jack.

'The agency was also under the illusion that she was missing, presumed dead. As you can see from her profile,' Tom added, pushing a sheet of paper across the table, 'we lost contact with her in 1989, when she ceased being a member of Ceauşescu's personal bodyguard. But we're now convinced that she works exclusively for Fenston.'

'That's one hell of a leap of logic,' suggested Jack, as a waiter appeared with a Tom Collins and another half pint of Guinness.

'Not if you consider the facts logically,' said Tom, 'and then follow them step by step,' he added, before sipping his drink. 'Um, not bad. After all, she and Fenston worked for Ceauşescu at the same time.'

'Coincidence,' said Jack. 'Wouldn't stand up in court.'

'It might, when you learn what her job description was.'

'Try me,' said Jack.

'She was responsible for removing anyone who posed a threat to Ceauşescu.'

'Still circumstantial.'

'Until you discover her chosen method of disposal.'

'A kitchen knife?' suggested Jack, not looking down at the sheet of paper in front of him.

'You've got it,' said Tom.

'Which, I fear, means that there is yet another undeniable link in your chain of logic.'

'What's that?' asked Tom.

'Anna is being lined up as her next victim.'

'No – there, fortunately, the logic breaks down, because Krantz was arrested in Bucharest this morning.'

'What?' said Jack.

'By the local police,' added Tom.

'It's hard to believe they got within a mile of her,' said Jack. 'I kept losing her even when I knew where she was.'

'The local police were the first to admit,' said Tom, 'that she was unconscious at the time.'

'Fill me in on the details,' said Jack impatiently.

'It seems, and reports were still coming through when I left the embassy, that Krantz was involved in a quarrel with a taxi driver, who was found to have five hundred dollars in his possession. The driver had his throat cut, while she ended up with a bullet in her right shoulder. We don't yet know what caused the fight, but as he was killed only moments before your flight took off, we thought you might be able to throw some light on it.'

'Krantz would have been trying to find out which plane Anna was on, after she made such a fool of herself in Tokyo, but that man would never have told her. He protected Anna more like a father than a taxi driver, and the five hundred dollars is a red herring. Krantz doesn't bother to kill people for that sort of money, and that was one taxi driver who never kept the meter running.'

'Well, whatever, Krantz is safely locked up, and with a bit of luck will spend the rest of her life in jail, which may not prove to be that long, as we're reliably informed that half the population of Romania would be happy to strangle her.' Tom glanced back down at his file. 'And it turns out that our taxi driver, one Colonel Sergei Slatinaru, was a hero of the resistance.' Tom took another sip of his drink before he added, 'So there's no longer any reason for you to worry about Petrescu's safety.'

The waiter reappeared to accompany them into the dining room.

'In common with most Romanians, I won't relax until

Krantz is dead,' said Jack. 'Until then, I'll remain anxious for Anna.'

'Anna? Are you two on first-name terms?' asked Tom as he took his seat opposite Jack in the dining room.

'Hardly, though we may as well be. I've spent more nights with her than any of my recent girlfriends.'

'Then perhaps we should have invited Dr Petrescu to join us?'

'Forget it,' said Jack. 'She'll be having dinner with Lady Arabella at Wentworth Hall, while we have to settle for the Wentworth Arms.'

A waiter placed a bowl of leek and potato soup in front of Tom and served Jack with a Caesar salad.

'Have you found out anything else about Anna?'

'Not a lot,' admitted Tom, 'but I can tell you that she called the New York Police Department from Bucharest airport. She asked them to take her name off the missing list, said she'd been in Romania visiting her mother. She also called her uncle in Danville, Illinois, and Lady Arabella Wentworth.'

'Then her meeting in Tokyo must have gone belly up,' said Jack.

'You're going to have to explain that one to me,' said Tom.

'She had a meeting in Tokyo with a steel tycoon called Nakamura, who has one of the largest collections of Impressionist paintings in the world, so the concierge at the Seiyo informed me.' Jack paused. 'She obviously failed to sell Nakamura the Van Gogh, which would explain why she sent the painting back to London, and even allowed it to be forwarded to New York.'

'She doesn't strike me as someone who gives up that easily,' said Tom, extracting another piece of paper from his file. 'By the way, the Happy Hire Company is also looking for her. They claim she abandoned one of their vehicles on the Canadian border, minus its front mud-guard, front and rear bumper, with not one of its lights in working order.'

'Hardly a major crime,' said Jack.

'Are you falling for this girl?' asked Tom.

Jack didn't reply as a waiter appeared by their side. 'Two steaks, one rare, one medium,' he announced.

'Mine's the rare,' said Tom.

The waiter placed both plates on the table, and added, 'Enjoy.'

'Another Americanism we seem to have exported,' grunted Tom.

Jack smiled. 'Did you get any further with Leapman?'

'Oh yes,' said Tom. 'We know a great deal about Mr Leapman.' He placed another file on the table. 'He's an American citizen, second generation, and studied law at Columbia. Not unlike you,' Tom said with a grin. 'After graduating, he worked for several banks, always moving on fairly quickly, until he became involved in a share fraud. His speciality was selling bonds to widows that didn't exist.' He paused. 'The widows existed, the bonds didn't.' Jack laughed. 'He served a two-year sentence at Rochester Correctional Facility in upstate New York, and was banned for life from working at a bank or any other financial institution.'

'But he's Fenston's right hand?'

'Fenston's possibly, but not the bank's. Leapman's name doesn't appear on their books, even as a cleaner. He pays taxes on his only known income, a monthly cheque from an aunt in Mexico.'

'Come on—' said Jack.

'And before you say anything else,' added Tom, 'my department has neither the financial resources nor the back-up to find out if this aunt even exists.'

'Any Romanian connection?' Jack asked as he dug into his steak.

'None that we're aware of,' said Tom. 'Straight out of the Bronx, and into a Brooks Brothers suit.'

'Leapman may yet turn out to be our best lead,' said Jack. 'If we could only get him to testify—'

'Not a hope,' said Tom. 'Since leaving jail, he hasn't even had a parking ticket, and I suspect he's a lot more frightened of Fenston than he is of us.'

'If only Hoover was still alive,' said Jack with a grin.

They both raised their glasses, before Tom added, 'So when do you fly back to the States? I only ask, as I want to know when I can return to my day job.'

'Tomorrow, I suppose,' said Jack. 'Now Krantz is safely locked up, I ought to get back to New York. Macy will want to know if I'm any nearer to linking Krantz with Fenston.'

'And are you?' asked Tom.

Neither of them noticed the two men talking to the maître d'. They couldn't have been booking a table, otherwise they would have left their raincoats in reception. Once the maître d' had answered their question, they walked purposefully across the dining room.

Tom was placing the files back in his briefcase by the time they reached their table.

'Good evening, gentlemen,' said the taller of the two men. 'My name is Detective Sergeant Frankham, and this is my colleague, Detective Constable Ross. I'm sorry to disturb your meal, but I need to have a word with you, sir,' he said, touching Jack on the shoulder.

'Why, what have I done?' asked Jack, putting down his knife and fork. 'Parked on a double yellow line?'

'I'm afraid it's a little more serious than that, sir,' said the detective sergeant, 'and I must therefore ask you to accompany me to the station.'

'On what charge?' demanded Jack.

'I think it might be wiser, sir, if we were not to continue this conversation in a crowded restaurant.'

'And on whose authority—' began Tom.

'I don't think you need to involve yourself, sir.'

'I'll decide about that,' said Tom, as he removed his FBI badge from an inside pocket. He was about to flick the leather wallet open, when Jack touched him on the elbow and said, 'Let's not create a scene. No need to get the bureau involved.'

'To hell with that, who do these people think—'

'Tom, calm down. This is not our country. I'll go along to the police station and sort this all out.'

Tom reluctantly placed his FBI badge back in his pocket, and although he said nothing, the look on his face wouldn't have left either policeman in any doubt how he felt. As Jack stood up, the sergeant grabbed his arm and quickly handcuffed him.

'Hey, is that really necessary?' demanded Tom.

'Tom, don't get involved,' said Jack in a measured tone.

Tom reluctantly followed Jack out of the dining room, through a room full of guests, who studiously carried on chatting and eating their meals as if nothing unusual was going on around them.

When they reached the front door, Tom said, 'Do you want me to come with you to the station?'

'No,' said Jack, 'why don't you stick around. Don't worry, I'm sure I'll be back in time for coffee.'

Two women stared intently at Jack from the other side of the corridor.

'Is that him, madam?'

'Yes it is,' one of them confirmed.

―◇―

When Tina heard her door open, she quickly flicked off the screen. She didn't look up, as only one person never bothered to knock before entering her office.

'I presume you know that Petrescu is on her way back to New York?'

'I'd heard,' said Tina, as she continued typing.

'But had you also heard,' said Leapman, placing both hands on her desk, 'that she tried to steal the Van Gogh?'

'The one in the chairman's office?' said Tina, innocently.

'Don't play games with me,' said Leapman. 'You think I don't know that you listen in on every phone conversation the chairman has?' Tina stopped typing and looked up at him. 'Perhaps the time has come,' Leapman continued, 'to let Mr Fenston know about the switch under your desk that allows you to spy on him whenever he's having a private meeting.'

'Are you threatening me, Mr Leapman?' asked Tina. 'Because if you are, I might find it necessary to have a word with the chairman myself.'

'And what could you possibly tell him that I would care about?' demanded Leapman.

'About the weekly calls you receive from a Mr Pickford, and then perhaps we'll discover who's playing games.'

Leapman took his hands off the table and stood up straight.

'I feel sure your probation officer will be interested to learn that you've been harassing staff at a bank you don't work for, don't have an office in and don't receive a salary from.'

Leapman took a pace backwards.

'When you come to see me next time, Mr Leapman, make sure you knock, like any other visitor to the bank.'

Leapman took another pace backwards, hesitated, then left without another word.

When the door closed, Tina was shaking so much she had to grip the armrests of her chair.

41

WHEN THE POLICE CAR arrived at the station, Jack was bundled out. Once he'd been checked in by the desk sergeant, the two detectives accompanied him downstairs to an interview room. DS Frankham asked him to take a seat on the other side of the table. Something else Jack hadn't experienced before. DC Ross stood quietly in one corner.

Jack could only wonder which one of them was going to play the good cop.

DS Frankham sat down, placed a file on the table and extracted a long form.

'Name?' began Frankham.

'Jack Fitzgerald Delaney,' Jack replied.

'Date of birth?'

'Twenty-second November, sixty-three.'

'Occupation?'

'Senior Investigating Officer with the FBI, attached to the New York field office.'

The detective sergeant dropped his pen, looked up and said, 'Do you have some ID?'

Jack produced his FBI badge and identity card.

'Thank you, sir,' said Frankham after he'd checked them. 'Can you wait here for a moment?' He stood and turned to his colleague. 'Would you see that Agent Delaney is offered a coffee? This may take some time.' When he reached the door he added, 'And make sure he gets his tie, belt and laces back.'

DS Frankham turned out to be right, because it was another hour before the heavy door was opened again and an older man with a weathered, lined face entered the room. He was dressed in a well-tailored uniform, with silver braid on his sleeve, epaulette, and the peak of his cap, which he removed to reveal a head of grey hair. He took the seat opposite Jack.

'Good evening, Mr Delaney. My name is Renton, Chief Superintendent Renton, and now that we have been able to confirm your identity, perhaps you'd be kind enough to answer a few questions.'

'If I can,' said Jack.

'I feel sure you can,' said Renton. 'What interests me, is whether you will.'

Jack didn't respond.

'We received a complaint from a usually reliable source that you have, for the past week, been following a lady without her prior knowledge. This is an offence in England under the 1997 Protection from Harassment Act, as you are no doubt aware. However, I feel sure you have a simple explanation.'

'Dr Petrescu is part of an ongoing investigation, which my department has been involved in for some time.'

'Would that investigation have anything to do with the death of Lady Victoria Wentworth?'

'Yes,' replied Jack.

'And is Dr Petrescu a suspect in that murder?'

'No,' replied Jack firmly. 'Quite the opposite. In fact, we had thought she might be the next victim.'

'Had thought?' repeated the chief superintendent.

'Yes,' replied Jack. 'Fortunately the murderer has been apprehended in Bucharest.'

'And you didn't feel able to share this information with us?' said Renton. 'Despite the fact that you must have been aware that we were conducting a murder enquiry.'

'I apologize, sir,' said Jack. 'I only found out myself a few hours ago. But I'm sure our London office planned to keep you informed.'

'Mr Tom Crasanti has briefed me, but I suspect only because his colleague was under lock and key.' Jack didn't comment. 'But he did go on to assure me,' continued Renton, 'that you will keep us fully informed of any developments that might arise in the future.' Once again, Jack didn't respond. The chief superintendent rose from his place. 'Good night, Mr Delaney. I have authorized your immediate release, and can only hope you have a pleasant flight home.'

'Thank you, sir,' said Jack, as Renton replaced his cap and left the room.

Jack had some sympathy with the chief superintendent. After all, the NYPD, not to mention the CIA, rarely bothered to let the FBI know what they were up to. A few moments later, DS Frankham returned.

'If you'll accompany me, sir,' he said, 'we have a car waiting to take you back to your hotel.'

'Thank you,' said Jack, as he followed the detective sergeant out of the room and up the stairs into reception.

The desk sergeant lowered his head as Jack left the building. Jack shook hands with an embarrassed DS Frankham before climbing into a police car that was parked outside the front door. Tom was waiting for him in the back.

'Just another case study for Quantico to add to its curriculum,' suggested Tom. 'This time on how to cause a major diplomatic incident while visiting one's oldest ally.'

'I must have brought a new meaning to the words "special relationship",' commented Jack.

'However, the condemned man is to be given a chance to redeem himself,' said Tom.

'What do you have in mind?' asked Jack.

'We've both been invited to join Lady Arabella and Dr Petrescu for breakfast at Wentworth Hall tomorrow morning, and by the way, Jack, I see what you mean about Anna.'

9/22

42

Jack emerged from the Wentworth Arms just after seven thirty to find a Rolls-Royce parked by the entrance. A chauffeur opened the back door the moment he saw him.

'Good morning, sir,' he said. 'Lady Arabella asked me to say how much she is looking forward to meeting you.'

'Me too,' said Jack, as he climbed into the back.

'We'll be there in a few minutes,' the chauffeur assured him as he drove out of the hotel entrance.

Half of the journey seemed to Jack to be from the wrought-iron gates at the entrance to the estate up the long drive that led to the hall. Once the chauffeur had brought the car to a halt, he jumped out and walked round to open the back door. Jack stepped out onto the gravel drive and looked up to see a butler standing on the top step, obviously expecting him.

'Good morning, sir,' he said, 'welcome to Wentworth Hall. If you would be good enough to follow me, Lady Arabella is expecting you.'

'"A usually reliable source,"' muttered Jack, but if the butler did overhear him, he made no comment as he led the guest through to the drawing room.

'Mr Delaney, m'lady,' announced the butler, as two dogs, tails wagging, padded forward to greet him.

'Good morning, Mr Delaney,' said Arabella. 'I think

we owe you an apology. You are so obviously not a stalker.'

Jack stared at Anna, who also looked suitably embarrassed, and then turned towards Tom, who couldn't remove the grin from his face.

Andrews reappeared at the door. 'Breakfast is ready, m'lady.'

◄○►

When she woke a second time, a young doctor was changing the dressing on her shoulder.

'How long before I can get out of here?' was her first question.

The doctor looked startled when he heard her voice for the first time – such a shrill, piping note didn't quite fit her legend. He remained silent until he'd finished cutting a length of bandage with his scissors.

'Three, four days at most,' he replied, looking down at her. 'But I wouldn't be in a hurry to get myself discharged, if I were you, because the moment I sign your release papers, your next stop is Jilava, which I think you're only too familiar with from your days serving the past regime.'

Krantz could never forget the barren, stone-walled, rat-infested building that she had visited every night in order to question the latest prisoners before being driven back to the warmth of her well-furnished dacha on the outskirts of the city.

'I'm told that the inmates are looking forward to seeing you again after such a prolonged absence,' added the doctor. He bent over, peeled an edge from the large dressing on her shoulder and paused. 'This is going to hurt,' he promised, and then in one movement, ripped it off. Krantz didn't flinch. She wasn't going to allow him that satisfaction.

The doctor dabbed iodine into the wound before placing a new dressing over it. He then expertly bandaged the shoulder and placed her right arm in a sling.

'How many guards are there?' she asked casually.

'Six, and they're all armed,' said the doctor, 'and just in case you're thinking of trying to escape, they have orders to shoot first and fill in any unnecessary forms later. I've even prepared an unsigned death certificate for them.'

Krantz didn't ask any more questions.

When the doctor left, she lay staring up at the ceiling. If there was any chance of escaping, it would have to be while she was still at the hospital. No one had ever managed to escape from Jilava penitentiary, not even Ceauşescu.

It took her another eight hours to confirm that there were always six guards, covering three eight-hour shifts. The first group clocked on at six o'clock, the second at two, and the night shift came on duty at ten.

During a long, sleepless night, Krantz discovered that the half-dozen guards on night duty felt they had drawn the short straw. One of them was just plain lazy and spent half the night asleep. Another was always sneaking off to have a cigarette on the fire escape – no smoking allowed on the hospital premises. The third was a philanderer, who imagined that he'd been put on earth to satisfy women. He was never more than a few paces from one of the nurses. The fourth spent most of his time grumbling about how much, or how little, he was paid, and his wife's ability to clean him out before the end of every week. Krantz knew that she could solve his problem if she was given the chance. The other two guards were older, and remembered her only too well from the past regime. One of them would have been happy to blow a hole right through her if she'd as much as raised her head from the pillow.

But even they were entitled to a meal break.

<o>

Jack sat down to a breakfast of eggs, bacon, devilled kidneys, mushrooms and tomatoes, followed by toast, English marmalade and coffee.

'You must be hungry after such an ordeal,' remarked Arabella.

'If it hadn't been for Tom, I might have had to settle for prison rations.'

'And I fear I am to blame,' said Anna. 'Because I fingered you,' she added with a grin.

'Not true,' said Tom. 'You can thank Arabella for having Jack arrested, and Arabella for having him released.'

'No, I can't take all the credit,' Arabella said, stroking one of the dogs, seated on each side of her. 'I admit to having Jack arrested, but it was your ambassador who managed to get him – what's the American expression? – sprung.'

'But there is one thing I still don't understand,' said Anna, 'despite Tom filling us in with all the finer details. Why did you continue to follow me to Wentworth once you were convinced I was no longer in possession of the painting?'

'Because I thought the woman who murdered your driver would then follow you to London.'

'Where she planned to kill me?' said Anna quietly. Jack nodded, but didn't speak. 'Thank God I never knew,' she said, pushing her breakfast to one side.

'But by then she'd already been arrested for murdering Sergei,' queried Arabella.

'That's right,' said Jack, 'but I didn't know that until I met up with Tom last night.'

'So the FBI had been keeping an eye on me at the same time?' said Anna, turning to face Jack, who was buttering some toast.

'For some considerable time,' admitted Jack. 'At one point, we even wondered if you were the hired assassin.'

'On what grounds?' demanded Anna.

'An art consultant would be a good front for someone who worked for Fenston, especially if she was also an athlete, and just happened to be born in Romania.'

'And just how long have I been under investigation?' asked Anna.

'For the past two months,' admitted Jack. He took a sip of coffee. 'In fact, we were just about to close your file when you stole the Van Gogh.'

'I didn't steal it,' said Anna sharply.

'She retrieved it, on my behalf,' interjected Arabella. 'And with my blessing, what's more.'

'And are you still hoping that Fenston will agree to sell the painting so that you can clear the debt, because if he did, it would be a first.'

'No,' said Arabella, a little too quickly. 'That's the last thing I want.'

Jack looked puzzled.

'Not until the police solve the mystery of who murdered your sister,' interjected Anna.

'We all know who murdered my sister,' said Arabella sharply, 'and if she ever crosses my path, I'll happily blow her head off.' Both dogs pricked up their ears.

'Knowing it is not the same as proving it,' said Jack.

'So Fenston has got away with murder,' said Anna quietly.

'More than once, I suspect,' admitted Jack. 'The bureau has had him under investigation for some time. There are four – ' he paused – 'now five murders in different parts of the world that have the Krantz trademark, but we've never been able to link her directly to Fenston.'

'Krantz murdered Victoria, and Sergei,' said Anna.

'Without a doubt,' said Jack.

'And Colonel Sergei Slatinaru was your father's commanding officer,' added Tom, 'as well as being a close friend.'

'I'll do anything I can to help,' said Anna, close to tears, 'and I mean anything.'

'We've had a tiny break,' admitted Tom, 'though we can't be sure it will lead us anywhere. When Krantz was taken into hospital to have the bullet removed from her shoulder, the only thing they found on her, other than the knife and a little cash, was a key.'

'But surely it will fit a lock in Romania?' suggested Anna.

'We don't think so,' said Jack, after devouring another mushroom. 'It has NYRC 13 stamped on it. Not much of a lead, but if we could find out what it opened, it might, just might, connect Krantz to Fenston.'

'So do you want me to stay in England while you continue your investigation?' asked Anna.

'No, I need you to return to New York,' said Jack. 'Let everyone know you're safe and well, act normally, even look for a job. Just don't give Fenston any reason to become suspicious.'

'Do I stay in touch with my former colleagues in his office?' asked Anna. 'Because Fenston's secretary, Tina, is one of my closest friends.'

'Are you sure about that?' asked Jack, putting down his knife and fork.

'What are you getting at?' asked Anna.

'How do you explain the fact that Fenston always knew exactly where you were, if Tina wasn't telling him?'

'I can't,' said Anna, 'but I know she hates Fenston as much as I do.'

'And you can prove it?' asked Jack.

'I don't need proof,' snapped Anna.

'I do,' said Jack, calmly.

'Be careful, Jack, because if you're wrong,' said Anna, 'then her life must also be in danger.'

'If that's the case, all the more reason for you to return to New York and make contact with her as soon as possible,' suggested Tom, trying to calm the atmosphere.

Jack nodded his agreement.

'I'm booked on a flight this afternoon,' said Anna.

'Me too,' said Jack. 'Heathrow?'

'No, Stansted,' said Anna.

'Well, one of you is going to have to change your flight,' suggested Tom.

'Not me,' said Jack. 'I'm not going to be arrested for stalking a second time.'

'Before I make a decision on whether to change flights,' said Anna, 'I'll need to know if I'm still under investigation. Because if I am, *you* can go on following *me*.'

'No,' said Jack. 'I closed your file a few days ago.'

'What convinced you to do that?' asked Anna.

'When Arabella's sister was murdered, you had an unimpeachable witness as your alibi.'

'And who was that, may I ask?'

'Me,' replied Jack. 'As I'd been following you around Central Park, you can't have been in England.'

'You run in Central Park?' said Anna.

'Every morning round the loop,' said Jack. 'Round the Reservoir on Sundays.'

'Me too,' said Anna. 'Never miss.'

'I know,' said Jack. 'I overtook you several times during the last six weeks.'

Anna stared at him. 'The man in the emerald-green T-shirt. You're not bad.'

'You're not so—'

'I'm sorry to break up this meeting of the Central Park joggers' club,' said Tom, as he pushed back his chair, 'but I ought to be getting back to my office. There's a stack of 9/11 files on my desk I haven't even opened. Thank you for breakfast,' he added, turning to Arabella. 'I'm only sorry that the ambassador had to disturb you so early this morning.'

'Which reminds me,' said Arabella, as she rose from her chair. 'I must get on with writing some humble-pie letters, my thanks to the ambassador and my apologies to half the Surrey police force.'

'What about me?' said Jack. 'I'm thinking of suing the Wentworth Estate, the Surrey police and the Home Office, with Tom as my witness.'

'Not a hope,' said Tom. 'I wouldn't care to have Arabella as an enemy.'

Jack smiled. 'Then I'll have to settle for a lift to the Wentworth Arms.'

'You got it,' said Tom.

'And now that I feel safe to join you at Heathrow,' said Anna, rising from her place, 'where shall we meet?'

'Don't worry,' said Jack. 'I'll find you.'

43

LEAPMAN WAS DRIVEN TO JFK to pick up the painting an hour before the plane was due to land. That didn't stop Fenston calling him every ten minutes on the way to the airport, which became every five once the limousine was on its way back to Wall Street with the red crate safely stowed in the trunk.

Fenston was pacing up and down his office by the time Leapman was dropped outside the front of the building, and waiting in the corridor when Barry and the driver stepped out of the elevator carrying the red crate.

'Open it,' ordered Fenston, long before the box had been propped up against the wall in his office. Barry and the driver undid the special clamps before setting about extracting the long nails that had been hammered firmly into the rim of the wooden crate, while Fenston, Leapman and Tina looked on. When the lid was finally prised open and the polystyrene corners that were holding the painting in place were removed, Barry lifted the painting carefully out of the wooden crate and leant it up against the chairman's desk. Fenston rushed forward and began to tear off the bubble wrap with his bare hands, until he could at last see what he'd been willing to kill for.

Fenston stood back and gasped.

No one else in the room dared to speak until he had offered an opinion. Suddenly, the words came tumbling out in a torrent.

'It's even more magnificent than I'd expected,' he declared. 'The colours are so fresh, and the brushwork so bold. Truly a masterpiece,' he added. Leapman decided not to comment.

'I know exactly where I'm going to hang my Van Gogh,' said Fenston.

He looked up and stared at the wall behind his desk, where a massive photograph of George W. Bush shaking hands with him on his recent visit to Ground Zero filled the space.

◦

Anna was looking forward to her flight back to the States, and the chance to get to know Jack a little better during the seven-hour journey. She even hoped that he would answer one or two more questions. How did he find out her mother's address, why was he still suspicious of Tina, and was there any proof that Fenston and Krantz even knew each other?

Jack was waiting for her when she checked in. Anna took a little time to relax with a man she couldn't forget had been following her for the last nine days, and investigating her for the past eight weeks, but by the time they climbed the steps to the aircraft, together for a change, Jack knew she was a Knicks fan, liked spaghetti and Dustin Hoffman, while Anna had found out that he also supported the Knicks, that his favourite modern artist was Fernando Botero, and nothing could replace his mother's Irish stew.

Anna was wondering if he liked fat women when his head fell onto her shoulder. As she was the cause of his not getting much sleep the previous night, Anna felt she was hardly in a position to complain. She pushed his head gently back up, not wishing to wake him. She began making a list of things she needed to do once she was back in New York, when Jack slumped back down onto her shoulder. Anna gave in and tried to sleep with his head there. She had once read that the head is one-seventh of your body weight and no longer needed to be convinced.

She woke about an hour before they were due to land to find Jack was still asleep, but his arm was now draped around her shoulder. She sat up sleepily and accepted a cup of tea from the stewardess.

Jack leaned across. 'Do you usually sleep with a man on the first date?' he asked, grinning.

'Only if he pays for dinner.'

'So what's the first thing you're going to do, now that you've miraculously risen from the dead?' he asked.

'Call my family and friends and let them know just how alive I am, and then find out if anyone wants to employ me. And you?'

'I'll have to check in with my boss and let him know I'm no nearer to nailing Fenston, which will be greeted with one of his two favourite maxims. "Raise your game, Jack," or "Step it up a notch."'

'That's hardly fair,' said Anna, 'now that Krantz is safely behind bars.'

'No thanks to me,' said Jack. 'And then I'll have to face up to an even fiercer wrath than the boss's, when I try to explain to my mother why I didn't call her from London and apologize for not turning up for her Irish stew night. No, my only hope of redemption is to discover what "NYRC" stands for.' Jack put a hand in his top pocket. 'After I'd checked out of the Wentworth Arms, I travelled on to the embassy with Tom, and thanks to modern technology, he was able to produce an exact copy of the key, even though the original is still in Romania.' He pulled the facsimile out of his top pocket and handed it across to Anna.

Anna turned the small brass key over in her hands. 'NYRC 13. Got any ideas?' she asked.

'Only the obvious ones,' said Jack.

'New York Racing Club, New York Rowing Club, anything else?'

'New York Racquet Club, but if you come up with any others, let me know, because I intend to spend the rest of the weekend trying to find out if it's any of those. I need to come up with something positive before I face the boss on Monday.'

'Perhaps you could slow down enough on your morning run to let me know if you've cracked it.'

'I was rather hoping to tell you over dinner tonight,' said Jack.

'I can't. I'm sorry, Jack, much as I'd love to, I'm having dinner with Tina.'

'Are you?' said Jack. 'Well, just be careful.'

'Six o'clock tomorrow morning suit you?' asked Anna, ignoring the comment.

'That means I'll have to set my alarm for five thirty, if we're going to meet up about halfway round.'

'I'll be out of my shower by then.'

'I'll be sorry to miss that.'

'By the way,' said Anna, 'can you do me a favour?'

◄○►

Leapman strode into the chairman's office without knocking.

'Have you seen this?' he asked, placing a copy of the *New York Times* on the desk and jabbing a finger at an article from the international section.

Fenston studied the headline: ROMANIAN POLICE ARREST ASSASSIN. He read the short article twice before speaking.

'Find out how much the chief of police wants.'

'It may not prove to be that easy,' suggested Leapman.

'It's always that easy,' said Fenston, looking up. 'Only agreeing a price will prove difficult.'

Leapman frowned, 'And there's something else.'

'What?'

'The Van Gogh. The painting ought to be insured, after what happened to the Monet.'

'I never insure my paintings. I don't need the IRS to find out how much my collection is worth, and in any case it's never going to happen twice.'

'It already has,' said Leapman.

Fenston scowled and didn't reply for some time.

'All right, but only the Van Gogh,' he eventually said. 'Make it Lloyd's of London, and be sure you keep the book value below twenty million.'

'Why such a low figure?' queried Leapman.

'Because the last thing I need is to have the Van Gogh with an asset value of a hundred million while I'm still hoping to get my hands on the rest of the Wentworth collection.'

Leapman nodded and turned to leave.

'By the way,' said Fenston, still looking down at the article, 'have you deposited Krantz's five hundred thousand yet?'

'No, I was planning to—'

'Then wait.' He looked up at Leapman and smiled. 'Until after she escapes.'

◄◦►

Krantz lay silently in her bed as she waited for the two am shift to report for duty. She had no way of telling the time other than by the change of guards. One guard had just returned from his meal break, so she calculated it must be about twenty minutes to two.

Time to carry out her nightly routine. Krantz pulled back the sheet, turned over on her side, and tucked her knees under her chin. She pushed two fingers up her rectum and slowly extracted a condom, from where even the most brazen of warders were loath to trespass. She undid the knot on top of the condom, and removed a wad of tightly wrapped hundred-dollar bills. She peeled off two, and hid them in her sling. She then carried out the whole exercise in reverse.

Krantz calculated that it must be ten to two.

She waited.

◄○►

Jack sat in the back of the taxi, looking out of the window.

The grey cloak of 9/11 still hadn't lifted from Manhattan, although New Yorkers rushing by no longer stared upwards in disbelief. Terrorism was something else the most frenetic city on earth had already learned to take in its stride.

Jack sat back and thought about the favour he'd promised Anna. He dialled the number she'd given him. Sam picked up the phone. Jack told him that Anna was alive and well, and that she had been visiting her mother in Romania, and he could expect her back that evening. Nice to start the day making someone feel good, thought Jack, which wasn't going to be the case with his second call. He phoned his boss to let him know that he was back in New York. Macy told him that Krantz had been taken to a local hospital in Bucharest to undergo an operation on her shoulder. She was being guarded round the clock by half a dozen cops.

'I'll be happier when she's locked up in jail,' said Jack.

'I'm told you speak with some experience on that subject,' said Macy.

Jack was about to respond, when Macy added, 'Why don't you take the rest of the week off, Jack? You've earned it.'

'It's Saturday,' Jack reminded his boss.

'So I'll see you first thing Monday morning,' said Macy.

Jack decided to text Anna next. *Told Sam U R on way home. Is he only other man in yr life?* He waited a couple of minutes, but there was no reply. He called his mother.

'Will you be coming home for supper tonight?' she asked sharply. He could almost smell the meat stewing in the background.

'Would I miss it, Ma?'

'You did last week.'

'Ah, yes, I meant to call you,' said Jack, 'but I was chasing a woman halfway round the world.'

'Is she a good Catholic girl?' was his mother's immediate response.

'No, mother,' Jack replied. 'She's a divorcee, three ex-husbands, two of whom died in mysterious circumstances. Oh, and she has five children, not all of them by the three husbands, but you'll be glad to know only four of the kids are on hard drugs – the other one's currently serving a jail sentence.'

'Does she have a regular job?'

'Oh yes, Ma, it's a cash business. She services most of her customers at the weekends, but she assures me that she can always take an hour off for a bowl of Irish stew.'

'So what does she really do?' asked his mother.

'She's an art thief,' said Jack, 'specializes in Van Gogh. Makes a huge profit on each assignment.'

'Then she'll be an improvement on most of your past girlfriends.'

'Goodbye, Mother,' said Jack. 'I'll see you tonight.'

He ended the call, to find there was a text from Anna, using her ID for Jack.

Switch your brain on, Stalker. Got the obvious R. UR 2 slow 4 me.

'Damn the woman,' said Jack. His next call was to Tom in London, but all he got was an answering machine saying, 'Tom Crasanti, I'm out at the moment, but will be back shortly, please leave a message.'

Jack didn't, as the cab was pulling up outside his apartment.

'That'll be thirty-two dollars.'

Jack handed the driver four tens, and didn't ask for any change and didn't get a thank-you.

Things were back to normal in New York.

◄○►

When Krantz heard the guard returning from his meal break, she calculated that it must be around one-forty. She waited for a few more minutes before she carried out her nightly routine.

She extracted the condom from her rectum, undid the knot, took out the wad of notes, peeled off two more hundred-dollar bills, tied the knot, replaced the condom, and waited. Krantz calculated that it must be around ten to two.

When Krantz heard the two o'clock shift come on duty, she felt confident that he would appear within moments. After all, he only had to bring her a glass of water, for which he received a packet of Silk Cut. Not a bad exchange rate.

It was usually about another twenty minutes before he sloped off for his first cigarette, such a killer. That was the cue for his partner to appear with a cheese sandwich, a diet coke and another packet of Silk Cut, for which he pocketed a hundred dollars. Even the Ritz wouldn't have charged such an outrageous mark-up. But then he was stupid as well as greedy, a combination she was counting on when it came to teaching him the real meaning of the words Silk Cut.

<o>

Even before Jack had showered and changed, he began to scour the New York telephone directory in search of NYRC. Other than the three Jack had already come up with, he couldn't spot Anna's 'obvious one'. He switched on his laptop and Googled the words 'new york racquet club'. He was able to retrieve a potted history of the NYRC, several photographs of an elegant building on Park Avenue and a picture of the present chairman, Darius T. Mablethorpe III. Jack was in no doubt that the only way he was going to get past the front door was if he looked like a member. Never embarrass the bureau.

Once Jack had unpacked and showered, he selected a dark suit with a faint stripe, a blue shirt and a Columbia tie for this particular outing. He left his apartment and took a cab to 370 Park Avenue. He stepped onto the sidewalk and stood staring at the building for some time. He admired the magnificent four-storey Renaissance revival architecture that reminded him of a palazzo, so popular with the Italians in New York at the turn of the century. He walked up the steps towards an entrance with the letters NYRC discreetly etched into the glass.

The doorman greeted Jack with, 'Good afternoon, sir,' holding the door open, as if he was a life-long member. He strolled into an elegant lobby with massive paintings on every available space of suitably attired former chairmen dressed in long white pants and blue blazers, sporting the inevitable racquet. Jack glanced up at the wide, sweeping staircase to see even more past chairmen, even more ancient; only the racquet didn't seem to have changed. He strolled up to the reception desk.

'May I help you, sir?' asked a young man.

'I'm not sure if you can,' Jack admitted.

'Try me,' he offered.

Jack took the replica key out of his pocket and placed it on the countertop. 'Ever seen one of these?' he asked.

The young man picked up the key and turned it over, staring at the lettering for some time, before he replied, 'No, sir, can't say I have. It could well be a safety deposit box key, but not one of ours.' He turned and removed a heavy bronze key from the board behind him. A member's name was etched on the handle, and 'NYRC' in red along the shaft.

'Any suggestions?' asked Jack, trying to keep any sign of desperation out of his voice.

'No, sir,' he replied. 'Not unless it was before my time,' he added. 'I've only been here for eleven years, but perhaps Abe might be able to help. He was here in the days when more people played racquets than tennis.'

'And the gentlemen only played racquets,' said an older man who appeared from an office at the back to join his colleague. 'And what is it that I might be able to help with?'

'A key,' said the young man. 'This gentleman wants to know if you've ever seen one like it,' he added as he passed the key to Abe.

Abe turned the key over in his hands. 'It's certainly not one of ours,' he confirmed, 'and never has been, but I know what the "R" stands for,' he added triumphantly, 'because it must have been, oh, nearly twenty years ago, when Dinkins was Mayor.' He paused and looked up at Jack. 'A young man came in who could hardly speak a word of English and asked if this was the Romanian Club.'

'Of course,' murmured Jack, 'how stupid of me.'

'I remember how disappointed he was,' continued Abe, ignoring Jack's muttered chastisement, 'to find the "R" stood for "Racquet". Not that I think he knew what a racquet was. You see, he couldn't read English, so I had to look up the address for him. The only reason I remember anything after all this time is because the club was situated somewhere on *Lincoln*,' he said, emphasizing the name of the street. He glanced at Jack, who decided not to interrupt a second time. 'Named after him, wasn't I?' he explained. Jack smiled at Abe, and nodded. 'Some place in Queens, I think, but I don't recall exactly where.'

Jack put the key back in his pocket, thanked Abe and turned to leave before he gave him the chance to share any more reminiscences.

-◇-

Tina sat at her desk, typing out the speech. He hadn't even thanked her for coming in on a Saturday.

Bankers must at all times be willing to set standards that far exceed their legal requirements.

The New York Bankers' Association had invited Fenston to deliver the keynote speech at their annual dinner, to be held at the Sherry Netherland.

Fenston was both surprised and delighted by the invitation, although he had been angling for it for some time.

The committee had been divided.

Fenston was determined to make a good impression

on his colleagues in the banking fraternity, and had already dictated several drafts of the speech.

Customers must always be able to rely on our independent judgement, confident that we will act in their best interests, rather than our own.

Tina began to wonder if she was writing a script for a bankers' sit-com, with Fenston auditioning for the lead. What part would Leapman play in this moral tale? she wondered. For how many episodes would Victoria Wentworth survive?

We must, at all times, look upon ourselves as the guardians of our customers' assets – especially if they own a Van Gogh, Tina wanted to insert – *while never neglecting their commercial aspirations.*

Tina's thoughts drifted to Anna, as she continued to type out Fenston's shameless homily. She had spoken to her on the phone just before leaving for the office that morning. Anna wanted to tell her about the new man in her life, whom she had met in the most unusual circumstances. They had agreed to get together for supper that evening, as Tina also had something she wanted to share.

And let's never forget that it only takes one of us to lower our standards, and then the rest of us will suffer as a consequence.

As Tina turned another page, she wondered just how much longer she could hope to survive as Fenston's personal assistant. Since she'd thrown Leapman out of her office, a civil word had not passed between them. Would he have her fired only days before she had gathered enough proof to make sure Fenston spent the rest of his life in a smaller room in a larger institution?

And may I conclude by saying that my single purpose in life has always been to serve and give back to the community that has allowed me to share the American dream.

This was one document Tina would not bother to retain a copy of.

The light on Tina's phone was flashing and she quickly picked up the receiver.

'Yes, chairman?'

'Have you finished my speech for the bankers' dinner?'

'Yes, chairman,' repeated Tina.

'It's good, isn't it?' said Fenston.

'It's remarkable,' responded Tina.

—◇—

Jack hailed a cab and told him Lincoln Street, Queens. The driver left the meter running while he looked up the address in his much-thumbed directory. Jack was halfway back to the airport before he was dropped off on the corner of Lincoln and Harris. He looked up and down the street, aware that the suit he'd carefully selected for Park Avenue was somewhat incongruous in Queens. He stepped into a liquor store on the corner.

'I'm looking for the Romanian Club,' he told the elderly woman behind the counter.

'Closed years ago,' she said. 'It's now a guest house,' she added, looking him up and down, 'but I don't think you'll wanna stay there.'

'Any idea of the number?' asked Jack.

'No, but it's 'bout halfway down, on the other side of the street.'

Jack thanked the woman, walked back out onto Lincoln and crossed the road. He tried to judge where the halfway mark might be, when he spotted a faded *Rooms for rent* sign. He stopped and looked down a short flight of steps to see an even more faded sign painted above the entrance. The letters *NYRC, founded 1919* were almost indecipherable.

Jack descended the steps and pushed open the creaking door. He stepped into a dingy, unlit hallway, to be greeted with the pungent smell of stale tobacco. There was a small, dusty reception desk straight ahead of him, and behind it, almost hidden from view, Jack caught a glimpse of an old man reading the *New York Post*, enveloped in a cloud of cigarette smoke.

'I need a room for the night,' said Jack, trying to sound as if he meant it.

The old man's eyes narrowed as he gave Jack a disbelieving look. Did he have a girl waiting outside? 'That'll be seven dollars,' he said, before adding, 'in advance.'

'And I'll also need somewhere to lock my valuables,' said Jack.

'That'll be another dollar – in advance,' repeated the man, the cigarette bobbing up and down.

Jack handed over eight dollars, in return for a key.

'Second floor, number three, and the safety deposit boxes are at the end of the corridor,' the man said, passing him a second key. He then returned his attention to the *New York Post*, the cigarette having never left his mouth.

Jack walked slowly down the corridor until he reached a wall lined with safety deposit boxes, which, despite their age, looked solid and not that easy to break into, even if anyone might have considered the exercise worthwhile. He opened his own box and peered inside. It must have been about eight inches wide, and a couple of feet deep. Jack glanced back towards the front counter. The desk clerk had managed to turn the page, but the cigarette still hadn't left his mouth.

Jack moved further down the corridor, removed the replica key from an inside pocket and, after one more glance towards the front desk, opened box 13. He stared inside and tried to remain calm, although his heart was pounding. He extracted one bill from the box and placed it in his wallet. Jack locked the box and put the key back in his pocket.

The old man turned another page and began to study the racing odds as Jack walked back onto the street.

He had to cover eleven blocks before he found an empty cab, but he didn't attempt to call Dick Macy until he'd been dropped back at his apartment. He unlocked the front door, ran through to the kitchen and placed the hundred-dollar bill on the table. He then recalled how deep and how wide the empty box had been, before attempting to calculate how many hundred-dollar bills must have been stuffed into box 13. By the time he called Macy, he'd measured a space out on the kitchen table and used several five-hundred-page paperbacks to assist him in his calculation.

'I thought I told you to take the rest of the weekend off,' said Macy.

'I've found the box that NYRC 13 opens.'

'What was inside?'

'Hard to be certain,' replied Jack, 'but I'd say around two million dollars.'

'Your leave is cancelled,' said Macy.

9/23

44

'GOOD NEWS,' declared the young doctor on the morning of the third day after he'd removed her sling. 'Your wound is almost healed, and I shall be advising the authorities that you can be transferred to Jilava penitentiary tomorrow.'

With those words the doctor had determined her timetable. He then changed her dressing and departed without another word. Krantz spent the rest of the morning going over her plan second by second. She slept soundly between the hours of three in the afternoon and nine that evening. After all, she only needed to be wide awake during the night shift.

'She's been no trouble all day,' Krantz heard one of the guards report when he handed over his keys to the night shift at ten o'clock.

Krantz didn't stir for the next four hours, as neither a packet of Silk Cut nor a hundred-dollar bill would have elicited as much as a smile from the two older guards. They couldn't wait to attend her funeral.

She didn't sleep.

◀◇▶

Anna left her apartment to set out on her morning run just before 6am. Sam rushed from behind his desk to open the door for her – a Cheshire cat grin hadn't left his face from the moment she'd arrived back.

Anna wondered at what point Jack would catch up

with her. She had to admit, he'd been in her thoughts a lot since they had parted yesterday, and she already hoped their relationship might stray beyond a professional interest.

'Beware,' Tina had warned her over supper. 'Once he's got what he wants, he'll move on, and it isn't necessarily sex that he's after.'

Pity, she remembered thinking.

'Fenston loves the Van Gogh,' Tina assured her. 'He's given the painting pride of place on the wall behind his desk.'

In fact, Tina had been forthcoming about everything Fenston and Leapman had been up to during the past ten days. However, despite gentle probing, hints and well-placed questions, by the time they left the restaurant a couple of hours later Anna was no nearer to finding out why Fenston had such a hold over her.

Anna couldn't help remembering that the last time she'd run round Central Park was on the morning of the eleventh. The dark grey cloud might have finally dispersed, but there were several other reminders of that dreadful day, not least the two words on everyone's lips, Ground Zero. She put aside the horrors of that day when she spotted Jack jogging on the spot under Artists' Gate.

'Been waiting long, Stalker?' Anna asked as she strode past him and up around the pond.

'No,' he replied once he'd caught up. 'I've already been round twice, so I'm treating this as a cooling-down session.'

'Cooling down already, are we?' said Anna, as she accelerated away. She knew she wouldn't be able to maintain that pace for long and it was only a few seconds before he was back striding by her side.

'Not bad,' said Jack, 'but how long can you keep it up?'

'I thought that was a male problem,' Anna said, still

trying to set the pace. She decided that her only hope would be to distract him. She waited until the Frick came in sight.

'Name five artists on display in that museum,' she demanded, hoping his lack of knowledge would compensate for her lack of speed.

'Bellini, Mary Cassatt, Renoir, Rembrandt and two Holbeins – More and Cromwell.'

'Yes, but which Cromwell?' asked Anna, panting.

'Thomas, not Oliver,' said Jack.

'Not bad, Stalker,' admitted Anna.

'You can blame it on my father,' said Jack. 'Whenever he was out on patrol on a Sunday, my mother would take me to a gallery or a museum. I thought it was a waste of time, until I fell in love.'

'Who did you fall in love with?' asked Anna as they jogged up Pilgrim's Hill.

'Rossetti, or, to be more accurate, his mistress Jane Burden.'

'Scholars are divided on whether he ever slept with her,' said Anna. 'And her husband – William Morris – admired Rossetti so much that they don't even think he would have objected.'

'Foolish man,' said Jack.

'Are you still in love with Jane?' asked Anna.

'No, that was my adolescent period, since then I've entered my modern period, and only fall for women whose breasts end up behind their ears.'

'So you must have been spending a lot of your time in MoMA.'

'Several blind dates,' admitted Jack, 'but my mother doesn't approve.'

'Who does she think you should be dating?'

'She's old-fashioned, so anyone called Mary who's a virgin, but I'm working on her.'

'Are you working on anything else?'

'Like what?' asked Jack.

'Like what R stands for,' said Anna, almost out of breath.

'You tell me,' said Jack.

'Romania would be my bet,' said Anna, the words puffing out intermittently.

'You should have joined the FBI,' said Jack, slowing down.

'You'd worked it out already,' said Anna.

'No,' admitted Jack. 'A guy called Abe worked it out for me.'

'And?'

'And both of you were right.'

'So where is the Romanian Club?'

'In a rundown neighbourhood in Queens,' replied Jack.

'And what did you find when you opened the box?'

'I can't be absolutely certain,' replied Jack.

'Don't play games, Stalker, just tell me what was in the box.'

'About two million dollars.'

'Two million?' repeated Anna in disbelief.

'Well, it might not be quite that much, but it certainly was enough for my boss to drop everything, stake out the building and cancel my leave.'

'What sort of person keeps two million in cash hidden in a safety deposit box in Queens?' asked Anna.

'A person who can't risk opening a bank account anywhere in the world.'

'Krantz,' said Anna.

'So now it's your turn. Did anything come out of your dinner with Tina?'

'I thought you'd never ask,' replied Anna, and covered another hundred yards before she said, 'Fenston thinks the latest addition to his collection is magnificent.

But, more important, when Tina took in his morning coffee, there was a copy of the *New York Times* on his desk, and it was open at page seventeen.'

'Obviously not the sports section,' said Jack.

'No, international,' said Anna, as she extracted the article from her pocket and passed it over to Jack.

'Is this a ploy to see if I can keep up with you while I read?'

'No, it's a ploy to find out if you can read, Stalker, and I can always slow down, because I know you haven't been able to keep up with me in the past,' said Anna.

Jack read the headline and almost came to a halt as they ran past the lake. It was some time before he spoke again. 'Sharp girl, your friend Tina.'

'And she gets sharper,' said Anna. 'She interrupted a conversation Fenston was having with Leapman, and overhead him say, *"Do you still have the second key?"* She didn't understand the significance of it at the time, but—'

'I take back everything I said about her,' said Jack. 'She's on our team.'

'No, Stalker, she's on *my* team,' said Anna, accelerating down Strawberry Fields as she always did for the last half mile, with Jack striding by her side.

'This is where I leave you,' said Anna, once they reached Artists' Gate. She checked her watch and smiled: 11 minutes 48 seconds.

'Brunch?'

'Can't, sadly,' said Anna, 'meeting up with an old friend from Christie's, trying to find out if they've got any openings.'

'Dinner?'

'I've got tickets for the Rauschenberg at the Whitney. If you want to join me, I'll be there around six, Stalker.'

She ran away before he could reply.

45

LEAPMAN HAD SELECTED a Sunday because it was the one day of the week Fenston didn't go into the office, although he'd already called him three times that day.

He sat alone in his apartment eating a TV dinner, and going over his plan, until he was certain nothing could go wrong. Tomorrow, and all the rest of his tomorrows, he would dine in a restaurant, without having to wait for Fenston.

When he'd eaten every last scrap, he returned to his bedroom and stripped down to his underpants. He pulled open a drawer that contained the sports gear he needed for this particular exercise. He put on a T-shirt, shorts and a baggy grey tracksuit that teenagers wouldn't even have believed their parents once wore, and finally donned a pair of white socks and white gym shoes. He didn't look at himself in the mirror. He walked back across the room, fell on his knees and reached under the bed to pull out a large gym bag that had the handle of a squash racket poking out of it. He was now dressed and ready for his irregular exercise. All he needed was the key, and a packet of cigarettes.

He strolled through to the kitchen, opened a drawer that contained a large carton of duty-free Marlboro and extracted a packet of twenty. He never smoked. His final act in this agnostic ritual was to place his hand under the drawer and remove a key that was taped to the base. He was now fully equipped.

He double-locked the front door of his apartment and took the stairs down to the basement. He opened the back door and walked up one flight, emerging onto the street.

To any casual passer-by, he looked like a man on the way to his squash club. Leapman had never played a game of squash in his life. He walked one block before hailing a yellow cab. The routine never varied. He gave the driver an address that didn't have a squash club within five miles. He sat in the back of the cab, relieved to find the driver wasn't talkative, because he needed to concentrate. Today, he would make one change from his normal routine, a change he'd been planning for the past ten years. This would be the last time he carried out this particular chore for Fenston, a man who had taken advantage of him every day for the last decade. Not today. Never again. He glanced out of the cab window. He made this journey once, sometimes twice a year, when he would deposit large sums of cash at NYRC, always within days of Krantz completing one of her assignments. During that time, Leapman had deposited over five million dollars into box 13 at the guesthouse on Lincoln Street, and he knew it would always be a one-way journey – until she made a mistake.

When he'd read in the *Times* that Krantz had been captured after being shot in the shoulder – he would have preferred that she'd been killed – he knew this must be his one chance. What Fenston would describe as a window of opportunity. After all, Krantz was the only person who knew how much cash was in that box, while he remained the only other person with a key.

'Where is it exactly?' asked the driver.

Leapman looked out of the window. 'A couple more blocks,' he said, 'and then you can drop me on the corner.' Leapman took the squash racket out of the bag and placed it on the back seat.

'Twenty-three dollars,' the driver mumbled as he came to a halt outside a liquor store.

Leapman passed three tens through the grille. 'I'll be back in five minutes. If you're still around, you'll get another fifty.'

'I'll be around,' came back the immediate reply.

Leapman grabbed the empty gym bag and stepped out of the cab, leaving the squash racket on the back seat. He crossed the road, pleased to find that the sidewalk was crowded with locals out shopping. One of the reasons he always chose a Sunday afternoon. He would never risk such an outing at night. In Queens, they'd be happy to mug him for an empty bag.

Leapman quickened his pace until he reached number 61. He stopped for a moment to check that no one was taking any interest in him. Why would they? He descended the steps towards the NYRC sign and pushed open a door that was never locked.

The caretaker looked up from his sedentary position and when he saw who it was, nodded – the most energetic thing he'd done all day – then turned his attention back to the racing page. Leapman placed the packet of Marlboro on the counter, knowing they would disappear before he turned round. Every man has his price.

He peered into the gloom of a corridor lit only by a naked forty-watt bulb. He sometimes wondered if he was the only person who advanced beyond the counter.

Despite the darkness of the corridor, he knew exactly where her box was located. Not that you could read the number on the door – like everything else, it had faded over the years. He looked back up the corridor; one of his cigarettes was already glowing in the darkness.

He took the key out of his tracksuit pocket, placed it

in the lock, turned it and pulled open the door. He unzipped the bag before looking back in the direction of the old man. No interest. It took him less than a minute to empty the contents of the box, fill the bag and zip it back up.

Leapman closed the door and locked it for the last time. He picked up the bag, momentarily surprised by how heavy it was, and walked back down the corridor. He placed the key on the counter. 'I won't be needing it again,' he told the old man, who didn't allow this sudden break in routine to distract him from his study of the form for the four o'clock at Belmont. He'd been fifty feet from a racing certainty for the past twelve years and hadn't even checked the odds.

Leapman walked out of the door, climbed back up the steps and into the light of Lincoln Street. At the top of the steps, he once again glanced up and down the road. He felt safe. He began to walk quickly down the street, gripping the handle of the bag tightly, relieved to see the cab was still waiting for him on the corner.

He had covered about twenty yards when, out of nowhere, he was surrounded by a dozen men dressed in jeans and blue-nylon windbreakers, FBI printed in bold yellow letters on their backs. They came running towards him from every direction. A moment later, two cars entered Lincoln, one from each end – despite its being a one-way street – and came to a screeching halt in a semi-circle around the suspect. This time passers-by did stop to stare at the tracksuited man carrying a sports bag. The taxi sped away, minus fifty dollars, plus one squash racket.

'Read him his rights,' said Joe, as another officer clamped Leapman's arms firmly behind his back and handcuffed him, while a third relieved him of his gym bag.

'You have the right to remain silent . . .' which Leapman did.

Once his Miranda rights had been recited to him – not for the first time – Leapman was led off to one of the cars and unceremoniously dumped in the back, where Agent Delaney was waiting for him.

—◇—

Anna was at the Whitney Museum, standing in front of a Rauschenberg canvas entitled *Satellite*, when her cellphone vibrated in her jacket pocket. She glanced at the screen to see that *Stalker* was trying to contact her.

'Hey,' said Anna.

'I was wrong.'

'Wrong about what?' asked Anna.

'It was more than two million.'

—◇—

Krantz listened as the clock on a nearby church tower struck twice. She lay still, suddenly alert, ready for a change in routine.

Within moments she heard the heavy key being rattled in the lock, followed by the door opening and the door closing. She didn't look up, all part of an established routine. The guard ambled across, placed a glass of water on her bedside table, removed the packet of Silk Cut, and left the room without a word passing between them. She heard the door close and the key turning in the lock.

She didn't move a muscle, a hundred-dollar bill in one hand, the doctor's scissors in the other.

Twenty-two minutes passed before she heard a key being pushed into the lock and the door opening for a second time. The door closed. The second guard walked more quickly across the room, and placed a cheese sandwich, a diet coke and another packet of Silk Cut on the bedside table. He turned to face the prisoner in anticipation.

A small fist slipped out from under the sheet, and the fingers slowly uncurled to reveal a hundred-dollar bill. The guard smiled. As he leant across to accept his reward, the note slipped from her fingers and floated to the ground.

The guard bent down to pick it up, and by the time he rose, a smile still on his face, Krantz was already crouched on the edge of the bed, waiting. He was just about to pocket the money when she grabbed his thick black hair in one hand, and with a well-practised movement sliced open his neck with the aid of the doctor's scissors in the other. Not the most efficient of instruments, but the only thing she'd been able to lay her hands on.

He sank to the ground, and lay in his own blood, while still clinging on to the hundred-dollar bill. Krantz leapt off the bed, quickly removed from his chain the one key she needed, ran to the door and locked it. She pulled the bed back, just a few inches, and looked up at the tiny open window. She was about to discover if she had taken one risk too many.

She ran the three paces from the door, jumped up onto the mattress, mounted the rail on the end of the bed, as if it were a parallel bar, swung herself up to a handstand and, turning like a pole vaulter, thrust her legs through the open window.

For a moment she found herself stuck halfway in and halfway out. Krantz turned herself sideways, wiggling her hips through the tiny gap, and thrust her arms forward, allowing her shoulders to follow. She ended up clinging on to the window ledge with her fingertips. Never look down, never hesitate. She released both hands, fell the two storeys, landing in a flowerbed, and rolled over as if she were dismounting from a high bar.

She was quickly up on her feet and running towards the high mesh wire fence that surrounded the hospital grounds, just as the smoker unlocked the door to see what had delayed his colleague.

Seconds later an alarm went off, and the hospital grounds were flooded with light, like a football pitch during an evening fixture. Krantz was only yards from her goal when she first heard the dogs. Never look back, it only slows you down.

Krantz leapt for the wire mesh as the first dog sprung after her, but he could only bark his raucous protests as the monkey-like figure deftly scaled the fence, straddled the barbed-wire summit and quickly slithered down the other side. The three guards reached the bottom of the fence, but none of them was willing to take the same route.

One of them pulled a gun as Krantz began to zigzag across the road. He took a first shot – close, but not close enough, and by the time he pulled the trigger a second time she had disappeared into the forest.

The young doctor knelt down, in a pool of blood, by the slaughtered guard, searching for the instrument of death.

He spotted his scissors under the bed, grabbed them and quickly tucked them into a jacket pocket. He looked up to see the smoker staring in disbelief at the position of the bed and the open window.

Then he remembered. She was an Olympic gymnast.

9/24

46

ONE OF ANNA'S golden rules when she woke in the morning was not to check the messages on her cellphone until she had showered, dressed, had breakfast and read the *New York Times*. But as she had broken every one of her golden rules during the past fortnight, she checked her messages even before she got out of bed. One from Stalker asking her to call, which made her smile, one from Tina – no message, and one from Mr Nakamura, which made her frown – only four words, 'Urgent, please call. Nakamura.'

Anna decided to take a cold shower before she returned his call. As the jets of water cascaded down on her, she thought about Mr Nakamura's message. The word urgent always made her assume the worst – Anna fell into the half-empty-glass category, rather than the half-full.

She was wide awake by the time she stepped out of the shower. Her heart was pounding at about the same pace as when she'd just finished her morning run. She sat on the end of the bed and tried to compose herself.

Once Anna felt her heartbeat had returned to as near normal as it was likely to, she dialled Nakamura's number in Tokyo.

'Hai, Shacho-Shitso desu,' announced the receptionist.

'Mr Nakamura, please.'

'Who shall I say is calling?'

'Anna Petrescu.'

'Ah yes, he is expecting your call.' Anna's heartbeat quickened.

'Good morning, Dr Petrescu.'

'Good afternoon, Mr Nakamura,' said Anna, wishing she could see his face and more quickly learn her fate.

'I've recently had a most unpleasant conversation with your former boss, Bryce Fenston,' continued Nakamura. 'Which I'm afraid' – Anna could hardly breathe – 'has made me reassess' – was she about to be sick? – 'my opinion of that man. However, that's not the purpose of this call. I just wanted to let you know that you are currently costing me around five hundred dollars a day as I have, as you requested, deposited five million dollars with my lawyers in London. So I would like to view the Van Gogh as soon as possible.'

'I could fly to Tokyo in the next few days,' Anna assured him, 'but I would first have to go to England and pick up the painting.'

'That may not prove necessary,' said Nakamura. 'I have a meeting with Corus Steel in London scheduled for Wednesday, and would be happy to fly over a day earlier, if that was convenient for Lady Arabella.'

'I'm sure that will be just fine,' said Anna. 'I'll need to contact Arabella and then call your secretary to confirm the details. Wentworth Hall is only about thirty minutes from Heathrow.'

'Excellent,' said Nakamura. 'Then I'll look forward to seeing you both tomorrow evening.' He paused. 'By the way, Anna, have you given any more thought to becoming the director of my foundation? Because Mr Fenston did convince me of one thing: you are certainly worth five hundred dollars a day.'

Although it was the third time Fenston had read the article, a smile never left his face. He couldn't wait to share the news with Leapman, though he suspected he'd already seen the piece. He glanced at the clock on his desk, just before ten. Leapman was never late. Where was he?

Tina had already warned him that Mr Jackson, an insurance assessor from Lloyd's of London, was in the waiting room, and the front desk had just called to say that Chris Savage of Christie's was on his way up.

'As soon as Savage appears,' said Fenston, 'send them both in and then tell Leapman to join us.'

'I haven't seen Mr Leapman this morning,' said Tina.

'Well, tell him I want him in here the moment he arrives,' said Fenston. The smile returned to his face when he reread the headline, KITCHEN KNIFE KILLER ESCAPES.

There was a knock on the door and Tina ushered both men into the office.

'Mr Jackson and Mr Savage,' she said. From their dress, it would not have been difficult to fathom which was the insurance broker, and which one spent his life in the art world.

Fenston stepped forward and shook hands with a short, balding man in a navy pinstriped suit and crested blue tie, who introduced himself as Bill Jackson. Fenston nodded at Savage, whom he had met at Christie's on several occasions over the years. He was wearing his trademark bow tie.

'I wish to make it clear from the outset,' began Fenston, 'that I only want to insure this one painting,' he said, gesturing towards the Van Gogh, 'for twenty million dollars.'

'Despite the fact that it might fetch five times that amount were it to come under the hammer?' queried

Savage, who turned to study the picture for the first time.

'That would, of course, mean a far lower premium,' interjected Jackson. 'That's assuming our security boys consider the painting is adequately protected.'

'Just stay where you are, Mr Jackson, and you can decide for yourself if it's adequately protected.'

Fenston walked to the door, entered a six-digit code on the key pad next to the light switch and left the room. The moment the door closed behind him, a metal grille appeared from out of the ceiling and eight seconds later was clamped to the floor, covering the Van Gogh. At the same time, an alarm emitted an ear-piercing sound that would have caused even Quasimodo to seek another vocation.

Jackson quickly pressed the palms of his hands over his ears and turned round to see that a second grille had already barred his exit from the only door in the room. He walked across to the window and looked down at the midgets hurrying along the sidewalk below. A few seconds later, the alarm stopped and the metal grilles slid up into the ceiling. Fenston marched back into the room, looking pleased with himself.

'Impressive,' said Jackson, the sound of the alarm still reverberating in his ears. 'But there are still a couple of questions I will need answered,' he added. 'How many people know the code?'

'Only two of us,' said Fenston, 'my chief of staff and myself, and I change the sequence of numbers once a week.'

'And that window,' said Jackson, 'is there any way of opening it?'

'No, it's double-glazed bulletproof glass, and even if you could break it, you'd still be thirty-two storeys above the ground.'

'And the alarm . . .'

'Connected directly to Abbott Security,' said Fenston. 'They have an office in the building, and guarantee to be on your floor within two minutes.'

'I'm impressed,' said Jackson. 'What we in the business call triple A, which usually means the premium can be kept down to one per cent or, in real terms, around two hundred thousand dollars a year.' He smiled. 'I only wish the Norwegians had your foresight, Mr Fenston, and then perhaps we wouldn't have had to pay out so much on *The Scream*.'

'But can you also guarantee discretion in these matters?' Fenston asked.

'Absolutely,' Jackson assured him. 'We insure half the world's treasures, and you wouldn't find out who our clients are, were you to break into our headquarters in the City of London. Even their names are coded.'

'That's reassuring,' said Fenston. 'Then all that needs to be done is for you to complete the paperwork.'

'I can do that,' said Jackson, 'just as soon as Mr Savage confirms a value of twenty million for the painting.'

'That shouldn't be too difficult,' said Fenston, turning his attention to Chris Savage, who was staring intently at the picture. 'After all, he's already assured us that the Wentworth Van Gogh is worth nearer one hundred million.'

'The Wentworth Van Gogh most certainly is,' said Savage, 'but not this particular piece.' He paused before turning round to face Fenston. 'The only part of this work of art that's original is the frame.'

'What do you mean?' said Fenston, staring up at his favourite painting as if he'd been informed that his only child was illegitimate.

'I mean just that,' said Savage. 'The frame is original, but the painting is a fake.'

'A fake?' repeated Fenston, hardly able to get the words out. 'But it came from Wentworth Hall.'

'The frame may well have come from Wentworth Hall,' said Savage, 'but I can assure you that the canvas did not.'

'How can you be so sure,' demanded Fenston, 'when you haven't even carried out any tests?'

'I don't need to carry out any tests,' said Savage emphatically.

'Why not?' barked Fenston.

'Because the wrong ear is bandaged,' came back the immediate reply.

'No it's not,' insisted Fenston, as he stared up at the painting. 'Every schoolchild knows that Van Gogh cut off his left ear.'

'But not every schoolchild knows that he painted the self-portrait while looking in a mirror, which is why the right ear is bandaged.'

Fenston slumped down into the chair behind his desk, with his back to the painting. Savage strolled forward and began to study the picture even more closely. 'What puzzles me,' he added, 'is that although the painting is undoubtedly a fake, someone has put it into the original frame.' Fenston's face burned with anger. 'And I must confess,' continued Savage, 'that whoever painted this particular version is a fine artist.' He paused. 'However, I could only place a value of ten thousand on the work, and perhaps – ' he hesitated – 'a further ten thousand on the frame, which would make the suggested premium of two hundred thousand seem somewhat excessive.' Fenston still didn't respond. 'I am sorry to be the bearer of such bad news,' concluded Savage as he walked away from the picture and came to a halt in front of Fenston. 'I can only hope that you haven't parted with a large sum, and, if you have, you know who is responsible for this elaborate deception.'

'Get me Leapman,' Fenston screamed at the top of his voice, causing Tina to come running into the room.

'He's just arrived,' she said. 'I'll tell him you want to see him.'

Neither the man from Lloyd's nor the Christie's expert felt this was the moment to hang around, hoping to be offered a cup of coffee. They discreetly left, as Leapman came rushing in.

'It's a fake,' shouted Fenston.

Leapman stared up at the picture for some time before offering an opinion. 'Then we both know who's responsible,' he eventually said.

'Petrescu,' said Fenston, spitting out the name.

'Not to mention her partner, who has been feeding Petrescu with information since the day you fired her.'

'You're right,' said Fenston, and turning towards the open door he hollered 'Tina' at the top of his voice. Once again, she came running into the room.

'You see that picture,' he said, unable even to turn round and look at the painting. Tina nodded, but didn't speak. 'Send that piece of shit back to Wentworth Hall, along with a demand for—'

'Thirty-two million, eight hundred and ninety-two thousand dollars,' said Leapman.

'And once you've done that,' said Fenston, 'you can collect all your personal belongings and make sure you're off the premises within ten minutes, because you're fired, you little bitch.'

Tina began shaking as Fenston rose from behind his desk and stared down at her. 'But before you leave, I have one last task for you.' Tina couldn't move. 'Tell your friend Petrescu that I still haven't removed her name from the missing, presumed dead list.'

47

ANNA FELT HER lunch with Ken Wheatley could have gone better. The deputy chairman of Christie's had made it clear that the unfortunate incident that had caused her to resign from Sotheby's was not yet considered by her colleagues in the art world to be *a thing of the past*. And it didn't help that Bryce Fenston was telling anyone who cared to listen that she had been fired for conduct unworthy of an officer of the bank. Wheatley admitted that no one much cared for Fenston. However, they felt unable to offend such a valuable customer, which meant that her re-entry into the auction house arena wasn't going to prove that easy.

Wheatley's words only made Anna more determined to help Jack secure a conviction against Fenston, who didn't seem to care whose life he ruined.

There wasn't anything suitable at the moment for someone with her qualifications and experience, was how Ken had euphemistically put it, but he promised to keep in touch.

When Anna left the restaurant, she hailed a cab. Perhaps her second meeting would prove more worthwhile. 'Twenty-six Federal Plaza,' she told the driver.

❖

Jack was standing in the lobby of the New York field office waiting for Anna some time before she was due to arrive. He was not surprised to see her appear a couple

364

of minutes early. Three guards watched Anna carefully as she descended the dozen steps that led to the entrance of 26 Federal Plaza. She gave her name to one of the guards, who requested proof of identity. She passed over her driver's licence, which he checked before ticking off her name on his clipboard.

Jack opened the door for her.

'Not my idea of a first date,' said Anna as she stepped inside.

'Nor mine,' Jack tried to reassure her, 'but my boss wanted you to be in no doubt how important he considers this meeting.'

'Why, is it my turn to be arrested?' asked Anna.

'No, but he is hoping that you will be willing to assist us.'

'Then let's go and bell the cat.'

'One of your father's favourite expressions,' said Jack.

'How did you know that?' asked Anna. 'Have you got a file on him as well?'

'No,' said Jack, laughing, as they stepped into the elevator. 'It was just one of the things you told me on the plane during our first night together.'

Jack whisked Anna to the nineteenth floor, where Dick Macy was waiting in the corridor to greet her.

'How kind of you to come in, Dr Petrescu,' he said, as if she'd had a choice. Anna didn't comment. Macy led her through to his office and ushered her into a comfortable chair on the other side of his desk.

'Although this is an off-the-record meeting,' began Macy, 'I cannot stress how important we at the bureau consider your assistance.'

'Why do you need *my* assistance?' asked Anna. 'I thought you had arrested Leapman and he was safely under lock and key.'

'We released him this morning,' said Macy.

'Released him?' said Anna. 'Wasn't two million enough?'

'More than enough,' admitted Macy, 'which is why I became involved. My speciality is plea-bargaining, and just after nine o'clock this morning, Leapman signed an agreement with the Southern District Federal Prosecutor to ensure that, if he fully cooperates with our investigation, he'll end up with only a five-year sentence.'

'But that still doesn't explain why you've released him,' said Anna.

'Because Leapman claims he can show a direct financial link between Fenston and Krantz, but he needs to return to their Wall Street office so he can get his hands on all the relevant documents, including numbered accounts, and several illegal payments into different bank accounts around the world.'

'He could be double-crossing you,' said Anna. 'After all, most of the documents that would implicate Fenston were destroyed when the North Tower collapsed.'

'True,' said Macy, 'but if he is, I've made it clear he can look forward to spending the rest of his life in Sing Sing.'

'That would quicken the pulse,' admitted Anna.

'Leapman's also agreed to appear as a government witness,' said Jack, 'should the case come to trial.'

'Then let's be thankful that Krantz is safely locked up, otherwise your star witness wouldn't even make it to the courthouse.'

Macy looked across at Jack, unable to mask his surprise. 'You haven't read today's final edition *New York Times*?' he asked, turning to face Anna.

'No,' said Anna, having no idea what they were talking about.

Macy opened the file, extracted an article and passed the clipping across to Anna.

Olga Krantz, known as the kitchen knife killer because of the role she played as an executioner in Ceauşescu's brutal regime, disappeared from a high-security hospital in Bucharest last night. Krantz, a slight figure, is thought to have used her gymnastic skills to escape through a tiny window on the second floor. One of the policemen who had been guarding her was later discovered with his . . .

'I'm going to be looking over my shoulder for the rest of my life,' said Anna, long before she'd reached the last paragraph.

'I don't think so,' said Jack. 'Krantz won't be in a hurry to return to America, now she's joined nine men on the FBI's most wanted list. She'll also realize that we've circulated a detailed description of her to every port of entry, as well as Interpol. If she were to be stopped and searched, she'd have some trouble explaining the bullet wound in her right shoulder.'

'But that won't stop Fenston seeking revenge.'

'Why should he bother?' asked Jack. 'Now that he's got the Van Gogh, you're history.'

'But he hasn't got the Van Gogh,' said Anna, bowing her head.

'What do you mean?' asked Jack.

'I had a call from Tina, just before I left to come to this meeting. She warned me that Fenston had called in an expert from Christie's so that he could have the painting valued for insurance. Something he's never done before.'

'But why should that cause any problems?' asked Jack.

Anna raised her head. 'Because it's a fake.'

'A fake?' both men said in unison.

'Yes, that's why I had to fly to Bucharest. I was

having a copy made by an old friend who's a brilliant portrait artist.'

'Which would explain the drawing in your apartment,' said Jack.

'You've been in my apartment?' said Anna.

'Only when I believed that your life was in danger,' said Jack quietly.

'But—' began Anna.

'And that also explains,' jumped in Macy, 'why you sent the red box back to London, even allowing it to be intercepted by Art Locations and delivered on to Fenston in New York.'

Anna nodded.

'But you must have realized that you'd be found out in time?' queried Jack.

'In time, yes,' repeated Anna. 'That's the point. All I needed was enough time to sell the original, before Fenston discovered what I was up to.'

'So while your friend Anton was working on the fake, you flew on to Tokyo to try and sell the original to Nakamura.'

Anna nodded.

'But did you succeed?' asked Macy.

'Yes,' said Anna. 'Nakamura agreed to purchase the original self-portrait for fifty million dollars, which was more than enough for Arabella to clear her sister's debts with Fenston Finance while still holding on to the rest of the estate.'

'But now that Fenston knows that he's in possession of a fake, he's bound to get in touch with Nakamura and tell him what you've been up to,' said Jack.

'He already has,' said Anna.

'So you're back to square one,' suggested Macy.

'No,' said Anna with a smile. 'Nakamura has already

deposited five million dollars with his London solicitors, and has agreed to pay the balance once he's inspected the original.'

'Have you got enough time?' asked Macy.

'I'm flying to London this evening,' said Anna, 'and Nakamura plans to join us at Wentworth Hall tomorrow night.'

'It's going to be a close-run thing,' said Jack.

'Not if Leapman delivers the goods,' said Macy. 'Don't forget what he has planned for tonight.'

'Am I allowed to know what you're up to?' asked Anna.

'No, you are not,' said Jack firmly. 'You catch your plane to England and close the deal, while we get on with our job.'

'Does your job include keeping an eye on Tina?' asked Anna quietly.

'Why would we need to do that?' asked Jack.

'She was fired this morning.'

'For what reason?' enquired Macy.

'Because Fenston found out that she was keeping me informed of everything he was up to while I was chasing halfway round the world, so I fear that I've ended up putting her life in danger as well.'

'I was wrong about Tina,' admitted Jack, and looking across at Anna added, 'and I apologize. But I still can't make out why she ever agreed to work for Fenston in the first place.'

'I have a feeling I'll find out this evening,' said Anna. 'We're meeting up for a drink just before I leave for the airport.'

'If you have any time before take-off, give me a call. I'd be fascinated to know the answer to that particular mystery.'

Anna nodded.

'There's another mystery I'd like to clear up before you leave, Dr Petrescu,' said Macy.

Anna turned to face Jack's boss.

'If Fenston is in possession of a fake, where's the original?' he demanded.

'At Wentworth Hall,' Anna replied. 'Once I'd retrieved the painting from Sotheby's, I grabbed a cab and took it straight back to Arabella. The only thing I came away with was the red box and the painting's original frame.'

'Which you took on to Bucharest so that your friend Anton could put his fake into the original frame, which you hoped would be enough to convince Fenston that he'd got his hands on the real McCoy.'

'And it would have stayed that way if he hadn't decided to have the painting insured.'

No one spoke for some time, until Macy said, 'And you carried out the whole deception right in front of Jack's eyes.'

'Sure did,' said Anna with a smile.

'So let me finally ask you, Dr Petrescu,' continued Macy, 'where was the Van Gogh while two of my most experienced agents were having breakfast with you and Lady Arabella at Wentworth Hall?'

'Plead the Fifth Amendment,' begged Jack.

'In the Van Gogh bedroom,' replied Anna, 'just above them on the first floor.'

'That close,' said Macy.

◄○►

Krantz waited until the tenth ring, before she heard a click and a voice enquired, 'Where are you?'

'Over the Russian border,' she replied.

'Good, because you can't come back to America while you're still regularly appearing in the *New York Times*.'

'Not to mention on the FBI's Most Wanted list,' added Krantz.

'Fifteen minutes of fame,' said Fenston. 'But I do have another assignment for you.'

'Where?' asked Krantz.

'Wentworth Hall.'

'I couldn't risk going back there a second time—'

'Even if I doubled your fee?'

'It's still too much of a risk.'

'You may not think so when I tell you whose throat I want you to cut.'

'I'm listening,' she said, and when Fenston revealed the name of his next victim, all she said was, 'You'll pay me two million dollars for that?'

'Three, if you manage to kill Petrescu at the same time – she'll be staying there overnight.'

Krantz hesitated.

'And four, if she's a witness to the first throat being cut,' added Fenston.

A long silence followed, before Krantz said, 'I'll need two million in advance.'

'The usual place?'

'No,' she replied, and gave him a numbered account in Moscow.

◄◦►

Fenston put the phone down and buzzed through to Leapman.

'I need to see you – now.'

While he waited for Leapman to join him, Fenston began jotting down headings for subjects he needed to

371

discuss: *Van Gogh, money, Wentworth estate, Petrescu.*
He was still scribbling when there was a knock on the
door.

'She's escaped,' said Fenston the moment Leapman
closed the door.

'So the *New York Times* report was accurate,' said
Leapman, hoping he didn't appear anxious.

'Yes, but what they don't know is that she's on her
way to Moscow.'

'Is she planning to return to New York?'

'Not for the moment,' said Fenston. 'She can't risk it
while security remains on such high alert.'

'That makes sense,' agreed Leapman, trying not to
sound relieved.

'Meanwhile, I've given her another assignment,' said
Fenston.

'Who is it to be this time?' asked Leapman.

Leapman listened in disbelief as Fenston revealed
who he had selected as Krantz's next victim, and why it
would be impossible for her to cut off their left ear.

'And has the impostor been dispatched back to
Wentworth Hall?' asked Fenston, as Leapman stared up
at the blown-up photograph of the chairman shaking
hands with George W. Bush following his recent visit to
Ground Zero, which had been returned to its place of
honour on the wall behind Fenston's desk.

'Yes. Art Locations picked the canvas up this afternoon,' replied Leapman, 'and will be returning the fake
to Wentworth Hall sometime tomorrow. I also had a
word with our lawyer in London. The sequestration
order is being heard before a judge in chambers on
Wednesday, so if she doesn't return the original by then,
the Wentworth estate automatically becomes yours, and
then we can start selling off the rest of the collection
until the debt is cleared. Mind you, it could take years.'

'If Krantz does her job properly tomorrow night, the debt will never be cleared,' said Fenston, 'which is why I called you in. I want you to put the rest of the Wentworth collection up for auction at the earliest possible opportunity. Divide the pictures equally between Christie's, Sotheby's, Phillips and Bonhams, and make sure you sell them all at the same time.'

'But that would flood the market, and be certain to bring the prices down.'

'That's exactly what I want to do,' said Fenston. 'If I remember correctly, Petrescu valued the rest of the collection at around thirty-five million, but I'll be happy to raise somewhere between fifteen to twenty.'

'But that would still leave you ten million short.'

'How sad,' said Fenston, smiling. 'In which case I will be left with no choice but to put Wentworth Hall on the market and dispose of everything, right down to the last suit of armour.' Fenston paused. 'So be sure you place the estate in the hands of the three most fashionable agents in London. Tell them they can print expensive colour brochures, advertise in all the glossy magazines and even take out the odd half-page in one or two national newspapers, which will be bound to cause further editorial comment. By the time I finish with Lady Arabella, she'll not only be penniless but, knowing the British press, humiliated.'

'And Petrescu?'

'It's just her bad luck that she happens to be in the wrong place at the wrong time,' said Fenston, unable to hide a smirk.

'So Krantz will be able to kill two birds with one stone,' said Leapman.

'Which is why I want you to concentrate on bankrupting the Wentworth estate, so that Lady Arabella suffers an even slower death.'

'I'll get on to it right away,' said Leapman as he turned to leave. 'Good luck with your speech, chairman,' he added as he reached the door.

'My speech?' said Fenston.

Leapman turned back to face the chairman. 'I thought you were addressing the annual bankers' dinner at the Sherry Netherland tonight.'

'Christ, you're right. Where the hell did Tina put my speech?'

Leapman smiled, but not until he had closed the door behind him. He returned to his room, sat down at his desk and considered what Fenston had just told him. Once the FBI learned the full details of where Krantz would be tomorrow night, and who her next intended victim was, he felt confident that the district attorney's office would agree to reduce his sentence by even more. And if he was able to deliver the vital piece of evidence that linked Fenston to Krantz, they might even recommend a suspended sentence.

Leapman removed a tiny camera, supplied by the FBI, from an inside pocket. He began to calculate how many documents he would be able to photograph while Fenston was delivering his speech at the annual bankers' dinner.

48

AT 7.16PM, LEAPMAN switched the light off in his office and stepped into the corridor. He closed his door, but didn't lock it. He walked towards the bank of elevators, aware that the only office light still shining was coming from under the chairman's door. He stepped into an empty elevator and was quickly whisked to the ground floor. He walked slowly across to reception and signed out at 7.19pm. A woman standing behind him stepped forward to sign herself out as Leapman took a pace backwards, his eyes never leaving the two guards behind the desk. One was supervising the steady flow of people exiting the building, while the other was dealing with a delivery that required a signature. Leapman kept retreating until he reached the empty elevator. He backed in and stood to one side so that the guards could no longer see him. He pressed button 31. Less than a minute later, he stepped out into another silent corridor.

He walked to the far end, opened the fire exit door and climbed the steps to the thirty-second floor. He pushed the door slowly open, not wanting to make the slightest sound. He then tiptoed down the thickly carpeted corridor until he was back outside his own office. He checked to confirm that the only light came from under the chairman's door. He then opened his own door, stepped inside and locked it. He sat down in the chair behind his desk and placed the camera in his pocket, but did not turn on the light.

He sat alone in the darkness, and waited patiently.

◄○►

Fenston was considering a loan application from a Michael Karraway, who wanted to borrow fourteen million to invest in a group of provincial theatres. He was an out-of-work actor with few stage credits to his name. But to his credit he had an indulgent mother, who had left him a Matisse, *View from the Bedroom*, and a thousand-acre farm in Vermont. Fenston studied a transparency of a young nude looking out of a bedroom window and decided that he would instruct Leapman to draw up a contract.

Fenston tossed the application to one side and began thumbing through the latest Christie's catalogue. He paused at a reproduction of Degas's *Dancer Before a Mirror*, but turned the page once he had seen the low estimate. After all, Pierre de Rochelle had supplied him with a Degas, *The Dancing Instructor*, at a far more reasonable price.

He continued to study the prices of each picture, a smile regularly appearing on his lips when he realized how much his own collection was increasing in value. He glanced up at the clock on the corner of his desk: 7.43pm. 'Shit,' he said, aware that if he didn't hurry he was going to be late for his own speech at the bankers' dinner. He picked up the catalogue and walked quickly to the door. He entered a six-digit code on the pad next to the light switch, stepped out into the corridor and closed his door. Eight seconds after he'd locked it, he heard the security grilles slam into place.

On the ride down in the elevator, Fenston was fascinated to see the low estimate for Caillebotte's *Street*

Sweepers. He had acquired the larger version for half that price from a client he had recently bankrupted. When the doors slid open, he walked quickly across to reception and signed himself out. 7.48pm.

As he strolled through the lobby, he could see his driver waiting for him at the bottom of the steps. He kept his thumb stuck in the catalogue as he climbed into the back seat. He was annoyed when he turned the next page and came across Van Gogh's *Reapers in the Field*, low estimate, $27 million. He swore. It wasn't in the same class as the *Self-portrait with Bandaged Ear*.

'Excuse me, sir,' said the driver, 'but are you still going to the bankers' dinner?'

'Yes, so we'd better get a move on,' said Fenston, and he turned another page of the catalogue.

'It's just that . . .' said the driver, picking up a gold-embossed card from the passenger seat.

'That what?' said Fenston.

'That the invitation says dinner jacket.' He turned and passed the card back to his boss.

'Shit,' said Fenston, dropping the catalogue onto the seat beside him. Tina would normally have put out his dinner jacket rather than leave it hanging in the closet. He jumped out of the car, even before his driver could open the back door, and took the steps up to the entrance of the building two at a time, quickly bypassing reception, not bothering to sign back in. He hurried towards a waiting elevator and pushed the button for the thirty-second floor.

When he stepped out of the elevator, the first thing he noticed as he walked down the corridor was a beam of light coming from under his office door. He could have sworn he'd switched the light off after he'd set the alarm, or had he become so engrossed in the catalogue that he simply forgot? He was about to enter the code on the pad by his door, when he heard a noise coming from inside.

Fenston hesitated, wondering who it could be. He didn't move as he waited to find out if the intruder was aware of his presence. They didn't stir, so he retraced his steps, slipped into the adjoining office and quietly closed the door. He sat down in his secretary's chair and began to look for the switch; Leapman had alerted him to the fact that Tina could observe everything that was taking place in his office. After searching for some time, he located the switch under the desk. He flicked it across and the little screen in the corner lit up, giving him a clear view of the interior of his office. Fenston stared in disbelief.

Leapman was sitting at his desk, a thick file open in front of him. He was slowing turning the pages, sometimes stopping to study an entry more carefully, while occasionally extracting a sheet, laying it on the table and photographing it with what looked like a high-tech camera.

Several thoughts flashed through Fenston's mind. Leapman must be collecting material, so that he could at some later date blackmail him. He was peddling information to a rival bank. The IRS had finally put the squeeze on him and he'd made a deal to sacrifice his boss in exchange for immunity. Fenston settled for blackmail.

It soon became clear that Leapman was in no hurry. He had obviously chosen this particular time with some thought. Once he had finished one file, he methodically returned it to its place and selected another. His routine didn't alter: search slowly through the contents of the file, select certain items to study more carefully, and then occasionally extract a page to be photographed.

Fenston considered his alternatives, before finally settling on something he considered worthy of Leapman.

He first wrote down the sequence of events that would be required to ensure he wasn't caught. Once he was confident that he had mastered the order, he flicked up a switch to stop all outgoing or incoming calls from his office. He sat patiently at his secretary's desk until he saw Leapman open another thick file. He then slipped back into the corridor, coming to a halt in front of his office. Fenston went over the order in his mind and, once he was satisfied, stepped forward. He first entered the correct code, 170690, on the pad by the door, as if he was leaving. He then turned his key in the lock and silently pushed open the door no more than an inch. He then immediately pulled it closed again.

The deafening alarm was automatically set off, but Fenston still waited for eight seconds until the security grilles had clamped firmly into place. He then quickly entered last week's code, 170680, opened the door a second time and immediately slammed it closed.

He could hear Leapman running across the room, clearly hoping that by entering the correct code he could stop the alarm and cause the grilles to slide back into the ceiling. But it was too late, because the iron grilles remained resolutely in place and the overpowering cacophony continued unabated.

Fenston knew that he had only seconds to spare if he was to complete the sequence without being caught. He ran back to the adjoining office and quickly scanned the notes he'd left on his secretary's desk. He dialled the emergency number for Abbott Security.

A voice announced, 'Duty officer, security.'

'My name is Bryce Fenston, chairman of Fenston Finance.' He spoke slowly, but with authority. 'The alarm has been triggered in my office on the thirty-second floor. I must have entered last week's code by mistake, and I just wanted to let you know that it's *not* an emergency.'

'Can you repeat your name, sir?'

'Bryce Fenston,' he shouted above the noise of the alarm.

'Date of birth?'

'Twelve six fifty-two.'

'Mother's maiden name?'

'Madejski.'

'Home zip code?'

'One zero zero two one.'

'Thank you, Mr Fenston. We'll get someone up to the thirty-second floor as quickly as possible. The engineers are currently responding to an incident on the seventeenth floor, where we have someone stuck in an elevator, so it might be a few minutes before they get to you.'

'No hurry,' said Fenston casually, 'there's no one else working on this floor at the moment, and the office won't open again until seven tomorrow.'

'It's sure not going to take us that long,' the guard promised him, 'but with your permission, Mr Fenston, we'll change your category from emergency to priority.'

'OK by me,' shouted Fenston above the deafening noise.

'But there will still be an out-of-hours call-out charge of five hundred dollars.'

'That sounds a bit steep,' said Fenston.

'It's standard in a case like this, sir,' came back the duty officer's reply. 'However, if you were able to report to the front desk in person, Mr Fenston, and sign our alarm roster, the charge is automatically cut to two fifty.'

'I'm on my way,' said Fenston.

'But I have to point out, sir,' continued the duty officer, 'that should you do that, your status will be lowered to routine, in which case we couldn't come to your assistance until we've dealt with all other priority and emergency calls.'

'That won't be a problem,' said Fenston.

'But you can be confident that whatever other calls we have outstanding, we still guarantee that yours will be sorted out within four hours.'

'Thank you,' said Fenston. 'I'll come straight down and report to the front desk.'

He replaced the receiver and walked back into the corridor. As he passed his office, he could hear Leapman pounding on the door like a trapped animal, but he could only just make out his voice above the shrill scream of the alarm. Fenston continued on towards the elevators. Even at a distance of some fifty feet he still found the piercing drone intolerable.

Once he'd stepped out of the elevator on the ground floor, he went straight to the front desk.

'Ah, Mr Fenston,' said the security guard. 'If you'll sign here, it will save you another two hundred and fifty bucks.'

Fenston slipped him a ten-dollar note. 'Thanks,' he said. 'No need to rush, I'm the last one out,' he assured them as he hurried out of the front door and back down the steps.

As he stepped into his waiting car, Fenston glanced up at his office. He could see a tiny figure banging on the window. The driver closed the door behind him and returned to the front seat, puzzled. His boss still wasn't wearing a dinner jacket.

49

JACK DELANEY parked his car on Broad Street just after nine thirty. He switched on the radio and listened to 'Cousin Brucie' on FM101.1, as he settled back to wait for Leapman. The venue for their meeting had been Leapman's choice, and he'd told the FBI man to expect him some time between ten and eleven, when he would hand over their camera containing enough damning evidence to ensure a conviction.

Jack was suspended in that unreal world somewhere between half awake and half asleep when he heard the siren. Like all law-enforcement officers, he could identify the different decibel pitch between police, ambulance and fire department in a split second. This was an ambulance, probably coming from St Vincent's.

He checked his watch: 11.15pm. Leapman was running late, but then he had warned Jack that there could be over a hundred documents to photograph, so not to keep him to the minute. The FBI technical boys had spent some considerable time showing Leapman how to operate the latest high-tech camera, so he could be sure to deliver the best results. But that was before the phone call. Leapman had rung Jack's office a few minutes after seven to say that Fenston had told him something that would prove far more damning than any document. But he didn't want to reveal the information over the phone. The line went dead before Jack could press him. He would have been more responsive if it hadn't been his experience that plea-bargainers always claim they have new information that will break the case wide open, and therefore the FBI should reconsider the length of their sentence. He knew his boss wouldn't agree to that unless the new evidence clearly showed an unbreakable link in the chain between Fenston and Krantz.

The sound of the siren was getting louder.

Jack decided to get out of the car and stretch his legs. His raincoat felt crumpled. He'd bought it from Brooks Brothers in the days when he wanted everyone to know that he was a G-man, but the higher up the ranks he climbed, the less he wished it to be that obvious. If he was promoted to run his own field office, he might even consider buying a new coat, one that would make him look more like a lawyer or a banker – that would please his father.

His mind switched to Fenston, who by now would have delivered his speech on Moral Responsibility for Modern Bankers, and then to Anna, who was halfway across the Atlantic on her way to meet up with Naka-mura. Anna had left a message on his cellphone, saying she now knew why Tina had taken the job as Fenston's PA, and the evidence had been staring her in the face. The line had been busy when she called, but Anna said she'd phone again in the morning. It must have been when Leapman was on the line. Damn the man. Jack was standing on a New York sidewalk in the middle of the night, tired and hungry, while he waited for a camera. His father was right. He should have been a lawyer.

The siren was now only a couple of blocks away.

Jack strolled down to the end of the road and peered up at the building in which Leapman was working, somewhere on the thirty-second floor. There was a row of blazing lights about halfway up the skyscraper, other-

wise the windows were mostly dark. Jack began to count
the floors, but by the time he'd reached eighteen he
couldn't be sure, and when he counted thirty-two, it just
might have been the floor that was blazing with lights.
But that didn't make any sense, because on Leapman's
floor, there should only have been a single light. The last
thing he would have wanted was to draw attention to
himself.

Jack looked across the road to watch an ambulance
come to a screeching halt in front of the building. The
back door burst open and three paramedics, two men
and a woman dressed in their familiar dark blue uniforms, jumped out onto the sidewalk. One pushed a
stretcher, the second carried an oxygen cylinder, while
the third held a bulky medical bag. Jack watched them
as they charged up the steps and into the building.

He turned his attention to the reception desk, where
one guard – pointing to something on his clipboard –
was talking to an older man dressed in a smart suit,
probably his supervisor, while the second guard was
occupied on the telephone. Several people strolled in
and out of the elevators, which wasn't surprising, as they
were in the heart of the city where finance is a 24-hour
occupation. Most Americans would be asleep while
money was changing hands in Sydney, Tokyo, Hong
Kong and now London, but there always had to be a
group of New Yorkers who lived their lives on other
people's time.

Jack's train of thought was interrupted when an elevator door opened and the three paramedics reappeared,
two of them wheeling their patient on the stretcher, while
the third was still holding onto the oxygen cylinder. As
they walked slowly but purposefully towards the entrance,
everyone in their path stood aside. Jack strolled up the
steps to take a closer look. Another siren blared in the

distance, on this occasion the droning pitch of the NYPD, but it could be going anywhere at that time of night, and in any case Jack was now concentrating on the stretcher. He stood by the door as the paramedics came out of the building and carried their patient slowly down the steps. He stared at the pallid face of a stricken man, whose eyes were glazed over as if they'd been caught in the blaze of a headlight. It wasn't until he'd passed him that Jack realized who it was. He had to make an instant decision. Did he pursue the ambulance back to St Vincent's, or head straight for the thirty-second floor? The police siren now sounded as if it could be heading in their direction. One look at that face and Jack didn't need to be told that Leapman wasn't going to be speaking to anyone for a very long time. He ran into the building with the sound of the police siren no more than a block or two away. He knew he had only a few minutes before the NYPD's finest would be on the scene. He paused at the reception desk for a moment to show them his FBI badge.

'You got here quickly,' said one of the guards, but Jack didn't comment as he headed for the bank of elevators. The guard wondered how he knew which floor to go to.

Jack squeezed through the elevator doors just as they were about to close, and jabbed at the button marked 32. When the doors opened again, he looked quickly up and down the corridor to see where the lights were coming from. He turned and ran towards some offices at the far end to find a security guard and two engineers in red overalls, along with a cleaner, standing by an open door.

'Who are you?' demanded the security guard.

'FBI,' said Jack, producing his badge but not revealing his name as he strode into the room. The first thing he saw was a blown-up photograph of Fenston shaking hands with George W. Bush, which dominated the wall behind the desk. His eyes moved quickly around the room until they settled on the one thing he was looking for. It was in the centre of the desk, resting on a pile of spread-out papers beside an open file.

'What happened?' demanded Jack authoritatively.

'Some guy got himself trapped in this office for over three hours and must have set the alarm off.'

'It wasn't our fault,' jumped in one of the engineers, 'we were told to downgrade the call, and we've got that in writing, otherwise we would have been here a lot sooner.'

Jack didn't need to ask who had set off the alarm and then left Leapman to his fate. He walked over to the desk, his eyes quickly scanning the papers. He glanced up to find all four men staring at him. Jack looked directly at the security guard. 'Go to the elevator, wait for the cops, and the minute they turn up bring them straight back to me.' The guard disappeared into the corridor without question and headed quickly towards the elevators. 'And you three, out,' was Jack's next command. 'This may be a crime scene, and I don't want you disturbing any evidence.' The men turned to leave, and in the split second their backs were turned, Jack grabbed the camera and dropped it into one of the baggy pockets of his trench coat.

He picked up the phone on Fenston's desk. There was no dialling tone, only a continuous buzzing noise. Someone had disconnected the line. The same person who triggered the alarm, no doubt. Jack didn't touch anything else in the room. He stepped back into the corridor and slipped into the adjoining office. A screen was fixed to the corner of the desk and was still relaying images from inside Fenston's office. Fenston had clearly not only witnessed Leapman's actions, but had enough time to set in motion the most diabolical revenge.

Jack's eyes moved across to the switchboard. One lever was up, illuminating a flickering orange light, indicating that the line was busy. He must have cut Leapman off from any hope of contacting the outside world. Jack looked down at the desk where Fenston would have been sitting when he planned the whole operation. He'd even written out a list to make sure he didn't make a mistake. All the clues were there for the NYPD to gather and evaluate. If this had been a *Columbo* investigation, the switch, the handwritten list left on the desk and the timing of the alarm going off would have been quite enough for the great detective to secure a conviction, with Fenston breaking down and confessing following the last commercial break. Unfortunately, this wasn't a made-for-TV movie, and one thing was certain, Fenston wasn't going to break down, and would never consider confessing. Jack grimaced. The only thing he had in common with Columbo was the crumpled raincoat.

Jack heard the elevator doors open and the words, 'Follow me.' He knew it had to be the cops. He turned his attention back to the screen on the desk as two uniformed officers marched into Fenston's office, and began to question the four witnesses. The plainclothes men wouldn't be far behind. Jack walked out of the adjoining office and headed silently towards the elevator. He'd reached the doors when one of the cops came out of Fenton's office and shouted, 'Hey, you.' Jack jabbed at the down button and turned sideways, so the officer couldn't see his face. The moment the doors opened, he quickly slipped inside. He kept his finger pressed on the button marked L and the doors immediately closed. When they opened on the ground floor thirty seconds later, he jogged past reception, out of the building, down the steps, and headed in the direction of his car.

Jack jumped in and started the engine, just as a cop

came running round the corner. He swung the car in a circle, mounted the sidewalk, drove back onto the road, and headed for St Vincent's Hospital.

—◦—

'Good afternoon, Sotheby's.'

'Lord Poltimore, please.'

'Who shall I say is calling, madam?'

'Lady Wentworth.' Arabella didn't have to wait long before Mark came on the line.

'How nice to hear from you, Arabella,' said Mark. 'Dare I ask,' he teased, 'are you a buyer or a seller?'

'A seeker after advice,' replied Arabella. 'But if I were to be a seller . . .'

Mark began to make notes as he listened to a series of questions that Arabella had obviously prepared carefully.

'In the days when I was a dealer,' Mark replied, 'before I joined Sotheby's, the standard commission was 10 per cent up to the first million. If the painting was likely to fetch more than a million I used to negotiate a fee with the seller.'

'And what fee would you have negotiated, had I asked you to sell the Wentworth Van Gogh?'

Mark was glad Arabella couldn't see the expression on his face. Once he'd recovered, he took his time before suggesting a figure, but quickly added, 'If you were to allow Sotheby's to put the picture up for auction, we would charge you nothing, Arabella, guaranteeing you the full hammer price.'

'So how do you make a profit?' asked Arabella.

'We charge a buyer's premium,' explained Mark.

'I already have a buyer,' said Arabella, 'but thank you for the advice.'

9/25

50

KRANTZ TURNED the corner of the street, relieved to find the pavement so crowded. She walked for about another hundred yards before stopping outside a small hotel. She glanced up and down the road, confident that she was not being followed.

She pulled open the swing doors that led into the hotel and, looking straight ahead, walked past reception, ignoring the concierge, who was talking to a tourist who sounded as if he might come from New York. Her gaze remained focused on a wall of deposit boxes to the left of the reception desk. Krantz waited until all three receptionists were fully occupied before she moved.

She glanced behind her to make sure no one had the same purpose in mind. Satisfied, she moved quickly, extracting a key from her hip pocket as she reached box 19. She turned the key in the lock and opened the door. Everything was exactly as she had left it. Krantz removed all the notes and two passports, and stuffed them in a pocket. She then locked the door, walked out of the hotel and was back on Herzen Street, without having spoken to anyone.

She hailed a taxi, something she couldn't have done in the days when the communists were teaching her her trade. She gave the driver the name of a bank in Cheryomushki, sat in the back and thought about Colonel Sergei Slatinaru – but only for a moment. Her one regret was that she hadn't succeeded in cutting off his left ear. Krantz would like to have sent Petrescu a little memento of her visit to Romania. Still, what she had in mind for Petrescu would more than make up for the disappointment.

But first she had to concentrate on getting out of Russia. It might have been easy to escape from those amateurs in Bucharest, but it was going to be far more difficult finding a safe route into England. Islands always cause a problem; mountains are so much easier to cross than water. She'd arrived in the Russian capital earlier that morning exhausted, having been constantly on the move since discharging herself from the hospital.

Krantz had reached the highway by the time the siren went off. She turned to see the hospital grounds bathed in light. A truck driver who made love to her twice, and didn't deserve to die, smuggled her across the border. It took a train, a plane, another three hundred dollars and seventeen hours before she eventually made it to Moscow. She immediately headed for the Isla Hotel, with no intention of staying overnight. Her only interest was in a safety deposit box that contained two passports and a few hundred roubles.

While she was marooned in Moscow, Krantz had planned to earn a little cash, moonlighting while she waited until it was safe to return to America. The cost of living was so much cheaper in the Russian capital than New York, and that included the cost of death. $5,000 for a wife, $10,000 for a husband. The Russians hadn't yet come to terms with equal rights. A KGB colonel could fetch as much as $50,000, while Krantz could charge $100,000 for a mafia boss. But if Fenston had transferred the promised two million dollars, tiresome wives and husbands would have to wait for her return. In fact, now that Russia had embraced free enterprise, she might even attach herself to one of the new oligarchs and offer him a comprehensive service.

She felt sure one of them could make use of the three million dollars stashed away in a safety deposit box in Queens, in which case she would never need to return to the States.

The taxi drew up outside the discreet entrance of a bank that prided itself on having few customers. The letters G and Z were chiselled in the white marble cornice. Krantz stepped out of the cab, paid the fare and waited until the taxi was out of sight before she entered the building.

The Geneva and Zurich Bank was an establishment that specialized in catering to the needs of a new breed of Russians, who had reinvented themselves following the demise of communism. Politicians, mafia bosses (businessmen), footballers and pop stars were all small change compared to the latest superstars, the oligarchs. Although everybody knew their names, they were a breed that could afford the anonymity of a number when it came to finding out the details of what they were worth.

Krantz walked up to an old-fashioned wooden counter, no lines, no grilles, where a row of smartly dressed men in grey suits, white shirts and plain silk ties waited to serve. They wouldn't have looked out of place in either Geneva or Zurich.

'How may I assist you?' asked the clerk Krantz had selected. He wondered which category she fell into – the wife of a mafia boss, or the daughter of an oligarch. She didn't look like a pop star.

'One zero seven two zero nine five nine,' she said.

He tapped the code into his computer, and when the figures flashed up on the screen he showed a little more interest.

'May I see your passport?' was his next question.

Krantz handed over one of the passports she had collected from the Isla Hotel.

'How much is there in my account?' she asked.

'How much do you think there should be?' he replied.

'Just over two million dollars,' she said.

'And what amount do you wish to withdraw?' he asked.

'Ten thousand in dollars, and ten thousand in roubles.'

He pulled out a tray from under the counter and began to count out the notes slowly. 'We haven't dealt in this account for some time,' he ventured, looking up at his screen.

'No,' she agreed, 'but you will be seeing a lot more activity now that I'm back in Moscow,' she added without explanation.

'Then I look forward to being of service, madam,' the clerk said, before passing across two bundles of notes neatly sealed in plastic wallets, with no hint of where they had come from, and certainly no paperwork to suggest a transaction had even taken place.

Krantz picked up the two wallets, placed them in an inside pocket and walked slowly out of the bank. She hailed the third available taxi.

'The Kalstern,' she said, and climbed into the back of the cab in preparation for the second part of her plan.

Fenston had kept his part of the bargain. Now she would have to keep hers if she hoped to collect the second two million. She had given a moment's thought to keeping the two million and not bothering to travel to England. But only a moment's thought because she knew that Fenston had kept up his contacts with the

KGB, and they would have been only too happy to dispose of her for a far smaller amount.

When the taxi came to a halt ten minutes later, Krantz handed over four hundred roubles and didn't wait for any change. She stepped out of the cab and joined a group of tourists who were peering in at a window, hoping to find some memento to prove to the folks back home that they had visited the wicked communists. In the centre of the window was displayed their most popular item: a four-star general's uniform with all the accessories – cap, belt, holster and three rows of campaign medals. No price tag attached, but Krantz knew the going rate was $20. Next to the general stood an admiral, $15, and behind him a KGB colonel, $10. Although Krantz had no interest in proving to the folks back home that she had visited Moscow, the kind of person who could lay their hands on the uniforms of generals, admirals and KGB colonels could undoubtedly acquire the outfit she required.

Krantz entered the shop and was greeted by a young assistant. 'Can I help you?' she asked.

'I need to speak to your boss on a private matter,' said Krantz.

The young girl looked uncertain, but Krantz just stared at her until she finally said, 'Follow me,' and led her customer to the back of the shop, where she tentatively knocked before opening the door to a small office.

Sitting behind a large wooden desk, littered with papers, empty cigarette cartons and a half-eaten salami sandwich, sat an overweight man in a baggy brown suit. He was wearing an open-necked red shirt that looked as if it hadn't been washed for several days. His bald head and thick moustache made it difficult for Krantz to guess his age, although he was clearly the proprietor.

He placed both hands on the desk and looked wearily up at her. He offered a weak smile, but all Krantz noticed was the double-chinned neck. Always tricky to negotiate.

'How can I help?' he asked, not sounding as if he was convinced she was worth the effort.

Krantz told him exactly what she required. The proprietor listened in astonished silence and then burst out laughing.

'That wouldn't come cheap,' he eventually said, 'and could take some considerable time.'

'I need the uniform by this afternoon,' said Krantz.

'That's not possible,' he said with a shrug of his heavy shoulders.

Krantz removed a wad of cash from her pocket, peeled off a hundred-dollar bill and placed it on the desk in front of him. 'This afternoon,' she repeated.

The proprietor raised his eyebrows, although his eyes never left Benjamin Franklin.

'I may just have a possible contact.'

Krantz placed another hundred on the desk.

'Yes, I think I know the ideal person.'

'And I also need her passport,' said Krantz.

'Impossible.'

Another two hundred dollars joined the Franklin twins.

'Possible,' he said, 'but not easy.'

Krantz placed a further two hundred on the table, making sextuplets.

'But I feel sure some arrangement could be made,' he paused, 'at the right price.' He looked up at his customer while resting his hands on his stomach.

'A thousand if everything I require is available by this afternoon.'

'I'll do my best,' said the proprietor.

'I feel sure you will,' said Krantz. 'Because I'm going to knock off a hundred dollars for every fifteen minutes after –' she looked at her watch – 'two o'clock.'

The proprietor was about to protest, but thought better of it.

51

When Anna's taxi drove through the gates of Wentworth Hall, she was surprised to see Arabella waiting on the top step, a shotgun under her right arm and Brunswick and Picton by her side. The butler opened the taxi door as his mistress and the two Labradors walked down the steps to greet her.

'How nice to see you,' said Arabella, kissing her on both cheeks. 'You've arrived just in time for tea.'

Anna stroked the dogs as she accompanied Arabella up the steps and into the house, while an under-butler removed her suitcase from the front of the taxi. When Anna stepped into the hall, she paused to allow her eyes to move slowly round the room, from picture to picture.

'Yes, it is nice to still have one's family around one,' said Arabella, 'even if this might be their last weekend in the country.'

'What do you mean?' asked Anna apprehensively.

'Fenston's lawyers delivered a letter by hand this morning, reminding me that should I fail to repay their client's loan in full by midday tomorrow, I must be prepared to pension off all the family retainers.'

'He plans to dispose of the entire collection? 'said Anna.

'That would appear to be his purpose,' said Arabella.

'But that doesn't make sense,' said Anna. 'If Fenston were to place the entire collection on the market at the same time he wouldn't even clear his original loan.'

'He would, if he then put the hall up for sale,' said Arabella.

'Fenston's obviously expecting you to hand over the Van Gogh.'

'I'll not give Victoria's murderer that satisfaction,' said Arabella. 'So we can only hope that Mr Nakamura remains infatuated with Van Gogh, because frankly he's my last hope.'

'Where is the masterpiece?' asked Anna as Arabella led her through to the drawing room.

'Back in the Van Gogh bedroom, where he's resided for the past hundred years –' Arabella paused – 'except for a day's excursion to Heathrow.'

While Arabella settled herself in her favourite chair by the fire, a dog on each side of her, Anna strolled around the room, reminding herself of the Italian collection, assembled by the fourth earl.

'Should my dear Italians also be forced to make an unexpected journey to New York,' said Arabella, 'they shouldn't grumble. After all, that appears to be no more than an American tradition.'

Anna laughed as she moved from Titian to Veronese and to Caravaggio. 'I'd forgotten just how magnificent the Caravaggio was,' she said, standing back to admire *The Marriage at Cana*.

'I do believe that you are more interested in dead Italians than living Irishmen,' said Arabella.

'If Caravaggio was alive today,' said Anna, 'Jack would be following him, not me.'

'What do you mean?' asked Arabella.

'He murdered a man in a drunken brawl. Spent his last few years on the run, but whenever he arrived in a new city, the local burghers turned a blind eye as long as he went on producing magnificent portraits of the Virgin Mother and the Christ child.'

'Anna, you're an impossible guest, now come and sit down,' said Arabella as a maid entered the drawing room carrying a silver tray. She began to lay up for tea by the fire.

'Now, my dear, will you have Indian or China?'

'I've always been puzzled,' said Anna, taking the seat opposite Arabella, 'why it isn't Indian or Chinese, or India or China?'

For a moment, Arabella was silenced, saved only by the entry of the butler.

'M'lady,' said Andrews, 'there's a gentleman at the door with a package for you. I told him to take it round to the tradesman's entrance, but he said he couldn't release it without your signature.'

'A sort of modern-day Viola,' suggested Arabella. 'I shall have to go and see what this peevish messenger brings,' she added. 'Perhaps I will even throw him a ring for his troubles.'

'I feel sure the fair Olivia will know just how to handle him,' rejoined Anna.

Arabella gave a little bow, and followed Andrews out of the room.

Anna was admiring Tintoretto's *Perseus and Andromeda* when Arabella returned, the cheerful smile of only moments before replaced by a grim expression.

'Is there a problem?' asked Anna, as she turned round to face her host.

'The peevish fellow has sent back my ring,' replied Arabella. 'Come and see for yourself.'

Anna followed her into the hall, where she found Andrews and the under-butler removing the casing of a red crate that Anna had hoped she had seen for the last time.

'It must have been sent from New York,' said Arabella, studying a label attached to the box, 'probably on the same flight as you.'

'Seems to be following me around,' said Anna.

'You appear to have that effect on men,' said Arabella.

They both watched as Andrews neatly removed the bubble wrap to reveal a canvas that Anna had last seen in Anton's studio.

'The only good thing to come out of this,' said Anna, 'is that we can transfer the original frame back onto the masterpiece.'

'But what shall we do with him?' asked Arabella, gesturing towards the impostor. The butler gave a discreet cough. 'You have a suggestion, Andrews?' Arabella enquired. 'If so, spit it out.'

'No, m'lady,' Andrews replied, 'but I thought you would want to know that your other guest is proceeding up the drive.'

'The man clearly has a gift for timing,' said Arabella, as she quickly checked her hair in the mirror. 'Andrews,' she said, reverting to her normal role, 'has the Wellington Room been prepared for Mr Nakamura?'

'Yes, m'lady. And Dr Petrescu will be in the Van Gogh room.'

'How appropriate,' said Arabella, turning to face Anna, 'that he should spend his last night with you.'

Anna was relieved to see Arabella so quickly back into her stride, and had a feeling that she might prove a genuine foil for Nakamura.

The butler opened the front door and walked down the steps at a pace that would ensure he reached the gravel just as the Toyota Lexus came to a halt. Andrews opened the back door of the limousine to allow Mr Nakamura to step out. He was clutching a small square package.

'The Japanese always arrive bearing a gift,' whispered Anna, 'but under no circumstances should you open it in their presence.'

'That's all very well,' said Arabella, 'but I haven't got anything for him.'

'He won't expect something in return. You have invited him to be a guest in your house, and that is the greatest compliment you can pay any Japanese.'

'That's a relief,' said Arabella as Mr Nakamura appeared at the front door.

'Lady Arabella,' he said, bowing low, 'it is a great honour to be invited to your magnificent home.'

'You honour my home, Mr Nakamura,' said Arabella, hoping she'd said the correct thing.

The Japanese man bowed even lower, and when he rose came face to face with Lawrence's portrait of Wellington.

'How appropriate,' he said. 'Did the great man not dine at Wentworth Hall the night before he sailed for Waterloo?'

'Indeed he did,' said Arabella, 'and you will sleep in the same bed that the Iron Duke slept in on that historic occasion.'

Nakamura turned to Anna and bowed. 'How nice to see you again, Dr Petrescu.'

'And you too, Nakamura San,' said Anna. 'I hope you had a pleasant journey.'

'Yes, thank you. We even landed on time, for a change,' said Nakamura, who didn't move as his eyes roamed around the room. 'You will please correct me, Anna, should I make a mistake. It is clear that the room is devoted to the English school. Gainsborough?' he queried, as he admired the full-length portrait of Catherine, Lady Wentworth. Anna nodded, before Nakamura moved on. 'Landseer, Morland,

Romney, Stubbs, but then, I am stumped – is that the correct expression?'

'It most certainly is,' confirmed Arabella, 'although our American cousins wouldn't begin to understand its significance. And you were stumped by Lely.'

'Ah, Sir Peter, and what a fine-looking woman – ' he paused – 'a family trait,' he said, turning to face his host.

'And I can see, Mr Nakamura, that your family trait is flattery,' teased Arabella.

Nakamura burst out laughing. 'With the risk of being taken to task a second time, Lady Arabella, if every room is the equal of this, it may prove necessary for me to cancel my meeting with those dullards from Corus Steel.' Nakamura's eyes continued to sweep the room, 'Wheatley, Lawrence, West and Wilkie,' he said before his gaze ended up on the portrait propped up against the wall.

Nakamura offered no opinion for some time. 'Quite magnificent,' he finally said. 'The work of an accomplished hand – ' he paused – 'but not the hand of the master.'

'How can you be so sure, Nakamura San?' asked Anna

'Because the wrong ear is bandaged,' replied Nakamura.

'But everyone knows that Van Gogh cut off his left ear,' said Anna.

Nakamura turned and smiled at Anna. 'And you know only too well,' he added, 'that Van Gogh painted the original while looking in a mirror, which is why the bandage ended up on the wrong ear.'

'I do hope that someone is going to explain all this to me later,' said Arabella as she led her guests through to the drawing room.

52

Krantz returned to the shop at 2pm, but there was no sign of the proprietor. 'He'll be back at any moment,' the assistant assured her, without conviction.

Any moment turned out to be thirty minutes, by which time the assistant was nowhere to be seen. When the owner did eventually show up, Krantz was pleased to see that he was carrying a bulky plastic bag. Without a word being spoken, Krantz followed him to the back of the shop and into his office. Not until he'd closed the door did a large grin appear on his fleshy lips.

The proprietor placed the carrier bag on his desk. He paused for a moment, then pulled out the red outfit Krantz had requested.

'She may be a little taller than you,' he said with a half apology, 'but I can supply a needle and thread at no extra charge.' He began to laugh, but ceased when his customer didn't respond.

Krantz held the uniform up against her shoulders. The previous owner was at least three or four inches taller than Krantz, but only a few pounds heaver; nothing – as the proprietor had suggested – that a needle and thread wouldn't remedy.

'And the passport?' asked Krantz.

Once again the proprietor's hand dipped into the carrier bag, and, like a conjuror producing a rabbit out of a hat, he offered up a Soviet passport. He handed over the prize to Krantz and said, 'She has a three-day layover, so she probably won't discover that it's missing until Friday.'

'It will have served its purpose long before then,' Krantz said, as she began to turn the pages of the official document.

Sasha Prestakavich, she discovered, was three years younger than her, and eight centimetres taller with no distinguishing marks. A problem that a pair of high-heeled shoes would solve, unless an overzealous official decided to carry out a strip search and came across the recent wound on her right shoulder.

When Krantz reached the page where Sasha Prestakavich's photo had once been, the proprietor was unable to disguise a satisfied smirk. For his next trick, he produced from under the counter a Polaroid camera.

'Smile,' he said. She didn't.

A few seconds later an image spewed out. A pair of scissors appeared next and the proprietor began to cut the photograph down to a size that would comply with the little dotted rectangle on page three of the passport. Next, a dollop of glue to fix the new holder in place. His final act was to drop a needle and thread into the carrier bag. Krantz was beginning to realize that this was not the first occasion he had supplied such a service. She placed the uniform and the passport back in the carrier bag, before handing over eight hundred dollars.

The proprietor checked the wad of notes carefully.

'You said a thousand,' he protested.

'You were thirty minutes late,' Krantz reminded him as she picked up the bag and turned to leave.

'Do come and visit us again,' suggested the proprietor as she retreated, 'whenever you're passing through.'

Krantz didn't bother to explain to him why, in her

profession, she never saw anyone twice, unless it was to make sure they couldn't see her a third time.

Once she was back on the street, she only had to walk for a couple of blocks before she came across the next shop she required. She purchased a pair of plain black high-heeled shoes – not her style, but they would serve their purpose. She paid the bill in roubles and left the shop carrying two bags.

Krantz next hailed a taxi, gave the driver an address and told him the exact entrance where she wished to be dropped off. When the cab drew up by a side door marked 'Staff Only', Krantz paid the fare, entered the building and went straight to the ladies' room. She locked herself in a cubicle, where she spent the next forty minutes. With the aid of the needle and thread supplied by the proprietor, she raised the hemline of the skirt by a couple of inches, and made a couple of tucks in the waist, which wouldn't be visible under the jacket. She then stripped off all her outer garments before trying on the uniform – not a perfect fit, but fortunately the company she was proposing to work for was not known for its sartorial elegance. Next she replaced her sneakers with the recently acquired high heels, before dropping her own clothes into the carrier bag.

When she finally left the ladies' room, she went in search of her new employers. Her walk was a little unsteady, but then she wasn't used to high heels. Krantz's eyes settled on another woman who was dressed in an identical uniform. She walked across to the counter and asked, 'Have you got a spare seat on any of our London flights?'

'That shouldn't be a problem,' she replied. 'Can I see your passport?' Krantz handed over the recently acquired document. The company's representative looked up Sasha Prestakavich's details on the company database. According to their records, she was on a three-day layover. 'That seems to be in order,' she eventually said, and handed her a crew pass. 'Be sure that you're among the last to check in, just in case we have any latecomers.'

Krantz walked across to the international terminal, and once she'd been checked through customs, hung around in duty free until she heard the final boarding call for flight 413 to London. By the time she arrived at the gate, the last three passengers were checking in. Once again her passport was checked against the company database before the gate officer studied his screen and said, 'We've got seats available in every class, so take your pick.'

'Back row of economy,' Krantz said unhesitatingly.

The gate official looked surprised, but printed out a boarding card and handed the little slip over to her. Krantz walked through the gate, and boarded Aeroflot's flight 413 to London.

53

ANNA WALKED SLOWLY down the wide, marble staircase, pausing for a moment at every two or three steps to admire another master. It didn't matter how often she saw them . . . she heard a noise behind her, and looked back towards the guest corridor to see Andrews coming out of her bedroom. He was carrying a picture under his arm. She smiled as he hurried away in the direction of the back stairs.

Anna continued to study the paintings on her slow progress down the staircase. As she stepped into the hall she gave Catherine, Lady Wentworth another admiring look, before she walked slowly across the black-and-white marbled-square floor towards the drawing room.

The first thing Anna saw as she entered was Andrews placing the Van Gogh on an easel in the centre of the room.

'What do you think?' said Arabella, as she took a pace back to admire the self-portrait.

'Don't you feel that Mr Nakamura might consider it a little . . .' ventured Anna, not wishing to offend her host.

'Crude, blatant, obvious? Which word were you searching for, my dear?' asked Arabella as she turned to face Anna. Anna burst out laughing. 'Let's face it,' said Arabella, 'I'm strapped for cash and running out of time, so I don't have a lot of choice.'

'No one would believe it, looking at you,' said Anna

as she admired the magnificent long rose silk-taffeta gown and diamond necklace Arabella was wearing, making Anna feel somewhat casual in her short black Armani dress.

'It's kind of you to say so, my dear, but if I had your looks and your figure, I wouldn't need to cover myself from head to toe with other distractions.'

Anna smiled, admiring the way Arabella had so quickly put her at ease.

'When do you think he'll make a decision?' asked Arabella, trying not to sound desperate.

'Like all great collectors,' said Anna, 'he'll make up his mind within moments. A scientific survey has recently shown that men decide whether they want to sleep with a woman in about eight seconds.'

'That long?' said Arabella.

'Mr Nakamura will take about the same time to decide if he wants to own this painting,' she said, looking directly at the Van Gogh.

'Let's drink to that,' said Arabella.

Andrews stepped forward on cue, proffering a silver tray that held three glasses.

'A glass of champagne, madam?' he enquired.

'Thank you,' said Anna, removing a long-stemmed flute. When Andrews stepped back, her gaze fell on a turquoise and black vase that she had never seen before.

'It's quite magnificent,' said Anna.

'Mr Nakamura's gift,' said Arabella. 'Most embarrassing. By the way,' she added, 'I do hope I haven't committed a *faux pas* by putting it on display while Mr Nakamura is still a guest in my home?' She paused. 'If I have, Andrews can remove it immediately.'

'Certainly not,' said Anna. 'Mr Nakamura will be flattered that you have placed his gift among so many other maestros.'

'Are you sure?' asked Arabella.

'Oh yes. The piece survives, even shines in this room. There is only one certain rule when it comes to real talent,' said Anna. 'Any form of art isn't out of place as long as it's displayed among its equals. The Raphael on the wall, the diamond necklace you are wearing, the Chippendale table on which you have placed the vase, the Nash fireplace and the Van Gogh have all been created by masters. Now I have no idea who the craftsman was who made this piece,' continued Anna, still admiring the way the turquoise appeared to be running into the black, like a melting candle, 'but I have no doubt that in his own country, he is considered a master.'

'Not exactly a master,' said a voice coming from behind them.

Arabella and Anna turned at the same time to see that Mr Nakamura had entered the room. He was dressed in a dinner jacket and bow tie that Andrews would have approved of.

'Not a master?' queried Arabella.

'No,' said Nakamura. 'In this country, you honour those who "achieve greatness", to quote your Bard, by making them knights or barons, whereas we in Japan reward such talent with the title "national treasure". It is appropriate that this piece has found a home in Wentworth Hall because, of the twelve great potters in history, the experts acknowledge that eleven have been Japanese, with the sole exception of a Cornishman, Bernard Leach. You failed to make him a Lord or even give him a knighthood, so we declared him to be an honorary national treasure.'

'How immensely civilized,' said Arabella, 'as I must confess that recently we have been giving honours to pop stars, footballers and vulgar millionaires.' Nakamura laughed, as Andrews offered him a glass of champagne.

'Are you a national treasure, Mr Nakamura?' enquired Arabella.

'Certainly not,' replied Nakamura. 'My countrymen do not consider vulgar millionaires worthy of such an honour.'

Arabella turned scarlet, while Anna continued to stare at the vase, as if she hadn't heard the remark. 'But am I not right in thinking, Mr Nakamura, that this particular vase is not symmetrical?'

'Quite brilliant,' replied Nakamura. 'You should have been a member of the diplomatic corps, Anna. Not only did you manage to deftly change the subject, but at the same time you raised a question that demands to be answered.'

Nakamura walked straight past the Van Gogh as if he hadn't noticed it and looked at the vase for some time before he added, 'If you ever come across a piece of pottery that is perfect, you can be confident that it was produced by a machine. With pottery, you must seek *near* perfection. If you look carefully enough, you will always find some slight blemish that serves to remind us that the piece was crafted by a human hand. The longer you have to search, the greater the craftsman, for it was only Giotto who was able to draw the perfect circle.'

'For me, it *is* perfection,' said Arabella. 'I simply love it, and whatever Mr Fenston manages to prise away from me during the coming years, I shall never allow him to get his hands on my national treasure.'

'Perhaps it won't be necessary for him to prise anything else away,' said Mr Nakamura, turning to face the Van Gogh as if he'd seen it for the first time. Arabella held her breath while Anna studied the expression on Nakamura's face. She couldn't be sure.

Nakamura glanced at the picture for only a few seconds before he turned to Arabella and said, 'There are times when it is a distinct advantage to be a vulgar millionaire, because although one may not aspire to being a national treasure oneself, it does allow one to indulge in collecting other people's national treasures.'

Anna wanted to cheer, but simply raised her glass. Mr Nakamura returned the compliment, and they both turned to face Arabella. Tears were flooding down her cheeks.

'I don't know how to thank you,' she said.

'Not me,' said Nakamura, 'Anna. Because without her courage and fortitude, this whole episode would not have been brought to such a worthwhile conclusion.'

'I agree,' said Arabella, 'which is why I shall ask Andrews to return the self-portrait to Anna's bedroom, so that she can be the last person to fully appreciate the painting before it begins its long journey to Japan.'

'How appropriate,' said Nakamura. 'But if Anna were to become the CEO of my foundation, she could see it whenever she wished.'

Anna was about to respond when Andrews re-entered the drawing room and announced, 'Dinner is served, m'lady.'

◄◦►

Krantz had chosen to sit in the back of the aircraft so that few of the passengers would notice her, only the crew. She needed to be adopted by one of them long before they touched down at Heathrow. Krantz took her time as she tried to work out which of her new colleagues would fulfil that purpose.

'Domestic or international?' asked the senior stewardess, soon after the aircraft had reached its cruising height.

'Domestic,' replied Krantz with a smile.

'Ah, that's why I haven't seen you before.'

'I've only been with the company for three months,' said Krantz.

'That would explain it. My name's Nina.'

'Sasha,' said Krantz, giving her a warm smile.

'Just let me know if you need anything, Sasha.'

'I will,' said Krantz.

Trying to relax when she couldn't lean on her right shoulder meant that Krantz remained awake for most of the flight. She used the hours getting to know Nina, so that by the time they landed, the senior stewardess would unwittingly play a role in the most crucial part of her deception. By the time Krantz finally fell asleep, Nina had become her minder.

'Would you like to go up front, Sasha?' Nina asked once the captain had instructed the crew to take their seats and prepare for landing. 'Then you can disembark immediately after the doors are opened.'

Krantz shook her head. 'It's my first visit to England,' she said nervously, 'and I'd prefer to be with you and the rest of the crew.'

'Of course,' said Nina. 'And if you'd like to, you can also join us on the minibus.'

'Thank you,' said Krantz.

Krantz remained in her seat until the last passenger had left the aircraft. She then joined the crew as they disembarked and headed in the direction of the terminal. Krantz never left the chief stewardess's side during the long walk down endless corridors, while Nina offered her opinion on everything from Putin to Rasputin.

When the Aeroflot crew finally reached passport control, Nina guided her charge past the long queue of passengers and on towards the exit marked CREW ONLY. Krantz tucked in behind Nina, who didn't stop chatting even when she'd handed over her passport to the official. He slowly turned the pages, checked the photograph and then waved Nina through. 'Next.'

Krantz handed over her passport. Once again, the official looked carefully at the photograph and then at the person it claimed to represent. He even smiled as he waved her through. Krantz suddenly felt a stab of pain in her right shoulder. For a moment, the excruciating feeling made it difficult for her to move. She tried not to grimace. The official waved again, but she still remained fixed to the spot.

'Come on, Sasha,' cried Nina, 'you're holding every-one up.'

Krantz somehow managed to stumble unsteadily through the barrier. The official continued to stare at her as she walked away. Never look back. She smiled at Nina, and linked her arm in hers as they headed towards the exit. The official finally turned his attention to the second officer, who was next in line.

'Will you be joining us on the bus?' asked Nina, as they strolled out of the airport and onto the pavement.

'No,' said Krantz. 'I'm being met by my boyfriend.'

Nina looked surprised. She said goodbye, before crossing the road in the company of the second officer.

'Who was that?' her colleague asked, before climbing onto the Aeroflot bus.

54

'WASN'T THERE anything on the film that would assist us?' asked Macy.

'Nothing,' replied Jack, as he looked across the desk at his boss. 'Leapman had only been in the office for long enough to photograph eight documents before Fenston's unscheduled appearance.'

'And what do those eight documents tell us?' Macy demanded.

'Nothing we didn't already know,' admitted Jack, as he opened a file in front of him. 'Mainly contracts confirming that Fenston is still fleecing customers in different parts of the world, who are either naive or greedy. But should any of them decide it would be in their best interests to sell their assets and clear the debt with Fenston Finance, I suspect that's when we'll end up with another body on our hands. No, my only hope is that the NYPD has gathered enough evidence to press charges in the Leapman case, because I still don't have enough to slap a parking ticket on him.'

'It doesn't help,' said Macy, 'that when I spoke to my opposite number this morning, or to be more accurate he spoke to me, the first thing he wanted to know was did we have an FBI agent called Delaney, and if so, was he on the scene of the crime before his boys arrived.'

'What did you tell him?' asked Jack, trying not to smile.

'I'd look into the matter and call him back.' Macy

paused. 'But it might placate them a little if you were willing to trade some information,' he suggested.

'But I don't think they have anything we aren't already aware of,' responded Jack, 'and they can't be that optimistic about pressing charges while Leapman is still out for the count.'

'Any news from the hospital about his chances of recovery?' asked Macy.

'Not great,' admitted Jack. 'While he was in Fenston's office he suffered a stress stroke caused by high blood pressure. The medical term is aphasia.'

'Aphasia?'

'The part of Leapman's brain that affects his speech has been irreparably damaged, so he can't speak. Frankly, his doctor is describing him as a vegetable, and warned me that the only decision the hospital will have to make is whether to pull the plug and let him die peacefully.'

'The NYPD tell me that Fenston is sitting solicitously by the patient's bedside.'

'Then they'd better not leave them alone for more than a few moments,' said Jack, 'because if they do, the doctors won't need to make the decision as to who should pull the plug.'

'The NYPD also wants to know if you removed a camera from the crime scene.'

'It was FBI property.'

'Not if it was evidence in a criminal enquiry, as you well know, Jack. Why don't you send them a set of the photos Leapman took and try to be more cooperative in the future? Remind them that your father served twenty-six years with the force – that should do the trick.'

'But what do they have to offer in exchange?' asked Jack.

'A copy of a photograph with your name on the back.

They want to know if it meant anything to you, because it sure didn't to them, or me,' admitted Macy.

The supervisor pushed two prints across his desk and allowed Jack a few moments to consider them. The first was a picture of Fenston shaking hands with George W. Bush when he visited Ground Zero. Jack recalled the blown-up version that was hanging on the wall behind Fenston's desk. He held up the picture and asked, 'How come the NYPD has a copy of this?'

'They found it on Leapman's desk. He was obviously going to hand it over to you yesterday evening, along with an explanation of what he'd written on the back.'

Jack looked at the second print and was considering the words, *Delaney, this is all the evidence you need*, when the phone on Macy's desk buzzed.

He picked it up and listened. 'Put him on,' said Macy as he replaced the receiver and flicked a switch that would allow them both to follow the conversation. 'It's Tom Crasanti, calling from London,' said Macy. 'Hi, Tom, it's Dick Macy. Jack's in the office with me. We were just discussing the Fenston case, because we're still not making much headway.'

'That's why I'm calling,' said Tom. 'There's been a development at this end, and the news is not good. We think Krantz has slipped into England.'

'That's not possible,' said Jack. 'How could she hope to get through passport control?'

'By posing as an Aeroflot stewardess, it would seem,' said Tom. 'My contact at the Russian embassy called to warn me that a woman had entered Britain using a fake passport under the name of Sasha Prestakavich.'

'But why should they assume Prestakavich is Krantz?' asked Jack.

'They didn't,' said Tom. 'They had no idea who she was. All they could tell me was that the suspect befriended Aeroflot's chief stewardess while on their daily flight to London. She then fooled her into accompanying her through passport control. That's how we got to hear of it. It turns out that the co-pilot asked who the woman was, and when he was told that her name was Sasha Prestakavich, he said that wasn't possible because he travelled with her regularly, and it certainly wasn't Prestakavich.'

'That still doesn't prove it's Krantz,' pressed Macy.

'I'll get there, sir, just give me time.'

Jack was glad his friend couldn't see the look of impatience on the boss's face.

'The co-pilot,' continued Tom, 'reported to his captain, who immediately alerted Aeroflot's security. It didn't take them long to discover that Sasha Prestakavich was on a three-day layover, and her passport had been stolen, along with her uniform. That set alarm bells ringing.' Macy began tapping his fingers on the desk. 'My contact at the Russian embassy called me in the new entente-cordiale spirit of post 9/11,' said Tom, 'having already briefed Interpol.'

'We are going to get there, aren't we, Tom?'

'Any moment, sir.' He paused. 'Where was I?'

'Taking calls from your contact in the Russian embassy,' said Jack.

'Oh, yes,' said Tom. 'It was after I'd given him a description of Krantz, about five foot, around a hundred pounds, crew cut, that they asked me to fax over a photograph of her, which I did. He then forwarded a copy of the photograph to the co-pilot at his London hotel, who confirmed that it was Krantz.'

'Good work, Tom,' said Macy, 'thorough as always, but have you come up with any theory as to why Krantz would chance going to England at this particular time?'

'To kill Petrescu would be my bet,' said Tom.

'What do you think?' asked Macy looking across his desk at Jack.

'I agree with Tom,' replied Jack. 'Anna has to be the obvious target.' He hesitated. 'But what I can't work out is why Krantz would take such a risk right now.'

'I agree,' said Macy, 'but I'm not willing to put Petrescu's life at risk while we try to second-guess Krantz's motives.' Macy leant forward. 'Now listen carefully, Tom, because I'm only going to tell you this once.' He quickly began to turn the pages of his Fenston file. 'I need you to get in touch with – just give me a moment,' he said as he turned over even more pages. 'Ah, yes, here it is, Chief Superintendent Renton of the Surrey CID. After reading Jack's report, I got a clear impression that Renton is a man used to making tough decisions, even taking responsibility when one of his subordinates has screwed up. I know you've already briefed him on Krantz, but warn him that we think she's about to strike again, and the target could well be someone else at Wentworth Hall. He won't want that to happen twice on his watch, and rub in that the last time Krantz was captured, she escaped. That will keep him awake at night. And if he wants to have a word with me at any time, I'm always on the end of a line.'

'And do pass on my best wishes,' added Jack.

'That should settle it,' said Macy. 'So, Tom, step it up a notch.'

'Yes, sir,' came back the reply from London.

Macy flicked off the speaker phone. 'And, Jack, I want you to take the next flight to London. If Krantz is even thinking about harming Petrescu, let's make sure we're waiting for her, because if she were to escape a second time, I'll be pensioned off and you can forget any thoughts of promotion.'

Jack frowned but didn't respond.

'You look apprehensive,' said Macy.

'I can't see why a photo of Fenston shaking hands with the President is *all the evidence you need* –' he paused – 'although I think I've worked out why Krantz is willing to risk returning to Wentworth Hall a second time.'

'And why's that?' asked Macy.

'She's going to steal the Van Gogh,' said Jack, 'then somehow get it to Fenston.'

'So Petrescu isn't the reason Krantz has returned to England.'

'No, she isn't,' said Jack, 'but once Krantz discovers she's there, you can assume that she'll consider killing Anna a bonus.'

55

LIGHTING-UP TIME was 7.41pm on September 25th.
Krantz didn't appear on the outskirts of Wentworth until
just after eight.

Arabella was at the time accompanying her guests
through to the dining room.

Krantz, dressed in a black skin-tight tracksuit, circled
the estate twice before she decided where she would
enter the grounds. It certainly wasn't going to be through
the front gates. Although the high stone walls that
surrounded the estate had proved impregnable when
originally built to keep invaders out, particularly the
French and Germans, by the beginning of the twenty-
first century wear and tear, and the minimum wage,
meant that there were one or two places where entry
would have been simple enough for a local lad planning
to steal apples.

Once Krantz had selected her point of entry, she
easily climbed the weakened perimeter in a matter of
seconds, straddled the wall, fell and rolled over, as she
had done a thousand times following a bad dismount
from the high bar.

Krantz remained still for a moment as she waited for
the moon to disappear behind a cloud. She then ran
thirty or forty yards to the safety of a little copse of trees
down by the river. She waited for the moon to reappear
so that she could study the terrain more carefully, aware
that she would have to be patient. In her line of work,

impatience led to mistakes, and mistakes could not be rectified quite as easily as in some other professions.

Krantz had a clear view of the front of the house, but it was another forty minutes before the vast oak door was opened by a man in a black tail coat and white tie, allowing the two dogs out for their nightly frolic. They sniffed the air, immediately picking up Krantz's scent, and began barking loudly as they bounded towards her. But then she had been waiting for them – patiently.

The English, her instructor had once told her, were an animal-loving nation, and you could tell a person's class by the dogs they chose to share their homes with. The working class liked greyhounds, the middle classes Jack Russells and cocker spaniels, while the nouveaux riches preferred a Rottweiler or German shepherd to protect their newly made wealth. The upper classes traditionally chose Labradors, dogs quite unsuited for protection, as they were more likely to lick you than take a chunk out of you. When Krantz was told about these dogs, it was the first time she had come across the word 'soppy'. Only the Queen had corgis.

Krantz didn't move as the two dogs bounded towards her, occasionally stopping to sniff the air, now aware of another smell that made their tails wag even faster. Krantz had earlier visited Curnick's in the Fulham Road and selected the most tender pieces of sirloin steak, which would have been appreciated by those guests now dining at Wentworth Hall. Krantz felt no expense should be spared. After all, it was to be their last supper.

Krantz laid the large juicy morsels around her in a circle and remained motionless in the centre, like a dumb waiter. Once Brunswick and Picton came across the meat, they quickly tucked into their first course, not showing a great deal of interest in the human statue in the centre of the circle. Krantz crouched slowly down on one knee and began to lay out a second helping, wherever she saw a gap appear in the circle. Occasionally the dogs would pause between mouthfuls, look up at her with doleful eyes, tails wagging if anything more enthusiastically, before they returned to the feast.

Once she had laid before them the final delicacy, Krantz leant forward and began to stroke the silky head of Picton, the younger of the two dogs. He didn't even look up when she drew the kitchen knife from its sheath. Sheffield steel, also purchased from the Fulham Road that afternoon.

Once again, she gently stroked the head of the chocolate Labrador, and then suddenly, without warning, grabbed Picton by the ears, jerked his head away from the last succulent morsels and, with one slash of the blade, sliced into the animal's throat. A loud bark was quickly followed by a shrill yelp, and in the darkness Krantz could not see the large black eyes giving her a pained expression. The black Labrador, older but not wiser, looked up and growled, which took him a full second. More than enough time for Krantz to thrust her left forearm under the dog's jaw, causing Brunswick to raise his head just long enough for Krantz to slash out at his throat, though not with her usual skill and precision. The dog sank to the ground, whimpering in pain. Krantz leant forward, pulled up his silken ears and with one final movement finished off the job.

Krantz dragged both dogs into the copse and dumped them behind a fallen oak. She then washed her hands in the stream, annoyed to find her brand-new tracksuit was covered in blood. She finally wiped the knife on the grass, before replacing it in its sheath. She checked her watch. She had allocated two hours for the entire operation, so she reckoned she still had over an hour before those in the house, occupied with either serving or being served, would notice the dogs had not returned from their evening constitutional.

The distance between the copse and the north end of the house Krantz estimated to be a hundred, perhaps a hundred and twenty yards. With the moon throwing out such a clear light, if only intermittently, she knew that there was only one form of movement that would go unobserved.

She fell to her knees before lying flat on the grass. She first placed one arm in front of her, followed by one leg, the second arm, then the second leg, and finally she eased her body forward. Her record for a hundred yards as a human crab was seven minutes and nineteen seconds. Occasionally, she would stop and raise her head to study the layout of the house so that she could consider her point of entry. The ground floor was ablaze with light, while the first floor was almost in darkness. The second floor, where the servants resided, had only one light on. Krantz wasn't interested in the second floor. The person she was looking for would be on the ground floor, and later the first.

When Krantz was within ten yards of the house, she slowed each movement down until she felt a finger touch the outer wall. She lay still, cocked her head to one side and used the light of the moon to study the edifice more carefully. Only great estates still boasted drainpipes of that size. When you've performed a somersault on a four-inch-wide beam, a drainpipe that prominent is a ladder.

Krantz next checked the windows of the large room where the most noise was coming from. Although the heavy curtains were drawn, she spotted one affording a slight chink. She moved even more slowly towards the noise and laughter. When she reached the window, she pushed herself up onto her knees until one eye was in line with the tiny gap in the curtain.

The first thing she saw was a man dressed in a dinner jacket. He was on his feet, a glass of champagne in one hand as if proposing a toast. She couldn't hear what he was saying, but then she wasn't interested. Her eyes swept that part of the room she could see. At one end of the table sat a lady in a long silk dress with her back to the window, looking intently at the man delivering the impromptu speech. Krantz's eyes rested on her diamond necklace, but that wasn't her trade. Her speciality was two or three inches above the sparkling gems.

She turned her attention to the other end of the table. She almost smiled when she saw who was eating pheasant and sipping a glass of wine. When Petrescu retired to bed later that night, Krantz would be waiting for her, hidden in a place she would least expect to find her.

Krantz glanced towards the man in the black tailcoat who had opened the door to let the dogs out. He was now standing behind the lady wearing the silk gown, refilling her glass with wine, while other servants removed plates and one did nothing more than scrape crumbs from the table into a silver tray. Krantz remained absolutely still while her eyes continued to move around the room, searching for the other throat Fenston had sent her to cut.

'Lady Arabella, I rise to thank you for your kindness and hospitality. I have much enjoyed trout from the River Test, and pheasant shot on your estate, while in the company of two remarkable women. But tonight will remain memorable for me for many other reasons. Not least, that I will leave Wentworth Hall tomorrow with two unique additions to my collection – one of the finest examples of Van Gogh's work, as well as one of the most talented young professionals in her field, who has agreed to be the CEO of my foundation. Your great-grandfather,' said Nakamura, turning to face his hostess, 'was wise enough in 1889, over a century ago, to purchase from Dr Gachet the self-portrait of his close friend, Vincent Van Gogh. Tomorrow, that masterpiece will begin a journey to the other side of the world, but I must warn you, Arabella, that after only a few hours in your home, I have my eye on another of your national treasures, and this time I would be willing to pay well over the odds.'

'Which one, may I ask?' said Arabella.

Krantz decided that it was time to move on.

She crept slowly towards the north end of the building, unaware that the massive corner stones had been an architectural delight to Sir John Vanbrugh; to her they formed perfectly proportioned footholds to the first floor.

She climbed up onto the first-floor balcony in less than two minutes, and paused for a moment to consider how many bedrooms she might have to enter. She knew that while there were guests in the house there was no reason to think any of the rooms would be alarmed, and because of the age of the building, entry wouldn't have caused much difficulty for a burglar on his first outing. With the aid of her knife, Krantz slipped the bolt on the window of the first room. Once inside, she didn't fumble around for a light but switched on a slim-line pen torch, which illuminated an area about the size of a small television screen. The square of light moved across the wall, illuminating picture after picture, and although Hals, Hobbema and Van Goyen would have delighted most connoisseurs' eyes, Krantz passed quickly over them in search of another Dutch master. Once she had given cursory consideration to every painting in the room, she switched off the torch and headed back to the balcony. She entered the second guest bedroom as Arabella rose to thank Mr Nakamura for his gracious speech.

Once again Krantz studied each canvas, and once again none brought a smile to her lips. She quickly returned to the parapet, as the butler offered Mr Nakamura a port and opened the cigar box. Mr Nakamura allowed Andrews to pour him a Taylor's 47. When the butler returned to his mistress at the other end of the table, Arabella declined the port, but rolled several cigars between her thumb and forefinger before she selected a Monte Cristo. As the butler struck a match for his mistress, Arabella smiled. Everything was going to plan.

56

KRANTZ HAD COVERED five bedrooms by the time Arabella invited her guests to join her in the drawing room for coffee. There were still another nine rooms left to consider, and Krantz was aware that not only was she running out of time, but she wouldn't be given a second chance.

She moved swiftly to the next room, where someone who believed in fresh air had left a window wide open. She switched on her torch, to be greeted by a steely glare from the Iron Duke. She moved on to the next picture, just as Mr Nakamura placed his coffee cup back on the side table and rose from his place. 'I think it is time for me to retire to bed, Lady Arabella,' he said, 'in case those dull men of Corus Steel feel I have lost my edge.' He turned to Anna. 'I look forward to seeing you in the morning, when we might discuss over breakfast any ideas you have for developing my collection, and perhaps even your remuneration.'

'But you have already made it clear what you think I am worth,' said Anna.

'I don't recall that,' said Nakamura, looking puzzled.

'Oh yes,' said Anna, with a smile. 'I well remember your suggestion that Fenston had convinced you that I was worth five hundred dollars a day.'

'You have taken advantage of an old man,' said Nakamura with a smile, 'but I shall not go back on my word.'

Krantz thought she heard a door close, and without giving Wellington a second look returned quickly to the balcony. She needed the use of her knife to secure entry into the next room. She moved stealthily across the floor, coming to a halt at the end of another four-poster bed. She switched on the torch, expecting to be greeted by a blank wall. But not this time.

The insane eyes of a genius stared at her. The insane eyes of an assassin stared back.

Krantz smiled for the second time that day. She climbed up onto the bed and crawled slowly towards her next victim. She was within inches of the canvas when she unsheathed her knife, raised it above her head and was about to plunge the blade into the neck of Van Gogh, when she remembered what Fenston had insisted on, if she hoped to collect four million rather than three. She switched off her torch, climbed down from the bed onto the thick carpet and crawled under the four-poster. She lay flat on her back and waited.

As Arabella and her guests strolled out of the drawing room and into the hallway, she asked Andrews if Brunswick and Picton had returned.

'No, m'lady,' the butler replied, 'but there are a lot of rabbits about tonight.'

'Then I shall go and fetch the rascals myself,' muttered Arabella and, turning to her guests, added, 'Sleep well. I'll see you both at breakfast.'

Nakamura bowed before accompanying Anna up the staircase, again stopping occasionally to admire Arabella's ancestors, who gazed back at him.

'You will forgive me, Anna,' he said, 'for taking my time, but I may not be given the opportunity of meeting these gentlemen again.'

Anna smiled as she left him to admire the Romney of Mrs Siddons.

She continued on down the corridor, coming to a halt outside the Van Gogh room. She opened the bedroom door and switched on the light, stopping for a moment to admire the portrait of Van Gogh. She took off her dress and hung it in the wardrobe, placing the rest of her clothes on the sofa at the end of the four-poster. She then turned on the light by the side of the bed and checked her watch. It was just after eleven. She disappeared into the bathroom.

When Krantz heard the sound of a shower, she slid out from under the canopy and knelt beside the bed. She cocked an ear, like an attentive animal sniffing the wind. The shower was still running. She stood up, walked across to the door and switched off the bedroom light, while leaving on the reading light by the side of the bed. She pulled back the covers on the other side of the bed and climbed carefully in. She took one last look at the Van Gogh, before neatly replacing the blanket and cover over her head and finally disappearing under the sheet. Krantz lay flat and didn't move a muscle. She was so slight that she barely made an impression in the half light. Although she remained secreted under the sheets, she heard the shower being turned off. This was followed by silence. Anna must have been drying herself, and then she heard a switch being flicked off – the bathroom light, followed by the sound of a door closing.

Krantz extracted the knife from its tailor-made sheath and gripped the handle firmly as Anna walked back into the bedroom. Anna slipped under the covers on her side of the bed and immediately turned on one side, stretching out an arm to switch off the bedside light. She lowered her head on to the soft goose-feather pillow. As she drifted into those first moments of slumber, her last thought was that the evening could hardly have gone better. Mr Nakamura had not only closed the deal, but offered her a job. What more could she ask for?

Anna was drifting off to sleep when Krantz leant across and touched her back with the tip of her forefinger. She ran the finger tip down her spine and onto her buttocks, coming to a halt at the top of her thigh. Anna sighed. Krantz paused for a moment, before placing her hand between Anna's legs.

Was she dreaming, or was someone touching her, Anna wondered, as she lay in that semi-conscious state before falling asleep. She didn't move a muscle. It wasn't possible that someone else could be in the bed. She must be dreaming. That was when she felt the cold steel of a blade as it slipped in between her thighs. Suddenly Anna was wide awake, a thousand thoughts rushing through her mind. She was about to throw the blanket back and dive onto the floor, when a voice said quietly but firmly, 'Don't move. Not a fucking muscle; you have a six-inch knife between your legs, and the blade is facing upwards.' Anna didn't move. 'If you as much as murmur, I'll slit you up from your crotch to your throat, and you'll live just long enough to wish you were dead.'

Anna felt the steel of the blade wedged between her thighs and tried hard not to move, although she couldn't stop trembling.

'Follow my instructions to the letter,' said Krantz, 'and you might just live.'

Anna didn't, and knew that if she was to have the slightest chance of survival, she would have to play for time. 'What do you want?' she asked.

'I told you not to murmur,' repeated Krantz, moving the knife up between Anna's thighs until the blade was a centimetre from the clitoris. Anna didn't argue.

'There is a light on your side of the bed,' said Krantz. 'Lean across, very slowly, and turn it on.'

Anna leant over and felt the blade move with her as she switched on the bedside light.

'Good,' said Krantz. 'Now I'm going to pull back the blanket on your side of the bed, while you remain still. I won't be removing the knife – yet.'

Anna stared in front of her, while Krantz slowly pulled the covers back on her side of the bed.

'Now pull your knees up under your chin,' said Krantz, 'slowly.'

Anna obeyed her order, and once again felt the knife move with her.

'Now push yourself up onto your knees and turn to face the wall.'

Anna placed her left elbow on the bed, pushed herself up slowly onto her knees and inched round until she was facing the wall. She stared up at Van Gogh. When she saw his bandaged ear, she couldn't help remembering the last act Krantz had performed on Victoria.

Krantz was now kneeling directly behind her, still gripping firmly onto the handle of the knife.

'Lean slowly forward,' said Krantz, 'and take hold of the painting on both sides of the frame.'

Anna obeyed her every word, while every muscle in her body was trembling.

'Now lift the picture off its hook and lower it slowly down onto the pillow.'

Anna managed to find the strength to carry out her command, bringing the portrait to rest on top of the pillows.

'Now I'm going to remove the knife from between your legs very slowly, before placing the tip of the blade on the back of your neck. Don't give a second's thought to any sudden movement once the blade has been removed, because should you be foolish enough to attempt anything, let me assure you that I can kill you in less than three seconds, and be out of the open window in less than ten. I want you to think about that for a moment before I remove the blade.'

Anna thought about it, and didn't move. A few seconds later, she felt the knife slide out from between her legs, and a moment later, as promised, the tip of the blade was pressed against the nape of her neck.

'Lift the picture up off the pillow,' ordered Krantz, 'then turn round and face me. Be assured the blade will never be less than a few inches away from your throat at any time. Any movement, and I mean any movement that I consider unexpected, will be your last.'

Anna believed her. She leant forward, lifted the picture off the pillow and moved her knees round inch by inch, until she came face to face with Krantz. When Anna first saw her, she was momentarily taken by surprise. The woman was so small and slight she even looked vulnerable, a mistake several seasoned men had made in the past – their past. If Krantz had got the better of Sergei, what chance did she have? The strangest thought passed through Anna's mind as she waited for her next order. Why hadn't she said yes when Andrews offered to bring her up a cup of cocoa before she retired to bed?

'Now I want you to turn the picture round so that it's facing me,' said Krantz, 'and don't take your eye off the knife,' she added as she pulled back the blade from her throat and raised it above her head. While Anna turned the picture round, Krantz kept the knife in line with her favourite part of the anatomy.

'Grip the frame firmly,' said Krantz, 'because your friend Mr Van Gogh is about to lose more than his left ear.'

'But why?' cried Anna, unable to remain silent any longer.

'I'm glad you asked,' said Krantz, 'because Mr Fenston's orders could not have been more explicit. He wanted you to be the last person to see the masterpiece before it was finally destroyed.'

'But why?' Anna repeated.

'As Mr Fenston couldn't own the painting himself, he wanted to be sure that Mr Nakamura couldn't either,' said Krantz, the blade of the knife still hovering inches from Anna's neck. 'Always a mistake to cross Mr Fenston. What a pity that you won't have the chance to tell your friend Lady Arabella what Mr Fenston has in mind for her.' Krantz paused. 'But I have a feeling he won't mind me sharing the details with you. Once the painting has been destroyed – so unfortunate that she couldn't afford to insure it, such a false economy, because that's when Mr Fenston will set about selling off the rest of the estate until she has finally cleared the debt. Her death, unlike yours, will be a long and lingering one. One can only admire Mr Fenston's neat and logical mind.' She paused again. 'I fear that time is running out, both for you and Mr Van Gogh.'

Krantz suddenly raised the knife high above her head and plunged the blade into the canvas. Anna felt the full force of Krantz's strength as she sliced through Van Gogh's neck, and with all the power she could muster, continued the movement, until she had completed an uneven circle, finally removing the head of Van Gogh and leaving a ragged hole in the centre of the canvas. Krantz leant back to admire her handiwork, and allowed herself a moment of satisfaction. She felt she had carried out her contract with Mr Fenston to the letter, and now that Anna had witnessed the whole spectacle, the time had come for Krantz to earn the fourth million.

Anna watched as Van Gogh's head fell onto the sheet beside her, without a drop of blood being spilt. As Krantz sat back to enjoy her moment of triumph, Anna brought the heavy frame crashing down towards her head. But Krantz was swifter than Anna had anticipated and was able to quickly turn, raise an arm and deflect the blow onto her left shoulder. Anna jumped off the bed as Krantz cast the frame to one side and pushed herself back up. Anna managed to rise and even take a step towards the door before Krantz leapt off the bed and dived at her, thrusting the tip of the blade into her leg as Anna attempted another step. Anna stumbled and fell, only inches from the door, blood spurting in every direction. Krantz was only a pace behind as Anna's hand touched the handle of the door, but it was too late. Krantz was on her before she could turn the handle. Krantz grabbed her by the hair and pulled Anna back down onto the floor. Krantz raised the knife above her head, and the last words Anna heard her utter were: 'This time it's personal.'

Krantz was about to perform a ceremonial incision when the bedroom door was flung open. Not by a butler carrying a cup of cocoa, but by a woman with a shotgun under her right arm, her hands and shimmering silk gown covered in blood.

Krantz was momentarily transfixed as she looked up at Lady Victoria Wentworth. Hadn't she already killed this woman? Was she staring at a ghost? Krantz hesitated, mesmerized, as the apparition advanced towards her. Krantz didn't take her eyes off Arabella, while still holding the knife to Anna's throat, the blade hovering a centimetre from her skin.

Arabella raised the gun as Krantz eased slowly backwards, dragging her quarry across the floor towards the open window. Arabella cocked the trigger. 'Another drop of blood,' she said, 'and I'll blow you to smithereens. I'll start with your legs, and then I'll save the second cartridge for your stomach. I can promise you a slow, painful death, and I will not be calling for an ambulance until I'm convinced there's nothing they can do to help you.' Arabella lowered her gun slightly and Krantz hesitated. 'Let her go,' she said, 'and I won't fire. You have my word.' Arabella broke the barrel of her gun, and waited. She was surprised to see how terrified Krantz was, while Anna remained remarkably composed.

Without warning, Krantz let go of Anna's hair and threw herself sideways out of the open window, landing on the balcony. Arabella snapped the barrel closed, raised the gun and fired all in one movement, blowing away the Burne-Jones window and leaving a gaping hole. Arabella rushed over to the smouldering gap and shouted, 'Now, Andrews,' as if she was ordering a beat at a pheasant shoot to commence. A second later, the security lights floodlit the front lawn so that it looked like a football field with a single player advancing towards goal.

Arabella's eyes settled on the diminutive black figure as she zigzagged across the lawn. Arabella raised the gun a second time, pulled the butt firmly into her shoulder, took aim, drew a deep breath and squeezed the trigger. A moment later Krantz fell to the ground, but still somehow managed to crawl on towards the wall.

'Damn,' said Arabella, 'I only winged her.' She ran out of the room, down the stairs and shouted long before she reached the bottom step, 'Two more cartridges, Andrews.'

Andrews opened the front door with his right hand and passed her ladyship two more cartridges with his left. Arabella quickly reloaded before charging down the front steps and onto the lawn. She could just about make out a tiny black figure as it changed direction towards the open gate, but Arabella was beginning to make ground on Krantz with every stride she took. Once she was satisfied that Krantz was within range, she came to a halt in the middle of the lawn. She raised her gun and nestled it into her shoulder. She took aim and was about to squeeze the trigger when, out of nowhere, three police cars and an ambulance came speeding through the gates, their headlights blinding Arabella so that she could no longer see her quarry.

The first car screeched to a halt at her feet, and when Arabella saw who it was that climbed out of the car, she reluctantly lowered her gun.

'Good evening, chief superintendent,' she said, placing a hand across her forehead as she tried to shield her eyes from the beam that was focused directly on her.

'Good evening, Arabella,' replied the chief superintendent, as if he had arrived a few minutes late for one of her drinks parties. 'Is everything all right?' he asked.

'It was until you turned up,' said Arabella, 'poking your nose into other people's business. And how, may I ask, did you manage to get here so quickly?'

'You have your American friend, Jack Delaney, to thank for that,' said the chief superintendent. 'He warned us that you might require some assistance. So we've had the place under surveillance for the past hour.'

'I didn't require any assistance,' said Arabella, raising her gun again. 'If you'd given me just a couple more minutes, I'd have finished her off, and been quite happy to face the consequences.'

'I have no idea what you're talking about,' said the

chief superintendent, as he returned to his car and switched off the headlights. The ambulance and the other two police cars were nowhere to be seen.

'You've let her get clean away, you fool,' said Arabella, raising her gun for a third time, just as Mr Nakamura appeared by her side in his dressing gown.

'I think that Anna—'

'Oh my God,' said Arabella, who turned and, not bothering to wait for the chief superintendent's response, began running back towards the house. She continued on up the steps, through the open door, before dashing up the staircase, not stopping until she reached the guest bedroom. She found Andrews kneeling on the floor, placing a bandage expertly around Anna's leg. Mr Nakamura came running through the door. He stopped for a moment to catch his breath before he said, 'For many years, Arabella, I have wondered what took place at an English country-house party.' He paused. 'Well, now I know.'

Arabella burst out laughing, and turned towards Nakamura, to find him staring at the mutilated canvas on the floor by the side of the bed.

'Oh my God,' repeated Arabella, when she first set eyes on what was left of her inheritance. 'That bastard Fenston has beaten us after all. Now I understand why he was so confident that I'd be forced to sell off the rest of my collection, even finally relinquishing Wentworth Hall.'

Anna rose slowly to her feet and sat on the end of the bed. 'I don't think so,' she said, facing her host. Arabella looked puzzled. 'But you have Andrews to thank for that.'

'Andrews?' Arabella repeated.

'Yes. He warned me that Mr Nakamura would be leaving first thing in the morning if he was not to be late for his meeting with Corus Steel and suggested that if I didn't want to be disturbed at some ungodly hour, perhaps it might be wise for him to remove the painting during dinner. This would not only allow his staff to transfer the frame back onto the original, but also give them enough time to have the picture packed and ready before Mr Nakamura departed.' Anna paused. 'I put it to Andrews that you might not be too pleased to discover that he had flouted your wishes, while I had clearly abused your hospitality. I think I recall Andrews's exact words,' said Anna. '"If you were to allow me to replace the masterpiece with the fake, I feel confident that her ladyship would be none the wiser."'

It was one of the rare occasions during the past forty-nine years that Andrews had witnessed the Lady Arabella rendered speechless.

'I think you should fire him on the spot for insubordination,' said Nakamura, 'then I can offer him a job. Were you to accept,' he said, turning to Andrews, 'I would be happy to double your present salary.'

'Not a hope,' said Arabella, before the butler was given a chance to respond. 'Andrews is one national treasure I will never part with.'

9/26

57

MR NAKAMURA woke a few minutes after six, when he thought he heard the bedroom door close. He spent a few moments thinking over what had taken place the previous evening, trying to convince himself it hadn't all been a dream.

He pushed back the sheets and lowered his feet onto the carpet, to find a pair of slippers and a dressing gown had been left by the side of the bed. He placed his feet in the slippers, put on the dressing gown and walked to the end of the bed, where he'd left his dinner jacket, evening dress shirt and the rest of his clothes on a chair. He had intended to pack before leaving, but they were no longer there. He tried to recall if he had already put them in his suitcase. He opened the lid to discover that his dress shirt had been washed, ironed and packed, and his dinner jacket was pressed and hanging up in his suit carrier.

He walked into the bathroom to find the large bath three-quarters full. He placed a hand in the water: the temperature was warm, but not hot. Then he recalled the bedroom door closing. No doubt with just enough force to wake him, without disturbing any other guest. He took off his dressing gown and stepped into the bath.

◄○►

Anna came out of the bathroom and started to get dressed. She was putting on Tina's watch when she first saw the envelope on the bedside table. Had Andrews delivered it while she was in the shower? She felt sure it hadn't been there when she woke. *Anna* was scrawled on it in Arabella's unmistakable bold hand.

She sat on the end of the bed and tore open the envelope.

WENTWORTH HALL

September 26th, 2001

Dearest Anna,

Queen Elizabeth the First awarded my pirate ancestor for his courage and enterprise with gold. It is therefore only right that, having been responsible for saving the family bacon . . .

Anna burst out laughing at the quaint English expression, causing two slips of paper to fall out of the envelope and onto the floor. Anna bent down to pick them up. The first was a Coutts cheque made out to *Anna Petrescu* for one million pounds. The second . . .

—◦—

Once Nakamura was dressed, he picked up his cellphone from the bedside table and dialled a number in Tokyo. He instructed his finance director to deposit the sum of forty-five million dollars by electronic transfer with his bank in London. He wouldn't need to brief his lawyers, as he had already given them clear instructions to transfer the full amount to Coutts & Co in the Strand, where the Wentworth family had maintained an account for over two centuries.

Before leaving the room to go down to breakfast, Mr Nakamura paused in front of the portrait of Wellington. He gave the Iron Duke a slight bow, feeling sure that he would have enjoyed last night's skirmishes.

As he walked down the marble staircase, he spotted

Andrews in the hall. He was supervising the moving of the red box, which contained the Van Gogh with its original frame restored. The under-butler was placing the crate next to the front door so that it could be loaded into Mr Nakamura's car the moment his chauffeur appeared.

Arabella bustled out of the breakfast room as her guest reached the bottom step.

'Good morning, Takashi,' she said. 'I do hope that, despite everything, you managed some sleep.'

'Yes, thank you, Arabella,' he replied, as Anna limped down behind him.

'I don't know how to thank you,' said Anna.

'Sotheby's would have charged me a lot more,' said Arabella without explanation.

'And I know that Tina—' began Anna, when there was a firm rap on the front door. Nakamura paused, as Andrews walked sedately across the hall.

'Probably my driver,' Nakamura suggested as the butler pulled open the oak door.

'Good morning, sir,' Andrews said.

Arabella swung round and smiled at her unexpected guest.

'Good morning, Jack,' she said. 'I hadn't realized you were joining us for breakfast. Have you just popped across from the States, or have you spent the night at our local police station?'

'No, Arabella, I did not, but I'm told that *you* should have done,' replied Jack with a grin.

'Hello, my hero,' said Anna, giving Jack a kiss. 'You arrived just in time to save us all.'

'Not quite fair,' chipped in Arabella, 'as it was Jack who tipped off the local constabulary in the first place.'

Anna smiled and, turning to Nakamura, said, 'This is my friend, Jack Fitzgerald Delaney.'

'No doubt christened John,' suggested Mr Nakamura as he shook hands with Jack.

'Correct, sir.'

'Names chosen by an Irish mother, or perhaps you were born on the twenty-second of November 1963?'

'Guilty on both counts,' admitted Jack.

'Very droll,' said Arabella, as she led her guests through to the breakfast room, and Anna explained to Jack why she had a bandage round her leg.

Arabella invited Nakamura to take the place on her right. Gesturing to Jack, she said, 'Come and sit on my left, young man. There are still one or two questions that I need answered.' Jack eyed the devilled kidneys as he picked up his knife and fork. 'And you can forget any thought of food,' Arabella added, 'until you've explained why I'm not on the front page of the *Daily Mail* following my heroic efforts last night.'

'I have no idea what you're talking about,' said Jack, as Andrews poured him a cup of black coffee.

'Not you, as well,' said Arabella. 'It's no wonder so many people believe in conspiracy theories and police cover-ups. Now do try a little harder, Jack.'

'When I questioned my colleagues at MI5 this morning,' said Jack, placing his knife and fork back on the table, 'they were able to assure me that no terrorists had entered this country during the past twenty-four hours.'

'In other words, she got clean away,' said Anna.

'Not exactly,' said Jack, 'but I can tell you that a woman of approximately five foot, weighing around a hundred pounds, with a gunshot wound, spent the night in solitary at Belmarsh prison.'

'From which no doubt she will escape,' suggested Arabella.

'I can assure you, Arabella, that no one has ever escaped from Belmarsh.'

'But they'll still end up having to send her back to Bucharest.'

'Unlikely,' said Jack, 'as there's no record of her ever entering the country in the first place, and no one will be looking for a woman in that particular prison.'

'Well, if that's the case, I'll allow you to help yourself to a small portion of mushrooms.'

Jack picked up his knife and fork.

'Which I can highly recommend,' said Mr Nakamura, as he rose from his place, 'but I fear I must now leave you, Arabella, if I am not to be late for my meeting.'

Jack put down his knife and fork for a second time, as everyone left the table to join Mr Nakamura in the hall.

Andrews was standing by the front door, organizing the packing of the red box into the trunk of a Toyota limousine, when Arabella and her guests walked into the hall.

'I think,' said Mr Nakamura, turning to face Arabella, 'that to describe my short visit to Wentworth Hall as memorable would be a classic example of English understatement.' He smiled, before taking one last look at Gainsborough's portrait of Catherine, Lady Wentworth. 'Correct me if I am wrong, Arabella,' he continued, 'but isn't that the same necklace as you were wearing at dinner last night?'

'It is indeed,' replied Arabella with a smile. 'Her ladyship was an actress, which would be the equivalent today of being a lap dancer, so heaven knows from which of her many admirers she acquired such a magnificent bauble. But I'm not complaining, because I certainly have *her* to thank for the necklace.'

'And the earrings,' said Anna.

'Earring, sadly,' said Arabella, touching her right ear.

'Earring,' repeated Jack as he looked up at the

painting. 'I'm so dumb,' he added. 'It's been staring me in the face all the time.'

'And what exactly has been staring you in the face all the time?' asked Anna.

'Leapman wrote on the back of a photograph of Fenston shaking hands with George W. Bush: "This is all the evidence you need".'

'All the evidence you need for what?' asked Arabella.

'To prove that it was Fenston who murdered your sister,' replied Jack.

'I fail to see a connection between Catherine Lady Wentworth and the President of the United States,' said Arabella.

'Exactly the same mistake as I made,' said Jack. 'The connection is not between Lady Wentworth and Bush, but between Lady Wentworth and Fenston. And the clue has always been staring us in the face.'

Everyone looked up at the Gainsborough portrait.

After a long silence, Anna was the first to speak.

'They're both wearing the same earring,' she said quietly. 'I also missed it completely. I even saw Fenston wearing the earring on the day he fired me, but I just didn't make the connection.'

'Leapman immediately realized its significance,' said Jack, almost rubbing his hands together. 'He'd worked out that it was the vital piece of evidence we needed to secure a conviction.'

Andrews coughed.

'You're quite right, Andrews,' said Arabella. 'We mustn't keep Mr Nakamura any longer. The poor man has suffered quite enough family revelations for one day.'

'True,' said Mr Nakamura. 'However, I would like to congratulate Mr Delaney on a remarkable piece of detection.'

'Slow, but he gets there in the end,' said Anna, taking his hand.

Mr Nakamura smiled as Arabella accompanied him down to his car, while Jack and Anna waited on the top step.

'Well done, Stalker. I agree with Mr Nakamura, that wasn't a bad piece of detective work.'

Jack smiled and turned to face Anna. 'But how about your efforts as a rookie agent? Did you ever discover why Tina—'

'I thought you'd never ask,' said Anna, 'though I must confess I also missed several clues that should have been obvious, even to an amateur.'

'Like what?' asked Jack.

'A girl who just happens to support the 49ers as well as the Lakers, has a considerable knowledge and love of American art, whose hobby was sailing a boat called *Christina* that had been named after the owner's two children.'

'She's Chris Adams's daughter?' said Jack.

'And Chris Adams Jr's sister,' said Anna.

'Well that explains everything.'

'Almost everything,' said Anna, 'because not only did Tina Adams lose her home and the boat after her brother had his throat cut by Krantz, but she also had to drop out of law school.'

'So Fenston finally crossed the wrong person.'

'And it gets better,' said Anna. 'Tina changed her name from Adams to Forster, moved to New York, took a secretarial course, applied for a temping job at the bank and waited for Fenston's secretary to resign – a fairly regular occurrence – before she stepped into the breach.'

'And held on to her position until she was fired last

week,' Jack reminded her, as Nakamura bowed low to Arabella before climbing into the back of his limousine.

'And even better news, Stalker,' continued Anna as she returned Mr Nakamura's wave. 'Tina downloaded every document that might implicate Fenston onto her personal computer. She kept everything, from contracts to letters, even personal memos that Fenston thought had been destroyed when the North Tower collapsed. So I have a feeling that it won't be that long before you can finally close the file on Mr Bryce Fenston.'

'Thanks to you and Tina,' said Jack. He paused. 'But she still lost everything.'

'Not everything,' said Anna, 'because you'll be happy to know that Arabella has given her a million dollars for the part she played in saving the Wentworth estate.'

'A million dollars?' said Jack.

'Not to mention the million pounds she's presented to me, "for the labourer is worthy of his hire" was how Arabella expressed it in her letter.'

'St Luke,' said Jack. '"And in the same house remain, eating and drinking such things as they give: for the labourer is worthy of his hire."'

'Impressive,' said Anna.

'And I didn't even get breakfast.'

'Well, perhaps I'll take pity on you, Stalker, and let you join me for lunch in first class on the flight home.'

Jack turned to Anna and smiled. 'I'd much rather you came to dinner with me on Saturday evening.'

'Your mother's Irish stew night?' said Anna. 'Now that's better than first class. I'd certainly be up for that.'

'But before you agree, Anna, there's something I have to tell you,' said Jack as Mr Nakamura's car disappeared down the drive and out of the gates.

'And what's that?' asked Anna, turning back to face him.

'My mother is under the illusion that you've already been married three times, you have five children, not necessarily by the three husbands, four of them are on hard drugs and the other one is currently serving a jail sentence.' He paused. 'She also thinks that you work in a far older profession than art consultancy.'

Anna burst out laughing. 'But what will you tell her when she discovers that none of it's true?'

'You're not Irish,' said Jack.

AUTHOR'S NOTE

Although Van Gogh cut off part of his left ear with a razor following a row with Gauguin, it still remains a mystery why his right ear is covered with a bandage in both self-portraits.

Art historians, including Louis van Tilborgh, Curator of Paintings at the Van Gogh Museum, are convinced that the artist painted the picture while looking in a mirror.

Tilborgh points out that Van Gogh wrote to his brother, Theo, on 17 September 1888, after buying a mirror 'to help him with his work' (letter number 685 in the 1990 edition of Van Gogh's letters, and number 537 in the 1953 (English) edition of his correspondence).

The mirror was left at Arles when the artist moved on to Saint-Rémy. However, Van Gogh wrote another letter to J. Ginoux (11 May 1890, 634a in the English edition, 872 in the Dutch edition), asking Ginoux to 'take good care of the mirror'.

Van Gogh is known to have painted two self-portraits with bandaged ear. One can be viewed at the Courtauld Institute at Somerset House in London. The second remains in a private collection.

café illuminé sur la terrasse par une grande
lanterne de gaz   dans la nuit bleue
avec un coin de ciel bleu étoilé
Le troisième tableau de cette semaine
est un portrait de moi même presque
décoloré des tons cendrés
sur un fond véronèse pâle
J'ai acheté exprès un miroir assez bon
pour pouvoir travailler d'après moi même
a défaut de modèle car si j'arrive à pouvoir
peindre la coloration de ma propre tête ce
qui n'est pas sans présenter quelque
difficulté je pourrai bien aussi peindre
les têtes des autres bonshommes et
bonnes femmes
La question de peindre les scènes de nuit
sur place et la nuit même m'intéresse
énormément Cette semaine je n'ai absolument
rien fait que peindre et dormir
et prendre mes repas. Cela veut dire
des séances de douze heures de
6 heures et selon et puis des
sommeils de 12 heures d'un seul
trait aussi

From Van Gogh's letter to his brother, Theo, 17 September 1888

A TIMELINE OF BESTSELLERS IN THE AUCTION WORLD, 1980–2005

Year	Artist / Title	Price / US$
1980	TURNER *Juliet and Her Nurse*	7,000,000
1981	PICASSO *Yo Picasso*	5,800,000
1982	BOTTICELLI *Giovanni de Pierfrancesco de Medici*	1,400,000
1983	CÉZANNE *Sucrier, poires et tapies*	4,000,000
1984	RAPHAEL *Chalk Study of a Man's Head and Hand*	4,400,000
1985	MANTEGNA *Adoration of the Magi*	10,500,000
1986	MANET *La rue Mosnier aux paveurs*	11,100,000
1987	**VAN GOGH *IRISES***	53,900,000
1988	PICASSO *Acrobate et jeune arlequin*	38,500,000
1989	PICASSO *Yo Picasso*	47,900,000
1990	**VAN GOGH *PORTRAIT DU DR GACHET***	**82,500,000**
1991	TITIAN *Venus and Adonis*	13,500,000
1992	CANALETTO *The Old Horse Guards*	17,800,000
1993	CÉZANNE *Nature morte: les grosses pommes*	28,600,000
1994	DA VINCI Codex Hammer	30,800,000

1995	PICASSO *Angel Fernandez de Soto*	29,100,000
1996	John F. Kennedy's rocking chair	453,500
1997	PICASSO *Le Rêve*	48,400,000
1998	**VAN GOGH *PORTRAIT DE L'ARTISTE SANS BARBE***	**71,500,000**
1999	CÉZANNE *Rideau, cruchon et compotier*	60,500,000
2000	MICHELANGELO *The Risen Christ*	12,300,000
2000	REMBRANDT *Portrait of a Lady, Age 62*	28,700,000
2001	KOONS *Michael Jackson and Bubbles*	5,600,000
2002	RUBENS *The Massacre of the Innocents*	76,700,000
2003	ROTHKO *No. 9 (White and Black on Wine)*	16,400,000
2004	RAPHAEL *Madonna of the Pinks*	*62,700,000*
2004	**PICASSO *Garçon à la pipe***	**104,000,000**
2004	VERMEER *A Young Woman Seated at the Virginals*	30,000,000
2004	WARHOL *Mustard Race Riot*	15,100,000
2005	**GAINSBOROUGH *PORTRAIT OF SIR CHARLES GOULD***	**1,100,000**
2005	**YUAN DYNASTY VASE**	**27,600,000**

Source: *Art & Auction*, September 2005

ACKNOWLEDGEMENTS

I would like to thank the following people for their invaluable help and advice with this book: Rosie de Courcy, Mari Roberts, Simon Bainbridge, Victoria Leacock, Kelley Ragland, Mark Poltimore (Chairman, nineteenth- and twentieth-century paintings, Sotheby's), Louis van Tilborgh (Curator of Paintings, Van Gogh Museum), Gregory DeBoer, Rachel Rauchwerger (director, Art Logistics), the National Art Collections Fund, Courtauld Institute of Art, John Power, Jun Nagai and Terry Lenzner.

Jeffrey Archer